READER'S DIGEST
SELECT EDITIONS

READER'S DIGEST
SELECT EDITIONS

The condensations in this volume
are published with the consent of the authors
and the publishers © 2006 Reader's Digest.

www.readersdigest.co.uk

The Reader's Digest Association Limited
11 Westferry Circus Canary Wharf London E14 4HE

For information as to ownership of
copyright in the material of this book,
and acknowledgments, see last page.

Printed in Germany
ISBN 0 276 44106 0

**SELECTED AND CONDENSED
BY READER'S DIGEST**

THE READER'S DIGEST ASSOCIATION LIMITED, LONDON

CONTENTS

Provence, with its sunbaked lavender fields and lovely picturesque towns, is the backdrop for a murder that baffles Daniel Jacquot of the Cavaillon crime squad. Even when an arrest is made, he suspects they've got the wrong man. The truth is more deeply buried and goes back to events that happened during the war. While locals with long memories provide clues, it takes the arrival of a visitor with extraordinary sensory powers, to help Jacquot to a breakthrough.

It starts one hot night in New York, with Jack Reacher sipping espresso outside a café and watching the world go by. But that all changes when he's approached by a stranger who tells him he's just witnessed the handover of a large ransom. What's more, wealthy businessman Edward Lane is asking for his services—at any price—to help find the kidnap victims. By the time Reacher gleans that the enigmatic Mr Lane has his own dark secrets, the ex-military policeman is in way too deep to change his mind.

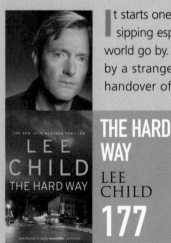

MARLEY & ME

JOHN GROGAN

321

Topping the New York best-seller charts for thirteen weeks, this book has taken America by storm and is now set to charm Britain. When John Grogan and his wife decided to get a dog, they looked for a gentle, placid animal, easy to train. What they got instead was Marley, an out-of-control but totally lovable Labrador, who brought chaos, laughter and joy into their lives. Even non-dog-lovers will find themselves won over by the exuberant Marley's antics.

Ever since his international blockbuster, *Kane and Abel*, achieved record sales, Jeffrey Archer has been hailed as one of Britain's top storytellers. For this new novel, he's drawn on his personal interest in art and collecting to produce a typically inventive story with a neat twist in the tail. Settle back and enjoy the ride as you're whisked across the world to New York, Bucharest and Tokyo, in the footsteps of a young art historian trying bravely to outwit a powerful and ruthless collector.

FALSE IMPRESSION

JEFFREY ARCHER

433

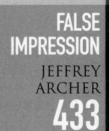

Jacquot and the Angel

MARTIN O'BRIEN

St Bedard's beautiful old square is
silent on summer afternoons,
apart from the gentle splashing of
the fountain and the low murmur
of local chatter.
It's the kind of place where everyone knows everyone else's business,
and where there are few secrets.
But when Dr Martner, a local
German resident is killed,
long-buried secrets are exactly
what Inspector Jacquot
must unearth.

PROLOGUE

Église St-Jean, Cavaillon, Provence: June 1944

It was a cart, clattering over the cobbles in the street below, that woke Sandrine. She came to with a start, wincing at the tightness in her neck, the stiffness of her shoulders. She took in the dusty boards, the panels of slatted wood, and knew immediately where she was, registering with a jolt of annoyance the soft grey light where before there'd been chill, inky darkness.

She'd fallen asleep. Some time in the night, in the belfry of Église St-Jean, she'd let her cheek rest against her sleeve, closed her eyes.

Sandrine eased herself into a sitting position and peered through the slats at the cobbled courtyard of the *Kommandantur* across the street. She looked at the watch he had given her. A little past five. Soon they would come up from the cells and she would see him one last time.

There had been six of them left alive and four taken by the bridge on the road to Brieuc. Somehow she and Bonaire had been missed in the sudden, sweeping beams of torchlight, in all the barking and the shouts, the pop of sidearms and the crackle of machine-gun fire. Side by side when the ambush came, they had managed to sink back down the bank and follow the river's course until they were far enough away to stop and catch their breath. Downstream they heard the sound of trucks passing, along the road from Brieuc, the juddering of brakes and the clatter of tailgates swinging down.

The Germans had been waiting for them. They knew.

As the young Bonaire began to sob, Sandrine had felt the first great wring of loss, as though some part of her had been wrenched away and left by the bridge. He was alive, that was all she knew. But taken.

High in the belfry, Sandrine shivered. It had been a long night. She'd come to the church the previous evening, attended Benediction, and according to plan, as she made to leave, she'd slipped through the curtain near the font and climbed the winding steps that led to this lookout. She'd made herself as comfortable as possible, eaten her bread and cheese, and waited.

Now, with so little time left, cold and alone, Sandrine thought only of him.

And then the steps came, the soft scuffing of boots on stone. She pressed her forehead against the slats, finding the best angle as the first soldiers stepped into the courtyard, rifles slung from their shoulders. Ten men, dressed in shadowy *feldgrau* uniforms, gathering near the centre. Cigarettes were dug for and a match flared in cupped hands, darting like a firefly as it was offered round. They'd done this many times before, at this same hour. Just another way to start the day.

An officer strode into the courtyard. Sandrine could make out the peaked hat, the short field jacket and jodhpurs. She didn't need to see the twin shafts of lightning on the man's collar to know he was SS.

The soldiers flicked away their cigarettes, snapped themselves upright.

The minutes ticked by. And then they were there, the men, stepping out from the passageway, one by one, attended by armed guards. Grion the Corsican was first, stooped and limping. Next was Jean-Pierre, the electrician from Barjas who rigged their explosives and, behind him, the boy Druout from Chant-le-Neuf. Then, last in line, pausing to gaze up at a sky he would never see again—came Albert.

Albert. She wanted to run to him, take him away from that terrible place and hold on to him for ever. Instead she watched him start forward after his comrades, casting round with his single eye as though weighing up the odds on some last-minute dash for freedom.

But there was no chance of that. Not this time. Not in this place.

The four men crossed the yard of the *Kommandantur*, dressed only in the shirts and trousers they had worn beneath their coats on the night of the attack. Each man's hands were tied behind his back.

One by one they filed past the officer and soldiers, and disappeared below the parapet that cut off from Sandrine's view the bullet-pocked wall and the wooden stakes where they would be tied.

Unslinging their rifles, the men in the firing squad lined up. The officer shouted something, then the soldiers lifted their Mausers, took aim and fired.

Puffs of smoke, muzzle flashes. And then a short, sharp clapping of shots that ricocheted off the walls of the *Kommandantur*.

Above her, pigeons rattled off the belfry roof, wings flapping, whirling away into the morning sky. And in her wooden nest, forehead pressed against the slats, Sandrine let the tears slide silently down her cheeks.

I

As Madame Ramier would tell anyone who asked, it was not a morning she would likely ever forget.

It was a Wednesday, the last in February, a bleak, beleaguered time in the country round St Bédard-le-Chapitre when the ground is as hard as iron and the vines are as bare and brown as a beetle's legs, a time when clouds can gather in a moment and press down with such malign intent that people start to believe the sun has gone for ever.

That was how it had been for the last few days, the widow Ramier would tell you, low clouds screwed down tight as a lid over the rooftops of St Bédard and the slopes of the Brieuc valley. But some time in the early hours, those clouds had slipped away. Now, at a little after eight o'clock, a pale sun peered into a sky as blue as cobalt and brittle as butterscotch.

That was how it was—bright and sharp, chill and crisp—the morning Odile Ramier found the first body.

Her day had begun like any other, sitting at the kitchen table in the house she shared with her sister Adeline. Listening to the boards creak overhead as Adeline moved around her bedroom, Madame Ramier had no idea—no idea at *all*, she would say later—what that winter morning held in store. Just the usual round of chores at the Martners' place, she'd supposed—polishing, vacuuming and dusting her way through their old farmhouse.

She fetched her moped from the cupboard under the stairs, and wheeled it down the hallway. Reaching for her coat and scarf, she called out '*à tout à l'heure*' to her sister, and manoeuvred herself through the front door.

Outside—scarfed, gloved and snugly buttoned up—she tugged on a helmet and goggles, mounted the bike, tipped it off its stand, and started to pedal as it picked up speed down the slope. When the engine caught, she stopped pedalling, sank her chin into her collar and turned left at the bottom of the square, leaving St Bédard along the Chant-le-Neuf road.

Twenty-three minutes later, red-cheeked and breathless, Odile Ramier returned to St Bédard, shoulders bent over the handlebars as though this position might provide some small measure of extra speed. Coming to an abrupt halt at the town's gendarmerie, she let the moped drop to the ground and hurried up the steps to report her discovery.

IT WAS, EVERYONE in St Bédard agreed, the most dreadful thing. No one had seen its like since the last days of the Occupation. By the end of that Wednesday morning four bodies had been found, but, as later reported in the national press, there were five deaths in all.

Dr Josef Martner and his wife, Jutta, had lived for ten years on the lower slopes of the Brieuc valley, four miles north of St Bédard along the road to Chant-le-Neuf. The couple, both German, had bought an old farmhouse and twenty hectares of land after selling their house in Paris, renovated the property, then added an extension to its eastern flanks. Built in the same stone as the original building, it enclosed a pretty courtyard set with terra-cotta pots, a small fountain and a pond. Part of this extension, comprising one entire side of the courtyard, was a lofty, temperature-controlled hot-house in which the doctor nurtured a celebrated collection of orchids.

It was in their first-floor bedroom that the couple had died in their bed, killed by a volley of shotgun blasts. Downstairs, in the doctor's hothouse, lay their daughter Ilse, also dispatched with a fusillade of close-range shots.

The fourth body, that of Ilse's seventeen-year-old daughter Kippi, was found outside the house, halfway along the drive leading to the road. Judging by the position of her left shoe, a yellow espadrille, some twenty metres behind the body, and given the shell casings found midway between body and shoe, it appeared that the killer had chased Kippi, caught up with her when she lost the shoe, stopped, aimed and fired. Having brought her down, the killer had walked up and finished the job at close range.

The fifth death was only revealed later, during autopsy, and leaked to the press by someone in the pathologist's office. According to this source, the blonde youngster had been three months pregnant.

In the initial crime report filled out that day at the St Bédard gendarmerie, sixty-eight-year-old Odile Ramier stated that she had found Kippi's body at approximately 8.55 in the morning. When asked why she'd come back to town, rather than go on to the Martners' home and phone from there, she had given the desk sergeant a withering look and replied: 'Do I look crazy? Miss Kippi had been shot. Maybe her killer was still in the house.'

FORTY MINUTES LATER, old Sergeant Lanclos, accompanied by his corporal, Frenot, arrived at the Martner property and found the first body exactly where Madame Ramier had told them they would.

The two policemen left their car between the body and the road, then walked on down to the house, taking the precaution of drawing their guns.

The front door of the farmhouse was half open. Lanclos pushed it with his boot and stepped cautiously inside, followed by Frenot.

Standing just inside the front door, Lanclos noticed a large crater, pitted with a halo of tiny holes, that decorated the wall above Frenot's head. It was clear that a heavy-calibre shell had done the damage, littering the floor with chips of masonry and plaster.

The policemen made their way along the hallway, checking the living room, dining room and the doctor's study. Nothing appeared to be out of place.

In the kitchen, it was a different story. Here they found an upturned chair and a floor dusted with plaster and scattered with the shredded remains of onions, garlic and herbs. On the kitchen table were larger scabs of plaster and splinters of lath brought down from the ceiling by a shotgun blast.

Lanclos peered through the window. It was the first time he had visited the house since the farmer Taillard had lived there, and he marvelled at the changes that had been made: the old farmyard where chickens had clucked was now enclosed by the three wings of the extension—a utility room and sun lounge to the left, guest quarters opposite, and the hothouse to the right, its glass roof and side whitewashed to protect the interior from direct sunlight.

It was there, with water from the sprinkler system dripping off the leaves, that Lanclos and Frenot found the body of Kippi's mother.

At this point, Frenot hurried back to their car to call up Regional Crime in Cavaillon while Lanclos prowled through the adjoining guest wing. Both ground and first floors were empty, though each showed signs of recent occupation. In the two guest bedrooms, the double beds had their winter quilts pushed back, pillows crumpled into comfortable shapes.

Back in the main house, Lanclos climbed the stairs to a landing with three doors leading off it. He opened the first: an airing cupboard. The second gave on to a marble-floored bathroom. Beyond the twin basins, in the far corner, was another door. Lanclos guessed that this would lead to the master bedroom, but he kept to the landing, making his way along it until he reached the last of the three doors. Noting the shell casings on the floor, he paused a moment and sniffed. The smell of cordite was strong here, hot and coppery, but laced with another, more sinister scent.

Only once before had Sergeant Lanclos smelt anything like it, as a small boy standing by the bridge at the Brieuc turning, its verge lined with a row of crumpled bodies, a dozen Resistance fighters and six Germans. The soldiers' corpses had been separated from the *résistants*, but their blood was puddled together in the space between them, a scarlet pool reeking of the butcher's slab.

Lanclos shuddered as he reached forward and pushed open the door.

Blood. Splashed across the walls at the head of the bed, pooling darkly on the stone floor, and soaked into the matted mess of quilt and down feathers that only partly concealed the remains of the good doctor and his wife.

Lanclos was sick on his way back to the car. Frenot was leaning against the passenger side, his usual ruddy complexion drained of colour.

The two policemen looked at each other without a word. Down in the valley, along the Brieuc road, beyond the bridge and the St Bédard turning, they could hear the first, distant wail of police sirens.

2

Chief Inspector Daniel Jacquot of the Cavaillon Regional Crime Squad was four blocks from his office when Frenot's call reached the switchboard at police HQ.

Eleven minutes later, as he turned into the car park at the back of the town's gendarmerie, the first person he saw was his assistant Jean Brunet, pulling on a coat and briefing a group of gendarmes. A police van, its twin blue lights revolving, stood nearby. A moment later, the gendarmes climbed into the van and Brunet, spotting Jacquot's car, hurried over.

Jacquot leaned across and opened the passenger door. 'So? What's up?'

As Jacquot turned his car and followed the police van through the courtyard's stone-pillared gates, Brunet briefed his superior. A message had come through from St Bédard-le-Chapitre: two bodies so far, maybe more, found in the old Taillard farmhouse. The place was owned by a German couple. Name of Martner, Josef and Jutta. Retired. Resident, not visiting. Apparently, the two bodies were the Martners' daughter and granddaughter.

'Cause of death?' asked Jacquot, following the police van.

'Looks like gunshot,' replied Brunet.

As he overtook the police van, Jacquot frowned. This was not how he'd planned his day. Claudine's daughter, Midou, had been staying with them and he'd promised her a farewell lunch at Chez Gaillard. There seemed little chance now that he'd make the date. As they left town, Jacquot called Claudine and left a message warning her he'd likely be held up, and that she and Midou should go on without him. He'd get there if he could.

Twenty minutes later they turned into the Martner driveway with the police van close behind. In the rearview mirror, Jacquot saw the van stop and two gendarmes clamber out to secure the entrance with a roll of blue and yellow scene-of-crime tape. Fifty metres further on, round a curve in the drive, he pulled up beside an old police Peugeot. Standing beside it were two gendarmes, a sergeant and corporal.

The sergeant snapped off a salute when he saw Jacquot. Buttoning the collar of his jacket and taking his kepi from the Peugeot's bonnet, Lanclos led them round the car to the first body, now covered in Frenot's police cape.

Jacquot knelt and lifted a corner. 'Is this how you found her?' he asked, getting to his feet.

'Yes, Chief,' replied Lanclos. 'Just covered the body, you know. It looks like the granddaughter. Kippi, she's called.'

'How many more?'

'Three, Chief. Grandparents and Kippi's mother, Ilse. In the house.'

'Show me. How you found them. Exactly what you did. Each step of the way.' And then, turning to Brunet: 'Have the boys spread out and check the vines—fifty metres either side of the drive to start with.'

'Yes, boss,' said Brunet, and he hurried away back up the drive.

Sergeant Lanclos led Jacquot down to the house, pointing out the shell casings and lone espadrille and filling him in on the discovery: the cleaning woman, Odile Ramier; her report at the gendarmerie in St Bédard.

The house, Jacquot noted, was like many converted *mas* in the region, the same golden stone, the same shutters and low-pitched roof of bleached rose tiles. But appearances were deceptive. It might still look like the farm it once had been, but Jacquot had seen enough of these conversions to know that its renovated interior would be spacious.

Parked outside the house, on a circle of gravel, was a green BMW estate.

'The Martners'?' asked Jacquot.

'That's right,' replied Lanclos.

'Does the daughter have a car?'

Lanclos looked uncertain. 'A Volkswagen, I think. Probably in the garage.' Lanclos pointed to a pair of barn doors at the end of the building.

Jacquot walked over, tried the doors then peered through a gap in the planking. In the gloom he could make out the grille and headlights of a black Golf saloon, and a German registration.

Gravel crunching underfoot, he rejoined Lanclos at the front door.

'The door was open?' Jacquot asked. 'Like this?'

'Just as you see it, Chief.'

Jacquot nodded. No sign of forced entry. Either the door had been left unlocked or the killer had had his own set of keys. Or maybe the Martners had let him in.

Pointing out the damage to the wall inside the house, Lanclos led Jacquot along the hallway, showed him the living room, the dining room and the doctor's study, then stepped into the kitchen.

Jacquot looked around. Despite the hole in the ceiling, the upturned chair and the plaster, lath, garlic and onions that littered the table and the floor around it, the kitchen was a homely, lived-in space.

'We found the light on,' Lanclos said, 'but the cooker was off. Looks like someone was getting some breakfast.'

On the work surface beside the sink stood a butter dish, a mound of grated cheese, a box of eggs, pepper and salt, and a glass mixing bowl. Two eggs had been broken into the bowl, their cracked shells tossed into the sink. A frying pan with a pat of butter in it had been placed on the hob.

Jacquot moved round the table and came to the upturned chair. Beneath, darkening the tiled floor, was a smear of what looked like oil. He bent down. Put a finger to it. Sniffed. Tasted. Olive oil.

He stood up and looked across at Lanclos. 'Where are the bodies?'

Lanclos pointed to the hothouse door. 'Through there, Chief.'

The door the sergeant indicated was half open, and Jacquot stepped through into a narrow vestibule and then through a second open door into what he could only have described as a miniature rain forest.

'Quite something, eh?' Lanclos whispered behind him.

Quite something indeed, thought Jacquot, gazing up into a canopy of branches that pressed against a whitewashed glass roof maybe twelve metres above their heads. And at ground level the undergrowth was dense and dark, a jungle landscape pillared with palms and giant ferns. So thick was this ground cover and so convoluted the path they now followed that it was difficult to estimate the size of the hothouse. Its furthest reaches were lost in a green, shadowy gloom.

And the heat. Incredible. A hundred degrees, had to be, thought Jacquot, feeling the sweat creep in like a warm, wet tide beneath his clothes.

Somewhere near the middle of the doctor's hothouse, Lanclos stopped at a tiny glade set with gorgeously coloured blooms. 'Orchids,' he said. 'My nephew did a school trip here, told me all about it. "The German's Jungle", they call it. Apparently the doctor was a real prof about orchids.'

Jacquot nodded again. 'And the bodies?'

'This was the second we found, Chief,' replied Lanclos, pushing aside a screen of pointed leaves. 'Far as we can tell, it's the girl's mother, Ilse.'

Jacquot knelt and leaned forward to inspect the body more closely. Like the daughter in the driveway there seemed little left above the shoulders.

'Watch that pollen, Chief,' warned Lanclos, pointing out a spray of fat, bulbous flowers hanging perilously close to the shoulder of his coat. 'The devil to get out,' he continued, brushing at a smear of gold on his own sleeve. 'Stains something dreadful, it does.'

Leaving through a second set of double doors at the far end of the hothouse, Lanclos led Jacquot into the doctor's laboratory, its workbench furnished with a computer, a microscope and a wooden trug of tuberish roots. Set against the wall, a half-dozen shelves were filled with books and files.

'Did they live here? The daughter and granddaughter?' asked Jacquot, following Lanclos through another set of doors into the guest wing, where they climbed the stairs to the bedrooms. 'Or just visiting?'

'Just visiting, Madame Ramier said.'

Back in the guest living room, Jacquot pulled a handkerchief from his coat pocket and tried the French windows to the central courtyard. They were locked. 'Any other doors this side of the house? To the outside?' he asked.

'Four, Chief. But they're all locked. Bolted too.'

From the guest living room, following the circuit of the courtyard, they stepped into the sun lounge, through a utility room and into the kitchen once more. Stepping around the mess of plaster and shredded vegetables, they made their way back down the hallway to the front door.

'The other bodies?' asked Jacquot.

'This way, Chief. Up here,' said Lanclos, making for the stairs.

'A moment, please,' said Jacquot, putting out a hand to hold him back. 'When you first went up, did you go by the wall or the banister?'

'The banister, Chief,' Lanclos replied. 'But I didn't touch it, sir.'

'So go on up, just as you did. Show me.'

As instructed, Lanclos climbed the stairs.

Up on the gallery landing, the sergeant stood aside as Jacquot pushed open the first two doors, just as Lanclos had done. Then Jacquot moved along the landing, stepping round the shell casings, pushing open the last door with the toe of his boot.

He paused in the doorway, taking it all in: the built-in wardrobes; the shuttered windows; the connecting door to the bathroom; the shell casings on the floor; the bloodied bedclothes; and the lumpy, silent shapes beneath.

When, finally, Jacquot went in, Lanclos stayed where he was, watching the man's every move. Under his kepi, his scalp prickled with excitement. So this is Ponytail, he thought, as Jacquot paused in the middle of the room, turned slowly, running his fingers through the curve of black hair that had earned him the nickname, the ponytail that was definitely not regulation but that no one 'upstairs' had ever managed to do anything about. Lanclos had recognised Jacquot the moment he pulled himself from the car—the jeans, the cowboy boots, the 5,000-franc topcoat. And the ponytail, of course.

Everyone on the Force had heard of Ponytail. The stories from Marseilles, the busts, the action, pictures in the papers, rumours of dubious practices and a quiet transfer to the country. And that try, all those years ago. That run. Beating those *anglais* on their own turf. A legend on and off the pitch. But they'd never met. No reason to, until this.

'You didn't say anything about dogs,' said Jacquot, standing by a wicker basket by the bed.

'Dachshunds,' replied Lanclos, looking at the bloody remains half in, half out of the basket. 'They had a pair of them. I didn't think . . .'

Abruptly Jacquot turned on his heel and strode back out of the bedroom. On the landing, he paused and the sergeant saw the younger man's eyes light on the banister. He walked over to it, bent down and sighted along it to the front door. Straightening up, he ran a finger along the top, and then beneath it, between the posts. He nodded, then took a couple of steps back and looked again, eyes squinting, down into the hall.

Lanclos watched intently, though he hadn't for the life of him the vaguest idea what Ponytail was doing.

Jacquot turned and caught Lanclos's eye. 'So. Let's go.'

BY THE TIME Jacquot and Lanclos got back to their cars, the forensics team had arrived. There were seven of them, togged up in white boots and jump-suits. Jacquot nodded to the man in charge, Guy Fournier, his bald skull still brown from the previous summer, his ears reddening from the cold.

Already Fournier's team had isolated Kippi, setting up a tentlike wind-break round her body. And two men were already lugging their silver cases down the Martners' driveway to begin work on the other bodies.

'It's messy,' said Jacquot, walking over to Fournier.

'When isn't it?' said Fournier, shaking Jacquot's hand. 'I'll get you an initial report as soon as I can. Tomorrow some time. Details later, I'm afraid.'

Jacquot left them to it. From here on in, he knew, it was nothing but grind—straightforward forensic procedure. Hours bent over the bodies, hours searching the surrounding land, hours dusting for prints, making inventories, taking photographs. But with Fournier in charge, it would be a thorough job. The man would miss nothing, and he'd have that report on Jacquot's desk when he said he would.

But for now Jacquot had seen all he needed.

A single killer, he decided, as he tossed Brunet his car keys and got into the passenger seat. Despite the body count, this was someone working alone. Of that, for no reason beyond a familiar twist in his gut, Jacquot was certain. And, soon enough, Guy Fournier would confirm it.

A lone killer with a pocketful of cartridges and a shotgun.

On the journey back to Cavaillon, the two men stayed silent, as usual. Brunet had worked with Jacquot long enough to know that his boss liked to fix the progression of the crime in his mind as soon as possible, preferably on the way back to the office, and did not take kindly to interruptions.

And that was exactly what Jacquot was doing, sorting his initial observations into some kind of order, a sequence.

First of all—a single killer. And then, man or woman?

At this early stage Jacquot favoured a man. It seemed unlikely that a woman would have the strength and ferocity to fire off what looked like close to twenty rounds, as well as chase two of the victims before gunning them down. Also, had the killer been a woman, the daughter or granddaughter might have attempted to confront her, to reason or struggle with her, instead of fleeing. Which was why they'd both been shot in the back.

So, let's say a man, thought Jacquot, just for argument's sake. A tall man, taller at any rate than most women. On the steep staircase leading to the Martners' bedroom, Jacquot had observed dirt from the driveway on every second step. The murderer had climbed those stairs two at a time—not the way a woman would have done it, or the way that short-ass Sergeant Lanclos had done it during the re-enactment.

And judging by the position of the dirt on the stairs, the intruder had stayed close to the wall, to avoid the creak of old wood, maybe. In so doing, his shoulder had brushed against two of the ascending line of small floral prints that decorated it, pushing them slightly out of alignment, at a height equal to Jacquot's own shoulder. And Jacquot was a shade over six feet tall.

Also, Jacquot was in no doubt, the Martner bedroom was where the killer had been headed—the grandparents were the first to die. Because if he'd gone up there last, the Martners would have been woken by the sound of gunshots below, would have been up and maybe already phoning the police. Also, any dirt that the killer had brought in on his shoes would have been dispersed around the ground floor.

Jacquot decided that the murders had taken place in the dark, just before dawn, when Ilse, the Martners' daughter, had gone to the kitchen, switched on the light and started to prepare breakfast—for herself, just the two eggs. Jacquot felt that it must have been Ilse in the kitchen. Younger women like Kippi, like Claudine's daughter Midou, all tousled hair and sleep-swollen faces, were rarely seen before breakfast was on the table.

And Jacquot was certain that, when Ilse came from the guest wing to prepare her breakfast, the killer had already entered the premises, through the Martners' front door. And that by the time Ilse switched on the kitchen lights, the killer was already creeping along the landing towards the Martners' bedroom. Had Ilse come down any earlier, the killer would surely have dealt with her first. But he'd gone straight upstairs, nothing to divert or distract him. It seemed unlikely that he had known anyone else was up.

If, indeed, he had known anyone else was in the house. There was, after all, just the one car in the driveway. The Martners' BMW.

So the sequence of events started in the Martners' bedroom. Hearing shots, Ilse had come running down the hall just as the killer stepped out of her parents' bedroom, breaking the gun to eject the spent cartridges.

The killer sees the daughter below, snaps the gun closed, raises it to fire but hits the barrel on the underside of the banister, hard enough to leave an angled dent on an otherwise smooth surface. By the time he'd wrestled the gun clear of the rails, he had had time only for a wild shot that went high, cratering the plaster way above head height.

Although he wasn't a parent, Jacquot was certain that Ilse's first thoughts would have been for her daughter, most likely still in her bedroom in the guest wing. Her overwhelming instinct, Jacquot was sure, would have been to protect Kippi, to warn her. This was why Ilse had turned back into the house and not out through the open front door in an effort to escape.

So, down the hallway, through the kitchen she had raced, with the killer in pursuit, which was when maybe she realised that she'd made a mistake, that she should have gone the other way, through the front door, to lead the killer away from her daughter. But by now it was too late. She was trapped. All possible exits, save the front door, locked and bolted.

In these short, frantic moments the killer had caught up with Ilse, maybe trying to hide herself in the hothouse, and this time he found his target. So far as Jacquot had been able to determine, the first shot had been fired from a distance, had hit the woman's shoulder and sent her sprawling. The second, third and fourth had been delivered at close range. One merciless shot after another. When the first would probably have done the job.

And then? Had the killer heard something? The sound of running feet?

Or maybe Ilse had called out her daughter's name, trying to warn her. That would have been her second mistake. Alerting the killer. Unless he already knew there was someone else in the house. A fourth family member. Had he come to kill them all?

By this time, Kippi would have been wide awake, roused by the gunshots. She'd have flung on the dressing gown they'd found her in, grabbed her espadrilles, then dashed downstairs to see what was going on, only to hear her mother's screams and then the second volley of gunshots from the hothouse.

Three options would have presented themselves to the girl, Jacquot decided: go and see what was happening; find a good hiding place; or get the hell out of there. She'd gone for the third option, dashing through the sun lounge, the utility room and into the kitchen—away from the hothouse where she'd heard the shots, heading for the front door.

Only the killer, doubling back through the hothouse to get away himself or to cut her off, had rushed into the kitchen at exactly the same moment.

The smear of olive oil on the floor and the upturned chair, the way the ceiling plaster, lath, onion skins and herbs covered one section of the kitchen floor and table, furthest away from the hothouse doors, told the story here. As Jacquot read it, the killer had slipped on the oil, crashed into the chair and, falling backwards, pulled the trigger, loosing off another wild shot that shredded the onions and garlic hanging from a beam. Giving Kippi just enough time to hightail it out of the kitchen and out of the house.

Which was where she, too, had made a fatal error. Instead of going for the cover of the vines, or for the line of trees at the back of the house, she'd kept to the driveway, heading for the road. It was here, crucially, that she lost her espadrille. It was all the killer needed to catch her up.

The killer had fired, pitching the girl forward, then walked up to the body to finish her off with another unnecessary volley of shots.

That, in Jacquot's opinion, was the way it had happened.

But it was not the whole story. Jacquot may have established the how. What he needed was the why. And then he'd maybe find out who.

There was, however, one thing he was absolutely certain about. This had been a premeditated act. Nothing random here. No chance encounter. No burglary gone wrong. Someone had come to the Martner house with the express intent to kill. And the whole thing smacked of something personal. There was anger and hatred in the commission of this crime. An almost palpable sense of revenge. A settling of accounts.

But was it just the elder Martners he was after? Or the whole family? Had he reckoned on the daughter and granddaughter being in the house?

There was something else. The killer didn't seem particularly comfortable with a gun. There was something clumsy in the way he'd used it—banging the barrel against the banister in his haste, losing his balance in the kitchen and blasting off at the ceiling; and using so many shells when half the number would have done.

A jolt shook Jacquot out of his theorising as Brunet drove over the ramp and up through the gates into Cavaillon Police Headquarters.

Walking across the car park to the main entrance, Jacquot told Brunet what he wanted. Everything there was to know about the Martners. Back before they had come to France. The whole story. And bank accounts—money was always a good place to start when you were looking for a motive. And statements from anyone who knew them; they must have had a lawyer, a doctor, friends, acquaintances. And send some of the boys up to St Bédard. Liaise with Lanclos. House to house. The usual.

As they took the lift to the fourth floor, Brunet nodded. He knew the drill.

In his office, Jacquot shrugged off his coat, slid into the chair behind his desk and went through his messages. There was one from Claudine: if he could join them for lunch, fine; if not, well, they understood.

Jacquot glanced at his watch. A little after 1 p.m. There was everything to do, and nothing to do. He looked through his window at the blue sky and witch-hat belfry of Église St-Jean.

Brunet was on the phone in the outer office when Jacquot strode past, pulling his overcoat back on and winding the scarf round his neck. Brunet put his hand over the mouthpiece. 'Chief?'

'I'll be back by three. If something urgent comes up, you can find me at Gaillard's.'

WHILE JACQUOT, Claudine and Midou enjoyed their farewell lunch at Brasserie Chez Gaillard, St Bédard buzzed with news of the murders.

After making her statement at the gendarmerie, Madame Ramier had gone straight home, startling Adeline with her unexpected return.

No, she explained to her sister, she hadn't been sacked by the Martners. And no, she was not feeling ill. Although, come to think of it, she said, a glass of cognac might help to settle her nerves. At which point, Adeline hurried off to fetch the bottle from the living room.

And so, with the two of them seated at the kitchen table, a fresh log hissing in the hearth, Odile Ramier told her story for the second time that morning.

After more cognac had been poured, Adeline said that someone should put a call through to Curé Foulard, to advise him that his services would be required at the Martner house and that he should go there with the blessed sacrament without delay. Indeed, she would take it upon herself to do just that.

Telling Odile she should go and rest for half an hour, Adeline went to the living room, closed the door and sat down beside the telephone. And she did not leave it at the *curé*. For the next forty minutes she passed on to her wide circle of friends and acquaintances the story of her sister's shocking discovery.

The success of her news service was brought home to Adeline later that morning when, calling at the *pharmacie* to pick up her prescription, she was buttonholed by Madame Héliard and informed of the discovery before she had time to tell the story herself.

As she stepped out onto Place Vausigne in the centre of St Bédard, Adeline realised that if Madame Héliard knew about the murders then undoubtedly the whole town would know about them too.

By Wednesday lunchtime that was certainly the case. At the Chaberts' flower shop, the Fontaine des Fleurs, the Widow Blanc whispered the facts to Denise Chabert much as she had heard them over the phone from Adeline Séguin, with only a few embellishments. At the *tabac*, further down the road, Marc Tesserat reported to his wife Christine that six body bags had been delivered to the Martner house. And at the grocery, Clotilde Lepantre, standing on the pavement among baskets of kale and sacks of potatoes, repeated Madame Héliard's account to each of her customers, with the added detail that the police had started digging for more bodies.

Across the square, in the Mazzelli family's Bar de la Fontaine, Clotilde's husband, Claude, pushing up the sleeves of his purple shell suit and belly-ing up to the bar with his various cronies, repeated the version he'd heard from his wife. In Claude's possession, the story included the fact that the two younger women had been found naked.

It wasn't until Corporal Frenot went to Mazzelli's, to muster volunteers for a wider sweep of the Martner property planned for that afternoon, that the true facts of the case were finally established.

Shortly after lunch, the local press arrived. In a battered Audi, Roland Lucas, from the Cavaillon weekly paper, and his photographer sidekick Bernard-André Marchal pulled up at the Martner property but got no further than the taped driveway entrance.

Undeterred, they headed back to St Bédard and parked outside Mazzelli's bar in the square. Lepantre was still pontificating, and the town's grocer warmed to Lucas's offer of a large brandy and the company of a man who actually wanted to write down what he had to say.

While Marchal took a picture of Lepantre, Lucas moved on to Aldo Mazzelli, the bar's owner. A larger man than Lepantre, if that was possible, with a fine head of curly black hair, thick black brows and a nose the size and shape of a ripening aubergine, Mazzelli needed little prompting.

Lucas was scribbling away in his spiral-bound notebook, recording Mazzelli's recollections of the Martners—'quiet peoples, kept themself to themself'—when Mazzelli's son, Tomas, shouted from the doorway, 'TV's here,' and everyone's attention was directed at the square. A large white van bearing the France 3 logo was pulling up beside the boules pitch.

No one in St Bédard had seen a TV outside-broadcast operation before and so, by the time the cameraman had shouldered his videocam outside the gendarmerie, a small crowd had gathered. When the camera light came on, Tomas Mazzelli and his friend Eric Chabert, standing at the front, were reminded of the night lights at Cavaillon stadium when the A team played.

Sergeant Lanclos stood on the gendarmerie steps, nervously straightening his jacket as the interviewer, a tall brunette in a belted camel overcoat and leather boots, began her introduction.

'There is a sense of stunned disbelief in the picturesque old town of St Bédard today, following the discovery early this morning of four bodies . . .'

At the edge of the crowd, one of St Bédard's older residents, Simon Dumé, spat into the gutter. 'All this fuss for a bunch of Krauts,' he said, to no one in particular. 'You ask me, someone's done us all a big favour.'

BY THE TIME Jacquot returned from his lunch at Chez Gaillard, three green incident folders were sitting in the centre of his desk. The first contained the initial crime-report statement from Madame Odile Ramier, faxed through from the gendarmerie in St Bédard. Nothing that Jacquot didn't know already. The second contained photocopies of the Martners' bank accounts, faxed through from Crédit Agricole in Cavaillon, copies of credit-card statements, phone records for the last quarter, and a typed list of names, addresses and phone numbers, including those for the Martners' lawyer and doctor. Jean Brunet had been busy.

Inside the third folder were a dozen or more sheets of paper. The first bore the letterhead of the Cavaillon Regional Crime Squad: Brunet's faxed request to the German authorities for information concerning four deceased German nationals: Josef and Jutta Martner, and Ilse and Kippi Brauer. Beneath this were pages of photocopied official documents from Munich's Criminal Investigation Bureau and Federal Intelligence Service, and from the Public Records Bureau in Zürich.

As he studied the file, Jacquot wondered how Brunet had found out the daughter's married name so quickly, why the German and Swiss authorities had come back so promptly, and what a retired doctor living in St Bédard could have done to merit so much information from such quarters.

Leaning forward, Jacquot buzzed through to the outer office. A moment later Brunet knocked and entered.

'Brauer? How . . . ?' asked Jacquot, holding up the file as Brunet pulled out a chair, swung it between his legs and sat down, arms across its back.

'Driver's licence, passport, even a letter,' replied Brunet. 'All in the daughter's handbag, boss. I called Fournier at the house and had him check it out. He found it in the guest wing. Ilse Brauer. Husband's name Gunther. Swiss national. Kippi is their only child.'

'And do you happen to know where Herr Gunther Brauer is?'

'His letter came from New York. He's been there a month. A Treasury Bond analyst for the Swiss government seconded to Credit Suisse. I'm afraid we can count him out.'

Jacquot sighed. The first dead end. 'When's he due back?'

'Our Swiss colleagues are liaising with the bank. Someone will break the news to him when he gets in to work this morning, New York time. He should be on a plane out of there by late tonight. Tomorrow maybe.'

'Good work, Jean. I should go to lunch more often.'

'I just wish it was all so straightforward,' replied Brunet. 'Have you read the report yet?'

'Not yet. Just your enquiry fax. Flicked through the rest.'

'When you have, you'll see what I mean.' Brunet got to his feet and headed for the door. 'My bet is high-ranking visitors any day now.' With a nod and a grin, he was gone.

Jacquot turned his attention back to the file. The first few pages contained smudged copies of birth and marriage certificates.

Josef Otto Rupperich Martner, born Hamburg, August 1920.

Jutta von Diepenbroek, born Munich, February 1926.

Martner and von Diepenbroek, married Munich, September 1949.

Ilse Martner, born Munich, April 1951.

Martner and Brauer, married Zürich, October 1976.

Kirsten Jutta Brauer, born Zürich, October 1980.

So far, so ordinary, thought Jacquot, flipping back the pages. Except, except . . . Something familiar. Something he was missing.

And then, like a light switched on in a darkened room: the names. Big names. Von Diepenbroek! Jutta Martner's father. And Brauer! Ilse's husband; Kippi's father.

Jacquot turned to the following pages. Security clearances, personal resumés, a selection of blurred press cuttings. And anxious requests from the Swiss and German authorities for further information. Soonest.

Oh, *merde*, thought Jacquot. Brunet was right. Big guns, for sure.

IT DIDN'T TAKE LONG for the initial mood of excitement at the macabre events to turn sour and sombre. Murders. Blood. And a killer on the loose. In St Bédard of all places.

Marc Tesserat at the *tabac*, setting out his postcard racks the morning after the murders, was probably the first to notice it. An hour later than usual, the blinds were still down on Lepantre's grocery store and the Bulots' *charcuterie*. The Chaberts had still to set out their flower racks, and not a single table had been moved out onto Mazzelli's terrace. Only the smell of baking bread from Doriane's ovens in the street behind the square suggested that someone other than himself was at work.

By lunchtime not even the happy chatter of the fountain could lighten the mood. The boules pitch was empty when normally a game would be in progress, and a cold, unfriendly breeze riffled its way through the trees. On the steps of the *pharmacie*, Madame Héliard and the Widow Blanc conferred, while further down the square Adeline Séguin and Clotilde Lepantre did the same. When a pair of police vans pulled up outside the gendarmerie, all four stopped their whispering and turned in that direction as a dozen gendarmes clambered out to continue their house-to-house enquiries.

Only old Dumé seemed unmoved. Standing outside the Fontaine des Fleurs, he turned to Eric, the Chaberts' son, and said: 'Wasn't so long ago, my son, and they'd have given the killer a medal.'

'Before my time,' replied Eric, with a mournful look.

3

The big guns that Jacquot and Brunet had been expecting made their appearance three days after the discovery of the bodies.

Jacquot was at home when the call came through from HQ, in the bath, suds to his chin and a Cesaria Evora track on the headphones.

Claudine knew he'd never hear the low buzz of his mobile phone so she reached across the bed, where she'd been reading, snug and content after his Saturday-morning caresses, picked up the mobile and answered it. She recognised Brunet's voice. 'He's in the bath, Jean. Hold on, I'll get him for you.' Reluctantly she slid from the warmth of the bed, pulled on a dressing gown and padded across their bedroom to the adjoining bathroom.

The room was hot and steamy. In a scroll-top bath in the centre, Jacquot lay stretched out, elbows over the edge of the tub, head resting on a towel. His eyes were closed and his lips pum-pum-pummed to the beat of the music. Claudine knelt and tugged the hanging ponytail. He sat up abruptly, and a wave of soapy water surged over the edge of the bath.

She held out the mobile to him. 'It's Jean.'

Jacquot slipped off his headphones and took the phone. 'Yes, Jean?'

As he listened, he watched Claudine take the towel, drop it on the floor and move it round with her foot, mopping up the overflow and tut-tutting as she did so, revealing her long brown legs with each sweep, the tie of her dressing gown dancing across the taut skin of her thighs.

'A Chief Inspector Gastal is on his way down from Lyon with two gentlemen from the German authorities,' Brunet was saying. 'Hans Dietering from the Federal Intelligence Service and Frank Warendorf from Federal Criminal Investigation's Munich office.'

Jacquot sat up straighter. Heavyweights. Bigger guns than they'd expected. And then that other name. Gastal? Surely it couldn't be. Not Alain Gastal. From Marseilles. But it had to be. That was where they'd posted him. To Lyon. Gastal. Of all people. *Merde*.

'This Gastal phoned Mougeon,' continued Brunet. 'Told him to organise things. Said he wanted you and Rochet and everything we have so far.'

Mougeon was one of the desk sergeants at Cavaillon and Georges Rochet was the station head, Jacquot's immediate boss. Jacquot could imagine Rochet's annoyance at being called in on a Saturday. Not that he was too happy about it himself. There was a match that afternoon and he'd been looking forward to it—lunch with Claudine, a tumbler of Armagnac, a fat cigar and his feet up in front of the TV. Wales versus France.

And why the rush? Surely this could wait till Monday. They still hadn't received the full forensic report from Fournier's office, or the post-mortem findings from Pathology. All they had were the bare details.

'Where are you now?' asked Jacquot.

'I got in a few minutes ago. Thought I'd get everything organised.' Brunet lived in town, in a flat near Headquarters.

'Good. When are they expected?'

It was a two-hour drive from Lyon, so maybe there was still time for a late breakfast with Claudine before he had to leave. She had finished wiping the floor and had come to sit on the edge of the bath. The front of her dressing gown had loosened and the skin between her breasts shone, beaded with moisture from the heat and exertion.

Maybe breakfast in bed, thought Jacquot.

'The storm's a beauty,' replied Brunet, clearly holding back bad news. 'It's sure to slow them down.'

Jacquot's heart fell. 'When are they expected?' he asked again, now certain there'd be no time for breakfast. Or anything else.

'Half an hour, at the outside.'

'*Merde*,' said Jacquot, and broke the connection.

Claudine watched him step from the bath, reach for a towel and start to dry himself. He might be fifty, she thought, but he still had a good body. Firm and trim and strong enough, she well knew, to sweep her off her feet and carry her upstairs. She smiled. He was also a gentle man, an easy man to love. She remembered the first time they'd met, in that gallery in Marseilles, the off-duty *flic* buying one of her paintings, not knowing that she was the artist. And then the second time their paths crossed, a year later, here in Cavaillon, when he had raised her hand to his lips. He had been irresistible then—even before she properly knew him—and was irresistible still.

Claudine leaned forward and ran her fingers across Jacquot's wet backside. 'It's cassoulet for dinner. And then me. So don't be late home.'

'I could make it back for lunch, if I'm lucky.' He knew there was little chance of that.

So did she. 'Dinner will do fine. Anyway, I like you when you're hungry. Maybe me first and then the cassoulet. Work up an appetite.'

PEELING POTATOES at the kitchen table, Florence Picard looked up with a start as the first pellets of rain smacked against the windows of the Château de Vausigne. There was a storm brewing.

Maybe, she thought, a good blow would help clear the air. It certainly needed clearing. Overcast one day, sun the next, then clouds again the day after. All this chopping and changing. It set your teeth on edge.

Except Florence knew it wasn't just the weather that was bothering her. The last few days had been . . . uncomfortable. Everything out of sorts.

When Monique, the girl from the village who came in to help three days a week, had clattered down the kitchen steps on Wednesday afternoon and told her the news, the de Vausignes' housekeeper had had to sit down and have the girl fetch her a glass of Pineau des Charentes. Murder? In St Bédard? No, it wasn't possible, surely.

But of course it was. There it was on the radio, in the paper, on TV. Four murders—not half a dozen kilometres from the gates of the chateau. Just along the road. The nearest house.

That Wednesday, when she'd finished the Pineau, Florence had gone straight to the apartment above the kitchen and changed into black. It was the least she could do, a mark of respect. Not that there'd be black upstairs. Indeed, it was almost as if the news of the Martners' deaths hadn't filtered through to the Comte and Comtesse—even with everything in the papers and on TV. But, then, that was how it had always been. The Martners might have been neighbours, but not once, in the ten years they'd lived there, had the doctor and his wife ever set foot in the chateau. Of course, being German didn't help. But Florence knew it wasn't just a question of nationality. It was class, too. A retired dentist? *Mais non.*

JACQUOT DROVE FASTER than normal. Not just for the sake of his visitors from Lyon and Munich, but for himself. He liked the way the old Peugeot held to the curving lane that led down from Claudine's house, rows of bare vines flashing past. Not that driving fast along it was that risky. A few hundred metres behind the house—an old olive mill that Claudine had been carefully renovating since her mother died—the lane petered out into a grassy track leading up into the hills. And where it joined the Rocsabin to Barjas road a couple of kilometres down the slope, the *sans issue* sign ensured a certain privacy. Also, there was a point a few metres from the gate where it was possible to see the entire length of the lane spooling down to the valley. Since there were no turn-offs and no other houses, Jacquot knew he could always push the old Peugeot. It was a kind of private speedway.

When he reached Cavaillon HQ he pulled into the courtyard and parked beside a large black Mercedes. Brunet's big guns had beaten him to it.

Pulling up his collar, Jacquot hefted himself from the car, ran through the pelting rain and up the steps into the main hall of the gendarmerie. Brunet was waiting for him with Mougeon at the duty sergeant's desk.

'They arrived five minutes ago,' said Brunet. 'Went straight up to Rochet's office.'

The two men headed for the lift, Jacquot tugging off his raincoat. The lift bell pinged and the doors slid open. They got in.

'What are they like, the Germans?' asked Jacquot as the lift doors opened at the fourth floor and he and Brunet stepped out.

'Very pleasant,' said Brunet lightly. 'I think you'll like them.'

Walking a step ahead, Jacquot missed his assistant's grim little smile, but the moment they entered Rochet's office he knew that Brunet had been having him on. He didn't like the look of the visitors one little bit.

The three men sitting at Rochet's desk looked businesslike and, for a Saturday, faultlessly turned out. Creases were sharp, shoes buffed and tie knots set just so in stiff white collars. All three wore suits, the toad Gastal's ridiculously double-breasted, the ribbon of the Légion d'honneur tucked neatly into his buttonhole.

'Ah, Daniel, sorry to drag you in on a Saturday, but we need to brief our friends here,' said Rochet, a tall, gentle man for whom Jacquot had great regard. 'I believe you already know Chief Inspector Gastal?'

Of course Jacquot knew Alain Gastal. His old partner. As slippery as a skinned grape, a gunslinger street cop with dubious friends turned rising star at the Lyon offices of the Direction Générale de la Sécurité Extérieure. The man Jacquot had worked with in Marseilles for just two weeks—long enough to know that there would never be anything close to friendship, just a barely civilised brew made up of Jacquot's usually quiet restraint and Gastal's dangerous self-interest.

In Marseilles, three years earlier, that fragile brew had finally boiled over. A drugs bust had gone wrong, two hundred kilos of cocaine went missing, and Gastal had put Jacquot in the frame. When he realised what Gastal was up to, Jacquot had taken a swing in the commissioner's office and broken his partner's nose. They hadn't seen each other since.

But somewhere along the line, it was clear that Gastal had picked up some clout. Three weeks after their spat, Jacquot had been reassigned to

Cavaillon to work out his pension, a long way from any fast track, while Gastal found himself transferred to the DGSE in Lyon. Although they shared the same rank, Gastal's posting gave him a nominal superiority, which Jacquot had no doubt his old partner would use to the full.

A few years younger, Jacquot had told Claudine that morning, as he pulled on his coat at the front door. And ten times snottier. Dangerous, too.

Claudine, still in her robe, had leaned up to kiss him goodbye and, with their lips still touching, had said that Gastal, whoever he was, couldn't possibly know a woman who would do what she planned to do to Jacquot when he got home that evening.

Looking at Gastal now, for the first time in three years, Jacquot reckoned that Claudine was right. Which made him feel just that little bit better. He was also glad he'd gone no further than jeans and polo neck for the meeting, unconcerned by Gastal's disapproving once-over. And pleased, too, that he'd kept his weight. At forty-six, Gastal may have been a sharp operator in Marseilles, but the good life in Lyon had fattened him up, an accomplishment only narrowly camouflaged by the shiny double-breasted suit.

The two men shook hands, Gastal with an oily smile, Jacquot with a brief nod. Gastal made a point of staying seated.

'Danny. Always a pleasure.'

'Alain.' Jacquot smiled amiably, then turned to his companions.

Unlike Gastal, the two Germans had risen to their feet. The first, introduced with a wave of the hand by Gastal as Frank Warendorf, chief inspector from Munich Criminal Investigation Bureau, was a tall, heavyset man with wavy, mouse-coloured hair, the thickest eyebrows and blackest eyes that Jacquot had ever seen, and a sharp little smile that cut creases into his cheeks. He also wore glasses so delicate that Jacquot only noticed them when the light from Rochet's desk lamp flashed across the lenses.

His colleague, Hans Dietering, was as tall as Warendorf but slimmer, with a gym-trained figure. His rust-coloured hair was as sparse as Gastal's, but to compensate he'd cultivated a thin, clipped moustache, a strip of red sandpaper that rode above slightly gapped front teeth and a cleft chin. Both men, Jacquot decided, looked exactly how ambitious senior policemen should look: tightly Teutonic, corporate, disciplined and, he guessed, ruthlessly efficient and unimaginative. And for all their comradely politeness, their slim smiles and standing to shake his hand (Dietering accompanying the act with the faintest click of heels and a stiff bow), Jacquot had no doubt that it wouldn't take them long to get as far up his nose as Gastal had.

'Messieurs, welcome to Cavaillon,' nodded Jacquot, indicating that there was no need for them to stand. Pulling up a chair, he caught Brunet's eye. His assistant looked away studiously.

When everyone was comfortable, Gastal got the ball rolling. Dietering and Warendorf, he explained, had flown down from Munich the night before. Warendorf would be returning that evening but Dietering would be staying on as an observer.

'Observer?' asked Jacquot lightly.

'I'm booked in at the Novotel,' said Dietering before Gastal could reply. 'I'm here to help in whatever way I can. For as long as it takes.'

And report back to Gastal and Warendorf every move I make, thought Jacquot grimly, but noted that the man's voice was warmer than he'd expected, and his tone surprisingly deferential.

'Of course,' continued Warendorf, 'it goes without saying that the jurisdiction and direction of the case remain yours, but Hans here will be on hand whenever you need him. There are,' he added, 'certain security implications, I'm sure you'll appreciate.'

'This is not political,' said Jacquot. 'It's not an assassination, you know. It's a domestic, pure and simple. Someone just—'

'Nevertheless,' interrupted Warendorf, 'the Bureau would like to be involved, whatever the nature of the . . . ah, assault turns out to be. Frau Martner was very well connected, through her father. As is her daughter's husband, Herr Brauer. So, why don't we see what you've got so far?'

And with that, they set to work.

It was past two o'clock when Rochet suggested some lunch. For the first time since he'd set eyes on Gastal, Jacquot's spirits lifted. He was starving. He was about to get to his feet—maybe a late table at Chez Gaillard, with a nice chilled bottle of red Sancerre?—when Warendorf suggested they send out for sandwiches. There was much to be done, after all.

Warendorf looked across at Gastal, who nodded agreement.

'Good idea, just the thing,' said Gastal, though Jacquot suspected he didn't mean a word of it. Gastal loved his food.

Jacquot tried to catch Rochet's eye, but the older man avoided the look. 'Of course. Sandwiches,' said Rochet. 'Brunet, could you call Mougeon and have him rustle up something from the canteen?'

Jacquot clenched his teeth. No lunch. No rugby. No wonder he didn't like Germans.

It was getting dark by the time the meeting finally broke up. Sheltering from the rain at the top of the steps to the car park, the six men pulled up their collars and shook hands. Gastal and Warendorf were driving back to Lyon, and Rochet had to hurry if he was going to make the first act of *Der Rosenkavalier* in Orange. As for Brunet, he'd pulled a cape over his head, slipped on his cycle clips and was snapping down the catches on his helmet.

The Novotel for Dietering, thought Jacquot. A Saturday night. A stranger in town. He looked at the overnight case at Dietering's feet and knew there was nothing else he could do.

His teeth were clenched tighter than a vice, but he managed to speak through them all the same: 'Ever tried cassoulet, Hans?'

OLD DUMÉ SAT at a table by the door of Mazzelli's, watched the rain slant through the streetlights in the square and listened to the chat across the room. They were all there, hunched round the bar: Lepantre, in a gaudy shell suit; Bulot, twisting his butcher's whiskers; Mazzelli, perched on his favourite corner stool, a cigarette clamped between pudgy fingers; Tesserat, tapping his tin of pastilles on the zinc bar; and Fernand Chabert, stirring the ice in his pastis with a long spoon. Behind the bar, Tomas leaned back against the Gaggia and thumbed his way through a GameBoy, glancing up every now and then to see if any glasses needed topping up.

Sergeant Lanclos, in civvies, had left the bar a few minutes earlier after fielding their questions as to progress in the Martner investigation. Now, in full possession of the latest facts, the five of them debated what had perplexed everyone in St Bédard. Who could have done such a thing?

'It's not no one from round 'ere,' said Mazzelli. He had lived in St Bédard as long as any of them, but hadn't lost his fruity Italian accent. 'They not 'ave many friends, I grant you, but I don't think of any enemies either.'

'I'll tell you one thing,' said Lepantre. 'Whoever did it, they'll never find him. No way those cops from Cavaillon are going to crack this one. Load of schoolboys coming round asking their damn-fool questions. No, no, no. They're free and clear, whoever did it. Long gone by now.'

'So you don't reckon it's someone local, then?' asked Bulot.

Lepantre shook his head. 'You ask me, it's professional. A hit. Mafia, maybe. Or one of those German outfits—Baader-something. But I'll tell you this. There's money at the root of it. You'll see.'

'But you heard the sergeant,' said Bulot. 'There's nothing stolen. And all that money in the kitchen drawer. Thousands, that's what he said.'

'What I mean is,' said Lepantre, 'there's money maybe owed and not repaid. A debt not honoured. That sort of thing. Look at what they spent on Taillard's place, doing it up. And the holidays. All over the place they were. And he's a dentist? What dentist earns that kind of money, eh? Tell me that. They borrowed too much, somewhere shady, and couldn't pay it back.'

'But why the child?' asked Chabert quietly. 'Why kill the child?'

'I'll tell you why,' said Tesserat. 'Because the girl recognised the killer.'

Mazzelli looked doubtful. 'So what you're sayin', you think the killer come from round here?'

'Not necessarily,' replied Tesserat. 'Maybe it's someone from where they lived before. Someone catching up with them, tracking them down.'

'You're all of you wrong, is my opinion.'

It was Dumé by the window, digging out the bowl of his pipe with a matchstick. The men at the bar turned in his direction.

'They was Krauts,' Dumé went on quietly. 'There's people still remember . . . You ask me, it's a settling of accounts. It's for what they did back then. Martner? He's one of them. And old enough. You mark my words, there's something he probably done come home to roost. And good riddance,' added Dumé, picking up his stick from the back of his chair and making for the door. 'Good riddance to the lot of them, is what I say.' And pulling open the door he stepped out into the hammering rain.

THERE HAD ALWAYS been the slim possibility that Hans Dietering would decline Jacquot's invitation to share Claudine's cassoulet. It wouldn't have taken the greatest skills of deduction on Dietering's part for him to realise that Jacquot was simply being polite.

But rather than decline, the man had said he would be delighted. And please, he said, as they hurried through the rain to Jacquot's car, now that they'd be working together, to call him Hans.

'Daniel,' said Jacquot. 'Or Dan. Whichever you wish.'

'Daniel for now,' replied Hans, snapping on his seat belt and loosening his tie with a 'do-you-mind?'.

Jacquot responded that he had no objection, and tried, as he pulled out of the gendarmerie, to work out which of them held the higher rank. Not that Hans appeared to care.

Five minutes later, as they approached a garage on the outskirts of town, Dietering asked him to pull in, jumped from the car and returned from the garage shop a few minutes later with a paper cone of flowers, a box of almond sweets and a bagged bottle.

'For your wife,' he explained, turning to drop the gifts on the back seat. 'And for us, too,' he added, opening the bag to reveal a bottle of what Jacquot knew was the most expensive Armagnac on the shelves.

'That's very kind of you,' said Jacquot, not bothering to correct Dietering about Claudine being his wife.

Later, Jacquot reckoned Claudine must have seen them getting out of the car, for when she opened the front door she showed not the least surprise or irritation that he had company. And taking in his apologetic there-was-nothing-I-could-do grimace behind Dietering's back, she'd made more of their unexpected guest than she might otherwise have done, to cover Jacquot's gentle annoyance and let him know she didn't mind the intrusion.

And of course the flowers, almond *calissons* and Armagnac helped.

That evening, contrary to expectation, Hans Dietering proved a most entertaining guest. Apologising to Claudine for his intrusion, he wasted no time in making himself thoroughly agreeable.

When Claudine led them through into the living room, he had stepped down into the old mill room to admire the watercolour landscapes—studies of the Montmirail hills, fields of lavender, a church spire above pantiled roofs—that Claudine had painted for her summer exhibition in Aix.

While Jacquot watched his colleague, he tried to decide whether Dietering's behaviour was sincere enthusiasm or practised charm. Despite himself, he had to admit that it seemed like the former. The man looked genuinely impressed with the way Claudine had done the place up, and at no time did Jacquot get the sense that he was thinking, Some coop for a cop. Which was what most people would have thought.

Three years earlier, after the Gastal business in Marseilles, Jacquot had arrived in Cavaillon without a friend in the world and with a blot on his copybook as big and black as a Périgord truffle. Most of his colleagues down south had reckoned on his resigning rather than take up a dead-end posting in Cavaillon. But for Jacquot, resignation had never been an option. He liked his job, and Marseilles or Cavaillon made little difference. With a philosophical shrug and only six years to run to a full pension, he had packed a bag and headed north.

And had met Claudine. For the second time. The sales assistant he'd wondered about in that gallery in Marseilles. The one who'd painted that lemon on a plate he kept in his study. As far as he was concerned, leaving Marseilles for Cavaillon had turned out to be the best thing he'd ever done.

While Claudine made things ready in the kitchen—a salad of chicken livers to precede the cassoulet—Jacquot pulled the cork from a bottle of Chablis she'd left on ice by one of the sofas. As he poured the wine and passed a glass to Dietering, the German asked about the house's history.

Standing there by the fire, a chilled glass of wine in hand, Jacquot found himself warming to Dietering. Somewhere between police HQ and home the man had lost his polished stiffness. His voice had become less curt, while the thin red moustache, Jacquot now decided, rather suited him. Without his tie and jacket, slipped off with his raincoat, Dietering fitted into their home as comfortably as an old friend. He could tell a good wine when he tasted one and he'd nodded appreciatively when Jacquot selected Stan Getz as a background soundtrack.

By the time Claudine called them through to the kitchen, Jacquot was pleased that he'd invited the man to join them for supper.

At the kitchen table, when Claudine passed him a steaming bowl of cassoulet, Dietering had immediately broken off telling them about the arrival three months earlier of his first child to concentrate on the food. Which, Jacquot knew, was the kind of behaviour Claudine appreciated. A man who stopped talking about something as important as family to taste something, savour it. Which he did, shaking his head in disbelief at the first mouthful, as though he'd never had better.

It was way past midnight when Dietering finally got up to leave, the taxi he'd insisted on ordering haloed with silvery rain in the driveway. Standing on the front steps, he had taken Claudine's hand and raised it to his lips, tipping his head but keeping his eyes on hers, accompanying the display with the lightest of heel clicks.

'It's been a long time since you kissed my hand,' said Claudine later, as she and Jacquot folded themselves into their bed, snuggling into each other.

'I've moved on,' he whispered. 'Found more interesting places,' and she felt his hand on her hip, pulling her round to him.

JACQUOT QUICKLY discovered that Hans Dietering was as agreeable at work as he had been as a guest in their home, far more useful than a mere observer, and far less the nuisance he had feared.

With Brunet out of the office coordinating a wider sweep for the murder weapon in the Martner grounds and taking statements in and around St Bédard, Dietering was quick to fill his place, happy to take on even the most menial jobs—a hands-on, let's-not-bother-with-office-protocols approach that Jacquot thoroughly approved of.

Without being asked, Dietering had photos of the murder scene and victims copied and distributed among the investigating team and, once he'd discovered the way Jacquot liked his coffee, always arrived at the office with two polystyrene cups from the café on the corner. He even wrote briefing statements for the press, always seeking Jacquot's approval before sending them out. Most important, however, was that at no time in the four weeks they ended up working together did Dietering ever question Jacquot's handling of the case, or his sense of direction.

It had begun with the doctor's orchids.

Jacquot had started thinking about them that Saturday night after Dietering left for the Novotel. Which was maybe why he'd woken the following morning with an image of the hothouse in his head.

'The German's Jungle', Lanclos had called it. School parties visited. It was a remarkable place. Jacquot had seen nothing like it, save at zoos and botanical gardens. Why, the heating alone must have cost a fortune.

It was that thought, as he buttered a croissant at the kitchen table on Sunday morning, that brought him up short. For Jacquot suddenly realised that there was nothing he could remember seeing in the Martners' financial records to account for the expense of maintaining the hothouse.

And what about the travelling? Four trips in the last couple of years, according to Brunet, who'd gone through the Martners' passports. To the Philippines. Borneo. Papua New Guinea. Malaysia. All expensive outings. More than a month away each time. Presumably in search of orchids.

And not a single one of those trips, Jacquot was certain, had shown up as a debit in either their bank-account or credit-card records.

By the time Jacquot got into the office on Monday morning, he knew that the first thing he wanted to do was go back to the Martner place and take a closer look at that hothouse. He looked at his watch. It wasn't even eight yet. He picked up the phone and put a call through to the Novotel.

Ten minutes later he was pulling out of the hotel car park with Dietering snapping on his seat belt.

'I thought you ought to have a look at the Martner place,' explained Jacquot, as they eased up into the hills above Cavaillon. 'No point working on the case if you're not familiar with the scene-of-crime. I'll give you the quick tour, then you can root about by yourself.'

At the entrance to the Martner driveway, Dietering leapt from the car to lift the police tape, then rejoined Jacquot. A minute later Jacquot stopped the car halfway down the drive and the two men got out.

'The first body was found here,' said Jacquot, pointing to the telltale depression in the gravel. 'The granddaughter, Kippi Brauer.'

Leaving the car where it was, the two men made their way to the house. Down in the valley, a ribbon of mist marked the river and on the crests of the hills a capping of snow showed against a blue horizon.

'Typical Provençal house,' explained Jacquot, as the Martner place came into view—breadcrust-coloured walls, blue shuttered windows and, just visible above the sloping tiled roof, the painted glass canopy of the hothouse. 'Hundreds like them in these parts. Used to be a farm.'

Dietering looked around appreciatively at the view. 'Nice place,' he said. 'Must have cost something.'

'Three million francs,' said Jacquot. 'According to the construction firm the Martners brought in, they spent another million doing it up. Total, about the same amount they got for their house in Paris.' He pulled the front-door keys from his pocket. 'The door was open when we got here. But no keys in the lock. And no sign of forced entry.'

'So either the door was unlocked and the killer just walked in, or he . . .'

'Who said it's a he?' asked Jacquot, fitting the key into the lock, turning it and pushing the door open.

'It just feels like a he,' replied Dietering. 'Wouldn't you say?'

Jacquot shrugged and stepped aside, letting his companion go first.

Although the house had changed, signs of violence still remained. The bodies might have been removed, the plaster on the hall floor swept away and the kitchen tidied up, but the hallway wall and kitchen ceiling were still cratered by shotgun blasts; light switches, door frames and handles were all smudged with the grey print powder left by Fournier's boys, and the floors were taped with tiny white squares where shell casings had been retrieved.

Just as Lanclos had done with him, Jacquot led Dietering on a tour of the house. Then, leaving him to snoop around by himself, Jacquot went back downstairs and made his way to the hothouse. Pulling off his coat and draping it over his shoulder, he wandered along the gravel path, breathing in the warm, loamy smell of hot soil, treading between the woodchip beds and bending beneath low, overhanging branches.

At the far end, he pushed through the double doors leading to Martner's lab and felt the temperature drop by about twenty degrees. He looked round at the equipment: Dolenz electronic weighing scales, powerful Apple Mac computer and Zeiss microscope. Everything top-of-the-range, pretty much brand new, and pricey. He reckoned there wouldn't be much change from

100,000 francs. As hobbies go, a pretty expensive one. Equipment, heating, travel. It all added up. But where had the money to pay for it all come from?

Five minutes later, Jacquot found Dietering in the doctor's study, flipping through a magazine taken from a shelf of similar magazines. '*Herr Doktor* took his flowers very seriously,' he said. 'Every book you see—orchids, orchids, orchids. Every magazine . . .' He gestured with the one he held. 'An expensive pastime, I believe.'

'Funny you should say that,' replied Jacquot.

FOR THE NEXT three days—after establishing from Sudelec that the Martners' quarterly heating bills were close to four times the domestic average during the winter months and always settled in cash over the counter at Sudelec's office in Aix; that the cost of the doctor's equipment considerably exceeded Jacquot's estimate; and that the Martners' foreign trips were paid for, as Jacquot had guessed, in cash, through a travel agent in Avignon—he and Dietering followed the orchid trail, visiting suppliers and nurseries whose names they had sourced from the doctor's laboratory Rolodex.

'Cash,' said a Monsieur Thibault, who ran a nursery-supply outlet in Salon and looked sad when he learned that this particular customer would not be returning. 'Always cash.'

Another supplier outside Orange, Pierre Salvaudon, told the same story. 'He just came in, bought what he wanted and left,' he said, returning the photo that Dietering had handed him. 'I never knew his name.'

'Always cash?' asked Jacquot.

Salvaudon thought for a moment, then nodded. 'Cash.'

When Dietering asked how much the doctor had spent with him each year, Salvaudon looked a little nervous. As had his colleague in Salon.

Jacquot wasn't surprised. In every business he'd ever heard of, cash had a way of disappearing from balance sheets. So the two policemen agreed that double the amount Thibault and Salvaudon had suggested would probably be a more realistic evaluation. And a very substantial sum it was too.

Yet there was still no sign of where the money had come from.

'Maybe,' suggested Dietering, 'Martner was selling his orchids to other collectors for cash and not declaring the income.'

Which was how they came to visit the half-dozen collectors in the region whose names Dietering gleaned from a collectors' website. All of them had heard of Martner and two had met him.

'I visited him once,' said Paul Marquand, a retired banker whose home in the hills outside Aix had been extended, like the Martners' place, to provide space for his collection. It was, Jacquot noted, a smaller version of Martner's hothouse. And while the blooms Marquand proudly pointed out looked suitably extravagant, they were not a patch, even to Jacquot's untutored eye, on those belonging to the doctor.

'He invited you?' asked Dietering.

Marquand shook his head. 'No, no. I just dropped by. We'd never met but we'd heard of each other, you know. It was . . . astonishing. I couldn't believe what I saw there. The most fabulous colours, shapes, textures. Quite remarkable. He had a magnificent set of *sanderens* that I'd never seen so heavily laden. Like a waterfall. A cascade. And the fragrance!'

'How much would flowers like that be worth, Monsieur?' asked Dietering.

'I would have paid him ten thousand francs. Just for one.'

'You offered?' asked Jacquot.

Marquand nodded. 'Of course. Who wouldn't? And there was enough there to spare, I can tell you.'

'But he wouldn't sell to you?'

'He just laughed, shook his head—"Nooooo, noooo, noooo, M'sieur."'

'Did you ever hear of him selling to other collectors?' asked Dietering.

'Never. Not Martner,' replied Marquand, emphatically. 'What was his was his. Just ask Balou. He would've loved to get his hands on them.'

The next morning, at the Jardins Balou a few miles outside Lucat, one of the largest nurseries in the region, the owner, Gaston Balou, told them all he could about orchids and the Martner collection. A small, chubby man in his fifties, he had been working with orchids for twenty years, he said, selling them in his nursery to cover his own collecting costs.

'It was remarkable, really,' Balou told them in his office, its bookshelves sagging, the windowsills, filing cabinets and desk covered with pots of thickly leafed tubers and delicate flowering stems. 'I couldn't believe it when I saw what Dr Martner was doing. He'd started hybridising terrestrials and epiphytes with fantastic results. He could have made a lot of money. But he never sold a single plant. I know collectors who contacted him, asked if he'd be willing to sell. Me too. But he never did.'

'So what kind of money are we talking about, Monsieur?' asked Dietering.

'Hard to say, but blooms like his can make up to four thousand dollars a stem. Often more. Especially the ones he had. Some I'd never seen before.'

'And what kind of costs would be involved in creating these new strains, and keeping them in that hothouse environment?' asked Jacquot.

Balou blew out his cheeks. '*Pfeu!* I only saw his place the one time, you understand, but it was the business, I can tell you.' He shook his head. 'Say three hundred thousand a year?'

Back at HQ, Jacquot asked Dietering to call a number Balou had given them—a Dr Clemens of the Palmgarten Institute in Hamburg. According to Balou, Clemens was as high up the orchid tree as it was possible to get.

Fifteen minutes later, Dietering set the phone in its cradle. 'As Balou told us, Martner's is a most important collection. According to Clemens, his research notes alone would be worth their weight in gold. As for the flowers, Clemens said it would be difficult to put a value on them. He says it is essential they are cared for until a new home can be found.'

It was at that very moment, a full week after the discovery of the bodies, that Herr Brauer—husband, father and son-in-law of the deceased—appeared in Jacquot's office.

4

They'd been expecting a visit from Herr Brauer but no one knew when. According to the Swiss authorities, he'd returned from the States to the family home in Zürich on the Friday following the murders.

Normally, a surviving family member would have been brought in for questioning and to provide formal identification of the bodies at the earliest opportunity. But since there were no features left to recognise on any of the victims, it was agreed that photos would be taken—of a tattoo on Kippi's ankle, a constellation of moles on Ilse Brauer's thigh, the rings on Madame Martner's left index finger, and a watch that the doctor had been wearing—and faxed through to Zürich for Herr Brauer to identify.

A statement from Herr Brauer accompanied the formal confirmation of identity that he faxed back three hours later. There was a brief note taken by the Swiss authorities giving his whereabouts at the time of the murders—New York—along with his sworn testimony that he could think of no reason for such a brutal act, no one with a grudge against the family.

Police authorities in Zürich also confirmed that Herr Brauer had had no idea his daughter was pregnant, adding that they had started interviewing Kippi's friends in an attempt to trace the father of her unborn child.

Now Herr Brauer was here, ushered into Jacquot's office by Sergeant Mougeon. Tall, with thin brown hair neatly parted, dressed in polo neck, grey flannels and loafers, and wrapped in a green loden coat that seemed a size too large for him, Brauer looked utterly diminished by his loss. His eyes were reddened behind oval, wire-framed spectacles, and his shoulders were stooped. He was accompanied by a lawyer, Pierre Boudit, of Boudit Frères in Zürich, shorter by six inches than any of them, and rounder too.

After introductions had been dealt with and coffee declined, there was a pause while Dietering darted into the squad room to bring in more chairs, at the same time covering the glossy black-and-whites of the murder scene and victims pinned to the incident board. After indicating that Herr Brauer and his lawyer should make themselves comfortable, Dietering expressed his condolences in German. Then Jacquot took over, bringing their visitors up to date on the progress of the investigation—no real leads as yet. But he managed to make it sound better than it was.

When he had finished, Brauer nodded but made no comment.

'Tell me,' continued Jacquot, 'did your wife visit her parents often?'

'Maybe once or twice a year,' replied Brauer.

'And whenever your wife came here, your daughter came too?'

'Of course. I am away a lot . . . and Kippi is . . .' Brauer took a breath, steadied himself. 'Kippi was too young to be left on her own. Anyway, Josef and Jutta loved their granddaughter. And she them.'

'And you, Herr Brauer, did you ever visit? Here in Provence?'

Across Jacquot's desk, Brauer shook his head. 'No. Never.'

'So when did you last see your parents-in-law, Dr Martner and his wife?'

Brauer gave it thought. 'Some time ago now. At least five years.'

'Tell me, did you get on with your wife's parents?'

Brauer took a breath, sighed. 'No, I did not.'

'Might I ask why?'

'Soon after they moved here from Paris . . . I discovered they had borrowed money from us. From my wife.'

'A lot of money?'

'At least a hundred thousand francs,' replied Brauer. 'I told my wife it must stop. I was not prepared to subsidise their extravagances. They had their own investments. If the returns were not enough, they should have economised.'

'These "extravagances" . . .'

'Their lifestyle, if you like. The holidays . . .'

Jacquot nodded. 'And was this loan . . . repaid?'

'Not that I am aware of. I never asked my wife about it again. It was enough for me that she gave her word that no further payments would be made. Whether the money was repaid was her concern.'

Jacquot decided to change tack. 'Tell me, Herr Brauer, did you have any idea that your daughter was pregnant?'

'No idea at all. It was a shock.'

'Did your wife know?'

Brauer sighed. 'Apparently. I found a letter addressed to my wife . . . when I got home. It was from a clinic. The Brücke. It is well known.'

'Your wife had arranged for the pregnancy to be terminated?'

'It appears that that would be the case. Yes.'

'And did your daughter have a boyfriend? A particular friend?'

Brauer shook his head. 'Not that I am aware of. Although . . .'

'Although?'

'Kippi was at a difficult age. Seventeen. She was starting to live her own life and did not particularly . . . communicate with us . . .'

Jacquot nodded again. 'Well, thank you for your cooperation, Herr Brauer. I know how difficult all this must be. You have been most helpful.'

For a moment no one moved, no one spoke.

And then the lawyer, Boudit, piped up: 'I wonder, Chief Inspector, whether it would be possible for my client to visit the Martner property?'

AN HOUR LATER, Monsieur Boudit, Dietering and Jacquot made themselves comfortable in the Martners' living room while Brauer prowled the house. They could hear cupboard doors opening and closing, drawers sliding. And once, from the kitchen, a pitiful sobbing. Jacquot and Dietering looked at each other, wondering whether one of them should go to comfort the man, but Boudit shook his head and they remained where they were.

When Brauer finally joined them, he thanked them for their patience and then, turning to his lawyer, rattled off a volley of Swiss German.

Jacquot looked at Dietering, who shrugged, meaning, as Jacquot sensed, that it was of no great significance.

When Brauer had finished, the round, squat Boudit turned to the two detectives and began speaking in a high-pitched wheeze: 'Herr Brauer wishes to make arrangements for his wife's and daughter's belongings to be sent home to Zürich. If that is acceptable to you, Monsieur?'

Jacquot nodded. The property was no longer a secure scene-of-crime, he told the lawyer. 'And the house? The cars? Those items belonging to Herr

Brauer's parents-in-law?' he asked, already aware from talks with the Martners' local lawyer that there were no beneficiaries beyond Brauer.

Once again Monsieur Boudit spoke for his client. 'Herr Brauer has instructed me to ask that the property be put on the market as soon as you have everything you need. As for the contents, there are certain items that my client would like to keep—albums, photos, family things. A list will be provided. As for the rest, it can be disposed of locally, at auction. Of course, if anything still has some pertinence to the investigation . . .'

Jacquot shook his head. The house could be cleared.

'There has been some damage done to the property.' Boudit coughed diplomatically. 'If you have no objection, Monsieur, we would like the house repaired and repainted prior to it being offered on the market.'

'I have no objections,' replied Jacquot. 'And Dr Martner's orchids?'

Monsieur Boudit's brow knotted. 'Orchids?'

It was clearly the first Boudit had heard about orchids. Even Brauer looked puzzled.

'Dr Martner was an authority on orchids,' explained Jacquot. 'One of Germany's foremost taxonomists and an expert hybridiser. I am reliably informed that the doctor's collection, along with his library, forms a most valuable legacy. If it stays here uncared-for . . .'

Boudit conferred with his client, who shrugged, as though the orchids were of no interest. Then Boudit turned back to Jacquot. 'We will make enquiries as to the best course of action and my office will be in touch. For the time being, I will make arrangements locally for the collection to be cared for in whatever way is appropriate.'

A few days later, Jacquot found out what Herr Brauer had decided to do. According to a letter from Boudit Frères, the collection would remain in place until the sale of the property, at which time Martner's orchids, library and research notes would be shipped to Dr Clemens at the Palmgarten Institute in Hamburg, which would make a significant contribution to a charity of Herr Brauer's choice in return for the collection. In the meantime, the Martner hothouse would be monitored by the Dassy Nursery in Aix.

FOR TWO WEEKS following Brauer's visit, the investigation ground on with little real progress. Soon, pretty well everyone within a ten-kilometre radius of the Martner property had been interviewed regarding their whereabouts at the time of the murders and questioned about any relationship they might have had with a member of the family.

In St Bédard there were a number of such relationships. The Martners had held accounts at Lepantre's grocery, the Bulots' *charcuterie* and with the baker Doriane. Each account was overdue for payment. Then there was Eric Chabert at the Fontaine des Fleurs, who'd worked as Martners' gardener when Denise and her husband Fernand could spare him. And the Martners had often dined at the Parmentiers' *auberge*, most recently that last weekend, for a birthday celebration. All of them had seemed in good spirits. It was the same story three doors down at Au Broc Fontaine, the antiques dealer André Ribaud reporting that Jutta Martner was a regular visitor.

Brunet and his squad of gendarmes had managed to establish that most people in the picturesque old town of St Bédard—save early risers like Tomas Mazzelli, Eric Chabert and Georges Doriane—had been in bed when the murders took place some time between five and seven in the morning. Or in the bath, or shaving, or getting ready for work or, in Claude Lepantre's case, engaged in his morning constitutional. Impossible to verify any of them one way or the other.

As for friends, it seemed the Martners had kept to themselves. Their address book provided no real leads and no one the police interviewed would volunteer more than a passing acquaintance with the family.

Which surprised Dietering. 'Ten years here and no friends? No dinner parties? No lunches?' he said, driving Jacquot back to Cavaillon after they had called on the heating engineer in Avignon who'd installed the doctor's hothouse system.

'You have to remember,' said Jacquot, 'they weren't from round here.'

'You mean they were German.' Dietering accompanied the remark with a smile, red moustache twitching as he glanced across at his passenger.

Jacquot shrugged. 'We're not known for our warm welcome, Hans. It takes time in these parts. And ten years? A tick of the clock, my friend.'

'It didn't take you ten years.'

'Maybe the Martners didn't have my charm,' replied Jacquot lightly.

What he wanted to say, what he felt, he kept to himself. Memories were long hereabouts. People hadn't forgotten. Especially the old ones.

'Could it be the war?' It was as though Dietering had read his mind.

Jacquot shifted in his seat. 'At the last count there were more than two hundred German families living in Provence,' he began, 'excluding the Côte d'Azur. And there are a further fifteen hundred, Hans, who maintain properties here and in the Languedoc. They stay for a month in the summer, a week at Christmas, and rent out the rest of the time. Then there are the tourists. More than a quarter of a million German visitors last summer. A month. And that's just hotel records. There may have been many thousands more putting up at *chambres d'hôtes* and the like, or coming on business. In and out the same day. But in the last seven years, excluding the World Cup, only seventy-three German nationals have been the victims of crime in Provence. And only six of those were fatalities. Most of them drug-related.'

Jacquot might not have remembered the figures exactly, but they were roughly what Brunet had come up with a few days after the murders, when Jacquot had been considering the nationality issue.

'Believe me, Hans,' Jacquot continued. 'The Martners were not killed because they were German.' But the moment the words were out of his mouth he felt a twist of discomfort, knowing somehow that, despite the statistics, the words didn't quite ring true. He knew all too well what people felt about the Germans, even after more than half a century.

'Anyway, how about dinner?' he said, keen to change the subject. 'Claudine's got a *gigot*. She said to ask you.'

'She could be offering burnt toast,' replied Hans, pulling into Headquarters, 'and I would still find it impossible to decline. So. Yes. Thank you.'

THAT FIRST NIGHT when he shared their cassoulet hadn't been the only time Dietering had visited the Jacquot home. He'd become a regular and increasingly welcome guest, joining Jacquot and Claudine for supper on several occasions. If he'd stayed in town at weekends, it would probably have been more often. But with a new family back home, Dietering had persuaded his superiors to agree to a five-day week rather than a permanent posting to Cavaillon. That meant flying out of Marseilles each Friday evening and back again on Monday morning. Which was when, Jacquot was certain, he submitted his progress reports. And from the moment Dietering had joined the team, there'd been no questioning from Lyon of the handling of the case. Which could only mean that he was reporting back favourably.

This had been confirmed the previous week, when Jacquot and his boss, Rochet, had shared a lift together. Although Rochet knew that the Martner investigation was going nowhere fast, he was clearly grateful that the right noises were being made by their German friend. According to Rochet, Gastal and the German authorities were well pleased with the way things were going, the leads that were being pursued—interesting angles, they'd said. And although everyone now seemed to agree that the murders looked less and less likely to have been political, Dietering remained at his post.

That evening, as the two detectives joined the queue of traffic out of Cavaillon, Jacquot brought up the question of reports.

Dietering hesitated. 'I tell them everything we do,' he said at last. 'I may have . . . coloured our leads and our progress on the case, but I have always said the truth. As I see it.' He glanced at Jacquot. 'Also, anything that keeps your esteemed colleague Herr Gastal off our backs is, like an invitation from you and Claudine to dinner, a pleasure quite impossible to resist.'

Jacquot was stunned at this disclosure. 'You don't like him, then?'

'Do you?'

'As a matter of fact . . . not one little bit. We used to work together.'

'You have my sympathy,' said Dietering. 'He is not a man I would like at my side in a difficult situation. And you know something else? There's nothing I dislike more than a fat policeman. In a smart suit.'

That evening the two men drank more Armagnac than they should have, and Dietering, instead of taking a taxi back to his hotel, passed out on the sofa.

The following morning, arriving at the office an hour late, tongues dry, heads hammering, they discovered that, three weeks and two days after the murders, the Martner case had taken a new turn.

WHEN JACQUOT and Dietering entered the office, Brunet was standing at his desk, hand clamped over his phone. 'A man called Benedict. Says he knows you, Chief. Says he's found a gun.'

It took a moment or two for the information to sink in, skimming like a pebble over a foggy lake of Armagnac. Jacquot squinted. That name. Benedict. Not Max Benedict? It couldn't be.

He took the phone. 'Jacquot,' he said, more briskly than he felt.

'Why, Chief Inspector. *Quel plaisir*. Such a long time.'

Three years, thought Jacquot, recognising the low, bourbony drawl, remembering the last time he'd heard it in that bar off Marseilles's Vieux Port, the day he had packed his bags and come north.

'And such a small world,' continued Benedict. 'I heard you'd been transferred but I had no idea we'd end up in the same place.'

'You live round here?'

'About four miles west of Rocsabin. A little farm I found a few years back. I've been letting it out, but I moved back in last week.'

Which explained why Jacquot had seen no statement from Max Benedict. With a house so close to St Bédard, he'd certainly have been interviewed in the days following the murders if he'd been in residence.

'My colleague tells me you've found a gun,' said Jacquot.

'I have indeed. I'm looking at it now.'

'And you are . . . where?'

'A hundred metres off the Brieuc road. On the border, if I'm not mistaken, of the Martner property.'

OF ALL THE PEOPLE to find the murder weapon it had to be a journalist, thought Jacquot, as he and Dietering sped out of Cavaillon.

And not just any journalist. Max Benedict. *The* Max Benedict.

A lean, rangy Texan, bald as a boule, suspiciously single and in his sixties, Benedict specialised in high-society crime—scandal by any other name—and was a master at getting stories. He and Jacquot had met in Marseilles where Benedict had covered the murder of an American heiress.

Three years later, Benedict was back in Jacquot's life.

He was sitting beneath an olive tree when Jacquot and Dietering arrived. They'd parked by the black Chevy SUV he'd told them to look out for in a layby and had followed the path he'd described, climbing up through stony scrub and wild olive trees, both wishing they'd drunk a little less the night before.

'Over here,' came Benedict's voice over the barking of dogs, somewhere ahead, close enough for him to have heard their approach but still hidden among the trees.

The next minute the path opened out into a clearing and there he was, legs stretched out in front of him, ankles crossed, back resting against the trunk of an olive tree. The bald brown head was nestled in the sheepskin collar of an expensive leather jacket, the blue eyes twinkled behind tortoiseshell spectacles. A pair of Weimaraners strained on their leashes towards Jacquot and Dietering.

'Mailer, Vidal. Behave yourselves. *Taisez-vous.*'

'Monsieur Benedict,' said Jacquot, wincing from the climb.

'Why, how nice to meet again, Chief Inspector,' said Benedict. His French was slow and precise, the words ghosted with a Texan drawl. And then, eyes straying to Dietering, 'I don't believe we've met.'

Dietering introduced himself.

'Dietering? Germans working with the French,' said Benedict, with a wry smile. 'My, my. What is the world coming to? Herr Dietering, a pleasure.'

'You said you'd found a gun,' said Jacquot.

'I have. I was with the dogs, on my way to town, when Mailer here got caught short. I stopped the car to let him out and he just chased off. So of course I had to follow—and I brought Vidal with me. I managed to get Mailer on the leash and I was just walking through this little glade, back to the car, when I saw it.'

Jacquot and Dietering looked around. The ground was hard and bare, the dry spear-tip leaves on the trees rattling lightly with the breeze. A pale sun left thin trails of light between the branches.

'And it is where exactly, Monsieur?' asked Dietering.

'Why, right above my head, Herr Dietering. In the branches.'

And there it was, hanging over Benedict's head, the wooden stock caught in a fork of the tree, the barrel supported by a branch. It looked as though it had been hurled there from a distance rather than placed deliberately.

'It's the gun that killed the Martners, isn't it?' said Benedict, as Dietering stepped forward and, using the end of his scarf as a makeshift glove, eased the weapon free of the branches. 'Oh, come on, Chief Inspector,' he continued. 'You know I'll find out soon enough. Why not spare yourself all my phone calls? You know what a pest I can be.'

When Dietering had pulled the gun clear, he snapped open the breech. Two empty shell casings flew from the barrels. Using the other end of his scarf he picked up the casings, then he looked at Jacquot and nodded. The same make and gauge as the others.

'Should I call Brunet?' asked Dietering, looking round the area.

Both men knew that three weeks' weather, along with the herd of goats they could hear bleating somewhere above them, not to mention Benedict and the Weimaraners, would have compromised the site. But they both knew, too, that there was still a possibility that something might be found, something that might point them to the killer.

'No need for Brunet,' replied Jacquot. 'Have Mougeon send out a couple of men to search the area. Fifty metres all round. The roadside too. Tell them to look out for any tracks or paths between here and the Martner place.'

Tucking the gun under his arm and pocketing the shell casings, Dietering pulled out his mobile and tapped in the number.

'Well? What do you say?' said Benedict.

'I say, thank you, Monsieur, for bringing this to our attention.' No matter how hard Jacquot tried to dislike Benedict there was something disarming about the man—and he rather enjoyed sparring with him.

'And?' said Benedict, scrambling to his feet, brushing off his Levi's. 'Go on, Chief Inspector. You can tell me. It *is* the Martner gun, isn't it?'

'Maybe, Monsieur. Who can say?'

Dietering pocketed his mobile. 'Mougeon's sending out a couple of men. Do we have any tape in the car to mark the tree?'

Jacquot shook his head.

'Then I'll leave my scarf,' said Dietering, passing the gun to Jacquot who cradled it against his chest.

With the scarf tied to a branch, Jacquot and Dietering started back.

'It's a grand story, you know. Just my sort of thing,' said Benedict, following behind them, the dogs straining at their leashes. 'Well-connected German couple and family killed in a bloody massacre.'

The men and the dogs broke through the last of the olive trees, scrambled down the bank and out onto the lay-by.

While Jacquot stowed the gun in the boot, Dietering hefted some stones into a pile to mark the path for Mougeon's men. He flagged them with an old carrier bag he found in the ditch.

'Get the accreditation, Monsieur Benedict,' said Jacquot, settling himself behind the wheel, 'and, as always, I will be happy to oblige.' He snapped on his seat belt, then started the engine. Dietering slid in beside him.

And with that, Jacquot's old Peugeot lurched off, leaving Benedict looking after him, a canny smile playing across his features.

IT DIDN'T TAKE long to get the results from Ballistics.

Dietering and Jacquot had just returned from a late canteen lunch when Brunet came into the office.

'It's the gun, all right,' he said, handing Jacquot the report. 'And there are prints, too, badly deteriorated but maybe enough to run a match. One thumb and a partial finger.'

'And the serial number?' asked Jacquot. 'The owner of the gun?'

TWENTY MINUTES LATER, Jacquot and Dietering drove out of Cavaillon along the Brieuc road. At the St Bédard turning, they crossed the old stone bridge, climbed up to the hilltop settlement and squeezed through the battlemented west gate.

'Busy,' said Dietering, as they drove along the lower end of Place Vausigne. The Friday market was in full swing, the square filled with tented stalls.

'Come summer, you can't move here on a Friday,' said Jacquot. 'It's one of those places they put on all the travel posters. *La vraie Provence*.'

They followed the sign for Chant-le-Neuf. A few minutes later, six kilometres on from the Martner property, they pulled off the road and drove between the stone pillars and through the wrought-iron gates that Brunet had described to them. After a hundred metres or so, the wooded driveway sloped down past alternating terraces of fig and olive to the pantiled, turreted roof of the Château de Vausigne.

Dietering whistled. 'They should photograph this for their posters too.'

Occupying a small bowl of land a few hundred metres from the road, concealed from passing traffic by a pelt of pine, holm oak and cypresses, the chateau was an impressive sight. Built in southern style, it had a tiled roof that lay almost flat, pegged out between four corner turrets, its windows were bracketed with blue-grey shutters and its pale limestone walls looked soft enough to spread on bread. The wisteria was yet to bloom from a tangle of thick branches that wove round the shutters and covered the lower half of the house.

Jacquot took the car out of gear and let it coast down the slope, gravel crunching as they swung through a final border of palms and boxed orange trees into the chateau's forecourt.

As they got out of the car, the front door opened and an elderly gentleman in a striped waistcoat appeared. A green apron was tied round his waist and his shirtsleeves were rolled up past bony elbows. He wore a pair of white cotton gloves and held a silver plate in one hand, a cloth in the other. He came down the steps to greet them, walking carefully, one step at a time.

'Inspectors Jacquot and Dietering from Cavaillon, to see the Comte de Vausigne,' said Jacquot. 'We are not expected.'

The old man nodded. 'Please, Messieurs, if you would follow me.'

Slowly, laboriously, he climbed back up the steps, then stood aside, ushering Jacquot and Dietering into a stone-flagged anteroom large enough to accommodate a long oak table. He put aside the plate and cloth, took their coats and laid them on a high-backed tapestried chair. Then he limped ahead of them down a stone-walled corridor and showed them into a library.

'If you will wait a moment, I'll let the Comte know that you are here,' he told them, and with that he inclined his head and left the room.

While they waited, Dietering strolled around, looking at the paintings, the furnishings. 'You know something, Daniel, the house looks so great from outside, but inside it is a little—'

At which point the old manservant reappeared and asked them to accompany him.

'A little what?' asked Jacquot, as they followed him down the hall.

'A little worn, tatty. *Schäbig*, we would say in German. Not cared for.'

Before he could say any more, a door was opened and a voice like crystal, pure and brittle, rang out: 'Messieurs, good afternoon. And how can we be of assistance?'

Hélène de Vausigne stood behind her husband, hands resting on the back of his armchair. Back straight as a peppermill, shoulders squared and turned slightly away, her head was tilted upwards as though the eyes needed the bridge of the nose to take aim.

Her husband, Gilles, legs crossed, put down the paper he was reading and smiled lazily in their direction. He looked as lean and haughty as his wife, narrow features tanned and lined, hair lustrously waved. He was, Jacquot judged, a man who enjoyed taking care of his appearance.

'Monsieur, Madame,' said Jacquot, then introduced himself and Dietering.

'Please, Messieurs, make yourselves comfortable.' The Comtesse waved to a matching pair of daintily upholstered chairs.

The two policemen sat down with frightening creaks, and tried to make themselves comfortable. It was no easy task.

Jacquot wondered which of them to address. He settled for the Comte, whose name was on the gun licence. 'I believe you own a Beretta shotgun, Monsieur,' he began.

Which was a mistake. Clearly Madame did the talking in this house.

'Four actually, a mixture—twelve, sixteen and twenty bores.'

'It's the twenty bore we're interested in,' said Jacquot.

'You're not going to tell me you've found it,' said the Comtesse.

Jacquot was startled. 'Did you know the gun was missing, Madame?'

'Why of course,' she replied, eyes twinkling with delight. 'We reported it stolen. When was it, my dear? Back in November?'

The Comte nodded. 'November, yes. Some time around then.'

It was the first time he'd spoken, a low, silky drawl as lazy as his smile.

'There was a break-in,' continued the Comtesse, fingering her pearl necklace. 'Nothing of any real value taken—my husband's wallet, a portable TV and video, a CD player. A few other trinkets. And the gun, of course.'

The Comte waved across the room. 'They came in through that terrace door there. Smashed a window pane and forced the lock. Glass all over the place. We called Lanclos in St Bédard and he came out, took all the details.'

Jacquot groaned. A twenty-bore shotgun had been reported stolen and three months later the same gauge shotgun had been used in a murder. And Lanclos hadn't thought to connect the two—even as coincidence.

Jacquot heard Dietering cough and felt the slightest pressure against his sleeve as his colleague nudged him. The Comtesse was looking at him, head cocked to one side. She must have asked him something.

'Madame was wondering when she could have the gun back?' prompted Dietering.

'You see, it has sentimental value,' she explained. 'I bought it for my husband on his fiftieth birthday.'

'Of course, Madame. As soon as we have finished with it,' said Jacquot.

'Finished with it? I'm afraid I don't follow.'

'We have reason to believe the Beretta was used in a crime, Madame,' said Dietering. 'A murder.'

'Not the Martners?' asked the Comtesse, making the connection.

Dietering nodded. 'I regret . . .'

'But that's dreadful,' said the Comtesse softly. 'I'm not so sure that I want it back now. Not after . . . that.' She looked stricken at the thought.

'Did you know the family?' asked Jacquot, catching her eye.

'The Martners? Only the name. We never actually met. We knew they lived nearby but . . .' The Comtesse let the words hang, looking with a gently complicit smile at Jacquot. 'We told that to the police when they questioned us after the murders.'

Jacquot nodded and turned to her husband. 'Might I ask where you keep your guns, Monsieur?'

The Comte pointed to a door by the fireplace. 'In my study. I'll show you.' He heaved himself out of his chair, indicating that they should follow.

With a polite nod to the Comtesse, and with much creaking from their chairs, the two detectives got to their feet and followed him. The study had a snug, clubby feel, its walls decorated with the heads of boar and deer.

The Comte took a ring of keys from his desk drawer, unlocked a cabinet and pulled open the doors. It was lined with scarlet baize and the guns were lined up in a chained rack. The Comte selected another key from the bunch and undid the clasp, sliding the chain through the trigger guards, then he stepped aside. The wooden stocks glowed a deep, burred mahogany from frequent polishing, the gunmetal barrels glinted a malevolent blue-black. There were twelve spaces but only eleven guns.

'How many people know about this gun cabinet?' asked Jacquot.

'My wife, son, the staff,' replied the Comte, 'and any friends who come to stay and like to shoot.'

'And the keys? Do you always keep them in that drawer?'

'Not always. In the drawer . . . on the desk . . . It depends.'

'And where did you find the keys, after you discovered the break-in?'

'Still in the padlock,' the Comte replied. 'The chain was on the floor.'

'Was it only the gun that was taken, or cartridges too?' asked Dietering.

'Oh, yes. Cartridges too. Three or four boxes, I seem to recall.'

'And where do you keep the ammunition?' continued Jacquot.

'The drawer there,' said the Comte, pointing below the rack.

Jacquot slid it open. Inside were a dozen boxes and a few loose cartridges—the same make and colour as the casings collected at the Martner's.

'You do a lot of shooting, Monsieur?' asked Jacquot.

'Now and again, Chief Inspector. But not as much as I used to.'

'Anyone else?'

'Eric the gardener—rabbits, crows, mostly. And then, as I said earlier, there are friends who maybe fancy a walk around the estate.'

'Your wife?'

'Used to, a fine shot as well. But not now.'

'And your son?'

'Antoine? Not so often. He lives in Paris now. But he's a good shot when the mood takes him.'

'And you are the keyholder? There are no copies for the cabinet?'

'Yes, and no.'

'So when your gardener, say . . .'

'If he needs a gun, he'll ask Picard, who'll ask me.'

'You get him the gun yourself?'

'If I'm here. Otherwise I leave it to Picard.'

'Does he have a preference? Your gardener? Twelve bore? Twenty bore?'

The Comte shrugged. 'I don't recall. Whichever comes to hand, usually.'

'And who cleans the guns, Monsieur?' asked Dietering.

'Picard.'

'And how often?'

'Whenever a gun is used. He's meticulous. Always. Without fail.'

Back in the morning room the Comte eased into his chair, as though exhausted by the questions. Jacquot and Dietering remained standing.

'Is there anything else we can do to help, Chief Inspector?' asked the Comtesse, patting her husband's shoulder.

'As a matter of fact, there is,' replied Jacquot. 'We will need to take fingerprints. From you and your staff. Purely for the purpose of elimination. I'm sure you understand.'

'I see . . . Well, I suppose if you must, you must.'

'And your staff? Who exactly . . . ?'

'Well, there's Picard, of course,' she replied, 'and his wife, Florence, our cook and housekeeper. They have an apartment above the kitchen.'

'And how long have they worked here?'

'As long as I can remember, Chief Inspector. As for the others, there's Monique, our maid who comes in three times a week, and the gardener, Eric, both of them from St Bédard.'

'And how long have Monique and Eric been with you?' asked Jacquot.

'Monique, about five years now, Eric, a year, maybe two. He's a little . . .' The Comtesse spread her hands. 'A little slow, but a good worker. Picard speaks highly of him, and the garden is always immaculate.'

Forty minutes later, Jacquot and Dietering pulled away from the house and followed the drive up the hillside. In Dietering's briefcase was a set of prints from the de Vausignes, Picard and his wife, and Monique. As for the gardener, Eric Chabert, no one seemed to know where he was. Jacquot decided to have Brunet call in on the gardener at his home in St Bédard.

ACCORDING TO LANCLOS'S report, which Jacquot called up from Records after dropping Dietering at the airport for his weekend flight home, the break-in at the chateau had happened exactly as the de Vausignes had described it. November 26, at night. Nothing taken beyond a wallet containing 6,000 francs, a TV, video and CD player. And the gun and cartridges. To all appearances it seemed to have been a simple but professional break-in. Whoever had done it had left no fingerprints at the scene, no footprints in the garden, and no one had heard a thing.

Jacquot tossed the report on his desk, swung round in his chair and wondered about the 6,000 francs. Somehow he doubted that the de Vausignes would leave that kind of cash lying around. What was the word Dietering had used to describe the interior of the chateau? *Schäbig*. Shabby, down-at-heel. The curtains were threadbare, the paint was flaking, the floorboards dulled and the carpets worn to the weave. A wad of 6,000 francs? No, no, no. Jacquot didn't think so. As for the TV, video and CD player, he was willing to bet his pension they'd been stacked upstairs, window-dressing contrived by the de Vausignes to increase the value of their insurance claim.

Which meant, so far as Jacquot could see, that it was the gun the intruder had come for. Which meant, more than likely, that the man who had broken into the de Vausignes' home in November was the same man who, three months later, had slaughtered the Martner family.

IT WAS DIETERING, fresh off the flight from Munich, who took the call at a little after eleven o'clock on Monday morning. 'The prints,' he said, coming through into Jacquot's office. 'We have a match.'

The prints—a partial right index finger on the trigger guard and a smudged thumb on the underside of the barrel—belonged to Eric Chabert, the de Vausignes' gardener. As far as Jacquot was concerned, it would have been astonishing if his prints had not been found—or those of Picard, or the Comte, or even the Comtesse. But for want of anything better to do, he called up all the information they could source. It didn't take long.

Name: Eric Gérard Chabert. Nineteen. Only child.

Parents: Fernand and Denise Chabert, owners of the flower shop Fontaine des Fleurs on Place Vausigne, St Bédard-le-Chapitre.

Education: École du Clos, Cavaillon. Poor academic results.

Employment: worked at his parents' shop, and part-time gardener at the Château de Vausigne. And at Mas Taillard—the Martners' home.

Previous convictions: none.

The gendarme who'd taken Chabert's statement the day after the murders was hauled in. His name was Barlisse and he looked uncomfortable standing there at Jacquot's desk.

'Eric Chabert. Impressions, please,' asked Jacquot.

Barlisse looked blank.

'St Bédard. The flower shop. You interviewed him,' Jacquot prompted.

The man thought for a moment, then nodded. 'Yes, I remember. Good-looking kid,' he replied. 'Well-built. But not the sharpest knife in the drawer. You know those village types—live at home, love their *mamans*.'

'Girlfriends? Boyfriends?' continued Jacquot.

'Seemed straight to me, boss. Shouldn't have had too much trouble with the girls, but nothing serious I heard about.'

'What did he think of the Martners?'

'He said they left him pretty much to his own devices. The doctor wasn't bothered with the garden, only the hothouse. Sometimes Chabert picked up supplies for him, but usually it was Madame Martner who dealt with him.'

'And where did he say he was at the time of the murders?'

'Having breakfast. Getting the shop ready.' The gendarme dug in his pockets and pulled out his notebook, scrabbled through the pages.

Jacquot continued. 'And what time did he get up that morning?'

Barlisse ran a finger down a page in his notebook. 'Six. As usual.'

'Anyone vouch for his whereabouts?'

'He shared a cigarette with Tomas Mazzelli,' replied Barlisse, glancing at his notes. 'Around seven, Mazzelli said.'

'But until then, Chabert was on his own?'

Barlisse thought for a moment, then nodded. 'That's all we got, boss.'

And that was it. Everything to go on—and nothing.

Two days after confirming the print, Jacquot gave the nod. Early evening, midweek, a good time to go calling. Chabert was having supper with his parents in the back parlour of the Fontaine des Fleurs when Brunet and three gendarmes knocked on the front door to bring him in to Cavaillon Police Headquarters for questioning.

CHABERT LOOKED UP when Jacquot, Dietering and Brunet came into the interview room, his anxious eyes darting between them. He had short blond hair, all awry as though he'd been running his fingers through it, a broad, honest face, bulky shoulders and large, strong hands. The hand-knitted sweater he wore was tight across the chest, and the cuffs and collar of his white shirt were grubby. He sat at a Formica-top table in the centre of the room, and seemed confused, uncertain. Which was why they'd left him alone for the last two hours, save visits from Mougeon with coffee from the machine.

As planned, Brunet took a seat across from Chabert, while Dietering and Jacquot settled in chairs by the window. Brunet shot his cuffs, shrugged his shoulders inside his sports jacket and loosened his tie. Only then did he open the file he'd brought with him, shuffling through its contents. He closed the file and sighed deeply. Next he pulled a pen from his pocket. Rolled it in his fingers. Removed the cap. Then placed the pen on the table, positioning it just so. Jacquot had seen the performance many times.

Like others before him, Chabert was mesmerised.

Brunet sighed again. Then, leaning across the table, he switched on the tape, introduced himself, gave the names of the other officers present and began the questions. The same ones they'd asked on the door-to-door.

Straight into it. Just like that. Questions. One after another.

Then again. Just as fast. Then a third time, moving about a bit, skipping the order, coming back to things. 'You said earlier . . .' and 'But I thought you said . . .' Trying to throw the boy.

But four times through and Chabert's story seemed to hold: where he was at the time of the murders; what he was doing; how the Martners treated him; what he thought of them; what he did for them. Not a step wrong. The doctor. His wife. The daughter, Ilse Brauer.

And then Kippi.

Chabert had trouble with the name. A catch in the voice, a clearing of the throat, a swift cuff across the eyes.

Brunet sensed something. 'Tell me about Kippi,' he probed. 'Pretty girl, wasn't she? I've seen the photos. Beautiful.' He leaned forward. 'How often did she visit? You see much of her? You ever go out with her? Take her into town?' He moved his elbows forward, dropped his voice. 'You and Kippi have something going on together, Eric? Yeah? You did?'

Brunet sat back and slapped the table, which made Chabert and Dietering jump. Not Jacquot: he'd known it was coming.

'Not bad,' said Brunet, chuckling darkly, as though considering the prospect of making love to a girl like Kippi. He reached into a pocket, pulled out a tiny silver tube, unscrewed the lid and shook out a toothpick. When the tube was back in his pocket, he set to work. On his teeth. And Chabert.

'And then what? Don't tell me. She gives you the boot. Over. *Fini*. Just when things are getting good. Is that how it was? Is that how it happened?'

Which was when Chabert put his elbows on the table, hands to his face, and began to weep. 'I didn't know she was pregnant. I didn't. I swear it.'

Brunet waited a beat, working on a tooth, then removed the toothpick and went on. 'Why should you? Why should you know she was pregnant?'

'I didn't.'

'I mean, why would she tell you? Come on, Eric. She might have been banging you, but you are just the gardener, right?' Another beat, and then: 'I mean, hey, it wasn't going anywhere, was it? Surely you knew that?'

Chabert shook his head, but his hands with their dirt-rimmed nails stayed where they were. A bunch of hair stood up at his fingertips.

Brunet gave it a few more moments.

'You loved her, didn't you?'

No reply. Head in hands.

'You loved her like you never loved anyone in your life, right? You didn't want to lose her, did you?'

Silence.

'Did you?'

The head shook. A mournful, muffled, 'No,' rose from behind the hands.

'And it's driving you crazy. I mean, you haven't seen her since, what? New Year? The last time she's here, right? And now, here she is giving you the heave-ho. Party's over, *liebchen*. Let's call it a day. Thanks for the memory.'

'If I had known . . . If only I had known . . .' he whimpered.

5

It was old Dumé who saw her first. On the last Sunday in May. During his favourite walk. It began at the lower end of the square, along a pavement that led to St Bédard's west gate, an arch of honeyed stone rising above the road like a giant keyhole. Beyond this gate, the countryside began: hillsides ribbed with vines, fields rustling with early maize and, down in the valley, the black ribbon of road that led from the heights of Rocsabin to Brieuc and Cavaillon.

In the cool shade of the arch, Dumé paused. It was maybe ten metres to the first of the plane trees that lined the far side of the road. He'd be out in the sun for those ten metres and Dumé knew it would be hot. Today was the first white sky of the year, any blue long since bleached away.

As he'd expected, the sun clamped down the moment he stepped from the arch. Gripping his stick he made for the nearest tree as fast as his old canvas boots would carry him. As he reached its shade, he felt a dampness in his armpits and an ache in his chest. Tomorrow, he decided, catching his breath, he'd leave his walk for later in the day.

From tree to tree, from one puddle of shade to the next, Dumé made his way along the road, surrounded by the ticking of insects and the scent of hot dust and wild fennel. Behind him the crumbling walls of St Bédard were soon hidden by the trees, and ahead he could see now where the road began its first gentle descent. After a few more steps the valley opened up before him, its distant heights scabbed with limestone bluffs, slopes freckled with olive trees and the course of its river piped with poplar and linden.

Dumé turned off along a path between the vines. About twenty metres along it stood a copse of twisted olives where he liked to sit, on the low stone wall that terraced them into the hillside, with nothing but the hum of crickets and the occasional flutter of a bird to keep him company.

Propping his stick against the wall, Dumé sat down and felt in his pockets for his pipe and pouch. Carefully, he pulled out a wad of tobacco, loaded it into the bowl and tamped it down with a finger. With his second match, the tobacco caught and, lips pop-pop-popping on the stem of the pipe, Dumé pocketed the pouch and matches and looked back towards the road.

It was then, through a curl of blue tobacco smoke, that something caught his eye, down in the valley, a flash of sun on metal. He waited for it to show itself again, and when it failed to do so he knew it wasn't a car, or it would have passed the St Bédard turn by now.

Moments later, he caught another movement, closer than he'd expected, something streaking towards the St Bédard bridge, pulling out to negotiate the turning off the Brieuc road . . . A bicycle. Had to be.

Dumé kept his eyes on the slope of the road. Whoever was riding the bicycle would be forced to stand up from the saddle after the first hundred metres, and then it was uphill all the way. A long, hard push. He followed the route in his mind's eye: past the memorial—'*Tués par les Allemands, le 8 juin 1944*'—through a tunnel of chestnuts, round the first long turn to the left, then a steep climb, with the valley dropping away to one side.

Maybe he'd dozed in the warm, chirruping afternoon shade. Dumé couldn't decide. But the next thing he knew, the bike was there, the rider leaning into the slope, pushing up towards St Bédard.

Dumé peered between the vines and watched it approach. There were panniers at either side of the back wheel, a saddlebag above the rear mud-guard and a large wicker basket on the handlebars.

Was the rider a boy or a girl? Dumé wondered. A man or a woman? All he could make out was a bob of black hair, a short-sleeved brown shirt, creased shorts that came to the knee and socks tucked round boots.

It was a boy, Dumé decided. And then he revised that opinion, for the legs were too narrow and smooth, the arms too long and thin, and the line and curve of the body altogether softer. It was a girl.

As the road began to level, she stopped and looked ahead, gauging what was left of the gradient. Dumé nodded. She could start riding now, even with the weight she was carrying. And that was what she did, stepping across the bike—a woman's model—lifting a foot to a pedal.

And in that pause, she turned in his direction, caught his eye—and waved to him. A big, strong wave, an extravagant, happy gesture.

Then she was off, weaving left and right until the front wheel steadied with the power from her legs. A moment later she had passed from sight.

Dumé's heart was beating fast. He pulled his beret from his head, feeling across his scalp the heat of the sun and the cool of the shade in a single instant, and shivered.

'*Bon Dieu*,' he said, to the leaves above his head. 'That's interesting.'

And, without knowing precisely why, he started after her, out of the shade of the olive trees, between the vines and back the way he had come.

'I REALLY THINK I should stay,' said Denise Chabert, unpinning her hat, lifting it off and placing it on the parlour table.

Fernand Chabert, putting away the last of the lunch plates, turned to her and managed a smile. The poor woman looked worn out, he thought, at the end of her tether. But he knew she didn't mean what she said about staying in St Bédard, knew there was only one place she wanted to be right now. And that was in Lyon. At Eric's side, or as close as she could manage, for all the days or weeks—however long it took—that lay ahead before the trial.

'It won't be much longer, *chérie*. You shouldn't worry so.'

'I know, I know,' she replied, in a tight, strained little voice. 'It's just they said midday. And midday's midday. Even on a Sunday. He should be here by now, that's all . . .'

She sat down at the parlour table, pushing aside the hat. She was fifty-two, a little stout now in the shoulders and hips, but with the same strong hands and long fingers that, Fernand knew, could grasp the stems of twenty tulips tightly enough to cut away the ends with a single, straight slice.

'I just want it all to be over,' she whispered, holding back the tears. 'I want him home again. I want it . . . like it was.'

'It will be, I promise. You'll see,' replied Fernand, with a strength and a certainty that he didn't altogether feel.

She sniffed and gave him a tearful smile, then turned once more to the clock on the wall as if it would hasten the arrival they were waiting for.

THAT SUNDAY, the Chaberts had missed Sunday mass. 'I couldn't face them. Not today,' Denise had said to Fernand.

Not that the Chaberts had anything to fear from the congregation of St Bédard. In those dreadful days after the police had come for Eric, everyone had rallied round. Curé Foulard had been first to call by, with gentle words, the evening they returned from Cavaillon after being told their son would not be coming home with them. And then, as news spread about Eric being held for the Martner murders, friends and neighbours all made a point of visiting the shop, offering support.

A mistake, they all said. Ridiculous! Eric, a killer? Whatever next? It'll soon be sorted out, you'll see.

The Chaberts might have anticipated these small kindnesses from their neighbours, but there was no way they could have been prepared for the letter that arrived from Gilles de Vausigne, informing them that a distinguished cousin, Maître Messain of Lyon, would be contacting them shortly regarding Eric's defence and that he and the Comtesse had taken it upon themselves to settle the fees in advance.

Such an unexpected profession of faith in their son's innocence had stunned the Chaberts. The boy was only their gardener, a four-afternoons-a-week handyman, who'd been with them just a couple of years. Such a generous offer seemed inconceivable.

That Sunday morning Denise had prepared a light lunch, which they had eaten in silence, the two of them expecting at any moment the man from the agency to arrive. Midday, Sunday, the agency had said.

Fernand supposed the word 'midday' allowed some leeway. Their train for Lyon didn't leave until five, so there'd be plenty of time to do what needed to be done. Show him the cold store, the hothouse; run him through the suppliers, the orders and account books. Explain the locks, the old Citroën van, the house. It wouldn't take long.

But Denise would not settle. Midday was midday in her book—twelve o'clock sharp—and after their lunch she'd taken to going through to the shop to peer through the slats in the metal grating that was rolled down over the window. Once, Fernand heard her unlock the front door to look out.

'Old Dumé out for his stroll,' he heard her say. And then, as she came back to the parlour: 'It's too hot. He should wait for evening.'

'Why don't we have some coffee?' suggested Fernand eventually, getting up from the table. Truth be told, he was now as troubled and anxious as his wife and desperate to fill the time.

Out in the kitchen he poured two cups from the pot brewing on the stove and brought them through to the table.

Which was when the stranger arrived. The girl.

Afterwards, in the taxi to Cavaillon, they talked about her.

'I thought they said a man,' Denise said. 'What did she say her name was?'

'Buhl,' replied her husband. 'Marie-Ange Buhl. A stand-in. The man they were going to send was ill. We were lucky they found someone.'

'Do you think she'll manage all on her own?' asked Denise.

'Of course she will. Don't fret, my darling. Everything will be fine.'

'She was beautiful, wasn't she?' said Denise. 'What I wouldn't give to see their faces tomorrow.'

'Maybe I should stay, help her out,' Fernand said, smiling at his wife.

She looked at him, uncertain again. Then saw his smile and smiled too, her first real smile for many days. In the bouncing rear seat of the taxi, she slipped her arm through his. 'Don't even think about it, Monsieur Chabert.'

THAT FIRST MONDAY in June, Marie-Ange Buhl awoke in Eric Chabert's bed. Without moving, she felt him there, all the warm hollows and soft depressions, the unfamiliar angles and unlikely curves. Over the years, he'd given the bed his form, moulded its surface, a set of unfamiliar contours, which Marie-Ange had fitted to the shape of her own body. Now, rubbing the sleep from her eyes, she stretched slowly, limbs unfolding under the crumpled sheet, all tousled black hair and sleepy face.

Here, at the front of the house, above the topmost branches of the trees in the square, with only thin cotton curtains to cover the window, the room grew light early. Marie-Ange liked that. She'd woken to the brooding of doves and the scratch of their claws on the roof tiles, the first chirruping of sparrows, a clattering of footsteps across the cobbles in the square and the distant splash of the fountain.

Shifting up in his bed, resting on her elbows, Marie-Ange looked around. A boy's room still, she decided, not quite a man's. Sparsely furnished, as she'd expected, but still cosy in an under-the-eaves way. And oddly out of kilter: the uneven walls, the casement window crookedly recessed in the slope of the roof, the bare boards tipping away from the window. There was something precarious about it all, like being in a nest at the top of a tree.

Of course, she'd been shown to the spare room the previous afternoon, at the back of the house. She'd professed herself delighted with it. But after the Chaberts had left, Marie-Ange had moved her things one floor up, into Eric's room, stripped off her clothes and run a bath in the bathroom across the landing, looking forward to a hot soak.

While the bath filled, she had explored her new home, from Eric's bedroom at the top of the house to the kitchen and parlour behind the shop, feeling the old place surrender its secrets one by one as she padded round in his dressing gown, feet bare, fingers trailing.

Although the house was warm that late Sunday afternoon, there were certain places—on the top landing outside Eric's room, in the room she'd chosen not to sleep in, and between the parlour and kitchen—where the skin puckered on her shoulders, arms and belly. It was a familiar sensation and Marie-Ange was not unduly perturbed.

She heard a rising battery of words in the parlour—not the Chaberts' voices—and the sound of a slap still echoing between dresser and table; a cool, regretful note of departure in the spare room; and on the top landing outside Eric's bedroom, a terrible, haunting melancholy. Not that any of this surprised Marie-Ange: the house was old—it had maybe 300 years of domestic history. She'd have been amazed if it had been any different.

Back in the bathroom, she'd spent an hour in the hot soapy water. Head resting where his head had rested, she'd listened through the open door to the Sunday-evening sounds of St Bédard that he would have heard: the tap of boules, the scrape of a chair at the bar across the square, the church bell tolling, a motorbike accelerating away along the road to Brieuc. And in the silences between, always there, the splashing of the fountain.

After her bath, Marie-Ange had decided to go for a walk, to explore this hilltop town, but by the time she unpacked her bags she'd thought better of it. Instead, still naked, she'd lain down on Eric's bed and watched the window darken. It was the last thing she remembered.

Now, she pushed herself up and slid from his bed. Drawing apart the curtains, she looked across the rooftops, the sky a pale lilac shot with shifting bars of rose and lavender, a dawn breeze wafting from the open casement.

It was all just as she'd imagined it.

WHATEVER THE TIME of year, St Bédard woke early.

The baker Georges Doriane, driving in from Chant-le-Neuf, was always the first to appear. Parking his car behind the gendarmerie on that first Monday in June, he hurried across Place Vausigne, hands deep in his jacket pockets, hair a nimbus of grey like a dandelion gone to seed.

He loved the early-morning stillness of St Bédard, the way his sabots rang out over the cobblestones and those welcoming scents of hot brick and warm dough when he unlocked the bakery door and pushed it open, pinging the bell on the spring that his grandfather had put up.

Doriane was a fourth-generation baker whose great-grandfather had secured premises a block back from the square behind what was now Mazzelli's bar, and rapidly established a reputation that none of his successors had in any way diminished—the Doriane brioches, croissants, baguettes and extravagant *pâtisseries* were still celebrated throughout the region and still baked in the same brick ovens in the basement.

Georges Doriane had worked these ovens six days a week for twenty years. And every year some salesman would call by in the hope of selling him the latest gas or electric installation. But Doriane had never given in. Dressed in singlet and baggy whites, his face, shoulders and arms ghosted with flour and rivered with sweat, he'd tell them wearily that if the old wood-burning ovens had been good enough for his father, for his father's father and for a generation before that, then they were good enough for him.

WOKEN BY DORIANE'S sabots clattering on the cobbles outside his bedroom window, Tomas Mazzelli swung out of bed, pulled on jeans and a T-shirt and then, so as not to disturb his parents, padded down the back stairs in bare feet, carrying a trainer in each hand. He pushed through the bead curtain that separated the bar from the Mazzellis' private quarters, leaned against the zinc bar to pull on his trainers, then switched on the Gaggia.

As the metal flanks of the coffee machine began to tick with heat, Tomas unbolted the terrace doors, folding them back into their pillared recesses. With the square still deeply shadowed but filled with the first scents of fresh-baked bread from Doriane's, he hosed off the terrace, chasing away the cigarette ends and spilt-drink stains from the night before, then set out tables and chairs. When the red light was glowing on the Gaggia, he returned to the bar to make himself a cup of strong black coffee.

He gave himself the usual double measure, then took the cup, helped himself to a cigarette from the packet his father always left by the till and sat down at one of the inside tables. It was his moment, his time away from the watchful eye of his father. He stretched out his legs, crossed his ankles and lit the cigarette.

Tomas was nineteen, beefily built like his father, with broad enough shoulders, he hoped, to see him promoted to the Cavaillon A rugby team in the coming season, along with his teammate, Eric Chabert. And that was all Tomas wanted right now, a place in the Cavaillon senior scrum and enough money to keep up payments on the Suzuki trail bike he kept in the back yard.

He was stubbing out his cigarette, wondering if he dare take another, when he glanced up and saw her. Just a glimpse, a movement at the window at the top of the house across the square. A shape, lit by a streak of sun. He tipped forward for a better view, but the moment was gone. Just the open window and a stirring of curtains in the breeze.

Tomas got up from his seat, went behind the bar and helped himself to a second cigarette. Back at the table he lit it, finished the last of his coffee and tried to convince himself that he hadn't just seen a naked girl at his friend's bedroom window.

SITTING AT THE TABLE in the Chaberts' parlour, Marie-Ange read the instructions that Monsieur Chabert had left her and sipped her coffee.

The first page contained information on opening and closing times, the various suppliers and their delivery times, and a list of useful telephone numbers: Denise Chabert's sister in Lyon where they would be staying for the duration of the trial; Sergeant Lanclos at the gendarmerie (Marie-Ange remembered the name from the first press cuttings she'd collected); the local plumber, electrician and garage mechanic; and the refrigeration people in Cavaillon in case something went wrong with the cold store.

The second page listed the Chaberts' regular clients, their orders and delivery details. There were only three standing accounts she would need to deal with. On Tuesday, Thursday and Saturday mornings she must deliver the table and room decorations for the Fontaine Dorée across the square; on Wednesday afternoons (half-day closing) take four boxes of canna lilies to the funeral parlour in Brieuc; and on Saturday afternoons put together those blooms that wouldn't last the following week for the *curé*.

It was all quite straightforward, though Monsieur Chabert had made it seem far more complicated than it was. She supposed, correctly, that it had been his nerves. Madame Chabert had been on edge too, telling her that they'd expected her earlier. She'd apologised, explained that the agency had told her she should get there in the early afternoon.

It had been strange meeting the Chaberts. After all this time, Marie-Ange had felt that she knew them. When Monsieur Chabert answered the door— a tall, angular man with sharp blue eyes and dark, tilting eyebrows—she'd recognised him immediately from TV and newspaper photographs. His wife was equally familiar. As she followed them round the house, the shop, cold store and hothouse, she'd wanted to explain that she could find her way round, that there was no need for their anxiety. But she'd said nothing, let them walk and talk her through it, which, she knew, was what they wanted.

Marie-Ange tucked Monsieur Chabert's instructions away in a drawer of the dresser. Then, taking the keys, she went through to the stores at the back of the house. It was time to prepare the Fontaine des Fleurs.

IF TOMAS MAZZELLI was the first to see Marie-Ange, it was Adeline Séguin, with one of her sister's terrines, who was the first to speak to her.

Planning to steal a march on her sister, whose discovery of the Martner bodies three months before still rankled, Adeline had left the house a little before eight, bound for Doriane's. But instead of using the gate at the bottom of their garden and taking the short cut, she'd deliberately opted for the square. She bade good day to her neighbour Marc Tesserat as he set up his postcard racks outside the *tabac*, nodded a greeting to Delphine Bulot laying out her pâtés and sausages in the Charcuterie Bulot's window, and paused at Ribaud's antiques shop, pretending to look at something on display but actually inspecting the reflection in his darkened window of the Fontaine des Fleurs through the trees.

Half an hour earlier than usual, the Chaberts' shop was open. Its metal grille was rolled up, its window panels folded back, and beneath the shop's striped awning its display shelves were laden with blooms, more than Adeline had ever seen, arranged in tiered ranks that were larger, grander and more extravagant than anything Denise Chabert had ever achieved.

Having taken the short cut home from Doriane's to tell her sister the news, Adeline was now back on the pavement in front of the Chaberts' shop, holding a china dish covered with a damp cloth.

'Hello, dear. Is Madame Chabert at home?'

The girl was standing with her back to Adeline, a hose in her hand, directing the finest spray the gun attachment would deliver over the flowers in the display rack.

When she turned and smiled, Adeline's heart seemed to miss a beat.

It was marvellous, Adeline told her sister when she got home again, this young woman set against the flowers, lost to her shoulders in the blooms, surrounded by rainbow clouds of colour from the sun catching the spray . . .

But what did she look like? her sister Odile prodded.

Oh, such a beauty, replied Adeline. Like a painting. And she started counting off on her fingers what she could remember of the newcomer. Let me see, she began . . . Her hair is short, and very dark, almost black, like a shiny cap. High, strong cheekbones. And deep black eyes. Or maybe brown. So dark you can't really tell. Elegant, continued Adeline. And tall. She holds herself well. Somehow very grown-up, wise for her years.

And how old is she, do you suppose? asked Odile.

Young, Adeline replied. In her twenties. And then: No, no, older than that. Oh, goodness. I couldn't really say for sure. One minute she looks so young, the next she seems . . .

And what did she say? continued Odile.

The girl had said, 'I'm so sorry, Madame. The Chaberts have gone away. To Lyon. They left yesterday. I'm looking after the shop. Maybe I can help?'

'Oh, how silly of me,' Adeline had replied. 'Of course they have. How forgetful I'm becoming. You see, well, usually on a Monday morning, I bring over . . .' She had lifted the china dish. 'Just a small terrine my sister, Odile, makes. It's a favourite of Denise's . . .'

Adeline had suddenly felt oddly flustered. She'd known very well that the Chaberts had left the previous day, just as she'd known that her sister's terrine was usually delivered on a Thursday—but, she told Odile, she'd never anticipated such a small distortion of the truth causing her so much . . . well, discomfort. All the time there was this beautiful girl, giving her the most charming smile, those dark eyes looking right through her, their owner somehow seeming to know she'd been telling a fib.

'Perhaps . . . since you've just moved in,' she had stammered, offering the dish, 'you might like to . . .'

'How kind,' the girl had said, squeezing between the blooms and stepping out onto the pavement. She put down the hose, wiped her hands on the blue apron she was wearing and took the dish. Clasping it to her, she lifted a corner of the cloth. 'Goodness, it looks delicious.'

And then, Adeline told her sister, the girl had held out her hand, long and straight, fingers together. 'I'm Marie-Ange. Marie-Ange Buhl.'

Is that all? asked Odile. Did you say anything else? Did she?

I told her my name, replied Adeline.

'Adeline Séguin. I live with my sister, Odile. Across the square. There.'

And then, she told Odile, this Marie-Ange reached into the display of flowers and picked out the most glorious blossom, snipped the stem with her scissors, and gave it to me. Here, look. It's perfect.

As her sister turned it admiringly in her gloved fingers, Adeline found a small vase and filled it with water. Then she placed the flower in it and set it on the kitchen table. Just perfect.

NOT LONG AFTER a flushed Adeline Séguin retreated across the square with her flower, Sergeant Lanclos left Frenot in charge of the gendarmerie and headed up to the Fontaine des Fleurs. He was going to introduce himself to the new arrival, just as he'd promised Fernand he would. Take a look at the fellow, get his measure.

Lanclos came to a halt where Adeline had stood and peered into the shop's shadowy interior. A shape rose from behind the counter and came towards him. She'd removed the blue apron, and the flowery print dress she wore seemed to cling and whisper round her as though it were a part of her.

'*Bonjour*, Monsieur.'

Like Adeline before him, Lanclos took a moment to collect his thoughts. This was not what he'd expected. 'Mademoiselle,' he replied, touching his fingers to the peak of his kepi. 'Mademoiselle . . . ?'

'Buhl. Marie-Ange Buhl.' She held out her hand, and Sergeant Lanclos took it. It made his own seem large and rough and hamlike.

'Lanclos, from the gendarmerie.'

'Ah, Sergeant Lanclos. Of course. I have you on my list.'

Lanclos looked uncertain. 'List?'

'Monsieur Chabert. He gave me a list of all the important people I'd need to get to know.'

Lanclos let the word 'important' settle warmly on his chest. 'Of course. I was just . . . you know . . . passing, as it happens, thought I'd call by, see how everything was going. Anything you needed.'

'How kind, Monsieur.'

And Marie-Ange smiled the smile she had given Adeline and, like Adeline before him, Lanclos felt a curious coil of discomfort as though he'd been caught out somehow, seen through.

'I've some coffee in the back,' Marie-Ange continued. 'Will you join me?'

And though he'd already drunk enough coffee that morning to float a battleship, Lanclos saw no reason not to take another.

IT WAS THE RINGING of the telephone that finally brought him to his senses.

Lanclos had sat at the counter for what seemed like a few minutes, sipping his coffee while Marie-Ange snipped away at the stems of flowers, yet when he glanced at his watch, Lanclos was astonished to see that he'd been there closer to forty minutes, breathing in a heady mix of scents he'd never noticed when the Chaberts ran the shop.

He dragged his eyes from the tight rise and swell of the girl's breasts as she cradled the phone to her shoulder, and he waited until the call was over before he got to his feet. 'Well, Mam'selle, I'd best be going . . .'

'Then I'll join you,' she said, taking a pen and notebook from the counter. 'I'm on my way to Madame Parmentier's. It's across the square, isn't it?'

'That's right,' said Lanclos, leading the way out of the shop. Then he stopped and turned. 'But you're not leaving the shop unattended?'

'Oh, it'll be fine, Sergeant. Don't you worry,' she said.

Lanclos was pretty sure he should worry—some of these tourists—but somehow he felt he needn't, not this morning, not in this company, and together they crossed the square to the Auberge de la Fontaine Dorée.

CAROLINE PARMENTIER was sitting at a table in the dining room, checking Doriane's monthly bill, when she'd looked up and spotted Sergeant Lanclos lumbering across the terrace. And there beside him was the girl she'd been speaking to on the phone, the one looking after the Chaberts' shop. She was certain of it. As Lanclos confirmed the fact with introductions, Caroline felt a great weight lift from her shoulders. A dozen reservations for lunch already and the annual dinner of the Confrèrie des Amis du Vin booked for that evening. And not a flower in the place, those from the weekend being well past their prime, despite Denise Chabert's assurances the previous week that they would last. After she had tried to revive them with a little trimming and some fresh water, Caroline had given up hope and taken them to the bins. Which was when she'd called the Fontaine des Fleurs.

Of course, she had no reason to suppose Denise's replacement would prove any more accommodating. Yet now, less than an hour later, here was this delightful girl, full of energy and enthusiasm, with half the job done already.

'It sounds an awful lot,' said Caroline Parmentier, as Marie-Ange jotted notes in her book. 'Are you quite sure you can manage it all?'

Marie-Ange looked up. 'Not a problem, Madame. I have some irises just about to bloom that will look great in Reception, some cornflowers for the bar, and black-eyed Susan for the bedside tables. Also, there's a dozen or so small bouquets I've nearly finished—daisies, jonquils and gypsophila—they'll look just glorious in here.' Marie-Ange closed her notebook. 'I could bring some over before lunch, if you like, and the rest this evening?'

And that was that.

Thank you, God, thought Madame Parmentier, as she watched Marie-Ange make her way to the Fontaine des Fleurs.

IT WAS A LITTLE after seven in the evening, at the end of her first day, when Marie-Ange rolled down the metal grille on the Fontaine des Fleurs and snapped the padlock into place. In the shop's shuttered gloom, the air heavy with the scent of flowers, she pulled out the chair from behind the counter and put up her feet on an upturned bucket.

It felt like the first moment she'd had to herself all day, which, despite her fatigue, was the way Marie-Ange liked it. Busy, busy, busy—no time to think beyond the flowers, the customers and her new neighbours, all of whom had found some pretext to introduce themselves, take a look at the newcomer. Just as she'd known they would.

First, the old lady, Adeline Séguin; then the policeman Lanclos. Delphine Bulot from the *charcuterie* had visited with a little sliced sausage and a *crottin* at lunch; the grocer's wife, Clotilde Lepantre, had then dropped by to ask if she had any ten-franc pieces for change when she could more easily have called at the *tabac*. After lunch, that sweet little man with the white shoes, the pink cords and the stripy shirt—André Ribaud, from the antiques shop—came looking for some flowers for his window display. She'd recommended some zinnias, creamy white, and he'd been delighted. Just what he'd been looking for, he told her, and offered one of his *crème abricots* as a thankyou. From Doriane's, he'd told her. In the street behind Mazzelli's. A billion calories, but who cared?

The strangest of her visitors, however, came later in the day: the lady from the *pharmacie*, Madame Héliard, tall and hunched, with a widow's peak and beetling brows. Marie-Ange had been ringing up a sale when she made her appearance, black cardigan over white dispenser's uniform.

'Broken aspirins,' the pharmacist began, when Marie-Ange's customers were out of earshot, holding out a paper bag across the counter. 'Not for you, of course. For the flowers. Denise swears by them.' And then, with a curt little nod: 'I'm Madame Héliard. From the *pharmacie*.'

Of all her visitors, Madame Héliard was the only one who brought up the real reason why Marie-Ange was looking after the Chaberts' shop.

'Poor dears. Simply dreadful,' she said, giving a little shudder.

'You mean the murders? Their son, Eric?'

Madame Héliard narrowed her eyes. 'You know about . . . all that?'

'The agency told me.' Marie-Ange squared up the wedge of wrapping paper on the counter between them. 'The Chaberts must be so worried.'

Madame Héliard nodded. 'It was a shock, that's for sure. No one could credit it. Eric of all people. Such a good, quiet boy. He must have—'

She cut herself short as a couple came into the shop and approached the counter. 'But I ought to be getting back,' she said regretfully.

Marie-Ange reached for one of her potpourri sachets, leaned across the counter and pressed it into Madame Héliard's hands. 'In return for the aspirins,' she said.

For a moment, Madame Héliard looked quite taken aback, but then her surprise softened into a smile. 'Why, how kind,' she said, sniffing at the tiny purse of petals, leaves, bark and seeds. 'Such a glorious scent.'

Madame Héliard wasn't the only one who thought so. By the end of her first day, Marie-Ange had sold a half-dozen, and by the time she had finished off the Parmentier order—the posies for bedside tables, and some ribboned sprigs of lavender for the *toilettes*—she was down to her last three.

Loading the Parmentiers' order onto a trolley, she'd trundled it across to the Fontaine Dorée and helped a beaming Madame Parmentier set them out.

'Have you eaten?' Caroline Parmentier asked and, without waiting for an answer, showed Marie-Ange through to the kitchen. 'We overdid it on the *poulet* and *rognons* for the Confrèrie, so there's no shortage. Please. I insist.'

Suddenly famished, nothing to eat since breakfast save André Ribaud's *crème abricot*, Marie-Ange sat on a stool in the *auberge* kitchen, while an attentive Michel Parmentier cut her a slice of truffled *foie gras*. Then he splashed some cognac into a pan of tumbling *rognons*, set them aflame with a whoosh and a billow, and gave them a final shuffle.

Now, an hour later, here she was, back at the shop with her feet up on a bucket and her stomach groaning. She looked at the laden flower trolleys waiting to be wheeled out to the storerooms but decided they could wait. She pushed herself out of her seat, went upstairs and had a bath, then pulled on a pair of jeans, a T-shirt and trainers.

A little night air might do the trick, she decided. That and a hot *chocolat*, if they had it, at the bar across the square.

MARIE-ANGE was Mazzelli's last customer. He'd been about to call Tomas in from the back yard to shut up shop when he saw her coming across the square. In his direction.

Mazzelli needed only one look to know who she was. The Chaberts' replacement. And coming in for a nightcap by the look of it. So he made himself busy behind the bar, pretending not to see her until she'd pulled out a stool and climbed onto it. When he turned to take her order, he felt as if the breath had been snatched from his lungs.

Tomas had been right, and so was every man who'd expressed an opinion that day in his bar. A vision. Radiance. They hadn't got the half of her. And without being able to do anything about it, Aldo felt his eyes widening.

'Signorina,' he managed, with what little breath he had left. 'Aldo Mazzelli,' he continued, attempting composure, extending a pudgy hand.

'Marie-Ange,' she replied, taking his hand and shaking it.

'Marie-Ange,' he repeated, looking to the ceiling as though the sound of the name would bring forth angels. 'A beautiful name. Welcome to St Bédard. And what can I get for you this evening, *per favore*?'

'A *chocolat*? You do them?'

'Only the best in the south,' Aldo replied, turning back to the Gaggia, selecting the superior cocoa and adding an extra spoonful to the mixing tumbler. 'You lookin' after the Chabert place?' he asked over his shoulder, pouring in the full-cream milk and whooshing it up under the steamer.

Marie-Ange nodded.

'Nasty business,' Mazzelli intoned, shaking his head. 'And couldn't have happened to nicer people.' He reached for a mug, poured the *chocolat* and turned back to the bar. 'There. The house speciality, young lady.'

Marie-Ange took a sip. 'Delicious.'

'So, anyway. What you think of our little community, eh?'

'It's just how I imagined it,' Marie-Ange replied. 'Only nicer.'

Mazzelli beamed, then turned to the shelves behind him, selected a bottle and whisked two glasses between them. The bottle was uncorked and the liquor poured before his visitor had a chance to say anything.

'There you go,' he said, pushing a glass towards her. 'A little something to keep the *chocolat* company.' He tipped his glass for a toast. Their glasses chinked. 'So, here's to the Fontaine des Fleurs. And new friends.'

'New friends,' replied Marie-Ange, closing her eyes as the grappa scalded its way down her throat.

Aldo watched. Not a cough, not a splutter. Just the closed eyes. Not bad, he thought, and smiled wickedly to himself. Tomas would have a stroke when he came in from mending his bike and saw the two of them at the bar chatting away. As for the wife, Tira, she'd gone to bed an hour ago, blessed be the mothers of all the saints, and would be fast asleep by now.

'So? Busy day?' he asked, loosening his collar, pushing back his hair.

'You could say,' said Marie-Ange, picking up the *chocolat*, cupping the mug in her hands and licking at the froth with the tip of her tongue.

A shiver passed through Mazzelli's limbs. Taking up the bottle for a second shot, he pulled the cork with a squeaky plop.

'No, no, please,' she protested, covering her glass with her hand. 'I couldn't. There's so much to do at the shop . . .'

Which was the moment that Tomas came in from the back yard. He rocked to a halt when he saw who his father was talking to.

Aldo slid him a look, then turned back to Marie-Ange. 'Oh, you not to worry about that. Tomas here will lend you a hand, won't you, Tomas? Tomas,' he continued, noting with pleasure his son's open mouth, 'meet Marie-Ange, from the flower shop.'

Five minutes later, having held up his hand when Marie-Ange made to pay for the *chocolat*, Aldo Mazzelli watched the two of them cross the square. Nice girl, he thought. A real cracker.

He chuckled. Wait till Tomas got back and took a look at that face of his, a smear of grease from the Suzuki slanting across his cheek from nose to ear. That'll teach him, thought Aldo. Way out of his league anyhow.

WITHIN A MONTH of Marie-Ange's arrival, everyone who lived and worked on the Place Vausigne had something to say about her. Among the men there was only the one opinion shared, greedily, like a glass of beer in the middle of a desert: she was an angel, a stunner, a gem.

As for the women of St Bédard, they were split. While Madame Héliard and the sisters Adeline and Odile had only good words to say about her, the rest were not so certain. Caroline Parmentier loved Marie-Ange's flower arrangements but she also knew what her husband was like. The same held true of Delphine Bulot. She might have persuaded her husband to decorate their window display with the wreaths of tarragon and myrtle that Marie-Ange had made, but she didn't miss the look in her husband's eye when the newcomer called by a few days later with some twists of vine for the shelf edgings. Clotilde Lepantre and Tira Mazzelli both acknowledged with a grim chuckle that neither of their husbands would resist much temptation.

As for the shop, everyone in the square agreed that it had never looked prettier. New varieties, new arrangements and each morning a fresh display—cacti and flowering succulents one day, everything red the next. Or blue, or purple, or pink. And the racks in front of the shop repositioned daily to show the blooms to best effect. Within a fortnight the place had been transformed. And the fragrance . . .

By the end of the month, almost every house on the square had one of Marie-Ange's potpourri sachets. And no one needed telling that the *curé*'s new altar decorations were Marie-Ange's handiwork: great sheaves of canna lilies and irises stepped around the altar, ropes of blood-red roses tumbling from the cross, banks of nasturtium woven into the Communion rail and fist-sized knots of wild lavender and rosemary at the end of every pew.

Little wonder, then, that everyone in St Bédard was talking about the new girl at the Fontaine des Fleurs.

Which was how Hélène de Vausigne came to hear of her.

IT WAS PICARD who delivered the summons, early one morning. By the time Marie-Ange came down for breakfast, he and the de Vausignes' Citroën 11 Légère were long gone, with only the envelope on the mat to tell of their passing. She picked it up, read her name and slipped it into her apron pocket. Only later, when the shop was open, the flowers set out to her satisfaction, leaves and blooms winking with droplets of spray, did she retrieve the envelope, slit it open and pull the letter free: an invitation to the Château at five o'clock that afternoon. No need to reply. Signed simply 'Hélène de Vausigne'.

Of course, Marie-Ange had read about the de Vausigne family. Their shotgun, their gardener, their neighbours. *Le Figaro* had done a big spread the week she had arrived in St Bédard, the story written by a journalist called Benedict, who'd actually found the murder weapon and lived nearby. There'd been a picture of the Comtesse, looking sad yet resigned.

All in all, Marie-Ange decided, driving back to St Bédard after dropping in with the week's takings at Crédit Agricole in Cavaillon, she was rather looking forward to the encounter.

Back at the shop, she went upstairs and ran a bath. While it filled, she went to her room, swung open Eric's wardrobe and fingered her way through half a dozen summer frocks, settling on a floral-sprigged outfit with high neck, tight bodice and elbow-length sleeves.

An hour later, tucking the folds of her skirt into the saddle, she pushed her bike away from the pavement outside the Fontaine des Fleurs and free-wheeled across the square, waving to Adeline before swinging left at the bottom of the square and heading for Chant-le-Neuf.

A few kilometres later, when she pulled in through the open gates of the chateau, she was neither too hot nor too tired, though she felt an unexpected shiver course through her as she swooped down the drive and the first of the chateau's four corner turrets showed through the trees.

At precisely four fifty-nine she pulled the bell chain.

'Marie-Ange Buhl,' she said, when Picard opened the door.

The old man's eyes narrowed. 'You are expected, Mam'selle.'

GILLES DE VAUSIGNE had spent the day at leisure. As he spent almost every one of his days. He liked it that way. He was seventy-one, after all.

That morning, as usual, he'd risen late, had Picard lay out cream linen trousers, a blue cotton shirt and yellow silk cravat, then soaked in his bath, pleasurably contemplating his forthcoming visit to Aix. Afterwards, dressed in a silk gown and velvet slippers, he'd shaved and taken clippers and dye brush to his thickening eyebrows.

On his way downstairs, Gilles had knocked at his wife's door and called her name. No answer. He pushed open the door and looked in. As expected. Long gone. Just that dreadful cloying scent of hers still heavy in the air, despite the open windows. He wondered how long she'd been up. Since they slept in separate rooms, it was difficult to know.

Breakfast done, he'd strolled the terrace, looking out over the land that spread down the valley and across to the distant blue slopes of the Luberon.

A generous holding to be sure. But there was one thing missing: the sea.

As plain Gilles Sallère, the Comte had spent his childhood roaming Brittany's rocky headlands and beaches. He remembered it as a dozen dreamy seaside years, which ended abruptly when his father drowned in a sailing accident and the creditors came calling. Dispossessed of their small *manoir*, his mother, Béatrice, had leased a set of rooms in Deauville, where, stalking its gaming tables, she'd chanced upon the recently widowed Edouard de Vausigne, softly seduced him and promptly accepted his invitation to move south. Here to St Bédard. The Château de Vausigne. No sea in sight. Even now, sixty years on, Gilles missed the briny green swell of it.

At a little after midday, the Comte took lunch in the small dining room, where his stepfather's great-grandfather had entertained Napoleon on his way to Elba, at the same round rosewood table where he now sat. The trouble was, he thought, as Florence ladled out a bowl of consommé, the history was all rather boring, especially the way Hélène went on about it. The title he'd given her might not have been a blood title, but it was a title all the same. And for Hélène de Vausigne, that was all that mattered.

Gilles rang the bell at his side. Florence reappeared with a plate of cutlets, swapped it for the empty soup bowl and retreated to the kitchen. As he ate, Gilles wondered at his wife. Extraordinary woman, he mused. Bold and decisive. But cold as a winter snap. He tried to remember the last time he'd gone to her room and not been sent packing. Their son, Antoine, was what? Thirty-seven? Gilles chuckled to himself. Soon after that, he reckoned. Astonishing she'd ever got pregnant in the first place. Some southerner, he thought, compared with the others who'd come his way since.

Gilles sometimes wondered if Hélène knew of his straying, but he guessed not. Never a word, never a look to hint that she was on to him. And he was always discreet, of course.

He pushed away the remains of his lunch, then finished his wine. Coffee in the library, he decided, and maybe a small brandy. Hélène wouldn't be back before five, so there was time. Apparently the girl looking after the Chaberts' place was coming to discuss flowers for the party.

Gilles was dozing in his chair when Picard knocked on the library door, entered and announced that a Marie-Ange Buhl was in the morning room.

He started up and looked at his watch. Five o'clock. How time flew.

'Is my wife back?' he asked, heaving himself from his chair and straightening his cravat in the mirror above the fireplace.

'Not as yet, sir.'

'Better bring her in here then,' he said gruffly.

As Marie-Ange was shown through into the library, she could see a pair of crossed legs and a newspaper, which, at a cough from Picard, was lowered with a rustle.

'Mademoiselle Buhl,' said Picard. 'From the village, sir.'

As Picard retreated, Marie-Ange watched the Comte put aside the paper, haul himself from his armchair and come across the room to shake her hand. As his hand touched hers it was as if a spill of cold water had trickled down her spine. For a moment she thought she would faint.

'Mademoiselle, a pleasure,' he said, eyes raking over her, his hand keeping hers to draw her into the room. 'What a delight.' He gestured to the sofa. 'Please, do take a seat,' he said. 'I'm afraid Hélène . . .'

And then, as he prepared to sit beside her, his eyes registered a slow sadness as the library door swung open. His wife had returned.

Marie-Ange turned as the Comtesse pushed the door closed behind her and tumbled an armful of ledgers and an attaché case onto a chair.

'Ah, Hélène. You're here at last. My dear, this is . . .' Gilles turned back to Marie-Ange, questioningly, although she knew he remembered the name.

'Buhl, Madame,' she said, getting to her feet, pulling the thin material of her dress away from her body, holding out her hand. 'Marie-Ange Buhl, from the Fontaine des Fleurs. You sent a note.'

'Of course, so good of you to come.' Hélène de Vausigne shook her hand, then went to her husband and kissed his cheek. 'So sorry I'm late, darling. Have you been looking after Mademoiselle Buhl? I do hope so.' And then, turning back to Marie-Ange: 'So. The anniversary.'

'Anniversary?'

'Fifty years together. A half-century, doesn't that sound terrible? The first weekend in August. It's to be quite big,' said Hélène, almost regretfully. 'More people than we anticipated. So we've decided on the ballroom and the terrace, with a marquee on the back lawn. And a dozen house guests as well. Rather a lot to get done, I'm afraid. I was rather hoping you could help?'

'I should be delighted,' replied Marie-Ange.

'*Très bien, très bien*. Shall I show you round? No time like the present.'

'Of course,' said Marie-Ange, gathering herself. She turned to the Comte and held out her hand.

'Mademoiselle,' he said. 'It's been a pleasure.' He was tempted to raise her hand to his lips but he made do with a tight little handshake. Such a remarkable young woman, he thought to himself. Such a perfect body.

6

rack! Crack-crack! Crack-crack, crack!
'That was what it sounded like, you know. Sharp, like stones hit together. But louder than you might expect. Maybe a dozen shots, single and overlapping . . . So quick. So fast. Over. Like that . . .'

The old lady sat in her chair by the window. She paused, nodded, fingers gripping the blanket they had tucked round her legs, and wondered again if anyone heard what she had to say.

'But the echo, that was the worst, you know. Not just a dozen shots, but a hundred, a thousand, fading, till there was nothing left but silence.'

If she could have cried, she would have. But all the tears were gone, years ago, her eyes dry and dim now. 'That's when I knew he was gone.' Her mouth trembled. 'They shot him, you know. *Rat-a-tat-a-tat.* Just like that. I watched it all. I saw. And I will never forget.'

The old woman's head nodded. Her eyes closed.

Later—ten minutes, an hour, another day, she couldn't tell—she opened her eyes, lifted her head from the pillow, then let it sink back. What was the use? She was in her room, that was all she knew. She could smell the jasmine curling round her window.

'We were betrayed,' she said, for she sensed that somebody was there, sitting beside the bed. 'Someone . . . talked. The Boches were waiting for us. "*Hande hoche!*" they said. And there they were.' Her eyes widened, staring back into the past. 'Rising out of the mist. A clatter of boots. Running. Shouts. Firing. There was nothing we could do. The game was up.'

She felt a hand take hers, stroke her crooked knuckles.

'We called him . . . Stéphane. Stéphane,' she repeated gently. 'But we knew that wasn't his real name. It was safer that way. Me? My name was Rose. Never Sandrine. Only Stéphane knew my real name. And I his.'

Somewhere she could hear a bell, a distant murmur of voices.

'Someone talked, you see. And that was that. All over,' she sighed.

And then she felt a sleeve brush her cheek, felt a finger touch her forehead, this way, that, leaving something cool, slick. And a voice, soft, lilting, sad, caring. Familiar words. Church words.

'All over . . .' she whispered. 'All over . . .'

JACQUOT SAT in cloudless late July sunshine. It was late morning, and Place Vausigne was bustling with life. Women with shopping bags, shopkeepers in their doorways, a couple of old-timers watching a game of boules, and a party of rickety American tourists mopping their brows after the climb from the coach park on the lower levels, looking round and realising that it had been worth the effort. The crescent of teetering town houses set at either side of the church, the pastel-wash façades, wrought-iron balconies and sun-pinked Provençal roofs following in stepped lines the slope of the hill on which St Bédard stood. It was just as the guidebooks had said.

Jacquot watched them make for the *tabac* and gather round the postcard racks. There was an urgency about them—so little time before their coach moved on. And in another hour, Jacquot knew, it would all close down. There would be just the sparrows swooping through the trees and the clatter of lunchtime plates from the shade of the *auberge* parasols.

Across the road, St Bédard's fountain splashed like a baby in the bath—the lapping water at its mossy edges flashing and winking in sunlight that was hard as diamonds in the open, dappled and shifting in the leafy shade where Jacquot sat. Behind him, inside the Bar de la Fontaine, there was the muted sound of a jukebox.

Jacquot sipped his beer, wiped away the froth with the back of his hand, then put down the glass. He lit a cigarette and took it all in, putting names to the faces of the people who lived and worked in St Bédard.

It wasn't easy. Brunet and his boys had done the house-to-house during those days following the murders. They'd probably remember who was who. Jacquot had just read through their reports.

Time and again. Over and over. Yet three weeks into Eric Chabert's trial, he knew that something was missing. Something was not ringing quite true.

Through the trees, a flash of black caught his eye, and he turned to see the *curé* dart across the square, sidestepping the corner of the boules pitch, soutane snapping at his ankles. And there, on the far side of the square, stood the Fontaine des Fleurs. In the shade beneath its awning, a customer was pointing out blooms in the display and a girl was reaching for them, collecting the stems in a bouquet. The last time he'd been in St Bédard, Jacquot had asked about her. Came from an agency, he was told, looking after the Chaberts' shop while Monsieur and Madame were away in Lyon.

She'd be there a while, Jacquot had thought.

As he sat there in the sunshine, he remembered his own day in court, at the end of the second week. His moment in the witness box. Hunched over folded arms beside his bloated counsel, Maître Messain, Eric Chabert had never once looked up as Jacquot testified . . .

'Excuse, M'sieur . . .'

It was the owner of the bar. Aldo Mazzelli, with a frosted glass of beer in one hand and a saucer of olives in the other. He set both down in front of Jacquot, slicing the air with the hand that had held the saucer, palm down, as though to deflect any argument, before Jacquot could reach for his pocket. 'M'sieur, a pleasure. And an honour. It really is you.' Mazzelli reached for Jacquot's hand and shook it. And then looked away, summoning the memory. 'Twick-en-ham. Those English thugs against France. Injury time. I never forget it. Inside,' he said, thumbing back to the interior of the bar. 'All of us round the TV. No one speaks. No one breathes. And then— oouff—from nowhere . . . *Assolutamente formidabile.*'

Jacquot nodded. Thanked him for the beer and olives. It was very kind.

Sometimes, still, he was recognised. All these years later. A drink. An autograph. He'd grown used to it. Sometimes he liked it too.

And all for sixteen seconds' work.

As he picked up an olive and popped it into his mouth, time concertinaed. Jacquot was back there.

A low, steely sky, sheets of freezing rain pelting down through the flood-lights, the English pitch a churn of mud. And Jacquot, substitute flanker, sitting it out on the bench, groaning with every English try, flooding with hope when his teammates fought back to bring the game level. And then, with only minutes to go, England two points up, the coach told him to warm up. He was going on. He couldn't believe it—playing for France. The moment he'd been waiting for. A minute later his stomach rolled, his heart vaulted and the crowd roared him onto the pitch. They roared again two minutes later when, springing from an English scrum on the French five-metre line, Jacquot found the ball in his arms and the field ahead clear to the English posts. All he had to do was run.

For sixteen seconds Jacquot galloped down that pitch, waiting for the tackle he knew had to come. Which it did, as he closed on the English posts, a desperate lunge that sent him sliding across the English line.

All these years, and people still remembered that winning try, in injury time, against the English, at Twickenham. And sometimes, too, they bought him a drink.

'My son plays,' Mazzelli was saying. 'Cavaillon A's next season. So he tells me. Who knows?'

'A good team. We never liked Cavaillon when I played with Béziers,' replied Jacquot.

'Ah, those Béziers boys. You had to be tough, eh?'

Jacquot nodded. Only he hadn't been quite tough enough.

That last game against Toulouse. He'd been selected for a second outing in his country's colours—against Wales—and was playing this local match cautiously. Until the second half, when he got caught in a ruck and the second row forward on his own side had stamped down on his heel and snapped his Achilles tendon. Jacquot's career on the rugby field was over. Thirty years old. One cap. Sixteen seconds of glory.

'Well, as I was saying, an honour and a privilege,' concluded Mazzelli.

And he was gone, weaving his way between the tables to report the conversation to his pals, to confirm that it was indeed Daniel Jacquot. Number Six. Flanker. Twickenham. The try. The man. Here at the Bar de la Fontaine.

Jacquot sighed. All these years later, here he was, marooned in a back-end posting in the Vaucluse. Another six years to a full pension and nothing more challenging than a furniture-warehouse fire to investigate.

But it wasn't all downside. There was always the glorious, captivating, wonderful Claudine, painter and sculptor. If he hadn't met up with her again after that first time in Marseilles, he really would have gone crazy. But some things were meant to be. Like the business in Marseilles and then ending up here. The very place she lived. Fate. And thank God for it.

Still Jacquot made no move to go, even though he knew he should be in Rocsabin, sifting his way through the charred remains of a burnt-out warehouse. Sitting here on the terrace of the Bar de la Fontaine in St Bédard, for the third time in as many weeks, he felt oddly distracted. But he knew, somehow, that he was in the right place. Doing the right thing.

DRIVING TO ROCSABIN later, Jacquot acknowledged that, like his other visits to St Bédard, this latest outing had failed to comfort him. There was no getting away from it, he thought as he took the bends and the sun flashed across his windscreen. The Chabert case. Try as he might, he just couldn't shake it.

Which had as much to do with his own worming intuition as with the letter in his pocket. And the others in his desk drawer.

The first letter had arrived a week after Eric Chabert's arrest, after Dietering had returned to Munich. The envelope bore an Alsace frank and was addressed: *L'Inspecteur 'Martner'*. After Jacquot's name had appeared in the papers in connection with the case, the letters that followed had all been correctly addressed. Letters from Île-de-France, Brittany, Poitou-Charentes. All in the same hand, a girlish slant. With the *Private and Confidential* heavily underlined.

The letters were brief. The message clear.

You have the wrong man.

It was a message that coincided exactly with Jacquot's feeling. Eric Chabert was not—could not be—the Martners' and Brauers' killer.

It was at the end of that first session with Brunet, after they'd found out about Eric and Kippi, that Jacquot realised they'd got it wrong. Right at the end, when Brunet switched off the tape and Mougeon came in to take the boy down to the cells.

He knew the moment Eric Chabert stood up. Sure he had access to the Comte's guns, sure he might shoot rabbits, be used to blood. And he certainly had the motive. It was just that . . . Eric Chabert wasn't tall enough.

No way, as he climbed the Martner staircase, could Chabert have knocked those floral prints out of line. No way, Jacquot was certain, unless the boy had done it with his head, and even then he'd have had to reach a bit.

And neither, more significantly, was Eric Chabert clairvoyant. Which he would have had to have been if he'd thought to steal the murder weapon in November. Kippi hadn't given him the push—hadn't provided him with a motive—until she and her mother had visited that last time, for Jutta Martner's birthday.

Like the orchids. Like the money. It just didn't add up.

But everyone else went for it. Rochet, Gastal, Warendorf, Brunet. They had their man. Confession or no confession, they had what they needed: access to the murder weapon; access to the same make of ammunition used; his prints on the weapon; and a DNA test confirming that the boy was the father. And motive, of course. The two letters.

When they found the letters, Jacquot knew it was all over. The note from Jutta Martner, discovered in a pocket in Chabert's overalls, terminating his employment, presumably after Ilse had told her mother that the boy had made Kippi pregnant. There was also the note from Kippi herself, dated four days before the killings, scrunched up behind the chest of drawers in Eric Chabert's bedroom, telling him to stop pestering her, she didn't want to see him any more.

They had enough to arrest. To secure a conviction. Nothing political. Nothing to worry about.

Even Dietering had seemed happy with the outcome. But, then, he had a wife and four-month-old baby to get home to. 'It adds up, Dan,' he said, as Jacquot drove him to the airport for the last time.

'He's not tall enough, Hans. I told you.'

Dietering shook his head. 'You mean the pictures on the stairs? He could have done it with the gun, running downstairs after the daughter.'

'And the shells?'

Dietering knew what Jacquot was getting at. Prints on the gun, but not on the shell casings?

'And the break-in. November?' continued Jacquot.

'He had to cover his tracks.'

'But in November, Hans, there were no tracks he needed to cover. He didn't know back then the girl was going to dump him, did he? The kid was in love, for God's sake.'

When they pulled up outside the departures hall, Dietering looked at him hard. 'You really don't believe it was this Chabert boy, do you?'

'No, Hans, I don't. Not Chabert. It just doesn't work for me.'

The two men got out of the car, the engine still running.

'Leave it,' said Dietering, as he pulled his bag from the back seat and closed the door. 'Things like this have a way of sorting themselves out.'

'I'm surprised to hear you say that, Hans.'

'In the end, Dan, there is always the truth,' he said, and reached out to shake Jacquot's hand.

'"In the end" can be a very long time,' replied Jacquot, taking his friend's hand, not to shake it but to draw the man towards him.

A hug. They'd parted on a hug. Which was good.

Leaning back in his seat, Jacquot felt the latest letter crumple in his pocket. No different from all the others he had received following Chabert's arrest. The same message: *You have made a mistake. Eric Chabert is innocent.* Each letter signed: *A Friend.*

No different in any respect. Except this last letter bore a Brieuc postmark. Someone was telling him something, and this time it wasn't just that Chabert was innocent. It was a plea: *Find me. I'm here. We need to talk.*

MARIE-ANGE BUHL crossed the cobbled yard at the Rocsabin stud and breathed in the scent of damp straw. She was still some distance from the stall but she could hear Pierrot stamping and snorting. He knew she was there.

Twenty minutes later, riding down the lane from the stud and through the gate that opened onto the slopes of the valley, she leaned forward, whispered, '*Allez-y*,' into Pierrot's flickering ears and touched her heels to his flanks. It was enough. They were off. In seconds the wind was batting through her hair, his mane whipping against her cheek and his hoofbeats thudding up inside her. She whooped with delight.

For the last three Wednesdays, Marie-Ange had come to Rocsabin in the afternoon and ridden Pierrot. It was André Ribaud who'd set it up, as a thankyou for the window displays Marie-Ange had helped him put together for Au Broc Fontaine. When she happened to mention that she loved riding, he'd taken her straight out to Rocsabin and introduced her to his lover, Didier Houssaye. And it was Houssaye who had introduced her to Pierrot.

According to Houssaye, none of the regulars would touch the old grey and the stud wouldn't dare let him out with a tourist. Spirited, mean-tempered when he wanted to be, Pierrot was just about the best ride at the stables, he'd told her. If you were up to it.

As usual, Pierrot had ridden fast for the first few minutes, galloping across the side of the valley, then he'd settled back into a gentle canter beside a field of sunflowers. Now he was pulling up as the land levelled.

Up ahead, Marie-Ange could see the river winking through the linden trees and poplars that marked its course. Pierrot was after the lush green shoots that lined the riverbanks. Try to keep him away from them, Marie-Ange had discovered, and you'd regret it. Give him his head, let him graze, and he'd pay you back in spades.

They followed the river until Pierrot found what he was looking for—a gentle, muddy slope between the trees. He slithered down the bank and into the water. Stepping delicately among the pebbles, he headed downstream. Ten metres on, Marie-Ange loosened the reins and his neck swooped down to a bright girdle of shoots and buds.

These flowers, Marie-Ange knew, made the sweetest *tisane*. She leaned down and picked a few handfuls, intending to make something up for Agnès Héliard, to ease her bones and help her sleep at night. Then, after a gentle walk along the riverbank, she decided to go as far as the large oak, where the river turned towards Cavaillon and the first three arches of St Bédard's bridge came into view. That was where she'd turn Pierrot back for Rocsabin. She knew if she went any closer to the bridge, the skin on her arms would pucker into shivery life and she'd get that dry, dusty taste in her mouth. And Pierrot wouldn't like it either. He'd stamp and snort and skitter and pull at his bit. The one time they'd got too close, he'd almost unsaddled her.

Not a nice place, the bridge that led to St Bédard. She'd glimpsed its coppery memorial from her bike the day she arrived, and she passed it every time she drove to and from Brieuc. But she'd never stopped to read the inscription. She didn't need to. What she heard there told her all she needed to know.

The stuttering of guns, shouting, the revving of engines and the clatter of boots. Panic, desperation and fear . . .

'THERE'S A BODY,' said Brunet, when Jacquot arrived at the smoking remains of the HacheGee furniture warehouse in Rocsabin.

Jacquot frowned. This was not what he'd expected. Another insurance job, he'd decided on his way out there, the owners looking to make something from a business that was not performing. Jacquot had been to the warehouse when he first arrived in Cavaillon, bought a desk and bookshelves for his cramped apartment because someone had told him there was always a sale on. Arson almost certainly, he'd decided. But he hadn't figured on a body.

'Name?'

Brunet shook his head. 'Fournier's there now. In the office at the back. What's left of it.'

He led Jacquot between the fire engines assembled in the front car park. They skirted the edge of the smouldering ruin and turned into the back yard. According to Brunet, the fire had been called in at 12.27 a.m. and had taken most of the night to subdue. Now, everything was running with water.

'Through here, boss,' said Brunet, stepping through what remained of a doorway.

Fournier was on his knees, sifting through a mound of ash, the sleeves and legs of his white forensic suit smeared with black. He looked round when Jacquot came in and got to his feet. 'Don't ask,' he said. 'Impossible to tell anything right now. If we hadn't spotted the wristwatch, she'd have been cleaned out of here with the rest of this mess.'

'She?'

'Seems likely. It's a woman's watch. Still working, would you believe?'

Jacquot looked at the cindery mound where Fournier had been working. At first he could see nothing but a coal-black square, but as his eyes adjusted he was able to make out a kind of pattern to the chaos: the twisted metal legs of a desk, its wooden surface reduced to a wrinkled sheet of carbon; a tumble of blistered metal filing cabinets; the puddling melt of a computer monitor; and there, between desk and cabinets, what looked like a chair, tipped over, its charred metal frame outlining a familiar form. The two objects appeared attached, spoonlike in their closeness: the bunched curve of a body, the crook of an elbow, a glimmer of metal, rounded and calcified like the bodies they had found at Pompeii, baked to a crisp.

Odd, thought Jacquot, sitting at your desk in the middle of the night, with the building burning around you. Heart attack? Suicide?

'Who runs the place?'

'Guy called Joel Filbert,' replied Brunet.

'What's his story?'

'Holiday. Corsica. Been away a week.'

'He the owner?'

Brunet shook his head. 'A Madame Grace Bartolomé. Lives out at Lucat the other side of Rocsabin. According to one of the staff, she's on a buying trip. Back later today.'

Or maybe lying there at his feet, thought Jacquot grimly. 'Tell me about the fire,' he said, turning to Fournier.

'Deliberate, no question,' said the forensics man. 'Petrol all over . . .'

Before he could say anything more, a fireman stepped up behind them, yellow helmet in hand, short hair standing up in sweaty spikes, face smeared with soot. The three men turned to him.

'*Un autre*,' he said, pointing across the blackened, smoking interior.

Jacquot and Brunet exchanged glances. Another body.

Fournier bent down for his bag and they followed the fireman, picking their way through a landscape of tangled metalwork, shifting ash and flame-quilted timbers to the front of the warehouse.

When they reached the fireman's colleagues, one of Fournier's team was there already, shooting off a roll of film. Jacquot looked where the camera was pointed. This time he had no trouble identifying the shape. The clothes might be scorched to the body, the features blackened beyond recognition, but the shoes were unmistakable: a man's, one foot crossed over the heel of the other as though the victim had tripped and fallen.

Fournier got down on his knees and opened his case. 'It's going to take a while,' he said, to Jacquot. 'I'll be able to give you more when we get them out of here. Tomorrow some time,' he said.

Out in the car park, Jacquot paused in the sunshine. 'So, how do you see it?' he asked Brunet, nodding back at the warehouse.

'We're missing a third party, boss. There's someone else involved. Has to be. Does the deed—a bullet, a blow to the back of the head—then starts the fire to cover his trail. Can't see it any other way.'

'Security cameras?'

'The fire got to the film before we did.'

'Sprinklers?'

'Active, but not enough to do the job. The blaze was way too strong. And the alarms weren't tripped until the fire reached the main hall.'

They watched Fournier walk to his car and open the boot. In the smouldering remains of the warehouse, two of his white-suited colleagues were laying out blue plastic body bags.

'I've asked the local boys to handle Rocsabin,' Brunet continued. 'Door to door. And interview the staff, too.'

Jacquot looked at the half-dozen cars parked in the bays.

Brunet knew what he was thinking. 'Four accounted for, boss. Mougeon's checking the other two.'

Jacquot glanced at his watch. A little after four. 'Seems about all we can do right now. Why don't we call it a day?' he said. 'Sleep on it.'

Brunet brightened. He hadn't expected to get away so early.

Jacquot gave him a look and Brunet's lips flickered close to a smile. Clearly his assistant had something else on his mind. Jacquot should have known: the haircut, the new jeans and tie . . .

'See you tomorrow, then,' said Brunet, eager to be gone before something else cropped up that might detain them.

'*À demain, oui*,' replied Jacquot, with a smile, getting into his car.

7

Sounds and voices. That was what Marie-Ange heard. Like some far-off signal picked up on a radio, something from the furthest reaches of the dial, beyond the usual frequencies. And always accompanied by an icy dance of shivery skin, like Pierrot's flanks when a horsefly settled, and that dry, dusty taste on her tongue.

And it always happened in the same way, in a deepening silence that seemed to isolate her, as though she'd put her fingers into her ears. Distant sounds and voices floating in that only she could hear. Like the whispering in the Chaberts' home, the sobbing on the top floor of the Fontaine Dorée, and like that evening, sitting out on Mazzelli's terrace, when everything around her had grown quiet. And in that silence, in the tree closest to her, the creaking of a branch and the tightening squeak of a rope as though some hefty weight was suspended from it . . .

Then, of course, there was the Martner place. The reason she'd come south.

Marie-Ange had gone there the first time with the representative from Agence Florale in Aix, an older lady whose voice had dropped away into an indistinct whisper the moment the front door closed behind them, at the very edge of a silence that had wrapped round Marie-Ange like a smothering blanket, muffling the woman's words.

On her left were the stairs, where her eyes were drawn up to the last of the three doors on the landing; ahead, the hallway, where she felt an urgent desire to run, to push past her companion as though her life depended on it; then the kitchen, filled with a desperate panic; and finally the hothouse, dense and stifling with memories. And out of the silence, at a bend in the gravel path, the terrible blasts of a shotgun, battering her ears with a percussive force that made her want to duck down, among the rich green foliage.

'Are you all right, dear?' the woman had asked, and the silence was gone.

'Fine,' Marie-Ange had replied, the dryness in her mouth giving her words an awkward thickness. 'Just fine.'

And the two of them had walked on.

They were neither pleasant nor unpleasant, these 'moments', but over the years Marie-Ange had grown used to them, learned to accommodate them.

She had been eleven when they had begun, in the house in Metz where the Buhl family moved in the winter of 1983, when her father, an administrator for French Railways, had been transferred there. The house overlooked the Metz marshalling yards, a landscape of sheds, sidings and rails.

The first night in her new room she fell asleep quickly, lulled by the sounds beyond her window—the distant rattle of coupling chains, the sliding clang of doors, the hiss of released steam—too exhausted by the excitement of moving to be surprised that there should be so much activity at night.

On her second night, however, no matter how hard she tried, Marie-Ange simply couldn't sleep. She tossed and turned, listening to the endless shunting to and fro, the rattle of box-car doors being pulled open and slammed shut, the bark of dogs and distant voices.

At last she gave up on sleep and went to the window. The moment she parted the curtains, her skin crawled with shivers and her mouth turned as dry and dusty as the thin carpet beneath her feet.

For there was nothing there. Nothing to see but the moon glinting off the rails and the distant lights of the main station. No movement. Nothing below her in the yards. Yet still the sounds continued, receding gently until all she was left with was an icy puckering of skin that raced up her neck and over the top of her head, tightening at her hairline.

If she'd been confused when she was eleven, she knew what was going on by the time she was fourteen. She'd read the books, seen the films, and knew now that she was different, more sensitive to her surroundings, more aware. Most often this 'awareness' presented as nothing more than a kind of intuition, about people, places—a certainty that someone was not telling the truth, or that something had happened at a particular place. But sometimes, as with the marshalling yards of Metz, her 'awareness' manifested itself more dramatically. And that isolating silence was her only warning.

But it was only ever sounds and voices. She never saw anything. Or anyone.

Until Kippi.

It was March, a bitter wind sweeping a sleety rain along the streets of Metz. But in the polythene-lined tunnels of the Jardins Gilbert where Marie-Ange worked, it was close and humid.

It was shortly after nine in the morning, as she was potting a tray of seedlings, that she became aware of someone at her side, talking to her. At first she thought it was Pascale, off for a cigarette and wanting company.

So she shook her head, no, then realised it couldn't be Pascale, because he had left for a nursery in St Maxime the week before.

Marie-Ange noticed then how quiet everything was—no radio from along the bench, no sound from the wind and rain blustering against the sides of the polytunnel. But she didn't stop work, just glanced round.

A young girl, a teenager, blonde, talking to her, telling her something. In German. Over and over. Something about a young man.

'*Ein Junge. Ein Junge, den ich liebe. Er ist Französe. Er ist Gärtner.*'

A gardener. Something about a young man who was a gardener.

And then, in French, so softly that Marie-Ange had to strain to hear: '*Pas lui. Pas lui.*'

And then the girl seemed to drift behind her. And not be there any more.

That was when Marie-Ange did stop working, fingers icy in her rubber gloves, expecting to be frightened but relieved to find that she wasn't. Rather, she felt an odd elation. It was just like the voices, only much more real. More . . . exhilarating.

It was another week before she put it together, reading a newspaper story about a killing in Provence, the arrest of a suspect. The moment she saw the picture that accompanied the report, she knew that the man in the photograph was not the murderer. She couldn't explain how she knew this, but when she reached the final paragraph, where she read what the suspect did for a living, she knew she was right. He was a gardener.

And that was when Marie-Ange made the connection with the girl in the polytunnel, knew instantly what her 'visitor' had been telling her.

The young man, the gardener, he is not the killer.

That evening, she had started writing her letters.

It wasn't the first time that Marie-Ange had 'worked' with the police. A year earlier, she'd heard about a local woman who'd jumped to her death from a fourth-floor window. She couldn't say what made her go to the street where the woman lived, but when she got there she knew immediately that the woman hadn't jumped. Or fallen. She'd been pushed. The silence was as deep as ever and the iciness gripped her as she walked up and down the street, as sharp and piercing as anything she'd ever felt.

That night she'd written to the policeman heading the investigation. 'It's not a suicide, it's not an accident,' she wrote. 'It's murder.'

And then, from somewhere she couldn't identify, the words just came to her. Details. Shadowy, sketchy, but unmistakable. There is a man, she wrote. Tall, fifties. With a beard. He bore a grudge. He wanted revenge. But it didn't turn out the way he wanted. Things got out of hand. He didn't mean to kill, just to frighten.

'He's a teacher,' she added, at the end of the letter, almost as an afterthought, looking at the word, knowing she was right.

And that was exactly what he turned out to be. A week later, a fifty-six-year-old man was arrested for the woman's murder and the newspapers gave his profession as teacher.

Of course, no mention of her letter was made in the press coverage that followed, so Marie-Ange couldn't say for sure whether her involvement or straightforward detective work had led to the man's arrest. All she knew for certain was that they had the right man. And when, a few days later, she returned to the street where the woman died, the chill had gone. Just as the sounds from the Metz marshalling yards had stopped when she learned what had happened a half-century earlier, down there among the sidings, in the lines of steaming, wailing box-cars and rattling cattle wagons headed east for Germany, Poland and the camps.

And now she was sending letters again. From Île-de-France, Brittany, Poitou-Charentes, from the various garden centres she was sent to by

Agence Florale, the outfit Pascale had told her about, working two weeks here, a week there, a month somewhere else, filling holiday shoes mostly.

'Dear Monsieur Jacquot,' her letters began. 'You may remember . . .'

And although she had nothing more to add, no details like the Metz case, she continued to send the letters. Simply stating that the gardener Chabert was innocent. They had the wrong man.

And then, at the beginning of May, working at a nursery in Angoulême, she had read in the newspapers that a trial was imminent, and known in an instant that letters weren't enough.

That same day she'd called Agence Florale and requested a transfer to the Fontaine des Fleurs, in St Bédard.

Yes, the agency said, they were aware of that posting but they'd already put a man in place. But for some reason, when she put down the phone, Marie-Ange felt no sense of loss. Things, she was certain, would work out.

And, of course, they had. In the last week of May, the agency had called her back. Their original placement was unable to make it. Something had cropped up and he'd had to back out. If she was still interested . . .

Three days later, Marie-Ange was pushing her bike up the hill to St Bédard. The place where Eric Chabert lived.

AFTER LEAVING ROCSABIN, with the sun settling over the distant Alpilles, Jacquot turned into the Martner property, coasted down the drive and pulled up in the gravelled forecourt.

And there was the horse. A grey. Tethered in the shade.

Jacquot climbed out of the car and looked around. Someone passing by? Someone working the vines? He gazed across the slope of the hill but could see no one. He turned back to the house. The front door was closed and the windows shuttered. Apart from the buzz of insects and the grey's occasional nickering, there was nothing to be heard.

At least it wasn't a burglary, Jacquot decided. Who ever heard of a housebreaker making their getaway on horseback? Or breaking into an empty house, come to that. Apart from the hothouse collection, all the Martners' belongings had been put into storage, placed with an auction house in Avignon or moved back to Zürich. The place was empty. Nearly five months after the murders, Herr Brauer had still to achieve a sale.

Jacquot walked to the Martners' front door, feeling in his pocket for the key. He slipped it into the lock and immediately felt resistance. Already unlocked. He pressed down the latch and the door swung open.

Whoever owned the horse, he decided, was probably in the house.

In the old days, in Marseilles, Jacquot would have kept his hand near his gun, every sense keening. Now he just stepped inside, wiped his boots on the mat and shouted, 'Anybody there?' That was the way it was in the Vaucluse. After three years, he'd grown used to it. As for his gun, it was back at HQ, in the drawer with the letters.

Jacquot closed the door behind him and stood in the shadows at the bottom of the stairs, listening, waiting for a reply, for someone to make an appearance. But no one did. There was not a sound.

He made his way down the hall and called again, but still no answer. In the kitchen, he noticed the courtyard shutters were open and tried to recall if they'd been that way the last time he'd visited. Since Eric Chabert's arrest he'd been to the house a couple of times on his own, walking through these rooms, searching for something he couldn't quite put his finger on.

From the kitchen he turned right, and opened the first of the double doors leading to the hothouse. He closed it behind him, reached forward, opened the second door and stepped into the stifling heat. It was like a warm, wet blanket that crept under his collar, seeped into his shirt and made his linen trousers cling to his thighs. Feeling a bead of sweat trickle into the small of his back, he peeled off his jacket and swung it over his shoulder, then followed the gravel path snaking between the trees and banks of foliage.

Suddenly he came to a halt. Something was very different. A few weeks before, the hothouse had seemed drab, February's radiant blooms reduced to a steaming, vegetative green. Now, suddenly, there was colour again—pinks and reds, blues and greens, the softest creams and purples, the petals of a thousand blooms speckled and striped.

Maybe it was the season for orchid blooms, he thought, for it was more glorious here than he could ever remember, more colourful and luxuriant than any of the collections that he and Dietering had visited on their orchid trail. The place felt alive with growth. The flowers looked . . . sexy—gloriously, gaudily sexy. And weaving through the drenching air was their fragrance—soft and subtle one moment, hot and spicy the next.

Jacquot looked about in amazement, and for the first time he began to understand the fascination—the obsession—that must have gripped the good doctor. No wonder Martner had been loath to sell anything.

He moved on, heading in the direction of the doctor's lab. About halfway through the hothouse, he rounded a bend and stopped in his tracks. A pace or two ahead, at the side of the path, a stepladder had been set up. On the ground beside it were a box of tools and a trug loaded with browned, twisted clippings. Whoever had been working there had placed the ladder beside a cascade of orchids, a three-metre shawl of pink and white slipper-like blooms, the most magnificent flowers Jacquot had ever seen. He was tempted to reach up a hand to touch them, just to see if they were real.

'*Vanda curvifolium cristata*. Very striking, don't you think?'

The voice came from behind him. He spun round.

She was wearing jodhpurs, riding boots and a man's white cotton shirt, which billowed round her waist. Her hair was tucked behind her ears and her cheeks had a rosy glow. She seemed not the least surprised to find him there.

'They come from southern India,' she continued, 'but the poor things have no scent. So strange, for such a beautiful bloom.'

'Jesus, you scared me,' said Jacquot, without thinking. And then: 'Who are you? What are you doing here?' Although he knew the answers already. It was the girl running the Chaberts' shop.

'Marie-Ange Buhl,' said the girl. 'I'm looking after the Fontaine des Fleurs in St Bédard. My agency asked me to take on this extra job, looking after the hothouse. It's beautiful, don't you think?'

Reaching past him, she swept away a tangle of cobwebs from the branch of an overhanging fern. As she did, Jacquot smelt the horse, hay and cooled sweat on her. She turned back to him and held his eyes. 'And you are?'

'Chief Inspector Daniel Jacquot. Cavaillon Regional Crime Squad.'

She gave him a closer look, a grin hovering on her lips. 'Didn't I see you in St Bédard this morning? With Aldo, at Mazzelli's?'

Jacquot nodded. 'I go there sometimes. It's a good place to have a beer.'

Another appraising glance. 'So, what brings you here, Chief Inspector?'

'Scene of crime,' he replied. 'A few months back. Sometimes I call by.'

'The Martner family.'

'You know about it?'

'Of course I know about it, Chief Inspector. I'm filling in for the Chaberts while they're away. Living in their house. Not to mention looking after the doctor's collection. I'd have to be pretty dim not to know about it, don't you think? It's all anyone ever talks about.' Then she frowned. 'But surely it's all over and done with? The investigation, I mean.'

Jacquot shrugged, left it at that.

The frown eased, disappeared. She looked around her. 'Tell me, Chief Inspector, do you know anything about orchids?'

'I know they're expensive.'

She laughed, and Jacquot felt every nerve-ending sing. It was the most beautiful laugh he'd ever heard.

'Oh, they're much more than that,' replied Marie-Ange, looping a fall of hair behind her ear. 'Would you like the tour?'

'My mother always said an education was a fine and noble thing,' replied Jacquot, trying to regain some sense of composure.

'Your mother was a wise woman,' said Marie-Ange, stepping past him, her arm brushing his. 'Come with me.'

She led the way deeper into the hothouse, pausing to point out the blooms—the names tripping off her tongue. Since the path was too narrow for them to walk side by side, Jacquot kept a pace or two behind her.

'The word "orchid" comes from the Greek,' she was telling him. '*Orkhis*. It means . . . testicle. Not the flower you understand, but the tuber. Look, here.' She pointed to some browning, oval balls peeping through the soil, each one tipped with a tiny green spear.

Jacquot nodded, not sure how to respond.

'Orchids are one of the largest flowering-plant families on earth,' she continued, 'found on every continent except Antarctica. So far, more than thirty thousand species have been identified, but there may be many thousands more to discover.' She reached up to touch the petals closest to her. '*Phalaenopsis deliria*. One of my favourites. First hybridised in the nineteenth century by an English grower called John Dominy. Look here, you see? From the *delenatii*, he's captured the frilled edge of the petals, and from the *casteria* that peachy colouring at the tips. Which is what hybridising is all about—years of trial and error to produce a flower like this.'

'You seem to know a great deal about it,' Jacquot said.

'I studied plant hybridisation at college,' she replied, turning her back on him and walking ahead. 'Orchids were my speciality. It wasn't much, but I always thought it was enough. Until I came here.' She stopped, looked back over her shoulder, turned towards him. 'These . . .' She gestured to the plants around them. 'Well, these are different.'

Jacquot suspected that she knew he'd been looking at her figure, the way she moved. He felt oddly flustered.

'Exquisite,' she said. 'Don't you think?'

Another unnerving look. Jacquot managed a nod.

'I'm not an expert,' she continued, 'but Dr Martner could have taught Dominy a thing or two. He's done some incredible work here. He must have travelled, brought back specimens to experiment with. Just look,' she said, lifting a stem looping down to her right, letting the flowers rest in the palm of her hand. '*Zygopetalum aspasia violacea*. It flowers only twice a year— July and late December, never more than ten days each time. A real collector's orchid, and a perfect specimen for hybridising. The colour of the throat, there, you see?' She took her eyes off the orchid and looked straight at Jacquot. 'Have you ever seen a colour like that? Such a shape?'

Again Jacquot felt flustered, this young woman rendering him as soft and stupid as a starstruck teenager.

'Where this plant is found, in the rain forests of Brazil, there are many like it fighting for attention, for some insect to come and pollinate them. It is up to each flower to create its own, unique enticement. And this one is the greatest seductress of them all.' She paused for a moment, then let the stem of blooms slide from her hand. 'I think it is the sexiest flower I know. You should only give it to someone you love. Or someone you want.'

'Maybe you could write the name down for me,' said Jacquot, reaching into his jacket pocket for a pen and paper, passing them to her.

She grinned. 'Of course.' Then, after a beat: 'Had you anyone in mind?'

'Oh, yes. Yes, I have someone in mind.'

She cocked her head, as though wanting to know more.

'A friend. It's her birthday in a few weeks.'

'But the blossom will be gone by then,' said Marie-Ange.

'Christmas, then,' he said, nodding for her to write the name anyway.

She smiled, then started writing. When she had finished, she folded the paper and handed it back with the pen. 'Well, Chief Inspector, I must get on.' She held out her hand and he took it. 'It was good to meet you.'

'And you, too, Mademoiselle. Thank you for the tour.'

'I enjoyed it as much as you,' replied Marie-Ange, eyes twinkling.

Ten minutes later, sitting in his car, Jacquot pulled the paper from his pocket and unfolded it. And gave a grunt of laughter. She'd written the orchid's name in capitals.

AFTER LEAVING the Martner house, Jacquot drove straight home. On the way, he called the office and left a message for Brunet to see in the morning. 'Any information you can get on Marie-Ange Buhl. Start with Brauer's lawyer. Boudit. Which agency he used for the Martner hothouse job. Anything.'

When Jacquot opened his front door he heard muffled sobbing coming from the kitchen. He knew immediately it was Claudine. His first thought was Midou, Claudine's daughter. Something had happened to Midou. His heart vaulted into his throat. He hurried down the hallway and pushed through the door into the kitchen.

Claudine was sitting at the table, head in hands, shoulders shaking, a tangle of auburn hair hanging round her wrists. At the end of the table the portable TV combo they kept in the kitchen was playing a video, a silent black and white film of a girl doing cartwheels in a garden. Jacquot had seen it before. It was an old family film of Claudine, aged ten, performing for her aunt, a frail figure clapping in a garden chair. Beside the television was a tin box, its glossy black paint chipped and scratched. It looked like an old deed box, the letters *J.E.* painted on the lid in curling copperplate.

Jacquot pulled out a chair and sat beside Claudine, reaching for her hand, which she gave him gratefully, looking up with a tearful smile that told him that, whatever was wrong, it was suddenly bearable with him there, that all she wanted was sympathy, love, a hug. He breathed a sigh of relief. Not Midou, then. He took Claudine in his arms and felt a hot, wet cheek press against his neck and the heave of her body as a fresh spring of sobs arrived.

'There, there,' he said, brushing the hair from her face where the tears had plastered it to her skin. 'Now tell me. What's wrong, my darling?'

Claudine took a deep breath, 'It's Tantine . . .'

Tantine. The old lady in the video. The last of Claudine's family. Sandrine Eddé. Seventy-nine, eighty. Somewhere around there. For the last four years she'd been cared for by the Sisters of Laune, in a seventeenth-century abbey run as a private hospice in the hills above Salon.

'She died this morning,' sniffed Claudine, pulling a tissue from the box by her elbow and blowing her nose. 'They called at lunchtime. I went over straight away. Saw her. She looked . . . at peace, at last.'

'I guess we knew it was coming,' said Jacquot gently. 'And maybe it's better this way.'

Four years earlier, while Jacquot was still in Marseilles, Tantine had lived with Claudine and Midou, in a self-contained ground-floor apartment off the kitchen, which Claudine now used as a studio. It was there, one morning, that Claudine had found her aunt, on the floor of her bathroom, breathing but unconscious. Claudine had called an ambulance and the old lady had been rushed to hospital. It was a stroke, the doctors told Claudine, from which it was unlikely her aunt would ever fully recover.

But Claudine would have none of it. It was a *tristesse de coeur*, a sadness of the heart that had finally got the better of the old lady. For as long as Claudine could remember, Tantine had suffered from it. The war, she'd told

Jacquot the first time she took him to Laune to meet her aunt. Something had happened then that had emptied her heart. Afterwards Tantine hardly ever spoke.

And now that hollow place in her heart engulfed her.

Jacquot remembered the abbey's silent cloisters, the cracked bell that rang out the Angelus twice a day with a single, discordant note. And the old lady. Tantine. He remembered standing in the doorway of her room while Claudine made the introductions. Back then, there still seemed to be some tatters of understanding, and Jacquot recalled the way the old lady looked at him, in astonishment—the ponytail, the cowboy boots, the jeans—as though she was wondering where her niece could have found such a specimen.

Claudine pulled another tissue from the box and blew her nose. 'I asked that she be buried at Laune. The *abbesse* said there would be no problem. The service has been set for Monday. Is that all right?'

'Of course,' said Jacquot. 'I will be there.'

On the TV, the video had ended and static filled the screen. Jacquot leaned over and switched it off, then reached across to the deed box.

'Tantine's,' said Claudine. 'They gave it to me. All her private things. She kept it under the bed. Here and at the *abbaye*. She never liked to be far from it, but I never saw it open.'

Jacquot pulled it towards him, tried the lid.

'It's locked,' she said. 'One of the nuns was certain she'd seen a key for it and they said they'd look. They promised to call when they found it.'

Jacquot lifted it and shook it gingerly. There was something heavy and loose inside. When he tipped the box, he could feel it slide with the tilt.

He ran his fingers over the copperplate script. 'J.E. Any ideas?'

Claudine nodded. 'Jacqueline Eddé, Tantine's mother. My grandmother.'

LATER, AFTER a supper of sausage, bread, cheese and wine, they went to bed, Claudine wriggling herself into the contours of Jacquot's body, pulling his arm round her waist and holding it tight, as though to stop it straying. He understood that she just wanted to feel him there, nothing more.

'I love you, Monsieur Jacquot,' he heard her whisper in a sleepy voice.

'And I love you too, Mademoiselle Eddé.'

For half an hour or more, he listened to her small, sad sighs and felt her gentle sobbing and held her close. But when, finally, she fell asleep, Jacquot slipped silently from their bed and, in darkness, tiptoed downstairs.

He couldn't help himself. And Claudine need never know.

He closed the kitchen door behind him and switched on the light, then made straight for the deed box. He sat in front of it to examine the lock. Then he pulled open the table drawer to look for a paperclip, sorting through household odds and ends until he found one.

He prised the clip apart and began to shape it as he'd learned to do long ago, not with the police but in his wild, ruffian days with the Chats de Nuit gang in Marseilles—breaking into cars, apartments, anything with a lock.

Some things you never forget, he thought, as he poured a drop of olive oil onto the wooden table and dipped the end of the paperclip into it. Tilting the box, he inserted it into the lock and played for a connection. He felt the obstruction he was looking for, gently applied pressure and the mechanism clicked into place. He put down the paperclip, wiped his hands on his night-shirt and lifted the lid.

He wondered when the box had last been opened. Years ago, judging by the smell seeping from the canvas that was carefully wrapped round the box's contents. Folding it back and draping it over the sides of the box, the first thing Jacquot saw was a dirty piece of oiled chamois, which he knew contained a gun, the loose weight he'd felt sliding around. That was what had brought him down to the kitchen: the gun, and the frustrating prospect of having to wait to know for sure.

He lifted the bundle from the box and unwrapped it. It was a service revolver, a Smith & Wesson, handgrip and body blackened. Given the chips along its bevelled barrel it looked as though someone had painted it. So the barrel wouldn't glint in the sunshine? In moonlight? Jacquot broke the weapon. The six chambers were empty.

What on earth was a frail old woman doing with a gun? And then he recalled Claudine telling him about Tantine's work with the Maquis, the Resistance. Pictures of her from those distant days hung in the living room, and there were photos in the family albums: a self-possessed, beautiful young woman, who had held the camera's eye firmly, unflinching, challeng-ing, even when she was laughing. It ran in the family, thought Jacquot. Claudine was no different. Self-assured, defiant, up for anything.

Laying the gun carefully on the table, he turned back to the deed box, and removed a thin sheet of stiff canvas to reveal the rest of the contents.

First out was a man's wristwatch with a strap of military webbing, a cracked glass and fat luminescent numerals. Jacquot turned it over. Engraved on the back were the letters '*à SE de AV*'. To Sandrine Eddé, it had to be. From 'AV'.

Jacquot placed the watch beside the gun, then lifted out a neatly folded handkerchief embroidered in one corner with the same *AV* initials. He put it aside, then brought out another layer of canvas, revealing beneath it a tightly squared fold of paper, which crinkled stiffly when he opened it, its creases brown with time, its corners split with overuse.

It was an old survey map, showing an area from the northern bank of the Durance river across the Luberon hills to the Vaucluse plateau, and from Cavaillon in the west to Manosque in the east. There were no contour lines, no colour to indicate forests or flats, just a cobwebbing of routes, and place names printed in small or large capitals according to size of population. Beside a number of them, scratched in thin pencil marks, were what could only be times and dates—PERTUIS: *3 a.m. 6/iv/43*; CÉRESTE: *midnight 16/v/43*; ROUSSILLON: *5 a.m. 14/iii/43*; BARJAS: *3 a.m. 28/iv/44*.

Jacquot refolded the map and laid it on the table. It was just as Claudine had said. The war. *Résistants*. The Maquis. Direct action. Dating, so far as he could tell, from Manosque in February 1943 to St Bédard in June 1944. Fourteen notations, fourteen separate strikes. In sixteen months.

The next documents confirmed it, a wad held together with twine. Jacquot slipped the knots and spread out the papers on the table. First an identity card, the picture of Sandrine in the top left-hand corner clearly recognisable. What drew Jacquot's attention, however, were the personal details, written in what he could only assume was Tantine's hand. Both date and place of birth looked OK, but the name was different: Rose Valence.

There was a second identity card, this time for a man named Stéphane Beaumont. The photo showed a youngish man in an open-necked shirt. He wore spectacles with one lens clear and the other blackened. '*Aveugle d'un oeil*', Jacquot saw in the space for distinguishing features. Blind in one eye.

False papers. They could be nothing else.

Jacquot put them to one side, picked up the last documents and unfolded them one by one. What he saw brought a whistle to his lips. Stiff vellum pages with crested letterheads and extravagant seals. Awards for gallantry to Sandrine Eddé: Médaille de la Résistance, 5 October 1945; Croix de la Libération and L'Ordre de la Libération, 14 February 1946; Chevalier de la Légion d'honneur, 17 April 1946.

And here, one after another, the justificatory reports: 'planned and carried out several dangerous and vital missions with total disregard to her own safety'—Colonel Hugo Rascousse (Renard), Head of Network F2; 'provided information of the greatest importance at great risk to herself'—

Lieutenant Colonel Jacques Mazin, Head of the Fighting France Service.

Jacquot laid down the documents, turned back to the box and lifted out a small velvet bag. It was weighty. He untied the knot that secured it and shook the contents into his palm.

Medals, four of them, the gold and silver catching the kitchen light, the milled edges still sharp, the colours of the silk ribbons only slightly faded.

So Claudine had not been exaggerating. Tantine had had a colourful— and dangerous—past. Jacquot tipped the medals back into the bag and retied the knot. By now he was about halfway through the deed box. He was about to lift out a pack of letters tied with string when a hand reached down and picked up the gun.

It was Claudine. He hadn't heard a thing. Hadn't heard the stairs creak or the kitchen door open. Caught fair and square. Too long away from Marseilles, he thought.

Claudine sat down beside him, hefting the Smith & Wesson. 'Well, well, Tantine,' she said, in a who-would-have-thought-it tone. And then, looking at Jacquot, an eyebrow arching: 'So you found yourself a key?'

Jacquot picked up the paperclip. 'You could say.'

She gave him an admonishing smile.

Jacquot felt a lift of relief. She wasn't angry.

'And?' she asked.

'Looks like mementoes from the war.'

Claudine put down the gun and reached for the handkerchief, ran her thumb across the embroidered initials, then picked up the watch and turned it over. 'The same initials.'

'Do they mean anything to you?'

'Perhaps.' She picked up the identity cards, studied the pictures. 'It was always said that there'd been a man in her life. In the war, you know? I remember Maman telling me how much in love they were. He sounded like a fairy-tale prince. But then, when I was older, I learned he was real. A Resistance fighter. That he was captured and shot by the Germans. In Cavaillon. Actually, in what is now your car park. At police headquarters.'

'Police headquarters? He was shot there? Where I work?'

Claudine nodded. 'From November 1942, the Germans used your building as their *Kommandantur*, their regional headquarters. Gestapo too. You didn't know?'

Jacquot shook his head. 'I've only been here three years, remember? And what about the name? AV?'

'That I do not know. Tantine never spoke of him. And my mother was so much younger, you see. Ten years, I think. They were never confidantes . . .'

Claudine reached into the box for the pack of letters that Jacquot had been about to pick up, undid the string bow and let them spill onto the table. Some were in envelopes, others simply folded. Only a few bore stamps. Jacquot and Claudine took one each.

'Love letters,' said Jacquot, after he had read a single page. '"*Ma chère Dédé*". Eddé? Sandrine?' He turned the letter over. 'No signature.'

Beside him, Claudine's lips flickered with the words. 'It's so beautiful. And so sad.' Her voice caught. 'Listen,' she said, and began to read: '"My darling Dédé. It is only two days since we met at Bonaire's yet it seems like a year. A lifetime. You looked so calm, so strong, so beautiful . . ."' Claudine's voice quivered again and she took a deep breath. '"In all my life I have never known anyone like you, never been so proud of someone, never been so happy, so complete. My heart breaks with love for you. One day, all this will be over and we will be together. Always. Albert."'

'Albert . . . The "A" in "AV", I assume. But Albert who?'

Claudine reached for another envelope, and as she lifted it a photo slid free, its edges creased, its surface a sun-faded sepia. She picked it up, looked at the two figures and turned it over. '*Voilà*,' she said. '"Albert de Vausigne. July 1943". And that's Tantine in the picture too.'

Jacquot reached for the picture and studied it. Sandrine with her head resting against the shoulder of a tall young man, his arm clasped in hers. Stéphane Beaumont. No doubt about it. The man in the ID card. The man with the spectacles. Jacquot turned the photo over and read the name. Only here he was Albert de Vausigne, forsaking the spectacles in favour of an eye patch, angled rakishly across his forehead, lost among blond curls.

'Familiar?' asked Claudine, sensing his interest.

Jacquot nodded. 'You could say. The family lives near St Bédard. The Comte and Comtesse de Vausigne. On the road to Chant-le-Neuf.'

'They're brothers, Albert and the present Comte?' asked Claudine.

'Stepbrothers, I think,' said Jacquot, trying to remember what Brunet had told him when they had found the Beretta and traced it to the de Vausignes. 'Albert was the heir. His mother died in the thirties, and the old Comte married again. Someone from Brittany. The second wife had a son, Gilles, by a previous marriage, younger than Albert. The old man adopted him.'

He put the photo beside the letters and tipped up the box to look inside. He reached in and pulled out a newspaper dated June 1944. In the bottom corner of the front page he found a single paragraph reporting the execution of four Resistance fighters in Cavaillon. No names were given.

But Jacquot was certain he knew one of the names. Stéphane Beaumont. Albert de Vausigne. The cause of Tantine's *tristesse de coeur*. Had to be.

He handed the newspaper to Claudine, and while she read the report he looked back into the box. It was empty. Jacquot pulled out the canvas envelope to make sure, and as he did so a half-dozen silvery bullets, nestled in the folds of the canvas, dropped out and thudded onto the faded pink cover of a school exercise book. Jacquot picked up the shells, the same calibre as the revolver, then turned to the exercise book and flipped through it.

Every page was written on. Different-coloured ink. Different pens. But only one word. Over and over again.

Rocsabin.

8

It was widely agreed at police HQ that Jean Brunet was a tomcat. He even had the look of a tomcat: always a little ruffled in the mornings, a tad fatigued, and every now and then altogether far too pleased with himself.

Like this morning, Jacquot decided. Brunet came into Jacquot's office carrying a file and wearing a satisfied smirk. 'Marie-Ange Buhl,' he said, sliding the dossier across Jacquot's desk. 'As requested.'

Jacquot, as usual, was impressed. He may have taken most of the morning off to be at home with Claudine, but the moment he sat at his desk, Brunet was there with the information he'd requested the previous evening.

'Anything I should know?' asked Brunet, nodding at the file.

Jacquot knew what his assistant was getting at. He wondered whether he should involve Brunet in a case they'd put to bed months before. Finally he reached into his pocket, pulled out the latest letter and handed it over.

His assistant read it through. 'You think this could be the Buhl girl?'

Jacquot shrugged. 'Maybe. Maybe not. They never say anything new. Just that we got the wrong man.'

Brunet held up the letter. 'This isn't the first?'

Jacquot opened his desk drawer, pulled out the others he'd received, all with the same handwriting.

Brunet whistled. 'You want me to keep an eye on her?'

'You don't have enough on your plate?'

Brunet gave Jacquot a kind of I-can't-think-what-you're-getting-at look.

'Mademoiselle Gaillard?' Jacquot prompted. 'Suzi? At the brasserie?'

'Aaah,' replied Brunet, as though finally making the connection, then he pushed out his bottom lip and nodded, as though giving the matter due consideration. And then, as though recalling some pleasurable little detail, he gave that smile of his, the smile that always won them over. Even Claudine said she loved Brunet's smile. He might be a little short, she told Jacquot, when she first met his assistant, but there was something about him. The way he moved, the snappy way he dressed. And, of course, that smile.

Jacquot couldn't see it, but he had no doubts about Brunet's score card. His assistant had never failed to get his girl in the three years they'd worked together. He guessed it was the way Brunet went about things. Like his interview technique. Determined, single-minded. There was the usherette at the Ritz in Cavaillon, the insurance assessor from Aix, some nurse at the hospital . . . Jacquot had a problem keeping track of them all. And now Suzi Gaillard at the brasserie. Only the owner's daughter, for God's sake.

Yet, somehow, Brunet still managed to be about the best assistant Jacquot had ever come across. He might stagger home at dawn, but he'd be at his desk, ready for anything, when Jacquot arrived—with whatever it was that Jacquot had asked for. And a lot else besides.

Jacquot moved on. 'Anything on the fire at Rocsabin?' he asked.

Brunet took a chair. 'Let's just say there have been developments.'

'I like developments. What kind?'

'Looks like the open-and-shut variety. Well, as good as. Like I said, there's a third party. No question. Both victims shot. Fournier called it in this morning. And the first body's been identified as Grace Bartolomé, the warehouse owner. Early fifties. Married. No kids. A looker, they say. They're matching dental records for confirmation.'

'Identified? How?'

'The watch. One of the staff recognised it. Last night, after we left.'

'Husband? What's he got to say for himself?'

'Not a lot,' replied Brunet. 'Which is why I'm saying open and shut. On account of Monsieur Guy Bartolomé having shot himself in the head.'

Jacquot's eyes widened. 'You're kidding?'

'After they identified the watch, one of the Rocsabin boys went out to Lucat where the Bartolomés live. Locked tight. No one home. So this morning, first thing, they go out there again. Still no answer. But there's a dog howling in the front room, pawing the window. So they force the lock and there he is. Sat at the kitchen table, gun in his hand.'

'And the gun belongs to?'

'Registered to Madame Bartolomé. A pearl-handled twenty-two. Three bullets fired. Ballistics are working on it, but if you ask me . . .'

'Any note?'

'No. But they found an empty petrol can in the boot of his car.'

'What do we know about him?'

'Used to be a teacher at the Rocsabin *lycée*. Retired early. Health reasons.'

'Which were?'

'He had a breakdown. Four months in a clinic outside Grenoble.'

'So this Guy Bartolomé discovers his wife's playing around . . .'

'And decides to do something about it. Catches them at the warehouse. Sorts them out. Torches the place to cover any trail he may have left. But when he gets back home, he goes to pieces. Tops himself.'

'What about the second body. Any names?'

'Nothing yet. Except the shoes. Handmade. Badly burnt, of course, but Fournier found a maker's mark. Some place in Aix. I've got one of our boys down there checking it out. Course, we might not have to wait that long.'

'You got something else?'

'Maybe.'

'The cars in the yard?'

'We traced both. The Peugeot belongs to a Louis Simon,' began Brunet. 'He runs a travel shop in Cavaillon, but lives out in Rocsabin, pretty much next door to the warehouse. According to Simon, the manager, Filbert, lets him leave his car overnight in the warehouse car park sometimes.'

'And the other car?'

'Aaah. The Citroën. A beauty—1952 Traction-Avant 11 Légère. Immaculate condition, you wouldn't believe . . .'

'And the owner?'

Brunet smiled. 'Just the Comte de Vausigne.'

JACQUOT HAD BRUNET drive him out to the chateau. Through the open window the wind was warm, buffeting Jacquot's fingers as he tapped them against the car door and reviewed the evidence. Brunet was right. Tracing the shoe would confirm it, but Jacquot was certain they already knew the identity of the second body found among the ruins.

According to Fournier, who'd phoned in just as Jacquot and Brunet were leaving the office, a set of keys had been found in the dead man's pocket, one of which unlocked the Citroën. There was even an overnight case in the boot. And a pair of shoes with the same maker's mark. It had to be the Comte.

Watching the vines flash by, Jacquot tried to get a fix on Gilles de Vausigne, recalling the time they'd met, when he and Dietering had gone out to the chateau to ask about the gun Benedict had found. Somewhere in his early seventies, Jacquot guessed, but still a good-looking man, tall, tanned and aristocratic, even if he wasn't family blood. The kind of man who took care of his appearance. The kind of man a fifty-year-old woman like Madame Bartolomé might take a shine to.

As they passed through the Château gates, Jacquot sighed. This was not going to be an easy call.

By the time they'd climbed out of the car, Picard had appeared on the front steps. When they reached him, Jacquot explained that they'd made no appointment, but Picard assured them that the Comtesse was around. He led them into the chateau and showed them to the library.

'Looks like they've had the decorators in,' said Brunet, as Picard closed the door behind him. 'About time, you ask me.'

Jacquot looked around. Brunet was right. The scuffed paintwork, fading drapes and threadbare upholstery that Dietering had pointed out were no more. The room had been given a makeover.

Before Jacquot could reply, the door swung open and a young man strode in, stopping in his tracks as though surprised to find anyone there. He wore a pair of pressed jeans, a blue Lacoste polo shirt and boat shoes on bare feet. He was tall, tanned and fit-looking. In his late thirties, Jacquot judged, with his mother's manner and his father's features.

'And you are?' he demanded, looking them over.

Brunet made the introductions. The young man nodded.

'And you are?' asked Jacquot back, already knowing the answer.

'Antoine de Vausigne,' he said, and swung the door wider, indicating that they should leave the room. 'If you don't mind, I have a phone call to make.'

'Just the one phone, is there?' asked Jacquot.

Before the young man could answer, Picard reappeared. He gave de Vausigne a deferential nod, then informed Jacquot and Brunet that the Comtesse would see them now.

'Monsieur,' said Brunet, as he passed de Vausigne at the door.

Jacquot simply nodded on his way out.

The door closed abruptly behind them.

Picard led them to the end of the corridor, and ushered them into the Comtesse's study. Sitting at a desk, Hélène de Vausigne was tapping away at a laptop computer. She was dressed in a tailored silk blouse and jeans, and she gave them a questioning look.

'Chief Inspector Jacquot, isn't it? And . . . I'm so sorry . . .?'

'Brunet. Inspector Jean Brunet.'

'Of course, yes.' She looked hard at Brunet. 'Aren't you the gentleman who took our statements? Back in . . . when was it? February or March?'

'That's correct, Madame. You have a good memory.'

'So, please, do have a seat, Messieurs,' she said, sweeping her hand towards a sofa while she repositioned herself to face them. A suitably attentive smile was switched on. 'Now, tell me, how can I be of help? Is it something to do with the trial? Our gardener, Chabert?'

Brunet shook his head. 'No, Madame. Something else entirely. I believe you own a 1952 Citroën 11 Légère. Registration number—'

'That's correct. No need to quote the number, it's the only 'fifty-two Légère in the *département*.' She looked from Brunet to Jacquot, then back again. 'And?'

'And do you happen to know where that car is at the moment, Madame?' asked Jacquot, taking over from Brunet.

The Comtesse turned to him. 'Of course I do,' she replied. 'It is in Aix. The Hôtel Pigonnet. My husband is staying there for a few days. On business. He drives down every few weeks to see his lawyer.'

'And when did your husband leave for Aix, Madame?'

'Why, Monday afternoon.'

'And have you spoken to him since then?'

'No, I haven't. There's no need. He's back tonight.'

'Not without his car, Madame,' broke in Brunet.

'You're being very mysterious, Chief Inspector. Has the car been stolen?' Then the Comtesse looked alarmed. 'Has there been an accident?'

'Not an accident, Madame,' said Jacquot. 'We just need to account for your husband's Citroën. Why it's in Rocsabin when you say it's in Aix.'

'In Rocsabin? But that's ridiculous.' She swung round to the desk, opened a drawer and found her address book. 'Let me call the hotel. I'm sure we can sort all this out,' she said, riffling through the pages.

She found a number, dialled and waited for the connection. 'Hello. Hôtel Pigonnet? . . . I wonder if I could speak to the Comte de Vausigne . . .'

Jacquot folded his hands in his lap. He knew how this was going to end.

The Comtesse looked suddenly perplexed. 'Are you sure? . . . That's right, Monday evening . . . Three days.' There was a pause. 'I see. Yes. Thank you.'

She put down the receiver and straightened her back. 'It appears that my husband spent only the one night in Aix. According to the hotel he checked out on Tuesday evening.' She cleared her throat. 'Perhaps, Chief Inspector, you would be so kind as to tell me what all this is about.'

'You may be aware, Madame, that early on Wednesday morning, a little after midnight, a fire broke out at a furniture warehouse in Rocsabin . . .'

'Yes, yes, I saw it on the news yesterday. The HacheGee warehouse. A dreadful business. I've been calling Grace all day.'

Jacquot sat forward. 'You know Madame Bartolomé?'

'Of course I know her. For some years now. We're partners. HacheGee— Hélène and Grace. My husband and I have a stake in the business.'

'A stake, Madame?'

'The warehouse is built on family land. In addition to rent, we take a small percentage of profits as non-executive directors . . .'

'Might I ask when you last saw Madame Bartolomé? Or spoke to her.'

'Last week. Thursday. Why? What is all this about, Chief Inspector?'

'As you already know, Madame, the warehouse was destroyed. What you will not know is that Madame Bartolomé perished in that fire.'

The Comtesse shook her head. 'You can't be serious? Surely not.'

'I'm afraid there's no doubt, Madame. I am very sorry.'

'Does Guy know? Grace's husband? I must call him. Poor, poor man. He'll be devastated.' The Comtesse reached for the phone.

'I'm afraid, Madame, he knows already. In fact, it would appear from our enquiries that it was Monsieur Bartolomé who started the fire, and is, as far as we can establish, responsible for his wife's death.'

'But that's ridiculous, Chief Inspector. He couldn't possibly—'

'May I ask why you say that, Madame?'

'Because he loved her, to distraction.' The Comtesse frowned. 'But what has all this to do with my husband? And his car?'

Jacquot took a deep breath. 'Your husband's Citroën has been found in Rocsabin, in the warehouse car park . . . As well as Madame Bartolomé, a second victim was found. So far we have been unable to confirm identity but . . .' Jacquot paused, spread his hands. He might not like the woman but he felt sympathy for her. 'Given the presence of your husband's car, and a set of keys to that car found on the second body, and having failed as yet to establish your husband's whereabouts, there seems a strong likelihood . . .'

The Comtesse swallowed hard, took a breath and let it out in a low moan that grew by degrees into a rising wail of grief.

The study door swung open, and in an instant Antoine was at his mother's side, getting down on his knees to wrap her in his arms, his eyes fixing hard on Jacquot and Brunet over her heaving shoulders.

THE MOMENT they arrived back at Cavaillon HQ, Jacquot asked Brunet to put a call through to Aix to confirm the Comte's hotel reservation and departure details. 'Find out whether he was on his own,' added Jacquot, heading for his office. 'Also, whatever you can get on the de Vausignes.'

He closed the door behind him and started up his computer. There was something he wanted to check out. He pulled the keyboard towards him, typed an email and, with a click of the mouse, sent it off.

Turning away from the computer, he noticed the file that Brunet had brought in earlier that morning, the one on Marie-Ange Buhl. He skimmed through photocopied brochure details about Agence Florale, part of the FranceFleurs organisation. The third page was a copy of a fax from Boudit Frères' offices in Zürich, instructing the agency to supply care to the hothouse of Josef Martner. According to the records on the following page, Agence Florale had put the Dassy Nursery in Aix in charge of the hothouse. The arrangement had lasted until June, when the Dassy Nursery had contacted Agence Florale to say they were no longer able to do the job: the hothouse collection needed more specialised care.

Jacquot flipped to the fifth page, a copy of the agency's personnel file for Mademoiselle Buhl. The final page gave a record of her employment, a list of gardens and nurseries in different parts of the country where the agency had placed her. In the last six months, she had worked in a half-dozen different locations—Alsace, Île-de-France, Brittany, Poitou-Charentes . . .

The significance of these postings was not lost on Jacquot.

TWO DAYS AFTER the fire at Rocsabin, Marie-Ange turned the Chaberts' delivery van off the Chant-le-Neuf road towards the Château de Vausigne. As she coasted down past the terraces of vine and fig, she saw a blue Mercedes saloon pull out of the chateau's forecourt and head up the drive towards her. The car, she knew, belonged to the Comtesse's son, Antoine, but Picard was at the wheel, with the Comtesse in the back seat. She was wearing a black veil and sunglasses.

As the two cars came abreast, the Mercedes slowed, the driver's window slid down and Picard said would she please wait at the house until the Comtesse returned. It wouldn't be long, he assured her. An hour at most.

News of the Comte's death had reached St Bédard the previous day. It was old Dumé who had filled Marie-Ange in on the details.

Parking the van at the side of the chateau, near the basement entrance to the kitchens, Marie-Ange skipped down the steps, tapped on the door and found Florence sitting by the range, shelling peas.

The Comtesse was devastated, reported the housekeeper, as Marie-Ange helped herself to coffee. She'd taken to her bed the moment the policemen left. Nothing to eat. Just her pills and Antoine at her side until the call from police HQ that morning. Madame was needed in Cavaillon to identify certain personal belongings found at the fire.

Florence was in no doubt that the party would be cancelled. And then, realising what this would mean, she settled a sympathetic eye on Marie-Ange. 'All that work, *ma jolie*. For nothing.'

Marie-Ange sighed. All that work, indeed. Since her initial meeting with the Comtesse, Marie-Ange had come to the chateau twice a week, scaffolding the ballroom with trelliswork for the weave of jonquils and honeysuckle they'd agreed on, devising floral arrangements for the marquee, and advising the Comtesse on decorations for the bedrooms that had been spring-cleaned for the arrival of friends and family.

Yet not a *sou* to show for it, nothing to cover the orders she'd made or the time spent at the chateau. And as if that wasn't enough, she'd had to endure every one of her estimates being questioned by the Comtesse as though they were targets to be shot at rather than the best quote for the work involved.

It wasn't only the woman's meanness that Marie-Ange had had to contend with. Whenever the Comtesse was out of the house, her husband had always contrived to be around, with his scraggy neck and gaudy cravats, following her with his greedy little eyes and always on hand to steady her ladder as she climbed up to secure the trelliswork.

And now it was the son she had to deal with: Antoine, down from Paris to stay through the festivities, a younger version of the father—the wavy hair, the shiny lower lip, those same hungry eyes licking over her like a cold, wet tongue. A film producer, apparently, though no one in St Bédard could say what kind of films he produced.

Finishing her coffee, Marie-Ange decided that while she was waiting she might as well start dismantling the decorations in the ballroom.

Leaving Florence to her peas, she climbed the kitchen stairs and pushed through the service door that led into the main house. Halfway across the hall she suddenly stopped, as though someone had caught her sleeve. Normally the chateau's interior was cool whatever the heat outside, kept so by metre-thick walls and flagstoned floors. But now, it seemed, the cool had sharpened to a chill, making the skin on the back of her neck pucker.

There was something else, too—a cindery smell. Compelled by some impulse she couldn't quite place, Marie-Ange turned and headed for the staircase leading to the chateau's upper floors. With the Comtesse and Picard at police HQ in Cavaillon, Florence busy with her peas in the kitchen and Antoine, according to the old housekeeper, still in his bed in the guest cottage by the pool, she had the house to herself.

Yet as she climbed the wide stone sweep of stairs, Marie-Ange felt a rising certainty that something was about to happen, and she began to prepare herself for the cloak of silence that preceded one of her 'moments'.

But there was nothing. No sounds. No enveloping silence or dry, dusty taste in her mouth. Just the distant smell of burning to draw her on.

At the top of the staircase, she paused. To the right, she knew from her visits with the Comtesse, were six of the chateau's guest bedrooms, and to the left a suite of rooms she had not yet visited, the private quarters of the de Vausignes. It was to these that Marie-Ange made her way, turning down the corridor as though led by the hand, scalp prickling, skin shivering, the smell of burning stronger with every step.

SCRATCHING THE TRIANGLE of hair on his chest, Antoine de Vausigne stood in his boxers and peered through the windows of the guest cottage.

Beyond the reflection of his tousled hair and puffy, sleep-creased face, he watched the swallows dive at the still surface of the swimming pool. It might be close to midday, but the new Comte was still sleepy enough not to be able to decide whether to shower first or to swim.

Antoine turned and walked over to the small kitchenette, which was divided from the living room by a narrow breakfast bar. While the coffee percolated, he found his wallet, pulled out a fold of paper and tipped some of its contents onto the smooth Formica top. With the back of a spoon he crushed the lumpy white powder and then, with its handle, arranged the cocaine into a ragged line. He picked up the same 200-franc note he'd used the night before, rolled it into a tube, then took the line up in a single snort.

Antoine had brought the coke from Paris. Four grams in a single fold. A week later there wasn't much left. He wasn't too concerned: he could always get more in Cavaillon. Not as good, of course, but not as pricey either.

Sniffing contentedly, Antoine squeezed his eyes shut, then opened them wide. He poured himself coffee and looked around the room. It was furnished simply in Provençal rental style. His bedroom in the main house was far more comfortable, but at least here he was certain of some privacy. The last time Antoine had stayed, the old man had walked into his bedroom without so much as a tap on the door at exactly the moment that Antoine entered the willing loins of his latest star turn. God knows how long the old man had stood there, taking in the scenery.

Now, of course, there was no old man to bother about. Burnt to a crisp. Tough break. Antoine tossed back the last of his coffee and smiled. He'd had it coming—him and his ladyfriend. Another few years and the pair of them would have bled the family dry. Now all Antoine had to do was cope with his mother. She'd taken the news very badly. Which was a bore. Things were happening in Paris and he wanted to get moving. He'd wait another week, he decided, but then he'd have to have a serious chat with her. He wondered if she knew what the old man had been up to. His *petites affaires*. He thought not. The old boy had always been discreet.

Antoine opened the French windows and wandered naked to the pool. It was surrounded by a screen of firs, and although the house was no more than a hundred metres distant there was no sign of it except the topmost tiles of one of its four towers.

As he stood there, he heard the Mercedes start up, at the front of the house. Picard taking his mother into Cavaillon. She'd called him earlier, saying the Citroën was still not back from Rocsabin and could she have Picard drive her in the Mercedes? The police had phoned to ask if she'd come into town, identify the old man's personal effects.

Perfect timing, thought Antoine to himself. And holding his nose like a little boy, he pushed up and away from the side of the pool, hugged his legs to his chest and dropped like a bomb into the cold, blue water.

Forty minutes later, dressed in shorts and sports shirt, he strode through the trees and up to the house. With Maman and Picard out of the house, and old Florence hobbling round the kitchen, he had the run of the place. Hands in pockets, he crossed the terrace, stepped through the French windows and headed across the hall. He'd start with those cuff links of his father's . . .

Heading for his parents' apartments, he climbed the stairs and turned to the left when he reached the landing. Which was when he noticed something out of place: a sweet scent he didn't recognise. Certainly not his mother's. Younger, fresher . . . some kind of flower, he thought, following it down the corridor. Monique, perhaps? Was this one of her days at the chateau?

The door to his parents' suite was open, and Antoine pushed through into the small living room they shared. From here, two doors led to their separate bedrooms and bathrooms. He was about to head for his father's door when he heard the creak of the *armoire* in his mother's bedroom.

Easing off his shoes, he stole across the living room and peered through the gap between door and frame. And there, standing in front of his mother's *armoire*, he saw a woman.

The long brown legs and the floral print dress were immediately familiar. Not Monique, but the town florist who'd been working in the ballroom. But what on earth was she doing up here? Looking for something to steal?

Antoine crept round the door and into his mother's bedroom, expecting the girl to turn, suddenly aware that there was someone in the room.

But she didn't. Instead, still with her back to him, she reached up to the top shelf, and touched one of his mother's hatboxes.

Enjoying the thrill of being there without her knowing it, Antoine sat quietly on the edge of his mother's bed and watched her.

MARIE-ANGE WAS PUZZLED. The silence she'd been expecting, the distant sounds and voices, had failed to materialise. Even the scent of burning had faded. Yet something was holding her here in the de Vausignes' private quarters, a sense that she was where she was supposed to be. It was, she realised, the same feeling she had had when she made her way to that street in Metz after reading about the woman's 'suicide'.

The comtesse's bedroom was large and brightly sunlit, occupying a corner of the chateau at the front of the house, where one of its four turrets provided a semicircular canopied space in which she'd set her dressing table. The windows to either side had been thrown open, looking out over the gravelled courtyard and terraces.

For an instant Marie-Ange felt guilty. What on earth was she doing, prying through the Comtesse's bedroom like a common criminal? What on earth had possessed her?

But if she couldn't explain it, neither could she resist it, the lure to go on, to be there, waiting for something to happen. Whatever it might be.

Comforting herself that she would hear the Mercedes returning from Cavaillon, and easily have enough time to get downstairs before the

Comtesse reached the front door, Marie-Ange moved to the bed, a wide *bateau lit* covered with a quilted pink satin counterpane. On each side stood a delicate empire chest, with a single drawer and small cupboard.

It was easy to tell which side of the bed Madame la Comtesse slept on. The left-hand chest had a small alarm clock set for six, a pot of moisturiser and a biography of Napoleon by Edmond Lévy. Marie-Ange searched the bedside table's drawer and cupboard, both equipped with tiny keys but unlocked. Finding nothing of interest, she went round to the other side of the bed and did the same.

Or tried to. On this side, both drawer and cupboard were locked. Marie-Ange went back to the first table and pulled out the two keys. It was a long shot, but it might work. And it did. The two bedside chests shared the same keys. With a tiny click, the drawer lock gave and she slid it open.

At first it looked empty, nothing but a few hairpins. Then she noticed a narrow rectangle of white with some writing on it. She slid it towards her, picked it up and read: '*AV et PR, Rocsabin. Fêtes de Noël, décembre 1937.*'

Turning it over, she saw it was a black and white photo of a young man and an older man standing together by a fireplace. The younger man looked to be in his early twenties, eyes twinkling with merriment, mouth curled into a grin, a hand pushing back a fall of wavy blond hair. He had, Marie-Ange decided, that eager, expectant expression you have when you begin to understand what the world has to offer.

The older man, without a doubt, was the Comtesse's father—he had the same thin lips, black eyes and that haughty set to the chin and eyebrows. With a well-upholstered stomach stretching the buttons of his waistcoat, he looked as if he might have been a jovial sort of a fellow. But in that instant of the flash he looked anything but jovial: there was something anxious at the back of his eyes, as though he were uncomfortable with his young companion.

Marie-Ange put the photo back, slid the drawer closed and relocked it. Then, settling in front of the cupboard, she fitted the second key into the lock and turned it. With a thin, resisting squeak, the door opened.

Inside was a stack of leather-spined ledgers. But what caught Marie-Ange's attention was a brown envelope wedged between them and the side of the cupboard. The flap had not been sealed, which meant that the contents were clearly visible: a meaty wad of emerald-green 500-franc notes, bound at either end with rubber bands. She lifted the envelope, felt the weight: 50,000, she estimated. Easily. For someone who quibbled over a few hundred francs, it was an astonishing amount of cash to keep in a bedside cupboard.

Tight-fisted old crow, thought Marie-Ange, as she replaced the envelope, locked the cupboard and put the keys back where she'd found them.

Which was when a bird, perched on a windowsill overlooking the side of the house, suddenly took flight, chattering away into the trees. Marie-Ange's heart lurched and her legs turned to water. If she'd been watching a scene like this in the movies, she'd be saying, 'Get out of there! Now!'

But she bottled up her fear and continued her search. With a volley of squeaks, she eased open the door of a tall, panelled *armoire* and looked inside. Above her, the top shelf was packed with hatboxes. Below this, a single rail held a selection of clothing, and at knee level there was a shelf and a pair of deep drawers. Tipping the hatboxes to gauge their weight and quickly discounting them, she ran her eyes along the line of clothes, then bent down, pushing them aside to see into the *armoire*'s depths.

It was at exactly that moment that a pair of hands grabbed her round the waist and heaved her backwards.

Frantically she tried to pull free, twisting and turning, reaching behind her for something to get at. But she was held too tightly, one of her assailant's hands now reaching up to cup a breast, fingers spreading round it. And, unbelievably, laughter, as though this was some kind of game.

She pulled at the hand on her breast, trying to lever it away, only to have the other hand reach down, slide between her legs, hoisting her back to where she knew the bed stood.

Marie-Ange jerked her hips to one side, squirming away from the fingers between her thighs, feeling as she did so a familiar stiffness press against her hip. Half turning in an attempt to beat off her assailant, she lost her balance, and the two of them fell back onto the bed.

From beneath her the laughter was cut short by a winded '*ouuff*' and the hands released her. Taking advantage of the spring in the mattress, Marie-Ange leapt away, panting, and spun round to confront her attacker.

'What the hell do you think you're doing?' she screamed.

On the bed, Antoine pushed himself up on an elbow. 'And what the hell, *exactly*,' he replied, 'do you think you're doing, Mam'selle? Sneaking around in my mother's—'

Which was the moment that a voice floated up to them. 'Marie-Ange? Where are you, Marie-Ange?'

It was Florence.

'I've made lunch. Some soup. Come quick.'

Which was just what Marie-Ange did.

9

Jacquot watched Hélène de Vausigne's blue Mercedes draw away from the steps of the Cavaillon gendarmerie and breathed a sigh of relief.

It had been gruelling watching the Comtesse identify her late husband's belongings. When it was over, Jacquot had offered his condolences. She'd thanked him, tried a brave smile, but then turned away quickly, busying herself with her sunglasses and veil. When she turned back she'd regained her composure, her mouth grim and tight. Jacquot might not like the woman but he felt for her in her loss.

Five minutes after Picard had settled her in the back of the Mercedes and driven off, Jacquot headed to his office. The phone began to ring the moment he reached his desk.

'You have mail.' The clipped tones from a thousand miles north were unmistakable. Jacquot couldn't help smiling at the familiar voice. He turned to his computer screen. The envelope icon in the top right-hand corner was blinking.

'I have indeed,' he said, opening the file. 'Thanks, Hans. I'm very grateful.'

'So you still haven't given it up, Dan?' asked Dietering.

'They reckon another week or so for the trial. So, still time,' replied Jacquot, setting the file to print.

'And then?'

'If the ball comes your way, you play it,' he said.

'And has it?'

'Not so far. But you never know,' he replied, watching the pages spill out of the printer. 'Anything interesting? About the Martners?'

Brunet came round the door, dropped a file onto his desk and returned to his office. Jacquot pulled the file towards him. The name '*de Vausigne*' was scrawled across its cover.

'Since I'm not sure what you are looking for, it's difficult to say,' replied Dietering, 'but I did what you asked. Every obituary I could find.'

A few minutes later, after they'd said their farewells and hung up, Jacquot scooped up the pages from the printer, picked up the file Brunet had brought him and went through to the outer office.

'I'll be gone for an hour or two. Back by three latest.'

Brunet glanced up and nodded. 'Anything you need?'

'Spare file for this?' Jacquot held up the sheaf of print-out.

Brunet pulled one from a drawer and handed it over. 'Anything else?'

Yes, thought Jacquot, there was something else, but in this particular instance Brunet wouldn't be able to help. What he needed was space to think, somewhere without the constant interruptions. 'Nothing, thanks,' he replied and, swinging his jacket over his shoulder, he headed for the door.

There was only one place he knew . . .

OFF CAVAILLON'S MAIN square, a brisk seven-minute walk from Jacquot's office, there was an unremarkable alleyway, a canyon of tall, tilting buildings rising to a band of blue sky, so close at the top that, leaning out of a window on one side, it seemed you could touch the fingers of someone leaning from the other side.

Low doors furnished with brass knockers led into these narrow, teetering houses, and lace-covered windows concealed their shadowy interiors from the cobbled passageway that ran between them. Most of the houses were private residences, the exceptions being an antiquarian bookseller, a carpenter's workshop that filled the passageway with the scent of freshly sawn wood and, halfway down on the left-hand side, Jacquot's favourite restaurant, Brasserie Chez Gaillard. Jacquot pushed through the door.

'Monsieur Jacquot. A pleasure, as always,' said the brasserie's owner, Laurent Gaillard, darting forward from the bar to shake the chief inspector's hand. 'A little lunch?'

'Afternoon, Laurent. No lunch today but a small table if you have one. And a *café calva* to clear the head.'

'Of course—please,' replied Laurent, leading Jacquot through the bar into a restaurant humming with chat and the clink of glass and cutlery.

The room was low, and closely beamed with a dozen tables crowded into a space not big enough for ten. In the middle of the room, Laurent's daughter, Suzi, was taking an order. She gave Jacquot a nod and a smile that told Jacquot there was no need to be concerned on her behalf, a smile that said, 'I can handle that tomcat of yours.' And as Jacquot nodded back, he knew she could. Maybe this time Brunet had met his match.

'How's the family?' asked Jacquot, as Laurent steered him to a corner table in the back.

'Oh, fine, just fine,' said Laurent, glancing up at the portrait gallery of Gaillard *patrons* who'd run this brasserie before him. 'Although the old man gets more curmudgeonly by the day. It takes all our wits to keep him out of the kitchen. That, and a sharp knife.' Laurent laughed, and pulled out a chair for Jacquot. 'Please, make yourself at home. *Café calva, tout de suite.*'

While Laurent hurried away, Jacquot shrugged off his jacket and re-arranged the tabletop to make room for his two files. His office outside his office, he thought contentedly. He pulled up his chair, rested his forearms on the table and opened the first file, the one from Dietering.

There were more than a dozen pages, a raft of obituaries for the Martners, taken from both German and Swiss publications. Obituaries. Such a mine of information. And someone else did all the work for you, found all those interesting little snippets that, more often than not, a police inquiry failed to uncover.

There was only one problem. As he leafed through the pile, Jacquot soon discovered that every single obituary was written in German. It was only when he reached the last three pages that his spirits lifted. A typewritten report from Dietering, God bless him, and in passable French as well:

Dear Dan

As requested, every obituary I could lay my hands on. Most, as you will see, are for the doctor, but his wife and daughter also feature. In case your German isn't up to it (!) I give you a short précis.

Martner, Josef. Father in shipping insurance, mother did not work. Although Martner's birth certificate says Hamburg, he was actually born in the family home at Quickborn, about twenty minutes from the city. Attended all the right schools, did passably well, and in 1939 started a medical internship at Heidelberg University. Halfway through the course his father died and Martner switched to dentistry. In 1942 he got called up and was seconded to the Abwehr in your newly occupied Southern Zone, France. As a medical orderly.

According to Die Welt, he was posted first to Toulouse and then— you will like this, Dan—to Cavaillon. Small world—huh?

Jacquot felt a sudden twist of excitement. A small world indeed, he thought, nodding his thanks as Laurent put down a double espresso and a vast *balon* of Calvados. He read on:

It was in Cavaillon that Martner ended his war, captured by the Allies, August 1944. Imprisoned Aix-Luynes for eighteen months, released without charge and repatriated.

So much for the blameless. Now for the fortunate.

Two years after returning to Germany, Martner got his licence to practise dentistry and, in 1949, married the only child of widower Ludwig von Diepenbroek, who was Minister for internal reconstruction after the war and rose to second secretary during the Adenauer years. According to the wife's obituary, the old man was against the marriage at first, but he came round. Seven years later, he died and Jutta inherited over two million Deutschmarks in today's currency.

Less than six months later, Martner's mother died and left him the family home in Quickborn. They sold the house in Hamburg and started travelling—all tropical destinations: the Far East particularly, but also South and Central America. Anything up to six months away. Purpose of travel? Botanical expeditions.

By the end of the seventies, the Martners tired of travelling and settled in Germany. Or maybe they didn't tire, exactly. As we already know from their tax submissions, their capital had decreased dramatically—inflation, one or two bad investments—and they had to rein in. But the new Germany no longer seemed to their liking. They moved to Paris, and then, in 1987, they went south. We know the rest.

As for their daughter, Ilse, she was at boarding school in Switzerland while the parents travelled. Worked for Bertelsmann, the German publisher, after graduation. Met Gunther Brauer, son of Helmut Brauer, the Swiss finance minister, on a skiing holiday in Zermatt. They married in Zürich. Ludwig would have approved.

So, that's it. I'm sorry if it's what you already know. But maybe these few extra details will help.

If you need anything else, call.

Jacquot finished the last of his coffee and took a gulp of the *calva*, quietly giving thanks for Dietering. Without his colleague's covering report, he'd have been wading through this for days. He was also grateful for the way Dietering saw it. Now that *was* interesting. 'Blameless'. 'Fortunate'. Those were the words that stayed in Jacquot's head. The second was certainly true—a safe middle-class upbringing, a secure war and an advantageous marriage. But Jacquot wasn't so sure about the first. Blameless. No, it couldn't be. There was something in his past—maybe in Toulouse, or here in Cavaillon—that they hadn't found.

'Another *café*, Monsieur?' Laurent was at his side. 'Another *calva*?'

Jacquot gazed at him, then at his watch. 'Is it too late for a little lunch?'

'*Jarret?*'

'If you have it.'

Laurent gave him a we'll-hunt-around-see-if-we-can't-find-you-something look, and was gone. Jacquot knew better than to ask about wine: seconds later Laurent was back with a *pichet* of his favourite Côtes du Rhône.

As Jacquot tasted the wine, he looked around him, taking it all in: local businesspeople, housewives leaning close over their coffee and petits fours to exchange gossip, and a sprinkling of tourists.

'Ah, Monsieur Jacquot,' said Marthe Gaillard, Laurent's wife and Suzi's mother, a large tureen clasped to her bosom as she planted a kiss on his cheek. 'How are you?' she asked, ladling the soup into his bowl. 'And Claudine?'

Jacquot made all the right noises. Madame Gaillard set the tureen on the table: 'You help yourself, yes? *Et bon appétit.*' And she was gone.

Bread roll broken, glass refilled, spoon in hand, the meal began. If you'd asked Jacquot after lunch what he'd eaten, he'd have probably remembered. You didn't easily forget a Gaillard meal. But as he ate it—the *soupe au potiron*, the *jarret*, a *salade frisée*, some cheese, a slice of pear, more coffee, another Calvados, all he could think of was Martner, tracing in his mind the man's life, from a cradle in Hamburg to a deathbed in St Bédard. Save just the one detail, there was absolutely no pattern to the man's life that Jacquot could detect beyond the normal.

Save that one small detail—the only thing out of place. In 1943, Josef Martner finds himself stationed in Cavaillon.

And nearly fifty years later Josef Martner comes back.

A childhood home Jacquot could understand, a pleasant place to play out one's final years. But choosing somewhere you've spent two years of your life as part of an occupying army? Even if it was in Provence.

That was what surprised Jacquot.

Then, of course, there was the money. By 1987, the year they had come south, it was clear there were problems. As Dietering had said, interest on the Martner's capital had dwindled to maybe 300,000 francs a year, after tax. Hardly the kind of money to subsidise the extravagant lifestyle they were used to but, with the property in Provence covered by the sale of their home in Paris and enough left over to fix the place up, there remained just about enough to live carefully.

Yet from the moment Martner arrived in Provence, his fortunes had turned. There might not have been much in the bank, but he and his wife had lived well. How, thought Jacquot, had they done it? How had the doctor been able to underwrite his orchids and his hothouse? And the BMW? And the travel? Where had the money come from? Nowhere were there any record of withdrawals to account for it all. Everything paid for in cash. Cash. Cash. Cash. And over the years a lot of it.

Which was why, Jacquot was certain, someone had decided to kill them. Not because of this unrequited-love twaddle they'd used to put the kid Chabert in the dock. This was about money.

But where was the missing link? The war? Martner's time in Toulouse? In Cavaillon? Something he'd done? People he knew? Jacquot groaned.

And then, 'A grand family once,' came a gravelly voice beside him. 'A sham now.'

Jacquot looked up. It was old man Gaillard, Laurent's father, a halo of white hair, purple nose and ponderous jowls, as solemn and disapproving as his portrait on the wall. His pouchy, red-rimmed eyes were fixed on the table, on the second of Jacquot's two files.

'The de Vausignes.' He gestured at the name with the handle of his stick. 'I knew the old Comte, Edouard. Came here, you know. Oh, yes. Fine man. Real upper class—*ancien*. Noble. And his son, Albert. I knew him too. One of the first to fight back, you understand my meaning? *Un homme de la première heure.*'

'I didn't know that, M'sieur,' Jacquot lied smoothly, sitting back to show he was ready for a chat, but knowing there was little point in inviting the old man to sit. Jacquot had offered a chair, just the one time, and had been roundly informed why such a thing could not be. Jacquot was a guest, the Gaillards his hosts. It would never do to mix the two.

'*Beh oui,*' continued old Gaillard. 'No one like him. Some of the things it turned out he did! And we never knew,' he said. 'Like a shadow he was. You'd never have guessed. Until they caught him. Three weeks with the Gestapo. Then they shot him. That was when we found out. Heard the stories. Set up, he was. So they say. Some action out on the Brieuc road.'

'Set up?'

'There were rumours. Only rumours. No one knew for sure.'

'What about you? What do you think?'

The old man shook his head. 'Back then, towards the end of the war, things happened it's best to forget.'

'Albert was married, wasn't he?' lied Jacquot, knowing full well that he hadn't been.

'Albert de Vausigne? No, M'sieur!' The old man shook his head vehemently, but then a twinkle lit his eye. 'There was one, though. Blonde. A beauty. They were always together, came here a few times. Her name was . . .'

Sandrine, thought Jacquot. Sandrine Eddé. Or maybe Rose Valence.

The old man looked at the floor, brows furrowed, wrestling with the handle of his stick. 'No, it's gone. Anyway,' he continued, 'they were tight.' You could see it. Which didn't please everyone, I can tell you.'

'Albert's father didn't approve?'

'No, no, no, M'sieur. The Comtesse. The one now. Set her sights on Albert the day they met. Thought she had a chance. *Bof,* some chance! But it's only when that blonde turns up, she sees her goose is cooked. And then, what do you know? Albert's dead and she's married the stepbrother.'

'Gilles de Vausigne?'

'That's the one.' Gaillard sniffed. 'Got what she wanted in the end.'

'Got what she wanted?'

'The title, of course! What else? At Rocsabin they had the land; at St Bédard they had the title. She might not have got the man she wanted, but at least she got the title. Course they've frittered the land away—sold it off, here, there—until there's pretty much nothing left. And the son? *Bof.* Low class. With pretensions. Not the true *gratin*, not by a long chalk.'

But Jacquot wasn't listening any more. He was leafing through the file that Brunet had given him. He sensed that he'd stumbled on something, a piece in the jigsaw puzzle there wasn't even space for.

The name, the name, the name. And there it was. The second page.

Rocsabin. Hélène de Vausigne, née Rocsabin.

MARIE-ANGE LAY in Eric's bath, the twin islands of her knees all that showed above a blanket of *bain moussant*. But she knew what lay beneath. The scarlet tracks of that pig Antoine's fingers on her breast, and the dull red rash at the side of her neck where his bristly mouth had rubbed against her skin. She'd run the water as hot as she could bear. But still she shivered.

What concerned her now was not that Antoine would tell his mother what he had found her doing, but that he would threaten her with exposure to have what he wanted. She'd have to watch her step when she visited the chateau, stay out of his way if she wanted to avoid a repeat performance.

How she'd got through the afternoon, she couldn't imagine. How she finished her soup, managed the chitchat with Florence, she'd never know.

And then, just when she'd decided to get out of the house and back to St

Bédard, they'd heard the Mercedes pull into the courtyard, the sound of Picard's boots on the steps down to the kitchen.

The Comtesse was waiting for her in the ballroom.

Which was where, having crept across the hallway, on the lookout for Antoine, Marie-Ange had found her.

'I regret, Mademoiselle, that we must forgo our planned festivities,' the Comtesse had told her. 'It's the Comte's funeral we have to arrange now,' she continued, with steel in her voice. 'And as usual there's a great deal to do and very little time. I'll help, if you don't mind. Best to stay busy.'

For the rest of that afternoon, the two of them had dismantled the flower frames that Marie-Ange had erected. But for a few directions, the whole job was done in silence.

And not once had Antoine made an appearance.

Now Marie-Ange heaved herself from the bath, wrapped herself in a towel and went to her room to dress. A pair of jeans and a rollneck sweater high enough to cover the rash on her neck. Afterwards she curled up in Monsieur Chabert's chair in the parlour and watched TV.

Remote in hand, she flicked through the options—news, a chat show, a football match—and settled for the last half of the film *Léon*. She'd seen it before. But it didn't matter. It would take her mind off her horrible day.

The next thing she knew the film was over. Another football match was on. She'd dozed off, and it took her a few moments to remember where she was and what she'd gone to sleep thinking about.

She frowned. Her eyes strayed to the screen. The referee in his black strip. Whistle in hand. Looking at his watch. The end of the match? she wondered. And then—the watch, the referee's watch, something about it. She felt for her own, twisted the strap, held it up to the light from the TV, examined it.

Something. She knew it for sure. Something to do with a watch. That was what she'd been thinking about when she fell asleep. A watch. But now, the image had lost something. Which annoyed her. It would be harder to make whatever connection there was to make.

Switching off the television, Marie-Ange stood up. She'd sleep on it.

But first, maybe, a breath of fresh air. And a *chocolat* at Mazzelli's.

As SHE STEPPED out onto the pavement, Marie-Ange saw that the square was still busy, lights glinting and winking in the trees, cars parked outside the Fontaine Dorée, people out for a stroll. She headed to Mazzelli's, found a table on the terrace and made herself comfortable.

Tomas appeared with a tray bearing her *chocolat*. She'd ordered it so often, usually at this time of night, that there was now no need for her to say anything. As soon as they saw her coming, they reached for the cocoa.

She thanked Tomas and watched him turn back to the bar. Which was when she saw old Dumé step out onto the terrace, take a look at the shifting sky, sniff the air. As Tomas passed him, he said something to the lad, then turned in her direction.

Of all the people in St Bédard, Dumé had been the hardest nut to crack. At first all she'd managed to get from him were grunts and nods. But gradually he'd softened, and had started stopping by to talk to her whenever he passed the shop. Now he pulled over a chair from a neighbouring table and sat down, positioning his stick between his legs.

'So, the party's off then, at the chateau,' he began.

She nodded. 'The Comtesse told me this afternoon.'

Dumé gave her a sly, sideways look. 'She pay you yet for your trouble, you'll excuse my asking?'

Marie-Ange shook her head. She'd meant to say something that afternoon but, sensing the Comtesse's grief, she'd put off raising the subject of money. Even if the old crow did have a bundle of cash in her bedside cupboard . . .

Dumé nodded. 'Always been mindful of money, that one,' he confided. 'Always on the lookout for extra cash. Like trying to hoist our rents. But she can't do it and she knows it.'

Over Dumé's shoulder, Marie-Ange saw Tomas coming back to their table. On his tray was a carafe of water and a glass of pastis for her companion.

'How come? The rents, I mean,' asked Marie-Ange.

'It was the old Comte. Edouard,' said Dumé, accepting the pastis from Tomas, dribbling some water into the glass and sipping it. 'Anyone living in the square at the end of the war, he gave 'em life terms, rent increases set at one per cent below the national rate, never more than two per cent increase per annum. Nothing she can do about it. Set in stone, it is. Till the day I dies.'

'How long have you lived here, Simon?'

'Born here,' replied Dumé. 'Nineteen fifteen. Over there. Next generation and it's all change. Then she can charge what she fancies. Or sell.'

'I thought the de Vausignes had money.'

'They've got a title sure enough, but money? No. Spent that. Or as good as. They've enough to see them through, if you asks me. If they watches theirselves. I mean, you just got to look at the place, the chateau. The last few years they've let things slip. A place like that . . . you got to maintain it or you loses it. Would never have happened with the real de Vausignes.'

'The real de Vausignes?'

'The original family. Been there centuries, they had. This lot, they're not of the blood. Married into it. Took it over. The Comte, the one just gone, he's the stepson, right? Legally adopted, but nothing to do with the old boy.'

'Tell me,' said Marie-Ange, taking this in, thinking of the photo in the Comtesse's bedside table, 'do the initials "AV" mean anything to you?'

'AV?' repeated Dumé. 'Up at the chateau, you mean? Albert. Must be. Edouard's son. Albert de Vausigne.'

'And "PR"?'

Dumé gave her another sideways look. 'What's with all the initials?'

'A photograph I saw in the chateau. In the library,' she added. 'Two men, one young, one older, but just initials. AV. PR. I wondered . . .'

'Large man? Red cheeks?' Dumé pinched his lip with his fingers.

Marie-Ange nodded.

'Paul Rocsabin. Has to be. Her ladyship's father. He and Albert used to go hunting, out with the dogs. Old man Rocsabin was always getting the boy up there on one pretext or another. The major reason being that he wanted the young feller to notice his daughter, Hélène.'

'And did he?' Judging by the photo—the fall of hair, the eyes, that devil-may-care grin—the Comtesse must certainly have noticed him.

'Not a chance. There was someone else for him. One of his gang.'

'Gang?'

Dumé put down his drink and felt for his pouch and pipe. He tamped down the tobacco and lit a match, held it over the bowl and looked at her over his cupped hands. 'The Maquis, Mam'selle. The AAC. *Aux Armes, Citoyens*. That's what we called it in these parts. Back in the war.' He took a puff and the tobacco crackled. 'There was a lot of us in those days, up in the hills, sleeping rough, cutting a power line or two. I was twenty-seven when I started, but young de Vausigne was in it from the beginning.'

'And this girl . . .' prompted Marie-Ange.

Dumé nodded. 'They was in the same team, see, Albert and this girl. Tight as ticks they were.'

'Did you ever meet her?'

'Once or twice. Joined forces for an action in, let's see now . . . Pertuis, I think. A rail line. Another time at Roussillon. They was always up front, the two of them. In charge, you know.'

'So what happened to them?' asked Marie-Ange.

'Him, he was shot. Caught by the Boches on the Brieuc road and put against a wall.'

'Is that the sign by the bridge?' asked Marie-Ange, knowing it had to be.

'The memorial? That's right. That's where it happened. You could hear the shooting from here. All hell breaking loose. I wasn't in on that one or I might not be here now. A dozen *résistants* killed and six Krauts. There was reprisals, of course. As well as the four they executed, they took three men from Chant-le-Neuf, three from Rocsabin and two from here in St Bédard. Hung 'em up right there.' Dumé nodded at the trees across the road.

Marie-Ange looked up at the trees and remembered the sounds she'd heard during her first week in St Bédard—the creak of branches, the stretched squeaking of a rope. So that was what it was, she thought, knowing now she'd never hear the sound again.

'And the girl?' she asked. 'Albert's friend? What happened to her?'

'Got away, so I heard. Never heard a thing more about her. But she must have been gutted.' Between puffs at his pipe, Dumé continued his story: 'Word was someone grassed 'em up. Told the Krauts what they was planning. That road there, you see, from Cavaillon to Brieuc, was a well-used transport route for the Boches. Lot of traffic, there was. Usually night-time. The plan was to ambush a load of arms. Albert de Vausigne had brought in some back-up, more than he usually had. Which was where, some say, the leak came from. Someone he'd wanted in, but they couldn't make it. Or didn't show. I mean, you don't squeal to the Boches about an op you're taking part in, eh? And so far as I knows, only the two got away. The woman, Albert's girl, and a young lad from Barjas. Name of Bonaire.'

'Could it have been him? The one who grassed?'

'Bonaire? Not a chance. He hated the Krauts. The reason he joined up was his old man had been sent to Drancy.'

'So who do you think blew the whistle?' she asked.

'Who knows?' said Dumé, rising to his feet. 'It was a long time ago. People don't seem to be interested any more. And what difference would it make?'

Quite a lot, thought Marie-Ange, not knowing why she should think it.

THAT WEEKEND, a summer mistral hurtled down from the north.

People said how they hated this wind, how it depressed them, made them ill-tempered and out of sorts. But Jacquot loved it—the power, the bluster, the self-confidence. Raw and delinquent, it swept down the Rhône valley like a barroom brawler looking for a fight.

It was the wind that woke Jacquot on the day of Tantine's funeral—or, rather, a downstairs window that had been left unlatched the night before.

A few desultory pelts of rain slapped against the glass as he secured it. Outside, the sky was low on the hilltops and grey as granite, the spindly tops of the cypresses whipping this way and that, the driveway filled with leaves from the olive trees, spinning and pirouetting across the gravel.

It was, thought Jacquot, as good a day as any for a funeral.

The service had been scheduled for four o'clock that Monday afternoon in the chapel at the Abbaye de Laune. At a little after two, Jacquot left the office, went home and changed into a dark suit. Then, with Claudine beside him, he drove the forty kilometres to Laune.

They parked in the abbey's gravelled forecourt, surprisingly full for a weekday afternoon, and made their way to the chapel where the *abbesse* was waiting for them at the door.

Her hands were tightly clasped and she seemed relieved to see them. 'I tried to call, but there was no reply,' she began apologetically.

Claudine looked at her anxiously, thinking something had gone wrong.

'There was just the one caller, you see, an old gentleman, asking about the arrangements. The time, you know. The day. So of course I told him. I didn't think to mention it to you. He must have passed it on,' she said, stepping forward and pushing open the door. 'It's just that the chapel is so small. There's so little room. And we never expected so many people.'

Claudine and Jacquot looked through the open door into the chapel.

Instead of the small, private ceremony they'd anticipated, every seat was taken, the pews packed as tightly as a jar of anchovies, the side aisles crowded with wheelchairs and those who'd arrived too late for a seat. From the doorway it was almost impossible to see Sandrine's coffin, covered in a tasselled *drapeau tricolore* by the altar. Which also surprised them: they had made no arrangements for any decoration other than their wreath. As they made their way down the central aisle, accompanied by the low hum of an organ, and the odd cough and shuffling of feet, line after line of ancient faces turned in their direction.

'Who are all these people?' whispered Claudine, as they slid into the front pew, which had been kept free for them.

'How should I know? Maybe it was that notice of yours in the papers.'

The day after Tantine's death Claudine had posted it in the local paper and in *Le Monde*. She'd had Jacquot read it before faxing it off. It was simple and to the point.

On 22 July, at the Abbaye de Laune, Salon,
Sandrine Eddé passed away in her sleep, aged 79.
A patriot. A fighter for freedom.
Our beloved Tantine.
On vit ensemble, on meurt tout seul.

Less than a week since that announcement, a crowd of people had turned up to show that you don't die alone. Or, at least, die forgotten.

The service was brief: a whispered litany of prayers and benedictions from the *curé*, the formal responses from the congregation, and a single psalm, which had every voice in the congregation a beat or two behind the organist.

As the *curé* gave the final blessing and the first notes of a Bach *Sanctus* that Tantine had loved filled the chapel, a half-dozen men, all in their seventies but still sprightly-looking, stepped from their pews and gathered round the coffin, medals sagging from their suit lapels.

And then Jacquot knew who the mourners were. Old soldiers to a man. All her old comrades. From the war. Come to see her off.

Taking their order from one of their number, a man with a wide shock of white hair and the ribbon of the Croix de Guerre in his buttonhole, they hoisted the coffin onto their shoulders and slow-marched out of the chapel.

So much, thought Jacquot, for the wheeled gurney the *abbesse* had promised when he'd asked about burial arrangements, and the abbey gardeners who'd double as pallbearers.

As the coffin was borne away, he and Claudine followed it, acknowledging the sad smiles and nods of commiseration they received as they passed through the congregation. In the last pew Jacquot saw an old boy lift his hand and salute as the coffin passed, tears welling in his eyes.

Outside, the mistral was waiting for them. As the cortège filed out, hands reached for hats as it bore down on them, tugging at trouser legs, coats and the flag draped over the coffin, lifting its tasselled edge and slapping it against the wood panels. Jacquot expected to see it lift off and sail through the air at any moment, but as they passed beneath the archway leading to the graveyard he noticed that someone had tacked the flag to the wood.

Much the same forethought had been employed at the graveside, where a pair of high trestles had been set beside the grave. The pallbearers had simply to walk either side and lower the coffin a few centimetres to take the weight off their shoulders.

In short order, the flag was removed, folded and presented to Claudine, canvas straps were looped through the coffin's handles and a dozen men joined the pallbearers and took the strain as the trestles were removed.

They've done this before, thought Jacquot as, gradually, the straps were played out and the coffin was lowered into the ground.

Afterwards, when he and Claudine turned from the grave, a tall, distinguished-looking gentleman with a thin cover of grey hair stepped forward, introduced himself. 'Colonel Hugo Rascousse,' he said, shaking their hands, extending his condolences.

Jacquot remembered the name from the citations in Sandrine's deed box. Renard. Head of Network F2.

He fell into step beside them, the wind whipping around them, and the three of them followed the other mourners from the cemetery.

'We never knew what happened to her,' the colonel explained. 'After the executions she just disappeared. No one knew where she'd come from and no one knew where she went. It was like that, after the war. But then, last week, Bonaire read the notice. Captain Henri Bonaire, the lead pallbearer with the white hair? He fought alongside your aunt. As did I on many occasions. He called me and the others. The word was passed round. We should have got in touch, I know, to ask your permission. We didn't think the chapel would be so small.'

'It was so good of you to come,' Claudine managed to say when they reached their car. 'Tantine would have been so . . . touched.'

'We could have filled your little chapel a dozen times over, Madame,' replied Rascousse, 'but many of us are old now and could not make the journey. I can assure you, though, that they will be thinking of her in their hearts today. Those who are left. In that terrible time when our country was taken from us, there were a few, like your aunt, who refused to compromise their honour or surrender their country. Without fear for her safety, she did everything in her power to turn the tide of war. And many of the men here today owe her their lives. Including me. She was a very courageous woman, Madame. One of the bravest.'

By this time, tears were streaming down Claudine's face and she clung to Jacquot as though to a rock in a stormy sea.

'I think . . .' began Jacquot.

'Please forgive me, Monsieur, Madame,' said Rascousse, his hand reaching out to touch Claudine's arm. 'It was just . . . It is important for you to know the kind of woman Sandrine Eddé was. She will never be forgotten.'

And with that he bowed his head and walked away.

10

It had been a busy week for Marie-Ange. For the last five days she'd spent every evening in St Bédard's church, arranging the floral decorations for the Comte de Vausigne's funeral.

On Monday, Picard had helped her bring the trelliswork from the chateau and by Tuesday night they'd secured it to the walls and the columns of the church. On Wednesday, the blooms she'd ordered for the de Vausignes' anniversary party had been delivered—lilies, jonquils, anemones, irises, peonies, marguerites, asters, all tightly budded creams, golds and whites—and she soaked their stems overnight in buckets of water diluted with Indian ink. By Thursday evening, when she and Tomas wheeled the flowers to the church, every petal was veined with black.

As far as Marie-Ange was concerned, working in the church had distinct advantages over the chateau. There was little risk of bumping into Antoine de Vausigne, and the church seemed to be the only place in St Bédard where the wind was kept at bay. She'd heard of the mistral, but it was the first time she'd ever been in it. And she hated it from the very first gusts.

Until the previous week, the Vaucluse countryside had captivated her. It was the sweetest place she'd ever been. But now she couldn't hear anything save the endless moaning and whistling of the wind. The grit and dust it carried found its way into her eyes, nose, ears, prickling across her scalp, gathering at the corners of her mouth. It went on, day after hot, muggy, dusty, blustery day, until Marie-Ange was just about ready to scream.

The mistral was still blowing on Saturday morning when St Bédard, but for Mazzelli's bar and the Parmentiers' *auberge*, closed down at midday. It was Gilles de Vausigne's funeral that afternoon, and customers were gently shooed from premises around the square as Clotilde Lepantre, the Bulots, Madame Héliard, André Ribaud and the Tesserats latched their shutters and rolled down their blinds as a mark of respect.

Inside the church, Marie-Ange made the final adjustments—pruning, dead-heading—then sat in one of the pews and wondered if he would come.

The policeman. Jacquot.

He had to come. She was sure of it. The Comte had been murdered, after all. And a woman too. Six murders in six months, in this tiny corner of

Provence. Seven deaths in all, counting Monsieur Bartolomé's suicide.

Marie-Ange had decided, after their meeting in the Martner hothouse, that she would confide in Jacquot. There was something strangely familiar about the man, as though the letters she'd been writing to him for the last four months had somehow drawn them together. The time had come to pool resources. She didn't need anyone to tell her that Jacquot was as uncomfortable with the Chabert case as she was. Maybe between them they could get to the bottom of it, because she was getting nowhere by herself. Just a raft of psychic messages she couldn't decipher—something to do with the war. Something to do with the memorial by the bridge . . .

Talk was, the trial was winding up. And things were not looking good for Eric Chabert. Time was getting short.

Marie-Ange was in no doubt that Jacquot was someone she could trust. Their meeting in the hothouse had confirmed it. The fact that he was there at all. And the way his eyes cast about, as though he was looking for some clue, something he'd missed the first time round.

And the times she'd seen him at Mazzelli's. Sitting in the sunshine. Thinking things through. Looking ill at ease . . . He wasn't at all what she'd expected. The policeman in Metz had been thin as a stick of celery, bald, glasses, with a dreadful belted raincoat. This was a different animal. This one looked . . . cool, handsome. And judging by the way she'd flustered him in the hothouse—all that playful flirting—he didn't seem to know it. Which made him seem even more attractive.

She liked a lot of things about him: the way his green eyes settled on her, kindly, etched with a spray of laugh lines; those big hands of his, holding out the notebook for her. And she even liked the ponytail. It was not the way a man his age should wear his hair. But it suited him. She wondered how old he was—late forties, maybe fifty. A good age. And in good condition too. For a moment she felt a tiny bolt of envy for the woman he loved, the woman whose birthday it was, the one for whom he would buy an orchid.

That was something else that impressed her. His honesty. Telling her there was a woman in his life. When men met Marie-Ange, the last thing they did was volunteer information about wives or girlfriends.

She was thinking how nice it must be to have a man like that come home every night when the great door of the church creaked open, a shaft of daylight split the shadows and the first of the mourners arrived.

Surrendering her seat, Marie-Ange made her way to the back of the church, taking up position behind the christening font, watching the arrivals as they made their way down the aisle. A few dress uniforms, frock coats, an official sash or two, black suits and overcoats, top hats, veils and gloves.

But no ponytail. No Jacquot.

It was only when the bishop, attended by the Curé Foulard, had begun the mass that the church door winced open once more. Marie-Ange peered through the gloom and there he was, slipping down the side aisle.

Marie-Ange felt a stir of excitement. It was beginning.

THE MISTRAL seemed to have lost some of its punch by the time Jacquot arrived in St Bédard, to find the balconies hung with snapping black ribbon and the fountain wreathed with garlands of rustling black taffeta, all of which, a day or two earlier, the wind would have snatched away.

He had only just made it. For the last three days he'd been in Aix, providing Claudine with moral support as she made the final arrangements for the opening of her summer exhibition. That morning, she'd delayed Jacquot longer than he'd intended in their room at the hotel . . .

But he had reached St Bédard in time, and now he was sitting at a table on Mazzelli's terrace, looking over the crowd that had gathered. He got to his feet as the plumed horses and glinting glass-sided hearse bearing Gilles de Vausigne on his final journey turned into the square.

Gilles, Comte de Vausigne. Edouard's adopted son. Second in line to the de Vausigne title. Was he the one who'd gone to the Germans all those years ago, the one who'd set up his stepbrother? It seemed to fit. Gilles betrays his stepbrother to secure the title and his future. Only Martner finds out about it. At the *Kommandantur* where he worked, or after the war in a cell in Aix-Luynes. And puts the screws on him all these years later. Pay me or else. Is that where the doctor's unexplained fortune had come from? Cash provided by the Comte de Vausigne to keep his secret safe? Until finally the Comte grew tired of the blackmail, and decided to do something about it?

Certainly de Vausigne had had good reason to betray his stepbrother. And he was tall enough to climb the Martner stairs two by two, and to knock those pictures out of line. But could a man in his seventies have recovered from that fall in the Martners' kitchen? Enough to chase a young girl out of the house and up the drive? And would a man with a dozen guns in his cabinet be so clumsy with his weapon of choice? Jacquot didn't think so.

The Comte's hearse clattered over the cobbles and drew up at the steps of St Bédard's church. As a rank of pallbearers in sashed top hats and tailcoats stepped forward to draw out the coffin, one final car came to a halt at the church steps. It was the de Vausignes' Citroën 11 Légère, Picard ramrod straight at the wheel, the bonnet strung with black ribbon. Jacquot watched as the new Comte helped his mother from the back seat.

Or could it be that Albert had been betrayed by the Comte's wife, Hélène de Vausigne? *Née* Rocsabin. The name Tantine had written a thousand times, page after page, in that old notebook. Maybe it had been the Comtesse whose treachery Martner had witnessed all those years ago.

But if Albert had been the man she loved, as old man Gaillard had implied, how could she have countenanced betraying him to the Gestapo? As Jacquot watched the Comtesse climb the church steps, supported by her son, one thing was certain. There was no way the Comtesse could have been the Martners' killer. Too old now, too frail, for that terrible killing spree.

Finishing his beer and dropping some coins on the table, Jacquot left Mazzelli's and made his way to the church. At the top of the steps he pulled open one of the doors and slipped into the dark interior.

The first thing he noticed was the overwhelming scent of flowers. Roped through the Communion rail, wound round the stone pillars, set in floral chains on the pulpit and decorating the end of every pew, a mass of blooms seemed to cover every inch of the church. Even the Comte's portrait, standing on an easel at the altar steps, was framed with flowers. And every bloom, every petal he could see, was veined with black.

'Indian ink,' came a whisper from behind him.

Jacquot looked round to find Marie-Ange Buhl standing at his shoulder. He'd wondered whether he'd bump into her again.

'You're late, by the way,' she continued, looking past him to the coffin.

'Miss Buhl. You were expecting me?'

'Marie-Ange, please.' She turned back to him. 'I'd have been surprised if you hadn't made an appearance.'

'And I you, Miss Buhl,' he replied. 'From Alsace, from Île de France, Brittany, Poitou-Charentes. And most recently, of course, Brieuc.'

'So you've found me out, Chief Inspector. Bravo. And I suppose now you want to have a few words with me?'

'I most certainly do,' replied Jacquot.

TEN MINUTES LATER they were sitting in Mazzelli's bar. The terrace had been packed, as though the Comte's funeral was some kind of tourist spectacle, so they'd come inside and found a table wedged in a far corner.

Marie-Ange watched him order a beer and a glass of white wine, and wondered whether she'd been right to make a move. She knew they were on the same side. But would he understand what she was going to say?

As Tomas moved off to fetch their drinks, Jacquot gave Marie-Ange a long, cool look. He wasn't sure where to start, had no idea what to expect. But he knew it would be an interesting exchange.

'So, Marie-Ange. Tell me about Eric Chabert.'

'What's to tell?' she replied lightly. 'You have the wrong man.'

Jacquot nodded, as though they were both agreed on that. Then, quietly: 'You have proof? I should remind you that withholding information from the police in the course of their investigations is a criminal offence.'

She sensed that their meeting wasn't going to be quite as straightforward as she had hoped. Had she underestimated him? He was a policeman after all. She shifted in her seat, slipped a fall of hair behind her ear.

'It is all I have, Chief Inspector, but it's enough for me.'

Tomas brought their drinks and she reached for her wine, sipped it. Jacquot did the same with his beer.

They put their drinks down on the table, played with their glasses like gamblers fingering their chips. Jacquot broke the silence between them.

'You understand, Marie-Ange, we need more than . . . intuition,' he began, with a patient smile. 'Next week the jury will be sent out to consider the evidence and reach a verdict. It does not look good for Monsieur Chabert. So, what makes you think he's innocent?'

'I saw his picture in the paper. And I knew. Just like that. This man did not kill the Martners. Sometimes that's all it takes, you know. A photograph. A name. A place. Without any warning, you know something. Without question. It's a kind of . . . clarity.'

Jacquot nodded. 'You said "sometimes".'

Which surprised her. He was taking it in, still reserving judgment. Which was why she continued, explaining things from the beginning. So there'd be no misunderstanding. About the marshalling yards of Metz, the raised voices on that fourth-floor balcony in the street where the woman died, the scream that ended with that dreadful thud.

'It's like echoes,' she said, anxious to make it as comprehensible as she could. 'Things from the past that find their way into my present. And stay there until I acknowledge them, understand them. Sometimes these . . . echoes are loud and strong, sometimes they're just distant. But however they present themselves, I know they mean something. Like now. With Eric Chabert. Unfinished business.'

'I have to say—' began Jacquot, not really sure what he wanted to say.

'I know, I know . . . It all sounds crazy,' she interrupted. 'If you don't believe me, call the policeman in Metz. Fayard was his name. Ask him about the letters he received. About the teacher. He'll tell you.'

But still Jacquot looked unconvinced, so she decided to go one step further and tell him about seeing the murdered girl in the nursery in Metz.

'To be completely accurate,' she said quietly, 'it wasn't just the photo in the paper that started this. It began with a young girl. The first time . . . I've ever seen anything.'

'So now you see things,' said Jacquot, and immediately regretted it. He had seen her flinch. To cover he said: 'And this was . . . ?'

For a while Marie-Ange said nothing, debating whether to go on, sliding a finger up and down the icy side of her glass.

'Please,' encouraged Jacquot, surprising himself.

'March,' she replied, relenting. 'In Metz. I was working at a nursery. In one of the hothouses. Suddenly I felt someone beside me. Heard a voice.'

'The girl just . . . appeared?'

Marie-Ange nodded.

'A ghost?'

'I suppose . . .'

'And what did she say? This . . . girl,' said Jacquot quietly.

The way he asked the question, the way he leaned forward, speaking so softly, made Marie-Ange feel better. She'd said enough to scare off most people, but he was still there, listening. She'd been right about him.

'She was speaking in German, and she said "*Gärtner*". Gardener. And then she switched to French. Not so good French, but I knew what she was saying. '*Pas lui. Pas lui.*' The words meant nothing to me. Until the day I opened the paper and saw that picture. Read the story. That's when I knew who she'd been talking about. Eric Chabert.'

'And what did she look like, this girl? Do you remember?'

'Young. Blonde. Skinny. Not as tall as me. I seem to remember a dressing gown, pyjamas . . .'

Jacquot nodded. Kippi had been wearing pyjamas and a dressing gown when they found her on the Martners' driveway. But Marie-Ange could have read those details in a paper, or guessed them.

'The strange thing was,' Marie-Ange continued, 'she was wearing only one shoe. An espadrille.'

Jacquot's scalp tightened, and he shivered. No one outside the investigation knew about the espadrille. There was no way Marie-Ange could have known that. Unless she'd been there. Or unless she was telling the truth.

'The granddaughter, Kippi,' Jacquot said at last.

Marie-Ange smiled. She knew she'd said something important, something that had made him believe her. 'That's what I guessed.'

'So you started writing letters.'

'Yes.'

'And came here to St Bédard. To do what, exactly?'

'Well, if Chabert didn't kill the Martners, then who did?' she said. 'I thought, being close to the scene, maybe something would become clear.'

'And has it?'

'I don't know yet. I feel . . . near something. I mean, I know that I'm in the right place. That I'm close. But right now?' She shrugged, looked almost forlorn. 'I just cannot say.'

Then, for an instant, she remembered the Comtesse's bedroom, something catching her eye, something at the edge of her vision, something important. But the next instant it was gone. Out of reach.

'Let me ask you something,' she said. 'You do believe me, don't you?'

'About your voices? Or about Chabert?'

'Both.'

'I don't necessarily disbelieve the first—your voices. But I certainly believe, like you, that Eric Chabert . . . may be innocent.'

'And what makes you think that?'

Jacquot shrugged, not wanting to give too much away. 'Inconsistencies.'

Marie-Ange waited, held his eye.

'First . . . Eric isn't tall enough to be the killer.' Jacquot didn't bother to explain how he knew that. So he was pleased to see her nod, which encouraged him to go on. 'Second. Prints on the gun, but none on the shell casings. It doesn't add up. What? He wears gloves to load, but not to shoot?'

She nodded again. She understood. 'Anything else?'

'Whoever killed the Martners was not comfortable with a gun.' Jacquot spread his hands. 'He was clumsy—hit a banister trying to take a shot, fired off another wild round in the kitchen. Eric Chabert wouldn't have done that.'

Marie-Ange frowned. 'He?'

Jacquot smiled. 'That's my guess. Also, the murder weapon was stolen in November, three months before the murders. But in November Eric had no reason to think about murder. He was in love with Kippi, and he hadn't yet been sacked or rejected.'

'And?'

Jacquot paused. This would be more difficult. This was thinner ice.

'In 1942,' he began, 'Josef Martner was called up and posted to France. After serving in Toulouse he was transferred here, to Cavaillon, as a medical orderly with the Abwehr.'

'It's strange you should mention the war,' Marie-Ange put in.

'How so?'

'Just a feeling I have. Something I can't shift. To do with the war.'

Jacquot took this in. 'Anyway, after the war, Martner gets repatriated, marries well and lives well. Gives up work and travels all over. But the money doesn't last. He and his wife don't have the same financial freedom they once enjoyed, and after a few years in Hamburg and Paris, making ends meet, they move south. After forty years, Martner comes back to Provence, buys a home near Cavaillon, and starts to live well again. Money to spare.'

'So? What does all this mean?'

'Call it a theory,' replied Jacquot, eager now to put into words what had filled his head since leaving the Brasserie Chez Gaillard the previous week. 'But I believe that Martner found something out when he worked here in Cavaillon, during the war. And then, much later, when things got a little difficult for him, he remembered what he'd seen or heard during the war and came back to put it into play.'

'Put it into play?'

'Blackmail. Someone with something to hide. Someone who'd be prepared to pay for his . . . discretion. It's the only way to explain the money.'

'And that money is . . .?'

'The money we can't account for. When Martner moved down here with his wife they had enough to get by. But not enough to cover the expenses he was running up. His hothouse, equipment, trips abroad. Everything paid in cash. And nothing in the records to show where it came from.'

'And this is money that has nothing to do with Eric Chabert?'

Jacquot shook his head. 'Nothing whatever. Which is the main reason I believe the boy is innocent. There's someone else mixed up in this. And I believe it's got something to do with the war. And Albert de Vausigne.'

Marie-Ange nodded, as though agreeing with every word.

'You know about de Vausigne?' asked Jacquot, noting her reaction.

'Simon Dumé. He lives here in St Bédard. He told me about it. Back in the war there was some kind of ambush on the Brieuc road, near the bridge. He says someone told the Germans about it, betrayed de Vausigne.'

Jacquot was taken aback. 'Did this Dumé know who?'

Marie-Ange shook her head.

'Well, it's my bet Martner knew. He saw someone at the *Kommandantur* or overheard something. Or maybe he found something out when he was in prison after the war, before he was repatriated. Forty years later, when he needed money, he got in touch, put on some pressure. Which is, I'm increasingly certain, how he ended up dead. His wife, daughter'—Jacquot shrugged—'they were just in the way. It was Dr Martner the killer was after.'

'So do you have a suspect?'

Jacquot sidestepped. 'I know someone who would certainly have benefited from Albert's death, someone who had motive, means and opportunity to betray him. But he could never have killed the Martners.'

'You're talking about the Comte, aren't you?' asked Marie-Ange.

'What makes you think that?'

'He was the stepson. If his stepbrother had inherited the title, what was there left for him? What kind of future?'

Jacquot nodded.

'Anyone else? Any other suspects?' Marie-Ange lifted her glass and finished her wine. 'The Comtesse, for example?'

Jacquot frowned. 'Why do you ask that?'

'Because . . . there is another voice I've heard.' Marie-Ange paused. 'A new one. I've heard it twice so far. Just this last week. Working in the church. A lovely, lonely, soft voice. A woman's voice. Elegant. Elderly, I'd say.'

'And what does this new voice say?' asked Jacquot, feeling the hairs on the back of his neck start to rise.

Marie-Ange put down her glass. 'Just one word,' she replied. 'Over and over again. "Rocsabin".'

SUNDAY MORNING the sky was bright and clear, a watery blue. It had rained hard in the night, but for the first time in a week the low ceiling of racing, pewter-coloured clouds had gone, the mistral barnstorming its way south, out into the ocean.

Jacquot drove east into the Luberon hills with all the windows down, the rush of air as fresh and clean as the sky above. It felt as though Provence had been washed, rinsed and hung out to dry in the sparkling sunshine.

The house he was looking for was easy to find, exactly where the old lady had said. To the left of a twelfth-century church, at the end of a narrow cobbled path. A green door set in a high wall.

Jacquot parked in the village square, in the shadow of the church, and followed the path on foot. It was walled on both sides, a passage of flaky gold stone that rose above his head, tightening the further he went. When he came to the green door, where the alley ended, he opened it as he'd been instructed to do and stepped into their garden.

Jacquot had phoned the evening before, after calling Hugo Rascousse. When the colonel heard what he wanted, he'd given Jacquot the number.

The wife had answered the phone, cautious at first, but after Jacquot mentioned Tantine's funeral and Rascousse's name, she had become more animated. Her husband was out just then, she told him, but they would be happy to see him the following day, for lunch.

Closing the door behind him, Jacquot found himself in a flagstoned courtyard bordered by terracotta pots—oranges and lemons alternating with great blooms of hibiscus and mimosa. In front of him stood a low stone house with butter-yellow walls, ivy weaving round turquoise shutters, and the peaks of the Grand Luberon rising above the pantiles.

An old woman, kneeling on a stuffed sack, was weeding a flowerbed by the front door. When she heard the latch she turned, shaded her eyes and got painfully to her feet. She wore a straw hat trimmed with a blue band, thick gloves and a housecoat tied round the middle.

'Monsieur Jacquot?'

Jacquot walked across and held out his hand. 'Madame Bonaire?'

She pulled off a glove. 'That's me,' she replied, and shook his hand, eyes twinkling in the leathery folds of her tanned face, taking in Jacquot's ponytail, pointed boots and leather jacket with an easy smile. 'You'll find Henri out back with his bees. Lunch in twenty minutes.'

Leading him round the side of the house and down a path shaded with hoops of jasmine, she stopped at an open doorway and pointed ahead. '*Là-bas*,' she said, then patted his arm and disappeared into the kitchen.

Jacquot crossed a terrace set with chairs and a wooden table in the shade of an old olive tree, and stepped down onto a strip of sloping lawn edged with oleander bushes and linden trees. At the far end, a wall of gold limestone rose above a line of brightly coloured beehives. The lid of one had been removed, and an old man, in shorts and singlet, his head covered with a black netted hat, was bent over the open hive.

Ten metres away, Jacquot stopped, not wanting to get too close, and coughed politely. The old man turned, waved and reached down for the lid. He replaced it carefully, then came up the slope.

'Monsieur Jacquot,' he said, rolling up the veil of netting and pulling off his hat. 'I didn't recognise the name, but I remember you from the funeral.'

'And I you, Monsieur.' Which Jacquot did. The shock of white hair was unmistakable. The man who had led the pallbearers at Sandrine's funeral, the one who'd presented Claudine with the flag from the coffin.

They shook hands. 'Come,' Bonaire said. 'Let's get ourselves a drink.'

On the terrace, Madame Bonaire was setting out a jug of wine, a bottle of rum and three glasses. She pulled the cork from the rum and poured three tots, taking hers and heading back inside.

When she was gone the two men settled themselves at the table.

'I am sorry I did not have an opportunity to speak with you and your wife at the funeral,' Bonaire said, 'to say how sorry I was for your loss. So many old faces. And I knew Rascousse would speak for all of us. She was a fine, fine woman.' He raised his glass. 'To Sandrine.'

'Sandrine,' echoed Jacquot.

They put their glasses down. 'So, Monsieur. What can I do for you?'

'Actually it's "Chief Inspector". I am a policeman.'

'Aha! I should have known. The boots, the hair. Signs of rank nowadays, *non*? So, how can I be of help, Monsieur Chief Inspector?'

'It's about Sandrine,' said Jacquot. 'I believe you worked with her in the Resistance?'

'For two years. We hid out together. Ten, twelve of us. Up there in the hills. I didn't know her real name then. Only afterwards. She was . . .' Bonaire looked to the sky. 'Rose. That was it.'

'There was one action I wanted to know about particularly,' said Jacquot. 'On the Brieuc road, near St Bédard?'

Bonaire grunted. 'I know the place. Of course. Not likely to forget it. Rose, Sandrine. We were the only two made it out. The rest. Gone.'

From the kitchen came a rattle of plates, and a moment later Madame Bonaire appeared carrying a large tray. She laid it on the table and distributed a selection of thick faience plates: slices of sausage, a mound of homemade *rillettes*, a heap of radishes, a bowl of wrinkled olives, a basket of bread, three apples and a wedge of goat's cheese. A Luberon lunch.

'So. Help yourself, Monsieur,' she said, sitting between the men.

'And some wine, Monsieur,' continued Bonaire, flourishing the jug in front of Jacquot till he had to toss back the last of the rum and hold out his glass. 'From our own vines,' he said, splashing a pale rosé into Jacquot's glass, then his wife's, then his own. 'So. *Santé.*'

For the next thirty minutes they ate, and talked about the season, the crops. When Madame Bonaire had cleared the dishes and gone inside for some coffee, Jacquot switched back to Sandrine.

'They say there was an informer . . .'

Bonaire shifted uncomfortably. 'That's what they said. That's what I heard. Two or three names.'

At that moment Madame Bonaire reappeared with the coffee, set out the cups and poured. 'Names?' she asked.

'The war, *ma chère*. Monsieur Jacquot wants to know about the war. Collaborators. Informants.'

'Oh, they were everywhere,' she said, passing round the sugar.

'Like I said,' continued Bonaire, taking two lumps, 'two or three names at least. But in those days, you wanted to get someone into trouble, settle a grudge maybe, you gave any name you chose. Just to make mischief. It didn't have to be true.' Bonaire caught his wife's questioning look. 'St Bédard. Monsieur Jacquot wanted to know about it.'

'It was her,' said Madame Bonaire, her lips tightening. 'You know it as well as I.'

'Denise, we do not know that. We cannot be sure. There were many mistakes made after liberation. Many innocent people . . .'

'I tell you it was her. Jealous, she was. Everyone knew it. That's why she did it. To get rid of Sandrine. She and Albert . . . well . . .'

'And who exactly is "she"?' asked Jacquot, knowing the answer.

Madame Bonaire looked at her husband. He made to shake his head but seemed to know it would do no good.

'Hélène Rocsabin,' she said. 'Still lives there, I hear. The nerve. Not that anyone would know. Not now. But back then? Oh, there was talk. But she was canny. Kept her head down. A woman scorned, Monsieur. You know the saying. Believe me, there is nothing you men should be more afraid of.'

Later, after Jacquot made his farewells, Bonaire saw him to the gate.

'You shouldn't listen too much to my wife. It's just rumour. About the lady. Who knows?'

The two men shook hands and Jacquot turned to leave.

'It's strange, you know,' called Bonaire after him. 'After all this time . . . You're not the first to come round asking about that night at the bridge.'

'I'm not?'

Bonaire shook his head. 'No, no. Just last week. A girl. Very . . . You know what I mean. A real Marianne.'

WHEN JACQUOT ARRIVED home, a black Chevy SUV was parked in the drive. He knew it from somewhere but couldn't place it . . . And then he saw the dogs, tied to the shoe scraper outside Claudine's front door. Weimaraners.

He was wondering what could possibly have brought Max Benedict out here on a Sunday afternoon when the front door opened and the man himself stepped out. Behind him stood Claudine.

'Chief Inspector, how good to see you again,' said Benedict, reaching over the dogs to shake Jacquot's hand. Then, turning to Claudine, 'Madame, a delight to meet you at last.' He gave a small bow, then turned back to Jacquot. 'I wondered, Chief Inspector, if I might have a word?'

Jacquot caught Claudine's eye. 'A moment. I'll be back.'

Claudine understood, closed the door.

After Benedict had untied the dogs, the two men walked to the SUV. Benedict opened the tailgate and the dogs leapt in.

'You have a fabulous place here,' he said. 'I must have driven past the lane a thousand times but I never suspected there was anything up here.'

'The sign puts people off,' replied Jacquot, wondering how Benedict had got the address, but not surprised that he had. The man was a journalist, after all. 'I read your piece on the Martners, by the way,' he prompted.

Benedict looked surprised. 'I'm honoured. And? What did you think?'

'Pretty fair, on the whole. Nicely written . . .'

The story had appeared in the weekend section of *Le Figaro*. Brunet had brought it into the office around the time Chabert's trial started. It began, of course, with Benedict's own role in the story, finding the murder weapon. After that he'd described the police investigation and arrest with surprising accuracy, given that Jacquot had made sure that all Benedict's enquiries were rerouted to Public Affairs and his access limited to press calls only.

'But,' continued Jacquot, 'you didn't seem . . . convinced.'

'You're right,' said Benedict. 'I *wasn't* convinced. Eric Chabert? Why on earth would he do such a thing? Because the girl drops him? Because he gets the sack? No. The boy may be a bit dim, but he's not stupid. There's something else going on here. Which reminds me . . . The reason I dropped by.'

Aha, thought Jacquot. 'And that might be?'

'The Rocsabin fire. I think I might have something of interest.'

'Which is?'

'On the night of the fire I was driving home from a dinner party in Barjas. I was on the back road between Barjas and Lucat, a little after midnight, when a car hurtled round that hairpin—you know the one, by the chapel?—and hit my wing mirror. Twenty minutes later, I'm out on the ter-race with a nightcap when I hear fire engines tearing up the valley road and see the sky above Rocsabin aglow.'

'Did you happen to see who was driving the car?'

'Regrettably not. It all happened so quickly.'

'And did you notice the make and model?'

'A Mercedes, I think. Not new. A saloon. Blue.'

'You could see the colour?'

'I have a scrape of its paint on my mirror. Right there,' said Benedict, pointing to the wing mirror, which was slightly buckled. 'You can see it,' he continued, as Jacquot bent down to look. 'A light blue. It seemed to me that a car racing away from Rocsabin like that might have something to do with the fire. Which is why I took the liberty of calling by on a Sunday.'

Jacquot felt in his pockets, found some paper, folded it into a makeshift envelope and stooped down to scrape some flakes of paint into it. 'And the reason you didn't report this earlier?' he asked, closing the envelope and slipping it into his pocket. 'The Rocsabin fire was more than a week ago.'

'I called you from the airport first thing the morning after. Thought it might be important. Left a message but you never called back.'

Jacquot remembered a message slip with Benedict's name and a mobile-phone number. There'd been no message, no sense of urgency, but he'd called back anyway, from Aldo Mazzelli's bar, on his way out to Rocsabin. He hadn't been able to get through, and hadn't bothered to try again.

'Airport?' he asked, changing the subject.

'On my way to New York. Work. Arrived back late last night to discover it's not just a fire any more. It appears you have another murder on your hands. And the Comte de Vausigne, no less.'

'A double murder. There was a woman too.'

'The Comtesse must be devastated,' said Benedict, opening the driver's door and climbing into the Chevy. He gave Jacquot a look, but Jacquot knew better than to volunteer any more information.

'I'm grateful for your interest,' said Jacquot, closing the door on him.

Benedict smiled. 'You'll let me know if I can be of any further assistance?'

'Be sure of it.'

Benedict started the engine and turned out of the drive. A hand appeared from the driver's window and waved. Jacquot waved back.

He might have had trouble placing the black Chevy, but Jacquot had no trouble placing a blue Mercedes.

11

First thing on Monday morning, Picard opened the door to find Jacquot and Brunet on the chateau steps.

'I'd like to see Antoine de Vausigne,' said Jacquot.

Picard stepped aside for them to enter, then showed them across the hall to the garden terrace. 'The Comte is staying in the summerhouse. By the pool. Just follow the path.' He pointed across the lawn to a stone archway set in a low wall. 'I'll call through to let him know you're coming.'

Antoine, dressed in swimming shorts and shiny with suntan oil, was spread out on a lounger reading a manuscript when Jacquot and Brunet appeared through the trees. He pushed up his sunglasses as they skirted the pool, watched them for a moment, then let the glasses drop back into place.

'Good day, Monsieur de Vausigne,' said Jacquot. Inside the cottage he could hear a phone ringing. Picard.

Antoine flicked through the remaining pages of the screenplay, then let it drop to the flagstones. 'Comte, Monsieur. *Comte* de Vausigne.'

Jacquot spread his hands as if apologising for his forgetfulness.

'So what is it I can do for you, Chief Inspector?' asked Antoine, reaching for the packet of cigarettes between his legs, lighting one, then dropping lighter and packet onto the discarded screenplay.

'First of all, please accept our condolences on the death of your father.'

'Thank you, Chief Inspector. That's very kind of you.' Antoine sniffed lightly, pulling at his nose with thumb and forefinger, then continued: 'So, what can I do for you now that you have delivered your condolences?'

'You are the owner of a blue Mercedes, Monsieur?' Jacquot began.

'That's right,' he replied sharply, noting the 'Monsieur'. 'What of it?'

'We believe it may have been involved in a traffic accident.'

'Believe what you wish, Chief Inspector,' said Antoine.

Jacquot considered this. 'Is your car here, Monsieur?' he asked.

'It is.'

'Perhaps you would be kind enough to show us.'

Antoine de Vausigne sighed deeply. Getting to his feet, he slid on slippers, snatched up a dressing gown and, with no indication that they should follow him, set off round the side of the guest cottage down a narrow path to a stone-built garage. The Mercedes was outside it, beneath the trees.

'*Voilà*, Chief Inspector. One blue Mercedes, although it doesn't look to me like it's been involved in any accident.'

'Would you mind?' asked Brunet, starting to examine the vehicle.

'Be my guest.' Antoine dropped his cigarette and ground it out.

Brunet walked round the car, examining the bodywork. As he came round the boot, he stopped by the back passenger door, ran his hand along the edge of the roof, then gave Jacquot a nod.

Jacquot joined him, followed by Antoine.

'And this, Monsieur?'

It was easy to miss, but an inch above the car's back door the metal trim had been flattened and a long, thin scratch had removed a layer of paint.

The new Comte's face clouded. He leaned past Jacquot and ran his fingers over the damage. '*Merde*, how did that get there?' he snapped.

'So you're saying you have no knowledge of this damage?' asked Jacquot, knowing that he didn't. The annoyance was just too genuine. No one could act it that well. De Vausigne might be a spoilt, unbearable little *crapaud*, but he wasn't lying. There was no way he could have driven the Mercedes and not felt the impact of Benedict's wing mirror. If, indeed, it had been Antoine's Mercedes involved. It seemed certain, but they'd have to wait for the tests on Benedict's sample to confirm it. Even then, there was no reason to assume that the Mercedes and its driver, whoever it might turn out to be, had had anything to do with the fire or the murders. With Guy Bartolomé's suicide and that incriminating can of petrol in the boot of his car, the case had already been closed. But still . . .

Stepping away from the car, Antoine shook his head. 'That's exactly what I'm saying. No idea at all. Must have been done in town. Some incompetent *salaud* getting too close. How on earth should I know?'

'Maybe,' said Jacquot, nodding. 'I wonder if you would mind telling me where you were on the evening the accident was reported?'

'Which was when?'

'Nearly two weeks ago, Monsieur. The night of the fire at Rocsabin.'

Antoine looked surprised. 'The night of the fire? Well, I was here the whole time. Here in the summerhouse. With my mother. Having dinner. I cooked. Picard and his wife had the night off.'

'And the dinner ended when?'

'My mother likes to get to bed early. I walked her back to the house about ten thirty, elevenish.'

'And the car was where?'

'I don't know. Up at the house, I think. In the courtyard. I can't remember.'

'So you don't always park the car here, Monsieur?' asked Jacquot.

'No. Not always. It depends whether I'm going to the house, or coming here. Whether I use the front or the back drive. Sometimes I park it here. Sometimes I leave it at the house. It's not that long a walk, Chief Inspector.'

'And the evening of the dinner?' continued Jacquot. 'You saw your mother home and . . .'

'I saw her up the garden steps and left her at one of the terrace doors. I did not go round to the front. Which was why I didn't actually see my car in the courtyard. I just assumed it was there. Or here.'

'Could the car have been taken without your knowledge, Monsieur?' asked Brunet.

'Well, if it was involved in this accident, it must have been, mustn't it?'

'Would you hear the car from your cottage if someone was driving it away?'

'Depends. You'd need the engine to get up the front drive, but the back drive over there'—Antoine gestured through the trees—'why, you could easily coast it.'

'With your permission,' said Jacquot. 'I'd like some of our boys to come up, take a look at the car? If that's all right? Say this afternoon?'

Antoine shrugged. 'If you think it necessary.'

Jacquot thanked him, then paused, seemed to consider something. 'Tell me, when you came back to the summerhouse after seeing your mother home, what then, if you don't mind my asking? Watched TV? Listened to some music? Went to bed?'

Antoine smiled. 'Not exactly, Chief Inspector.'

'You had company?'

'Correct.'

'Would you mind telling me the name of your companion?'

'To make sure I'm telling the truth? You don't really imagine I'd kill my own father, surely?'

Jacquot demurred, said nothing.

'Her name is Frankie Alzon,' Antoine replied.

Beside him, Brunet cleared his throat.

'She's a nurse at the hospital in Cavaillon. Charming girl. She came out here after her shift. Round eleven. She loves films. Writes these little scenarios for me. Which she acts in.' He smiled. 'And you know something? She really is very good.'

AFTER LEAVING Antoine by the pool, Jacquot and Brunet crossed the lawn and climbed the terrace steps to the chateau. Picard was waiting for them at the French windows. He looked perturbed.

'I'm so sorry, Monsieur,' he began. 'I tried to call the Comte but got no answer. Did you manage to find . . .?'

'Yes, yes, no problem,' said Jacquot. 'But I wonder,' he continued, stepping past Picard into the hallway, 'since we're here, whether it might be possible to have a few words with the Comtesse?'

'If you'll wait here a moment, sir, I'll see if I can find her.'

Moments later he was back. 'If you'd care to follow me, Messieurs, Madame la Comtesse will see you in the morning room.'

The Comtesse was standing by the fireplace, looking elegant in black. Picard announced them and withdrew, closing the door behind him.

'Chief Inspector. Inspector Brunet,' she said, nodding in their direction.

'Madame,' Jacquot began, 'I'm sorry to bother you again at this time but I would be most grateful if I could ask you a few questions.'

'I believe I have told you all I know,' she replied.

'As far as the Rocsabin incident, and your husband, yes. But I'd like to speak to you about something else entirely. To do with the war.'

Hélène de Vausigne crossed to a sofa and sat down. She gestured for them to take a seat opposite and gave Jacquot an intrigued by-all-means-carry-on look as he made himself comfortable.

'Your maiden name is Rocsabin, is it not?'

'That is correct.'

'And during the war,' Jacquot continued, 'you lived at Rocsabin?'

'That is also correct. Until the very last days, when the Germans requisitioned the chateau and moved us out.'

'I didn't know that,' said Jacquot.

Hélène de Vausigne nodded. 'They needed a good defensive position. And Rocsabin was certainly that. The Germans held the Allies there for ten days. Until the big guns were brought up. And that was that.' She looked around the room. 'We stayed here, my mother, my father and I. With Béatrice and Edouard. Close enough to hear it all. I remember going back with my parents, after the fighting was over. And the chateau was gone. Just rubble. And that was how it stayed for years . . . until we cleared the land and built the furniture warehouse. Exactly there.'

'So your family, the Rocsabins, and the de Vausignes were friends, as well as neighbours?'

'That is correct. It was always hoped that I would marry Gilles de Vausigne. The two families, you know . . .'

'Gilles? Not Albert?'

Hélène de Vausigne started. 'Certainly not Albert. At first, of course. When we were growing up, we saw a lot of each other. But later it became clear that we had little in common. And then, after Albert's father remarried, Gilles arrived on the scene . . .' For a moment it looked as though the memory might bring on tears, but she steeled herself. 'I really can't see what this is about, Chief Inspector,' she said, managing a helpful smile.

Brunet shifted in his seat, also uncertain where all this was going.

'Just trying to clear a few things up,' replied Jacquot. 'Did you know that Albert de Vausigne fought with the Resistance?'

Hélène de Vausigne sighed patiently. 'In those days, in this part of the world, almost every young man fought in the Resistance. Or, at least, that was what they liked to tell you. Still do, some of them.'

'And women too.'

The Comtesse looked at her hands. 'I helped where I could,' she replied.

'Women like Sandrine Eddé?'

The Comtesse gave the name some thought, trying to place it, then shook her head.

'You might have known her as Rose Valence?' said Jacquot. 'Her *nom de guerre*, if you like.'

'No, no. I'm sorry. I do not recognise either name. But that means nothing. There were many groups then, many outfits.'

'Sandrine Eddé worked with Albert de Vausigne. In the same group.'

Hélène de Vausigne considered this. 'Maybe,' she replied. 'It's possible.'

Jacquot nodded. If what old man Gaillard and the Bonaires had told him was true, then the Comtesse had to be lying. She must have known, or known of, Sandrine Eddé. Or Rose Valence.

'You say you worked for the Resistance?' he continued.

'Now and then. Running messages. That sort of thing. I was young. A girl. Sixteen, seventeen. The Germans didn't pay me much attention.'

'In June 1944 there was an incident near here, on the Brieuc road. By the St Bédard bridge. Maybe you recall?'

'Of course I recall,' she replied sharply.

'Did you play any part in this action?'

'I did not.'

'But you knew about it.'

The Comtesse nodded. 'Albert told me about it. I knew it was coming. I was not happy. I had a feeling about it. I tried to dissuade him.'

'Why was that? What feeling?'

'A couple of months earlier, Albert's team had carried out a similar operation between Brieuc and Barjas on the same transport route. It had been very successful. They had liberated a substantial cache of arms and ammunition. As a result, the Germans were on the lookout. It was too soon to repeat the operation. That's what I told Albert. But he wouldn't listen. He said the Germans would never expect a second strike in the same place. And anyway, they'd made up their minds.'

' "They"?'

Hélène de Vausigne raised a hand to her mouth, cleared her throat. 'The planners. Albert and the planners. He told me they wouldn't change it.'

'Does the name Rascousse mean anything to you?'

Hélène de Vausigne shook her head. 'Rascousse? No.'

'Colonel Hugo Rascousse was in charge of Resistance fighters here in the south. He was known by the code name Renard. He told me that the operation at the St Bédard bridge failed because someone betrayed them.'

'I've heard that said. But I do not believe it,' said the Comtesse firmly. 'They were pushing their luck, that's all. I really don't see where this is leading, Chief Inspector. I mean, this was fifty years ago. What possible—?'

Jacquot cut her off. 'At the end of 1943, a medical orderly called Josef Martner was posted to Cavaillon.'

Hélène de Vausigne stiffened.

Jacquot continued: 'Nearly forty years later Dr Martner returned, bought a house here, retired.'

'Many Germans do,' she replied, calmer now.

'Now, Dr Martner was not a rich man,' continued Jacquot, 'but he lived a life he really could not afford. What I want to know is . . . how did he manage that trick?'

'And how do you suppose I can help you with that?' replied the Comtesse crisply. 'I never knew the man.'

'And there, you see, is my problem, Madame,' said Jacquot. 'Because I believe you did know him. Maybe not that well during the war, but certainly in recent years. In fact, I'd say you got to know him very well indeed.'

'Preposterous!' Hélène de Vausigne got to her feet and started for the door. 'I think, perhaps, it's time you left, Chief Inspector.'

'Not quite,' replied Jacquot, keeping his seat, certain now that he was on the right track, the scent stronger than ever. 'Unless, of course, you'd like to continue this conversation at Headquarters.'

The Comtesse gave him a withering look. 'Please don't threaten me, Chief Inspector.'

Jacquot spread his hands but said nothing.

'What is it you want to know?' she said quietly, returning to the sofa.

'I want to know if Dr Martner was blackmailing you.'

The silence stretched away. Birds were trilling in the garden, the *cigales* hummed, somewhere a dog barked.

When the words came, they were soft, resigned. 'Yes, he was.'

'Because he knew what you did in the war? How you passed on certain information to the Germans? Collaboration?'

The word hit her like a slap. The word that made the blackmail possible.

'He knew, didn't he? Martner. He knew you were the one who told the Germans about the action at the bridge.'

Hélène de Vausigne looked at her hands, twisting them in her lap. She said nothing for a moment, then turned to the French windows as though the past was waiting for her on the terrace, waiting for her to acknowledge it.

'When I went to the Germans,' she began, 'I was shown into a colonel's office. I forget his name. He was having his teeth checked. At his desk, boots on the table, a white bib round his neck. He made no attempt to dismiss the orderly, just made me say everything in front of them both. The orderly was there the whole time. Forty years later he introduced himself.'

'And is that why you killed him?' asked Jacquot, knowing that she had not. She certainly wasn't strong enough to handle that shotgun—not for twenty-odd shots' worth. And he couldn't see her recovering too quickly from that fall in the kitchen, or chasing Kippi up the drive.

'No! I did not. That is not true.' The Comtesse looked outraged. But then, slowly, the anger passed and a smile played across her lips. 'Though I can't deny that it was welcome news.' She sighed. 'All that money.'

'How much did you pay him?'

'Over the years? A fortune. Twice, three times a year. A hundred thousand here, fifty thousand there. Whatever he needed. For his holidays or his blessed plants.' She cast around the room. 'Paintings, silver, family things. Even land. I had to sell so much. But now I don't have to pay another sou. Thanks to someone else, to whom I shall always remain immensely grateful.'

Hélène de Vausigne pinned Jacquot with a cool, implacable stare. 'And now, I think, you had better leave, Chief Inspector.'

The two men got to their feet, and Jacquot followed Brunet to the door. As Brunet opened it, Jacquot turned to the Comtesse. She was standing by the sofa, her back to them, staring out of the window.

'What I can't understand,' said Jacquot, 'is why you betrayed the man you loved. Because it was Albert you loved, wasn't it? Not Gilles.'

Hélène de Vausigne turned to him, lifted her chin. Her voice was calm, accepting. 'Yes. It was Albert I loved. I always had. But I never meant him to die. That was not the plan. It was the woman, the name you said. She was the one I wanted out of the way. Without her . . .' The Comtesse sighed.

Jacquot said nothing. He sensed there was more to come.

'The night of the raid, Albert came to dinner. At Rocsabin. Later, when it was time for him to leave, after my parents had gone to bed, I . . . I made myself . . . available. I was certain I could get him to stay. But I couldn't. He wouldn't be persuaded. He just laughed. Gave me a hug. Told me I was his little sister. Which . . .' Her face hardened. 'Which. Made. Me. Hate. Him. Suddenly, right then, right there, I just didn't care any more.'

She felt for the sofa, lowered herself into it. 'I never saw him again.'

'Thank you, Madame.'

Outside the chateau, Jacquot strode ahead. He was strapping on his seat belt by the time Brunet got into the car.

'Mind telling me, boss, what on earth all that was about?'

'An opening shot,' replied Jacquot, starting the engine, looking over his shoulder as he turned the car. 'Just an opening shot.'

FRANKIE ALZON lived in a small *atelier* overlooking a corner of the market square in Cavaillon. Even at four in the afternoon, long after the stalls that lined the square had been taken down, the sweet scent of melons still hung in the air, the gutters littered with their discarded crescents.

'Maybe I should stay out of this,' suggested Brunet, as the two men climbed the stairs to the top floor of Alzon's building.

'Oh, I don't think so,' said Jacquot, savouring the prospect of seeing his assistant come face to face with an old acquaintance. Which was how Brunet had described Mademoiselle Alzon on their drive back to town.

When they reached her door, Jacquot held back so that Brunet had to knock. As they waited, Brunet straightened his tie, brushed back his hair. He looked distinctly unhappy, like a cat caught in a shower of rain.

When she opened the door, Frankie Alzon was tugging on a silk dressing gown. Her cheeks were flushed and a sheen of sweat covered her brow.

Over her shoulder, the doors to a tiny roof terrace were open. On the terrace were a towel and cassette player. A narrow square of sun slanted across the towel. Frankie Alzon had been sunbathing.

'Yes?' she said, pushing a wedge of blonde hair from her eyes.

Jacquot knew at once that Antoine hadn't phoned to warn her that the police might come calling. He was too sure of himself—and the facts—to bother. He knew that Frankie Alzon would back up his story.

'Inspector Jean Brunet,' said Brunet, showing his badge, 'and Chief Inspector Jacquot. Cavaillon police.'

'I know you, don't I?' she asked, then grinned. 'Jean Brunet, that's right. But I don't recall you being a policeman. Lawyer, wasn't it?'

Already Brunet was squirming. Jacquot stepped forward, taking gleeful pity on his assistant. 'Mademoiselle Alzon? I wonder if we might come in.'

She gave Jacquot a look, clearly liking what she saw. 'Sure,' she said, and stepped aside, closing the door behind them, squeezing past to show them through into a cramped little living room.

The apartment had a certain charm, Jacquot decided, as he and Brunet settled themselves on a sofa. The cast-iron fireplace was painted a deep crimson and filled with sunflowers, and the walls were hung with movie posters. He liked the smell of the place too: a warm pulse of garlic, perfume and cigarettes suspended in the kind of languid, ticking heat you get when you live in an attic and the sun's been hammering down all day.

Curling up in the room's single armchair, Frankie Alzon reached for a packet of cigarettes, lit up and gave them a mischievous 'Well?' look, her brown eyes switching between them, leaving them to make the play.

'We're investigating a traffic accident, Mam'selle, on the road to—' Jacquot got no further.

'A traffic accident? A chief inspector investigating a traffic accident?' She laughed. 'Hey, I mean, I know Cavaillon's quiet, but—'

'A traffic accident involving a car that might have been used in the commission of a crime,' explained Jacquot.

'You mean, like a getaway car? That sort of thing?'

'That sort of thing, yes.'

'So? What's it got to do with me? I haven't been in any accidents.'

'We believe the car in question may belong to a friend of yours.'

'Oh, yeah? Who?'

'Perhaps I could start by asking, Mam'selle Alzon, what you were doing on the evening of July the 21st? A Tuesday. Around, say, ten o'clock?'

She gave it no thought. 'Working. At the hospital. Twelve till ten. Never finish before ten thirty, though. Not in Casualty, you don't.'

'And afterwards?'

'Tuesday, let me see . . .' She smiled. 'I met up with a friend. Old friend. Bit of business. Bit of fun. You know?'

'And the friend's name, Mademoiselle?'

'Antoine de Vausigne. He lives the other side of St . . . Whatsit? Bédard,' she continued. 'Big old place. Beautiful.'

'And you arrived there at what time?'

'Say, a little after eleven? Around there. The time it takes from the hospital. I still had my uniform on . . .' She gave Jacquot a look.

He nodded. 'And you stayed how long?'

'Let's say the birds were singing when I left, Chief Inspector. Why? What's all this got to do with Antoine?'

'We believe the car involved in this incident may have belonged to him.'

'Oh, yeah? Well, I can tell you he wasn't doing any driving that night.'

'And did you see the Mercedes when you arrived at the house?'

Frankie tried to remember. 'Not that I recall.'

'You used the front or back drive to the chateau?'

'The back drive. Didn't want to disturb the old lady, Antoine's mum.'

And then, suddenly, Frankie Alzon pursed her lips, glanced at her watch, and Jacquot knew what she was thinking. Why was she bothering with all these questions when the sun was shining outside?

'Look,' she said, sharp and flinty now, 'I don't really see what all this has got to do with a car crash. I mean—'

'You're quite right, Mademoiselle.' Jacquot pushed himself to his feet. 'All just routine stuff, really. But thank you for your time.'

'Mmmmhh,' was all she said, a little disapprovingly, then she pulled herself out of the chair and showed them to the front door. 'Tell me,' she asked, opening the door for them, 'does Antoine know you're here?'

Jacquot turned in the doorway, holding up Brunet, who was forced to stand only inches away from her: 'Of course, Mademoiselle. It was Monsieur de Vausigne who gave us your name and address. How else . . . ?'

'OK, OK. It's just . . .'

'The sun is shining and time is short, n'est-ce pas?' said Jacquot.

'In one,' she replied, and smiled. Then, turning to Brunet, she let the smile fade as she looked him over. 'Always preferred doctors myself.' And with that she stepped back and closed the door.

IT WAS A LITTLE after ten, and thanks to Picard—Picard and the police—Antoine was late.

Someone from Cavaillon Police Headquarters had phoned that afternoon asking if they could collect his car and bring it in for a paint match.

Without the Mercedes, and having drunk a little too much wine by the pool, Antoine had had Picard drive him. Which was why he was running late. Despite a clear road, the old man had kept under eighty kilometres per hour the whole way.

Now, strolling into Place Véran, Antoine checked the name and address that Duc, his supplier, had given him. Panisse. A private club in this small square. He soon spotted the sign, a blue neon 'P' set above double doors, and was just a few steps away when one of the doors opened and a large man in an evening suit stepped out.

'M'sieur?' he asked, blocking Antoine's path.

'I'm not a member,' said Antoine. 'I've come to see Christophe. Duc sent me.'

'Please go on down, M'sieur,' said the heavy. 'Your friend is at the bar.'

Antoine's 'friend' was no such thing. They'd never even met. Duc had given him Christophe's number in case supplies ran low, and Antoine had called to set up the meet. When Antoine mentioned Duc, Christophe had had no trouble in accommodating him. Just as Antoine had no problem identifying his man as he trotted into Panisse's downstairs bar. Sitting on the furthest stool with his back against the wall, looking as if he owned the place, Christophe wore a sharp black suit and braided hair. Antoine walked over.

'It's in the car,' said Christophe, finishing his drink and sliding off the stool. 'We'll take a drive.'

A few minutes later, in a throaty BMW Z3, Christophe pointed to the glove compartment as they pulled out of the square and headed out of town.

'Half an ounce. As requested.'

Antoine pulled an envelope from his pocket. 'Nine thousand francs. As requested.'

Which was the moment the two men became aware of a flashing blue light appearing from nowhere and the rising, heart-stopping wail of a siren.

IF SHE HAD DRIVEN without headlights, Marie-Ange would still have found her way to Rocsabin. There was a full moon in a cloudless sky, so bright that the road she followed was as clear as a twisting white ribbon.

It was a little after ten when she parked the Chaberts' van in a side street beside Rocsabin's church. As she climbed out, she was suddenly glad of her wrap, tugging it round her shoulders.

Marie-Ange had no idea what she was looking for. But she knew she was there for a reason. Forty minutes earlier, she'd been crossing the square from Mazzelli's, thinking about her bed, when without warning she heard a voice whispering, over and over so it sounded like a single word: Rocsabinrocsabinrocsabin. She'd spun round, but there'd been no one there. Just the whispering. The old lady's voice again. Soft but urgent.

It wasn't the first time Marie-Ange had been to Rocsabin. She drove through the village every Wednesday afternoon on her way to the stables, and called there twice a week to deliver her table sets to the Restaurant Ravigote. But tonight was the only time she'd been there after dark.

Rocsabin was larger than St Bédard but not as pretty. The only thing the village had was its position, its elevation, which meant that one side of the main square, bordered by a low wall, was set above the Brieuc valley. Which was where Marie-Ange headed, to sit and gaze across at the twinkling lights of St Bédard and Chant-le-Neuf.

It was there, sitting on the wall, that she became aware of a cindery smell that reminded her of the scent in the Château de Vausigne the afternoon Antoine had caught her snooping. Without knowing why, she returned to her car and headed out of Rocsabin.

Five minutes later, she pulled into the car park of the HacheGee furniture warehouse and switched off the engine. For a minute or two she sat where she was. Through the windscreen, the blackened hulk of the warehouse rose ghostly grey in the moonlight. Around its perimeter a line of wire mesh fence panels had been put to keep out the curious.

Marie-Ange got out of the car and walked towards the fence, gravel crunching underfoot, a dog barking somewhere beyond the line of trees that edged the far side of the car park. The scent of burning was stronger here, which struck her as strange. With the mistral storming its way through the previous week, there should have been no smell at all.

It was at that moment that she felt an icy puckering across her skin and sensed a growing silence, a turning down of the ambient volume around her. She could still feel the gravel underfoot but she couldn't hear it so clearly now. Nor was the dog barking so loudly.

She waited. And then, out of the silence, came a distant *boom-boom-boom-boom-boom*, like a line of big guns firing, one after another, somewhere far away in the valley, followed, seconds later, by a whistling shriek of shells and a series of thunderous explosions, making her duck and crouch. It was as though a war had broken out. Yet everything she could see was still. Nothing moved. Nothing to explain the mayhem raging around her, the sound of falling stone, the splintering of wood, the shattering of glass, the acrid scent of cordite and the bitter, dusty taste in her mouth.

Marie-Ange walked to the fence and looped her fingers through the mesh, staring into the warehouse's charred interior. As she did so, the sounds diminished and the silence came again, deep and muffling. And then, behind her, she heard a vehicle pull into the car park.

She turned, expecting to see a sweep of headlights. The security people come to check the property, she thought. But there was nothing to see. Only the sound of a car door slamming, and footsteps on gravel, coming towards her, brushing past, only inches away.

It was then that the voices came—not words, just sounds—ringing out at her from the warehouse. A woman first—indignant, challenging, then pleading, low and desperate—cut short by a single gunshot. And then a man's voice—shocked, horrified—followed by a second shot.

In the silence that followed, Marie-Ange eased her fingers off the mesh and stepped away from the fence. From somewhere close at hand came the rising bark of the dog again, the whistling call of a nightjar and the rich, honeyed scent of night-flowering jasmine.

Whatever it was, she knew it was over.

JACQUOT FELT a great contentment settle round him. Feet up on the sofa, a glass of Armagnac at his side and a lulling tenor sax from João Gilberto in the shadows. It couldn't get much better than this, he thought, letting his mind stray to Claudine's warm body one floor above.

Which was when the phone rang. He peered at his watch in the light from a candle. A little after midnight. He reached out and picked it up.

It was Marie-Ange. 'I'm sorry to call you at home, Chief Inspector, but you said I could if it was important.' Her voice was low, troubled.

'Well, it is quite late, Marie-Ange.'

'Don't be cross, please. I did think about calling tomorrow but I just had to speak to you.'

Jacquot decided he didn't mind her calling at all. Even this late. Even at home. Even if it was work. 'So, what can I do for you?' he asked.

'I believe the Martner murders and the Rocsabin fire are related.'

Which gave Jacquot pause. It was one of the reasons he'd stayed up after

Claudine went to bed, thinking it through. Six murders in a ten-kilometre radius in only five months? If Chabert hadn't been in the dock, they'd have started comparing the two crimes, searching for similarities, parallels, patterns. Coincidences. There were certainly enough of those.

'How are they "related"? I see no similarity,' said Jacquot.

'It's difficult,' she said. 'Still not clear. But it's something to do with the de Vausignes.'

Jacquot shivered. Marie-Ange's timing was uncanny; the way she matched her thoughts so closely to his findings. 'I told you, Marie-Ange. It's not enough to believe something. In my line of work I have to have proof.'

It didn't stop her: 'Did you know that the Comtesse was in love with Albert de Vausigne?'

'Is that what Bonaire told you?' he asked, letting her know that he knew of her visit.

'Bonaire's wife. And the Comtesse was the one being blackmailed, wasn't she? Because she betrayed Albert. But she didn't kill the Martners.'

'Correct. The killer was a man, remember?'

'Did the Comte know what was going on? About the blackmail?'

'If he did, it didn't appear to worry him, or stop him dipping into the family pot whenever he got the chance.'

'And what about the son? Antoine? Did he know about the blackmail?'

'Not so far as we know,' replied Jacquot.

'Did he know the Martners?'

'I don't have that information in front of me. It would be on file.'

But he knew it wasn't. Antoine de Vausigne wouldn't have been interviewed after the Martner killings because he hadn't even been in St Bédard.

And then Jacquot heard a burst of breath down the line. 'Of course . . .' he heard her cry. 'Oh, God, of course, of course.'

'I'm still listening.'

'It's something I saw,' she said in a rush. 'Proof. What you want. To do with the Martners,' she continued. 'I've been trying to work it out. And right now, just this minute . . .'

'And that is?'

'The wristwatch. The green stain on the strap. It's a pollen stain. Very distinctive and very hard to get rid of. The more you try to remove it, the greater the damage. It spreads, settles, works its way in. It starts out yellow, but when it comes into contact with salt—the salt in—it turns green.'

'Salt?'

'Sweat, for instance.'

'And?'

'The point is this particular pollen comes from only one flower. An orchid. *Epidendrum longifolium radicans*. And the only place I know where you'll find it outside Honduras, Guatemala and the Jardins des Plantes in Paris is Dr Martner's hothouse. Now, in the right conditions, the *longifolium* flowers spectacularly. But only for a few weeks each year. In this part of the world, that would be around February. And the pollen is only secreted a matter of days before the flowers die. So if you have that pollen on your clothes, or on your watch strap, you must have been in Martner's hothouse right at the time when that particular flower secretes its pollen—the last few days of February. And if you say you weren't there, then you're lying.'

'So who does this watch belong to, Marie-Ange?'

'YOU HAVE A VISITOR,' said Brunet, when Jacquot arrived at the office the following morning, head still spinning from his conversation with Marie-Ange. 'An overnight guest, you might say. Brought in around midnight. Not a happy bunny.'

Jacquot took the charge sheet from Brunet and rocked back on his heels.

'Small world, or what?' said Brunet.

'Antoine de Vausigne?'

Jacquot skimmed through the charges—running a red light, resisting arrest, in possession of a so-far unidentified substance thought to be cocaine.

'There's more.' Brunet continued. 'They've finished with the Mercedes. The paint matches. And there's gravel in the tyre treads.'

'From the warehouse car park?'

'Looks like it. And traces of petrol in the boot. The fire was started with petrol, so the fire investigators say. And the Merc's a diesel.'

'Could be fuel for a lawn mower, chain saw?' Jacquot knew that any defence counsel worth his gown would argue the point in court and sow the necessary seed of doubt. But after last night's call from Marie-Ange, he knew they were getting close.

'Could be,' said Brunet.

Jacquot knew his assistant wasn't finished. 'And?'

'One of Fournier's boys found what he thinks might be a spot of blood. On the door sill. Driver's side. They're doing tests right now. If it *is* blood, I told them to run a match on Bartolomé and the Comte.'

Jacquot's stomach was turning cartwheels. 'Let's pay a call.'

THERE WERE TWO of them in the interview room. Antoine de Vausigne and his lawyer, Bernard Charron. The Comte, arms sprawled across the Formica table, was not at his best. He looked creased and needed a shave. In contrast, Charron was snappily dressed in a double-breasted suit, with a crisply ironed white shirt and shiny red tie.

'My client has nothing to say, Chief Inspector,' began Charron, when Jacquot and Brunet came into the room, getting to his feet as if the meeting was over before it had begun, buttoning his jacket.

'And *bonjour* to you, too, Maître Charron,' said Jacquot, pulling out a chair and settling himself. 'Please, there's no formality here.'

He pointed to a chair, and Charron had no option but to unbutton his jacket and sit down again. Jacquot glanced at de Vausigne then opened the file and pored over the charge sheet. Brunet stayed by the door, arms crossed.

'My client categorically denies these ludicrous charges,' said Charron.

'Of course he does,' replied Jacquot, looking up from the file and smiling. 'But, as I'm sure you'll appreciate, it is all rather out of our hands, I'm afraid. Wheels will turn. The usual thing. Although regarding last night's events your client is, of course, free to leave. Under your recognisance.'

Charron was taken aback. These kinds of negotiation were usually more strenuous.

But Jacquot continued: 'No, no. What I'd like to talk about this morning has nothing whatever to do with the possession of a class A substance.' Jacquot glanced at the test results, handed to him by Mougeon on their way down to the interview room, and now attached to the charge sheet. 'We've confirmed that by the way. Five fifteen-gram bags in all. Two in the glove compartment, the rest concealed in a door seal. Forty-eight per cent cocaine.' He smiled across the table at de Vausigne.

Who scowled back.

'And neither,' continued Jacquot, 'does it have anything to do with resisting arrest or—'

'I did not resist arrest,' snapped de Vausigne, making to rise, his bottom lip trembling with indignation. Charron put a hand on his arm. De Vausigne shook it off and cleared his throat. 'I was having a drink. The man offered me a lift home. Because you had my car. It's not my fault he ran a light or had drugs on him. How was I to know?'

'Please, Monsieur Le Comte,' his lawyer interrupted.

'Ah, yes, your car. Which is precisely what I would like to talk about.'

Charron turned to de Vausigne. 'Your car?'

'For your information, Maître Charron, our investigations have established that your client's car, a blue Mercedes, was involved in a motor incident, two weeks ago now—the paint match confirms it, by the way—on the road between Lucat and Rocsabin. Less than twenty minutes before a fire was reported at the HacheGee furniture warehouse. A warehouse in which your client's father was murdered. Of course, Monsieur de Vausigne has denied driving his car at that time and has kindly provided us with the name of a witness to confirm it.'

De Vausigne nodded, stretched back in his seat, hands behind his head.

'But we are still left with a car that is "taken" without your client's permission and involved in an accident, a car that may also have been involved in the commission of arson and murder. And a stolen car that is returned to the place from where it was taken. Extraordinary, don't you think? The car thief who returns the car.'

'Quite so,' said Charron, reaching for his briefcase, sliding away his notepad and pocketing his pen with a flourish. 'But if you have established that my client was otherwise engaged, then it would seem to me that . . .'

But Jacquot wasn't listening. 'Tell me, Monsieur,' he said, looking directly at de Vausigne, 'do you ever carry petrol in the boot of your car?'

'You are under no obligation to reply,' Charron interrupted, 'whatever all this is about. And I advise you most strongly—'

'Of course I don't carry petrol in the car,' said de Vausigne, paying his lawyer no heed. 'Why should I? It's a diesel engine.'

'No lawn mower? No chain saw?'

'Hardly, Chief Inspector. In Paris I live in a flat. And down here Picard handles all that.'

'Which means,' said Jacquot, 'that I regret to say we must keep your car a little longer than we expected, Monsieur. For further tests.'

'This is simply—' began de Vausigne.

'I am sure my client is only too happy to help the police in whatever way he can,' volunteered Charron, trying to smooth the waters.

'For which we are most grateful,' said Jacquot, getting to his feet. He went to the door and opened it. 'And now, Messieurs, if you'll follow me, we can sign all the relevant release papers and'—he smiled at de Vausigne—'see about having your property returned to you.'

At the property room behind the front desk, Jacquot called up de Vausigne's belongings. They arrived in a large sealed manilla envelope, which Brunet tore open, tipping out the contents. Wallet, watch, small change, silver bracelet, lighter, cigarettes. A bundle of 500-franc notes.

'You'll confirm all these are yours?' asked Brunet.

De Vausigne shot him a look and took possession of his belongings, distributing the lighter, cigarettes and change to various pockets, sliding the bracelet over his wrist, pushing the wad of notes into an inside pocket and strapping on the watch.

'If you'd sign for them, Monsieur,' said Brunet, offering him a pen.

De Vausigne took the pen and scrawled his name on the sheet.

'If that is all, Chief Inspector?' asked Charron.

Jacquot nodded, and de Vausigne and his lawyer left the building.

THREE HOURS LATER, Brunet came into Jacquot's office. The chief inspector was on the phone, boots on the windowsill, watching a flight of pigeons as they circled the belfry of Église St-Jean. Whoever it was he'd been talking to, Jacquot said thanks, bade them *adieu* and spun round to replace the phone.

'Results are through, boss,' said Brunet. 'Fournier confirms it's blood on the Merc's door sill. But it's not Bartolomé's, or the Comte's. Nor does it match the sample our police doctor took from de Vausigne last night.'

Jacquot knew where this was headed now. The puzzle was finally falling into place.

'Just out of interest they did a search. And found a match.'

Jacquot smiled, said just one word: 'Martner.'

Brunet looked astonished. 'Actually, the daughter. Ilse.'

12

Jacquot stepped from the lift into the underground garage at Cavaillon Police Headquarters and stood, taking it all in. No shadows here any more, thanks to the strip lighting. No smell of sweat and fear, just petrol fumes and oil. For a moment he wondered what Marie-Ange would make of the place. He had a feeling she wouldn't much like it. There'd be echoes here, all right. Lots of them. And none very pleasant.

Fifty years earlier Gestapo cells had occupied this lower level of the Cavaillon gendarmerie. Jacquot had seen the pictures, called them up from the planning-department archive after Claudine told him about the building's past. Long stone corridors, a webbing of overhead pipes, a line of narrow cells with stout wooden doors, iron hinges and barred viewing slots.

But now the old cells had gone, the gendarmerie's current 'holding rooms' relocated to the ground floor following a programme of renovation. Sections of the original building had been torn down and rebuilt, the cobbled courtyard with the horseshoe-shaped doorway and caged bulb above it had been laid with Tarmac, while the high stone wall that separated the gendarmerie from the street had been replaced by iron railings and an electronically controlled sliding gate.

Below ground—where the old cells and interrogation room had once been—a far-sighted planner had opened up the space and installed a garage and service facility for police vehicles. There were inspection pits, a fully equipped workbench along one wall and a glass-walled office in one corner—with a ramp sloping up to the new courtyard car park above.

Jacquot looked around. To his left a team of mechanics was still at work. Beyond, in the small glass-walled office, the chief mechanic, Plessis, was finishing his paperwork. He saw Jacquot and waved. They'd spoken on the phone and Plessis knew what was coming.

This underground area was also where suspect vehicles were examined by Fournier and the forensic boys. Suspect vehicles like Antoine de Vausigne's blue Mercedes, standing on a thick white plastic sheet under an overhead light just a few steps away.

Jacquot walked over to the car, and stooped to peer through the driver's window. The interior was as clean as a whistle, everything they'd found inside—scraps of paper, receipts, gum wrappers, empty drinks cans, pens, pencils, cassette tapes, the contents of the ashtray, glove compartment, door side-pockets and boot—ranged along a trestle table set clear of the vehicle.

Jacquot was inspecting the trim above the Mercedes' rear passenger door when a squeal of tyres turning down the ramp signalled the first arrival.

Showtime, he thought, and glanced at his watch. A little after six.

An hour earlier he'd sent Brunet, Mougeon and two squad cars to the Château de Vausigne—one team along the back drive to the guest cottage, one team to the main house. A couple of gendarmes had accompanied them as back-up. He'd told Brunet to come straight down to the garage when they returned rather than park in the yard outside. And here he was, with Antoine de Vausigne in the caged back seat.

First out of the squad car was Brunet. He nodded to Jacquot and opened the back passenger door. Leaning in, he took hold of de Vausigne's arm and hauled him out. As Jacquot had requested, the Comte had been handcuffed.

When de Vausigne saw Jacquot by the Mercedes, he tried to pull free, but Brunet kept a firm grip on him. 'This is a disgrace, Chief Inspector. How dare you treat me like this? I demand to see my lawyer.'

'A disgrace indeed,' replied Jacquot. 'But please don't fret, Monsieur. Your lawyer is on his way. I took the liberty of calling him on your behalf. My guess is you'll be keeping him pretty busy.'

Jacquot had hardly finished speaking when another squeal of tyres announced the second squad car's arrival. It pulled up beside them and Mougeon got out of the front passenger seat, then came round to open the rear door. A black trouser leg appeared, followed by a tiny curled hand. Mougeon took it gallantly and helped Hélène de Vausigne out. With a courteous nod she thanked him, then started when she saw her son.

'Antoine?'

Antoine looked equally surprised. 'Maman?'

Her eyes settled on the handcuffs. 'What on earth is going on here?'

'Madame,' said Jacquot, with the kind of stiff bow that Dietering would have been proud of, 'so good of you to spare the time.'

The Comtesse turned towards him. Her eyes narrowed and her chin rose. 'Whatever all this is about,' she said, 'I'd appreciate an explanation, Chief Inspector. We have friends for dinner this evening and—'

Behind them the lift doors pinged and rolled open. Jacquot turned, smiled. 'Ah, Maître Charron. Perfect timing.'

'Monsieur Le Comte? Comtesse?' said Charron, setting down his briefcase. He, too, saw the handcuffs and turned to Jacquot. 'What exactly . . .?' And then, recognising the Mercedes: 'Isn't this your car, Monsieur Le Comte?'

'It certainly is,' said Jacquot. 'And a remarkable car, too,' he continued. 'A 200D, 1966.' He nodded towards the mechanics. 'According to the boys, they're called Fintails. Bit heavy on the corners, but a very comfortable ride.'

'I trust we're not here to discuss motor cars,' said the Comtesse, icily.

'Oh, but we are, Madame. Particularly this one. As I said, a remarkable car. With a remarkable past.'

'Chief Inspector—' began Charron.

'Yes, indeed,' continued Jacquot, ignoring the lawyer. 'Quite remarkable. Used by not one but two killers. In the commission of not one, not two, but three separate crimes. Seven murders in all. Not many cars with that kind of background, wouldn't you agree, Maître Charron?'

Without waiting for an answer, Jacquot walked over to de Vausigne.

'Monsieur de Vausigne, tell me, if you would, how many times a year do you visit your parents?'

De Vausigne shrugged. 'Every couple of months. Something like that?'

'In November last year?'

Antoine looked to his mother. 'November? I don't think so.'

His mother shook her head in agreement.

'And February?' asked Jacquot. 'How about February?'

De Vausigne shifted uncomfortably. 'February? I don't . . .'

He turned to his mother. Again she shook her head.

Jacquot turned to the Comtesse. 'Madame, I am sure you will be delighted to hear that not only did we retrieve your shotgun, we have now apprehended the man who broke into your home last November and stole it.' He indicated de Vausigne with a sweep of his hand. 'Your own son, Madame. Hence the handcuffs. Hence Maître Charron.'

'Antoine? Why, that's ridiculous.'

'But that, Madame, is not all. Far, far from it.' Jacquot walked over to the evidence table, selected a piece of paper, then turned back to the Comtesse. 'For several years your nearest neighbours were Dr and Madame Martner of Mas Taillard, is that not so, Madame?'

'That is correct, Chief Inspector. As well you know.'

Jacquot turned to Antoine. 'Did you ever meet the doctor, Monsieur, or any member of his family?'

'Martner, you say?' Antoine shook his head. 'No, not that I recall.'

'And you never visited their house?'

'If I didn't know them—'

'You'd have had no reason to visit them at home. Of course. But you did know them, Monsieur, didn't you? And you did know what the good doctor was up to. And you did kill him, didn't you?'

There was a gasp from the Comtesse. 'No, Antoine. It's not possible.'

'And the rest of his family. With the gun that you stole from your parents' house. Driving this rather fine piece of German engineering,' continued Jacquot, patting the car's roof, 'leaving it in a lay-by off the Brieuc road to make your way on foot up to the Martner house. Is that not so?'

Antoine raised his eyes to the strip lights above their heads in a distracted manner, as though what Jacquot was saying was of no interest whatsoever.

'Which means, Monsieur, that you are now under arrest for the murders in February this year of Dr Josef Martner, his wife, Jutta Martner, their daughter Ilse and granddaughter Kippi.'

Hélène de Vausigne reached for her son, gripped his arm. 'This cannot be. Say it's not true, my darling. Tell me it's not true.'

'Why this is simply preposterous, Chief Inspector,' Charron began.

Jacquot turned to the lawyer and waved the piece of paper he'd taken from the evidence table. 'In which case, Monsieur Charron, your client will be able to explain this: a record from the traffic authority here in Cavaillon that a charge was levied on a car bearing this registration for failure to display a valid parking permit for Parc Boulevard Crillon. Dated last November, the day before the chateau break-in—a date that Monsieur de Vausigne can't seem to recall. Of course, there's also the small matter of blood on the door sill of Monsieur de Vausigne's car. Madame Brauer's blood, by the way. Oh, and animal blood too, on the accelerator pedal. Presumably the Martners' dachshunds.

'And then there's the pollen stain on Monsieur de Vausigne's watch strap.' Jacquot pointed at his handcuffed wrists, the green stain on the watch strap clearly visible. 'A stain from an orchid in Dr Martner's hot-house, an orchid that only blooms in February. Nor should we forget the matching fibres from his car rug on the murder weapon, and a matching twenty-bore shell found beneath the spare tyre.'

These last two 'facts' were untrue. Jacquot used them simply to load his case, to stretch and unsettle his suspect.

'On November the 26th last year, Monsieur de Vausigne, you stayed in Cavaillon with Mademoiselle Francine Alzon. She was working the late shift back then, at the hospital—midnight to ten. After she went to work and left you alone in her apartment, you drove out to the chateau and broke in, removing a Beretta twenty-bore from your father's gun cabinet.

'Three months later you returned to Cavaillon, the last week in February, and this time you used the gun you'd stolen from the chateau to kill Dr Martner and his wife. Regrettably their daughter and granddaughter had arrived a few days earlier for Madame Martner's birthday. You might not have intended to kill them, but they saw you. You had to shoot them too.'

'And what possible motive—?' began Charron.

'Motive?' repeated Jacquot, glancing across at Hélène de Vausigne, whose features were pinched with shock. 'Money, Maître Charron. Watching his inheritance bleed away. Putting an end to a costly blackmail.'

Jacquot walked back to the Mercedes and perched himself on the bonnet, stretching out his legs and crossing his ankles. 'What do you say, Madame? When did your son find out about Dr Martner?'

'I didn't know that he had,' replied the Comtesse.

'I suppose it must have been obvious,' Jacquot continued. 'Paintings, family silver, things going missing. Maybe even pressure to sell the chateau. A title without a chateau, Madame. Like land without a title, no? But it wasn't just the good doctor dipping his fingers into the family pot, was it, Madame?' continued Jacquot, walking over to her.

Hélène de Vausigne lifted her chin, half turned her head from Jacquot.

'Plessis,' called Jacquot over his shoulder. 'A chair, please.'

A moment later, Plessis appeared with a chair, placed it beside the Comtesse and wiped the seat with a cloth. Without a word, she sat down.

'Those trips your husband made to Aix,' Jacquot began again. 'Business? Property matters in Brittany? I don't think so, Madame. How long had the affair been going on? The latest one, that is, with Madame Bartolomé.'

'I don't know what you think you're suggesting, Chief Inspector—'

'I'm suggesting, Madame, that your husband was not in the habit of visiting Aix alone. He was usually accompanied on his "business" trips. According to the reservations manager at the Hôtel Pigonnet, room seventeen was reserved on a regular basis for the Comte and Comtesse de Vausigne.'

Hélène de Vausigne straightened her shoulders.

'A fine hotel,' continued Jacquot, 'and not cheap. Take room seventeen. Even in low season it's only a few sous short of two thousand francs a night. And you know what?' Jacquot took two photographs from his jacket pocket. 'When I showed the reservations manager your photograph, he didn't recognise you. But when I showed him this one, of Madame Bartolomé, he identified her immediately as the Comtesse de Vausigne.'

'This is preposterous. Gilles was—'

'Gilles was spending your money, Madame. Money that was, thanks to Dr Martner, in short supply. A suite at the Hôtel Pigonnet every month or so, tables at Le Prieuré, at Hiely . . .' Jacquot walked back to the Mercedes and placed the two photos on the bonnet, felt around in an inside pocket, pulled out a notebook, flipped it open and found a page. 'Ah, yes. Here we are. The Auberge de Cassagne, the Ermitage Meissonnier, and Hostellerie Les Frênes. Some of the best tables in Provence. And always tables for two. Several thousand francs in a matter of months. Quite the epicure, your husband.'

Hélène de Vausigne raised her brows disdainfully, studied her fingertips.

'And so generous too. Not just the size of the tips that the *maître d'*s remember, but all those gifts for Madame Bartolomé as well.' Jacquot consulted his notebook once more. 'A Rolex from Temps Perdu, a bracelet from Joailliers des Paumes, clothes from Gago . . . There was hardly a shop in Aix that I visited where they didn't recognise your husband's photo. Or Madame Bartolomé's. And everything he bought? Paid for in cash.'

Maître Charron's eyes were wide. He coughed, tried to collect himself. 'I think, Chief Inspector . . .'

But Jacquot was getting into his stride. The ball was in his hands and he was running for the line. He could feel his heart beating. 'So where did he get all that cash? Not from you, Madame. No, no. He got it from Grace Bartolomé. From the tills at the HacheGee warehouse.'

Jacquot slid the notebook back into his pocket. 'But let's go back to the night of the Rocsabin fire. You were having dinner with your son, and after he had seen you back to the house, instead of going to bed you borrowed his car, this fine old car, and drove out to the furniture warehouse for a show-down, taking the lower drive so there was no need to start the engine and alert your son. And on your return, you used the front drive, coasting down into the chateau's forecourt. Never a sound.'

'You have proof, of course, to back up these ridiculous allegations?' asked Hélène de Vausigne, gathering herself.

'Yes, Madame, I do. Shortly before six o'clock, before joining your son for dinner at the summerhouse, you made a telephone call. To the Hôtel Pigonnet. You left a message. The concierge found it for me. I was lucky. They keep copies, you know, for a week, sometimes longer. I have it here.' Jacquot brought out his wallet and slipped a piece of paper from it. '"HacheGee Warehouse,"' he read out. '"Eleven. Be there."'

Jacquot took the message slip to the Comtesse, held it out for her to read. She didn't bother to look, simply turned away her head. Jacquot slipped it back into his wallet.

'Of course, there's no signature,' continued Jacquot, 'but phone companies also keep records, Madame. Which is what this is . . .' He walked over to the evidence table and picked up a sheet of paper, returned to the Mercedes and laid it on the bonnet beside the photos. A column of figures was visible, one of the entries highlighted in green. Jacquot pointed to it. 'July the 21st. Five thirty-seven p.m. 42 59 02 90. That's Le Pigonnet's number. The time on your phone records and the time the message was received and noted at Le Pigonnet are the same.'

Hélène de Vausigne smiled, seemed relieved. 'You're quite right, Chief Inspector. I'd forgotten. I did call my husband at the hotel. But we spoke. I did not leave any . . . any message.'

'But when Inspector Brunet and I came to see you about your husband's car, the day after the fire, you said you hadn't spoken to him.'

'I'm sure you must be mistaken, Chief Inspector.'

'You may be right, Madame. But this message was handed to your husband shortly after that phone call, when he and . . . the "Comtesse" were on their way out to dinner. According to the concierge, they asked him to cancel the reservation and checked out soon after. Driving back to Rocsabin, it would appear. To the HacheGee warehouse. Where you met them, Madame.'

'I did no such thing.'

'And where you killed them. Using Madame Bartolomé's own gun, the gun she kept in her bag.'

'This is ridiculous, Chief Inspector. Really. How could I have known that Madame Bartolomé carried a gun?'

'The same way Joel Filbert, the warehouse manager, knew. He told me Madame Bartolomé never went anywhere without it, said she showed it to him on more than one occasion. Just as she probably showed it to you.'

The Comtesse was shaking her head. 'You're dreaming, Chief Inspector.'

'Chief Inspector,' began Charron. 'I really must object—'

But Jacquot held up a hand. He wasn't finished yet. Not by a long way. 'Now normally, in a situation like this, the killer would leave the gun at the scene of crime, maybe in the hand of one of the victims, hoping to persuade the police that they were looking at a tragic lovers' quarrel—murder, then suicide. With no murder weapon found at the warehouse, it was clear that someone else had been involved. But you never intended leaving the gun, did you? Much more convincing to implicate someone else. And who better than Guy Bartolomé? The retired *lycée* teacher, a wreck of a man, according to the doctor who treated Bartolomé after his breakdown.

'So after you started the fire you called in on Guy. And what did you do when you got there, apart from planting the empty petrol can? Well, you sat Guy Bartolomé down at the kitchen table and shot him with his wife's gun. Ensuring that the murders would be blamed on him, the wronged husband, who'd come home and shot himself rather than face the music.'

Hélène de Vausigne sat there, unmoved by Jacquot's conjectures. She was more resilient than he had given her credit for.

Photographs, phone records, hotel messages, shop receipts . . . All of it, Jacquot knew, was circumstantial. It was nothing without a confession. Yet she refused to give way, and he wondered if he'd have to play his final card. Tell the Comtesse where she was. The underground car park. What it had once been. The place where she'd sent Albert all those years ago. Weaken her resolve. Break her down.

And then, quietly, she said: 'He was going to leave me.'

Hélène de Vausigne glanced up at them—Brunet, Jacquot, Charron, Mougeon and, finally, Antoine—as though seeking understanding that what she had done was the only thing she could have done. 'They'd been planning it for months,' she continued. 'Grace was going to leave her husband, and Gilles told me we'd have to sell the chateau. Said he hated the place. Always had. Told me he was going to live by the sea.' The Comtesse took a deep breath. 'I simply couldn't countenance it. It was not . . . permissible.'

She smiled sadly at her son, reached a hand towards him. 'My darling, you would have lost everything. Don't you see? I had no—'

But before she could say another word, Antoine had pushed her hand aside, lunged forward and snatched Mougeon's gun from its holster. Two shots rang out. The first had Mougeon crumpling to the ground, gripping his left leg, the second shattered the rear indicator light on the Mercedes. As the shots thundered round the underground car park, Antoine turned and sprinted up the ramp into the courtyard above.

CLAUDINE EDDÉ stepped out of the art supply shop and felt a thrill of guilt course through her. She had spent far more than she had intended. The success of her show in Aix had made her bold. The last painting sold. A sellout. So she'd gone quite mad.

The proprietor had called that morning to say that Madame's order for the Series 7 cadmium reds and yellows had finally arrived from Sennelier's in Paris. At 200 francs a tube would have been bad enough, but Claudine had spotted the alizarin crimson and the viridian marked down, and then, wandering down a dusty side aisle, she'd seen the brushes. The Rafael Mangouste 24s. Making sure she couldn't be seen, she'd removed the cover from one of them and run her thumb over the bristles, then smoothed them against her cheek. That was all it had taken. Now, 3,000 francs poorer, she felt both dizzy and delighted with her extravagance.

Back in her car, she placed her precious brushes and paints on the passenger seat and snapped on her seat belt. She glanced at her watch. Nearly seven o'clock. She still hadn't told Daniel the news about Aix. He'd be so pleased. Maybe even take her to a celebration dinner. And he was so close, only a couple of blocks away. And she was heading in that direction anyway. She'd call at his office and surprise him.

IT WASN'T EASY running with handcuffs round your wrists and a gun in your hand, but Antoine was twenty metres clear. Halfway up the ramp to the entrance gate. There was just one problem. How far was he going to get with the handcuffs and the gun—running through the streets of Cavaillon?

And then, turning in between the stone pillars of the entrance gate, bouncing over the ramp, came a blue Citroën estate, with a woman at the wheel.

Antoine headed for the Citroën. He saw the woman frown, not sure what was happening. And then she spotted the cuffs and the gun.

But it was too late for her to do anything. He was there, wrenching the door open and throwing himself into the front seat. He slammed the door shut, then swivelled round in the seat, feeling something snap beneath him, and raised the gun to her head, double-handed.

'Drive!' he screamed. 'Get going! Now! Now!'

STAYING CLOSE to the wall, Jacquot moved up the ramp, slowing as the courtyard came into view, keeping low in case de Vausigne was waiting for him. He could hear Brunet and the gendarmes running up the ramp behind him.

Ahead, he spotted de Vausigne racing for the entrance gates. In another few seconds he'd be out on the street.

And then Jacquot saw a car turn in through the gates. Oddly familiar. A blue Citroën estate. A woman driving.

Claudine.

Jacquot knew exactly what was going to happen next. Antoine headed for the car. Seconds later he was there, hauling open the door and jumping in, pointing his gun at Claudine's head, screaming at her to drive, then looking over his shoulder as Jacquot came to a halt a few metres short.

'Any closer and I'll shoot. I swear it.'

'You shoot her and you lose your ride,' said Jacquot.

'Then I'll shoot you,' Antoine replied, turning the gun in his direction.

'Stay away! I'm fine,' Claudine pleaded.

Off to his left, Jacquot caught a glimpse of Brunet, working the control box beside the gate. With a rattle the gate began to slide across the entrance.

Antoine saw it too. 'Keep it open. Or I swear . . .' He waved the gun.

Jacquot turned, waved Brunet away from the controls. The gate stopped.

Inside the car, Antoine dug Claudine in the leg with the gun. 'Drive! Just drive—now! Go forward and turn!'

As Claudine wrestled with the gear stick, Jacquot thought about rushing the car. But he knew he'd never make it.

And now the car was moving, swinging round in a tight circle, Antoine keeping the gun on Jacquot every inch of the way.

As they drew level, Claudine tried a smile for Jacquot, but it didn't work. She looked terrified. And then she saw him raise his right hand to his left shoulder and sweep it down across his chest. Claudine frowned. He did it again. And then she understood.

'Let's go! Let's go!' screamed Antoine.

Gripping the steering wheel, Claudine started forward, gradually increasing her speed, then pushed down hard on the accelerator. The car surged forward, heading for the open gates, but at the last moment she swung the wheel to the left and threw up her hands as the gatepost bore down on them.

It took only a second or two for Antoine to realise what was happening. Desperately he snatched at the wheel to correct their course. But it was too late. The Citroën hit the pillar a little off-centre, hard enough to have the back wheels lift off the ground, hard enough for de Vausigne to lift off too, his chest slamming onto the dashboard, doubling him over, his head and shoulders splintering through the windscreen.

As Jacquot ran to the car, he could see that Antoine was no longer a threat, and the gun lying out of reach on the Tarmac.

But Claudine . . .

Held back by her seat belt, her head drooped onto her chest, a fall of hair concealing her face. But she was alive. He could hear her moaning.

'Claudine!' Jacquot tried to pull open her door but it was stuck fast. He reached in, carefully lifted back her hair. Her eyes were clenched tight shut, her wrist lay at an odd angle in her lap, but she was saying something.

Jacquot leaned closer.

'My brushes,' she cried. 'He's broken my brushes.'

EPILOGUE

Jacquot took the road for St Bédard, changing down a few gears for the first of the hairpins out of Rocsabin. It was a week since the de Vausignes' arrest and he had been out to see Max Benedict, to thank him for his help in the Martner killings and the Rocsabin fire and to provide—off the record, of course—an account of the de Vausignes' involvement, in case he was planning any further features. It seemed the least Jacquot could do.

The two of them had had lunch together on Benedict's terrace, an omelette, some salad and goat's cheese, a bottle of Bandol.

'Will he live? De Vausigne?' Benedict had asked.

'He'll live, but he won't be making any films for a while.'

'And Claudine?'

'She broke her wrist, cracked her collarbone.'

'I shall send her flowers.'

'She'd like that.'

Normally Jacquot would have driven back to Cavaillon the way he had come, but after lunch he'd decided to return via St Bédard. There was someone else he wanted to see. It was the first chance he'd had since news of the de Vausignes' arrest had broken. Seven days of bedlam had followed after the Chabert trial in Lyon was halted and the jury dismissed. On TV Jacquot had watched with quiet satisfaction as his old colleague Gastal, red-faced with fury, was mobbed by journalists outside the Palais de Justice, refusing to answer any questions, fighting his way down the steps to a waiting car.

In St Bédard, having parked behind the *mairie*, Jacquot made his way across the square to the Fontaine des Fleurs. They'd spoken on the phone, of course, but he was looking forward to thanking her in person. But as he drew closer, Jacquot saw that the grille was down, the shop shut.

Wednesday. Half-day closing.

At the door he rang the bell, heard it sound somewhere inside. But there was no answer. He turned and looked around the square.

Which was when André Ribaud walked by. 'The Chaberts will be back later today, Monsieur. If you're looking for Mademoiselle Buhl, then I am sorry to say she has gone. Closed the shop at lunch. Told me she'd write.'

ONLY OLD DUMÉ saw her leave.

From the cool, rustling shadows of the olive trees he watched the silvery spokes flash between the vines as she spun downhill, hair flying, shoulders thrust forward, feet on the pedals as the bike picked up speed on the long descent, cycling out of their lives and the life of St Bédard for ever.

We'll miss her, he thought sadly, and that's the truth. And he felt in his pockets for his pipe and tobacco.

MARTIN O'BRIEN

RD: How did you get the inspiration for _Jacquot and the Angel_?

MO'B: It was the character of Marie-Ange that started the ball rolling. I was doing a job in the South of France for a magazine and I saw this girl who was very, very striking. I thought of writing a short story about her and then I saw that the story could be bigger . . .

RD: Jacquot is an interestingly renegade detective. Why the ponytail?

MO'B: It suggests he doesn't care too much for authority. It's his way of saying I am who I am. I may be a policeman, but I'm not going to cut my hair _en brosse_!

RD: Are you a big Francophile?

MO'B: I love the country and, as travel editor for British _Vogue_ in the seventies, I went there often. As a family, we go there a lot in the holidays.

RD: Would you ever think of settling in France?

MO'B: Yes, in fact I'm hoping we'll be moving there next year. We are thinking of Languedoc or the area near Biarritz and the Spanish border.

RD: What appeals to you about the country?

MO'B: I just think it's a really stylish place. And I'm very fond of the French. I find them intriguing and I love their enjoyment of good food, good wine, music . . . Their enthusiasm, I suppose. If you can break through that slight iciness that you some-times get to begin with, they're marvellous, big-hearted people.

RD: How did your career progress?

MO'B: I left Oxford in 1973, went into the city as a trainee foreign exchange broker, and hated it from day one. I'm not numerate at all, so it was absolutely the wrong career move. I resigned on the first Friday and left the following week. I had always wanted to write, so I decided to give it a go. Not a good time to try to be a freelance journalist, because it was the winter of discontent and the TV networks were closing early . . . I had to get a job in a hamburger bar initally, while I sent round samples of my work. I was offered a job in the copy department of _Vogue_ and stayed for seven years.

RD: Why did you become a novelist and how long did it take you?

MO'B: Basically, I married late and when we moved down here to the country with a two-month-old baby, I realised that if I was to continue writing travel pieces I'd be away twenty or thirty weeks of the year and I didn't want to do that any more. So I struck a deal with my wife: she would continue her successful career in advertising while I stayed at home to look after the kids and write books. It took me about five years. I'd written three other books before *Jacquot and the Waterman* was published in 2005.

RD: What made you think of introducing orchids into *Jacquot and the Angel*?

MO'B: The book really started with the pollen from a particular orchid, which is the crucial clue. Also, I had a friend who had a huge conservatory filled with exotic plants. It cost him a fortune in heating bills, but it was such a wonderful place and it stuck in my mind. There was just something about orchids, too: the sheer glory of them . . .

RD: Your travel writing is now available on the Travel Intelligence website. Having written about so many wonderful destinations, what is the one journey that you'd most like to make?

MO'B: To cross the Atlantic. I wouldn't want to be crew or work too hard, but I just love the idea of being out there at night, the stars above you, a long way from land. I like the idea of sailing in a very comfy boat—with music and good food on board. I have a more romantic view of it than a skipper might.

THE AMAZING ORCHID

It was the Victorians who started the fashion for collecting these exotic blooms, sending plant-hunters all over the world in search of new species. No other plant family has so many varieties: today, there are nearly 30,000 species and 100,000 hybrids, or cultivars, on record—there is even one that grows entirely underground. The hothouse beauties prized by collectors such as Dr Martner in Martin O'Brien's novel, usually originate from tropical or sub-tropical climates; however, there are over 40 species native to Britain and Ireland, some of which grow in the wild. Visit: www.rbgkew.uk.org for more information on these fascinating plants.

A loner by nature, used to travelling light,
Jack Reacher is always ready to lend a
hand—and some muscle—to make
sure justice is done.
When he's hired by the enigmatic
Mr Lane to trace the kidnapper
of Lane's wife and daughter, he's
soon aware that working the clues
in his usual style is getting
him nowhere.
This is one Reacher is going to have
to unravel the hard way . . .

Chapter One

Jack Reacher ordered espresso, double, foam cup, and before it arrived at his table he saw a man's life change for ever. Not that the waiter was slow. Just that the move was slick. So slick, Reacher had no idea what he was watching. It was just an urban scene, repeated a billion times a day: a guy unlocked a car and got in and drove away. That was all.

But that was enough.

THE ESPRESSO HAD BEEN close to perfect, so Reacher went back to the same café exactly twenty-four hours later. Two nights in the same place was unusual for Reacher, but he figured great coffee was worth a change in his routine. The café was on the west side of Sixth Avenue in New York City, in the middle of the block between Bleecker and Houston. It occupied the ground floor of an undistinguished four-storey building. The café itself had low light and a dented chrome machine as hot and long as a locomotive, and a counter. Outside there was a single line of metal tables on the sidewalk behind a low canvas screen. Reacher took the same end table he had used the night before and chose the same seat. He got comfortable. His back was against the café's outside wall and left him looking east, across the sidewalk and the width of the avenue. He liked to sit outside in the summer, in New York City. Especially at night. He liked the electric darkness and the hot, dirty air and the blasts of noise and traffic and the crush of people. It helped a lonely man feel connected and isolated both at the same time.

He was served by the same waiter as the night before and ordered the same drink, double espresso in a foam cup. He paid for it as soon as it arrived and left his change on the table. That way he could leave exactly when he wanted to, without insulting the waiter. Reacher always arranged the smallest details in his life so he could move on at a split second's notice. He owned nothing and carried nothing. Physically he was a big man, but he cast a small shadow and left very little in his wake.

He drank his coffee slowly. He watched taxis flow north. Saw knots of young people heading for clubs. Saw a blue German saloon park on the block. Watched a compact man in a grey suit get out. Watched him thread between two sidewalk tables and head inside to where the café staff were clustered in back. Watched him ask them questions.

The guy was medium height, too solid to be called wiry, too slight to be called heavy. His hair was grey at the temples and cut short and neat. He kept himself balanced on the balls of his feet. His mouth didn't move much as he talked. But his eyes flicked left and right tirelessly. The guy was about forty, Reacher guessed, and furthermore he guessed he had got to be about forty by staying relentlessly aware of everything that was happening around him. He had seen the same look in elite infantry veterans who had survived long jungle tours.

Then Reacher's waiter turned and pointed straight at him. The compact man in the grey suit stared over. Reacher stared back, over his shoulder, through the window. The man in the suit mouthed *thank you* to the waiter. He stepped back out through the door and threaded his way down to Reacher's table. Reacher let him stand there while he made up his mind. Then he said 'Yes' to him, like an answer, not a question.

'Yes what?' the guy said back.

'Yes whatever,' Reacher said. 'Yes I'm having a pleasant evening, yes you can join me, yes you can ask me whatever it is you want to ask me.'

The guy sat down. 'Actually, I do have a question,' he said.

'I know,' Reacher said. 'About last night.'

'How did you know that?' The guy's voice was low and his accent was flat and clipped and British.

'The waiter pointed me out,' Reacher said. 'And the only thing that distinguishes me from his other customers is that I was here last night and they weren't.'

'Did you see a car last night?' the guy asked.

'I saw plenty of cars last night,' Reacher said.

'A Mercedes-Benz. Parked over there.' The guy pointed at a length of empty kerb by a fire hydrant on the other side of the street.

Reacher said, 'Silver, four-door saloon, an S420, New York vanity plates starting "OSC". Dirty paint, scuffed tyres, scrapes on both bumpers.'

'Did you see it leave?'

Reacher nodded. 'Just before eleven forty-five a guy got in and drove off.'

'It must have been closer to midnight.'

'Maybe,' Reacher said. 'Whatever.'

'Did you get a look at the driver?'

'I told you, I saw him get in and drive away.'

The guy stood up. 'I need you to come with me.'

'Where?'

'To see my boss.'

'Who's your boss?'

'A man called Lane.'

'You're not a cop,' Reacher said. 'That's my guess. You're not American. You're British. The NYPD isn't that desperate.'

'Most of us are Americans,' the British guy said. 'But you're right, we're not cops. We're private citizens.'

'What kind?'

'The kind that will make it worth your while if you give them a description of the individual who drove that car away.'

'Worth my while how?'

'Financially,' the guy said. 'Is there any other way?'

'Lots of other ways,' Reacher said. 'I think I'll stay right here.'

'This is very serious.'

'How?'

The guy sat down again. 'I can't tell you that,' he said. 'Mr Lane made it mission-critical that nobody knows. For very good reasons.'

'You got a name?' Reacher asked.

The guy stuck a thumb into the breast pocket of his jacket and slid out a single card. He passed it across the table. At the top it said: *Operational Security Consultants*.

'OSC,' Reacher said. 'Like the licence plate.' He smiled. 'You're security consultants and you got your car stolen?'

The guy said, 'It's not the car we're worried about.'

Lower down on the business card was a name: *John Gregory*. Under the name was a subscript: *British Army, Retired*. Then a job title: *Executive Vice-President*.

'How long have you been out?' Reacher asked.

'Of the British Army?' Gregory said. 'Seven years.'

'Unit?'

'SAS.'

'You've still got the look.'

'You too,' Gregory said. 'How long have you been out?'

'Seven years,' Reacher said.

'Unit?'

'US Army CID, mostly.'

Gregory looked up. Interested. 'Investigator?'

'Mostly.'

'Rank?'

'Major,' Reacher said. 'That's as far as I got.'

'Career problems?'

'I had my share.'

'You got a name?'

'Reacher.'

'You need work?'

'No,' Reacher said. 'I don't.'

'I was a sergeant,' Gregory said.

Reacher nodded. 'I figured. SAS guys usually are.'

'So will you come with me and talk to Mr Lane?'

'Seems like a lot of fuss over a stolen car.'

'This is not about the car.'

'So what is it about?'

'Life and death,' Gregory said. 'Right now more likely death than life.'

Reacher checked his cup. There was less than an eighth of an inch left, thick and scummy with espresso mud. He put the cup down.

'OK,' he said. 'So let's go.'

THE BLUE GERMAN SALOON turned out to be a new BMW 7 Series with OSC vanity plates. Gregory unlocked it with a remote and Reacher got in the front passenger seat. Gregory pulled out a silver cellphone.

'Incoming with a witness,' he said, clipped and British.

Gregory drove north on Sixth Avenue through Midtown to 57th Street and then two blocks west. He turned north on Eighth, through Columbus Circle, onto Central Park West and into 72nd Street. He stopped outside the Dakota Building.

'Nice digs,' Reacher said.

They got out together and another compact man in a grey suit stepped out of the shadows and stepped into the car and drove it away. Gregory led Reacher into the building and up in the elevator. The lobbies and the hallways were as dark and baronial as the exterior.

'You ever see Yoko?' Reacher asked.

'No,' Gregory said.

They got out on five and an apartment door opened. The lobby staff must have called ahead. The door was heavy oak, the colour of honey, and the warm light that spilled out into the corridor was the colour of honey too. There was a small square foyer open to a big square living room. The living room had cool air, yellow walls, low table lights, comfortable chairs and sofas. In it were six men, none of them sitting down. They were all silent. Three wore grey suits similar to Gregory's and three were in black jeans and black jackets. Reacher knew immediately they were all ex-military. They all had the look. The apartment itself had the desperate, quiet feel of a command bunker far from some distant point where a battle was turning to shit.

All six men turned and glanced at Reacher. Then five men glanced at the sixth, which Reacher guessed identified him as Mr Lane. The boss. He was half a generation older than his men. He was in a grey suit. He had grey hair, buzzed close to his scalp. He was maybe an inch above average height, and slender. His face was pale and full of worry. He was standing absolutely straight, racked with tension, with his fingertips touching the top of a table that held a telephone and a framed photograph.

'This is the witness,' Gregory said. 'He saw the driver.'

The man at the table moved towards Reacher, assessing him. He stopped a yard away and offered his hand.

'Edward Lane,' he said. 'I'm very pleased to meet you, sir.' His accent was American. Reacher said his own name and shook Lane's hand.

'Tell me what you saw,' Lane said.

'I saw a guy get in a car,' Reacher said. 'He drove it away.'

'I need detail,' Lane said.

'Reacher is ex-US Army CID,' Gregory said. 'He described the Benz to perfection.'

'Where were you?' asked Lane.

'In a café. The car was a little north and east of me, across Sixth Avenue. Maybe a twenty-degree angle, maybe ninety feet away.'

'Why were you looking at it?'

'It was badly parked. I guessed it was on a fireplug.'

'It was,' Lane said. 'Then what?'

'Then a guy crossed the street towards it. Through gaps in the traffic, at an angle. So most of what I saw was his back.'

'Then what?'

'He stuck the key in the door and got inside. Took off.'

'Going north obviously, this being Sixth Avenue. Did he turn?'

'Not that I saw.'

'Can you describe him?'

'Blue jeans, blue shirt, blue baseball cap, white sneakers. The clothing was old and comfortable. The guy was average height, average weight.'

'Age?'

'I didn't see his face. But he didn't move like a kid. He was at least in his thirties. Maybe forty.'

'How exactly did he move?'

'He was focused. And the way he held his shoulder, I think he might have had the key out in front of him, horizontally. Focused, and urgent.'

'Where did he come from?'

'From behind my shoulder, more or less.'

'Would you recognise him again?'

'Only by his clothes and his walk and his posture.'

'If he crossed through the traffic he must have glanced south to see what was coming at him. So you should have seen the right side of his face. Then when he was behind the wheel, you should have seen the left side.'

'He was white,' Reacher said. 'No facial hair.'

'It's not good enough,' Lane said.

'Didn't you have insurance?' Reacher asked.

'This is not about the car,' Lane said.

'It was empty,' Reacher said.

'It wasn't empty,' Lane said.

'So what was in it?'

'Thank you, Mr Reacher,' Lane said. 'You've been helpful.'

He turned and walked back to the table with the phone and the photograph. He stood beside it and spread his fingers again and laid the tips lightly on the polished wood, next to the telephone, like his touch might detect an incoming call before the electronic pulse started the bell.

'You need help,' Reacher said. 'Don't you?'

'I've got help,' Lane said. He gestured around the room. 'Navy SEALs,

Delta Force, Recon Marines, Green Berets, SAS. The best in the world.'

'You need a different kind of help. The guy who took your car, these folks can start a war against him, for sure. But first you need to find him.'

No reply.

'What was in the car?' Reacher asked.

'Tell me about your career,' Lane said.

'It's been over a long time. That's its main feature.'

'Final rank?'

'Major. Army CID.'

'Investigator?'

'Basically.'

'A good one?'

'Good enough.'

'110th Special Unit?'

'Some of the time. You?'

'Rangers and Delta. Started in Vietnam, ended in the Gulf the first time around. Finished a full colonel.'

'What was in the car?'

Lane looked away. Then he looked back, like a decision had been made. 'You need to give me your word about something,' he said.

'Like what?'

'No cops.'

Reacher shrugged. 'OK,' he said.

'Say it.'

'No cops.'

'No FBI, no nobody,' Lane said. 'We handle this. Understand? You break your word, I'll have you blinded.'

'My word is good,' Reacher said.

'Say you understand what I'll do if you break it.'

Reacher looked around the room. Took it all in. A desperate atmosphere and six Special Forces veterans, all as hard as nails, all looking right back at him, all full of unit loyalty and hostile suspicion of the outsider.

'You'll have me blinded,' Reacher said.

Lane picked up the framed photograph. He held it flat against his chest, so that Reacher felt he had two people staring back at him. Above, Lane's worried features. Below, under glass, a woman of breathtaking classical beauty. Dark hair, green eyes, high cheekbones and a bud of a mouth, photographed with expertise and printed by a master.

'This is my wife,' Lane said.

Reacher nodded. Said nothing.

'Her name is Kate,' Lane said. 'Kate disappeared yesterday morning. I got a call in the afternoon. From her kidnappers. They wanted money. That's what was in the car. You watched one of the kidnappers collect the ransom.'

Silence.

'They promised to release her,' Lane said. 'And it's been twenty-four hours. And they haven't called back.'

EDWARD LANE held the framed photograph like an offering and Reacher stepped forward to take it. He tilted it to the light. Kate Lane was beautiful. She was hypnotic. She was younger than her husband by maybe twenty years, which put her in her early thirties. In the picture she was gazing at something just beyond the edge of the print. Her eyes blazed with love. Her mouth seemed ready to burst into a smile.

'My Mona Lisa,' Lane said. 'That's how I think of that picture.'

Reacher passed it back. 'Is it recent?'

Lane propped it upright again. 'Less than a year old.'

'Why no cops? They usually do a good job.'

'No cops,' Lane said. 'You can do what they do.'

'I can't,' Reacher said. 'I don't have their resources.'

'You can make a start.'

'How much money did they want?' Reacher asked.

'One million dollars in cash,' Lane answered.

'And that was in the car? A million bucks?'

'In the trunk. In a leather bag.'

'OK,' Reacher said. 'They're going to call back. Let's all sit down. Start at the beginning. Tell me about yesterday.'

So Lane sat down and started to talk about the previous day. Reacher sat at one end of a sofa. Gregory sat next to him. The other five guys distributed themselves around the room.

'Kate went out at ten o'clock in the morning,' Lane said. 'She was heading for Bloomingdale's, I think.'

'You think?'

'I allow her some freedom of action. She doesn't supply me with a detailed itinerary. Not every day.'

'Was she alone?'

'Her daughter was with her.'

'*Her* daughter?'

'She has an eight-year-old by her first marriage. Jade.'

'She lives with you here?'

Lane nodded.

'So where is Jade now?'

'Missing, obviously,' Lane said.

'So this is a *double* kidnapping?' Reacher said.

Lane nodded again. 'Triple. Their driver didn't come back either.'

'You didn't think to mention this before?'

'Does it make a difference? One person or three?'

'Who was the driver?'

'A guy called Taylor. British, ex-SAS. A good man.'

'What happened to the car?'

'It's missing.'

'Does Kate go to Bloomingdale's often?'

Lane shook his head. 'Never on a predictable pattern. We do nothing regular or predictable. I vary her drivers, vary her routes.'

'Because? You got a lot of enemies?'

'My fair share. My line of work attracts enemies.'

'You're going to have to explain your line of work to me. You're going to have to tell me who your enemies are.'

'Why are you sure they're going to call?'

'I'll get to that,' Reacher said. 'Tell me about the first conversation. Word for word.'

'They called at four o'clock in the afternoon. It went pretty much how you would expect. You know, we have your wife, we have your daughter.'

'Voice?'

'Altered. One of those electronic squawk boxes. Metallic, like a robot in a movie. I asked them what they wanted. They said a million bucks. I asked them to put Kate on the line. They did, after a short pause.' Lane closed his eyes. 'She said, you know, help me.' He opened his eyes. 'Then the guy with the squawk box came back on and I agreed to the money. No hesitation. The guy said he would call back in an hour with instructions.'

'And did he?'

Lane nodded. 'At five o'clock. I was told to wait six hours and put the money in the trunk of the Mercedes you saw and have it driven down to the Village and parked in that spot at eleven forty exactly. The driver was to lock it up and walk away and put the keys through a mail slot in the front door of a certain building on the southwest corner of Spring Street and West Broadway. Then he was to walk south on West Broadway. Someone would move in behind him and collect the keys. If my driver stopped or even looked back, Kate would die. Likewise if there was a tracking device on the car.'

'Who drove the car down?' Reacher asked.

'Gregory,' Lane said.

'I followed the instructions,' Gregory said. 'To the letter.'

'How far of a walk was it?' Reacher asked him.

'Six blocks.'

'What was the building with the mail slot?'

'Abandoned,' Gregory said. 'It was empty, anyway.'

'How good was Taylor? Did you know him in Britain?'

Gregory nodded. 'Taylor was very good indeed.'

'OK,' Reacher said. 'There are some obvious early conclusions. The first conclusion is that Taylor is already dead. These guys clearly know you to some extent, and therefore we should assume they knew who Taylor was. They wouldn't keep him alive. Too dangerous.'

Lane asked, 'Why do you think they know me?'

'They asked for a specific car,' Reacher said. 'And they suspected you might have a million dollars in cash lying around. They asked for it after the banks were closed and told you to deliver it before the banks reopened. Not many even very rich people could comply with those conditions.'

Nobody spoke.

'And there are three of them,' Reacher said. 'One to guard Kate and Jade. One to watch Gregory while he walked south on West Broadway, on a cell-phone to a third who was waiting to move in and pick up the keys.'

Nobody spoke.

'And they're based a minimum two hundred miles upstate,' Reacher said. 'Let's assume the initial action went down before about eleven o'clock yesterday morning. But they didn't call for more than five hours. Because they were driving. Then they issued instructions at five o'clock for a ransom drop more than six hours later. Because two of them had to drive all the way back. Five, six hours, that's two hundred miles.'

'Why upstate?' Lane said. 'They could be anywhere.'

'Not south or west,' Reacher said. 'Or they would have asked for the ransom car south of Canal, so they could head straight for the Holland Tunnel. Not east on Long Island, or they would have wanted to be near the Midtown Tunnel. No, north on Sixth was what they wanted. That implies the George Washington Bridge, or the Henry Hudson and the Saw Mill, or the Triborough and the Major Deegan. Eventually they hit the Thruway, probably. They could be in the Catskills. A farm, probably. Certainly somewhere with a big garage or a barn.'

'Why?'

'They just inherited your Mercedes-Benz. Right after hijacking whatever Taylor drove to Bloomingdale's yesterday. They need a place to hide them.'

'Taylor was driving a Jaguar.'

'There you go. Their place must look like a luxury car lot by now.'

'Why are you so sure they're going to call back?'

'Because of human nature. Right now they're kicking themselves. They asked for a million dollars in cash, and you bagged it up without a moment's hesitation. You should have gambled and stalled. Because now they're saying, damn it, we should have asked for more. So they're going to hit you up for another chunk.'

Nobody spoke.

'Five million,' Reacher said. 'That's what they'll ask for next.'

'Is Kate safe?' Lane asked.

'Right now, she's safe,' Reacher said. 'She's their meal ticket. And you did the right thing, asking to hear her voice the first time. That set up a good pattern. The problem will come after they've had the last payment.'

'Good conclusions,' Lane said, to nobody in particular. 'Three guys, far away. Upstate. On a farm.'

Chapter Two

The phone rang at exactly one o'clock in the morning. Lane snatched it out of the cradle and said, 'Yes?' Reacher heard a faint voice from the earpiece, distorted. Lane said, 'Put Kate on the phone.' Then there was a pause, and then there was a woman's voice, panicked, breathy. It said just one word, and then it exploded in a scream. The scream died into silence and Lane screwed his eyes shut and the electronic robot voice barked six short syllables. Lane said, 'OK, OK,' and Reacher heard the line go dead.

Lane sat in silence, his breathing ragged.

'Five million dollars,' he said. 'How did you know?'

'It was the obvious next step,' Reacher said. 'One, five, ten, twenty. That's how people think.'

'You've got a crystal ball. I'm putting you on the payroll. Twenty-five grand a month, like all these guys.'

'This isn't going to last a month,' Reacher said. 'It can't.'

'I agreed to the money,' Lane said. 'I couldn't stall. They were hurting her.'

Gregory asked, 'Instructions later?'

'In an hour,' Lane said.

All around the room men settled back imperceptibly. Lane stared off into space.

'We need to talk,' Reacher said quietly. 'We should try to figure out who these guys are.'

'OK,' Lane said vaguely. 'We'll go to the office.'

He led Reacher out of the living room and through a kitchen to a maid's room in back. It had been fixed up as an office. Desk, computer, fax machine, phones, file cabinets, shelves.

'Tell me about Operational Security Consultants,' Reacher said.

Lane sat down in the desk chair. 'Not much to tell,' he said. 'We're just a bunch of ex-military trying to keep busy. Bodyguarding, mostly. Corporate security. Like that.'

There were two framed photographs on the desk. One was a smaller print of Kate's stunning picture from the living room. The other was of another woman, about the same age, blonde where Kate was dark, blue eyes instead of green. But just as beautiful.

'You're not convincing me, Mr Lane. Bodyguards don't make twenty-five grand a month.'

'My business is confidential,' Lane said.

'Not if you want your wife and daughter back.'

No reply.

'A Jaguar, a Mercedes and a BMW,' Reacher said. 'Plus a co-op in the Dakota. Plus lots of cash lying around. Plus half a dozen guys on twenty-five grand a month. Altogether big bucks.'

'All legal.'

'Except you don't want the cops involved.'

Lane glanced at the photograph of the blonde woman. 'That's not the reason.'

Reacher followed Lane's gaze. 'Who is she?'

'Anne,' Lane said. 'She was my first wife.'

'And?'

'You see, I've been through this before,' Lane said. 'Five years ago. Anne was taken from me. In just the same way. But back then I followed procedure and called the cops. The cops called the FBI.'

'And what happened?'

'The FBI screwed up somehow,' Lane said. 'They found her body a month later in New Jersey.'

Reacher said nothing.

'That's why there's no cops this time,' Lane said.

Reacher and Lane sat in silence for a long time. Then Reacher said, 'Fifty-five minutes. You should be ready for the next call.'

'You're not wearing a watch,' Lane said.

'I always know what time it is.'

Reacher followed him back to the living room. He guessed Lane wanted to take the call with his men around him. Maybe he needed the comfort. Or the support.

The phone rang right on time, at two o'clock in the morning. Lane picked it up. Reacher heard faint robot squawks. Lane said, 'Put Kate on,' but his request must have been refused, because then he said, 'Please don't hurt her.' He listened for a minute and said, 'OK.' Then he hung up.

'Seven o'clock in the morning,' he said. 'Same place, same routine. The blue BMW. One person only.'

'I'll do it,' Gregory said.

'We should all be there,' one of the others said. He was a small, dark American, whose eyes were as flat and dead as a hammerhead shark's. 'Ten minutes later we would know where she is. I can promise you that.'

'Apparently they know us,' Lane said. 'They would recognise you.'

'I could go,' Reacher said. 'They wouldn't recognise me.'

'Decision in one hour,' Lane said. He headed towards the master bedroom. *Gone to count out the money*, Reacher thought. He wondered what five million dollars looked like.

'How much money has he got?' Reacher asked.

'A lot,' Gregory said.

'He's down six million in two days.'

The guy with the shark's eyes smiled. 'We'll get it back,' he said. 'You can count on that. They'll be sorry they were ever born.'

Reacher glanced into the guy's empty eyes and believed every word he said. Then the guy stuck out his hand, abruptly. 'I'm Carter Groom,' he said.

The four other men introduced themselves with a quiet cascade of names and handshakes. Reacher tried to tie the names to faces. Gregory he already knew. A guy with a big scar over his eye was called Addison. The shortest guy among them was a Latino called Perez. The tallest was called Kowalski. There was a black guy called Burke.

'Lane told me you do bodyguarding and corporate security,' Reacher said.

Sudden silence. No reply.

'My guess is you guys were all operational noncoms. Fighting men. So I think your Mr Lane is into something else entirely.'

'Like what?' Gregory asked.

'I think he's pimping mercenaries,' Reacher said.

Groom shook his head. 'Wrong choice of words, pal,' he said. 'We're a private military corporation and we're legal. We work for the Pentagon, just like we always did, and just like you did, back in the day.'

'How many guys have you got?' Reacher asked. 'Just what's here?'

Groom shook his head. 'We're the A-team. Then there's a Rolodex full of B-team squad members. We took a hundred guys to Iraq.'

'Is that where you've been? Iraq?'

'And Colombia and Panama and Afghanistan. We go anywhere Uncle Sam needs us.'

'My guess is the Pentagon pays by cheque,' Reacher said. 'But there seems to be an awful lot of cash around here. Africa?'

No response.

'Whatever,' Reacher said. 'Not my business. All I need to know is where Mrs Lane has been. For the last couple of weeks.'

'What difference does that make?' Kowalski asked.

'There was surveillance,' Reacher said. 'Don't you think? I don't suppose the bad guys were just hanging out at Bloomingdale's on the off chance.'

'Mrs Lane was in the Hamptons,' Gregory said. 'With Jade, most of the summer. They came back three days ago.'

'Anything happen out in the Hamptons? Anything unusual?'

'A woman showed up at the door one day,' Gregory said.

'What kind of a woman?'

'Just a woman. Fat. Kind of heavyset. About forty. Long hair, centre parting. Mrs Lane took her walking on the beach. Then the woman left. I figured it was a friend on a visit.'

'Ever saw her before?'

Gregory shook his head.

'What did Mrs Lane and Jade do after they got back here to the city?'

'I don't think they did anything yet.'

'No, she went out once,' Groom said. 'Mrs Lane, I mean. On her own. I drove her. Staples.'

'The office supply store? What did she buy?'

'Nothing,' Groom said. 'I waited twenty minutes on the kerb, and she didn't bring anything out.'

'Weird place to browse. Did she take something in?' Gregory asked. 'Maybe she was returning something.'

'She had her tote,' Groom said. 'It's possible.' Then he looked up, beyond Reacher's shoulder. Edward Lane was struggling with a large leather duffle. *Five million dollars*, Reacher thought. *So that's what it looks like*. Lane dropped the bag on the floor.

'I need to see a picture of Jade,' Reacher said.

'Bedroom,' Lane said.

So Reacher followed him to the bedroom. It was painted a chalky off-white, as serene as a monastery and as quiet as a tomb. There was a cherry-wood kingsized bed. Matching tables at each side. A matching armoire. A matching desk, with a chair in front of it and a framed photograph sitting on it. It was a portrait of two people. On the right was Kate Lane. It was the same shot as in the living-room print. But the living-room print had been cropped to exclude the object of her affection, which was her daughter Jade. They were about to look at each other, love in their eyes, smiles about to break out on their faces. In the picture Jade was maybe seven years old. She had long dark hair, slightly wavy, as fine as silk. She had green eyes and porcelain skin.

'May I?' Reacher asked.

Lane nodded. Reacher picked the picture up and looked closer. The photographer had caught the bond between mother and child perfectly and completely. It was a great picture, although the print quality wasn't quite as good as the living-room copy. Maybe Lane's budget hadn't run to a custom hand-print where his stepdaughter was concerned.

'Very nice,' Reacher said. He put the photograph back on the desk. 'You mind if I check the desk?'

Lane shrugged and Reacher started with the bottom drawers. The left-hand drawer held boxes of stationery. The right-hand drawer was fitted with file hangers, and the contents related exclusively to Jade's education. She was enrolled at a private school. The cheques were all drawn on Kate Lane's personal account. The upper drawers held pens and pencils, envelopes, stamps, a chequebook. And credit-card receipts. But nothing very significant. Nothing recent. Nothing from Staples, for instance.

The centre drawer at the top held nothing but two American passports, one for Kate and one for Jade.

'Who is Jade's father?' Reacher asked.

'He's dead,' Lane said. 'He died of stomach cancer when Jade was three.'

'Who was he?'

'He owned a jewellery store. Kate ran it for a year, afterwards. She had been a model. That's where I met her. In the store. I was buying a watch.'

'Any other relatives?'

'Nobody that I ever met.'

Reacher closed the centre drawer. 'What was she wearing when she went out?' he asked.

'I'm not sure,' Lane said. 'We all left before her. Except Taylor.'

'May I see Jade's room?' Reacher asked.

Jade's room was all pale pastels and kids' stuff. Furry bears, china dolls, toys, games. A low bed. A low desk covered in drawings done with wax crayons on cheap paper. A small chair.

Nothing that meant anything to a military cop.

'I'm done,' Reacher said. 'I'm very sorry to intrude.'

He followed Lane back to the living room. Gregory and the five other soldiers were still in their places.

'Decision time,' Lane said. 'Do we assume Reacher was observed entering the building tonight? Or not?'

'I didn't see anyone,' Gregory said. 'And I think it's very unlikely. Round-the-clock surveillance would eat manpower.'

'I agree,' Lane said. 'So I think Reacher should be on the street at seven o'clock. And we should try a little surveillance of our own.'

Reacher nodded. 'I'll watch the front of the Spring Street building,' he said. 'That way I'll see one of them at least.'

'Surveillance only. Absolutely no intervention.'

'Don't worry.'

'They'll be there early,' Lane said.

'Don't worry,' Reacher said again. 'I'll leave right now.'

'Don't you want to know which building's the one you're supposed to be watching?'

'I don't need to know,' Reacher said. 'I'll see Gregory leave the keys.' Then he let himself out of the apartment, rode down in the elevator and walked out to the street. Headed for the subway at 72nd and Broadway.

THE WOMAN who was watching the building saw him go. She had seen him arrive with Gregory. She checked her watch and made a note of the time.

Reacher rode eleven stops south to Houston Street. Then he walked south on Varick. It was past three o'clock in the morning, three hours and forty minutes ahead of schedule. He walked along several blocks with the leisurely gait of a man with a place to go but in no hurry to get there. As he ambled past Spring he had a good view of the southwest corner. There was a narrow iron-fronted building with a dull red door set high. Three steps up to it. The upper storey windows were filthy and backed with some kind of a dark fabric. On the ground floor there was a single window, pasted over with faded building permits. There was a mail slot in the door.

That's the one, Reacher thought. *Got to be.*

He completed a circuit around the block. Walked south on West Broadway again and found a doorway on the east sidewalk. He lay down on his back, his head canted sideways like a somnolent drunk, but with his eyes half open and focused on the dull red door seventy feet away.

THE CLOCK in Reacher's head crept around to six in the morning. Down in the brick and iron canyons of SoHo it was still dark, but the sky above was already brightening. The night had been warm and Reacher hadn't been uncomfortable. So far he had seen no activity at the dull red door. But the early people were already out and about. Nobody was looking at him. He was just a guy in a doorway.

He figured whoever was coming would be in position soon. They clearly weren't fools. They would check rooftops and windows and parked cars for watching cops. But Reacher had never been mistaken for a cop. There was always something phoney about a cop who dresses down. Reacher was the real thing.

He had no watch but he figured when he saw Gregory it must have been between eight and nine minutes after seven o'clock. Eight or nine minutes was about right for the walk down from the fireplug on Sixth. So Gregory was right on time. He stopped outside the dull red door and walked up the three short steps. Then Reacher saw Gregory lift the mail slot's flap and shovel the keys through. Saw him walk away. Saw him make the right onto West Broadway. He didn't look back, he just played his part, trying to keep Kate Lane alive.

Reacher kept his eyes on the red door. Waited. Three minutes, he figured. Five million bucks was a lot of money. As soon as the one guy confirmed that Gregory was safely distant, the other guy would be in through the door.

One minute. Two minutes. Three minutes.

Nothing happened.

Reacher kept his eyes half closed but stared at the door so hard that its details etched themselves in his mind.

Six minutes. Eight. Nine. Nothing happened.

Reacher asked himself: Did they see me? He answered himself: Of course they did. Guys good enough to take down an SAS veteran were going to check the street pretty carefully. But were they worried? Answered himself: No, they weren't. People in doorways were like trash cans or mailboxes. And he was alone. Cops or FBI would have come in a group.

So what the hell was happening?

Nineteen minutes.

Reacher gave it up after twenty. Hustled north six blocks to the kerb with the fireplug. It was empty. No BMW.

REACHER HEADED BACK to Spring Street. He found Gregory on the sidewalk outside the dull red door.

'Well?' Gregory said.

'Nothing,' Reacher said. 'Nobody showed up. The car is gone.'

'How is that possible?'

'There's a back door,' Reacher said. 'That's my best guess.'

'We should check it out. Mr Lane will want the whole story.'

They found an alley entrance two buildings west. It was gated and chained. Above the gates was a single iron screen extending twenty feet in the air.

No way in.

Reacher stepped back and looked left and right. The target building's right-hand neighbour was a chocolate shop. There was a light on in back of the store. Reacher cupped his hands against the glass. Saw a small shadowy figure moving about. He banged on the door. The small figure turned around. It was a woman. Short, dark, young, tired. She opened the door against a thick steel chain.

'Department of Health,' Reacher said.

'You don't look like it,' the woman said. And she was right. Reacher had looked convincing as a bum in a doorway. He didn't look convincing as a bureaucrat. So he nodded at Gregory, in his neat grey suit.

'He's with the city,' he said. 'I'm with him.'

'I was just inspected,' the woman said.

'This is about the building next door,' Reacher said.

'What about it?'

'Rats,' Reacher said. 'I'm the exterminator. We've had reports.'

The woman went quiet.

'You got a key for the alley gate?' Gregory asked her.

The woman nodded. 'But you can use my back door.'

She led them inside through air intense with the smell of cocoa. The front of the store was dressed up for retail, and there was a working kitchen in back. Ovens, just now warming up. Vats of melting chocolate. A rear door, at the end of a short tiled hallway. Reacher and Gregory found themselves in a brick alley. The alley ran east to west across the block with a single gated exit on Thompson Street at one end and a right-angle dogleg to the gate they had seen on Spring at the other.

One ground-floor window. And a back door. It had a good, solid deadbolt.

Reacher turned back and headed for the kitchen.

'You ever seen anyone next door?' he asked.

'Nobody,' the chocolatier said. 'It's a vacant building.'

'Are you here every day?'

'From seven thirty in the morning. I fire up the ovens first thing, and I turn them off at ten in the evening. I'm out of here by eleven thirty. I'm regular as clockwork.'

'Seven days a week?'

'Small business. We never rest.'

Reacher nodded. 'Who's the owner next door?'

'I've got no idea,' the woman said. 'Check the building permits on the front window.'

'Thanks,' Reacher said.

'Want a chocolate?'

'Not on duty,' he said.

He and Gregory checked the target building's front window. There were a dozen permits pasted to the glass. All of them were long expired. But they still had phone numbers handwritten with a black marker pen. Gregory took out his small silver cellphone and took a picture with it.

He and Reacher walked back into the Dakota's lobby at eight thirty exactly. The woman who was watching made a note of the time.

THE BAD NEWS put Edward Lane on a knife edge. Reacher watched him struggling for control.

'Conclusions?' he asked. Like a demand. Like an entitlement.

'I'm revising my conclusions,' Reacher said. 'Maybe there aren't three guys. Maybe there are only two. One stays with Kate and Jade, the other comes to the city alone. He doesn't really need to watch Gregory walk away down West Broadway because he's planning on using the back door anyway.'

'Risky. Safer to be loose on the street.'

Reacher shook his head. 'They did their homework. The neighbour is in her building from seven thirty in the morning until eleven thirty at night. Which explains the times they chose. Seven o'clock this morning, before she arrived. Eleven forty the first night, after she left. Eleven forty is a weirdly precise choice of time. There had to be some reason for it.'

Edward Lane said nothing.

Reacher said, 'Or maybe there's only one guy. On his own. It's possible. If Kate and Jade are secured upstate. And maybe he wasn't in the alley at all. Maybe he was actually inside the building.'

Lane paced. But it was like he had been hit with a new consideration. Reacher had been expecting it. *Here it comes*, he thought.

'Maybe it's *four* guys,' Lane said. 'And maybe you're the fourth guy. Maybe that's why you were in that coffee shop the first night. You were watching your buddy's back.'

Reacher said nothing.

'It was you who elected to watch the front door this morning,' Lane said. 'Because you knew nothing would happen there. You should have watched the car. And you knew they were going to ask for five million more. You're one of them, aren't you?'

'Two questions,' Reacher said. 'Why would I have gone back to the coffee shop the second night? Nothing happened the second night. And if I was a bad guy why would I have told Gregory I had seen anything at all?'

'Because you wanted to worm your way inside where you could steer us wrong.'

Reacher looked down at Kate Lane's photograph.

'Pity,' he said. 'Your wife is a beautiful woman, Mr Lane. And her daughter is a lovely kid. And if you want to get them back, then I'm all you've got. Because like I said, these guys here can start a war, but they're not investigators.'

Nobody spoke.

'You know where I live?' Reacher asked.

'I could find out,' Lane said.

'You couldn't,' Reacher said. 'Because I don't really live anywhere. So if I choose to walk out of here today, you'll never see me again.'

Lane didn't answer.

'And therefore Kate. You'll never see her again either.'

Nobody spoke.

'I'm not here to steer you wrong,' Reacher said. 'If I wanted to steer you wrong, I'd have given you descriptions of two fantasy guys this morning. But I didn't. I came back here and told you I'm sorry that actually I'm not steering you anyplace yet. Because I am sorry about that. Really I am.'

Nobody spoke. Then Lane exhaled. 'I apologise,' he said. 'Please forgive me. It's the stress.'

Reacher said, 'No offence taken.'

Lane said, 'One million dollars to find my wife.'

'For me?' Reacher said. 'That's some raise. It was twenty-five grand a few hours ago.'

'Will you accept?' Lane asked.

'We'll talk about a fee afterwards,' Reacher said. 'If I succeed.'

'If?'

'I'm way behind the curve here. Success depends on how much longer we can keep this thing going.'

'Will they call back again?'

'Yes, I think they will.'

LANE WENT TO HIS OFFICE and five men went out for breakfast. Reacher stayed in the living room. Gregory stayed with him.

'Can you get her back?' Gregory asked.

'I don't know,' Reacher said. 'Usually this kind of a thing doesn't end happily. Kidnapping is a brutal business.'

'You think they were really in the building when I dropped the keys?'

'It's possible.'

'OK,' Gregory said. 'So how about this: that's their base. That's where they *are*. Not upstate.'

'It would be one hell of a double bluff,' Reacher said. 'So call those numbers. If possible, aim to have someone meet us with a key. But on the corner of Thompson. Out of sight. Just in case.'

REACHER LEFT GREGORY working with his cellphone on the sofa and wandered back through the kitchen to Lane's office. Lane was at his desk, and staring at the photographs in front of him. His two wives. Maybe both lost.

'Did the FBI find the guys?' Reacher asked. 'With Anne?'

Lane shook his head.

'But you found out later.'

'It became a threshold question,' Lane said. 'Who would do such a thing? At first I couldn't imagine anyone doing it. But clearly someone had, so I revised the threshold of possibilities downwards. But then everyone in the world seemed to be a possibility. It was beyond my understanding.'

'You surprise me. You move in a world where hostage-taking and abduction aren't exactly unknown.'

'But this was domestic,' Lane said. 'This was right here in New York City. And it was my wife, not me or one of my men.'

'But you did find the guys.'

'Did I?'

Reacher nodded. 'You're not asking me if I think it could be the same people, all over again. It's like you know for sure it isn't.'

Lane said nothing.

'How did you find them?' Reacher asked.

'Someone who knew someone heard some talk. Arms dealers.'

'What happened to the guys?'

'Let's just say I'm confident that this isn't the same people doing it again.'

'Have you heard any new talk?' Reacher asked.

'Not a word.'

'A rival in this business?'

'I don't have rivals in this business. And even if I did have rivals, they wouldn't do something like this. It would be suicide.'

Reacher said nothing.

'Will they call again?' Lane asked.

'I think they will.'

'What will they ask for?'

'Ten,' Reacher said. 'That's the next step.'

'That's two bags,' Lane said.

Reacher thought: *This guy is right now looking at a running total of seventeen million dollars, and he hasn't even blinked.*

'When will they call?' Lane asked.

'Drive time plus argument time,' Reacher said. 'Late afternoon, early evening. Not before.'

There was a quiet knock at the door and Gregory stuck his head in the room. 'I got what we need,' he said, to Reacher, not to Lane. 'The building on Spring Street? The owner is a bankrupt developer. One of his lawyer's people is meeting us there in a hour. I said we were interested in buying the place.'

'Good work,' Reacher said.

Chapter Three

The guy from the bankrupt developer's lawyer's office was a reedy paralegal of about thirty. Gregory gave him an OSC business card and introduced Reacher as a contractor whose opinion he valued.

'Is the building habitable?' Gregory asked.

'There's nobody in there right now,' the guy said. 'No water, no power, no gas, capped sewer. Also, there's another feature that makes it highly unlikely.'

He unlocked the Thompson Street alley gate. The three men walked to the target building's rear door.

'Wait,' Gregory said. Then he turned to Reacher and whispered, 'If they're in there, we could get them both killed right here.'

Reacher nodded and looked up and checked the windows. They were black with filth and dusty black drapes were drawn tight behind them. Street noise was loud. Therefore, their approach was still undetected.

'What makes you so sure there's nobody in there?' Reacher asked the lawyer's guy.

'I'll show you.' The guy shoved the key in the lock and pushed open the door. Then he raised his arm to stop Gregory and Reacher from crowding in too closely behind him. Because the feature that made current habitation of the building unlikely was that it had no floors. The back door was hanging open over a yawning ten-foot pit.

'See?' the lawyer's guy said. 'Not exactly habitable, is it?'

There was a ladder set next to the rear door. A nimble person could grasp the door frame and swing sideways and get on it and climb down. Then that person could pick his way forward to the front of the building and collect anything that had fallen the thirteen feet from the letter slot above.

Or, a nimble person could be already waiting down there and could catch whatever came through the slot.

'Who else has keys to this place?' Reacher asked.

'Everyone and his uncle, probably,' the guy said. 'It's been vacant nearly twenty years. The first thing you'll need to do is change the locks.'

'We don't want it,' Gregory said. 'We were looking for something ready to move into.'

'We could be flexible on price,' the guy said.

'A dollar,' Gregory said. 'That's all I'd pay for a dump like this.'

'You're wasting my time,' the guy said.

He pulled the door closed. Then he relocked it and walked back up the alley without another word. Reacher and Gregory followed him out to Thompson Street. The guy relocked the gate and walked away south.

'Not their base, then,' Gregory said. 'Just a dead drop for the car keys. Next time we should watch the alley.'

'I guess we should.'

Thirty-six minutes later the two men were back in the Dakota, and the woman who was watching the building had made another entry in her log.

REACHER DOZED on a sofa for a while, woke up and found himself all alone in the living room except for Carter Groom. The guy with the shark's eyes. He was sitting in an armchair, doing nothing.

'You pulled guard duty?' Reacher asked.

'You're not exactly a prisoner,' Groom said. 'You're in line to get a million bucks.'

'Did you drive her often?'

'My fair share.'

'When Jade was with her, how did they ride?'

'Mrs Lane always rode in the front. The kid in the back.'

'What were you, back in the day?'

'Recon Marine,' Groom said. 'First Sergeant.'

'How would you have handled the takedown at Bloomingdale's?'

'Only one way to do it clean,' Groom said. 'You'd have to keep all the action inside the car, before they even got out. Bloomie's is on the east side of Lexington Avenue. Lex runs downtown. So Taylor would pull over on the left and stop opposite the main entrance. Double parked. Whereupon our guy would grab the rear door and slide in right next to the kid. She's belted in behind her mother. Our guy puts a gun straight to the kid's head. That's game over, right there. Nobody on the street is worried. And Taylor would do what he's told from that point on. And what can he do anyway?'

'And then what?'

'Then our guy makes Taylor drive somewhere quiet. He shoots him, spine shot through the seat. He makes Mrs Lane dump him out. Then he makes her drive the rest of the way. He wants to stay in the back with the kid.'

Reacher nodded. 'That's how I see it.'

'Tough on Taylor,' Groom said. 'They haven't found his body yet.'

'You optimistic?'

Groom shook his head. 'It's not somewhere populated, that's all it means.'

'What was he like as a person?'

'Off duty he was gentle. He was good with the kid. Mrs Lane seemed to like him. Taylor was inner circle. He was good. I'm outer circle. I'm all business. I'm kind of stunted, in a social situation. I can admit it. I'm nothing, away from the action. Some of the others can be both.'

'Were you here five years ago?'

'For Anne? No, I came just after.'

AROUND A QUARTER TO FIVE in the afternoon, probably fifty-four hours since the snatch, Lane came back into the room and people started drifting in after him. Fifty-four hours was an incredibly long time for a kidnap to sustain itself. Most were over in less than twenty-four, one way or another.

The vigil around the phone started up again. Lane stood next to the table. The others grouped themselves around the room, all facing the same way.

In her apartment across the street the woman who had been watching the building picked up her telephone and dialled.

THE WOMAN across the street was called Patricia Joseph, Patti to her few friends, and she was dialling an NYPD detective named Brewer.

'There's a new character on the scene,' Patti said.

Brewer didn't ask who his caller was. He didn't need to.

'Who?'

'I don't have a name for him yet.'

'Description?'

'Very tall, heavily built, like a real brawler. Late thirties or early forties. Short fair hair, blue eyes. Green shirt, chinos. He showed up late last night.'

'One of them?' Brewer asked.

'He doesn't dress like them. And he's much bigger than the rest. But he acts like them. Almost certainly ex-military.'

'OK,' Brewer said. 'Good work. Anything else?'

'One thing,' Patti Joseph said. 'I haven't seen the wife or the daughter in a couple of days.'

INSIDE THE DAKOTA living room the phone rang at what Reacher figured was five o'clock exactly. Lane snatched the receiver out of the cradle. Lane said, 'Put Kate on,' and there was a long pause. Then a woman's voice, loud and clear. But not calm. Lane closed his eyes. Then the electronic squawk came back. Lane listened, his face working. Then the call ended.

Lane put the receiver back in the cradle. His face was half filled with hope, half filled with despair.

'They want more money,' he said. 'Instructions in an hour.'

'Maybe I should get down there now,' Reacher said. 'In case they change the time interval.'

But Lane was already shaking his head. 'They said they're changing the whole procedure.'

'Is Mrs Lane OK?' Gregory asked.

Lane said, 'There was a lot of fear in her voice.'

'What about the guy's voice?' Reacher asked. 'Word choice, word order, cadence. Is it an American or a foreigner?'

'It's an American,' Lane said. 'I think.' He closed his eyes and concentrated. 'Yes, American. Never any weird or unusual words. Just normal.'

'How much money?' Reacher asked. 'Ten?'

'Four and a half,' Lane said. 'That's what they want. In a bag.'

REACHER SPENT the remaining fifty-five minutes puzzling over the choice of amount. It was a bizarre figure. A bizarre progression. One, five, four and a half. Altogether ten and a half million dollars. It made no sense at all.

The phone rang right on time, at six in the evening. Lane picked it up and listened. He didn't speak. The instruction call lasted less than two minutes.

'This is the final instalment,' Lane said. 'After this, it's over. They promise I get her back.'

Too soon, Reacher thought. *Ain't going to happen.*

'One hour from now,' Lane said. 'One man leaves here alone with the money in the black BMW and cruises. He'll be carrying my cellphone and he'll be given a destination. He's to keep the line open from that point on so they know he's not conversing with anyone else. He'll drive to the destination. He'll find the Jaguar parked on the street there. The car that Taylor drove Kate in. He's to put the money on the back seat and drive away. Any tricks at all, and Kate dies.'

'They've got your cellphone number?' Reacher asked.

'Kate will have given it to them.'

'I'll be the driver,' Gregory said. 'If you want.'

'No,' Lane said. 'I want you here.'

'I'll do it,' Burke said. The black guy.

Lane nodded. 'Thank you.'

'Then what?' Reacher asked. 'How do we get her back?'

Lane said, 'After they've counted the money, there'll be another call. Here. The money is already bricked and banded and labelled. But they won't trust that. They'll break the bands and count the bills by hand. It will take some time.'

Reacher nodded. If the money was in hundreds, that would give them forty-five thousand bills. If they could count to a hundred every sixty seconds, that would take them four hundred and fifty minutes, which was seven and a half hours. Plus the drive time. A long night ahead, he thought.

'Office,' Lane said. 'Burke and Reacher.'

In the office Lane took a small silver Samsung phone out of a charging cradle and handed it to Burke. Then he disappeared, to his bedroom, maybe.

'Gone to get the money,' Burke said.

Reacher nodded. Gazed at the portraits on the desk. Anne Lane had long, blonde straight hair parted in the middle, like a model, or an actress. She had clear, guileless eyes and an innocent smile.

'No kids with Anne, right?' Reacher asked.

'No,' Burke said. 'Thank God.'

Lane came back awkwardly with a bulging leather bag. He dropped it on the floor and sat down at his desk.

'How long?' he asked.

'Forty minutes,' Reacher said.

'Go wait in the other room,' Lane said. 'Leave me alone.'

Burke picked up the bag, carried it to the foyer and dropped it near the door. Reacher took a seat and started counting off the minutes. Burke paced. Carter Groom drummed his fingers on the arm of a chair. Next to him Gregory sat quiet, all British reserve. Next to him was Perez, the Latino. Next to him was Addison, with the scarred face. Then Kowalski, taller than the others.

Reacher glanced at Kate Lane's picture next to the phone and went a little cold. She was closer to dead now than at any point in the last three days, and he knew it. He guessed they all knew it.

'Time,' Burke said at last. 'I'm going.'

'I'll carry the bag for you,' Reacher said.

They rode down in the elevator. A BMW was waiting. This one was black. Burke opened the rear door.

'Stick the bag on the back seat,' he said.

'I'm coming with you,' Reacher said. 'You know as well as I do there's not going to be any cute little Checkpoint Charlie scene in this story. She's not going to come towards us through the mist, smiling bravely, with Jade holding her hand. So we're going to have to get proactive.'

'What are you planning to do?'

'After you've switched the bag I'll get out around the next corner. I'll double back and see what I can see.'

'Lane will kill me.'

'He doesn't have to know anything about it. I'll say I went for a walk.'

'Lane will kill you if you screw it up.'

'My risk.'

'Kate's risk.'

'You still banking on the Checkpoint Charlie scenario?'

Burke paused. Ten seconds. Fifteen. 'Get in,' he said.

BURKE STUCK Lane's cellphone in a cradle on the BMW's dash and Reacher crawled into the rear footwell on his hands and knees.

'Don't hit any big bumps,' Reacher said.

'We're not supposed to talk,' Burke said. 'You see this?'

Reacher saw Burke pointing at a small black bud near his sun visor.

'Microphone,' Burke said. 'For the cell. Real sensitive.'

'Will I hear them? On a speaker?'

'On ten speakers,' Burke said.

'Where are we now?' Reacher asked.

'Fifty-seventh Street,' Burke said. 'Traffic is murder. I'm going to get on the West Side Highway and head south. My guess is they'll want us downtown somewhere. Street parking for the Jag would be impossible anyplace else.'

'What were you?' Reacher asked. 'Back in the day?'

'Delta,' Burke said.

'How would you have done the thing outside Bloomingdale's?'

'Quick and dirty inside the car. As soon as Taylor stopped.'

'That's what Groom said.'

'Groom's a smart guy, for a jarhead. You disagree?'

'No. But why would you have been at Bloomingdale's at all?'

'It's Mrs Lane's favourite store. She gets all her stuff there.'

'But who would have known that?'

Burke was quiet. 'That's a very good question,' he said.

The phone rang.

'Shut up now,' Burke said, and hit a button on the cell.

'Good evening,' a voice said.

The voice was so heavily processed that there would be no chance of recognising it again without the electronic machine.

'Who am I speaking with?' it asked. 'I want your name.'

Burke said, 'My name is Burke.'

The voice asked, 'Who's that in the car with you?'

'There's nobody in the car with me,' Burke said.

Reacher figured there might be a lie detector hooked up to the other end of the phone. Delta soldiers were taught to beat better tests than a person could buy retail on Madison Avenue. And after a second the voice calmly asked, 'Where are you now, Mr Burke?'

'Fifty-seventh Street,' Burke said. 'I'm heading west.'

'Take the West Side Highway. Go south.'

'Give me time,' Burke said. 'Traffic is real bad.'

'Stay on the line,' the voice said.

The sound of distorted breathing filled the car. It was slow and deep. *Unworried*, Reacher thought.

'I'm at 42nd Street now,' Burke said.

'Keep going,' the voice said. 'Just keep on driving.'

American, Reacher thought. *Not a big guy*. There was a lightness.

'Coming up on 24th Street,' Burke said.

Reacher thought, *We're going back to Greenwich Village*.

The voice asked, 'Where are you now?'

'Perry,' Burke said.

'Keep going. But stand by now.'

Reacher thought, *Stand by now? That's a military term.*

'Morton Street,' Burke said.

'Left turn in three blocks,' the voice said. 'On Houston.'

He knows New York City, Reacher thought. *He knows that Houston is three blocks south of Morton and he knows you say it House-ton, not like the place in Texas.*

Reacher felt the car slow.

'East on Houston now,' Burke said.

'Keep going,' the voice said.

'Sixth Avenue next,' Burke said.

The voice said, 'Take it.'

Burke turned left.

The voice said, 'Get in the right-hand lane. Now. You'll see your target on the right. The green Jaguar. Halfway up the block.'

Reacher thought: *It's right there on the same damn fireplug?*

The voice said, 'Stop and make the transfer.'

Reacher felt the transmission slam into park and he heard the click of the hazard lights start up. Then Burke's door opened. Ten seconds later the door next to Reacher's head opened. Burke leaned in and grabbed the bag. Then the door shut. Reacher heard the Jaguar's door open. Then he heard it shut again. He heard a faint hydraulic *thunk* from somewhere outside. Ten seconds after that Burke was back in his seat.

'The transfer is done,' he said. 'The money is in the Jaguar.'

The voice said, 'Goodbye.' The phone clicked off.

'Go now,' Reacher said. 'Turn right on Bleecker.'

Burke took off, accelerated twenty yards and jammed the brakes on. Reacher found the door handle, scrambled out and hustled back to the corner.

REACHER TURNED LEFT onto Sixth like a man walking home. Just blending in, which he was surprisingly good at, given that he was always a head taller than anyone else. He looked straight ahead and put the green Jaguar firmly in his peripheral vision. Checked left. Nothing. Checked right.

And saw a guy six feet from the driver's door.

It was the same guy he had seen the very first night. Same stature, same movements, same clothes. White, a little sunburnt, lean, chiselled, clean-shaven, jaw clamped, not smiling, maybe forty years old. Calm, focused, intent. The guy pulled the door and slid into the seat and started the engine and took a long glance over his shoulder at the traffic. Then he pulled out neatly and took off north. The guy flashed past, out of sight. Six seconds, beginning to end. Maybe less.

Reacher glanced around. There were no cabs coming. So he set out walking. He needed to walk off his frustration. He charged north on Sixth, fast and furious, and people moved out of his way like he was radioactive.

Twenty minutes and twenty blocks later he saw a Staples store on the opposite sidewalk. Windows full of office supply bargains. He crossed over. He didn't know which branch Carter Groom had taken Kate Lane to, but he figured chains carried the same stuff everywhere. He went inside and passed a corral where shopping trolleys were racked together. Beyond that on the left were the check-out registers. On the right was a print shop full of industrial-strength photocopiers. In front of him were about twenty narrow aisles with shelves that reached the ceiling, piled high with an intimidating array of stuff. He zigzagged through the store to the rear of the last aisle.

He had absolutely no idea at all of what Kate Lane might have been looking for.

He stood in a daze and watched a photocopier as big as a tumble drier at work spitting out copies. Then headed for the street.

Another twenty minutes later and he was at Bryant Park, eating a hot dog from a street vendor. Thirty-two more blocks north he was in Central Park, directly opposite the Dakota Building, stopped dead, face to face with Anne Lane, Edward Lane's first wife.

THE FIRST THING Anne Lane did was tell Reacher he was wrong. 'Anne was my sister,' she told him. 'We were very alike.'

'I'm sorry for staring,' Reacher said. 'And I'm sorry for your loss.'

'Thank you,' the woman said. 'I'm six years younger. Which means right now I'm the same age as Anne was, in Lane's photograph.'

'You look exactly like her.'

'I try to,' the woman said. 'It feels like I'm keeping her alive. Because I couldn't, back when it mattered.'

'How could you have kept her alive?'

'We should talk,' the woman said. 'My name is Patti Joseph.'

'Jack Reacher.'

'Come with me,' the woman said. 'We have to double back. We can't go too near the Dakota.'

She led him south through the park, to the exit at 66th Street. Then, north again, and into the lobby of a building at 115 Central Park West.

'Welcome to the Majestic,' Patti Joseph said.

The apartment was on the seventh floor. Its living-room window looked directly at the Dakota's entrance. There was a dining chair placed in front of the sill. On the sill was a notebook and a pen. And a Nikon camera with a long lens, and a pair of Leica 10x42 binoculars.

'Do you work for Lane?' Patti asked.

'No, I don't.'

'Did you know Lane in the service?'

'No, I didn't.'

Patti Joseph smiled.

'I thought not,' she said. 'Otherwise you wouldn't be there. I told Brewer, you're not one of them. You're too big for Special Forces.'

'I was an MP. Who is Brewer?'

'NYPD.' She pointed at the notebook. 'I do all this for him.'

'You're watching Lane and his guys? For the cops?'

'For myself, mostly. But I check in.'

'Why?'

'Because hope springs eternal.'

'Hope of what?'

'That he'll slip up, and I'll get something on him.'

Reacher glanced at the notebook. The last entry read: *2014 hrs. Burke returns alone, no bag, in black BMW OSC 23, enters TDA.*

'TDA?' Reacher asked.

'The Dakota Apartments. The building's official name.'

'You ever see Yoko?'

'All the time.'

'You know Burke by name?'

'Burke was around when Anne was there.'

'Why are you showing me all this?' Reacher asked.

'I decided to watch for new guys, and warn them,' she said.

'About what?'

'About what Lane is really like. About what he did.'

'What did he do?'

'I'll make coffee,' Patti said.

She ducked into a small kitchen and started fiddling with a machine. Pretty soon Reacher could smell coffee. He figured he could stay for a cup.

Patti called out, 'No cream, no sugar, right?'

'How did you know that?'

'I trust my instincts,' she said.

And I trust mine, Reacher thought, although he wasn't entirely sure what they were telling him right then.

'I need you to get to the point,' he said.

'OK,' Patti Joseph said. 'Anne wasn't kidnapped five years ago. That was just a cover story. Lane murdered her.' She brought Reacher black coffee in a mug and sat on the chair at the window. 'My sister Anne wasn't very obedient,' she said. 'But Edward Lane ran the marriage like a military operation and she couldn't handle it. The more she chafed, the more Lane demanded discipline. He's borderline mentally ill, I think. Psychotic.'

'What was she before?'

'A model. Just like the second wife.'

'What happened?'

'Between them they drove the marriage on the rocks. She wanted a divorce. I was all in favour of that. It was the best thing for her. But she tried to do the whole thing. Alimony, division of assets. I told her just to get the hell out. But she had brought money to the relationship. Lane had used it for part of his initial stake. Anne wanted her share back. It would have been a public humiliation for Lane, because he would have had to go out and find another investor. So he faked a kidnapping and had her killed.'

'The police were involved,' Reacher said. 'The FBI, too.'

Patti smiled, sadly. 'He made it seem very real.'

'You got any particular suspects in mind?' he asked.

Patti said, 'Nobody who's still in the A-team. But I don't think he would have used B-teamers.'

'So who?'

'A-team guys who aren't around any more. There were two. A guy called Hobart and a guy called Knight. Shortly after Anne died there was an operation overseas. Two men didn't come back. Those two.'

'That would be a coincidence,' Reacher said. 'Wouldn't it?'

'I think Lane made sure they didn't come back.'

Reacher said nothing.

'I know,' Patti said. 'The little sister is crazy, right?'

Reacher gazed at her. She didn't look crazy. She had long blonde hair, straight, just the same as Anne in the photograph. Big blue eyes, a button nose, a dusting of freckles, pale skin.

'How do you think it went down?' he asked.

'Knight drove Anne that day,' Patti said. 'He took her shopping. Waited. But she never came out of the store. Next thing anyone knew was a phone call four hours later. The usual. No cops, a ransom demand.'

'How much was the ransom?'

'A hundred grand.'

'But Lane did call the cops.'

Patti nodded. 'But only to cover his ass. The FBI tapped the phones and moved in on the ransom drop. Lane's story is that they were seen. But the whole thing was phoney. They waited, nobody showed up, because nobody was ever going to show up. So they brought the money home again. It was all a performance. Lane acted it all out and came home and gave the word that the cops had bought the story, that the FBI was convinced, and then Anne was killed.'

'Where was the other guy during all of this? Hobart?'

'He was off duty. He said he was in Philadelphia. But obviously he had been in the store, waiting for Anne to show.'

'Did you go to the cops at the time?'

'They ignored me,' Patti said. 'This was not long after the Twin Towers. Everyone was preoccupied.'

'What about this cop Brewer? Now?'

'He tolerates me. But I don't suppose he's doing anything about it.'

'You got any evidence against Lane at all?'

'No,' Patti said. 'None at all. All I've got is context and intuition.'

'Context?'

'Do you know what a private military corporation is really for? Fundamentally?'

'Fundamentally its purpose is to allow the Pentagon to escape Congressional oversight.'

'Exactly,' Patti said. 'They're not necessarily better fighters, better than people currently enlisted. Often they're worse. They're there to break the rules. Simple as that.'

'So what do you wish you had done to keep Anne alive?'

'I should have just got her out of there, penniless but alive.'

'What do you want me to do?'

'I want you to just walk away from him. For your own sake. Don't dirty your hands with his business.'

Silence for a moment.

'And he's dangerous,' Patti added.

'I'll be careful,' Reacher said. 'I always am. But I'll walk away on my own schedule.'

Patti Joseph said nothing.

'I'd like to meet with this guy Brewer,' Reacher said. 'Because if he's any kind of a cop he'll have checked with the original detectives and the FBI agents. He might have a clearer picture.'

'He usually comes over after I phone in a report.'

'You said he wasn't doing anything.'

'He just drops by, at the end of his shift. On his way home.'

'When does his shift end?' Reacher asked.

'Midnight. I'm not involved with him or anything,' Patti said, reading Reacher's face. 'He's lonely. I'm lonely. That's all.'

Reacher said nothing.

'Check my window,' Patti said. 'If Brewer's here, the light will be on. If he isn't, it won't be.'

Chapter Four

Reacher let himself out. He walked clockwise around her block for caution's sake. It was a quarter to ten in the evening. It was a perfect late-summer night. There was music in the park and probably baseball up in the Bronx or out at Shea. Reacher stepped inside the Dakota.

The lobby staff called up and let him go to the elevator. He got out and found Gregory waiting for him.

'We thought you'd quit on us,' Gregory said.

'Went for a walk,' Reacher said. 'Any news?'

'Too early.'

Reacher followed him into the apartment. Edward Lane was in the armchair next to the phone. Next to him, at the end of a sofa was an empty place. A dented cushion. Recently occupied by Gregory, Reacher guessed. Then came Burke. And Addison, and Perez, and Kowalski. Groom was leaning on the wall, facing the door, vigilant. *I'm all business*, he had said.

'When will they call?' Lane asked.

Good question, Reacher thought. *Or will you call them? And give them the OK to pull the triggers?*

But he said, 'They won't call before eight in the morning.'

Lane glanced at his watch. 'Ten hours from now.'

'Yes,' Reacher said.

'I did everything they asked,' Lane said, to nobody except himself.

Nobody replied.

HALFWAY THROUGH the second hour Lane looked at Reacher and said, 'There's food in the kitchen, if you want some.'

Reacher didn't want food. But he wanted to get the hell out of the living room. It was like they were all sitting around a deathbed. 'Thanks,' he said.

He walked into the kitchen. There were dirty plates and open containers of Chinese food on the countertop. He left them alone and sat on a stool. Glanced to his right at the open office door.

He listened. Nobody coming. He stepped inside the office. *Desk, computer, fax machine, phones, file cabinets, shelves.*

He started with the shelves.

There were phone books, and manuals for firearms, and a one-volume history of Argentina, and an atlas of the world. There was a Rolodex full of index cards with names and phone numbers and MOS codes on them. *Military Occupational Specialties.* Reacher flipped to *G* and looked for Carter Groom. Not there. Then *B* for Burke. Not there either. So clearly this was the B-team candidate pool. Some names had KIA or MIA notations. *Killed in Action, Missing in Action.*

Reacher touched the computer mouse. The dialogue box on the screen asked for a password. Reacher tried *Kate*. Access was denied. He tried *O5LaneE* for Colonel Edward Lane. ACCESS DENIED. He gave it up.

He moved on to the file cabinets.

There were four of them. Two drawers in each. Unlabelled. Unlocked. He slid the first drawer open. It had twin hanging rails with six file dividers made of thin yellow cardboard slung between them. All six were full of paperwork. Financial records. He closed the drawer.

He opened the bottom drawer on the left. Same yellow dividers. But they were bulky with the kind of big plastic wallets that come in the glove boxes of new cars. Instruction books, warranty certificates, service records. Some had valet keys. Some had spare keys and remote fobs. There were toll records. Receipts from gas stations.

Reacher closed the drawer. Glanced back at the door. Saw Burke standing there, silent, just watching him.

Burke didn't speak for a long moment. Then he said, 'I'm going for a walk.'

'I'll keep you company,' Reacher said.

Burke just shrugged. Reacher followed him out. They rode down in the elevator in silence. Stepped out to the street and turned east towards Central Park. Reacher looked up at Patti Joseph's window. It was dark. Therefore she was alone.

'That question you asked,' Burke said.

'What question?' Reacher said.

'Who knew Mrs Lane loved Bloomingdale's?'

'What about it?'

'I think there's inside involvement,' Burke said. He was as black as coal, a small man, about the size and shape of an old-fashioned Major League second baseman.

'What happened after Anne?' Reacher asked.

'With the guys who took her? No comment.'

'Did they admit it?'

'No,' Burke said.

The park loomed ahead of them, dark and empty. The music had finished.

'Where are we going?' Reacher asked.

'Doesn't matter,' Burke said. 'I just wanted to talk.'

'About the insider involvement?'

'Yes.'

'Who do you think it was?' Reacher asked.

'I have no idea,' Burke said, turning south.

'But who got tipped off?' Reacher asked. 'Not who did the tipping. I think that would be the more important answer. And I think that's what you want to tell me.'

Burke walked on in silence.

'I thought you wanted to talk,' Reacher said. 'Yet you don't have much to talk about. You as good as dragged me out here. Not because you're worried if I'm getting enough fresh air and exercise.'

Burke stayed quiet.

'You going to make me play Twenty Questions?'

'That might be the best way to do it,' Burke said.

'You think this is about the money?'

'No,' Burke said. 'Half the equation at best.'

'The other half of the equation being punishment?'

'You got it.'

'There's someone out there with a grudge against Lane?'

'Yes. More than one person,' Burke said.

'Two?'

'Yes.'

'What kind of a grudge?'

'What's the worst thing one man can do to another?'

'Depends who you are,' Reacher said.

'Exactly,' Burke said. 'So who are we?'

Reacher thought. 'Special Forces soldiers,' he said.

'Exactly,' Burke said again. 'So what don't we do?'

'You don't leave bodies behind on the battlefield.'

Burke said nothing.

'But Lane did. He left two bodies behind.'

Burke stopped on the north curve of Columbus Circle.

'So what are you saying?' Reacher asked. 'Someone's come out of the woodwork looking for revenge? On their behalf?'

Burke didn't answer. Reacher stared at him.

'You left two guys behind *alive*?'

'Not me,' Burke said. 'Not us. It was Lane.'

'Hobart and Knight,' Reacher said.

'You know their names. How? There's nothing about them in those file cabinets. Or in the computer. They've been erased. Like they never existed.'

'What happened with them?'

'They were wounded. According to Lane. We never saw them. They were in forward observation posts and we heard small-arms fire. Lane went up the line and came back and said they were hit bad and couldn't possibly make it. He said we couldn't bring them in. He said we'd lose too many guys trying. He flat ordered us to pull out. We left them there.'

'And what do you suppose happened to them?'

'We assumed they'd be taken prisoner. In which case we assumed their life expectancy would be about a minute and a half.'

'Why did you stick around afterwards? All this time?'

'I obey orders. And I let officers decide things. That's how it always was and that's how it always will be. That's a code.'

'Does he know they're back? Lane?'

'You're not listening,' Burke said. 'Nobody *knows* they're back. Nobody even knows if they're alive. I'm just guessing, is all.'

'Who would be talking to them? From the inside?'

'I don't know.'

'What were they?'

'Jarheads.'

'Like Carter Groom?'

'Yes,' Burke said. 'Like Carter Groom.'

Reacher said nothing.

'Marines hate that,' Burke said. 'They hate leaving guys behind.'

'So why does *he* stick around?'

'Same reason I do. Ours is not to reason why.'

'Maybe in the service,' Reacher said. 'Not necessarily in some half-assed private company.'

'Watch your mouth, pal. I'm earning you a million bucks. You find Hobart and Knight, you find Kate and Jade, too.'

'I don't need to watch my mouth,' Reacher said. 'If you've still got a code, then I'm still an officer. I can say what I like and you can stand there and take it and salute.'

Burke turned and headed back north. Reacher caught up and fell in beside him. Nothing more was said. Ten minutes later they turned into 72nd Street. Reacher glanced up. Patti Joseph's window was blazing with light.

REACHER SAID, 'You go on ahead. I'm going to walk some more.'

'Why?' Burke asked.

'You gave me things to think about. One more question,' Reacher said. 'Did Lane and Kate get along OK?'

'They're still married,' Burke said.

'What does that mean?'

'It means they get along OK.'

'As well as he got along with Anne?'

Burke nodded. 'About the same.'

'I'll see you later,' Reacher said.

Reacher watched Burke disappear inside the Dakota and then moved away from Patti Joseph's place. Routine caution.

THE DOORMAN at the Majestic called upstairs. Three minutes later Reacher was shaking hands with Brewer, the cop. Patti Joseph was in the kitchen, making coffee. She had changed into a dark trouser-suit, prim and proper. She came out of the kitchen with two mugs of coffee. She gave one to

Brewer and one to Reacher and said, 'I'll leave you guys to talk. Maybe easier if I'm not here. I'll go for a walk. Night-time is about the only time it's safe for me to be out.'

Then she left, with a nervous glance back, as if her future was at stake. Reacher took a better look at Brewer. He was everything anyone would expect a New York City detective to be, except a little taller, a little heavier, longer hair, more unkempt, more energetic. He was about fifty and prematurely grey.

'What's your interest here?' he asked.

'Lane wants to hire me,' Reacher said. 'And I heard Patti's story. So I want to know what I'm getting into.'

'What's your line of work?'

'I was in the army,' Reacher said.

'It's a free country,' Brewer said. Then he sat down on Patti Joseph's sofa like he owned it.

Reacher leaned on the wall. 'I was a cop once myself,' he said. 'Military police.'

Brewer shrugged. 'I guess I can give you five minutes,' he said.

'Bottom line,' Reacher said. 'What happened five years ago?'

'Nobody in the NYPD can tell you that,' Brewer said. 'If it was a kidnap, that's FBI business, because kidnapping is a federal crime. If it was a straightforward homicide, then that's New Jersey business, because the body was found on the other side of the George Washington Bridge. Therefore it was never really our case.'

'So why are you here?'

'Community relations. The kid is hurting, and she needs an ear. Plus she's cute and she makes good coffee.'

'Your people must have got copied in on the paperwork.'

Brewer nodded. 'There's a file,' he said. 'But the only thing anyone knows for sure is that Anne Lane died five years ago in New Jersey. She was a month decomposed when they found her. But there was a definitive dental identification. It was her.'

'Cause of death?'

'Fatal gunshot wound to the back of her head. Large-calibre handgun, probably a nine. She was out in the open. Rodents had been in and out the bullet hole. But it was probably a nine, probably jacketed.'

'Anything else at the scene?'

'There was a playing card. The three of clubs. Shoved down the back of her shirt. No forensics worth a damn, nobody knew what it meant.'

'So what do you think?' Reacher said. 'Kidnap or murder?'

Brewer yawned. 'You hear hoofbeats, you look for horses, not zebras. A guy calls in that his wife has been kidnapped, you assume it's true. And there were real phone calls, there was real cash money in a bag.'

'But?'

Brewer went quiet for a moment.

'Patti kind of sucks you in,' he said. 'You have to admit it's just as plausible the other way around.'

'Gut feeling?'

'I just don't know,' Brewer said. 'Which is a weird feeling for me. I mean, sometimes I'm wrong, but I always *know*.'

'So what are you doing about it?'

'Nothing. It's an ice-cold case outside of our jurisdiction.' Brewer took a pull on his mug of coffee, then asked again, 'What's your interest here?'

'Like I said.'

'Bullshit. Something's on your mind,' Brewer said. Then, 'One thing Patti told me. She hasn't seen the new Mrs Lane for a couple of days. Or the kid.'

Reacher said nothing.

Brewer said, 'Maybe she's missing and you're looking for parallels in the past.'

Reacher stayed quiet.

Brewer said, 'You were a cop, not a combat soldier. So now I'm wondering what Lane would want to hire you for.'

More silence. A long hard look, cop to cop.

'As you wish,' Brewer said. 'Like I said, it's a free country.'

Reacher finished his coffee and stood up. 'So what do you do with the stuff Patti calls in?'

'I pass it on,' Brewer said. 'To someone with an interest.'

'Who?'

'A private detective. A woman. She's cute, too. Older.'

'NYPD is working with private detectives now?'

'She's retired FBI. The lead agent on the Anne Lane case.'

'Does Patti know?'

Brewer shook his head. 'Better that she doesn't.'

'What's this woman's name?'

'I thought you'd never ask.'

REACHER LEFT Patti's apartment with two business cards. One was Brewer's and the other was an elegant item with *Lauren Pauling* engraved at the top and *Private Investigator* under the name. Then: *Ex-Special Agent, Federal Bureau of Investigation.* At the bottom was a downtown address, with phone numbers for land line, cell and email. It looked professional.

Reacher tossed Brewer's card in a trash can and put Lauren Pauling's in his shoe. It was close to one o'clock in the morning. He saw a cop car on Columbus Avenue. *Cops*, he thought. The word hung up in his mind like a twig on a swirling current catches on a river bank. He closed his eyes and tried to catch it. But it spun away again. He turned into the Dakota's lobby. The night doorman called upstairs. On five Gregory was already out in the corridor. Reacher followed him inside and Gregory said, 'Nothing yet. But we've got maybe seven more hours.'

Everyone was still in the living room.

'I need to sleep,' Reacher said. 'Three or four hours.'

'Use Jade's room,' Lane said.

Reacher nodded and headed off to Jade's room. The bed was way too small for a guy Reacher's size.

He took the pillow and the sheet and the comforter off the bed and made himself a bivouac on the floor. He cleared bears and dolls out of his way. The bears were all plush and new and the dolls looked untouched. He moved the desk to make room and all the papers fell off it. The drawings in wax crayon on cheap paper. Trees, like bright green lollipops on brown sticks, with a big grey building beyond. The Dakota, maybe. There was another of three stick figures, one much smaller than the others. The family, maybe. Mother, daughter, stepfather. Mother and daughter were smiling but Lane was drawn with black holes in his mouth like someone had punched half his teeth out. There was a picture of an airplane low in the sky. The plane's fuselage had three portholes with faces in them. The last picture was of the family again, but twice over. Two Lanes, two Kates, two Jades.

Reacher restacked the papers neatly. He set the alarm in his head for five in the morning. He closed his eyes, breathed once, and fell asleep.

REACHER WOKE as planned at five o'clock, still tired. He found Carter Groom in the kitchen, next to a big Krups coffee machine.

'Three hours to go,' Groom said.

Then Burke came in. He didn't say anything. He acted like the previous evening had never existed. Groom filled three mugs with coffee. Took one, and left the room. Burke took one and followed him. Reacher drank his sitting on the counter.

Time for ex-Special Agent Lauren Pauling's wake-up call.

He stopped in the living room on his way out. Lane was still in the same chair. Real or phoney, it was one hell of a display of endurance. Gregory and Perez and Kowalski were asleep on sofas. Addison was awake but inert. Groom and Burke were drinking their coffee.

'I'm going out,' Reacher said. 'Breakfast.'

Reacher turned right on 72nd and headed for Broadway. Nobody came after him. He found a payphone and dialled Pauling's cell.

She answered on the third ring. 'Hello?' she said.

Rusty voice, not sleepy, just not yet used today.

Reacher asked, 'You heard the name Reacher recently?'

'Should I have?' Pauling asked back.

'It will save us a lot of time if you just say yes. From Anne Lane's sister Patti, through a cop called Brewer.'

'Yes,' Pauling said. 'Late yesterday.'

'I need an early appointment,' Reacher said.

'You're Reacher?'

'Yes, I am. Half an hour, at your office?'

'You know where it is?'

'Brewer gave me your card.'

'Half an hour,' Pauling said.

And so half an hour later Reacher was standing on West 4th Street, with a cup of coffee in one hand and a doughnut in the other, watching Lauren Pauling walk towards him.

PAULING WAS an elegant woman of about fifty. Brewer had said *she's cute*, and he had been right. She was quite tall, dressed in a black pencil skirt. Black stockings, black shoes with heels. An emerald-green blouse that could have been silk. A rope of big fake pearls at her neck. Hair frosted gold and blonde. It fell in big waves to her shoulders. Green eyes that smiled.

'Jack Reacher, I presume,' she said.

Reacher shoved his doughnut between his teeth, wiped his fingers on his chinos and shook her hand. Then he waited as she unlocked her street door. Watched as she deactivated an alarm with a keypad in the lobby. She was right-handed. She used her middle finger, index finger, ring finger, index finger, without moving her hand much. *Probably 8461*, Reacher thought. *Dumb or distracted to let me see. Distracted, probably. She can't be dumb.*

Reacher followed her up to the second floor. She unlocked the door to a two-room suite. Waiting room first, and then a back room for her desk and two visitor chairs. Very compact, but the decor was good. A little bigger, it could have been a lawyer's place, or a cosmetic surgeon's.

'I spoke to Brewer,' she said. 'I called him at home after you called me. He's curious about your motives.'

Lauren Pauling's voice was low and husky. Reacher could have listened to it all day.

'Therefore I'm curious too,' she said.

Reacher sat down. She squeezed around the end of her desk. Sat down.

'I'm just looking for information.'

'But why?'

'Let's see if it leads me to where I need to tell you.'

'Brewer said you were a military cop.'

'Once upon a time.'

'Then you know you shouldn't be talking to me,' she said.

'Why not?'

'Because I'm not a reliable witness.'

'Why?'

'Think about it,' she said. 'If Edward Lane didn't kill his wife, then who the hell did? Well, *I* did, that's who. Through my own carelessness.'

Reacher said, 'Nobody scores a hundred per cent. Not in the real world.'

Pauling nodded. 'It's the sister. She's up there in that weird little eyrie all the time. She's like my conscience.'

'I met her.'

'She weighs on my mind.'

'Tell me about the three of clubs,' Reacher said.

Pauling paused, like a gear change.

'We concluded it was meaningless,' she said. 'There had been a book or a movie or something where assassins left calling cards. So we tended to get a lot of that at the time. But there was nothing in the databases about threes. Not much about clubs, either. We had people with brains the size of planets working on it. Nothing. So the three of clubs was designed to make us chase our tails. What we needed to know was who would want us to.'

'Did you look at Lane back then?'

Pauling nodded. 'We looked at him very carefully, and all his guys. Like, who knew him? Who knew he had money? Who even knew he had a wife?'

'And?'

'He's not a very pleasant man. He's borderline mentally ill. He has a psychotic need to command.'

'Patti Joseph says the same things.'

'She's right.'

'And you know what?' Reacher said. 'His men are a couple of sandwiches short of a picnic, too. They've got a psychotic need to be commanded. They're civilians, but they're holding fast to their old military codes. Like security blankets.'

'The Pentagon wasn't very forthcoming. But we noticed two things. Most of them had been around the block many times, but there were far fewer medals among them than you would expect. And most of them got general discharges. Not honourable discharges. Including Lane himself.'

Reacher nodded. 'It kind of explains why they stick with Lane. Where else are they going to get twenty-five grand a month with their records?'

'Is that what they get? Is that what Lane offered you?'

Reacher said nothing.

'What is he hiring you for?'

'We're not done with the information yet.'

'Anne Lane died, five years ago, in a vacant lot near the New Jersey Turnpike. That's all the hard data we'll ever have.'

'Gut feeling?'

'What's yours?'

Reacher shrugged. 'Brewer said something to me. He said he just didn't know, which was weird for him, he said, because whereas he was sometimes wrong, he always *knew*. And I'm exactly the same. I always know. Except this time I don't know.'

'I think it was a genuine kidnap,' Pauling said. 'I blew it.'

'How did you blow it?'

'I don't know.'

'So maybe it *was* an elaborate charade.'

'What's on your mind, Reacher?'

He looked at her. 'Whatever it was, it's happening again.'

Lauren Pauling sat forward in her chair and said, 'Tell me.' So Reacher told her everything, from the first double espresso in its foam cup, the anonymous driver driving the Benz away, to the drop-off at the exact same fire hydrant.

'If that's a charade it's unbelievably elaborate,' Pauling said.

'My feeling exactly,' Reacher said. 'And if it isn't real, I can't imagine who's doing it. He would need people he trusts, but there's nobody AWOL.'

'Were they getting along? Man and wife?'

'Nobody says otherwise.'

'So it's real.'

Reacher nodded. 'There's an internal consistency to it. The initial take-down must have depended on an inside tip, as to where Kate and Jade were going to be, and when. And they know exactly what cars he's got.'

'And what else?'

'Something that was nagging at me. Something about cops. I asked Lane to repeat what was said during the first phone call. And he did. And the bad guys never said *no cops*. Which suggests these people knew the story from five years ago. They knew Lane wouldn't go to the cops anyway.'

'That would suggest that five years ago was for real.'

'Not necessarily. It might only reflect what Lane put out there for public consumption. But there's one thing I can't make fit any scenario. Which is the initial takedown itself. The only viable method would have been quick and dirty inside the car, as soon as it stopped. Everyone agrees on that. And the problem is, Bloomingdale's is a whole block long. How could anyone have predicted exactly what yard of Lexington Avenue Taylor's Jaguar was going to stop on? And if they didn't predict it exactly right, then the whole thing would have fallen apart immediately.'

'So what are you saying?'

'I'm saying real or fake there's something wrong with this whole thing. I'm saying I can't get a handle on what happened. I'm saying for the first time in my life I just don't know.'

'So what are you going to do?'

'I'm going to have to do it the hard way,' Reacher said.

'What way is that?'

'It's what we called it in the service when we didn't catch a break. You know, start over at square one, re-examine everything, sweat the details.'

'Can I help?'

'I need to know about two guys called Hobart and Knight.'

Pauling nodded. 'Knight was the driver the day Anne was taken and Hobart was in Philadelphia. They died overseas.'

'Maybe they didn't die overseas. They were abandoned wounded but alive. I need to know what's likely to have happened to them.'

'You think they're alive? You think they're back?'

'I don't know what to think. But at least one of Lane's guys wasn't sleeping too well last night.'

'I met Hobart and Knight, you know. Five years ago. At the time of the investigation.'

'Did either of them look like the guy I saw?'

'Medium-sized and ordinary-looking? Both of them, exactly.'

'What are you going to do now?'

'I'm going back to the Dakota. Maybe we'll get a call and this whole thing will be over. But more likely we won't, and it's just the beginning.'

'Give me three hours,' Pauling said. 'Then call my cell.'

Chapter Five

By the time Reacher got back to the Dakota it was seven o'clock and dawn had given way to full morning. The sky was a pale, hard blue. Inside the apartment Reacher didn't need to ask whether the phone had rung. Clearly it hadn't. The tableau was the same as it had been hours earlier. Lane in his chair. Then Gregory, Groom, Burke, Perez, Addison, Kowalski, all silent, all morose, all arrayed here and there, staring into space, breathing low.

Lane turned his head slowly and looked straight at Reacher and asked, 'Where the hell have you been?'

'Breakfast,' Reacher said.

'I pay you to work.'

'You don't pay me at all,' Reacher said. 'I haven't seen dime one yet.'

'Is *that* your problem?' Lane asked. 'Money?'

Reacher said nothing.

'That's easily solved,' Lane said. He levered himself upright, like it was the first time he had moved in hours, which it probably was.

'Come,' he said. Reacher followed him to the master bedroom suite. Lane opened his closet. The narrower of the two doors. Inside was a another door. To the left of the inner door was a security keypad. Lane used his left hand. Index finger. Ring finger. Middle finger. Middle finger . . . *3785*, Reacher thought. *Dumb or distracted enough to let me see.* The keypad beeped and

Lane opened the inner door. Reached inside and pulled a chain. A light came on and showed a chamber maybe six feet by three. It was stacked with cube-shaped bales wrapped tight in heavy plastic. Foreign printing on the plastic.

The printing was French, and it said *Banque Centrale*. Money.

US dollars, bricked and banded and stacked and wrapped. Some cubes were neat and intact. One was torn open and spilling bricks.

Lane dragged the open bale out into the bedroom. Two slim bricks of cash fell out.

'Pick it up,' Lane said. 'It's yours. Take it.'

Reacher stood still.

Lane picked up a spilt brick. 'Take it.'

Reacher said, 'We'll talk about a fee if I get a result.'

'*Take it!*' Lane screamed. Then he hurled the brick straight at Reacher's chest. It struck above the breastbone, dense, surprisingly heavy. Lane picked up the other loose brick and threw it. It hit the same spot. '*Take it!*' he screamed again.

Then he bent down and plunged his hands into the plastic, started hauling out one brick after another. He threw them wildly. They hit Reacher in the legs, in the stomach, in the chest, in the head. Wild random salvos, ten thousand dollars at a time. A torrent. Then there were tears streaming down Lane's face and he was screaming uncontrollably, panting, sobbing, gasping: *Take it! Take it!* Then: *Get her back! Get her back! Get her back!* Then: *Please! Please!*

Smarting slightly from the multiple impacts, Reacher stood there, with hundreds of thousands of dollars littered at his feet, and he thought: *Nobody's that good an actor. This time it's real.*

Reacher walked back to the living room, while Lane calmed down. Lane followed a minute later quietly and calmly and sat down in his chair, like nothing at all had happened. He just sat and stared at the silent phone.

It rang just before seven forty-five. Lane snatched it out of the cradle and said 'Yes?' Then his face went blank. *Wrong caller*. He listened for ten seconds more and hung up.

'Who was it?' Gregory asked.

'Just a friend,' Lane said. 'Cops found a body in the Hudson River this morning. A floater. At the 79th Street boat basin. Unidentified white male, maybe forty years old. Shot once.'

'Taylor?'

'Has to be,' Lane said.

Gregory asked, 'So what do we do?'

'Now?' Lane said. 'Nothing. We wait here. We wait for the right phone call. The one we want.'

It never came. By a quarter to ten in the morning all the resolve had leaked out of Lane's body. He sank into the chair cushion and laid his head back and stared up at the ceiling.

'It's over,' he said. 'She's gone. Hasn't she?'

Nobody answered.

At ten o'clock Lane raised his head off the back of the chair and said, 'OK.' Then he said it again: 'OK.' Then he said, 'Now we move on. We seek and destroy. Justice will be done. Our kind of justice.'

Nobody spoke.

'For Kate,' Lane said. 'And for Taylor.'

Gregory said, 'I'm in.'

'All the way,' said Groom, and the others nodded.

'Thank you,' Lane said.

Then he sat forward, newly energised. He turned to face Reacher directly. 'Almost the first thing you ever said in this room was that these guys of mine could start a war against them, but first we had to find them.'

Reacher nodded.

'So find them,' Lane said.

REACHER STARTED at the same payphone he had used before. Took the card out of his shoe and dialled Lauren Pauling's cell. Said, 'It's real this time and they're not coming back.'

She said, 'Can you be at the United Nations in half an hour?'

REACHER SAW Lauren Pauling waiting for him in the middle of the First Avenue sidewalk. She looked good. She was ten years older than him but he liked what he saw.

'I called in a favour,' she said, walking towards him. 'We're meeting with an army officer who liaises with one of the UN committees.'

'On what subject?'

'Mercenaries,' Pauling said. 'We're supposed to be against them.'

'The Pentagon loves mercenaries.'

'But it likes them to go where it sends them. It doesn't like them to fill their downtime with unauthorised sideshows.'

'Is that where they lost Knight and Hobart? A sideshow?'

'Somewhere in Africa,' Pauling said.

'Does this guy have the details?'

'Some of them. He's reasonably senior, but he's new. He's not going to tell you his name and I haven't told him yours. That's the deal.'

'OK.'

Her cellphone chimed. She listened and looked around.

'We have to go to a coffee shop on Second,' she said. 'He'll follow.'

Pauling led Reacher to a booth in back and sat so she could watch the door. Reacher slid in next to her. He never sat any other way than with his back to a wall. Pauling waved to the waitress and mouthed *coffee* and held up three fingers. The waitress came over and dumped three heavy brown mugs on the table.

Reacher took a sip. Hot, strong and generic.

He made the Pentagon guy before he was even in through the door. Army, but not necessarily a fighting man. Maybe just a bureaucrat. Dull. Not old, not young, corn-coloured buzz cut, cheap blue wool suit, white button-down shirt, striped tie, shoes polished to a mirror shine. A different kind of uniform.

The guy paused and looked around. *Not looking for us*, Reacher thought. *Looking for anyone else who knows him. If he sees somebody, he'll fake a phone call and leave. He's not so dumb after all.*

But the guy evidently saw nothing to worry about. He walked on in and slid in opposite Pauling and Reacher. Up close Reacher saw that he was wearing a black crossed-pistols lapel pin.

'I don't have much for you,' the guy said. 'Private-enterprise Americans fighting overseas are rightly considered to be very bad news, especially when they go to fight in Africa. So this stuff is very need-to-know and, since it was before my time, I don't know much about it.'

'Where was it?' Reacher asked.

'I'm not even sure of that. Burkina Faso or Mali. It was the usual deal. Civil war. A scared government, a bunch of rebels. An unreliable military. So the government buys what protection it can on the international market.'

'Does one of those countries speak French?'

'As their official language? Both of them. Why?'

'I saw some of the money. In plastic wrap printed in French.'

'How much?'

'More than you or I would earn in two lifetimes.'

'US dollars?'

Reacher nodded. 'Lots of them.'

The guy said, 'The story that did the rounds was that Edward Lane took the money and ran.'

'But not everyone got out.'

The guy nodded. 'It seemed that way. Eventually we got a solid report that two Americans had been captured. A year later we got names. It was Knight and Hobart.'

'It surprises me that they stayed alive.'

'The rebels won. Anyone who had worked for the old regime was suddenly in big trouble. And a couple of Americans were like trophies. So they were kept alive. But they suffered very cruelly.'

'Anything about what happened in the end?'

'It's sketchy. One died in captivity, but the other one got out, according to the Red Cross. Some kind of humanitarian gesture that the Red Cross pushed for, to celebrate the fifth anniversary of the coup. They let out a whole bunch. Relatively recently. End of story. But then Immigration has a lone individual entering the US from Africa shortly afterwards on Red Cross documentation. Finally if you jump to the Veterans Administration, there's a report of someone just back from Africa getting the kind of remedial outpatient care that might be consistent with tropical diseases and some of the mutilations that Médecins Sans Frontières reported on.'

Reacher asked, 'Which one got out?'

'I don't know,' the guy said.

'I need his name,' Reacher said. 'And I need his address, from the VA.'

'That's a tall order,' the guy said. 'I would have to go way beyond my remit. And I would need a very good reason to do that.'

Reacher looked pointedly at his lapel and said, 'Ten-sixty-two.'

No reaction.

Reacher said, 'So don't be an asshole. Pony up, OK?'

Still nothing in the guy's face.

'I'll call Ms Pauling's cell,' he said. 'When, I don't know. But I'll get what I can as soon as I can.'

Then he slid out of the booth and walked straight to the door. Opened it and made a right turn and was lost to sight.

'What was that ten-sixty-two thing?' Pauling asked.

'He was wearing a military police lapel pin. MP is his day job. Ten-sixty-two is MP radio code for *fellow officer in trouble, requests urgent assistance*. So he'll help.'

'Then maybe you won't have to do it all the hard way.'

'Maybe. He seemed a little timid. Me, I'd have busted straight into some-body's file cabinet.'

'Maybe that's why he's getting promoted and you didn't.'

'A timid guy like that won't get promoted.'

'He's already a brigadier general,' Pauling said.

'That guy? He was kind of young, wasn't he?'

'No, you're kind of old. Everything's comparative.'

Reacher said, 'NYPD found an unexplained body in the river this morn-ing. White male, about forty. Lane got a call.'

'Taylor?'

'Almost certainly.'

'So what next?'

'We work with what we've got,' Reacher said. 'We adopt the theory that Knight or Hobart came home with a grudge.'

'How do we proceed?'

'With hard work,' Reacher said. 'I'm not going to hold my breath on get-ting anything from the Pentagon.'

'Want to talk it through? I was an investigator once. Think out loud. What doesn't fit?'

'The initial takedown. That doesn't work.'

'What else?'

'Everything.'

'That's too big,' Pauling said. 'Start small.'

'OK,' Reacher said. 'I got out of the black BMW after Burke had switched the bag into the Jaguar and I was surprised how fast the guy was into the driver's seat.'

'So what does that mean?'

'That he was waiting right there on the street.'

'But he wouldn't risk that. If he was Knight or Hobart, Burke would have recognised him in a heartbeat.'

'Maybe he was in a doorway.'

'Three times running? He used that same fireplug on three separate occa-sions. It would be hard to find appropriate cover each time. I've done that job many times. Including one special night five years ago.'

Reacher said, 'Give yourself a break.'

But he was thinking: *Appropriate cover.* Remembered thinking: *It's right there on the same damn fireplug?*

He put his coffee cup down, gently, slowly, and then he picked up Pauling's left hand with his right. Kissed it tenderly. Her fingers were cool and slim and fragrant.

'Thank you,' he said. 'Thank you very much.'

'For what?'

'He used a fireplug three times running. Why? Because a fireplug almost always guarantees a stretch of empty kerb. But he used the *same* fireplug each time. Why? Because he liked that one. But what makes a person like one fireplug more than another?'

'What?'

'Nothing,' Reacher said. 'What this guy had was a *vantage point* that he liked. He needed cover that was reliable and unobtrusive, late night, early morning and rush hour. We need to get down to Sixth Avenue and figure out where it was. Someone might have seen him.'

REACHER AND PAULING caught a cab and it took them all the way south to Houston and then west to Sixth. They got out on the southeast corner and glanced back at the empty sky where the Twin Towers used to be, and then they turned north together into a warm breeze full of trash and grit.

'So show me the famous fireplug,' Pauling said.

They walked north until they came to it, right there in the middle of the block. Fat, short, squat, upright. Pauling stood near the hydrant.

'Where would a military mind want to be?' she asked.

Reacher recited, 'A soldier knows that a satisfactory observation point provides an unobstructed view to the front and adequate security to the flanks and the rear. He knows it provides protection from the elements and concealment of the observers. He knows it offers a reasonable likelihood of undisturbed occupation for the full duration of the operation.'

'What would the duration be?'

'Say an hour maximum, each time.'

'How did it work, the first two times?'

'He watched Gregory park, then followed him down to Spring Street.'

'So he wasn't waiting inside the derelict building?'

'Not if he was working alone.'

'But he still used the back door?'

'On the second occasion, at least.'

'Have we definitely decided he was working alone?'

'Only one of them came back alive.'

'So where was his observation point?'

'West of here,' Reacher said. 'He wanted a full-on view. Nothing too oblique. Range, maybe up to a hundred feet.'

'Across the street?'

Reacher nodded. 'Middle of the block, or not too far north or south of it.'

'So set some limits.'

'A maximum forty-five-degree arc. That's twenty-some degrees north to twenty-some degrees south. Maximum radius, about a hundred feet.'

Pauling turned to face the kerb. She spread her arms out straight and forty-five degrees apart and held her hands flat and upright like mimed karate chops. Scoped out the view. A total of five establishments to consider. The centre three were possibilities. The one to the north and the one to the south were marginal. Her left hand was pointing at a flower store. Then came Reacher's new favourite café. Then came a picture framer. Then a double-fronted wine store. Her right hand was pointing at a vitamin shop.

'A flower store would be no good,' she said. 'It wouldn't be open at eleven forty at night.'

Reacher said nothing.

'The wine store was probably open,' she said. 'But it wouldn't have been at seven in the morning.'

Reacher said, 'Can't hang around in a flower store or a wine store for an hour at a time. And even the café would have been pretty risky. Three separate lengthy spells, someone would have remembered him.'

'So maybe he was just out on the street?'

'No protection from the elements and no concealment. Three times in a row. This part of town, he would have been afraid of getting busted for a drug dealer. Or a terrorist.'

'So where was he?'

'Reasonably high up. A Recon Marine wants an unobstructed view. And he can't guarantee that at street level. A panel truck could park right in front of him at the wrong moment.'

Lauren Pauling turned back to face the kerb and spread her arms again, this time raised at an angle. They bracketed the upper floors of the same five buildings. 'Where did he come from, the first time?' she asked.

'From south of me,' Reacher said. 'From my right. I was facing a little north and east, at the end table. But he was coming back from Spring Street then. No way of knowing where he had started out from.'

'But the last time, after Burke switched the bag, he must have been coming straight from the observation point, right?'

'He was almost at the car when I saw him.'

'From what direction?'

'Actually very similar to the first time,' he said to her.

Pauling brought her right hand south and chopped the air a fraction to the left of the café's most northerly table. That cut the view to half of the building with the flower store in it, and most of the building with the café in it. Above the flower store were three storeys of windows with vertical blinds behind them and printers and stacks of paper on their sills.

'Office suites,' Pauling said.

Above the café were three storeys of windows filled variously with faded drapes of Indian cloth, or macramé hangings, or suspended discs of stained glass. One had nothing at all. One was papered over with newsprint.

'Apartments,' Pauling said.

Between the flower store and the café was a blue recessed door. To its left was a dull silver box, with buttons and nameplates. Reacher said, 'A person who came out that door heading for the fireplug would have to cross north and east through the traffic, right?'

Pauling said, 'We found him.'

THE SILVER BOX to the left of the blue door had six black call buttons in vertical array. The top nameplate had *Kublinski* written very neatly in faded ink. The bottom nameplate clearly belonged to the caretaker and had *Super* scrawled with a black marker pen. The middle four were blank.

'Low rent,' Pauling said. 'Short leases. Transients. Except for Mr or Ms Kublinski.'

'They probably moved to Florida fifty years ago,' Reacher said. 'Shall we try the super?'

Pauling nodded and put an elegant nail on the super's call button and pressed. She was answered by a distorted burst of sound from the speaker.

'Federal agents,' Pauling called. Which was remotely true.

There was another burst of noise from the speaker and moments later the door opened to reveal a tall, gaunt man with a black knitted cap on his head.

'Yes?' he said. Strong Russian accent.

Pauling waved her business card long enough for some of the words to register. 'Tell us about your most recent tenant,' she said.

'Number five,' the guy said. 'One week ago. He responded to an advertisement in the *Village Voice*.'

'We need to see his apartment.'

'I'm not sure I should let you,' the guy said. 'There are rules in America.'

'Homeland Security,' Reacher said. 'The Patriot Act. There are no rules in America any more.'

The guy just shrugged. Headed for the stairs. Reacher and Pauling followed him in. Reacher could smell coffee coming through the walls from the café. There was no apartment number one or number two. Number four was the first door they came to, at the head of the stairs at the back of the building. Then number three was on the same floor, along a hallway at the front of the building. Number five was going to be directly above it, third floor, looking east across the street. Pauling glanced at Reacher, and Reacher nodded.

'The one with nothing in the window,' he said to her.

On the third floor they passed number six at the back of the building and walked forward towards number five. The smell of coffee had faded and been replaced by the universal hallway smell of boiled vegetables.

'Is he in?' Reacher asked.

The super shook his head. 'I only ever saw him twice. He's out now for sure. I was just all over the building fixing pipes.' He used a master key from a ring on his belt and unlocked the door. Pushed it open and stood back.

The apartment was completely empty.

Except for a single upright dining chair. It was the kind of thing you see for sale on the Bowery sidewalks, where the bankrupt restaurant dealers hawk seized inventory. It was set in front of the window and turned slightly north and east.

Reacher stepped over and sat down on the chair. The way his body settled put the fireplug across Sixth directly in front of him. He stood up again and turned a full circle. Saw a door that locked. Saw three solid walls. *A soldier knows that a satisfactory observation point provides an unobstructed view to the front and adequate security to the flanks and the rear. He knows it provides protection from the elements and concealment of the observers. He knows it offers a reasonable likelihood of undisturbed occupation for the full duration of the operation.*

Reacher turned to the super and said, 'Tell us about this guy.'

'He can't talk,' the super said.

'What, like he's a mute?'

'Not by birth. Because of a trauma.'

'Like something struck him dumb?'

'Not emotional,' the super said. 'Physical. He communicated by writing on a pad. He wrote that he had been injured in the service. But he had no visible scarring. And he kept his mouth tight shut all the time. Like he was embarrassed about me seeing something. And it reminded me very strongly of something I saw more than twenty years ago.'

'Which was?'

'I am Russian. For my sins I served with the Red Army in Afghanistan. Once we had a prisoner returned to us by the tribesmen as a warning. His tongue had been cut out.'

THE SUPER TOOK Reacher and Pauling down to his own apartment in the basement. He opened a file cabinet and found the current lease papers for apartment five. They had been signed exactly a week previously by a guy calling himself Leroy Clarkson. Which, as expected, was a blatantly phoney name. Clarkson and Leroy were the first two streets coming off the West Side Highway north of Houston, just a few blocks away.

'You don't see ID?' Pauling asked.

'Not unless they want to pay by cheque,' the super said. 'This guy paid cash.'

The signature was illegible.

The super gave a decent physical description, but it did nothing more than match what Reacher himself had seen. Late thirties, maybe forty, white, medium height and weight, no facial hair. Blue jeans, blue shirt, baseball cap, sneakers, all of them worn and comfortable.

'How long did he pay for?'

'A month. It's the minimum. Renewable.'

'This guy's not coming back,' Reacher said. 'You should go ahead and call the *Village Voice* now. Get them to run your ad again.'

REACHER AND PAULING came out of the blue door and stopped in at the café for espresso.

Pauling said, 'So he wasn't working alone. Because he couldn't have made the phone calls.'

Reacher didn't reply.

Pauling said, 'Tell me about the voice you heard.'

'American,' Reacher said. 'The machine couldn't disguise the words or the cadence or the rhythm. And he was patient. Intelligent, in command, in control, not worried. Familiar with the geography of New York City. Possibly military, from a couple of phrases. He wanted to know Burke's name, which suggests he's familiar with Lane's crew or he was calibrating a lie detector. The distortion was huge. But I felt he wasn't old. There was a lightness there.'

'Unworried and in command makes him sound like the prime mover here. Not like a sidekick.'

Reacher nodded. 'Good point.'

'So who the hell is he?'

'If your Pentagon guy hadn't told us different I'd say it was both Hobart and Knight, both still alive, back here together, working together.'

'But it isn't,' Pauling said.

'So whichever one came back picked up a new partner.'

'One that he trusts,' Pauling said. 'And he did it fast.'

Reacher gazed over at the hydrant.

'Would a remote clicker work at this distance?' he asked.

'For a car?' Pauling said. 'Maybe. Why?'

'After Burke switched the bag I heard a sound like car doors locking. I guess the guy did it from up in his room. He was watching. He didn't want to leave the money in an unlocked car for a second longer than he had to.'

'Sensible.'

'But you know what isn't sensible? Why was he up there and not the other guy? Why would the guy who can't talk go rent the apartment? Anyone who comes into contact with him isn't going to forget him in a hurry. And what's an observation point for? It's for command and control. But this guy couldn't even get on a cellphone.'

'Text messaging,' Pauling said. 'You can send written words by cellphone.'

'OK,' Reacher said. 'But I still don't see why they sent the guy who couldn't talk to meet with the building super.'

'Neither do I,' Pauling said.

Silence for a moment.

'What next?' Pauling asked.

'Hard work,' Reacher said. 'You up for it?'

'Are you hiring me?'

'No, you're volunteering. Because if we do this right you'll find out what happened to Anne Lane five years ago. No more sleepless nights.'

'Unless I find out five years ago was for real. Then I might never sleep again.'

'Life's a gamble,' Reacher said. 'It wouldn't be so much fun otherwise.'

Pauling was quiet for a long moment.

'OK,' she said. 'I'm volunteering.'

Reacher said, 'So go hassle our Soviet pal again. Get the chair. We'll walk it over to the Bowery and find out where it came from. Maybe the new buddy picked it out. Maybe someone will remember him.'

REACHER CARRIED the chair in his hand like a bag and he and Pauling walked east. South of Houston the Bowery had organised itself into a sequence of distinct retail areas. Like a string of official malls. There were electrical supplies, and used office gear, and industrial kitchen equipment, and restaurant front-of-house outlets. Reacher liked the Bowery.

Put the good stuff in the store window was the usual retail mantra. But on the Bowery the store windows were secondary to the sidewalk displays. And the chair in Reacher's hand wasn't the good stuff. So he and Pauling squeezed through the narrow doors and looked at the dusty items inside. They saw a lot of chairs. None looked very comfortable.

The fourth store was where they found what they wanted.

It was a double-width place that had chrome diner furniture out front and a bunch of Chinese owners in back. Behind the gaudy padded stools on the sidewalk, inside the store there were piles of old tables and sets of chairs stacked six high. At the back, hung high on a wall, were two chairs that were exact matches for the specimen in Reacher's hand.

'We shoot, we score,' Pauling said.

Reacher carried the chair to where a Chinese guy was sitting behind a table.

'You sold this chair.' Reacher held it up, then nodded towards the wall where its siblings hung. 'About a week ago.'

'Five dollars,' the old guy said.

'You're not understanding me. I don't want to buy it,' Reacher said. 'And it isn't yours to sell. I want to know who you sold it to.'

The old guy smiled. 'No, I'm understanding you very well. You want information about the purchaser of that chair. And I'm telling you that information always has a price. In this case, the price is five dollars.'

'Who bought it, a week ago?'

'Five dollars.'

'Two-fifty plus the chair.'

'You'll leave the chair anyway. You're sick of carrying it around.'

'I could leave it next door.'

For the first time the old guy's eyes moved. He glanced up at the wall.

Reacher saw him think: *A set of three is better than a pair.*

'Four bucks and the chair,' he said.

'Three and the chair,' Reacher said.

'Three and a half and the chair.'

'Guys, please,' Pauling said. She opened her purse. Took out a fat black wallet and snapped off a crisp ten from a wad as thick as a paperback.

'Ten dollars,' she said. 'And the damn chair. So make it good.'

'He couldn't talk,' the old man said. 'He just kept his mouth closed and gulped like a fish.'

'Description?' Reacher asked.

The old guy launched into the same run-down that the Sixth Avenue super had given.

The old man turned to Pauling and asked, 'Was my information helpful?'

'Maybe,' Pauling said. 'But it didn't add anything.'

'I'm sorry,' the old man said. 'You may keep the chair.'

'I'm sick of carrying it around,' Reacher said.

The old man inclined his head. 'As I thought. Please feel free to leave it.'

Pauling led Reacher out to the Bowery sidewalk, and the last he saw of the chair was a young guy hoisting it up on a pole and hanging it back on the wall next to its two fellows.

'The hard way,' Pauling said.

'Makes no sense,' Reacher said. 'Why are they sending the guy that can't speak to meet with everyone?'

'There must be something even more distinctive about the other one.'

'I hate to think what *that* might be.'

'Lane abandoned those two guys. So why are you helping him?'

'I'm not helping him. This is for Kate and the kid now.'

'They're dead.'

'In that case they need to be avenged, Pauling. Because it wasn't their fight. If Hobart or Knight had come after Lane directly, maybe I'd have been on the sidelines cheering him on. But he didn't. He came after Kate and Jade. And two wrongs don't make a right.'

'Neither do three wrongs.'

'In this case they do,' Reacher said.

'You never even met Kate or Jade.'

'I saw their pictures. That was enough.'

'I wouldn't want you mad at me,' Pauling said.

'No,' Reacher said back. 'You wouldn't.'

PAULING'S CELLPHONE must have vibrated because she pulled it out of her pocket before Reacher heard it ring.

She stopped on the sidewalk and said her name loudly over the traffic noise and then listened for a minute. Said thanks and snapped the phone shut.

'Some solid information. The location was Burkina Faso. It used to be called Upper Volta. It's a former French colony. Population thirteen million, with a GDP about a quarter of what Bill Gates is worth.'

'But with enough spare cash to hire Lane's crew?'

'Not according to my guy,' Pauling said. 'It's where Knight and Hobart were captured, but there's no record of their government contracting with Lane.'

'We need a name. We'll have to try something on our own. Our guy called himself Leroy Clarkson. Maybe it was because he lives over there.'

'Near Clarkson or Leroy?'

'A guy who was making good money before a five-year sentence in an African jail might already have owned a place there.'

Pauling nodded. 'We should stop by my office. Start with the phone book.'

THERE WERE a few Hobarts and half a page of Knights in the Manhattan White Pages but none of them were in the part of the West Village that would have made Leroy Clarkson an obvious pseudonym.

Pauling had other databases, but no unexplained Knights or Hobarts cropped up.

'He's been away five years,' Pauling said. 'Effectively he'll have dropped out of sight, won't he? Disconnected phone, unpaid utilities, things like that?'

'Probably,' Reacher said. 'But not necessarily. These guys are used to sudden travel. They usually set up automatic payments.'

'His bank account would have emptied out.'

Reacher nodded. 'He probably rented anyway. Landlord probably threw all his stuff on the sidewalk years ago.'

'So what do we do?'

'I guess we wait,' Reacher said. 'For your bureaucratic buddy. Unless we grow old and die first.'

But a minute later Pauling's phone went off again. She listened for a minute. Then she closed it slowly. 'We're not much older,' she said.

'What's he got?'

'Hobart,' she said. 'It was Hobart who came back alive.'

Chapter Six

Reacher asked, 'First name?'

Pauling said, 'Clay. Clay James Hobart.'

Reacher asked, 'Address?'

Pauling said, 'We're waiting on an answer from the VA.'

'So let's hit the phone books again.'

'I recycle my old phone books. I don't keep an archive. I certainly don't have anything from five years ago.'

'He might have family here. Who better to come back to?'

'There were seven Hobarts in the book.'

'Call them all,' Reacher said. 'Make like a VA administrator with a paperwork glitch.'

Pauling's cell buzzed again and the Pentagon guy came through with more information. She put it all down on a yellow pad.

'Hobart's address?' Reacher asked her.

'Not yet,' Pauling said. 'The VA is baulking.'

'So what did he have for us?'

'Lane is on an official Pentagon blacklist,' Pauling said.

'Why?'

'You know what Operation Just Cause was?'

'Panama,' Reacher said. 'Against Manuel Noriega. More than fifteen years ago. I was there, briefly.'

'Lane was there, too. He was still in uniform back then. He did very well there. That's where he made full colonel. Then he went to the Gulf the first time around and then he quit under a bit of a cloud. But not enough of a cloud to stop the Pentagon hiring him on as a private contractor. They sent him to Colombia. He took the beginnings of his present crew with him to fight one of the cocaine cartels. He took our government's money to do it, but when he got there he also took the target cartel's money to go wipe out one of their rival cartels instead. The Pentagon wasn't all that upset because one cartel is as bad as another to them, but they never really trusted Lane afterwards and never hired him again.'

'His guys said they'd been to Iraq and Afghanistan.'

Pauling nodded. 'But only as subcontractors. The Pentagon hired someone they trusted and that someone laid off some of the work to Lane. Since Colombia, Lane has been living off the crumbs from other men's tables. Big crumbs at first, but they're getting smaller. There's a lot of competition now. Apparently he got rich that one time in Africa but whatever is left from that payment is all the capital he's got.'

'Was he subcontracting in Burkina Faso too?' Reacher asked.

'He must have been,' Pauling said. 'Otherwise why isn't he in the records as a principal?'

'Was our government involved there?'

'It's possible. My official friend seems a little tense.'

Reacher nodded. 'That's why he's helping, isn't it? This is not one MP to another. This is a bureaucracy trying to control the situation. This is someone deciding to feed us stuff privately so we don't go blundering about and making a lot of noise in public.'

Pauling said nothing. Then her phone went off again. She listened for fifteen seconds and wrote a dollar sign, and then two numbers, and then six zeros on her pad. She clicked off the phone.

'Twenty-one million dollars,' she said. 'In cash. That's how rich Lane got in Africa.'

'You were right. Big crumbs.'

Pauling nodded. 'The whole deal was worth a hundred and five million US dollars from their government's central reserve.'

'OK,' Reacher said. 'What's half of twenty-one?'

'Ten and a half.'

'Exactly. Kate's ransom was precisely half of the Burkina Faso payment. It was a weird amount. But now it makes some kind of sense. Lane probably skimmed fifty per cent as his profit. So Hobart got home and figured he was entitled to Lane's share for his suffering.'

'Reasonable,' Pauling said.

'I would have wanted more,' Reacher said. 'I would have wanted all of it.'

Pauling's cell buzzed again. This time she wrote just three lines.

'We have his address,' she said. 'He lives with his sister. In a building on Hudson Street that I'm betting is on the block between Clarkson and Leroy.'

'A married sister,' Reacher said. 'Otherwise we would have found her name in the phone book.'

'Widowed. I guess she kept her married name.'

The widowed sister was called Dee Marie Graziano and she was right there in the phone book at an address on Hudson. Pauling dialled up a city tax database.

'Rent-stabilised,' she said. 'Been there ten years.' She copied Dee Marie's Social Security number and pasted it into a box in a different database. 'Thirty-eight years old. Marginal income. Doesn't work much. Her late husband was a Marine too. He died three years ago.'

Pauling opened Google and typed *Dee Marie Graziano*. Hit the return key. Glanced at the results and something about them made her click off Google and open LexisNexis. The screen rolled down and came up with a whole page of citations.

'Well, look at this,' she said. 'She sued the government. State and the Department of Defense.'

Pauling hit the print button and fed Reacher the pages. Dee Marie Graziano had waged a five-year campaign to find out what had happened to her brother Clay James Hobart. It had been a long, hard, bitter campaign.

'She was really going at it,' Pauling said. 'Wasn't she?'

'Like Patti Joseph,' Reacher said. 'This is a tale of two sisters.'

'The Pentagon knew Hobart was alive after twelve months. And they knew where he was. But they kept quiet for four years. They let this poor woman suffer.'

'What was she going to do anyway? Lock and load and go to Africa and rescue him single-handed? Bring him back to stand trial for Anne Lane's homicide?'

'There was never any evidence against him.'

Pauling went quiet.

'What?' Reacher said.

'We agree that Hobart picked up a new partner, right?' she said. 'As soon as he got back? One that he trusts, and real fast? Could it be the sister? Is it possible that the voice you heard on the phone in the car was a woman? You said there was a lightness to the voice.'

Reacher nodded. 'Yes, I did.'

'Therefore like a woman.'

'Maybe,' Reacher said. 'Gregory told me a woman showed up in the Hamptons. A fat woman. She and Kate talked.'

'Maybe it was Dee Marie. Maybe she was asking for money. Maybe Kate blew her off and that was the last straw.'

'This is about more than money.'

'But that doesn't mean this isn't at least partly about money,' Pauling said. 'Dee Marie's share would be more than five million dollars. She might think of it like compensation. A million dollars a year for being kept in the dark. For five years of stonewalling.'

'Maybe,' Reacher said again.

Pauling pulled a city directory off her shelf and checked the Hudson Street address.

'They're south of Houston,' she said. 'Between Vandam and Charlton. Not between Clarkson and Leroy. But they're only fifteen minutes from here.'

'They've got blood on their hands and money in their pockets, Pauling. They'll be in the Caymans by now.'

'So what do we do?'

'We head over to Hudson Street, and we hope like crazy that the trail is still a little bit warm.'

REACHER AND PAULING were coming from a position of weakness, in that neither of them was armed and Hobart had met Pauling twice after Anne Lane's disappearance. Pauling had interviewed Lane's whole crew at length after Anne Lane's disappearance. Balancing the disadvantages was Reacher's conviction that the Hudson Street apartment would be empty.

There was no doorman. It was a boxy five-storey tenement faced with dull red brick. It had a black door with an aluminium squawk box chiselled into the frame. Ten black buttons. *Graziano* was written neatly against 4L.

'Walk-up,' Pauling said. 'Central staircase. Long, thin, front-to-back apartments, two to a floor. Four-L will be on the fourth floor, on the left.'

Reacher hit every button except 4L's and said in a loud, slurred voice, 'Can't find my key.' The door buzzed twice and Pauling pushed it open.

Inside was a centre hallway with a staircase on the right.

'Now we wait,' Reacher said. 'At least two people are going to be sticking their heads out looking for whoever lost their key.'

Way above them in the gloom a door opened. Then closed again. Then another door opened. Thirty seconds later it slammed shut.

'OK,' Reacher said. 'Now we're good to go.'

He put his weight on the bottom tread of the staircase and it creaked loudly. Pauling started up behind him.

They walked through the third-floor hallway and turned and glanced up into the fourth-floor gloom. Reacher took the stairs two at a time to cut the number of creaks by half. Pauling put her feet near the edges of the treads where any staircase is quieter. They made it to the top.

Apartment 4L's door had been painted a dull green. There was a clouded spy lens about level with Reacher's chest.

Reacher put his ear on the crack where the door met the jamb. Listened, then straightened up. 'There's someone in there,' he whispered. He bent forward again. 'Straight ahead. A woman, talking.' Then he straightened up and stepped back. 'What's the layout going to be?'

'A short hallway,' Pauling whispered. 'Narrow, until it clears the bathroom. Then maybe it opens out to the living room. The back wall will have a window on the left into the light well. Kitchen door on the right. The kitchen will be bumped out to the back.'

Reacher nodded. Worst case, the woman was in the kitchen, down a straight line of sight to the door. Worse than worst case, she had a loaded gun next to her on the countertop.

'Wait there,' Reacher said. 'If you hear shooting, call an ambulance. If you don't, follow me in six feet behind.'

He took a step back. He was six feet five inches tall and weighed about two hundred and fifty pounds. His shoes were size twelve. The soles were heavy, composite items. The heels were a five-layer stack an inch and a quarter thick. Each shoe weighed more than two pounds.

'Stand by now,' Reacher whispered.

He put his weight on his back foot and stared at the cheap door and bounced like a high jumper, going for a record. Then he launched. One pace, two. He smashed his right heel into the door just above the knob and wood splintered and dust filled the air and the door smashed open and he continued running. Two paces put him in the centre of the living room. He stopped dead there. Lauren Pauling crowded in behind him.

The apartment was laid out exactly as Pauling had predicted. In the kitchen doorway stood a heavyset woman in a shapeless cotton shift. She had long brown hair parted in the centre. In one hand she held an open can of soup. Her eyes and her mouth were open wide in surprise.

In the living room, horizontal on the worn-out sofa, was a man.

This man was sick. Emaciated. He had no teeth. His skin glittered with fever. He had no hands. He had no feet.

Pauling said, *'Hobart?'*

There was nothing left that could surprise the man on the sofa. He moved his head and said, 'Special Agent Pauling. It's a pleasure to see you.'

He had a tongue. He could talk just fine.

Pauling looked at the woman. 'Dee Marie Graziano?'

'Yes,' the woman said.

Pauling turned back to Hobart. 'What the hell happened to you?'

'Africa,' Hobart said. 'Africa happened to me.'

He was wearing stiff new denims, dark blue, and a shirt. The sleeves and legs were rolled to clear the stumps of his wrists and his shins, which were all smeared with a clear salve of some kind. The amputations were crude and brutal, no stitching of the severed flesh, no reconstruction.

'What happened?' Pauling asked again.

'Long story,' Hobart said.

'We need to hear it,' Pauling said.

'Why? The FBI is here to help me now?'

'I'm not FBI,' Pauling said. 'Not any more.'

'So what are you now?'

'A private investigator.'

Hobart's eyes moved to Reacher's face. 'And you?'

'The same,' Reacher said. 'More or less.'

'I was making soup,' Dee Marie Graziano said.

Pauling said, 'Go ahead. Please.'

Reacher pushed the shattered door as far shut as it would go. When he got back to the living room Dee Marie was in the kitchen. Pauling was still staring at the man on the sofa.

'What happened to you?' she asked him for the third time.

'First he eats,' Dee Marie called.

HIS SISTER sat on the sofa next to him and fed him the soup slowly. From time to time Hobart started to raise one of his missing hands to wipe a dribble off his chin. He would look perplexed for a fleeting second and then rueful, as if he were amazed at how long the memory of simple physical routines endured even after they were no longer possible.

'Edward Lane,' Pauling said finally. 'When was the last time you saw him?'

'Five years ago,' Hobart said. 'In Africa.'

'What happened there?'

'I was taken alive. Not smart.'

'And Knight too?'

Hobart nodded. 'Knight too,' he said.

'How?' Reacher asked.

Hobart paused for a long moment.

'There was a civil war in Burkina Faso,' he said. 'There usually is. We had a city to defend. This time it was the capital. It's called Ouagadougou. We called it O-Town.'

'What happened there?' Pauling asked.

'All the action was to the northeast. The tree line was about a mile outside the city limit. Two roads in, like spokes in a wheel. We called them the One o'Clock Road and the Two o'Clock Road. Like the face of a wristwatch? The One o'Clock Road was the one the rebels were going to be using. Except they would be flanking it in the jungle. We wouldn't see them until they passed the tree line and came out in the open. They had a mile of open ground to cross and we had heavy machine guns.'

'So where was the problem?'

'We figured they'd be tracking the One o'Clock Road with half their force on the right shoulder and the other half on the left. We figured about two miles out the half that was on the right would wheel ninety degrees to its left and attempt an outflanking manoeuvre. But that meant that maybe five thousand guys would have to cross the Two o'Clock Road. We'd see them.

'Knight and I had been Recon Marines. So we volunteered to set up forward observation posts. Knight set up with a good view of the One o'Clock Road and I set up with a good view of the Two o'Clock Road. Plan was if they didn't attempt to outflank us we'd take them head-on and if we were making good progress with that our main force would join us. If their attack was heavy Knight and I would fall back to the city limit and set up a secondary line of defence there. And if I saw the outflanking manoeuvre in progress we'd fall back immediately and reorganise on two fronts.'

Reacher asked, 'So where did it all go wrong?'

'I made two mistakes,' Hobart said. He started wheezing.

'He has malaria and tuberculosis,' his sister said. 'You're tiring him.'

'Is he getting care?' Pauling asked.

'We have no benefits. The VA does a little. Apart from that I take him to the St Vincent's ER.'

'How? How do you get him up and down the stairs?'

'I carry him,' Dee Marie said. 'On my back.'

Reacher asked Hobart, 'What two mistakes?'

'There was an early feint,' Hobart said. 'About ten soldiers came out of the trees a mile ahead of Knight. They were going for death or glory. Knight let them run and then he dropped them all with his rifle. I couldn't see him. I crawled over to check he was OK.'

'And was he?'

'He was fine. When I got to Knight's position I realised I could see the Two o'Clock Road even better from his hole. Plus when the shooting starts it's always better to be paired up. So that was my first mistake. I put myself in the same foxhole as Knight.'

'And the second mistake?'

'I believed what Edward Lane told me.'

Reacher asked, 'What did Edward Lane tell you?'

'About thirty minutes after that first feint Lane showed up in Knight's foxhole. He seemed surprised to see me there too. He told me he had new intelligence that we *were* going to see men crossing the Two o'Clock Road but that they would be government troops coming in from the bush and circling around to reinforce us through the rear. Lane told me the higher the number the better, because they were all on our side.'

'And you saw them?'

'Thousands and thousands of them.'

'And then?'

'We sat tight. All day, and into the night. Then all hell broke loose. About five thousand guys just stepped out of the trees on the One o'Clock Road and started straight towards us. At the same time another five thousand stepped out of the bush just south of the four o'clock position and came straight at us. They were the same guys I had counted earlier. They were rebels. Lane's new intelligence had been wrong. Later I realised he had lied to me.'

'What happened?' Pauling said.

'The way I pieced it together afterwards, Lane and his troops had pulled out twelve hours before. He must have got back from his little visit with us and just hopped straight into his Jeep.'

Reacher said, 'What we need to know is why he did that.'

'That's easy,' Hobart said. 'Lane abandoned us because he wanted Knight dead. I just happened to be in the wrong foxhole, that's all.'

'Why did Lane want Knight dead?'

'Because Knight killed Lane's wife.'

PAULING ASKED, 'Did Knight confess that to you?'

At first Hobart didn't answer. Then he said, 'He confessed to about a thousand different things.' Then he smiled ruefully. 'You had to be there. Knight was out of his mind for four years. Me too, probably.'

'So how was it?' Pauling asked. 'Tell us.'

Dee Marie Graziano stood up. 'I don't want to hear this again. I can't hear this again. I'm going out.'

Pauling opened her purse and took out her wallet. Handed a sheaf of notes to Dee Marie. 'Get stuff,' she said. 'Food, medicine.'

'I don't like charity.'

'Then get over it,' Reacher said. 'Your brother needs everything he can get.'

'Take it, Dee,' Hobart said. 'Be sure to get something for yourself.'

Dee Marie shrugged, then took the money. Collected her keys and walked out. Reacher heard the front door open. The hinges squealed where he had damaged them.

'We should call a carpenter,' Pauling said.

'Call that Soviet super from Sixth Avenue,' Reacher said. 'I'm sure he moonlights.' He turned to Hobart. 'You're lucky to have a sister like that.'

'But it's hard on her,' he said.

'Tell us about Knight.'

With his sister gone, Hobart seemed to relax.

'It was one of those unique moments,' he said. 'I mean, you think you've been in deep shit before, and then you realise you have absolutely no conception of how deep that can really be. At first we didn't do anything. Then we just looked at each other and I guess we just took an unspoken decision to go down fighting. So we started firing. They just kept on coming, and we just kept putting them down. We started to have equipment problems, like they knew we would. When they sensed it, they all charged. OK, I thought, bring it on.' He closed his eyes and the little room went quiet.

'But?' Reacher said.

'They got to the lip of the hole and stopped. Some kind of an officer looked down at us and smiled. Black face, white teeth, in the moonlight. We'd just killed hundreds of their guys and we were about to be captured.'

'How did it go down?'

'The first few days were chaos. We were chained all the time. They had no jail facilities. They had nothing, really. But they fed us. Then after a week it was clear the coup had succeeded, so they all moved into O-Town proper and put us in a separate wing in the city prison. We figured they were negotiating with Washington.

'But evidently they gave up on Washington because they tossed us in with the others. And that was bad. Incredible overcrowding, filth, disease, no clean water, almost no food. We were skeletons within a month. Then they put us on trial.'

'You had a trial?'

'I guess it was a trial. I had no idea what they were saying. Then they found us guilty. I figured I was about as low as I could go. But I was wrong. I had a birthday.'

'What happened on your birthday?'

'They hauled out about a dozen guys. I guess we all shared the same birthday. They took us to a courtyard. First thing I noticed was a big bucket of tar on a propane burner. It was bubbling away. Then I saw next to the bucket was a big stone block, all black with blood. Then some big guard grabbed a machete and started screaming at the first guy in line. The guy next to me spoke a little English and translated for me. He said we had a choice. Three choices, actually. To celebrate our birthdays we were going to lose a foot. First choice, left or right. Second choice, short pants or long pants. It meant we could be cut above the knee or below. Third choice, we could use the bucket or not. The boiling tar seals the arteries and cauterises the wound. Choose not to, and you bleed out and die. Our choice.'

Nobody spoke.

Hobart said, 'I chose left, long pants, and yes to the bucket.'

FOR A LONG TIME the small room stayed quiet as a tomb.

Then Hobart said, 'Twelve months later on my next birthday I chose long pants, and yes to the bucket.'

Reacher said, 'They did this to Knight too?'

Hobart nodded. 'We thought we had been close before. But some things really bring you together.'

Pauling was white as a sheet. 'Knight told you about Anne Lane?'

'He told me he shot Anne Lane in New Jersey.'

'Did he tell you why?'

'He gave me a whole bunch of different reasons. Different day, different reasons. Sometimes it was that Lane was mad at her and asked him to do it. Other times he said he was working for the CIA. Once he said she was an alien from another planet.'

'Did he kidnap her?'

Hobart nodded. 'Drove her to the store, but didn't stop there. Just pulled a gun and kept on going, all the way to New Jersey. Killed her there.'

'Immediately?' Pauling asked.

Hobart said, 'Yes, immediately. She was dead a day before you ever even heard of her. There was nothing wrong with your procedures.'

'Were you really in Philadelphia?' Reacher asked.

'Yes, I was,' Hobart said. 'I had no idea what Knight was doing that day.'

'Who faked Anne's voice on the phone?' Pauling asked. 'Who set up the ransom drop?'

'Sometimes Knight would say it was a couple of his buddies. Sometimes he would say Lane took care of all of that.'

Pauling said, 'What was the truth about Anne Lane?'

Hobart smiled, sadly.

'The truth about Anne Lane?' he said. 'Believe me, I obsessed over it. Because, basically, it was responsible for what was happening to me. I think Lane set the whole thing up because Anne wanted a divorce and she wanted alimony. Lane's ego couldn't take it. So he had her killed.'

'Why would Lane want Knight dead if all he had done was act on Lane's own orders?'

'Lane was covering his ass and avoiding being in someone else's debt.'

'What happened to Knight in the end?' Reacher asked.

'His fourth birthday,' Hobart said. 'He didn't go for the bucket. He didn't want to go on. He just quit on me. Some damn jarhead he was.'

TEN MINUTES LATER the squawk box in the hallway sounded and Dee Marie asked for help carrying packages. Reacher went down and hauled four grocery bags back to the kitchen.

Reacher said to her, 'We heard that Kate Lane had a visitor in the Hamptons. Was it you?'

'We thought she should be told what her husband was capable of doing,' Dee Marie said.

'How did she react?'

'She listened. We walked on the sand and she listened.'

'How definite were you?'

'I said we had no proof. Equally I said we had no doubt. She took it all in. Didn't react much.'

'Did you tell her about your brother?'

'It's a part of the story. She listened to it.'

'What happened to your husband?'

'Iraq happened to Vinnie. A roadside booby trap. They told me he was killed instantly. But they always say that.'

REACHER LEFT DEE MARIE in the kitchen and stepped into the living room.

'What would the three of clubs mean to you?' he asked Hobart.

'Knight. Three was his lucky number. Club was his nickname in the Corps. Because of how he liked to party, and because of the pun on his name. Knight Club, nightclub, like that.'

'He left a playing card on Anne Lane's body. The three of clubs.'

'He did? He told me that. I didn't believe him.'

Dee Marie came back to the living room.

Reacher said, 'I need to know where you've been and what you've been doing for the last four days.'

Dee Marie answered. No hesitation. Just a slightly incoherent and therefore completely convincing pieced-together narrative account. The four days had started with Hobart in St Vincent's hospital for forty-eight hours with a severe malaria relapse. Dee Marie had stayed with him most of the time. Then she had brought him home in a taxi. They had been alone in the apartment since then, until their door had smashed open and Reacher had ended up in the middle of their living room.

'Why are you asking?' Hobart said.

'The new Mrs Lane was kidnapped. And her kid.'

'You thought I did it?'

'For a spell. We got a basic report on you and Knight. We heard about mutilations. No details. Then we heard about a guy with no tongue. We thought it was you.'

'No tongue?' Hobart said. 'I'd take that deal.'

'We apologise,' Pauling said.

'No harm, no foul,' Hobart said.

'And we'll help you if we can.'

'See to the woman and the child first.'

'We think we're already too late.'

'Don't say that. Where there's hope, there's life. Hope kept me going, five hard years.'

REACHER AND PAULING left Hobart and Dee Marie together on their battered sofa. They walked down four flights to the street and stepped into the afternoon shadows of a fabulous late-summer day. Traffic ground past on the street, slow and angry. Horns blared. Fast pedestrians swerved by on the sidewalk.

Reacher said, 'Eight million people. Eight million stories in the naked city.'

Pauling said, 'We're nowhere.'

Chapter Seven

'Wat now?' Pauling said.
'Back to the hard way. We wasted time. Wasted energy. My fault. I was stupid.'
'How?'
'Did you see how Hobart was dressed?' ·
'Cheap new denims.'
'The guy I saw driving the cars away was wearing old denims. Old, soft, warm, comfortable denims. No way was the guy just back from Africa. It takes ages to get jeans and a shirt looking like that. The guy I saw has been safe at home for five years doing his laundry.'
Pauling said nothing.
'You can split now,' Reacher said. 'You got what you wanted. Anne Lane wasn't your fault. You can sleep at night.'
'But not well. Because I can't touch Edward Lane. Hobart's testimony is meaningless. OK, Knight's dying declaration would be admissible because the court would assume he had no motive to lie on his deathbed. But there was no dying declaration. There were dozens of random fantasies spun over a four-year period. Hobart chose to back one of them, that's all.'
'So you settle for half a loaf. Patti Joseph, too. I'll drop by and tell her.'
'Would you be happy with half a loaf?'
'Not me. I'm not quitting. My agenda is getting longer by the minute.'
'I'll stick with it too.'
'I'll meet you at Patti Joseph's,' Reacher said. 'Two hours from now. We should travel separately.'
'Why?'
'I'm going to try to get killed.'

WHILE PAULING HEADED for the subway Reacher started walking north on Hudson, not fast, not slow. He crossed Morton, and Barrow, and Christopher. On West 10th he started zigzagging through the narrow tree-lined Village streets, east for a block, then north, then west, then north again. He made it to the bottom of Eighth Avenue and walked north for a spell and then started zigzagging again where the Chelsea side streets were quiet. He stopped in the lee of a brownstone's front steps and bent down and retied his shoes. Walked on. At West 23rd Street he turned east and then north again on Eighth. Patti Joseph and the Majestic lay a little more than two miles ahead in a dead-straight line, and he still had a whole hour to get there.

REACHER FOUND Pauling waiting in an armchair in the Majestic's lobby. She had freshened up. She looked good.

'I stopped by and asked that Russian super,' she said. 'He'll go over later tonight to fix the door.'

'Good,' Reacher said.

'You didn't get killed,' she said.

He sat down. 'Something else I got wrong,' he said. 'I've been assuming there was inside help from one of Lane's crew. But now I don't think so. Lane offered me a million bucks. Anyone watching from the inside would have to assume I was pretty well motivated. And I've shown them that I'm at least partially competent. But nobody has tried to stop me. I just spent two hours strolling through Manhattan. I gave whoever it might be a dozen chances to take me out. But nobody tried.'

'How could they have done this thing without inside help?'

'I have absolutely no idea.'

They checked in at the desk and then rode up to seven. Patti Joseph was out in the corridor. There was a little awkwardness. Patti had spent five years thinking Pauling had failed her sister. So there was ice to break. But the implied promise of news helped Patti thaw.

'So what's up?' Patti asked, as she walked to the kitchen to set up the coffee machine.

Ten minutes later Patti Joseph was in tears. Tears of grief, tears of relief, tears of closure. Tears of anger.

'Where is Knight now?' she asked.

'Knight died,' Reacher said. 'And he died hard.'

'Good. I'm glad. What are we going to do about Lane?'

'That remains to be seen.'

'I should call Brewer.'

'Brewer can't do anything. There's no evidence. Not the kind that a cop or a prosecutor needs.'

'Why are you here? In New York, in and out of the Dakota?'

Reacher said nothing.

'I'm not a fool,' Patti said. 'And I know that the day after I stop seeing

Kate Lane and Jade any more, you show up and people put bags in cars and you come here to interrogate Brewer about the last time one of Edward Lane's wives disappeared.'

Reacher asked. 'Why do you think I'm here?'

'I think he's done it again.'

Reacher looked at Pauling and Pauling shrugged like maybe she agreed Patti deserved to hear the story. So Reacher told her everything he knew. Told her all the facts, all the assumptions, all the questions, all the conclusions.

When he finished Patti stood up and stepped over to an armoire drawer and pulled out a packet of photographs. Tossed the packet into Reacher's lap. Close to the end of the stack he saw Dee Marie Graziano, coming out of the Dakota's lobby.

'That's Hobart's sister, am I right?' Patti said. 'That's when the Dakota doorman told her the family was in the Hamptons. Then she went out there.'

'So?'

'Kate Lane takes this weird woman walking on the beach, and she hears a fantastical story, but there's something about it that stops her from just dismissing it out of hand. Maybe enough to make her ask her husband for an explanation. In which case all hell would break loose. Suddenly Kate's as bad as Anne was.'

'Lane would have gone after Hobart and Dee Marie, too.'

'If he could find them. You only found them with help from the Pentagon.'

'Two questions,' Reacher said. 'If this is Anne all over again, why is Lane pushing me to help?'

'He's putting on a show for his men,' Patti said.

'Second question,' Reacher said. 'Who could be playing Knight's part this time around?'

Patti paused. 'It's an inconvenient detail,' she said. 'Because there's nobody missing.' Then she said, 'OK, I apologise. Maybe you're right. Just because it was fake for Anne doesn't mean it's fake for Kate. But just remember: you're not looking for a woman he loves. You're looking for a prize possession. This is like somebody stole a gold watch from him and he's angry about it.'

REACHER AND PAULING rode down to the Majestic's lobby in silence. They stepped out to the sidewalk. Early evening. Four lanes of traffic and lovers in the park. Dogs on leashes, tour groups.

Pauling asked, 'Where now?'

'Take the night off,' Reacher said. 'I'm going back to the lions' den.'

Pauling headed for the subway and Reacher headed for the Dakota. The doorman sent him up without making a call. Either Lane had put him on some kind of approved list or the doorman had grown accustomed to his face.

Reacher knocked and Kowalski opened up. He seemed to be alone. Reacher stepped inside.

'Where is everybody?' Reacher asked.

'Out shaking the trees,' Kowalski said.

'What trees?'

'Burke thinks we're being visited by ghosts from the past.'

'Knight and Hobart,' Reacher said. 'Waste of time. They died in Africa.'

'Not true,' Kowalski said. 'A friend of a friend of a friend called a VA clerk. Only one of them died in Africa.'

'Which one?'

'We don't know yet. But we'll find out. Everyone has a price. And a VA clerk's is pretty low.'

They moved to the deserted living room.

'Did you know them?' Reacher asked. 'Knight and Hobart?'

'Sure,' Kowalski said.

'So whose side are you on? Theirs or Lane's?'

'Lane pays me. They don't.'

Reacher headed for the master bedroom.

Kowalski said, 'Where are you going?'

'To count the money.'

'Is that OK with Lane?'

'He wouldn't have given me the combination if it wasn't.'

'He gave you the combination?'

I hope so, Reacher thought.

Reacher opened the closet door and entered *3785* on the keypad. There was an agonising second's wait and then the inner door's latch clicked.

Reacher pulled on the door and tugged on the light chain. A narrow walk space on the left, money on the right. Bales of it. All of them intact except for one that was half empty. Reacher dragged it out.

'You know how to count?' Reacher asked Kowalski.

'Funny man,' Kowalski said.

Reacher stepped back to the closet. Hefted an intact plastic bale off the top of the pile. On one face under the legend *Banque Centrale* there was smaller print that said *Gouvernement National, Ouagadougou, Burkina Faso*. Under that was printed: *USD 1,000,000*. Reacher saw Ben Franklin's face. Hundred-dollar bills. Ten thousand of them. A million bucks.

Altogether there were ten intact bales. And ten empty wrappers.

'Fifty packets,' Kowalski called from the bed. 'Ten thousand dollars each.'

It's five hundred grand. Total of ten and a half million still here, total of ten and a half million gone.

Original grand total, twenty-one million dollars.

Reacher led Kowalski to the office. He glanced around. At the computer. At the file drawers. Something about them nagged at him. Then a new thought struck him. Like an ice cube dropped down the back of his neck.

'What trees are they shaking?' he asked.

'Hospitals,' Kowalski said. 'We figure whoever is back has got to be sick.'

Silence for a moment.

'I'm going out again,' Reacher said. 'You stay here.'

Three minutes later he was at the payphone dialling Pauling's cell.

Pauling answered on the second ring. 'Jump in a cab and get over to Dee Marie's place. Lane and his guys are out scouting hospitals. They don't know which one came back yet. But it's only a matter of time before they hit St Vincent's and buy Hobart's address. So I'll meet you there. We're going to have to move them.'

He hung up and flagged a cab.

UP ON THE FOURTH FLOOR the apartment door still hung open on its splintered frame. Beyond it were voices in the living room. Dee Marie's and Pauling's. Reacher stepped inside. Pauling was wearing jeans and a T-shirt. Hobart was propped up on the sofa. He looked bad. But his eyes were blazing.

'Lane's coming here?' he asked.

'Maybe,' Reacher said. 'Can't discount the possibility.'

'So what are we going to do?'

'We're going to be smart. We're going to make sure he finds an empty apartment.'

Hobart nodded, a little reluctantly.

'Where should you be?' Reacher asked him. 'Medically?'

'Medically? I have no idea. I guess Dee Marie did some checking.'

Dee Marie said, 'Birmingham, Alabama, or Nashville, Tennessee. One of the big university hospitals down there. I got brochures. They're good.'

'We can't get him to Birmingham or Nashville tonight.'

'We can't get him there ever. The surgery alone could be over two hundred thousand dollars. The prostheses could be even more than that.' Dee Marie picked up two brochures from a small table and handed them over.

'Looks good,' Reacher said after a minute. He put them back on the table.

'Pie in the sky,' Dee Marie said.

'A motel tonight,' Pauling said. 'Somewhere close.'

Reacher stepped out the front door. Checked the stairwell. Nothing was happening. He came back inside and pulled the door as far closed as it would go. Turned left in the entry and walked to the bedroom.

He stepped to the window and glanced north. He glanced south. And saw a black Range Rover pulling in to the kerb.

Licence plate: OSC 19.

Reacher spun around, strode back to the living room.

'They're here,' he said. 'Now.'

'What do we do?' Dee Marie said.

'Bathroom,' Reacher said. 'All of you. Now.'

He stepped over to the sofa and lifted Hobart. Carried him to the bathroom and laid him gently in the tub. Dee Marie and Pauling crowded in after him.

'They shouldn't find you here,' Pauling said.

'Lock the door,' Reacher said. 'Sit tight and keep quiet.'

He stood in the hallway and a second later the intercom buzzed. He hit the button and said, 'Yes?' Heard a voice. 'VA visiting nurse service.'

Reacher smiled. *Nice*, he thought.

He hit the button again and said, 'Come on up.'

Then he walked back to the living room and sat down on the sofa to wait. Reacher heard loud creaking from the staircase. Three people, he guessed.

First into the living room was Perez, the tiny Latino guy.

Then Addison, with the knife scar above his eye.

Then Edward Lane himself.

'The hell are you doing here?' he asked.

'I beat you to it,' Reacher said.

'It was you who broke down the door?'

'I didn't have a key.'

'Where is Hobart?'

'In the hospital.'

'Bull. We just checked.'

'Not here. In Alabama, or Tennessee.'

'How do you figure that?'

'He needs specialised care. St Vincent's recommended one of those big university hospitals down south.'

Reacher pointed at the small table and Edward Lane picked up the shiny brochures. 'Which one?'

Reacher said, 'It doesn't matter. Hobart didn't kidnap Kate.'

'You think?'

'No, I know. You should have asked why he was at St Vincent's.'

'We did. They said malaria.'

'He's a quadruple amputee,' Reacher said. 'Can't walk, can't drive, can't hold a gun or dial a telephone.'

Nobody spoke.

'It happened in prison,' Reacher said. 'Back in Burkina Faso. The new regime had a little fun.'

Nobody spoke.

'After you all ran away and left him behind,' Reacher said.

'You don't know how it was,' Lane said.

'But I know how it is now,' Reacher said.

'I still want to find him,' Lane said.

'Why?'

No answer. *Checkmate*. Lane couldn't say why without admitting what he had asked Knight to do for him five years previously.

'I'm close,' Reacher said. 'I'll give you the guy.'

'When?'

'When you give me the money.'

'What money?'

'You offered me a million bucks.'

'To find my wife. It's too late now.'

'OK,' Reacher said. 'So I won't give you the guy.'

'I could have it beaten out of you.'

'You try that shit and I'll bend you over and I'll use Addison's head to hammer Perez up your ass like a nail.'

'I don't like threats.'

'This from the guy who said he'd have me blinded?'

Silence in the room.

'OK, a million bucks. When do I get the name?'

'Tomorrow,' Reacher said.

Lane nodded. Said to his men, 'Let's go.'

Addison said, 'Where's the bathroom?'

Reacher stood up, slowly. Said, 'Go home and use yours.'

'What?'

'You're not fit to piss in the same bowl as him. You left him behind.'

'You weren't there.'

'For which you can thank your lucky stars. I'd have kicked your ass and dragged you up the line by your ears.'

Lane took a step forward. 'The sacrifice was necessary to save the unit.'

Reacher looked straight at him. 'Sacrificing and saving are two different things. Now get these runts out of here,' he said.

Silence for a long moment. Nothing in Perez's face, a scowl on Addison's, shrewd judgment in Lane's eyes.

'The name,' Lane said. 'Tomorrow.'

'I'll be there,' Reacher said.

Lane nodded to his men and they trooped out. Reacher waited for the street door to bang and then he stepped back to the bedroom. Watched the Range Rover take off north. He walked to the bathroom.

'They're gone,' he said.

Reacher carried Hobart back to the sofa. Pauling looked down at the floor and said, 'We heard everything.'

Hobart said, 'You were minutes away from getting hurt bad. Lane doesn't hire nice people.'

'He hired you.'

'I'm not a nice person,' Hobart said. 'I fit right in.'

Reacher asked, 'Suppose it had been Perez and Addison in those forward OPs in Africa? Would you have left them there? Bottom line?'

'No way. And I sure as hell don't see how they could have left me there.'

Pauling said, 'We should move you.'

'No need now,' Dee Marie said. 'They won't come back. Right now this is the safest place in the city.'

Then the buzzer sounded and they heard a Russian accent on the intercom. The super from Sixth Avenue, come to fix the broken door.

'Now we're definitely OK,' Dee Marie said.

So Pauling paid the Russian and she and Reacher walked down the stairs to the street.

PAULING WAS QUIET and faintly hostile as they walked. Avoided looking even close to Reacher's direction.

'What?' Reacher asked.

'We heard everything from the bathroom. You signed on with Lane. You sold out. You're working for him now.'

'I wanted to test him,' Reacher said. 'I'm working for Kate and Jude. I still need proof it's for real this time. If it wasn't, he'd have backed off. He wants the guy. Therefore there is a guy.'

'I don't believe you. Lane's gambling. He's putting on a show for his men and gambling that he's smarter than you are.'

'But he had just found out that he's not smarter than I am. I found Hobart before he did.'

'Whatever, this is about the money, isn't it?'

'Yes,' Reacher said. 'It is.'

'At least you might try to deny it.'

Reacher smiled and kept on walking.

'What are you going to do with a million dollars? Buy a house? A car? A new shirt? I liked you. I thought you were better than this.'

He said, 'Pauling, give me a break.'

'Why would I?'

'Because first I'm going to pay you for your time and your services and your expenses, and then I'm going to send Hobart down to Birmingham or Nashville and get him fixed up right. I'm going to rent him a place to live and I'm going to give him some walking-around money. And then if there's anything left, then sure, I'll buy myself a new shirt.'

'Seriously?'

'Dead serious. He deserves it. That's for sure. And it's only right that Lane should pay for it.'

Pauling stopped walking. 'I'm sorry,' she said.

'Then make it up to me.'

'How?'

'Work with me. We've got a lot to do.'

'You told Lane you'd give him a name tomorrow.'

'I had to get him out of there.'

'Can we do it by tomorrow?'

'I don't see why not.'

'Where are we going to start?'

'I have absolutely no idea.'

THEY STARTED in Lauren Pauling's apartment. She lived in a small co-op on Barrow Street, near West 4th. Her apartment was painted mostly yellow and felt warm and friendly. There was an alcove bedroom, and a bathroom, and a kitchen, and a room with a sofa and a chair and a television set and a lot of books. There were small framed photographs of children, but Reacher knew without asking that they were nephews and nieces.

He sat on the sofa and rested his head back on the cushion. He liked a short and finite time to crack a problem.

Pauling called out for Indian food. The clock in Reacher's head crawled around to nine thirty. The sky outside the window turned from navy-blue to black and the city lights burned bright.

'Do that thing again,' Reacher said. 'The brainstorming.'

'OK,' Pauling said. 'What was the very first false note?'

Reacher closed his eyes and recalled the beginning. He recalled Gregory's walk in from the kerb.

He said, 'Gregory asked me about the car I had seen the night before and I told him it drove away before eleven forty-five, and he said no, it must have been closer to midnight.'

Pauling said, 'You don't wear a watch.'

'I'm usually pretty sure what time it is.'

'What was the next thing?'

Reacher said, 'Something about getting into Gregory's car. The blue BMW. Something rang a bell. In retrospect.'

'You don't know what?'

'No.'

'Then what?'

'Then we arrived at the Dakota. After that, everything was about the photograph.'

Pauling said, 'We need to take a break. I've got white wine.'

'You didn't blow it five years ago. You did everything right. We should take a minute to celebrate that.'

Pauling took a bottle out of the refrigerator and opened it. Filled two glasses.

She moved back to the sofa with the wine. Reacher asked, 'Did you quit because of Anne Lane?'

She said, 'Not directly. But ultimately, yes.'

Reacher stopped talking and watched her. She looked great. Reacher liked women as much as any guy but he was always ready to find something wrong with them. There was nothing wrong with Lauren Pauling. Nothing at all. That was for sure.

'Anyway, congratulations,' he said. 'Sleep well tonight.'

'Maybe I won't get the chance,' she said.

He could smell her fragrance. Subtle perfume, soap, clean skin. Her hair fell to her collarbone. She was slim and toned, except where she shouldn't be.

She said, 'Maybe we'll be working all night.'

He said, 'All work and no play makes Jack a dull boy.'

'You're not a dull boy,' she said.

'Thank you,' he said, and leaned forward and kissed her, just lightly, on the lips. Pulled her closer and kissed her harder.

'I don't usually do this,' she said, her mouth against his. 'Not to people I work with.'

'We're not working,' he said. 'We're taking a break.'

'We're celebrating. We're celebrating the fact that we're not Hobart or Kate Lane.'

'I'm celebrating the fact that you're you.'

'Older woman,' she said. 'We're worth it.'

He didn't answer. Just smiled and kissed her neck below her ear.

SHE RAISED her arms over her head and held the pose and he pulled her shirt off. She was wearing a tiny black bra. He raised his arms in turn and she knelt up on the sofa and hauled his shirt up over his head. She spread her hands like small starfish on the broad slab of his chest. Ran them south to his waist. Undid his belt. He unclipped her bra. Lifted her up and laid her down flat on the sofa and kissed her breasts. By the time the clock in his head was showing five past ten they were in her bed, locked together, making love with a kind of patience and tenderness he had never experienced before.

Afterwards they showered together and drank their wine and went back to bed. Reacher just floated, warm, spent, happy.

MUCH LATER Reacher woke to find Pauling's hands over his eyes. She asked him, 'What time is it?'

'Eighteen minutes to seven,' he said. 'In the morning.'

'You're unbelievable.'

'It's not a very useful talent. Saves me the cost of a watch, maybe.'

'What would it mean if Gregory was wrong about the time of the first ransom pick-up and you were right?'

He opened his mouth to say *I don't know*.

But then he stopped.

Because suddenly he saw what it would mean.

'You got a flashlight?' he asked.

'There's a small Maglite in my purse.'

'Put it in your pocket,' he said. 'Leave the purse at home. And wear some trousers.'

Chapter Eight

They walked, because it was a beautiful city morning. They took it slow, to time it right. They turned east on Spring Street at seven thirty exactly.

Reacher stopped outside the chocolate shop. Peered in. There was a light in the kitchen. He could see the owner moving about.

He knocked on the glass, loud, and she turned. Undid the locks and opened the door.

He asked, 'Can we come through to the alley again?'

The owner asked, 'Are you really exterminators?'

'Investigators,' Pauling said. She had a business card ready.

'What are you investigating?'

'A woman disappeared,' Reacher said. 'And her child.'

The owner asked, 'You think they're next door?'

'No,' Reacher said. 'Nobody's next door. This is just routine.'

Pauling and Reacher stepped inside. Pauling followed Reacher through the kitchen, down the hallway and out through the back door to the alley.

The rear of the abandoned building was exactly as Reacher had last seen it. He bent down. Took off his shoe and used the heel to break a ground-floor window. He put his shoe back on. Put his arm through the hole in the glass and groped around until he found the inside door handle. He unlocked it and withdrew his arm carefully.

'OK,' he said.

He opened the door to let Pauling get a good look.

'You up for a trip down the ladder?'

'Why me?'

'Because if I'm wrong I might just give up and stay down there for ever.'

Pauling craned in and took a look. She turned around and backed up to the void. Reacher took her right hand and she swung her left foot and left hand onto the ladder. Let Reacher's hand go and climbed down.

He saw her flashlight beam stab the gloom. She called, 'Where am I going?'

'The front of the building. Directly underneath the door.'

The flashlight beam levelled out.

Pauling reached the front wall, directly beneath the door.

'Look down now,' Reacher called. 'What do you see?'

The beam stabbed downwards. 'I see trash,' Pauling called.

Reacher called, 'Look closer.'

The flashlight beam traced a small random circle. Then a wider one. Then it stopped dead and held steady.

'OK,' Pauling called. 'Now I see. But how did you know?'

Reacher said nothing. Pauling bent down. Stood up again. In her right hand was the flashlight. In her left hand were two sets of car keys, one for a Mercedes-Benz and one for a BMW.

PAULING TOSSED the keys up to Reacher. Both sets were on chrome split rings. Both had a single large car key and a remote clicker. He put them in his pocket. Then he caught Pauling's arm and hauled her off the ladder to the safety of the alley.

'This whole thing with the mail slot was a pure decoy,' he said, closing the door and putting his arm back through the hole in the glass to lock it from the inside. 'The guy already had keys from the file cabinet in Lane's office.'

'So you were right about the time.'

Reacher nodded. 'The guy was in the apartment above the café. Looking out the window. He watched Gregory park at eleven forty and just came out and crossed Sixth Avenue and used the valet key from his pocket. Immediately, much closer to eleven forty than midnight.'

'Same thing with the blue BMW the second morning.'

'Exactly the same thing,' Reacher said.

'And that's why he specified the cars so exactly. He needed to match them with the stolen keys.'

'And that's why it bugged me later on. I realised that when Gregory let me into his car that first night, he used the remote thing from ten feet away, like anyone would. But the night before the other guy didn't do that with the Mercedes. Because he didn't have the remote. All he had was the valet key. Which also explains why he used the Jaguar for the final instalment. He wanted to be able to lock it from the other side of the street, as soon as Burke put the money in it. The only remote he had was for the Jaguar. He inherited it at the initial takedown.'

Pauling was quiet for a second. 'You're back to saying there was inside help. Aren't you?'

'The guy with no tongue. He's the answer to the whole ball game.'

PAULING AND REACHER were back in Pauling's office before nine.

'We need Brewer now,' Reacher said. 'And Patti Joseph.'

'Brewer's still asleep,' Pauling said. 'He works late.'

'Today he's going to work early. Because we need a definitive ID on that body from the Hudson River.'

'Taylor?'

'We need to know for certain it's Taylor. I'm sure Patti has got a photograph of him. Brewer could use it to make the ID for us.'

So Pauling called Patti Joseph. Patti confirmed that she had a file of photographs of all Lane's men. She agreed to pick out the best full-frontal and put it aside for Brewer to collect. Then Pauling called Brewer and woke him up. He was bad-tempered about it but he agreed to pick up the picture.

'Now what?' Pauling asked. 'Lane is expecting a name today.'

'Today lasts until midnight,' Reacher said. 'And there's something I need to check before we do anything else,' he said.

'What?' Pauling asked.

'The phone book first,' he said. 'T for Taylor.'

She hauled the Manhattan White Pages off the shelf and opened it on the desk. She asked, 'Initial?'

'No idea,' he said. 'Look for private individuals in the West Village.'

Pauling ended up with seven possibilities. West 8th Street, Bank, Perry, Sullivan, West 12th, Hudson and Waverly Place.

Reacher said, 'Start with Hudson Street. Check the city directory and find out what block that address is on.'

'It's exactly halfway between Clarkson and Leroy,' she said. 'What's going on here?'

'Your best guess?'

'The guy with no tongue knew Taylor? Lived with him? Was working with him? Killed him?'

Reacher said nothing.

'Wait,' Pauling said. 'Taylor was the inside man, wasn't he? He stole the valet keys. He stopped the car outside Bloomingdale's exactly where the other guy, the guy with no tongue, wanted him to. You were always worried about the initial takedown. That's the only way it could have worked.'

Reacher said nothing.

'What exactly is going on here?'

'We're sweating the details and we're working the clues. We're doing it the hard way. Next step, we go visit the Taylor residence.'

'Now?'

'It's as good a time as any.'

They walked. Second-storey air conditioners dripped condensation like fat raindrops. Vendors hawked fake watches and umbrellas. The city, in full tumult. Reacher liked New York more than most places. He liked the casual indifference of it all, the frantic hustle and the anonymity.

Taylor's number matched a brick cube sixteen storeys high. It had a plain entrance but a decent lobby. One lone guy behind a long desk.

'Approach?' Pauling asked.

'The easy way,' Reacher said. 'The direct approach.'

They pulled the street door and stepped inside. Reacher walked straight to the desk.

'Here's the deal,' he said. 'This lady will give you four hundred bucks if you let us into Mr Taylor's apartment.'

Concierges are human. And it was a well-chosen sum. It was big enough to feel like serious cash. And in Reacher's experience it created an irresistible temptation to bargain upwards towards five hundred. And in Reacher's experience once that temptation had taken hold the battle was won.

The guy paused, glanced left, glanced right. Saw nobody. Said, 'OK, I'll send a handyman.'

But you'll keep the cash for yourself, Reacher thought.

'Five hundred,' the guy said.

Reacher said, 'Deal.'

Pauling took her wallet from her purse, opened it and counted off five hundred-dollar bills and slipped them across the desk.

'Twelfth floor,' the concierge said. 'Turn left, go to the door at the end on the right. The handyman will meet you.' He pointed towards the elevator bank. Reacher and Pauling stepped over and pressed the UP arrow.

'You owe me a lot of money,' Pauling said, as the elevator door slid open.

'I'm good for it,' Reacher said. 'I'll be rich tonight.'

The elevator car stopped on twelve and the door slid back. They turned left and found the end door on the right, waited right outside.

Reacher asked, 'What's he paying for a place like this?'

'Rental?' Pauling glanced at the distance between doors to judge the size of the apartments and said, 'Small two-bedroom, maybe four grand a month. Maybe four and a quarter.'

'That's a lot.'

The elevator bell dinged and a man in a green uniform stepped off. The handyman. He walked up and unlocked Taylor's door, and stepped back.

Reacher went in first. The air inside was hot and still. There was a foyer the size of a phone booth and then a stainless-steel kitchen on the left and a coat closet on the right. Living room dead ahead, two bedrooms side by side away to the left. The kitchen and the living room were spotless. The decor was modern, restrained, tasteful, masculine. Classic pieces. There were lots of books, shelved alphabetically. A small television set. A large number of CDs.

'Very elegant,' Pauling said.

The bigger of the two bedrooms was spare, almost monastic. White walls, a king-sized bed, grey linens. The closet was full of suits and jackets and shirts and trousers grouped precisely by season and colour.

'This is amazing,' Pauling said. 'I want to marry this guy.'

Reacher moved on to the second bedroom. It was a small, plain, undecorated space. There was no light bulb in the ceiling fixture. The room held nothing but two narrow iron beds. There were used sheets on them. Dented pillows. The window was covered with a width of black fabric.

Reacher said, 'This is where Kate and Jade were hidden.'

Pauling examined the pillows. 'Long dark hairs,' she said.

Reacher walked back to the living room and checked the desk. Some personal papers, some financial papers. Taylor's first name was Graham. He was a UK citizen and a resident alien. There was a console telephone on the desk. It looked brand new. It had ten speed-dial buttons with paper strips next to them under plastic. The paper strips were marked with initials. At the top was L. For Lane, Reacher guessed. He hit the corresponding button and a 212 number lit up in a grey LCD window. He hit the other nine buttons one after the other. The grey window showed three 212 numbers, three 917 numbers, two 718s, and a long number with 01144 at the beginning. The 212s would all be Manhattan. Buddies, probably. The 917s would be cellphones. Maybe for the same set of guys. The 718s would be for Brooklyn. The long 01144 number would be for Great Britain. Family, maybe. The corresponding initial was S.

Reacher kept on pressing buttons on the phone for a while and then he finished up.

'You think there are doormen here twenty-four hours?' Reacher asked.

'I doubt it,' Pauling said. 'Not this far downtown. Mine aren't. They're probably part-time here. Maybe until eight.'

'Then that might explain the delays. He couldn't bring them in past a doorman. The first day, he would have had to wait hours. Then he kept the intervals going for consistency.'

'And to create an impression of distance.'

'That was Gregory's guess. He was right and I was wrong.'

Pauling asked, 'What next?'

'I'd like to meet with your Pentagon buddy again. Make him an offer.'

'What can we offer him?'

'Tell him we'll take Lane's crew off the board if he helps us out with one small piece of information. He'll take that deal.'

'Can we deliver that?'

'Sooner or later it's going to be them or us.'

So Pauling played phone tag around the UN building, looking for her friend. Reluctantly he agreed to meet in the same coffee shop as before, at three o'clock in the afternoon.

'Time is moving on,' Pauling said.

'It always does. Try Brewer again.'

But Brewer wasn't at his desk and his cell was off.

THEY WERE in the Second Avenue coffee shop forty minutes early.

'You've got a theory,' Pauling said to Reacher. 'Haven't you? Like a physicist. A unified theory of everything.'

'No,' Reacher said. 'Not everything. It's only partial. I'm missing a big component. But I've got a name for Lane.'

'What name?'

'Let's wait for Brewer,' Reacher said. He waved to the waitress. The same one as before. He ordered coffee. Same hot, strong, generic taste.

Pauling's phone buzzed thirty minutes before the Pentagon guy was due to show. She listened for a spell and then gave their location. Then she hung up.

'Brewer,' she said. 'Finally. He wants to talk face to face. He's meeting us here.'

'He's going to arrive at the same time as your guy.'

'My guy's not going to like that. I don't think he likes crowds.'

But Pauling's Pentagon friend showed up a little early.

'I'm concerned about your offer,' he said. 'I can't condone illegality.'

Reacher thought, *Be grateful for once in your miserable life.* But he said, 'I understand your concern, sir. And you have my word that no cop or prosecutor anywhere in America will think twice about anything that I do.'

The guy paused. 'So what do you want me to do?'

'I need you to check a passenger name against flight manifests out of this area during the last forty-eight hours.'

'Military?'

'No, commercial.'

'Which airport? What flight?'

'I'm not sure. I'd start with JFK. British Airways, United or American to London, England. I'd start with late evening the day before yesterday. Failing that, try Newark. No hits, try JFK again yesterday morning.'

'OK,' the guy said. Then he asked, 'Who am I looking for? One of Edward Lane's crew?'

Reacher nodded. 'A recent ex-member.'

'Name?'

Reacher said, 'Taylor. Graham Taylor. He's a UK citizen.'

The Pentagon guy left with a promise to liaise via Pauling's cellphone.

Pauling said, 'You didn't find Taylor's passport in his apartment. So either he's still alive or someone's impersonating him.'

Reacher said nothing.

Pauling said, 'Let's say Taylor was working with the guy with no tongue. Let's say they fell out over something, either what they did to Kate and Jade, or the money, or both. Then let's say one of them killed the other and ran, on Taylor's passport, with all the money.'

'Why would he use Taylor's passport?'

'Maybe he doesn't have one of his own. Many American citizens don't. Or maybe he's on a watch list. Maybe he couldn't get through an airport with his own name.'

'Passports have photographs.'

'Do you look like your passport photograph?'

'A little.'

Pauling said, 'A little is sometimes all you need. Going out, they don't care as much as when you're coming in.'

Reacher looked up and saw Brewer coming through the door. He sat in the spot the Pentagon guy had vacated.

He said, 'The body in the river was not the guy in Patti's photograph. Patti's guy is about five-nine and athletic and the floater was six-three and wasted.'

Pauling asked, 'Did he have a tongue?'

'A what?' Brewer said.

'We're looking for a guy who had his tongue cut out.'

Brewer looked straight at her. 'Then the floater ain't yours. He's got everything except a heartbeat.'

Reacher asked, 'Did you get an ID?'

Brewer nodded. 'From his fingerprints. He was a valuable NYPD snitch. Methamphetamine out of Long Island. He was due to testify.'

'Then we don't know anything about him,' Reacher said. 'He's completely unrelated.'

Brewer gave him a long hard look. 'You sure?'

Reacher nodded. 'I promise. I'm sorry we can't help.'

Brewer just shrugged. 'OK.'

'You still got Patti's photograph?' Reacher asked.

'Photographs,' Brewer said. 'She gave me two.'

They were in a standard white letter-size envelope. Brewer laid it on the table. Then he left. Reacher left the envelope unopened.

'What have we got?' he asked.

'Same as always. We've got Taylor and the guy who can't talk.'

Reacher shook his head. 'Taylor *is* the guy who can't talk.'

Pauling paused. Then she said, 'Because of his accent.'

Reacher nodded. 'Exactly. We've been saying nobody was missing, but by definition Taylor was missing from the start. And Taylor was behind this whole damn thing. He rented the apartment and he bought the chair. And he couldn't risk opening his mouth. Because he's English. He knew he had to be leaving a trail. And if whoever was tracking him heard all about an average-looking forty-year-old man with an English accent, they would have made him in a second as he was the last one to see Kate and Jade alive. It was the perfect piece of misdirection.'

'He did the same thing as Knight, five years ago. That's how the takedown worked. Open the envelope,' Pauling said. 'Confirm it.'

So Reacher slid the two photographs out, face down. Then he flipped the top picture over.

It was the guy he had seen twice before.

Taylor.

'No doubt about it,' Reacher said. 'That's the guy I saw first getting into the Mercedes and then the Jaguar.'

He turned the second picture over. It was a closer shot. This time the guy's mouth was open. He had terrible teeth. Some were missing.

'There you go,' Reacher said. 'He was concealing two pieces of evidence. His English accent, and his British dentistry.'

'Where is he now? England?'

'That's my guess. He flew home, where he feels safe.'

'With the money?'

'Checked luggage. Three bags.'

'Could he do that? With all the X-rays?'

'I don't see why not. I once had a lesson about paper money from an expert. It's mostly linen and cotton fibres. I think it would show up like clothing on an X-ray.'

Pauling slid the photographs across the table and butted them together side by side in front of her.

'It's a shame,' Reacher said. 'I liked him when I thought he was dead. Everyone spoke well of him.'

'Well, you've got a name to give to Lane,' she said. 'A unified theory of everything. Like a physicist. I don't see why you say it's only partial. Taylor did it all.'

'He didn't,' Reacher said. 'An American made the phone calls. He had a partner. That's why it's only a partial theory.'

'Lane won't settle for half a loaf. He's not going to pay.'

'He'll pay part. We'll get the rest when we tell him who the partner was.'

'How do we find out who the partner was?'

'The only sure way is to find Taylor and ask him.'

'In England?'

'If that's where your Pentagon buddy says he went. He could check for us who Taylor sat next to on the flight. There's a chance they flew together.'

So Pauling left a voicemail message for the Pentagon guy.

'What now?' she said.

'Wait for your guy to get back to you,' Reacher said. 'Then book us a car to the airport and flights to London, if that's where Taylor went. I'm betting

Lane will ask me to go over to do the advance work. Then he'll bring his crew over for the kill. And we'll deal with them there.'

Pauling looked up. 'That's why you promised no cop or prosecutor in America is going to think twice.'

Reacher kissed Pauling and headed for the subway. He was outside the Dakota before five in the afternoon.

But he didn't go inside. Instead he walked into Central Park, towards the John Lennon memorial. Near where Lennon was killed. Like most guys of his age, Reacher felt that the Beatles were part of his life. They were its soundtrack, its background. Maybe that was why he liked English people.

Maybe that was why he didn't want to do what he was about to do. But there was no doubt about it. Taylor was the bad guy.

Maybe there was just no joy in giving one bad guy to another. *But this is for Kate*, Reacher thought. *For Jade. For Hobart.*

He turned around and walked back out of the park.

EDWARD LANE fanned the two photographs of Taylor between his finger and his thumb and asked one simple question: 'Why?'

'Greed,' Reacher said. 'Or malice, or jealousy, or all of the above.'

'Where is he now?'

'My guess is England. I'll know soon.'

Lane said, 'He must have had a partner. Who was it?'

'You'll have to ask Taylor that.'

'I want you to find him for me.'

'I want my money.'

'Ten per cent now. The rest when I'm face to face with Taylor.'

'Twenty per cent now. Or I'm out of here.'

Lane said, 'OK, twenty per cent now. But you'll leave right now, too. Tonight. Then we'll follow you twenty-four hours later. The seven of us. We'll be at the Park Lane Hilton.'

'With the rest of the money?'

'Every cent. I'll show it to you when you meet us at the hotel and you tell us where Taylor is. I'll give it to you when I've got visual contact with him.'

'OK,' Reacher said. 'Deal.' And ten minutes later he was back in the subway, with two hundred thousand US dollars in a plastic Whole Foods shopping bag.

Reacher met Pauling at her apartment and gave her the bag and said, 'Take out what I owe you and hide the rest. It's enough to get Hobart started at least.'

Pauling opened the bag and peeled off some notes and put them on the kitchen counter. Then she refolded the bag and put it in the oven.

'I don't have a safe here,' she said.

She took four notes from the stack on the counter and handed them to Reacher. 'For new clothes,' she said. 'We leave for England tonight.'

'Your guy got back to you?'

She nodded. 'Taylor was on British Airways to London less than four hours after Burke put the money in the Jaguar.'

'Alone?'

'Apparently. He was seated next to some British woman.'

Reacher said, 'I don't need four hundred dollars for clothes.'

Pauling said, 'You do if you're travelling with me.'

Thirty minutes later Reacher was doing something he had never done in his life. He was buying clothes in a department store. He was in Macy's, in the men's department, in front of a cash register, holding a pair of grey trousers, a grey jacket, a black T-shirt, a black V-neck sweater, a pair of black socks and a pair of white boxer shorts. He shuffled to the head of the queue and paid. He showered and dressed back at Pauling's apartment and took his battered passport and Patti Joseph's photographs out of his old jeans and shoved them in his new trousers. Took his folding toothbrush and put it in his new jacket pocket. Then he waited with Pauling in the lobby until the car service showed up to take them to the airport.

Chapter Nine

Pauling had booked them business class on the same flight that Taylor had taken forty-eight hours previously. 'What's the strategy?' she asked.

'We'll find Taylor, Lane will take care of him, then I'll take care of Lane.'

'How?'

'I'll think of something.'

'What about the others?'

'If I think the crew will fall apart with Lane gone, then I'll leave the rest alone. But if one of them wants to step up to take over, I'll do him too. And so on, until the crew really does fall apart.'

'Taylor won't be easy to find,' she said.

'I've got a plan.'

'Tell me.'

'You know any British private investigators? Is there an international brotherhood?'

'There might be a sisterhood. I've got some numbers.'

'Local knowledge,' Reacher said. 'It's always the key.'

Pauling took a blanket from a stewardess and reclined her seat. Reacher watched her sleep for a while then he lay down too. He liked flying. Going to sleep in New York and waking up in London was a fantasy that could have been designed expressly for him.

THE STEWARDESS woke him to give him breakfast.

Then all kinds of signs went on to announce the start of their approach into Heathrow Airport.

Reacher put his forehead against the window and stared down. Saw the Thames, glittering in the sun like polished lead. Saw Tower Bridge, white stone, recently cleaned. He craned his neck and looked for St Paul's Cathedral. Saw the big dome, crowded by ancient winding streets. Saw the Houses of Parliament and Big Ben.

He said to Pauling, 'We need to find a quiet hotel. The kind of place where they don't look at your passport and they let you pay cash. Bayswater, maybe.'

He turned to the window again and saw a six-lane motorway with slow traffic driving on the left. Then the airport fence. The steward welcomed the passengers to London over the public-address system.

They filled in landing cards and had their passports stamped by an official. Pauling changed a wad of the O-Town dollars and they found the fast train to Paddington station. Convenient for the Bayswater hotels. They came out to the street in central London in the middle of the afternoon.

London was bright and fresh and cold.

Reacher carried Pauling's case and they walked south and east towards Sussex Gardens. From previous trips he recalled groups of terraced houses joined together into cheap hotels. Pauling rejected the first two places he found before understanding that there wasn't going to be anything better. So she gave up and agreed to the third. The desk guy was happy to take cash. There was no register. The bed was a queen with a green nylon counterpane.

'We won't be here long,' Reacher said.

'It's fine,' Pauling said.

She didn't unpack. Reacher sat on the bed while she washed. Then she came out of the bathroom and moved to the window, looked out over the rooftops.

'Nearly ninety-five thousand square miles,' she said. 'That's what's out there. Where do we start?'

'Let's call on the sisterhood,' Reacher said.

So Pauling fetched her purse and took out a small device. A Palm Pilot. She called up a directory and found a name and an address.

'Gray's Inn Road,' she said. 'Is that near here?'

'I don't think so,' Reacher said. 'I think that's east of here. Where the lawyers are. We can get there on the subway, I guess.'

She dialled the phone on the bedside table. Reacher listened to Pauling's end of the conversation. She explained who she was, and she asked for an appointment. Then she asked 'How does six o'clock suit you?' and then said 'OK, thank you,' and hung up.

Reacher said, 'The sisterhood comes through.'

'Brotherhood,' Pauling said. 'The woman whose name I had seems to have sold the business.'

They walked down to the tube station. It was a crowded six-stop ride. They came up out of Chancery Lane station at a quarter to six into full daylight and narrow streets that were choked with traffic. Black cabs, red buses, white vans, pavements thick with people.

They walked north on Gray's Inn Road, past a sign that said that Charles Dickens had lived nearby.

Pauling was checking doors for numbers. She spotted the one she wanted. It was a narrow maroon door with a glass fanlight. They checked the brass plates on the stonework. One was *Investigative Services Ltd.* Reacher pushed the door and found that it was open. They walked up two flights until they found the right door. It was standing open onto a square room with a desk. The occupant was a small man with thin hair.

'You must be the Americans,' he said.

'We're looking for someone,' Pauling said. 'He arrived from New York two days ago. He's English, and his name is Taylor.'

'Twice in one day,' the guy said. 'Your Mr Taylor is a popular person.'

'What do you mean?'

'A man telephoned from New York with the same enquiry. Wouldn't give his name. I imagined he was trying all the London agencies.'

Pauling turned to Reacher and mouthed, *Lane.*

She turned back to the desk. 'What did you tell him?'

'That there are sixty million people in Great Britain and that several hundred thousand of them are called Taylor. That without better information I couldn't help him.'

'And can you help us?'

'That depends on what extra information you have.'

'We have photographs.'

'They might help eventually. But not at the outset. How long was Mr Taylor in America?'

'Many years, I think.'

'Then it's hopeless,' the guy said. 'I work with databases. Bills, electoral registers, credit reports. If your Mr Taylor hasn't lived here for years he won't show up anywhere. I'm very sorry.'

Pauling shot Reacher a look that said: *Great plan.*

Reacher said, 'I've got a phone number for his closest relative.'

'WE SEARCHED Taylor's apartment in New York and we found a desk phone that had ten speed-dials programmed,' Reacher said. 'The only British number was labelled with the letter S. And if the relationship is fairly close, then Taylor won't have come back to Britain without at least letting them know.'

'What was the number?' the guy asked.

Reacher closed his eyes and recited the 01144 number he had memorised back on Hudson Street. The guy at the desk wrote it down.

'OK,' he said. 'We delete the international prefix, and we add a zero in its place. Then we fire up the old computer and we look in the reverse directory This will give us the address only, you understand. We'll have to go elsewhere to discover the identity of the person who lives there.' He hit several buttons and the screen came up with an address.

'Grange Farm,' he said. 'In Bishops Pargeter. Not far from Norwich, judging by the postcode.'

'Bishops Pargeter is the name of a town?'

The guy nodded. 'It'll be a small village, probably. In the county of Norfolk, in East Anglia. Farming country, very flat, windy, the Fens, north and east of here, about a hundred and twenty miles away.'

'Find the name.'

The guy opened up another database. 'The electoral register,' he said. 'Here we are. Two voters at that address. Mr Anthony Jackson, and let's see, yes, Mrs Susan Jackson. So there's your S. S for Susan.'

'A sister,' Pauling said. 'Married. This is like Hobart all over again.'

'Now then,' the guy said. 'Let's do a little something else. Not quite legal this time, but I'm among colleagues.' He opened a new database. 'The Department for Work and Pensions. The nanny state at work.' He entered Jackson's name and address and then added a complex keyboard command. 'Anthony Jackson is thirty-nine years old and his wife Susan is thirty-eight. Her maiden name was indeed Taylor. They have one child, a daughter, aged eight, with the unfortunate name of Melody.'

The guy scrolled up the screen. 'Melody seems to have been born in London.' He opened another site. 'The Land Registry,' he said. He entered the address. Hit a *Submit* command. The screen redrew. 'They bought the place in Bishops Pargeter just over a year ago. Which would suggest they're city folk heading back to the land.'

'Thank you,' Reacher said. 'We appreciate your help.' Then he said, 'Maybe you could forget all about this if the guy from New York calls again.'

'First come, first served,' the guy said. 'My lips are sealed.'

'Thank you,' Reacher said again. 'What do we owe you?'

'Oh, nothing at all,' the guy said. 'It was my pleasure entirely. Always happy to help a fellow professional.'

On the street Pauling said, 'All Lane has to do is check Taylor's apartment and find the phone and he's level with us. Those reverse directories are available online.'

'He won't find the phone,' Reacher said. 'And if he did, he wouldn't make the connection. Different skill set.'

'Are you sure?'

'Not entirely. So I erased the number.'

'So what next?'

'We're going to go to Bishops Pargeter to see Susan Jackson.'

REACHER AND PAULING walked from their hotel to Marble Arch to find a car rental office. Reacher had neither a driver's licence nor a credit card so he left Pauling to fill in the forms and went down Oxford Street to look for a bookstore. He found one that had a whole shelf of motoring atlases of Britain. The first three he checked didn't show Bishops Pargeter. *Too small*, he figured. Then he saw a cache of Ordnance Survey maps. He pulled all the Norfolk sheets off the shelf and tried them one by one. He found Bishops Pargeter on the fourth attempt. It was a crossroads hamlet about thirty miles south and west of Norwich.

He bought the map for detail and the cheapest atlas for basic orientation. Then he hiked back to the rental office and found Pauling waiting with the key to a Mini Cooper.

'A red one,' she said. 'With a white roof. Very cool.'

He said, 'I think Taylor might be there. With his sister.'

'Why?'

'His instinct would be to go hide somewhere isolated. And he was a soldier, so he'd want somewhere defensible. It's flat as a pool table there. I just read the map. He'd see someone coming from five miles away. If he's got a rifle he's impregnable. And if he's got four-wheel drive he's got a three-sixty escape route. He could just take off across the fields.'

'It's possible,' Pauling said. 'I guess. So what's our play?'

'Taylor was with Lane three years,' Reacher said. 'So he never met you and he never met me. He's not going to shoot every stranger who comes to the house.'

'We're going right to the house?'

Reacher nodded. 'At least close enough to scope it out.'

The rental guy brought the Mini Cooper out from a garage space and Reacher shoved the passenger seat hard against the rear bench and slid inside. Pauling got in the driver's seat and started the engine.

'Northeast,' Reacher said. 'On a highway called the M11.'

They made halting progress through the city until they found a wide road labelled the A10, which took them onto the M25. They hit it clockwise and two exits later they were on the M11, heading north and east for Cambridge, Newmarket and ultimately Norwich. Nine o'clock in the evening, and nearly dark.

The little Mini hummed along. The clock in Reacher's head crawled round to ten in the evening.

'I don't like anything about this whole situation,' he said. 'It feels wrong. I can't get past the feeling that I'm making a bad mistake.'

Much later they blew through a town called Fenchurch St Mary. The road narrowed. They saw a sign that said NORWICH 40 MILES. So Reacher switched maps and they started hunting the turn to Bishops Pargeter. The road signs were clear and helpful. But the longer names were abbreviated. Reacher saw a sign to B'SH'PS P'TER and they were two hundred yards past it before he figured out what it meant. So Pauling U-turned and went back. The smaller road was narrow and winding.

'How far?' Pauling asked.

'Maybe nine miles,' Reacher said. Then he looked out the car window.

'This is pointless,' he said. 'It's too dark. We're not even going to see the house, let alone who's living in it.' The map showed buildings about four miles ahead. One was labelled PH. He checked the legend.

'Public house,' he said. 'A pub. Maybe an inn. We should get a room. Go out again at first light.'

Pauling said, 'Suits me, boss.'

He realised she was tired. Travel, jet lag, unfamiliar roads, driving stress. 'I'm sorry,' he said. 'We overdid it.'

'No,' she said. 'We're right on the spot for the morning.'

Soon they saw a glow in the distance that turned out to be the pub's spotlit sign: 'The Bishop's Arms'. The pub looked warm and inviting.

Pauling slotted the tiny car between a dirty Land Rover and a battered saloon. Turned the motor off. Reacher carried Pauling's case to the pub's door. Dead ahead was a hotel reception counter made from dark old wood varnished to an amazing shine. It was unattended. To the left was a doorway marked *Saloon Bar*. It led to a room that seemed to be empty. To the right beyond the stairs was a doorway marked *Public Bar*. Through it Reacher could see a bartender and the backs of four drinkers hunched on stools. In the far corner he could see the back of a man sitting alone at a table.

Reacher dinged the bell. A long moment later the bartender came in. He was about sixty, large and florid.

'We need a room,' Reacher said to him.

'It'll cost you forty pound. But that's with breakfast.'

'Sounds like a bargain.'

'You want a room with a bath?'

Pauling said, 'Yes, a bath. That would be nice.'

She gave him four ten-pound notes and he gave her a brass key. Then he handed Reacher a pen and squared a register in front of him. Reacher wrote *J. & L. Bayswater* on the *Name* line. Then he checked a box for *Place of Business* rather than *Place of Residence* and wrote Yankee Stadium's street address on the next line. *East 161st Street, Bronx, New York, USA*. In a space labelled *Make of Vehicle* he scrawled *Rolls Royce*. Then he asked the bartender, 'Can we get a meal?'

'You're a little too late for a meal, I'm afraid,' the bartender said. 'But you could have sandwiches, if you like.'

'That would be fine,' Reacher said.

'You're Americans, aren't you? We get a lot of them. They come to see the old airfields. Where they were stationed.'

'Before my time,' Reacher said.

The bartender nodded sagely and said, 'Go on in and have a drink. Your sandwiches will be ready soon.'

The guy disappeared into the kitchen and Reacher stepped in through the door to the public bar. Five heads turned. The four guys at the bar looked like farmers. Red, weathered faces, thick hands.

The guy alone at the table in the corner was Taylor.

LIKE THE GOOD SOLDIER he was, Taylor kept his eyes on Reacher long enough to assess the threat level. Pauling's arrival behind Reacher's shoulder seemed to reassure him, and he turned back to his beer. Reacher led Pauling to a table on the other side of the room from Taylor and sat with his back to the wall and watched the farmers turn back to the bar. A moment later the bartender reappeared.

Reacher said, 'We should buy a drink.'

Pauling said, 'I guess I'll try the local beer.'

So Reacher got up and stepped over to the bar. He said, 'A pint of best, please, and a half for the lady.' He turned to the four farmers and added, 'And will you gentlemen join us?' Then he glanced at the bartender and said: 'And can I get yours?' Then the whole dynamic of the room funnelled towards Taylor as the only person as yet uninvited. Taylor looked up from his table as if compelled to and Reacher mimed a drinking action and called, 'What can I get you?'

Taylor looked back at him and said, 'Thanks, but I've got to go.' A flat British accent. Calculation in his eyes. But nothing in his face. A guileless half-smile. Then he got up and headed for the door.

The bartender pulled six and a half pints of best bitter and lined them up. Reacher paid. Then he picked his own up and carried Pauling's glass over to her, and the four farmers and the bartender all turned towards their table and toasted them. Reacher thought: *Instant social acceptance for less than thirty bucks.* But he said, 'I hope I didn't offend that other fellow somehow.'

'Don't know him,' one of the farmers said.

'He's at Grange Farm,' another farmer said. 'Must be, because I saw him drive up in Grange Farm's Land Rover.'

'Where's Grange Farm?'

'Down the road apiece. There's a family there now.'

'Ask Dave Kemp,' the third farmer said. 'He'll tell you all about them.'

Reacher said, 'Who's Dave Kemp?'

'Dave Kemp in the shop,' the third farmer said. 'In Bishops Pargeter. He'll know on account of the post office. Nosy bugger.'

'Is there a pub there?'

'This is the only pub for miles, lad. Why else do you think it's so crowded?'

Reacher didn't answer that.

'They're newcomers at Grange Farm,' the fourth farmer said. 'From London. Organic, they are.'

And that information seemed to conclude what the farmers felt they owed in exchange for a pint of beer.

'You were right,' Pauling said. 'Taylor's at the farm.'

'But will he stay there now?' Reacher said.

'I don't see why not. Your big, dumb, generous American act was pretty convincing.'

The sandwiches were good. Fresh, crusty homemade bread, butter, rare roast beef, creamy horseradish sauce, farmhouse cheese on the side. They ate them and finished their beers. Then they headed upstairs to their room. Reacher set the alarm in his head for six in the morning. First light. *Taylor will stay or Taylor will run, and either way we'll watch him do it.*

Chapter Ten

The view out the window at six the next morning was one of infinite misty flatness. The land was level and grey-green all the way to the far horizon. The trees had long, thin, supple trunks and round, compact crowns to withstand the winds.

Outside it was cold and their car was all misted over with dew. They climbed inside without saying much.

Grange Farm was bounded by ditches, not fences. Then came flat fields, neatly ploughed, dusted pale green with late crops recently planted. Closer to the centre were small stands of trees, then a large, handsome, grey stone house. Bigger than Reacher had imagined, it was more impressive than a mere farmhouse. In the distance to the north and the east of the house were five low barns. Three of them bordered three-sides of a square yard. Two stood alone.

The road they were driving on was flanked by the ditch that formed the farm's southern boundary. The driveway crossed the boundary ditch on a small, flat bridge and then ran north into the distance. The house itself was end-on to the road, a half-mile in. The Land Rover was parked between the back of the house and one of the stand-alone barns.

'He's still there,' Reacher said.

Pauling slowed. There was no sign of activity in the house. No light.

Pauling coasted to a halt and buzzed her window down. Outside was all silence and stillness.

'I guess all the world looked like this once,' Pauling said.

Then the silence was shattered by a shotgun. Reacher and Pauling both ducked, then scanned the horizon for smoke. Looking for incoming fire.

'Hunters?' Pauling asked.

Reacher listened hard. Heard nothing more.

'I think it was a bird scarer,' he said. 'They just planted a winter crop.'

'I hope that's all it was.'

'We'll come back,' Reacher said. 'Let's go find Dave Kemp in the shop.'

Pauling took off again. Bishops Pargeter was little more than an ancient stone church standing alone and a fifty-yard string of buildings along the road opposite. One of them was a general store and, because it sold newspapers, it was already open.

'The direct approach?' Pauling asked.

'A variant,' Reacher said.

They got out of the car into a stiff easterly wind. The village store felt warm and snug by comparison. There was a shuttered post-office window, a central section that sold food, and a newspaper counter at the far end. There was an old guy behind the counter.

'Are you Dave Kemp?' Reacher asked.

'That's my name,' the old guy said.

'I was told you were the man to ask. We're here to buy farms.'

'You're Americans, aren't you?'

'We represent a large agricultural corporation in the United States, yes. And we can offer very generous finders' fees. Generally we want good, well-run places that were recently bought up by amateurs. But we want them before they're ruined.'

'Grange Farm,' Kemp said. 'They're bloody amateurs. They've gone organic. It should be top of your list. They've bitten off more than they can chew there. And that's when they're both at home.'

'Grange Farm sounds like a good prospect,' Reacher said. 'But we heard that someone else is snooping around there too. He's been seen, recently.'

'Really?' Kemp said, excited, conflict in the offing. Then his face fell. 'No, I know who you mean. That's the woman's brother.'

'Are you sure about that?'

Kemp nodded. 'The chap came in here and introduced himself. Said his wandering days were over. He was posting a packet to America. Air mail. We had quite a nice chat.'

Pauling asked, 'What did he post to America?'

'He didn't tell me what it was. It was going to a hotel in New York. Addressed to a room, not a person.'

Reacher asked, 'Did you guess what it was?'

'It felt like a thin book,' Kemp said. 'Not many pages. A rubber band around it.'

'Didn't he fill out a customs declaration?'

'We put it down as printed papers. Don't need a form.'

'Thanks, Mr Kemp,' Reacher said.

'What about the fee?'

'If we buy the farm, you'll get it,' Reacher said.

THEY WENT BACK to the farmhouse. The place was still quiet, no lights.

'You were very plausible,' said Pauling. 'It fitted very well with last night. Assuming Kemp spreads the word, Taylor's going to put you down as a con man looking to make a fast buck.'

'I can lie with the best of them,' Reacher said. 'Sadly.'

Then he shut up fast because the farmhouse door was opening. He made out four figures emerging. Two big, one slightly smaller, one very small. Probably two men, a woman, and a little child.

'They're up,' he said.

Pauling said, 'I see them, but only just. Four people. It's the Jackson family and Taylor, right?'

'Must be.'

They all had things on their shoulders. Long poles.

'What are they doing?' Pauling asked.

'Those are hoes,' Reacher said. 'They're going to the fields to dig weeds.'

The tiny figures moved north, away from the road, just faint, remote blurs in the mist.

Reacher said, 'We've seen enough. The job is done. Let's get back to London and wait for Lane.'

THEY HIT COMMUTER TRAFFIC on the road to London. Lots of it.

Two hours into the ride they pulled off and got gas and Reacher changed places with Pauling, even though he wasn't on the paperwork. It seemed to him a minor transgression compared with what they had in mind for later.

The traffic moved on slowly, circulating like water around a bathtub drain, before yielding to the inexorable pull of the city: through St John's Wood, past Regent's Park, through Marble Arch and on to Park Lane. The Hilton Hotel was at the south end. They parked in a commercial garage at a quarter to eleven. Maybe an hour before Lane and his guys were due to check in.

'Want an early lunch?' Pauling said.

'Can't eat,' Reacher said. 'Too knotted up. I feel like I'm delivering Taylor to an executioner.'

'So walk away.'

'I can't. I want retribution for Kate and Jade and I want the money for Hobart. On top of that we have a deal with your Pentagon buddy. I have to deliver. But all things considered I think I'll skip lunch.'

Pauling asked, 'Where do you want me?'

'In the lobby. Watching. Then go get yourself a room somewhere else. Leave me a note at the Hilton's desk. Use the name Bayswater. I'll take Lane to Norfolk, Lane will deal with Taylor, I'll deal with Lane. Then I'll come back and get you. Then we'll go somewhere together. Bath, maybe. To the Roman spas. We'll try to get clean again.'

They went up a flight of steps to the lobby. Pauling detoured to a distant group of armchairs and Reacher walked to the desk. He stood in queue. Above a Xerox machine was a brass plaque that said: *By statute some documents may not be photocopied. Like banknotes*, Reacher thought.

'Edward Lane's party,' he said, when he got to the head of the queue. 'Have they checked in yet?'

The clerk tapped his keyboard. 'Not yet, sir.'

'When they get here, tell them I'm across the lobby.'

'Your name, sir?'

'Taylor,' Reacher said. He walked away and found a quiet spot. He was going to be counting eight hundred thousand dollars in cash and he didn't want an audience. A nearby family was watching him warily. Two kids and a mother. The mother looked tired and the kids looked fractious. Off an early flight and waiting for their room to be ready, he thought. She had unpacked half their stuff, trying to keep them amused. Colouring books, battered teddy bears, a doll missing an arm, video games. *Why don't you draw a picture of something you're going to see?* she was saying. Like therapy.

He turned away and watched the door.

He saw Perez walk in. Then Kowalski. Then Edward Lane himself. Then Gregory, and Groom, and Addison, and Burke. Roll-on bags, duffles. A little crumpled. But awake and alert. They looked like what they were: a group of Special Forces soldiers trying to travel incognito.

He watched them check in. Watched the clerk give Lane the message. Saw Lane turn around. Lane's gaze moved over the lobby. Onto Reacher's face. Lane nodded. All seven men hoisted their luggage again and eased their way through the crowds. Lane dropped one bag and kept hold of another and sat down opposite Reacher.

'Show me the money,' Reacher said.

'Do you know where Taylor is?'

Reacher nodded. 'I know where he is. I made visual contact twice. Last night, and then again this morning.'

'So tell me where he is.'

'Show me the money first.'

Lane said nothing. Reacher said, 'You called a bunch of London private eyes.'

Lane said, 'A man's entitled to save himself an unnecessary expense.'

'Did you get ahead of me?'

'No.'

'Therefore the expense isn't unnecessary.'

'OK,' Lane said. He placed a leather duffle on the floor and unzipped it. Reacher leaned down. The duffle was full of money.

Reacher put a fingernail under one of the paper bands. It was tight. Therefore full. There were four equal stacks of twenty bricks each. Total of eighty bricks. A hundred hundreds in each brick. Eighty times a hundred times a hundred was eight hundred thousand.

He lifted the edge of a bill and rubbed it between his finger and thumb. They were real. He could feel the engraving. He could smell the paper and the ink.

'OK,' he said, and sat back.

Lane zipped the duffle. 'So where is he?'

Reacher said, 'There are civilians there.'

'We won't be shooting,' Lane said. 'A bullet is too good for Taylor. We'll go in and we'll get him and we'll bring him out without harming a hair on his or anyone else's head. He'll tell us about his partner and then he'll die, slow and hard. So a gunfight is no good to me. Not because I care about noncombatants. But because I don't want any accidents with Taylor.'

'OK,' Reacher said.

'So where is he?'

Reacher paused. Thought about Hobart, and Birmingham, Alabama, and Nashville, Tennessee.

'He's in Norfolk,' he said. 'It's a county, north and east of here. About a hundred and twenty miles.'

'Where in Norfolk?'

'A place called Grange Farm.'

'Nearest big city?'

'It's about thirty miles south and west of Norwich.'

'Nearest town?'

Reacher didn't reply.

'Nearest town?' Lane asked again.

Reacher glanced at the reception desk. *By statute some documents may not be photocopied.* He heard the harassed mother's voice in his head: *Why don't you draw a picture of something you're going to see?* He looked at the kid's doll, missing an arm. Heard Dave Kemp's voice, in the country store: *It felt like a thin book.*

Lane said, 'Reacher?'

Reacher heard Lauren Pauling's voice in his mind: *A little is sometimes all you need. Going out, they don't care as much as when you're coming in.*

Lane said, 'Reacher? Hello? What's the nearest town?'

Reacher dragged his focus back, and he looked directly into Lane's eyes. He said, 'The nearest town is called Fenchurch St Mary. Be ready to leave in one hour. I'll come back for you.'

Then he stood up and concentrated hard on walking slowly across the lobby floor. He caught Pauling's eye. Walked out onto the sidewalk.

Then he ran like hell for the car park.

Reacher had parked the car, so he still had the keys. He blipped the door and wrenched it open and threw himself inside. Hurled the tiny car out of the parking space. He threw a ten-pound note at the barrier guy. He blasted up the ramp and shot straight across the oncoming traffic and jammed to a stop on the opposite kerb because he saw Pauling hurrying towards him. She slid inside and he took off again.

'North,' he said. 'Which way is north?'

'North is behind us,' she said. 'What the hell is going on?'

'Just get me out of town. Use the atlas. There's a city plan.'

Pauling turned pages, frantically. 'Go around Hyde Park Corner and back onto Park Lane. And please tell me exactly what the hell is going on.'

'I made a mistake,' Reacher said. 'Remember I told you I couldn't shake the feeling I was making a bad mistake? Well, I was wrong. It wasn't a bad mistake. It was a catastrophic mistake.'

'What mistake?'

'Tell me about the photographs in your apartment. Nieces and nephews, right?'

'Lots of them,' Pauling said.

'Tell me about their favourite toys. Their old favourites. When they were eight years old?'

'I guess a teddy bear or a doll. Something they'd had since they were tiny.'

'Exactly,' Reacher said. 'Something they loved. The kind of thing they would want to take on a journey. Like the family next to me in the lobby just now.'

'So?'

'What did those things look like?'

'When they were eight? They'd had them for ever by then. They looked like crap. All kids have toys like that.'

'Jade didn't. That's what was missing from her room.'

'What are you saying?'

'I'm saying that if Jade had been kidnapped on the way to Bloomingdale's I would have found all her favourite old toys still in her room afterwards. But I didn't.'

'But what does that mean?'

'It means Jade knew she was leaving. She packed.'

Reacher figured he was about two hours ahead of Edward Lane. It would take an hour for Lane to realise he had been ditched, and then it would take at least another hour for him to organise a pursuit.

Pauling said, 'Jade packed?'

'Kate packed too,' Reacher said. 'Just one thing. But her most precious thing. The photograph with her daughter. From the bedroom.'

'But you saw it,' Pauling said. 'She didn't take it.'

Reacher shook his head. 'I saw a photocopy. From Staples. It was very good, but not quite good enough.'

'But who packs for a kidnap?'

'They weren't kidnapped,' Reacher said. 'That's the thing. They were set free.'

They made it through Marble Arch and got green lights all the way past the Marylebone Road. Soon they were driving through the northern reaches of London, through Finchley and Swiss Cottage, towards Hendon. The M1 would carry them all the way to the M25, then clockwise to the M11.

'Kate believed Dee Marie,' Reacher said. 'Dee Marie told her about Anne, and warned her, and Kate believed her.'

Pauling said, 'You know what this means?'

'Of course I do.'

'Taylor helped them. He rescued them, and he hid them, and he risked his life for them. He's the good guy.'

Reacher nodded. 'And I just told Lane where he is.'

They joined the M1 motorway at its southern tip. Reacher hit the gas and forced the Mini up to ninety-five miles an hour.

Pauling said, 'What about the money?'

'Alimony,' Reacher said. 'We thought it was half of the Burkina Faso payment, but in Kate's eyes it was also half of their jointly owned property. She probably put money in, way back. That's what Lane seems to want his wives for. Apart from their trophy status.'

'Hell of a plan,' Pauling said. 'But they made mistakes.'

'They sure did. If you really want to disappear, you take nothing with you. Absolutely nothing at all. It's fatal.'

'Who helped Taylor? He had an American partner. On the phone.'

'It was Kate herself. They collaborated.'

'Did you really tell Lane where Taylor is?'

'As good as. I stopped myself from saying Bishops Pargeter just in time: said Fenchurch St Mary instead. But he'll work it out with the right map.'

Pauling was quiet for a second. 'We have to try to warn them. There's the sister to think about. And Melody.'

'Susan and Melody are perfectly safe.'

'How can you say that?'

'Ask yourself where Kate and Jade are.'

'I have no idea where they are.'

'You do,' Reacher said. 'You know exactly where they are. You saw them this morning.'

THEY TURNED OFF the highway at Newmarket and set out cross-country towards Norwich.

Reacher said, 'Think about the dynamic here. Why would Kate ask Taylor for help? How could she ask any of them for help? They're all insanely loyal to Lane.'

Pauling said, 'They already had a thing going.'

'That's the only way to explain it. And there were signs. Carter Groom said that Kate liked Taylor and that Taylor got on well with the kid.'

'Dee Marie showing up must have acted like a kind of tipping point.'

Reacher nodded. 'Kate and Taylor made a plan and put it into action. But first they explained it to Jade.'

'Big secret for a kid to keep.'

'She didn't exactly keep it,' Reacher said. 'She was worried about it. She straightened it out in her head by drawing it.'

'What picture?'

'There were four in her room. Kate didn't sanitise well enough. There was a big grey building with trees in front. I thought it was the Dakota from Central Park. Now I think it was the Grange Farm farmhouse. They must have shown her photographs. She got the trees just right. Like bright green lollipops on brown sticks. And then there was a picture of a family group. I thought the guy was Lane. But there was something weird about his mouth. Like half his teeth had been punched out. So it was Taylor. She drew her new family. Taylor, Kate and her.'

'And you think Taylor brought them here to England?'

'They needed a safe haven. Jade did a picture of three people in an airplane. Then she did one of two families together. Like double vision. I had no idea what it meant. But now my guess is that was Jackson and Taylor, and Susan and Kate, and Melody and herself. Her new extended family. Happy ever after on Grange Farm.'

'Doesn't work,' Pauling said. 'Their passports were still in the drawer.'

'That was crude,' Reacher said. 'Leaving them on show like that was a message. Hey, we're still in the country. Meaning actually they weren't.'

'How do you get out without a passport?'

'You don't. But you once said they don't look as closely on the way out.'

Pauling said, 'Susan and Melody.'

'Susan and Melody had flown to the States. They got all the correct entry stamps. Then they gave their passports to Kate and Jade. Then Taylor booked on British Airways. He was sitting next to a British woman on the plane. A buck gets ten she's on the passenger manifest as Mrs Susan Jackson. And another buck gets ten that next to her was Ms Melody Jackson. But they were really Kate and Jade Lane.'

'But that leaves Susan and Melody stuck in the States.'

'Temporarily,' Reacher said. 'What did Taylor mail back?'

'A thin book. Not many pages.'

'Two passports, bundled together with a rubber band. Mailed to Susan's New York City hotel room.'

'But when they leave they'll be exiting without having entered.'

Reacher nodded. 'It's an irregularity. But what are the people at JFK going to do about it? Deport them? That's exactly what they want.'

'Sisters,' Pauling said. 'Patti Joseph, Dee Marie Graziano, Susan Jackson. This whole thing has been about the loyalty of sisters.'

JOHN GREGORY was hitting the gas, too. He was at the wheel of a rented dark green seven-seater Toyota Land Cruiser. Edward Lane was next to him. Kowalski and Addison and Groom were on the rear bench. Burke and Perez were on the jump seats. They were joining the M11 at its southern tip, having blasted straight through central London to the northeast corner of the city.

THIS TIME Reacher saw the sign to B'SH'PS P'TER and slowed well in advance. It was close to two o'clock in the afternoon. The sun was high. A perfect English late-summer day. Almost.

Pauling said, 'What are you going to tell them?'

'That I'm sorry,' Reacher said. 'It might be the best place to start.'

'Then what?'

'Then I'll probably say it again.'

'Don't beat yourself up. They faked a kidnap. Don't blame yourself for taking it seriously.'

'I should have seen it,' Reacher said.

They passed the Bishop's Arms. They passed the ditch that marked Grange Farm's southern boundary.

Reacher slowed the car well before the small, flat bridge. Turned in wide and deliberate. Small vehicle, low speed. Unthreatening. He hoped.

The driveway was long and it looped through two curves. The beaten earth was muddy and less even than it had looked from a distance.

'Where is everybody?' Pauling said. 'Out hoeing?'

'You can't hoe for seven hours straight. You'd break your back.'

The driveway split thirty yards in front of the house. West, the formal approach to the front door. East, a shabbier track towards the barns. Reacher went east. The Land Rover wasn't there. The barn doors were closed.

Reacher braked gently and backed up. Took the wider driveway west. He stopped ten feet from the front door.

'What now?' Pauling asked.

'We knock,' Reacher said.

They walked together to the front door. It was a large slab of ancient oak, as black as coal. There was a twisted ring hinged in the mouth of a lion and positioned to strike down on a nail head as big as an apple. Reacher used it, twice. It resonated like a bass drum.

Reacher called, 'Taylor? Graham Taylor?'

No response.

No sound at all. Except for the shuffle of a tiny foot, thirty feet away. Reacher glanced to his left. Saw a small bare knee pull back around the far corner of the house.

'I saw you,' Reacher called. 'Come on out now. It's OK.'

No response.

A long moment later Reacher saw a small dark head peer out from around the corner. A small face, pale skin, big green eyes. A little girl, about eight years old.

'Hello,' Pauling called. 'What's your name?'

'Melody Jackson,' Jade Lane said.

'MY NAME IS LAUREN,' Pauling said. 'This man is Reacher.'

Jade nodded her head. She was instantly recognisable from the Xerox Reacher had seen at the Dakota apartment. She was wearing a summer dress, sleeveless, green seersucker stripes. She had white socks on, and thin summer sandals.

Pauling said, 'We're here to talk to the grown-ups. Do you know where they are?'

A voice said, 'One of them is right here, lady,' and Kate Lane stepped out from around the other corner of the house. She was pretty much unchanged from her photograph. Dark hair, green eyes, a bud of a mouth. Extremely, impossibly beautiful. She was maybe five feet nine inches tall, slim and willowy. She was wearing a man's flannel shirt. She looked great in it.

'I'm Susan Jackson,' she said.

Reacher shook his head. 'You're not, but I'm very glad to meet you anyway. And Jade, too.'

'Who are you?'

'My name is Reacher. Where's Taylor?'

'Who?'

Reacher took a step towards Kate. 'We don't have time for that, Kate. Can we talk? I don't want to upset your daughter.'

'She knows what's going on.'

'OK,' Reacher said. 'Edward Lane is an hour behind us. Maybe less.'

'Edward is here?' Kate said, real fear showing in her face. 'Edward is here in England? Already?'

Reacher nodded. 'Heading this way. He paid me to find Taylor.'

'So why warn us?'

'Because I just figured out it wasn't for real.'

Kate said nothing.

'Where's Taylor?' Reacher asked again.

'He's out,' Kate said. 'He went with his brother-in-law, Tony. To Norwich. For a part for the backhoe. They said we need to dredge some ditches.'

'When did they leave?'

'About two hours ago.'

'Let's all go inside,' Reacher said.

Kate seemed reassured by the presence of another woman. She opened the front door. Led them all in. The farmhouse had low beamed ceilings and small leaded windows. The kitchen was a large rectangular room. There were bright copper pans hanging from hooks, and sofas and armchairs and a fireplace big enough to live in and a huge old-fashioned range. There was a massive oak dining table with twelve chairs around it and a separate pine desk with a phone and stacks of papers.

Reacher said, 'I think you should get out, Kate. Right now. You and Jade. Until we see what happens.'

'How?' Kate asked. 'The truck isn't here.'

'Take our car.'

'I've never driven before. I've never even been here before.'

Pauling said, 'I'll drive you. Anywhere you want to go.'

'Does he know?'

'That it was all a sham? Not yet.'

'OK,' Kate said. 'Take us somewhere. Now. Please.'

She grabbed Jade's hand. No purse, no coat. She was ready to go, right there and then. Reacher tossed Pauling the Mini's keys and followed them all outside again.

'Wait,' Reacher said.

On the road a mile to the west he could see a dark green shape moving fast. Clean and polished and shiny, not filthy like the farm truck.

A mile away. Ninety seconds. No time.

'Everybody back in the house,' he said. 'Right now.'

KATE AND JADE and Pauling ran upstairs and Reacher headed for the southeast corner of the house and crept around to where he could get a look at the bridge over the ditch. He got there just in time to see a truck turn in. It was an old-style Land Rover Defender. Two guys in it. One of them looked like one of the vague shapes in the mist that Reacher had seen earlier that morning. Tony Jackson. The farmer. The other was definitely Taylor. The truck was the Grange Farm Land Rover, newly cleaned and polished. Clearly the Norwich itinerary had included a stop at the car wash.

Reacher ducked into the kitchen and shouted an all clear up the stairs. Then he went back outside. The Land Rover skidded to a halt between the back of the house and the barns. The doors opened and Jackson and Taylor climbed out. Jackson walked up to Reacher and said, 'Dave Kemp told me what you want. And the answer is no. I'm not selling.'

'I'm not buying,' Reacher said.

'So why are you here?'

Jackson was a lean and compact guy, not unlike Taylor. Same kind of English features. Lighter hair worn a little longer. Better teeth.

Reacher said, 'I'm here to see Taylor.'

Taylor stepped up and said, 'What for?'

'To apologise to you,' Reacher said. 'And to warn you.'

Taylor paused a beat. Then his eyes flicked left, flicked right, full of intelligence and calculation.

'Lane?' he asked.

'He's probably less than an hour away.'

'OK,' Taylor said. He sounded calm. Not surprised. Surprise was for amateurs. And Taylor was a professional. Precious seconds spent being surprised were precious seconds wasted.

'I saw you on Sixth Avenue,' Taylor said. 'When I was getting in the Jaguar. Didn't think much of it, but I saw you again last night. In the pub. So then I knew. I thought you'd be heading up to your room to call Lane. But it looks like he mobilised himself faster than I thought he would.'

'He was already en route.'

'Does he have this precise location?'

'More or less. I said Grange Farm. I stopped myself saying Bishops Pargeter. I said Fenchurch St Mary instead.'

'He'll find us in the phone book. There's no Grange Farm in Fenchurch. We're the nearest.'

'I'm sorry,' Reacher said.

'When did you figure it all out?'

'Just a little bit too late.'

'What tipped you off?'

'Toys. Jade packed her best toys.'

Taylor smiled. Bad teeth, but a lot of warmth there. 'She's a great kid,' he said. 'What are you, a private cop?'

'I was a US Army MP.'

'What's your name?'

'Reacher.'

'How much did Lane pay you?'

'A million bucks.'

Taylor smiled again. 'I'm flattered. And you're good. But it was always only a matter of time. The longer nobody found my body, the more people would get to thinking. But I thought I might have a couple of weeks.'

'You've got about sixty minutes.'

THEY GATHERED in the farmhouse kitchen for a council of war. Jade sat at the table and drew. First thing Taylor said was, 'Let's light the fire. It's cold in here. And let's have a cup of tea.'

Pauling asked, 'Do we have time for that?'

'The British Army,' Reacher said. 'They always have time for a cup of tea.'

Jackson didn't seem very worried, either. Just calm and competent.

'What were you, back in the day?' Reacher asked him.

'First Para,' Jackson replied.

The 1st Parachute Regiment. Air-mobile tough guys.

'Lane's got six guys with him,' Reacher said.

'The A-team?' Taylor asked. 'Used to be seven guys. Before I resigned.'

'Used to be nine guys,' Reacher said.

'Hobart and Knight,' Taylor said. 'Kate heard that story. From Hobart's sister.'

'Was that the trigger?'

'Partly. And partly something else. Hobart isn't the only one. Lane got a lot of people killed and wounded over the years. He doesn't do anything for them. Or their families.'

'Is that why you wanted the money?'

'The money is Kate's alimony. She's entitled to it. How she spends it is up to her. But I'm sure she'll do the right thing.'

Tony Jackson poured the tea, hot and sweet and strong, into five chipped and unmatched mugs.

'Do we have time for this?' Pauling asked again.

'Reacher?' Taylor said. 'Do we have time for this?'

'This is England. If it was Kansas, Dave Kemp's store would be selling rifles and ammunition. But this isn't Kansas. And no way could Lane bring anything in on the plane. So if he shows up now, he's unarmed.'

'But there have to be weapons available somewhere,' Pauling said.

Taylor nodded. 'All over the place. But it takes time to find them.'

'How much time?'

'Twelve hours minimum, I would guess. So, if Lane wants to lock and load first, he can't show up until tomorrow at the earliest. Plus, he likes dawn raids.'

'Are you armed here?' Reacher asked.

'This is a farm,' Jackson answered. 'Farmers are always prepared for vermin control.'

Something in his voice. Some kind of lethal determination. Reacher looked between him and Taylor. *Same kind of height, same kind of weight, same kind of generic English features.* Reacher got up and walked over to the phone. It was the old-fashioned type. No memory. No speed dials.

He turned back to Taylor. 'You wanted this,' he said. 'You used the name Leroy Clarkson. To point the way to your apartment.'

Taylor said nothing.

'You could have stopped Jade from bringing her toys. You could have told Kate to leave the photograph behind. Your sister Susan could have brought Tony's passport over for you. Then there would have been three Jacksons on the airplane manifest, not two Jacksons and a Taylor. Without your real name you couldn't have been followed back to England.'

Taylor said nothing.

'The phone in your apartment was new,' Reacher said. 'You bought it so that you could leave Susan's number in it.'

Taylor said nothing.

'You talked to Dave Kemp,' Reacher said. 'And he's the biggest gossip in the county. Then you hung out in the pub with a bunch of nosy farmers. Because you wanted to lay a clear trail. Because you wanted to bring Lane here for a showdown.'

Silence in the room.

Reacher said, 'You wanted to be on your home turf. And you figured this is an easy place to defend.'

Taylor nodded. 'He was a little faster than we expected. But yes, we wanted him to come.'

'Why?'

'You just said it. We wanted a showdown. Closure.'

'Why now?'

Kate Lane looked up from her chair by the fire.

'I'm pregnant,' she said.

IN THE SOFT LIGHT of the flames from the hearth, Kate's beauty was emphasised to the point of heartbreak. She said, 'When Edward and I first started fighting he accused me of being unfaithful. Which wasn't true then. He said if he ever caught me sleeping around he would show me how much it hurt him by doing something to Jade that would hurt me even more. I didn't take it seriously. But after hearing about Anne and Knight and Hobart I knew I had to take it seriously. By which time I really did have something to hide. So we ran.'

'With Lane right behind you.' Reacher turned to Jackson. 'You're not fixing the backhoe to dredge ditches, are you? You're fixing the backhoe to dig graves, aren't you?'

Taylor said, 'You got a problem with that?'

'No,' Reacher answered. 'I don't have a problem with that.'

'You keeping your million bucks?'

Reacher shook his head. 'I was going to give it to Hobart.'

'That's good,' Kate said. 'That frees up some of our money for the others.'

Taylor said, 'Ms Pauling? What about you? Do you have a problem?'

Pauling said, 'I ought to. I ought to have a huge problem. Once upon a time I swore an oath to uphold the law.'

'But?'

'I can't get to Lane any other way.'

'So we're in business,' Taylor said. 'Welcome to the party.'

After they finished their tea Jackson took Reacher into a small mudroom off the kitchen and opened a wall cupboard. In it were racked four Heckler & Koch G36 automatic rifles. The G36 was a modern design that had shown up in service just before Reacher's military career had ended. It was chambered for the standard 5.56mm NATO round and like most German weapons it looked very expensive and beautifully engineered.

Reacher asked, 'Where did you get these from?'

'I bought them,' Jackson said. 'From a bent quartermaster in Holland.'

'Got ammunition?'

Jackson opened another cupboard. Reacher could see the glint of black metal. A lot of it.

'We can't use more than three or four rounds. Too noisy.'

'How close are the cops?'

'Not very. Norwich. But people here have phones.'

'You could turn the bird scarer off for the day.'

Jackson nodded. 'Obviously. But it's part of the planning. Set to start firing at dawn. That's when we expect Lane to come.'

'If I had a sister and a brother-in-law I'd want them to be like you and Susan.'

'I go way back with Taylor. We were in Sierra Leone together. I'd do anything for him.'

'You OK with all of this? You've got roots here, literally.'

'We'll be OK. The G36 is pretty accurate. One round might do it.'

Jackson locked both cupboards. Reacher stepped back into the kitchen and sat down next to Taylor.

'Tell me about Gregory,' Reacher said.

'What about him?'

'Is he going to stand by Lane? Or you?'

'Lane, I think. Gregory always wanted an officer's commission, but he never got it. And then Lane made him a kind of unofficial lieutenant. Status at last. Plus he'll be offended that I didn't share my secret.'

'Does he know this area?'

Taylor shook his head. 'He's a Londoner, like me.'

'What about the others? Will any of them turn?'

'The best we can hope for is neutrality from Groom and Burke. And I wouldn't bet the farm on that.'

'How good are they? All of them, as a whole?'

'They're about as good as me. They used to be outstanding, and now they're well on the way to average. They don't train any more. Training is important.'

'Why did you join them?'

'The money,' Taylor said. 'Then I stayed with them because of Kate.'

They drew lots for the first round of lookout duty. Jackson and Pauling pulled the short straws. Jackson sat in the Land Rover at the back of the house and Pauling sat in the Mini at the front. That way each of them could cover a little more than one hundred and eighty degrees. Ninety seconds' warning if Lane came in by road, a little more if he came in across the fields.

Reasonable security. As long as the daylight lasted.

Chapter Eleven

The daylight lasted until a little after eight o'clock. By then Reacher was in the Land Rover and Kate Lane was in the Mini. Twilight rolled in fast, and with it came an evening mist that cut visibility to less than a hundred yards.

By eight thirty visibility was so marginal that Reacher slid out of the Land Rover and headed for the kitchen. Taylor appeared out of the gloom.

'Ten hours to go,' he said. 'We're safe until dawn.'

'You sure?' Reacher said.

'Not really.'

'We could take Kate and Jade someplace else.'

Taylor shook his head. 'Better if they stay. I don't want my focus split.'

Privately Reacher agreed with Taylor. Split focus was a bad thing. And it was possible that Lane's guys already had covert surveillance going. If so, they would have the roads covered. Looking for Taylor, primarily. But if they were given the chance to see that the females who were supposed to be Susan and Melody Jackson were actually Kate and Jade Lane, then the whole game would change.

They planned as they ate dinner. Agreed to set up two two-person watches, sequential, five hours each. That would take them through until dawn. Each would be armed with a loaded G36. The first watch would be Taylor and Jackson, and at half past one Reacher and Pauling would take over. Kate Lane would sit it out. The possibility that a hostile night-time reconnaissance probe might identify her was too much of a risk.

Reacher washed the dishes and Taylor and Jackson went outside with their G36s. Kate went upstairs to put Jade to bed. Pauling put logs on the fire. A half-hour later Kate Lane came downstairs again. Reacher figured it was possible to see she that was pregnant. Just.

He asked, 'Is Jade doing OK?'

'She's asleep now but she hasn't been sleeping great. The jet lag screwed her up. And she's a little nervous. And she doesn't understand why there are no animals here. She doesn't understand arable farming. She thinks we're hiding a whole bunch of cute little creatures from her.'

Reacher said, 'Tell me how the whole thing went down.'

'It was pretty easy, really. We did stuff in advance. Bought the voice machine, rented the room, got the chair, took the car keys.'

'Taylor did most of that, right?'

'But I had to buy the voice machine. Too weird if a guy who couldn't talk wanted one.'

'I guess.'

'Then I copied the photograph at Staples. That was tough. I had to let Groom drive me. It would have been too suspicious to insist on Graham all the time. But after that it was easy. We left for Bloomingdale's that morning and went straight to Graham's apartment instead. Just holed up there and waited. Then later we started the phone calls. Right from the apartment.'

'You forgot to say no cops.'

'I know. I was so nervous at first. I thought I'd blown it. But Edward didn't seem to notice. Then it got much easier later.'

'Why did you split the demands into three parts?'

'Because to ask for it all at once would have been too much of a clue. We thought we'd better let the stress build up. Then maybe Edward would miss the connection.'

'I don't think he missed it. But I think he misinterpreted it. He started thinking about the Africa connection.'

'Edward wanted to own me. Like a chattel. And he said if I was ever unfaithful he would hurt Jade. He said he would tie me up and make me watch him do it. You try to blot a thing like that right out of your mind. But I knew he was capable of doing it. They say you should never get between a lioness and her cub. I never really understood that before. Now I do.'

The room went as quiet as only the countryside can be. The flames in the fireplace flickered and danced.

Reacher asked, 'Are you planning on staying on here?'

'I hope to,' Kate said. 'Organic farming is going to be a big thing. Better for people, better for the land. Maybe we can expand a little.'

'Hard to picture you as a farmer.'

'I think I'm going to enjoy it.'

'Even when Lane is out of the picture completely?'

'In that case I guess we could go back to New York occasionally. But never to the Dakota apartment.'

'Anne's sister lives directly opposite the Dakota. She's been watching Lane every day for four years.'

Kate said, 'I'd like to meet her. And I'd like to see Hobart's sister again.'

'Like a survivors' club,' Pauling said.

Reacher walked to the window. Saw nothing but blackness. Heard nothing but silence.

'First we have to survive,' he said.

THEY KEPT THE FIRE GOING and dozed quietly in the armchairs. When the clock in Reacher's head hit one thirty in the morning he tapped Pauling on the knee and stood up and stretched. They headed outside together into the dead-of-night dark and cold. Reacher headed for the south end of the house.

He settled in and waited. After a minute his eyesight had adjusted and he saw that there was a little moonlight behind heavy cloud. Nobody would see him from a distance. But at night vision was not the sense that counted anyway. Hearing was primary.

He stepped forward two paces and stood still. Turned his head slowly and scoped out a two-hundred-degree arc all around him.

He would hear any human approach a hundred yards away.

Reacher, in the dark. Armed and dangerous. Invincible.

HE STOOD in the same spot for five straight hours. Nobody came. By six thirty in the morning there was a bright horizontal band of pink in the sky. Grey visibility was spreading westwards slowly, like an incoming tide.

The time of maximum danger.

Taylor and Jackson came out of the house carrying the third and fourth rifles. Reacher took up a new station against the rear façade of the house, facing south. Taylor mirrored his position against the front wall. Reacher knew that sixty feet behind them Jackson and Pauling were doing the same thing. Reasonable security.

For as long as they could bear to stay in position.

THEY STAYED in position all day long and well into the evening. Fourteen straight hours.

Lane didn't come.

One at a time they took short meal breaks and shorter bathroom breaks. Their eight-pound rifles started to feel like eight tons in their hands. Jackson turned the bird scarer back on.

Kate and Jade stayed in the house, out of sight. They made food and poured drinks. The sun burned through the mist and the day grew warm, and then it grew cold again in the late afternoon.

Lane didn't come.

Jade drew pictures. She drew the red Mini Cooper, she drew Pauling with her gun. She drew Reacher, taller than the house. Then she drew farm animals in the barns, even though she had been told that the Jacksons didn't have any.

Lane didn't come.

Jade took to asking everyone in turn if she could come outside and explore. Everyone in turn said no. On the third go-round Reacher heard her modify her request and ask Taylor if she could come out after dark, and he heard Taylor say maybe, like worn-down parents everywhere.

At eight thirty in the evening they all met in a loose huddle by the front door, shaky with fatigue.

Taylor said, 'He's waiting us out.'

'Therefore he's going to win,' Jackson said. 'We can't keep this up much longer.'

Pauling said, 'We have to assume he's armed by now.'

'He'll come tomorrow at dawn,' Taylor said.

'You sure?' Reacher asked.

'Not really. Three or four in the morning would work just as well.'

'Too dark,' Jackson said.

'If they've bought guns they could have bought night vision.'

'How would you do it?' Reacher asked Taylor.

'Three guys walk in from the north,' Taylor replied. 'The other four come up the driveway, maybe two in a car, lights off, high speed, with the other two flanking it on foot. Seven guys. We couldn't stop at least three of them getting inside. They'd get a hostage before we could react.'

'We'd get them before they got anywhere near the house,' Pauling said.

'Only if all four of us can stay awake and alert for the next eight hours. Or the next thirty-two hours.' Taylor sighed. 'Lane's in no hurry.'

'Time is on Lane's side, not ours,' Reacher said. 'This is a siege now. We're going to run out of food, and sooner or later all four of us are going to be asleep at the same time.'

'So we halve the guard,' Taylor suggested. 'One man south, one man north, the other two resting but ready.'

Reacher shook his head. 'No, it's time to get aggressive. I'm going to go find them. They've got to be holed up here somewhere.'

'Alone?' Pauling said. 'That's insane.'

'I have to anyway,' Reacher said. 'I didn't get Hobart's money yet. There's eight hundred grand out there. Can't let it go to waste.'

REACHER FETCHED the Ordnance Survey map from the Mini and looked at it with Jackson. Grange Farm and Bishops Pargeter were roughly in the centre of a wide triangle of empty space bounded to the east by the road that ran south from Norwich to Ipswich and to the west by the Thetford road. Elsewhere in the triangle were meandering tracks and isolated farm settlements. Some of the larger buildings were shown. The only one within any kind of a reasonable distance from Bishops Pargeter, and labelled PH, was the Bishop's Arms.

'Are they there, do you think?' Reacher asked.

Jackson said, 'If they stopped in Fenchurch St Mary first and then aimed for Bishops Pargeter afterwards, then that's the only place they could have passed. But nearer Norwich there are a lot of places.'

'I think they stayed close,' Reacher said.

'Then the Bishop's Arms could be it,' Jackson said.

Five miles, Reacher thought. *On foot, that's a three-hour round trip. Back by midnight.*

'I'm going to check it out,' he said.

He detoured via the mudroom and collected two spare magazines for his G36. Found Pauling's purse in the kitchen and borrowed her little Maglite. Folded the map and put it in his pocket. Then he huddled with the others in the dark outside the front door and agreed a password. He didn't want to get shot at when he arrived back. Jackson suggested *Canaries*, which was the Norwich soccer team's nickname, for its yellow strip.

'Are they any good?' Reacher asked.

'They used to be,' Jackson said. 'Twenty-some years ago, they were great.'

Them and me both, Reacher thought.

He started by walking north behind the house. Then he turned west, staying parallel to the road. There was a little leftover twilight in the sky. Ragged clouds with pale stars beyond. The dirt was soft and heavy underfoot. He carried his G36 by its handle, left-handed, ready to swing it up into position when needed.

The Grange Farm boundary was a drainage trench ten feet across with a muddy bottom six feet down. Reacher had to slide down the near bank, struggle through the mud, and then climb up the far bank again.

Two miles into the trip he was very tired. And behind schedule. He changed course and moved closer to the road. Found a tractor route through the next farmer's fields. He speeded up a little. He followed the tyre tracks until they turned abruptly north. Then he struck off through the fields again.

Five minutes before eleven o'clock he spotted the glow from the pub's sign. He kept well to the north of the road, just in case Lane had watchers out, until he was facing the back of the building from four hundred yards away. He saw small squares of harsh white fluorescent light. Kitchen or bathroom windows, he guessed.

He headed south, straight for the squares of light.

REACHER CIRCLED the building in the dark, clockwise, away from the spill of light from the windows.

The small, bright rooms in back were clearly gents' and ladies' washrooms. He rounded the corner and found there were no windows in the end wall to the east of the building. He rounded the next corner and peered into the public bar, east of the entrance. Reacher saw the same four farmers he had seen two nights previously. And the same bartender.

He moved on.

The car park had four cars in it. None of the cars was new. None of them was the kind of thing a Park Lane rental company could have produced in a hurry.

West of the entrance were three more windows, into the saloon bar.

Two nights previously the saloon bar had been empty. It wasn't empty any more. Now a single table was occupied. By three men: Groom, and Burke, and Kowalski. On the table in front of them Reacher could see the remains of a meal. And three half-full glasses. The room was warm and bright and inviting.

Reacher moved on.

Around the next corner there was a single window in the end wall to the west and through it Reacher got a different view of the saloon bar.

Reacher backtracked four short steps towards the front corner of the building. Invisible from any window. He dropped to his knees, and very carefully laid his rifle on the ground directly under the west-facing window. Nobody would find the rifle, unless they tripped over it. Then he shuffled south and stood up again and looped through the car park heading for the front door. Opened it up and stepped into the foyer. In front of him was the reception desk. To his right he could hear the bartender, working quietly in the public bar.

He turned the register and opened it up. Two nights previously, *J. & L. Bayswater*. The following night three guests had registered: C. Groom, A. Burke, L. Kowalski. *Make of Vehicle* had been given as Toyota Land Cruiser.

No Toyota Land Cruiser in the car park.

And where were Lane, Gregory, Perez and Addison?

He leafed back through the book and saw that the Bishop's Arms had a maximum of three rooms available. So assuming that Groom and Burke and Kowalski had been given a room each, there had been no room at the inn for the others. They had driven somewhere else.

Reacher went into the public bar. The bartender looked up at him and the four farmers nodded.

Reacher asked the bartender, 'Seven guys showed up yesterday. Three of them are here. Where did you send the other four?'

'I sent them to Maston Manor. She does bed and breakfast.'

'Where's that?'

'The other side of Bishops Pargeter. About six miles beyond.'

One of the farmers half turned and said, 'It's very nice. Classier than this place. I reckon they drew lots and the losers stayed here.'

His friends laughed. Bar-room humour, the same the world over.

'Thanks,' Reacher said. He headed back to the foyer. Stopped in front of the saloon-bar door. He put his hand on the knob. Paused a beat and then pushed the door open.

CARTER GROOM was facing the door. He looked up. Kowalski and Burke spun around and stared. Reacher stepped into the room and closed the door gently behind him.

'You've got some nerve,' Groom said.

Reacher moved towards the fireplace. Tapped the toes of his shoes against the hearth to shed some mud. Took a heavy iron poker from a hook and used the end to scrape dirt off his heels. Then he hung the poker back up. The three guys were just sitting there, waiting.

'The situation has changed,' Reacher said. He moved towards the west-facing window. He pulled out a chair from the table nearest to it and sat down, four feet and one pane of glass away from his rifle.

'Changed how?' Burke said.

'There was no kidnap,' Reacher said. 'It was faked. Kate and Taylor fell in love, they eloped. That was all. And they took Jade with them. But they had to dress the whole thing up, because Lane is a psychopath where his marriages are concerned. Among other things.'

'Kate's alive?' Groom said. 'Where?'

'Somewhere in the States, I guess.'

'So why is Taylor here?'

'He wants a showdown with Lane on his own turf.'

'He's going to get one.'

Reacher shook his head. 'That's a bad idea. He's on a farm, and it's surrounded by ditches too deep to drive through. So you'd be going in on foot. And he's got eight of his old SAS buddies with him, and his brother-in-law was a kind of Green Beret for the Brits, and he's brought in six of his guys, too. They've got Claymores on a hundred-yard perimeter and heavy machine guns in every window. They've got night vision and grenade launchers.'

'They can't possibly use them. This is England.'

'He's prepared to use them. Believe me. But actually he won't have to. Because four of the SAS guys are snipers. They've got PSG1s. Heckler & Koch sniper rifles. They'll drop you all three hundred yards out. Game over.'

The room went quiet. Kowalski picked up his drink and sipped. Then

Burke did, and then Groom. Kowalski was left-handed. Burke and Groom were right-handed. Reacher said, 'So your best play is to just forget it.'

Burke said, 'We can't just walk away.'

'You walked away in Africa,' Reacher said. 'You left Hobart and Knight behind, to save the unit. So now you should leave Lane behind, to save yourselves.'

Groom asked, 'Are you with Taylor?'

Reacher nodded. 'And I'm good with a rifle.'

'They stole all that money,' Burke said.

'Alimony. Asking for alimony is what got Anne Lane killed. Kate found that out.'

'That *was* a kidnap.'

Reacher shook his head. 'Knight offed her. For Lane, because Anne wanted out. That's why you all abandoned Knight in Africa. Lane was covering his ass. He sacrificed Hobart too because he was in the same observation post.'

'That's bullshit.'

'I found Hobart. Knight told him all about it. While they were busy getting their hands and feet cut off.'

Silence.

Burke looked at Groom. Groom looked at Burke. They both looked at Kowalski. There was a long pause.

'OK,' Burke said. 'I guess we could sit this one out.'

'Smart decision,' Reacher said. He got up and moved towards the door. Stopped at the hearth. Asked, 'Where are Lane and the others?'

Quiet. Then Groom said, 'There was no room here. They went up to Norwich. Some hotel up there.'

Reacher nodded. 'And when is he locking and loading?'

Another pause. 'Dawn the day after tomorrow.'

'What did he buy?'

'Submachine guns. MP5Ks, one each plus two spares. Ammunition, night vision, flashlights, various bits and pieces.'

'Are you going to call him? As soon as I'm gone?'

'No,' Burke said. 'He's not the kind of guy you call with this kind of news.'

'OK,' Reacher said. Then he stepped fast to his left and lifted the poker off its hook. Spun around and swung it hard and caught Carter Groom across the upper right arm. The bone shattered like a piece of dropped china. Groom opened his mouth but before any kind of a scream got out Reacher had broken Kowalski's left arm with a vicious backhanded blow.

Kowalski was left-handed. Burke and Groom were right-handed. Reacher knocked Kowalski out of his way with his hip and smashed Burke across the right wrist, pulverising every bone in there. Then he turned away and stepped to the fireplace and put the poker back on its hook.

'Just making sure,' he said. 'You didn't entirely convince me with your answers. Especially the one about Lane's hotel.'

Then he walked out of the saloon bar and closed the door quietly behind him. It was exactly eleven thirty-one in the evening, according to the clock in his head.

AT EXACTLY eleven thirty-two Edward Lane closed the Toyota's rear door on nine Heckler & Koch MP5K submachine guns, sixty thirty-round magazines of 9mm Parabellums, seven sets of night-vision goggles, ten flashlights, six rolls of duct tape and two long coils of rope. Then Gregory started the engine. Behind him on the rear bench were Perez and Addison, quiet and pensive. Lane climbed into the front passenger seat and Gregory took off west. Standard Special Forces doctrine called for dawn assaults, but it also called for the insertion of a small advance force for a period of surveillance.

AT EXACTLY eleven thirty-three by the clock on her bedside table Jade woke up. She sat up in bed for a spell. Then she swung her feet to the floor. Crossed the room and pulled back her curtain. It was dark outside. And she could go outside in the dark. Taylor had said so. She could go visit the barns, and find the animals she knew had to be there.

REACHER RETRIEVED his G36 at eleven thirty-four and set out to walk back on the road, which he reckoned would make the return trip faster, about seventy-five minutes total. He was tired, but content. Three trigger fingers out of action, the opposing force degraded to about fifty-seven per cent of its original capacity.

He walked on. Alone in the dark. Invincible.

THAT FEELING ENDED just after he had walked the length of the Grange Farm driveway and seen the dark and silent bulk of the house looming in front of him. He had called the password at least half a dozen times. At first quietly, and then louder.

Canaries, canaries, canaries.

He had got no response at all.

Chapter Twelve

Reacher raised his rifle to the ready position. *No point in having a weapon unless it's ready for instant use.* He stood absolutely still. Listened hard. Heard nothing.

Lane, he thought.

He wasn't surprised. Surprise was strictly for amateurs, and Reacher was a professional. He just walked away from the house. Making himself smaller as a target and improving his angle of view. The windows were all dark. Just a faint red glow from the kitchen. The remains of the fire. The front door was closed. Near it was the shape of the Mini Cooper. Canted down at the front, like it was kneeling.

He walked towards it, knelt down near the front bumper, and felt for the tyre. There were torn shreds of rubber and a vicious curled length of bead wire. He shuffled quietly to the other side. Same situation.

A front-wheel-drive car, comprehensively disabled.

He headed for the front door. It was closed but unlocked. He turned the handle. Pushed the door open. Raised the rifle. The house was dark. It felt empty. He checked the kitchen. The room looked exactly like he had left it, except there were no people in it.

He switched on the flashlight and clamped it in his left palm under the rifle's barrel. Used it to check all the other ground-floor rooms. All empty.

He crept up the stairs. The first room he came to was clearly Jade's. The bed had been slept in. No sign of the child herself.

The next room belonged to the Jacksons. There was a vanity table cluttered with cosmetics. There were framed photographs of a girl that wasn't Jade. Melody, Reacher guessed. A backhoe catalogue on one of the bedside tables. Jackson's bedtime reading.

No sign of Jackson.

The next room was Kate and Taylor's. An old double bed, an oak bedside table. Undecorated, like a guest room. The photograph was propped on a dresser. Kate and Jade, together. The original print. No frame.

He moved on. Then he stopped, halfway along the upstairs hallway.

Because there was blood on the floor.

It was a small, thin stain, a foot long, like flung paint. Suggestive of rapid movement. Reacher sniffed. There was a faint smell of gunpowder. He sighted down the hallway with the Maglite beam and saw an open bathroom door at the far end. A smashed tile on the back wall, at chest height.

So at least one wounded, Reacher thought as he eased down the stairs and back out into the night.

He circled the house, clockwise. The barns were distant and dark and quiet. The old Land Rover was collapsed on its rims, as he had been certain it would be. Four blown tyres. He walked past it and stopped against the south gable wall. Turned the Maglite off and stared into the darkness.

How had it happened?

He trusted Pauling because he knew her and he trusted Taylor and Jackson even without knowing them. Three professionals. Tired, but functioning. A long, perilous approach from the intruders' point of view. He should have been looking at four riddled bodies and a wrecked rental car.

So why wasn't he?

Distraction, he figured. As ever, the answer was in Jade's pictures. The animals in the barns. *She hasn't been sleeping great*, Kate had said. Reacher pictured the child waking, maybe around midnight, running out of the house into the imagined safety of the darkness, four adults scrambling after her, panic, a search, unseen watchers moving in. Taylor and Jackson and Pauling holding their fire in case they hit each other or Kate or Jade.

Lane recognising his own stepdaughter.

His own wife.

Reacher shivered once, a violent, uncontrollable spasm. He clicked the Maglite on and lowered the beam to light his way, and walked on down the driveway. After the first curve in the track he started to run. Towards he knew not where.

PEREZ FLIPPED HIS night-vision goggles into the up position on his forehead and said, 'OK, Reacher's gone.'

Edward Lane nodded.

He turned to Perez and said, 'Find a telephone. Call the Bishop's Arms. Tell the others to get here now.'

'We've got the truck,' Perez said.

'Tell them to walk,' Lane said.

Jackson said, 'Reacher will come back, you know.' He was the only one who could talk. The only one without tape on his mouth, even though his face was a mess where Lane had hit him.

Lane said, 'I know he'll come back. Worst case for us he'll walk six miles east and find nothing and walk back here again. It will take him four hours. You'll be dead by then. He can watch the child die, and then Ms Pauling, and then I'll kill him. Slowly.'

'You're insane,' Jackson said.

'I'm angry,' Lane said. 'And I think I have a right to be.'

Perez left.

REACHER RAN THROUGH the second curve in the driveway. Then he slowed a little. Then he stopped dead.

He killed the flashlight beam. Stood still and concentrated on the after-image of what he had just seen.

The mud showed tyre tracks. Three sets.

First, Tony Jackson's old Land Rover.

Second, the Mini Cooper's tyres.

The third set was a large, heavy vehicle, open treads, new and crisp. The kind of tyres a rented Toyota Land Cruiser would wear.

One set only. One way.

Lane was still on the property.

LANE HIT JACKSON again with his flashlight, hard, and Jackson went down.

Lane stepped up close to Kate. Eye to eye. He lit up the flashlight beam and held it just under her chin, shining it directly upwards, turning her exquisite face into a ghastly Halloween mask.

'Till death us do part,' he said. 'That's a phrase I take seriously.'

Kate turned her head away. Lane clamped her chin in his free hand and turned her head back.

'Forsaking all others,' he said. 'I took that part seriously too. I'm so sorry that you didn't.'

Kate closed her eyes.

REACHER KEPT ON WALKING to the end of the drive, over the bridge, east on the road, away from the farm, his flashlight on. He figured he needed to let them see him go. To see a small spectral night-vision figure strolling away.

He walked east for two hundred yards and clicked off the Maglite. Then he turned ninety degrees and hiked north across the shoulder and slid down the boundary ditch's nearside slope. Clawed his way up the far side with his rifle held one-handed high in the air. Then he ran, fast, straight north.

Two minutes later he was a quarter of a mile in. He paused to recover. Thumbed his fire selector to single shots. Then he put the stock against his shoulder and walked forward. Towards the barns.

Reacher, armed and dangerous. Coming back.

EDWARD LANE was still face to face with Kate. He said, 'I'm assuming you've been sleeping with him for years.'

Kate said nothing.

'I hope you've been using condoms. You could catch a disease from a guy like that.'

Then he smiled. A new thought. A joke. 'Or you could get pregnant.'

Something in her terrified eyes.

He paused. 'You're pregnant,' he said. 'You're pregnant, aren't you? I can tell.'

He put the flat of his hand on her belly and she pulled away hard against the post she was tied to.

'Oh man, this is unbelievable. You're going to die with another man's child inside you.'

Then he spun away. Stopped, and turned back.

'Can't allow that,' he said. 'Wouldn't be right. We'll have to abort it first.'

Kate closed her eyes.

'You're going to die anyway,' Lane said, like the most reasonable man in the world.

REACHER KNEW they were in a barn. Where else could they hide their truck? He knew there were five barns.

He started with the nearest, hoping to get lucky. But he didn't get lucky. Reacher put his ear on a crack between two boards and listened hard. Heard nothing inside. He put his eye on the crack and saw nothing. Just darkness.

He moved on to the second barn, hoping to get lucky. But the second barn was just as dark and quiet as the first. He moved on through the blackness, towards the three barns grouped around the yard. Stopped dead.

Because in the corner of his eye he saw light and movement, in the house. The kitchen window.

LANE TURNED to Gregory and said, 'We need an operating table. Find something flat. And turn the truck's lights on. I need to be able to see what I'm doing.'

REACHER MOVED FAST and quiet to the back door of the house. Waited. He could hear a voice through the door. A slight Hispanic accent. Perez, on the phone. Reacher reversed his rifle in his hands. Gripped the foregrip in front of the carrying handle.

Then he waited.

Two minutes later Perez stepped out into the night and turned to close the door behind him. Reacher swung. The sight block caught Perez in the temple. He was dead before he hit the ground.

LANE TURNED to Addison and said, 'Go find out what the hell Perez is up to. He should have been back by now.'

'Reacher's out there,' Jackson said. 'That's why Perez isn't back.'

Lane smiled. 'So what should I do? Go out and search? Not going to happen. Because right about now Reacher is walking past the Bishops Pargeter church.'

REACHER WAS CROUCHING outside the kitchen door, sorting through all the things that Perez had dropped. An MP5K with a thirty-round magazine and a ballistic nylon shoulder sling. A flashlight, now broken. Two kitchen knives, one serrated, one plain.

Reacher tucked one knife in his shoe. Picked up the MP5 submachine gun and slung it over his left shoulder.

Then he headed back north and east towards the barns.

Reacher, alone in the dark. Doing it the hard way.

REACHER STEPPED INTO the beaten earth yard. It was a little more than a hundred feet square, with barns on the north side, and the east, and the south. All three had tall sliding doors and tile roofs and wood wall planks, dull grey in the starlight.

No immediate way of telling which one was currently occupied.

He stood still. North or east, he guessed. Easier for the truck. He crossed the yard, slow and silent. He made it to the near left-hand corner of the north barn. Circled it, clockwise.

He came around to the right-hand front corner. He crept along the front wall and put his ear on the space between the door and the wall. Heard nothing. Saw no chink of light.

Wrong one, he thought.

He turned and glanced east. *Has to be*, he thought. He set off towards it.

He was twenty feet away when the door rolled back. A yard-wide bar of bright blue light spilled out. The Toyota four-wheel drive parked inside, its headlights on. Addison stepped out. His MP5 was slung over his shoulder. He turned to roll the door shut again. He got it to within six inches of closed, clicked on a flashlight and set off towards the house.

Reacher took a deep breath and fell in behind Addison, fast and silent.

Then the two figures merged in the dark. They stopped. The flashlight hit the dirt. Addison stumbled and went down, his throat ripped by the knife from Reacher's shoe.

Reacher was on his way even before Addison had stopped twitching. With an automatic rifle, two submachine guns. He walked on down to the house. Made his first port of call upstairs in the master bathroom. Then he stopped in the kitchen, at the hearth and at the desk. Then he came back out and walked towards the barns.

He stopped beside the eastern barn. Rejected the G36. It fired only single rounds or triples, and it fired them too slowly. So he laid the G36 on the ground and dropped the magazine out of Perez's MP5. Nine rounds left. Perez had been the designated trigger man. Which meant that Addison's magazine should still be full. Which it was. He put Addison's magazine in Perez's gun. A magazine he knew to be full, in a gun he knew to be working. A sensible step for a man who planned to live through the next five minutes. He breathed in, breathed out.

Showtime.

He sat on the ground with his back against the partly open door. Assembled the things he had brought from the house. A seventeen-inch length of ash bough, thick as a child's wrist. Three rubber bands. A tortoiseshell hand mirror.

He fixed the tortoiseshell handle to the ash bough with the rubber bands. Then he lay down flat and inched the bough forward. Towards the six-inch gap where the barn door stood open. Left-handed. He tilted the stick until he could see a perfect reflection of the view inside.

The mirror showed that the barn was strong and square because it had vertical timbers inside that held up the roof ridge and reinforced the timber peg rafters. There were twelve. Five of them had people tied to them. From left to right in the mirror Reacher could see Taylor, then Jackson, then Pauling, then Kate, then Jade. Their arms were pulled behind them and their wrists were tied behind the posts. Their ankles were tied together. They had duct tape across their mouths. All except Jackson.

But his mouth was a bloody mess. He wasn't standing.

It was Taylor who had been wounded. His shirt was soaked with blood, upper right arm. Pauling looked OK. Kate was as white as a sheet and her eyes were closed. Jade had slid down her post, head down, fainted maybe.

The Toyota had been backed in and turned so that it was hard up against the end wall on the left. Its headlights were turned full on.

Gregory was wrestling with some kind of a large, flat panel. An old door, maybe. Walking it across the floor of the barn.

Lane was standing in the middle of the floor, his right fist around his MP5's pistol grip and his left fist around the fore grip. His finger was on the trigger. He was facing the door. *Borderline mentally ill*, people had said. *Crossed that border long ago*, Reacher thought.

Gregory got the big flat panel front and centre and Reacher heard him say, 'Where do you want this?'

Lane answered, 'We need sawhorses.' Lane kicked Jackson in the ribs and asked him, 'Do you have sawhorses here?' and Jackson said, 'In the other barn,' and Lane said, 'I'll send Perez and Addison for them when they get back.'

'They're not coming back,' Jackson said. 'Reacher's out there and he's got them.'

'You're annoying me,' Lane said. But Reacher saw him glance towards the door. And he saw what Jackson was trying to do. He was trying to focus Lane's attention outside the barn. He was trying to buy time.

Then Reacher heard Lane walk just inside the door and scream, 'Reacher? You out there?'

Reacher waited.

Lane screamed, 'Reacher? You there? Listen up. Ten seconds from now, I'm going to shoot Jackson. In the thighs. He'll bleed out through his femoral arteries.'

Reacher waited.

'Ten,' Lane screamed. 'Nine. Eight.' His voice faded as he stalked back to the centre of the barn. Then Lane turned again and yelled, 'Seven. Six. Five.' Gregory was standing with the panel held vertical in front of him.

'Four,' Lane screamed.

Reacher considered taking the risk of sacrificing Jackson. One KIA out of five hostages wasn't excessive. He'd been given a medal for an outcome worse than that.

'Three,' Lane screamed.

But Reacher liked Jackson, and there were Susan and Melody to consider. Susan, the loyal sister. Melody, the innocent child. And there was Kate Lane's dream to think about, the new extended family farming together.

'Two,' Lane screamed.

Reacher dropped the mirror and extended his right arm like a swimmer and hooked his fingers around the edge of the door. Crawled backwards, fast, hauling the door with him. Opening it wide, the full twenty feet, staying out of sight.

Then he waited.

Silence inside the barn. He knew Lane's eyes were on the black void outside. Knew his ears were straining to hear something in the stillness. The oldest of all atavistic human fears. *There's something out there.*

Reacher heard a thump as Gregory dropped the panel. Then it was a foot race. From Lane's perspective the door had opened right to left, driven by some unseen agency. Therefore that agency was now outside and to the left. Reacher stood up and turned and ran counterclockwise around the barn. Three hundred feet, four turns, in about thirty seconds. An Olympic athlete would have done it in ten, but an Olympic athlete didn't need to be composed enough at the finish line to fire a submachine gun accurately.

Now he was outside and to the right.

Silence inside the barn. No movement. Reacher planted his feet and leaned his left shoulder on the wall, his elbow tucked in, his wrist turned, his hand on the MP5's front grip, lightly. His right index finger had already moved the trigger through its first eighth-inch of slack. His left eye was closed and his right eye had lined up both iron sights. He waited. Heard a soft footfall on the barn's concrete floor, four feet in front of him and three feet to his left. Saw a shadow in the spill of light. Saw the back of Lane's head, just a narrow arc like a crescent moon, craning out, peering left into the darkness. Reacher wanted to fire parallel with the barn, not into it. Moving his gun would put hostages in the line of fire. He had to let Lane come to him.

Lane came to him. Inched out, craning left. Inched out a little more. Into the MP5's sight. First, the right-hand edge of his skull. Then a larger sliver. Then the front sight was on the bony ridge at the back of his head. Dead-on centred.

For half a second he thought about calling Lane's name. Making him turn around. Telling him why he was about to die.

Then he thought about a fight. Man to man. Something ceremonial. Maybe something fairer.

Then he thought about Hobart, and he pulled the trigger.

A strange blurred purr, like a sewing machine or a distant motorcycle at a light. The empty thump of flesh and bone hitting concrete was clearly audible, muffled only by cotton and canvas clothing.

I hope Jade didn't see that, Reacher thought.

Then he stepped into the doorway. Gregory was looking left, but the shots that had killed Lane had come from the right.

'Shoot him,' Jackson said.

Reacher didn't move.

'Shoot him,' Jackson said again. 'Don't make me tell you what that table was for.'

Reacher risked a glance at Taylor. Taylor nodded. Reacher glanced at Pauling. She nodded too. So Reacher put three in Gregory's chest.

CLEANUP TOOK the rest of the night and most of the next day. Even though they were all bone-weary, by common consensus they didn't try to sleep. Except for Jade. Kate put her to bed and sat with her while she slept. The child had fainted early and had missed most of what had gone on and seemed not to have understood the rest. Reacher figured that if any ill effects arrived in the days to come she would work them out with crayons on paper.

Kate herself looked like she had been to hell and back. She had stared down at Lane's body for a long moment. Understood for sure that there was going to be no Hollywood moment where he reared up again, back to life. He had gone, utterly, completely and definitively. And she had seen it happen. That kind of certainty helps a person. She walked away from the corpse with a spring in her step.

Taylor's right triceps was all torn up. Reacher field-dressed the wound as best he could. But he was going to need attention. He decided to delay it by a couple of days. It seemed smart to distance an A&E visit from mayhem in the night.

Jackson was OK apart from cut eyebrows and some facial bruising and a split lip and a couple of loose teeth. Nothing worse than he had experienced half a dozen times before with 1st Para, he said.

Pauling was fine. Reacher had cut her ropes and she had torn the tape off her mouth herself and then kissed him hard. She seemed to have had total confidence that he would show up and work something out. He wasn't sure if she was telling the truth or flattering him. Either way he didn't mention how close he had come to walking away on some phantom pursuit. Didn't mention how lucky it was that a stray peripheral glance at the driveway's surface had fired some random synapse in his brain.

Reacher searched the Toyota and found Lane's leather duffle. The one he had seen before, in the Park Lane Hilton. The eight hundred thousand dollars was all there. Untouched. He gave it to Pauling for safekeeping. Then he sat on the floor, leaning back on the post that Kate had been tied to, six feet away from Gregory's corpse. He was calm. Just another night of business as usual in his long and violent life. He was used to it. And where some men might have agonised over justification, he spent his energy figuring out where best to hide the bodies.

They hid them in a ten-acre field near the northwest corner of the farm. Jackson fired up the backhoe. Started work immediately on a massive pit that needed to be thirty feet long, nine feet wide and nine feet deep, because they had decided to bury the cars as well.

Taylor was walking wounded so he was excused from heavy work. Instead he scoured the area for every piece of physical evidence he could find. Pauling scrubbed his blood off the upstairs hallway floor and replaced the shattered bathroom tile. Reacher piled the bodies inside the Toyota.

The sun had been up for hours before the pit was finished. Jackson had left a neat graded slope at one end and Reacher drove the Toyota down it and smashed it hard against the earth wall at the other end. Jackson drove the backhoe to the house and manoeuvred the Mini all the way to the pit and rolled it down the slope. Taylor threw the other items in the hole. Then Jackson started to fill it.

Reacher sat and watched. The sky was pale blue and the sun was watery. There were thin, high clouds and a mild breeze that felt warm. He watched Jackson work until the dirt hid the top of the cars, and then he walked away, slowly, back to the house.

EXACTLY TWELVE MONTHS LATER to the hour the field was dusted pale green with a brand-new winter crop. Tony and Susan Jackson and Graham and Kate Taylor were working the field next to it. Back at the house the nine-year-old cousins and best friends Melody Jackson and

Jade Taylor were watching Jade's baby brother, a healthy five-month-old boy named Jack.

Three thousand miles west of Grange Farm Lauren Pauling was in her Barrow Street apartment, drinking coffee and reading the *New York Times*. She had missed a piece inside the main section that reported the deaths of three newly arrived private military contractors in Iraq. Their names were Burke, Groom and Kowalski, and they had died two days previously when a land mine exploded under their vehicle outside Baghdad. But she caught a piece in the Metro section in which it was reported that the cooperative board at the Dakota Building had foreclosed on an apartment after twelve consecutive months of unpaid monthly maintenance. On entering the apartment they had found more than nine million dollars in a locked closet.

Six thousand miles west of Grange Farm, Patti Joseph was fast asleep in a waterfront condominium in Seattle, Washington. She was ten months into a new job as a magazine copy editor. Her perseverance and her relentless eye for detail made her good at it. She was seeing a local journalist. She was happy.

Far from Seattle, far from New York City, far from Bishops Pargeter, down in Birmingham, Alabama, Dee Marie Graziano was up early in a hospital gymnasium, watching her brother grasp his new metal canes and walk across the floor.

Nobody knew where Jack Reacher was. He had left Grange Farm two hours after the backhoe had shut down, and there had been no news of him since.

LEE CHILD

Born: 1954, Coventry
Homes: Manhattan, the South of France
Website: www.leechild.com

Lee Child's writing career started in 1995 with a bold gamble. He'd been working for Granada Television for many years when he was suddenly made redundant at the age of forty. He was determined not to get another corporate job, and when his wife, Jane, asked him what he was going to do, he recalls that he replied, '"Well, I'm going to be a novelist." She took it very well, really.'

He comments that in hindsight it does seems a rather crazy thing to have done. 'But I put all my time and energy into writing. I saw it as the best option I had. Looking back, it was incredibly risky.' Luckily, it was a gamble that paid off. Child's first novel, *Killing Floor*, was published in 1997 and quickly became an international best seller. He has published a novel a year since, all equally successful, and all featuring his maverick tough guy, Jack Reacher.

When it came to creating Reacher, Child was determined to buck the trend towards miserable or dysfunctional heroes. 'I wanted a happy-go-lucky guy. He has quirks and problems but, the thing is, he doesn't know he's got them. Hence no tedious self-pity. He's smart and strong, an introvert, but any anguish he suffers is caused by others.'

Reacher is an American through and through and the novels are set in the US: a difficult trick for the British Lee Child to pull off, although he says that the years of listening to American dialogue during his television career were a help. The decision to make Reacher American was partly driven by commercial realities—the US has a bigger fiction market—but also influenced by Child's love of America's wide open spaces.

When writing brought him the freedom to relocate to New York with his American wife, Child jumped at the chance. He hasn't lost touch with his roots, however. He's still a keen Aston Villa fan and drives a supercharged Jaguar on the American highways; built at the Brown's Lane plant, just thirty yards form the hospital where he was born.

Fans of the Reacher series will be pleased to learn that rights to *Killing Floor* have just been bought by Paramount, with Tom Cruise tipped to be the film's producer.

Marley
& Me

JOHN GROGAN

'A person can learn a lot from a dog, even a loopy one like ours. Marley taught me about living each day with unbridled exhuberance and joy, about seizing the moment and following your heart. And as he grew old and achy, he taught me about optimism in the face of adversity. Mostly, he taught me about friendship and selflessness and, above all else, unwavering loyalty.'

John Grogan

Preface

In the summer of 1967, when I was ten years old, my father caved in to my persistent pleas and took me to get my own dog. Together we drove in the family station wagon far into the Michigan countryside to a farm run by a rough-hewn woman and her ancient mother. The farm produced just one commodity—dogs. Dogs of every imaginable size and shape and age and temperament. They had only two things in common: each was a mongrel of unknown and indistinct ancestry, and each was free to a good home. We were at a mutt ranch.

'Now, take your time, son,' Dad said. 'Your decision today is going to be with you for many years to come.'

I immediately raced to the puppy cage. 'You want to pick one that's not timid,' my father coached. 'Try rattling the cage and see which ones aren't afraid.'

I grabbed the chain-link gate and yanked on it with a loud clang. The dozen or so puppies reeled backwards, collapsing on top of one another in a squiggling heap of fur. Just one remained. He was gold with a white blaze on his chest, and he charged the gate, yapping fearlessly. He jumped up and excitedly licked my fingers through the fencing. It was love at first sight.

I brought him home in a cardboard box and named him Shaun. He was one of those dogs that give dogs a good name. He effortlessly mastered every command I taught him and was naturally well behaved. I could drop a crust on the floor and he would not touch it until I gave the OK. He came when I called him and stayed when I told him to. Best of all, I trained him to pull me through the neighbourhood dog-sled-style as I sat on my bicycle, making me the hands-down envy of my friends.

He was with me when I smoked my first cigarette (and my last) and when I kissed my first girl. He was right there beside me in the front seat when I snuck out my older brother's car for my first joy ride.

Shaun was spirited but controlled, affectionate but calm. Relatives would visit for the weekend and return home determined to buy a dog of their own, so impressed were they with Shaun—or 'Saint Shaun', as I came to call him. It was a family joke, the saint business. Born with the curse of uncertain lineage, he was one of the tens of thousands of unwanted dogs in America. Yet by some stroke of good fortune, he became wanted. He came into my life and I into his—and in the process, he gave me the childhood every kid deserves.

The love affair lasted fourteen years, and by the time he died I was out of college and working across the state in my first real job. Saint Shaun had stayed behind when I moved on. It was where he belonged. My parents, by then retired, called to break the news to me. My mother would later tell me, 'In fifty years of marriage, I've only seen your father cry twice. The first time was when we lost Mary Ann'—my sister, who was stillborn. 'The second time was the day Shaun died.'

Saint Shaun of my childhood. He was a perfect dog. It was Shaun who set the standard by which I would judge all other dogs to come.

Chapter I

And Puppy Makes Three

We were young. We were in love. We were rollicking in those sublime early days of marriage when life seems as good as life can get. We could not leave well enough alone.

And so on a January evening in 1991, my wife of fifteen months and I ate a quick dinner together and headed off to answer a classified ad in the *Palm Beach Post*.

Why we were doing this, I wasn't quite sure. A few weeks earlier I had awoken just after dawn to find the bed beside me empty. I got up and found Jenny sitting in her bathrobe at the glass table on the screened porch of our little bungalow, bent over the newspaper with a pen in her hand.

There was nothing unusual about the scene. Not only was the *Palm Beach Post* our local paper, it was also the source of half of our household income. We were a two-newspaper-career couple. Jenny worked as a feature writer in the *Post*'s 'Accent' section; I was a reporter at the competing paper in the area, the South Florida *Sun-Sentinel*, based an hour south in Fort Lauderdale. We began every morning poring over the newspapers, seeing how our stories stacked up to the competition. We circled, underlined and clipped with abandon.

But on this morning, Jenny's nose was in the classified section. When I stepped closer, I saw she was feverishly circling beneath the heading 'Pets—Dogs'.

'Uh,' I said in that new-husband, still-treading-gently voice. 'Is there something I should know?'

'It's the plant,' she said, her voice carrying an edge of desperation.

'The plant?' I asked.

'That dumb plant,' she said. 'The one we killed.'

The one *we* killed? I wasn't about to press the point, but for the record it was the plant that *I* bought and *she* killed. I had surprised her with it one night, a lovely large dieffenbachia with emerald-and-cream variegated leaves. 'What's the occasion?' she'd asked. But there was none. I'd given it to her for no reason other than to say, 'Damn, isn't married life great?'

She had adored both the gesture and the plant. Then she promptly went on to nurture the poor thing to death. Jenny didn't exactly have a green thumb. Working on the assumption that all living things require water, but apparently forgetting that they also need air, she began flooding the dieffen-bachia on a daily basis.

'Be careful not to overwater it,' I had warned.

'OK,' she had replied, and then dumped on another gallon.

The sicker the plant got, the more she doused it, until finally it just kind of melted into an oozing heap. Now here she was, somehow making the cosmic leap of logic from dead flora in a pot to living fauna in the pet classifieds. *Kill a plant, buy a puppy.* Well, of course it made perfect sense.

I looked more closely at the newspaper in front of her and saw that she had drawn three fat red stars beside one ad. It read: 'Lab puppies, yellow. American Kennel Club purebred. All shots. Parents on premises.'

'So,' I said, 'can you run this plant-pet thing by me one more time?'

'You know,' she said, looking up. 'I tried so hard and look what happened. I can't even keep a stupid house plant alive. I mean, how hard is *that*? All you need to do is water the damn thing.'

Then she got to the real issue: 'If I can't even keep a plant alive, how am I ever going to keep a baby alive?' She looked as if she might start crying.

The Baby Thing, as I called it, had become a constant in Jenny's life and was getting bigger by the day. When we had first met, at a small newspaper in western Michigan, she was just a few months out of college, and serious adulthood still seemed a far distant concept. For both of us, it was our first professional job out of school. We ate a lot of pizza, drank a lot of beer and gave exactly zero thought to the possibility of someday being anything other than young, single, unfettered consumers of pizza and beer.

But years passed. We had barely begun dating when various job opportunities pulled us in different directions across the eastern United States. At first we were one hour's drive apart. Then we were three hours apart. Then eight, then twenty-four. By the time we both landed together in South Florida and tied the knot, she was nearly thirty. Her friends were having babies. Her body was sending her strange messages. That once seemingly eternal window of procreative opportunity was slowly lowering.

I leaned over and kissed her. 'It's OK,' I said. But I had to admit, she raised a good question. We both knew we wanted to one day have children, but was either of us really up for the job? Children were so . . . so . . . scary.

A little smile broke out on Jenny's face. 'I thought maybe a dog would be good practice,' she said.

AS WE DROVE through the darkness, heading out of town into the country, I thought through our decision to bring home a dog. It was a huge responsibility, especially for two people with full-time jobs. Yet we knew what we were in for. We'd both grown up with dogs and loved them immensely. When we were dating, long before children ever came on our radar, we spent hours discussing our childhood pets, how much we missed them and how we longed someday—once we had a house and some stability in our lives—to own a dog again.

Now we had both. We were together in a place we did not plan to leave anytime soon. And we had a house to call our very own.

It was a perfect little house on a perfect little quarter-acre fenced lot just right for a dog. And the location was just right, too, a funky city neighbourhood one and a half blocks off the Intracoastal Waterway separating West Palm Beach from the rarefied mansions of Palm Beach. At the foot of our street, Churchill Road, a linear green park and paved trail stretched for miles along the waterfront. It was ideal for jogging and bicycling. And, more than anything, for walking a dog.

The house was built in the 1950s and had an Old Florida charm—rough plaster walls, a fireplace, big airy windows, and French doors leading to our favourite space of all, the screened back porch. The yard was a little tropical haven, filled with palms and bromeliads and avocado trees. Dominating the property was a towering mango tree; each summer it dropped its heavy fruit with loud thuds that sounded, somewhat grotesquely, like bodies being thrown off the roof. We would lie awake in bed and listen: *Thud! Thud! Thud!*

We bought the two-bedroom, one-bath bungalow a few months after we returned from our honeymoon and immediately set about refurbishing it. On our first night in the house, we ripped up the carpeting and dragged it to the kerb. Where the carpet had been, we discovered a pristine oak plank floor. We painstakingly sanded and varnished it to a high sheen. Then we went out and blew the better part of two weeks' pay for a handwoven Persian rug, which we unfurled in the living room in front of the fireplace.

Once we got the joint just right, of course, it only made sense that we bring home a large, four-legged room-mate with sharp toenails, large teeth and limited English-language skills to start tearing it apart again.

'SLOW DOWN, dingo, or you're going to miss it,' Jenny scolded. We were driving through inky blackness across what had once been swampland, drained after World War II for farming and later colonised by suburbanites seeking a country lifestyle.

As Jenny predicted, our headlights soon illuminated a mailbox marked with the address we were looking for. I turned up a gravel drive that led into a large wooded property with a pond in front of the house. At the door, a middle-aged woman named Lori greeted us, a big, placid yellow Labrador retriever by her side.

'This is Lily, the proud mama,' Lori said after we introduced ourselves. Lily was just what we pictured a Lab would be—sweet-natured, affectionate, calm and breathtakingly beautiful.

'Where's the father?' I asked.

'Oh,' the woman said, hesitating for just a fraction of a second. 'Sammy Boy? He's around here somewhere.' She quickly added, 'I imagine you're dying to see the puppies.'

She led us through the kitchen out to a utility room that had been drafted into service as a nursery. Newspapers covered the floor, and in one corner was a low box with nine tiny yellow puppies clamouring to check out the latest strangers to drop by. Jenny gasped. 'Oh my,' she said. 'I don't think I've ever seen anything so cute in my life.'

We sat on the floor and let the puppies climb all over us as Lily happily bounced around. The deal I had struck with Jenny was that we would check the pups out, ask some questions, and keep an open mind as to whether to bring home a dog. 'This is the first ad we're answering,' I had said. 'Let's not make any snap decisions.' But thirty seconds into it, I could see there was no question that one of these puppies would be ours.

Lori was a back-yard breeder. She was a hobbyist, motivated by love of the breed. She owned just one female and one male. They had come from distinct bloodlines, and she had the paper trail to prove it. This would be Lily's second and final litter before she retired to the good life of a countrified family pet. With both parents on the premises, the buyer could see first-hand the lineage—although in our case, the father apparently was outside.

The litter consisted of five females, all but one of which already had deposits on them, and four males. Lori was asking $400 for the remaining female and $375 for the males. One of the males seemed particularly smitten with us. He was the goofiest of the group and charged into us, somersaulting into our laps and clawing his way up our shirts to lick our faces. He gnawed on our fingers with surprisingly sharp baby teeth and stomped clumsy circles around us on giant tawny paws that were way out of proportion to the rest of his body. 'That one there you can have for three-fifty,' the owner said.

A rabid bargain hunter, Jenny cooed, 'The little guy's on clearance!'

I had to admit he was darn adorable. Frisky, too. Before I realised what he was up to, the rascal had half my watchband chewed off.

'We have to do the scare test,' I said. Many times before I had recounted for Jenny the story of picking out Saint Shaun when I was a boy, and my father teaching me to make a sudden move or loud noise to separate the timid from the self-assured.

I stood up, turned away from the puppies, and then swung quickly back around, taking a sudden, exaggerated step towards them. I stomped my foot and barked out, 'Hey!' Only one plunged forward to meet the assault head-on. It was Clearance Dog.

'I think it's fate,' Jenny said.

'Ya think?' I said, scooping him up and holding him in one hand in front of my face, studying his mug. He looked at me with heart-melting brown eyes and then nibbled my nose. I plopped him into Jenny's arms, where he did the same to her. 'He certainly seems to like us,' I said.

And so it came to be. We wrote Lori a cheque for $350, and she told us we could return to take Clearance Dog home with us in three weeks when he was eight weeks old and weaned. We thanked her, gave Lily one last pat and said goodbye.

Walking to the car, I threw my arm around Jenny's shoulder and pulled her tight to me. 'Can you believe it?' I said. 'We actually got our dog!'

'I can't wait to bring him home,' she said.

Just as we were reaching the car, we heard a commotion coming from the woods. Something was crashing through the brush—and breathing very heavily. It sounded like what you might hear in a slasher film. Then in a flash the thing burst into the clearing and came charging in our direction, a yellow blur. A very *big* yellow blur. As it galloped past, we could see it was a large Labrador retriever. But it was nothing like the sweet Lily we had just cuddled with inside. This one was soaking wet and covered up to its belly in mud and burs. Its tongue hung out wildly to one side, and froth flew off its jowls as it barrelled past. In the split-second glimpse I got, I detected an odd, slightly crazed, yet somehow joyous gaze in its eyes.

Then, with the roar of a stampeding herd of buffalo, it was gone, around the house and out of sight. Jenny let out a little gasp.

'I think,' I said, queasiness rising in my gut, 'we just met Dad.'

Chapter 2

Running With the Blue Bloods

Our first official act as dog owners was to have a fight. It began on the drive home from the breeder's and continued in fits and snippets through the next week. We could not agree on what to name Clearance Dog. The battle culminated one morning before we left for work.

'*Chelsea?*' I said. 'That is *such* a chick name. No boy dog would be caught dead with the name Chelsea.'

'Like he'll really know,' Jenny said.

'Hunter,' I said. 'Hunter is perfect.'

'*Hunter?* You're kidding, right? What are you, on some macho sportsman trip? Way too masculine.'

'He's a male,' I said, seething. '*He's supposed to be masculine.*'

This was not going well. As we fought, Jenny absently walked to the stereo and pushed the play button on the tape deck. The lilting reggae strains of Bob Marley began to pulse through the speakers, having an almost instant mellowing effect on us both.

We had only discovered the late Jamaican singer when we moved to South Florida from Michigan. In the pulsing ethnic stew that was South Florida, Bob Marley's music, even a decade after his death, was everywhere. We heard it on the car radio as we drove down Biscayne Boulevard. We heard it as we sipped *cafés cubanos* in Little Havana and ate Jamaican jerk chicken in the immigrant neighbourhoods west of Fort Lauderdale.

The more we explored, the more we fell in love, both with South Florida and with each other. And always in the background, it seemed, was Bob Marley. He was the soundtrack for our new life in this strange, exotic place that was so unlike anywhere we had lived before.

At the exact same moment, in perfect unison, as if we had rehearsed it for weeks, we both shouted, 'Marley!'

'That's it!' I exclaimed. 'That's our name.'

Our fight was over. We had our new puppy's name.

WHILE WE COUNTED DOWN the days until we could bring Marley home, I belatedly began reading up on Labrador retrievers. I say *belatedly* because virtually everything I read gave the same advice: *Before* buying a dog, make sure you thoroughly research the breed so you know what you're getting into. Oops.

I was embarrassed to admit that Jenny and I had done almost no research before settling on a Labrador retriever. We chose the breed on one criterion alone: kerb appeal. We had often admired them with their owners down on the Intracoastal Waterway bike trail—big, dopey, playful galumphs that seemed to love life with a passion not often seen in this world.

Now, as I pored through books on the Labrador retriever, I was relieved to learn that our choice, however ill informed, was not too wildly off the mark. The literature was filled with testimonials about the Labrador's loving, even-keeled personality, its gentleness with children, its lack of aggression and its desire to please. Their intelligence and malleability had made them a leading choice for search-and-rescue training and as guide dogs for the blind. All this boded well for a pet in a home that would sooner or later most likely include children.

And yet the literature was filled with ominous caveats. Labs were bred as working dogs and tended to have boundless energy. They were highly social and did not do well left alone for long periods. They could be thick-skulled and difficult to train. They needed rigorous daily exercise or they could become destructive. Some were excitable and hard to control. They had what could seem like eternal puppyhoods, stretching three years or more. The long, exuberant adolescence required extra patience from owners.

And then I came across a sentence that struck fear in my heart. 'The parents may be one of the best indications of the future temperament of your new puppy. A surprising amount of behaviour is inherited.' My mind flashed back to the frothing, mud-caked banshee that came charging out of the woods the night we picked out our puppy. *Oh my*, I thought. The book counselled to insist, whenever possible, on seeing both the dam and the sire. My mind flashed back again, this time to the breeder's ever-so-slight hesitation when I asked where the father was. *Oh . . . He's around here somewhere.* And then the way she quickly changed the topic. It was all making sense. I said a silent prayer that Marley had inherited his mother's disposition.

Individual genetics aside, purebred Labs all share certain predictable characteristics. Physically, they are stocky and muscular, with short, dense, weather-resistant coats. Their fur can be black, chocolate brown, or a range of yellows, from light cream to a rich fox red. One of the Labrador retriever's main distinguishing characteristics is its thick, powerful tail, which resembles that of an otter and can clear a coffee table in one quick swipe. The head is large and blocky, with powerful jaws and high-set, floppy ears. Most Labs are about two feet tall in the withers, or top of the shoulders, and the typical male weighs sixty-five to eighty pounds, though some can weigh more.

But looks, according to the American Kennel Club, are not all that make a Lab a Lab. The club's breed standard states: 'True Labrador retriever temperament is as much a hallmark of the breed as the "otter" tail. The disposition is one of a kindly, outgoing, tractable nature, eager to please and non-aggressive towards man or animal. His gentle ways, intelligence and adaptability make him an ideal dog.'

An ideal dog! Endorsements did not come much more glowing than that. The more I read, the better I felt about our decision.

A WEEK BEFORE we were to bring our dog home, Jenny's sister called from Boston. She, her husband and their two children planned to be at Disney World the following week; would Jenny like to drive up and spend a few days with them? A doting aunt who looked for any opportunity to bond with her niece and nephew, Jenny was dying to go. But she was torn. 'I won't be here to bring little Marley home,' she said.

'You go,' I told her. 'I'll get the dog and have him all settled in and waiting for you when you get back.' I tried to sound nonchalant, but secretly I was overjoyed at the prospect of having the new puppy all to myself for a few days of uninterrupted male bonding.

A week later Jenny left for Orlando. That evening after work, a Friday, I returned to the breeder's house to fetch the new addition to our lives. When Lori brought my new dog out from the back of the house, I gasped audibly. The tiny, fuzzy puppy we had picked out three weeks earlier had more than doubled in size. 'He's a growing boy, isn't he?' Lori said cheerily. 'You should see him pack away the puppy chow!'

I leaned down and said, 'Ready to go home, Marley?' It was my first time using his new name for real, and it felt right.

In the car, I used beach towels to fashion a cosy nest for him on the passenger seat and set him down in it. But I was barely out of the driveway when he began wiggling his way out of the towels. He belly-crawled in my direction across the seat, whimpering as he advanced. At the centre console, Marley met the first of the countless predicaments he would find himself in over the course of his life. There he was, hind legs hanging over the passenger side of the console and front legs hanging over the driver's side. In the middle, his stomach was firmly beached on the emergency brake. His little legs were going in all directions, but he was grounded like a freighter on a sandbar.

Slowly, he began working his hind quarters into the air, his butt rising up until the law of gravity finally kicked in. He slalomed headfirst down the other side of the console, somersaulting onto my lap.

Man, was he happy—desperately happy. He quaked with joy as he burrowed his head into my stomach and nibbled the buttons of my shirt, his tail slapping the steering wheel like the needle on a metronome. *Thump. Thump. Thump.* When I cupped my hand over his head and massaged my fingers into his scalp, the beat exploded into a machine-gun rapid-fire samba. *Thumpthumpthumpthumpthump!*

'Wow! You've got rhythm!' I told him. 'You really are a reggae dog.'

When we got home, I led him inside and unhooked his leash. He began sniffing and didn't stop until he had sniffed every inch of the place. Then he sat back on his haunches and looked up at me as if to say, *Great digs, but where are my brothers and sisters?*

The reality of his new life did not fully set in until bedtime. Before leaving to get him, I had set up his sleeping quarters in the one-car garage attached to the side of the house. We never parked there, using it more as a storage room. The washer and dryer were out there, along with our ironing board. The garage was dry and comfortable and with its concrete floor and walls it was virtually indestructible. 'Marley,' I said cheerfully, leading him out there at bedtime, 'this is your room.'

I had scattered chew toys around, laid newspapers down in the middle of the floor, filled a bowl with water, and made a bed out of a cardboard box lined with an old bedspread. 'And here is where you'll be sleeping,' I said, and lowered him into the box. He was used to such accommodation but had always shared it with his siblings. Now he paced the perimeter of the box and looked forlornly up at me. As a test, I stepped back into the house and closed the door. I stood and listened. At first nothing. Then a slight, barely audible whimper. And then fully fledged crying.

I opened the door, and as soon as he saw me he stopped. I reached in and petted him for a couple of minutes, then left again. Standing on the other side of the door, I began to count. One, two, three . . . He made it seven seconds before the yips and cries began again. We repeated the exercise several times, all with the same result. I was tired and decided it was time for him to cry himself to sleep. I closed the door, walked to the opposite side of the house, and crawled into bed.

The crying continued. Even after I wrapped my pillow around my head, I could still hear it. I thought of him out there alone for the first time in his life, in this strange environment without a single dog scent to be had anywhere. The poor little thing. How would I like it?

I hung on for another half-hour before getting up and going to him. As soon as he spotted me, his face brightened and his tail began to beat the side of the box. I lifted the box with him in it and carried it into my bedroom, where I placed it on the floor tight against the side of the bed. I lay down on the very edge of the mattress, my arm dangling into the box. There, my hand resting on his side, feeling his rib cage rise and fall with his every breath, we both drifted off to sleep.

FOR THE NEXT three days I threw myself with abandon into our new puppy. I lay on the floor with him and let him scamper all over me. I wrestled with him. I used an old towel to play tug of war with him—and was surprised at how strong he was. He followed me everywhere—and tried to gnaw on anything he could get his teeth around.

Every half-hour or so I would lead him out into the back yard to relieve himself. When he had accidents in the house, I scolded him. When he peed outside, I placed my cheek against his and praised him in my sweetest voice. And when he pooped outside, I carried on as though he had just delivered the winning Florida Lotto ticket.

When Jenny returned from Disney World, she threw herself into him with the same utter abandon. As the days unfolded I saw in my young wife a calm, gentle, nurturing side I had not known existed. She held him; she caressed him; she played with him. She combed through every strand of his fur in search of fleas and ticks. She rose every couple of hours through the night—night after night—to take him outside for bathroom breaks. That more than anything was responsible for his becoming fully housebroken in just a few short weeks.

Mostly, she fed him. Following the instructions on the bag, we gave Marley three large bowls of puppy chow a day. He wolfed down every morsel in a matter of seconds.

Between meals Marley's reaction to any situation was the same: grab the nearest shoe or pillow or pencil—really, any item would do—and run with it. Some little voice in his head seemed to be whispering to him, 'Go ahead! Pick it up! Drool all over it! Run!'

Some of the objects he grabbed were small enough to conceal, and this especially pleased him. But when Marley had something to hide, he could not mask his glee. He would explode into a manic sort of hyperdrive. His body would quiver, his head would bob from side to side, and his entire rear end would swing in a sort of spastic dance. We called it the Marley Mambo.

'All right, what have you got this time?' I'd say, and as I approached he would begin evasive action, waggling his way around the room. When I would finally get him cornered and prise open his jaws, I never came up empty-handed. Always there was something he had plucked out of the trash or off the floor or, as he got taller, right off the dining-room table. Paper towels, wadded Kleenex, wine corks, chess pieces—it was like a salvage yard in there. One day I prised open his jaws to find my pay cheque plastered to the roof of his mouth.

WE QUICKLY fell into a routine. I started each morning by taking him for a brisk walk down to the water and back. After breakfast and before my shower, I patrolled the back yard with a shovel, burying his land mines in the sand at the back of the lot. Jenny left for work before nine, and I seldom left the house before ten, first locking Marley in the concrete bunker with a fresh bowl of water, a host of toys, and my cheery directive to 'be a good boy'. By twelve thirty, Jenny was home on her lunch break, when she would give Marley his midday meal and throw him a ball in the back yard until he was tuckered out. After dinner most evenings we walked together with him back down to the waterfront, where we would stroll along the Intracoastal as the yachts from Palm Beach idled by in the sunset.

Stroll is probably the wrong word. Marley strolled like a runaway locomotive. He surged ahead, straining against his leash with everything he had, choking himself hoarse in the process. We yanked him back; he yanked us forward. We tugged; he pulled, coughing like a chain smoker from the collar strangling him. When someone approached with another dog, Marley would bolt at them joyously, rearing up on his hind legs when he reached the end of his leash, dying to make friends. 'He sure seems to love life,' one dog owner commented, and that about said it all.

He was still small enough that we could win these leash tug of wars, but with each week the balance of power was shifting. He was growing bigger and stronger. It was obvious that before long he would be more powerful than either of us. We knew we would need to rein him in and teach him to heel properly before he dragged us to humiliating deaths beneath the wheels of a passing car. Our friends who were veteran dog owners told us not to rush the obedience regimen. 'It's too early,' one of them advised. 'Enjoy his puppyhood while you can.'

That is what we did. But we didn't let him totally have his way. We set rules and tried to enforce them consistently. Beds and furniture were off limits. Drinking from the toilet, sniffing crotches and chewing chair legs were actionable offences, though apparently worth suffering a scolding for. We worked with him on the basic commands—come, stay, sit, down—with limited success. Marley was young and wired, with the attention span of algae and the volatility of nitroglycerin.

Still, for all his juvenile antics, Marley was serving an important role in our home and our relationship. He was showing Jenny she could handle this maternal nurturing thing. He had been in her care for several weeks, and she hadn't killed him yet. Quite to the contrary, he was thriving.

As we grew more comfortable with the new member of our family, we became more comfortable talking about expanding our family in other ways. Within weeks of bringing Marley home, we decided to stop using birth control. That's not to say we decided to get pregnant, which would have been way too bold a gesture for two people who had dedicated their lives to being as indecisive as possible. Rather, we backed into it, merely deciding to stop trying *not* to get pregnant. We weren't trying for a baby; we were just going to let whatever happened happen. *Che sarà, sarà* and all that.

Frankly, we were terrified. We had several sets of friends who had tried for months, years even, to conceive without luck and who had gradually taken their pitiful desperation public. At dinner parties they would talk obsessively about doctor's visits and sperm counts, much to the discomfort of everyone else at the table. I mean, what were you supposed to say? 'I think your sperm counts sound just fine!' It was almost too painful to bear.

So as our friends announced their plans to try to get pregnant, we remained silent. Jenny was simply going to stash her birth-control prescription away in the medicine cabinet and forget about it. If she ended up pregnant, fantastic. If she didn't, well, we weren't actually trying anyway, now, were we?

Winter in West Palm Beach is a glorious time of year, marked by crisp nights and warm, dry, sunny days. After the insufferably long, torpid summer, most of it spent in air conditioning, winter was our time to celebrate the gentle side of the subtropics. We ate all our meals on the back porch, squeezed fresh orange juice from the fruit of the backy-yard tree each morning, tended a tiny herb garden, and picked hibiscus blooms to float in little bowls of water on the dining-room table.

On one of those gorgeous days in late March, Jenny invited a friend from work to bring her basset hound, Buddy, over for a dog playdate. We let the two dogs loose in the back yard, and off they bounded. Old Buddy wasn't quite sure what to make of this hyperenergised yellow juvenile who raced and ran tight circles around him. But he took it in good humour, and the two of them romped together for an hour before they both collapsed in the shade of the mango tree, exhausted.

A few days later Marley started scratching and wouldn't stop. Jenny dropped to her knees and began one of her routine inspections, parting his fur to see his skin below. After just a few seconds, she called out, 'Damn it! Look at this.' I peered over her shoulder just in time to see a small black dot dart under cover. We laid Marley flat on the floor and began going through every inch of his fur. Everywhere we looked we found fleas! Swarms of them. They were between his toes and under his collar and burrowed inside his floppy ears.

We had heard about Florida's legendary flea and tick problems. With no hard freezes, not even any frosts, the bug populations flourished. Jenny was freaked out; her puppy was crawling with vermin. Of course, we blamed Buddy without having any solid proof. Jenny had images of not only the dog being infested but our entire home, too. She grabbed her car keys and ran out the door.

A half-hour later she was back with a bag filled with chemicals. There were flea baths and flea powders and flea sprays and flea foams and flea dips. There was a pesticide for the lawn. There was a special comb designed to remove insect eggs.

My wife threw herself into the task with a vengeance. She scrubbed Marley in the laundry tub, using special soaps. She then mixed up the dip, which contained the same chemical, I noted, as the lawn insecticide, and poured it over him. As he was drying in the garage, smelling like a miniature chemical plant, Jenny vacuumed furiously and doused the inside of the house with flea killer. I doused the outside with it. 'You think we nailed the little buggers?' I asked when we were finally finished.

'I think we did,' she said.

Our multipronged attack on the flea population of 345 Churchill Road was a roaring success. We checked Marley daily and could find no sign of a flea anywhere. We checked the carpets, the couches, the curtains, the grass—nothing. We had annihilated the enemy.

Chapter 3

The Test Strip

A few weeks later we were lying in bed reading when Jenny closed her book and said, 'It's probably nothing.'

'What's probably nothing?' I said absently, not looking up from my book.

'My period's late.'

She had my attention. 'It is?' I turned to face her.

'It's been over a week. And I've been feeling weird, too.'

'Weird how?'

'Like I have a low-level stomach flu or something.'

'Do you think . . .' I began to ask.

'I almost didn't say anything,' Jenny said. 'I don't want to jinx us.'

That's when I realised just how important this was to her—and to me, too. We lay there side by side for a long while, saying nothing, looking straight ahead.

'We're never going to fall asleep,' I finally said.

'The suspense is killing me,' she admitted.

'Come on,' I said. 'Let's go to the drugstore and get a home test kit.'

We threw on shorts and T-shirts and opened the front door, Marley bounding out ahead of us, overjoyed at the prospect of a late-night car ride. He pranced on his hind legs by our tiny Toyota Tercel, hopping up and down, flinging saliva off his jowls, absolutely beside himself with anticipation. 'Geez, you'd think he was the father,' I said.

The pharmacy was open till midnight, and I waited in the car with Marley while Jenny ran in. The dog paced in the back seat, whining, his eyes locked on the front door of the pharmacy.

'Settle down,' I told him. 'I'm pretty sure she plans to return.' He responded by shaking himself off in a great flurry, showering me in a spray of dog drool and loose hair.

Jenny came back, a small bag in her hand, and a few minutes later we were home in the bathroom with the kit spread out on the side of the sink. I read the directions aloud. 'OK,' I said. 'First thing you have to do is pee in this cup.' The next step was to dip a skinny plastic test strip into the urine and then into a small vial of a solution that came with the kit. 'Wait five minutes,' I said. 'Then we put it in the second solution for fifteen minutes. If it turns blue, you're officially knocked up, baby!'

We timed off the first five minutes. Then Jenny dropped the strip into the second vial and said, 'I can't stand here watching it.'

We went into the living room and made small talk, pretending we were waiting for something of no more significance than the kettle to boil. But my heart was pounding wildly. If the test came back positive, our lives were about to change for ever. If it came back negative, Jenny would be crushed. An eternity later, the timer rang. 'Here we go,' I said. 'Either way, you know I love you.'

I went to the bathroom and fished the test strip out of the vial. No doubt about it, it was blue. As blue as the deepest ocean. A rich, navy-blazer blue. 'Congratulations, honey,' I said.

'Oh my God' was all she could answer, and she threw herself into my arms.

As we stood there by the sink, arms around each other, eyes closed, I gradually became aware of a commotion at our feet. I looked down and there was Marley, wiggling, head bobbing, tail banging the linen-closet door. When I reached down to pet him, he dodged away. Uh-oh. It was the Marley Mambo, and that could mean just one thing.

'What do you have this time?' I said, and began chasing him. He weaved into the living room, just out of reach. When I finally cornered him and prised open his jaws, at first I saw nothing. Then far back on his tongue, on the brink of no return, I spotted something. It was skinny and long and flat. And as blue as the deepest ocean. I reached in and pulled out our positive test strip. 'Sorry to disappoint you, pal,' I said, 'but this is going in the scrapbook.'

Jenny and I started laughing and kept laughing for a long time. Then she grabbed Marley by the front paws, lifted him up on his hind legs and danced around the room with him. 'You're going to be an uncle!' she sang. Marley responded by lunging up and planting a big wet tongue squarely on her mouth.

The next day Jenny called me at work, her voice bubbling. The doctor had officially confirmed the results of our home test. 'He says all systems are go,' she said.

The night before, we had counted back on the calendar, trying to pinpoint the date of conception. She was worried that she had already been pregnant when we went on our hysterical flea-eradication spree. Exposing herself to all those pesticides couldn't be good, could it? She raised her concerns with the doctor, and he told her it was probably not an issue. Just don't use them any more, he advised. He told her he'd see her back in his office in three weeks for a sonogram, an electronic-imaging process that would give us our first glimpse of the tiny foetus.

'He wants us to make sure we bring a videotape,' she said, 'so we can save our own copy for posterity.'

On my desk calendar, I made a note of it.

THE NATIVES will tell you South Florida has four seasons. Subtle ones, but distinct seasons nonetheless. Do not believe them. There are only two—the warm, dry season and the hot, wet one. It was about the time of the return to tropical swelter when we awoke one day to realise our puppy was a puppy no more. Marley had morphed into a gangly adolescent. At five months old, his body had filled out the wrinkles in its oversized yellow fur coat. His enormous paws no longer looked so comically out of proportion. His needle-sharp baby teeth had given way to fangs that could destroy a brand-new leather shoe in a few quick chomps. The timbre of his bark had deepened to an intimidating boom. When he stood on his hind legs, tottering around like a dancing Russian circus bear, he could rest his front paws on my shoulders and look me straight in the eye.

The first time the veterinarian saw him, he let out a soft whistle and said, 'You're going to have a big boy on your hands.'

We were not the only ones to notice the transformation. We could tell from the wide berth strangers gave him and the way they recoiled when he bounded in their direction that they no longer viewed him as a harmless puppy. To them he had grown into something to be feared.

This, we found, was not necessarily a bad thing.

Ours was what urban planners call a changing neighbourhood. Built in the 1940s and '50s and initially populated by retirees, it began to take on a gritty edge as the original homeowners died off and were replaced by a motley group of renters. By the time we moved in, the neighbourhood was again in transition, this time being gentrified by gays, artists and young professionals drawn to its location near the water and its funky, Art Deco architecture.

Our block served as a buffer between hard-bitten South Dixie Highway and the posh estate homes along the water. Dixie Highway was the original US 1 that ran along Florida's eastern coast and served as the main route to Miami before the arrival of the interstate. It was lined with a slightly decayed assortment of thrift stores, gas stations, fruit stands, diners and mom-and-pop motels from a bygone era.

On the four corners of South Dixie Highway and Churchill Road stood a liquor store, a twenty-four-hour convenience mart, an import shop with heavy bars on the window and an open-air coin laundry where people hung out all night, often leaving bottles in brown bags behind. Our house was in the middle of the block, eight doors down from the action.

The neighbourhood seemed safe to us, but there were telltales of its rough edge. Tools left out in the yard disappeared, and during a rare cold spell, someone stole every stick of firewood I had stacked along the side of the house. One Sunday we were eating breakfast at our favourite diner, sitting at the table we always sat at, right in the front window, when Jenny pointed to a bullet hole in the plate glass just above our heads and noted drily, 'That wasn't there last time we were here.'

Somehow, having Marley with us, and seeing how strangers eyed him so warily, gave us a sense of peace we might not have had otherwise. He was a big, loving dope of a dog whose defence strategy against intruders would surely have been to lick them to death. But the predators out there didn't know that. To them he was big, he was powerful, and he was unpredictably crazy. And that is how we liked it.

PREGNANCY SUITED JENNY WELL. She began rising at dawn to exercise and walk Marley. She prepared wholesome meals, loaded with fresh vegetables and fruits. She swore off caffeine and alcohol, not even allowing me to stir a tablespoon of cooking sherry into the pot.

We had vowed to keep the pregnancy a secret until we were confident the foetus was beyond the risk of miscarriage. But we were so excited that we dribbled out our news to one confidant after another, swearing each to silence, until our secret was no longer a secret at all.

I took time off work the morning of the doctor's appointment and, as instructed, brought a blank videotape so I could capture the first images of our baby. The appointment was to be part checkup, part informational meeting. We would be assigned to a nurse-midwife who could answer all our questions, listen for the baby's heartbeat, and show us its tiny form.

We arrived at 9.00 a.m., brimming with anticipation. The nurse-midwife, a gentle middle-aged woman, led us into an exam room and asked, 'Would you like to hear your baby's heartbeat?' Would we ever, we told her. We listened intently as she ran a sort of microphone hooked to a speaker over Jenny's abdomen. We sat in silence, smiles frozen on our faces, straining to hear the tiny heartbeat, but only static came through the speaker.

The nurse said that was not unusual. 'It depends on how the baby is lying. Sometimes you can't hear anything.' She offered to go right to the sonogram. 'Let's have a look at your baby,' she said breezily.

'Our first glimpse of baby Grogie,' Jenny said, beaming at me. The nurse-midwife led us into the sonogram room and had Jenny lie back on a table with a monitor screen beside it.

'I brought a tape,' I said, waving it in front of her.

'Just hold on to it for now,' the nurse said as she pulled up Jenny's shirt and began running an instrument the size and shape of a hockey puck over her stomach. We peered at the computer monitor at a grey mass without definition. 'Hmm, this one doesn't seem to be picking anything up,' she said in a completely neutral voice. 'We'll try a vaginal sonogram. You get much more detail that way.'

She left the room and returned moments later with a nurse named Essie who used a latex-covered probe to zoom in on what looked like a tiny sac in the middle of the sea of grey. With the click of a mouse, she magnified the image but despite the great detail, the sac just looked like an empty, shapeless sock to us. Where were the little arms and legs the pregnancy books said would be formed by ten weeks? Where was the head? Where was the beating heart? Jenny, her neck craned sideways to see the screen, asked the nurses with a little nervous laugh, 'Is there anything in there?'

I looked up to catch Essie's face, and I knew the answer was the one we did not want to hear. She replied in a controlled voice, 'Not what you'd expect to see at ten weeks.' I put my hand on Jenny's knee. We both continued staring at the blob on the screen, as though we could will it to life.

'Jenny, I think we have a problem here,' Essie said. 'Let me get Dr Sherman.'

As we waited in silence, I felt the blood rushing out of my head and heard buzzing in my ears. *If I don't sit down*, I thought, *I'm going to collapse.* I half sat on the edge of the examining bench, holding Jenny's hand.

Dr Sherman confirmed that the foetus was dead. 'We'd be able to see a heartbeat, no question,' he said. He gently told us that one in six pregnancies ends in miscarriage. Apparently remembering Jenny's worry about the flea sprays, he told us it was nothing we did or did not do. 'I'm sorry,' he said. 'You can try again in a couple of months.'

We both just sat there in silence. The blank videotape sitting on the bench beside us suddenly seemed like an incredible embarrassment, a reminder of our naive optimism. I asked the doctor, 'Where do we go from here?'

'We have to remove the placenta,' he said. He gave us the option of waiting over the weekend and returning on Monday for the procedure, which was the same as an abortion. But Jenny wanted to get it behind her, and so did I. 'The sooner the better,' she said.

'OK then,' Dr Sherman said. He gave her something to force her to dilate and was gone. Alone in the room, Jenny and I fell heavily into each other's arms and stayed that way until a light knock came at the door. It was an older woman we had never seen before. She carried a sheaf of papers. 'I'm sorry, sweetie,' she said to Jenny. 'I'm so sorry.' And then she showed her where to sign the waiver acknowledging the risks of uterine suction.

When Dr Sherman returned he was all business. He injected Jenny first with Valium and then Demerol. The procedure was quick. Later the nurse helped dress Jenny, and I walked her out of the office.

In the car, Jenny maintained a detached silence, gazing out the window. Her eyes were red but she would not cry. I searched for comforting words without success. Really, what could be said? We had lost our baby. Yes, I could tell her we could try again. I could tell her that many couples go through the same thing. But she didn't want to hear it, and I didn't want to say it. Someday we would be able to see it all in perspective. But not today.

When we arrived at the house, I helped Jenny inside and onto the couch, then went into the garage where Marley, as always, awaited our return with breathless anticipation. As soon as he saw me, he dived for his rawhide bone and begged me to try to snatch it from him.

'Not today, pal,' I said, and let him out the back door into the yard. He took a long pee and then came barrelling back inside, took a deep drink from his bowl, water sloshing everywhere, and careened down the hall, searching for Jenny. It took me a few seconds to mop up the spilt water and follow him into the living room.

When I turned the corner, I stopped short. I would have bet a week's pay that what I was looking at couldn't possibly happen. Our rambunctious, wired dog stood with his shoulders between Jenny's knees, his big, blocky head resting quietly in her lap. His tail hung flat between his legs, the first time I could remember it not wagging whenever he was touching one of us. His eyes were turned up at her, and he whimpered softly. She stroked his head a few times and then, with no warning, buried her face in the thick fur of his neck and began sobbing. Hard, unrestrained, from-the-gut sobbing.

They stayed like that for a long time, Marley statue-still, Jenny clutching him to her. I stood off to the side feeling like a voyeur intruding on this private moment. And then, without lifting her face, she raised one arm up towards me, and I joined her on the couch and wrapped my arms around her. There the three of us stayed, locked in our embrace of shared grief.

Chapter 4

Master and Beast

The next morning, a Saturday, I awoke at dawn to find Jenny lying on her side with her back to me, weeping softly. Marley was awake, too, his chin resting on the mattress, once again commiserating with his mistress. I got up and made coffee, squeezed fresh orange juice, brought in the newspaper. When Jenny came out in her robe minutes later, she gave me a brave smile as if to say she was OK now.

After breakfast, we decided to get out of the house and walk Marley down to the water for a swim. A large concrete breakwater and mounds of boulders lined the shore in our neighbourhood, making the water inaccessible. But if you walked a half-dozen blocks to the south, the breakwater curved inland, exposing a small white sand beach littered with driftwood— a perfect place for a dog to frolic.

When we reached the little beach, I wagged a stick in front of Marley's face and unleashed him. He stared at the stick as a starving man would stare at a loaf of bread. 'Go get it!' I shouted, and hurled the stick as far out into the water as I could. He cleared the concrete wall in one spectacular leap, galloped down the beach and out into the shallow water, sending up plumes of spray around him. This is what Labrador retrievers were born to do. It was in their genes and in their job description.

No one is certain where Labrador retrievers originated, but this much is known for sure: it was not in Labrador. These muscular, short-haired water dogs first surfaced in the 1600s in Newfoundland. There, the local fishermen took the dogs to sea with them in their dories, putting them to good use hauling in lines and nets and fetching fish that came off the hooks. The dogs' dense, oily coats made them impervious to the icy waters, and their swimming prowess, boundless energy, and ability to cradle fish gently in their jaws without damaging the flesh made them ideal work dogs for the tough North Atlantic conditions. They were then soon pressed into duty by island hunters to fetch game birds and waterfowl.

This was Marley's proud heritage, and it appeared he had inherited at least half of the retrieving instinct. He was a master at pursuing his prey. It was the concept of returning it that he did not seem to quite grasp. His general attitude seemed to be, *If you want the stick back that bad, YOU jump in the water for it.*

He came charging back up onto the beach with his prize in his teeth. 'Bring it here!' I yelled, slapping my hands together. He pranced over, his whole body wagging with excitement, and promptly shook water and sand all over me, taunting me to chase him. I made a few lunges, but it was clear he had both speed and agility on his side.

'You're supposed to be a Labrador retriever!' I shouted. 'Not a Labrador evader!'

What I had that my dog didn't have was an evolved brain that at least slightly exceeded my brawn. I grabbed a second stick and made a tremendous fuss over it. I held it over my head and tossed it from hand to hand. I could see Marley's resolve softening. Suddenly, the stick in his mouth, just moments earlier his most prized possession, had lost its cachet. My stick drew him in like a temptress. He crept closer and closer until he was just inches in front of me. 'Oh, a sucker is born every day, isn't he, Marley?' I cackled, rubbing the stick across his snout. He went cross-eyed trying to keep it in his sights.

I could see the little cogs going in his head as he tried to figure out how he could grab the new stick without relinquishing the old one.

'You know you want it,' I whispered. And did he ever. I could feel his grip loosening. And then he made his move. He opened his jaws to try to grab the second stick without losing the first. In a heartbeat, I whipped both sticks high above my head. He leapt in the air, barking and spinning, obviously at a loss as to how such a carefully laid battle strategy could have gone so badly awry.

'This is why I am the master and you are the beast,' I told him. And with that he shook more water and sand in my face.

I threw one of the sticks out into the water and he raced after it, yelping madly as he went. He returned a new, wiser opponent, refusing to come anywhere near me. He stood about ten yards away, stick in mouth, eyeing the new object of his desire, which just happened to be the old object of his desire, his first stick, now perched high above my head. I could see the cogs moving again. He was thinking, *This time I'll just wait right here until he throws it, and then he'll have no sticks and I'll have both sticks.*

'You think I'm really dumb, don't you, dog?' I said. I heaved back and with a great, exaggerated groan hurled the stick with all my might. Sure enough, Marley roared into the water with his stick still locked in his teeth. The only thing was, I hadn't let go of mine. Do you think Marley figured that out? He swam halfway to Palm Beach before catching on that the stick was still in my hand.

'You're cruel!' Jenny said, laughing.

When Marley finally got back onshore, he plopped down in the sand, exhausted but not about to give up his stick. I showed him mine, reminding him how far superior it was to his, and ordered, 'Drop it!' Then I repeated, 'Drop it!' It took several tries, but finally he did just that. And the instant his stick hit the sand, I launched mine into the air for him. We did it over and over, and slowly the lesson sank in. If he returned his stick to me, I would throw a new one for him. 'It's like an office gift exchange,' I told him. 'You've got to give to get.'

As Jenny and I walked home, I said, 'You know, I really think he's starting to get it.'

She looked down at Marley, plodding along beside us, his stick still clenched in his jaws. 'I wouldn't be so sure of that,' she said.

THE NEXT MORNING I again awoke before dawn to the sounds of Jenny softly sobbing beside me. 'Hey,' I said, and wrapped my arms around her. She nestled her face against my chest, and I could feel her tears soaking through my T-shirt.

'I'm fine,' she said. 'Really. I'm just—you know.'

I did know. I was trying to be the brave soldier, but I felt it, too, the dull sense of loss and failure.

Later that day I took Marley with me in the car to pick up a few groceries. On the way back, I stopped at a florist shop and bought a giant bouquet of flowers arranged in a vase, hoping they would cheer Jenny up. I strapped them into the seat belt in the back seat beside Marley so they wouldn't spill. As we passed the pet shop, I made the split-second decision that Marley deserved a pick-me-up, too. After all, he had done a better job than I at comforting the inconsolable woman in our lives. 'Be a good boy!' I said. 'I'll be right back.' I ran into the store to buy a rawhide chew for him.

When we got home a few minutes later, Jenny came out to meet us, and Marley tumbled out of the car to greet her. 'We have a little surprise for you,' I said. But when I reached in the back seat for the flowers, the surprise was on me. The bouquet was a mix of white daisies, yellow mums, assorted lilies and bright red carnations. Now, however, the carnations were nowhere to be found. I looked more closely and found the decapitated stems that minutes earlier had held blossoms.

I finally caught Marley, prised open his jaws and found the incontrovertible evidence of his guilt. Deep in his cavernous mouth was a single red carnation. The others presumably were already down the hatch. I was ready to murder him.

I looked up at Jenny and tears were streaming down her cheeks. But this time, they were tears of laughter. There was nothing left for me to do but laugh, too.

'That dog,' I muttered.

'I've never been crazy about carnations anyway,' she said.

Marley was so thrilled to see everyone happy and laughing again that he jumped up on his hind legs and did a break dance for us.

WHEN MARLEY was not quite six months old, we signed him up for obedience classes. God knew he needed it. Despite his stick-fetching breakthrough on the beach that day, he was a challenging student, dense, wild, distracted, a victim of his boundless nervous energy.

Our veterinarian told us about a local dog-training club that offered basic obedience classes on Tuesday nights in a parking lot. The teachers were unpaid volunteers from the club, serious amateurs who presumably had already taken their own dogs to the heights of advanced behaviour modification. The course ran eight lessons and cost fifty dollars, which we thought was a bargain, especially considering that Marley could destroy fifty dollars' worth of shoes in thirty seconds. At registration we met the woman who would be teaching our class. She was a stern, no-nonsense dog trainer who subscribed to the theory that there are no incorrigible dogs, just weak-willed owners.

The first lesson seemed to prove her point. Before we were fully out of the car, Marley spotted the other dogs gathering with their owners across the tarmac. A party! He leapt over us and out of the car and was off, his leash dragging behind him. He darted from one dog to the next, sniffing private parts. For Marley it was a festival of smells.

Meanwhile, the instructor was staring at us with a look that could not have been more withering. 'Take your place, please,' she said curtly, and when she saw both Jenny and me tugging Marley into position, she added, 'You are going to have to decide which of you is going to be trainer.' I started to explain that we both wanted to participate, but she cut me off. 'A dog,' she said definitively, 'can only answer to one master.' I began to protest, but she silenced me with that glare of hers. I slunk off to the sidelines with my tail between my legs, leaving Master Jenny in command.

This was probably a mistake. Marley was already considerably stronger than Jenny. Miss Dominatrix was only a few sentences into her introduction on the importance of establishing dominance over our pets when Marley decided the standard poodle on the opposite side of the class deserved a closer look. He lunged off, tugging Jenny across the parking lot. My wife looked amazingly like a water-skier being towed behind a powerboat. Everyone stared. I covered my eyes.

Marley wasn't one for formal introductions. He crashed into the poodle and immediately crammed his nose between her legs. I imagined it was his way of asking, 'So, do you come here often?'

After Marley had given the poodle a full gynaecological examination,

Jenny was able to drag him back into place. Miss Dominatrix announced calmly, 'That, class, is an example of a dog that has been allowed to think he is the alpha male of his pack.' As if to drive home the point, Marley attacked his tail, spinning wildly, and in the process he wrapped the leash around Jenny's ankles until she was fully immobilised. I winced and gave thanks that it wasn't me out there.

The instructor began running the class through the sit and down commands. It was too painful to watch. At one point I opened my eyes to see Jenny lying on the pavement face down and Marley standing over her, panting happily. Later she told me she was trying to show him the down command.

As class ended and Jenny and Marley rejoined me, Miss Dominatrix intercepted us. 'You really need to get control over that animal,' she said with a sneer. We retreated to the car in humiliation and drove home in silence, the only sound Marley's loud panting as he tried to come down from the high of his first classroom experience. Finally I said, 'One thing you can say for him, he sure loves school.'

THE NEXT WEEK Marley and I were back, this time without Jenny. When I suggested to her that I was probably the closest thing to an alpha dog we were going to find in our home, she gladly relinquished her brief title as master and commander.

The night's lesson was walking on heel, one I was especially keen on mastering. I was tired of fighting Marley every step of every walk. It was time he learned to trot placidly along by our sides. I wrestled him to our spot on the tarmac. Miss Dominatrix handed each of us a short length of chain with a steel ring welded to each end. These, she told us, were choke collars and would be our secret weapons for teaching our dogs to heel effortlessly at our sides. The choke chain was brilliantly simple in design. When the dog behaved and walked beside its master, the chain hung limply round its neck. But if the dog lunged forward, the chain tightened like a noose, choking the errant hound into gasping submission. It didn't take long, our instructor promised, before dogs learned to submit or die of asphyxia.

I started to slip the choke chain over Marley's head, but he saw it coming and grabbed it in his teeth. I prised his jaws open, got the chain out of his mouth and finally forced it over his head. Then, as instructed, I pushed his butt down into a sit position and stood beside him, my left leg brushing his right shoulder. On the count of three, I was to say, 'Marley, heel!' and step off with my left foot. If he began to wander off course, a series of minor corrections—sharp little tugs on the leash—would bring him back into line. 'Class, on the count of three,' Miss Dominatrix called out. 'One . . . two . . . three.'

'Marley, heel!' I commanded. As soon as I took my first step, he took off like a fighter jet from an aircraft carrier. I yanked back hard on the leash and he made an awful coughing gasp as the chain tightened around his airway. He sprang back for an instant, but as soon as the chain loosened, the momentary choking was behind him, ancient history in that tiny compartment of his brain dedicated to life lessons learned. He lunged forward again. I yanked back and he gasped once more. We continued like this the entire length of the parking lot, Marley yanking ahead, me yanking back, each time with increasing vigour. He was coughing and panting; I was grunting and sweating.

'Rein that dog in!' Miss Dominatrix yelled. I tried to with all my might, but the lesson wasn't sinking in. 'Here,' she said impatiently, holding out her hand. 'Let me show you.' I handed the leash to her, and she efficiently tugged Marley around into position, pulling up on the choke as she ordered him to sit. Sure enough, he sank back on his haunches, eagerly looking up at her. *Damn.*

With a smart yank of the lead, Miss Dominatrix set off with him. But almost instantly he barrelled ahead as if he were pulling the lead sled in the Iditarod. It looked as if he was going to pull her arm out of its socket. I should have been embarrassed, but I felt an odd sort of satisfaction. She wasn't having any more success than I was. My classmates sniggered, and I beamed with perverse pride. *See, my dog is awful for everyone, not just me!*

Miss Dominatrix shot me a look that told me I had crossed some invisible line and there would be no crossing back. Marley had publicly humiliated her. She handed the leash back to me and turned to the class as if this unfortunate little episode had never occurred.

When the lesson was over, she asked if I could stay behind for a minute. I waited with Marley as she fielded questions from other students. When the last one had left, she turned to me and said, 'I think your dog is still a little young for structured obedience training.'

'He's a handful, isn't he?' I said, feeling a new camaraderie with her now that we'd shared the same humiliating experience.

'He's simply not ready for this,' she said. 'He has some growing up to do.'

It was beginning to dawn on me what she was getting at. 'Are you trying to tell me—'

'He's a distraction to the other dogs.'

'—that you're kicking us out of class?'

'You can always bring him back in another six or eight months.'

'So you're kicking us out?'

'Yes,' she finally said. 'I'm kicking you out.'

Marley, as if on cue, lifted his leg and let loose a raging stream of urine, missing his beloved instructor's foot by mere centimetres.

SOMETIMES A MAN needs to get angry to get serious. I owned a beautiful, purebred Labrador retriever, a proud member of the breed famous for its ability to guide the blind, rescue disaster victims, assist hunters and pluck fish from roiling ocean swells. How dare Miss Dominatrix write him off after just two lessons? So he was a bit on the spirited side; he was filled with nothing but good intentions. I was going to prove that Marley was no quitter.

First thing the next morning, I had Marley out in the back yard with me. 'Nobody kicks the Grogan boys out of obedience school,' I told him. 'Untrainable? We'll see who's untrainable. Right?' He bounced up and down.

We started with the sit command, which I had been practising with him since he was a small puppy and which he already was quite good at. I gave him my best alpha-dog scowl, and in a firm but calm voice ordered him to sit. He sat. I praised. We repeated the exercise several times. Next we moved to the down command, another one I had been practising with him. He stared intently into my eyes, neck straining forward, anticipating my directive. I slowly raised my hand in the air and held it there as he waited for the word. With a sharp downward motion, I snapped my fingers, pointed at the ground and said, 'Down!' Marley collapsed in a heap, hitting the ground with a thud. He could not possibly have gone down with more gusto had a mortar shell just exploded behind him. Jenny, sitting on the porch with her coffee, noticed it, too, and yelled out, 'Incoming!'

After several rounds of hit-the-deck, I decided to move up to the next challenge: come on command. This was a tough one for Marley. The coming part was not the problem; it was waiting in place until we summoned him that he could not get. Our attention-deficit dog was so anxious to be plastered against us he could not sit still while we walked away from him.

I put him in the sit position facing me and fixed my eyes on his. As we stared at each other, I raised my palm, holding it out in front of me. 'Stay,' I said, and took a step backwards. He froze, staring anxiously, waiting for the slightest sign that he could join me. On my fourth step backwards, he could take it no longer and broke free, racing up and tumbling against me. I admonished him and tried it again. And again and again. Each time he allowed me to get a little farther away before charging. Eventually, I stood fifty feet across the yard, my palm out towards him. I waited. He sat, locked in position, a volcano ready to blow. I counted to ten. He did not budge. *OK, enough torture*, I thought. I dropped my hand and yelled, 'Marley, come!'

He made a beeline for me, a vacant, crazed look on his face. In the instant before impact I realised the pilot had left the wheelhouse. It was a one-dog stampede. I had time for one final command. 'STOP!' I screamed. *Blam!* He ploughed into me without breaking stride and I pitched backwards, slamming hard to the ground. When I opened my eyes a few seconds later, he was straddling me with all four paws, lying on my chest and desperately licking my face. *How did I do, boss?* Technically speaking, he had followed orders exactly. After all, I had failed to mention anything about stopping once he got to me.

Jenny peered out the kitchen window at us and shouted, 'I'm off to work. When you two are done making out, don't forget to close the windows. It's supposed to rain this afternoon.' I gave him a snack, then showered and headed off to work myself.

WHEN I ARRIVED HOME that night, Jenny was waiting for me at the door, and I could tell she was upset. 'Go look in the garage,' she said.

I opened the door into the garage and the first thing I spotted was Marley, lying on his carpet, looking dejected. His snout and front paws were caked in dried blood. Then my focus zoomed out and I sucked in my breath. The garage—our indestructible bunker—was a shambles. Throw rugs were shredded, paint was clawed off the concrete walls, and the ironing board was tipped over, its fabric cover hanging in ribbons. Worst of all, the doorway in which I stood looked as though it had been attacked with a chipper-shredder. Bits of wood were sprayed in a ten-foot semicircle around the door, which was gouged halfway through to the other side. Blood streaked the walls from where Marley had shredded his paws and muzzle.

Jenny's voice came from behind me. 'When I came home for lunch, everything was fine,' she said. 'But I could tell it was getting ready to rain.' After she was back at work, an intense storm moved through, bringing with it dazzling flashes of lightning and thunder so powerful you could almost feel it thump against your chest.

When she arrived home a couple of hours later, Marley, standing amid the carnage of his desperate escape attempt, was in a complete, panic-stricken lather. He was so pathetic she couldn't bring herself to yell at him.

Over dinner, we tried to put things in perspective. All we could figure was that, alone and terrified as the storm descended, Marley decided his best chance at survival was to begin digging his way into the house. He pursued his goal with a zealous efficiency I wouldn't have thought possible without the aid of heavy machinery.

When the dishes were done, Jenny and I went out into the garage where Marley, back to his old self, grabbed a chew toy and bounced around us, looking for a little tug-of-war action. I held him still while Jenny sponged the blood off his fur. Then he watched us, tail wagging, as we cleaned up his handiwork. We threw out the rugs and ironing-board cover, swept up the shredded remains of our door, mopped his blood off the walls and made a list of materials we would need from the hardware store to repair the damage—the first of countless such repairs I would end up making over the course of his life. Marley seemed positively ebullient to have us out there, lending a hand with his remodelling efforts.

'You don't have to look so happy about it,' I said, scowling, and brought him inside for the night.

Chapter 5

The Stuff Males Are Made Of

Every dog needs a good veterinarian. Every new dog owner needs one, too, mostly for the advice and reassurance. We had a few false starts finding a keeper, but then we stumbled upon the doctor of our dreams. His name was Jay Butan—Dr Jay to all who knew him—and he was young, smart and extraordinarily kind. In those early months, we kept him on speed dial and consulted him about the most inane concerns. When Marley began to develop rough scaly patches on his elbows, I feared he was developing some rare skin ailment. Relax, Dr Jay told me, those were just calluses from lying on the floor. One day Marley yawned wide and I spotted an odd purple discoloration on the back of his tongue. *Oh my God*, I thought. *He has cancer.* Relax, Dr Jay advised, it was just a birthmark.

Now, on this afternoon, Jenny and I stood in an exam room with him, discussing Marley's deepening neurosis over thunderstorms. We had hoped the chipper-shredder incident in the garage was an isolated aberration, but it turned out to be just the beginning of what would become a lifelong pattern of phobic behaviour. Despite Labs' reputation as excellent gun dogs, we had ended up with one who was mortally terrified of firecrackers, backfiring engines, and anything louder than a popping champagne cork. Thunder was a house of horrors all its own. Even the hint of a storm would throw Marley into a meltdown.

Dr Jay pressed a vial of small yellow pills into my hand and said, 'Don't hesitate to use these.' They were sedatives that would, as he put it, 'take the edge off Marley's anxiety.' The hope, he said, was that, aided by the calming effects of the drug, Marley would be able to cope more rationally with storms. Thunder anxiety was not unusual in dogs, he told us, especially in Florida, where huge boomers rolled across the peninsula nearly every afternoon during the summer months. Marley nosed the vial in my hands, apparently eager to get started on a life of drug dependency.

Dr Jay began working his lips as though he had something important to say but wasn't quite sure how to say it. 'And,' he said, pausing, 'you probably want to start thinking about having him neutered.'

'Neutered?' I repeated. 'You mean, as in . . .'

I must have winced, because he quickly added, 'It's painless, really, and he'll be a lot more comfortable.' Dr Jay knew all about the challenges Marley presented: the disastrous obedience training, the numskull antics, the destructiveness, the hyperactivity. And lately Marley, who was seven months old, had begun humping anything that moved, including our dinner guests. 'It'll just remove all that nervous sexual energy and make him a happier, calmer dog,' he said. He promised it wouldn't dampen Marley's sunny exuberance.

'I don't know,' I said. 'It just seems so . . . so final.'

Jenny, on the other hand, was having no such compunctions. 'Let's snip those suckers off!' she said.

'But what about siring a litter?' I asked. 'What about carrying on his bloodline?'

'I think you need to be realistic about that,' he said. 'Marley's a great family pet, but I'm not sure he's got the credentials he would need to be in demand for stud.' He was being as diplomatic as possible, but the expression on his face gave him away. It almost screamed out, *Good God, man! For the sake of future generations, we must contain this genetic mistake at all costs!*

I told him we would think about it, and with our new supply of mood-altering drugs in hand, we headed home.

IT WAS AT THIS SAME TIME, as we debated slicing away Marley's manhood, that Jenny was placing unprecedented demands on mine. Dr Sherman had cleared her to try to get pregnant again. She accepted the challenge with the single-mindedness of an Olympic athlete. The days of simply putting away the birth control pills and letting whatever might happen happen were behind us. In the insemination wars, Jenny was going on the offensive. And that meant I had a job to perform. That most joyous of acts overnight became a clinical drill involving basal-temperature checks, menstrual calendars and ovulation charts.

Jenny was used to my being game to go at the slightest hint of an invitation, and she assumed the old rules still applied. I would be, let's say, fixing the garbage disposal and she would walk in with her calendar in hand and say, 'I had my last period on the 17th, which means'—and she would pause to count ahead from that date—'that we need to do it NOW!'

The Grogan men have never handled pressure well, and I was no exception. It was only a matter of time before I suffered the ultimate male humiliation: performance failure. The more I worried about performing my husbandly duty, the less I was able to relax and do what had always come naturally. I began to live in mortal fear that my wife would, God forbid, ask me to have my way with her.

One morning when I was working in my newspaper's West Palm Beach bureau, just ten minutes from home, Jenny called from work. Did I want to meet her at home for lunch?

'Or we could meet at a restaurant somewhere,' I countered.

'Oh, c'mon,' she said. Then her voice lowered to a whisper and she added, 'Today's a good day. I . . . think . . . I'm . . . ovulating.' A wave of dread washed over me. *Oh, no. Not the O word.* I wanted to plead into the phone, *Please don't make me.* Instead I said as coolly as I could, 'Sure. Does twelve thirty work?'

When I opened the front door, Marley, as always, was there to greet me, but Jenny was nowhere to be found. I called out to her. 'In the bathroom,' she answered. 'Out in a sec.' I sorted through the mail, killing time, a general sense of doom hovering over me.

'Hey there, sailor,' a voice behind me said, and when I turned around, Jenny was standing there in a little silky two-piece thing. Her flat stomach peeked out from below the top, which hung precariously from her shoulders by two impossibly thin straps. Her legs had never looked longer. 'How do I look?' she said. She looked incredible, that's how she looked.

She scampered into the bedroom with me in pursuit. Soon we were on top of the sheets in each other's arms. I closed my eyes and could feel the magic returning. *You can do this, John.* I could feel her breath on my face. Hot, moist, heavy. *Mmmm, sexy.*

But wait. What was that smell? Something on her breath. Something at once familiar and foreign, not exactly unpleasant but not quite enticing, either. I knew that smell, but I couldn't place it. I hesitated. A food; yes, but what food? Not crackers. Not chips. Not tuna fish. I almost had it. It was . . . Milk-Bones?

Milk-Bones! That was it! *But why?* I wondered—and I actually heard a little voice ask the question in my head—*Why has Jenny been eating Milk-Bones?* And besides, I could feel her lips on my neck . . . How could she be kissing my neck and breathing in my face all at once? It didn't make any . . .

Oh . . . my . . . God.

I opened my eyes. There, inches from my face loomed Marley's huge head. His chin rested on the mattress, and he was panting up a storm, drool soaking into the sheets. 'Bad dog!' I shrieked, recoiling across the bed. 'No! No!' I frantically ordered. 'Go to bed! Go lie down!'

But it was too late. The magic was gone.

THE NEXT MORNING I made an appointment to take Marley in to have his balls cut off. I figured if I wasn't going to have sex for the rest of my life, he wasn't either. Dr Jay said we could drop Marley off before we went to work and pick him up on our way home. A week later, that's just what we did.

As Jenny and I got ready, Marley cannoned happily off the walls, sensing an impending outing. I began to feel pangs of guilt. The poor guy trusted us, and here we were secretly plotting to emasculate him. Did betrayal get any more treacherous than this?

'Come here,' I said, and wrestled him to the floor where I gave him a vigorous belly scratch. 'It won't be so bad. Sex is highly overrated.' Not even I, still rebounding from my run of bad luck the last couple of weeks, believed that. Who was I fooling? The poor dog was going to miss out on life's greatest pleasure. I felt horrible.

And I felt even worse when I whistled for him and he bounded out the door and into the car with utter blind faith. Jenny drove and I sat in the passenger seat. As was his habit, Marley balanced his front paws on the centre console, his nose touching the rearview mirror. Every time Jenny touched the brakes, he went crashing into the windshield, but Marley didn't care. He was riding shotgun with his two best friends. Did life get any better than this?

I cracked my window, and Marley began listing to starboard, trying to catch a whiff of the outdoor smells. Soon he had squirmed his way fully onto my lap and pressed his nose so firmly into the narrow crack of the window that he snorted each time he tried to inhale. *Oh, why not?* I thought. This was his last ride as a fully equipped member of the male gender; the least I could do was give him a little fresh air. I opened the window wide enough for him to stick his snout out. He was enjoying the sensation so much, I opened it further, and soon his entire head was out the window.

'John, he's making me nervous,' Jenny said.

'He's fine,' I answered. 'He just wants a little fresh—'

At that instant he slid his front legs out the window until his armpits were resting on the edge of the glass.

'John, grab him! Grab him!'

Before I could do anything, Marley was off my lap and scrambling out the window of our moving car. As his body slithered past me, I lunged for him and managed to grab the end of his tail with my left hand. Jenny was braking hard in heavy traffic. Marley dangled fully outside the moving car, suspended upside-down by his tail, which I had by the most tenuous of grips. My body was twisted around in a position that didn't allow me to get my other hand on him. Marley was frantically trotting along with his front paws on the road.

Jenny got the car stopped in the outside lane with cars lining up behind us, horns blaring. 'Now what?' I yelled. I was stuck. I couldn't pull him back in the window. I couldn't open the door. I couldn't get my other arm out. And I didn't dare let go of him or he would surely dash in the path of one of the angry drivers swerving around us.

Jenny put the flashers on and ran around to my side, where she grabbed him and held him by the collar until I could get out and help her wrestle him back into the car. Our little drama had unfolded directly in front of a gas station, and as Jenny got the car back into gear I looked over to see that the mechanics, who had all come out to take in the show, were laughing. 'Thanks, guys!' I called out. 'Glad we could brighten your morning.'

When we got to the clinic, I walked Marley in on a tight leash in case he tried any more smart moves. My guilt was gone. 'You're not getting out of this one, Eunuch Boy,' I told him. I turned him over to Dr Jay's assistant and said, 'Give him the works.'

That night when I picked him up, Marley was a changed dog. He was sore from the surgery and moved gingerly. His eyes were bloodshot and droopy from the anaesthesia, and he was still groggy. And where those magnificent crown jewels of his had swung so proudly, there was . . . nothing. Just a small, shrivelled flap of skin. The irrepressible Marley bloodline had officially and for ever come to an end.

OUR LIVES increasingly were being defined by work. Work at the newspapers. Work on the house. Work around the yard. Work trying to get pregnant. And, nearly a full-time vocation in itself, work raising Marley. In many ways, he was like a child, requiring the time and attention a child requires, and we were getting a taste of the responsibility that lay ahead of us if we ever did have a family. But only to a degree. Even as clueless as we were about parenting, we were pretty sure we couldn't lock the kids in the garage with a bowl of water when we went out for the day.

We hadn't even reached our second wedding anniversary and already we were feeling the grind of responsible, grown-up married life. We needed a vacation, just the two of us, far from the obligations of our daily lives. So I surprised Jenny one evening with two tickets to Ireland. We would be gone for three weeks. There would be no itineraries, no guided tours, no must-see destinations. Only a rental car, a road map and a guide to bed-and-breakfast inns along the way.

First we had a few duties to dole out, and at the top of the list was Marley. We quickly ruled out a boarding kennel. He was too young, too wired, too rambunctious to be cooped up in a pen. As Dr Jay had predicted, neutering had not diminished Marley's exuberance one bit. It did not affect his energy level or loony behaviour, either. Except for the fact that he no longer showed an interest in mounting inanimate objects, he was the same crazed beast. He was way too wild—and too unpredictably destructive when panic set in—to pawn off at a friend's house. What we needed was a live-in dog sitter, someone who was responsible, *very* patient, and strong enough to reel in seventy pounds of runaway Labrador retriever.

We made a list of every friend, neighbour and coworker we could think of, then one by one crossed off names. Eventually, we were left with just one name. Kathy worked in my office and was single and loved animals. She was athletic and liked to walk. She would be perfect. Best of all, she said yes.

The list of instructions I prepared for her couldn't have been more painstakingly detailed were we leaving a critically ill infant in her care. The Marley Memo ran six full pages, single-spaced.

I gave the instructions to Jenny and asked if there was anything I had forgotten. She took several minutes to read them and then looked up and said, 'What are you thinking? You can't show her this.' She was waving them at me. 'You show her this and you can forget about Ireland. She'll start running and won't stop until she hits Key West.'

But I've always believed in full disclosure, and show it to her I did. Kathy did flinch noticeably a few times, but she kept any misgivings to herself. Looking just a little green, but far too kind to renege on a promise, she held fast. 'Have a great trip,' she said. 'We'll be fine.'

IRELAND WAS EVERYTHING we dreamed it would be. Beautiful, bucolic, lazy. The weather was gloriously clear and sunny most days. As we had promised ourselves, we kept no schedules and set no itineraries. We simply wandered, bumping our way along the coast, stopping to stroll or shop or quaff Guinness or simply gaze out at the ocean.

As evening approached each day, we would begin looking for a place to spend the night. Invariably, these were rooms in private homes run by sweet Irish widows who doted on us, served us tea, turned down our sheets and always seemed to ask us the same question, 'So, would you two be planning to start a family soon?' And then they would leave us in our room, flashing back knowing, oddly suggestive smiles as they closed the door behind them.

Jenny and I became convinced there was a national law in Ireland that required all guest beds to face a large wall-mounted likeness of either the Pope or the Virgin Mary. Some places provided both. The Irish Celibate Traveller Law also dictated that all guest beds be extremely creaky, sounding a rousing alarm every time one of its occupants so much as rolled over.

It all conspired to create a setting that was about as conducive to amorous relations as a convent. We were in someone else's home—someone else's *very Catholic* home—with thin walls and a loud bed and statues of saints and virgins, and a nosy hostess.

Suddenly, sex seemed so . . . so . . . illicit. It was like being in high school again. To risk sex in these surroundings was to risk shameful humiliation at the communal breakfast table the next morning. It was to risk Mrs O'Flaherty's raised eyebrow as she served up eggs, asking with a leering grin, 'So, was the bed comfortable for you?'

Ireland was a coast-to-coast No Sex Zone. And that was all the invitation I needed. We spent the trip bopping like bunnies.

Still, Jenny couldn't stop fretting about her big baby back home. Every few days she would feed a fistful of coins into a payphone and call home for a progress report from Kathy. I would stand outside the booth and listen to Jenny's end of the conversation.

'He did? . . . Right into traffic? . . . You weren't hurt, were you? . . . Thank God . . . What? Your shoes? . . . Oh no! *And* your purse? . . . We'll certainly pay for repairs . . . Of course, we insist on replacing them . . . And he what? . . . Wet cement, you say? What's the chance of that happening?'

And so it would go. Each call was a litany of transgressions, one worse than the next, many of which surprised even us, hardened survivors of the puppy wars. Marley was the incorrigible student and Kathy the hapless substitute teacher. He was having a field-day.

When we arrived home, Marley raced outside to greet us. Kathy stood in the doorway, looking tired and strained. She had the faraway gaze of a shell-shocked soldier. Her bag was packed and sitting on the front porch, ready to go. We gave her gifts, thanked her profusely, and told her not to worry about the ripped-out screens and other damage. She excused herself politely and was gone.

'Poor Kathy,' Jenny said. 'She looked kind of broken, don't you think?'

'Shattered is more like it.'

'We probably shouldn't ask her to dog-sit for us again.'

'No,' I answered. 'That probably wouldn't be a good idea.'

Turning to Marley, I said, 'The honeymoon's over, Chief. Starting tomorrow, you're back in training.'

THE NEXT MORNING Jenny and I both started back to work. But first I slipped the choke chain around Marley's neck and took him for a walk. He immediately lunged forward, not even pretending to try to heel. 'A little rusty, are we?' I asked, and heaved with all my might on his leash, knocking him off his paws. He righted himself, coughed, and looked up at me with a wounded expression as if to say, *Kathy didn't mind me pulling.*

'Get used to it,' I said, and placed him in a sit position. 'OK, let's try this again,' I said. He looked at me with cool scepticism.

'Marley, heel!' I ordered, and stepped briskly off on my left foot with his leash so short my left hand was actually gripping the end of his choke chain. He lurched and I tugged sharply, tightening the stranglehold without mercy. 'Taking advantage of a poor woman like that,' I mumbled. 'You ought to be ashamed of yourself.' By the end of the walk, my grip on the leash so tight that my knuckles had turned white, I finally managed to convince him that I was the master and he was the pet. As we turned in to the driveway, my recalcitrant dog trotted along beside me, not perfectly but respectably. For the first time in his life he was heeling. 'Oh, yes,' I sang joyously. 'The boss is back.'

Several days later Jenny called me at the office. She had just been to see Dr Sherman. 'Luck of the Irish,' she said. 'Here we go again.'

Chapter 6

The Things He Ate

This pregnancy was different. Our miscarriage had taught us some important lessons. This time we kept our news the most closely guarded secret since D-Day. No one, not even our parents, was brought into our confidence.

We locked away all the chemical cleaners and pesticides. Jenny became a convert to the natural cleaning powers of vinegar, which was up to even the ultimate challenge of dissolving Marley's dried saliva off the walls. We found that boric acid, a white powder lethal to bugs and harmless to humans, worked pretty well at keeping Marley and his bedding flea-free.

Jenny rose at dawn each morning and took Marley for a brisk walk along the waterfront. I would just be waking up when they returned. My wife was the picture of health in all ways but one. She spent most days on the verge of throwing up. But she greeted each wave of nausea with what can only be described as gleeful acceptance, for it was a sign that the tiny experiment inside her was chugging along just fine.

Indeed it was. This time around, Essie took my videotape and recorded the first faint, grainy images of our baby. We could hear the heart beating, see its four tiny chambers pulsing. We could trace the outline of the head and count all four limbs. Dr Sherman popped his head into the sonogram room to pronounce everything perfect, and then looked at Jenny and said,

'What are you crying for, kid? You're supposed to be happy.' Essie whacked him with her clipboard and rolled her eyes at Jenny as if to say, 'Men! They are so clueless.'

When it came to dealing with pregnant wives, clueless would describe me. I gave Jenny her space, sympathised with her in her nausea, and tried my best to indulge her increasingly bizarre behaviour. I was soon on a first-name basis with the overnight clerk at the twenty-four-hour market as I stopped in at all hours for ice cream or apples or celery or chewing gum in flavours I never knew existed. 'Are you sure this is clove?' I would ask him. 'She says it has to be clove.'

As the pregnancy progressed, so did Marley's training. I worked with him every day, and now I was able to entertain our friends by yelling, 'Incoming!' and watching him crash to the floor, all four limbs splayed. If I barked stern orders, he would obey, sometimes even eagerly. But his default setting was stuck on eternal incorrigibility.

He also had an insatiable appetite for mangoes, which fell by the dozens in the back yard. Each weighed a pound or more and was so sweet it could make your teeth ache. Marley would stretch out in the grass, anchor a ripe mango between his front paws, and go about surgically removing every speck of flesh from the skin.

He ate other things as well: bath towels, sponges, socks, used Kleenex, combs. Handi Wipes were a particular favourite.

For Jenny's birthday I bought her an eighteen-carat gold necklace, a delicate chain with a tiny clasp, and she immediately put it on. But a few hours later she pressed her hand to her throat and screamed, 'My necklace! It's gone.' The clasp must not have been fully secured.

'Don't panic,' I told her. 'We haven't left the house. It's got to be here somewhere.' As we searched, I gradually became aware that Marley was squirming. When he noticed I had him in my sights, he began evasive action. *Oh, no*, I thought—the Marley Mambo. It could mean only one thing.

'What's that,' Jenny asked, panic rising in her voice, 'hanging out of his mouth?'

It was thin and delicate. And gold.

'No sudden moves,' she ordered, her voice dropping to a whisper. We both froze.

'OK, boy, it's all right,' I coaxed like a hostage negotiator on a SWAT team. 'We're not mad at you. We just want the necklace back.' Instinctively, Jenny and I began to circle him from opposite directions, moving with glacial slowness. It was as if he were wired with high explosives and one false move could set him off.

'Easy, Marley,' Jenny said in her calmest voice. 'Drop the necklace and no one gets hurt.'

Marley eyed us suspiciously, his head darting back and forth between us. We had him cornered, but he knew he had something we wanted. I could see him weighing his options.

Jenny and I glanced at each other and knew, without speaking, what to do. We had been through the Property Recovery Drill countless times before. She would lunge for the hindquarters, pinning his back legs to prevent escape. I would lunge for the head, prising open his jaws and nabbing the contraband. With any luck, we'd be in and out in a matter of seconds. That was the plan, and Marley saw it coming.

We were less than two feet away from him. I nodded to Jenny and silently mouthed, 'On three.' But before we could make our move, he threw his head back and made a loud smacking sound. The tail end of the chain, which had been dangling out of his mouth, disappeared. I forced his jaws open and pushed my whole hand into his mouth, down his throat. 'It's too late,' I said. 'He swallowed it.' Jenny began slapping him on the back, yelling, 'Cough it up, damn it!' But it was no use. The best she got out of him was a loud, satisfied burp.

Marley may have won the battle, but we knew it was just a matter of time before we won the war. Nature's call was on our side. Sooner or later, what went in had to come out. As disgusting as the thought was, I knew if I poked through his excrement long enough, I would find it.

And so I prepared Marley his favourite laxative—a giant bowl of dead-ripe sliced mangoes—and settled in for the long wait. For three days I followed him around every time I let him out, eagerly waiting to swoop in with my shovel. Instead of burying his piles in the sand at the back of the lot, I carefully placed each on a wide board in the grass and poked it with a tree branch while I sprayed with a garden hose, gradually washing the digested material away and leaving behind any foreign objects. I felt like a gold miner working a sluice and coming up with a treasure trove of swallowed junk, from shoelaces to guitar picks. But no necklace.

On the fourth day, my perseverance paid off. I scooped up Marley's latest deposit, repeating what had become my daily refrain—'I can't believe I'm doing this'—and began poking and spraying. I was about to give up when I spotted something odd: a small brown lump, about the size of a lima bean. It wasn't even close to being large enough to be the missing jewellery, yet clearly it did not seem to belong there. I pinned it down with my probing branch and gave the object a blast from the hose nozzle. As the water washed it clean, I got a glimmer of something exceptionally bright and shiny. Eureka! I had struck gold.

The necklace was impossibly compressed, many times smaller than I would have guessed possible. The strong stream of water began to loosen the hard wad, and gradually the lump of gold unravelled back to its original shape, untangled and unmangled. Good as new. No, actually better than new. I took it inside to show Jenny, who was ecstatic to have it back, despite its dubious passage. We both marvelled at how blindingly bright it was now. Marley's stomach acids had done an amazing job. It was the most brilliant gold I had ever seen. 'Man,' I said with a whistle. 'We should open a jewellery-cleaning business.'

Jenny went off to disinfect her recovered birthday present. She wore that gold chain for years, and every time I looked at it I had the same vivid flashback to my brief career in gold speculation. I had gone where no man had ever gone before. And none should ever go again.

YOU DON'T GIVE BIRTH to your first child every day, and so, when St Mary's Hospital in West Palm Beach offered us the option of paying extra for a luxury birthing suite, we jumped at the chance. The suites looked like upper-end hotel rooms, spacious, bright and well appointed. Just for Dad, a comfy couch folded out into a bed. Instead of standard-issue hospital food, 'guests' were offered gourmet dinners.

'Man, it's just like being on vacation!' I exclaimed, bouncing on the Dad Couch as we took a tour several weeks before Jenny's due date.

The suites catered to the yuppie set and were a big source of profits for the hospital, bringing in hard cash from couples with money to blow above the standard insurance allotment for deliveries. A bit of an indulgence, we agreed, but why not?

When Jenny's big day came and we arrived at the hospital, overnight bag in hand, we were told there was a little problem.

'A problem?' I asked.

'It must be a good day for having babies,' the receptionist said cheerfully. 'All the birthing suites are already taken.'

Taken? This was the most important day of our lives. What about the comfy couch and romantic dinner for two? 'Now, wait a second,' I complained. 'We made our reservation weeks ago.'

'I'm sorry,' the woman said with a noticeable lack of sympathy. 'We don't have a lot of control over when mothers go into labour.'

She made a valid point. It wasn't as if she could hurry someone along. She directed us to another floor, where we would be issued a standard hospital room. But when we arrived, the nurse at the counter had more bad news. 'Would you believe every last room is filled?' she said. No, we couldn't. Jenny seemed to take it in her stride, but I was getting testy. 'What do you suggest, the parking lot?' I snapped.

The nurse smiled calmly at me, apparently well familiar with the antics of nervous fathers-to-be, and said, 'Don't you worry. We'll find a spot for you.'

After a flurry of phone calls, she sent us down a long hallway and through a set of double doors, where we found ourselves in a mirror image of the maternity ward we had just left except for one obvious difference— the nurses were talking in Spanish to the patients.

Palm Beach County is known as a playground for the rich, but it is also home to huge farms that stretch across drained Everglades swamp. Thousands of workers, mostly from Mexico and Central America, migrate into South Florida each growing season to pick the peppers, tomatoes, lettuce and celery that supply much of the East Coast's winter vegetable needs. It seems we had discovered where the migrant workers came to have their babies. Periodically, a woman's anguished scream would pierce the air, followed by awful moans and calls of '*Mi madre!*'

The nurse led us into a small cubicle containing one bed, one chair and a bank of electronic monitors and handed Jenny a gown to change into. 'Welcome to the indigent ward!' Dr Sherman said brightly when he breezed in a few minutes later. 'Don't be fooled by the bare-bones rooms,' he said. They were outfitted with some of the most sophisticated medical equipment in the hospital, and the nurses were some of the best trained. Because poor women often lacked access to prenatal care, theirs were some of the highest-risk pregnancies. We were in good hands, he assured us as he broke Jenny's water. Then, as quickly as he had appeared, he was gone.

Indeed, as the morning progressed and Jenny fought her way through ferocious contractions, we discovered we were in very good hands. The nurses were seasoned professionals who exuded confidence and warmth. I stood helplessly by, trying my best to be supportive, but it wasn't working.

At one point Jenny snarled at me through gritted teeth, 'If you ask me one more time how I'm doing, I'm going to RIP YOUR FACE OFF!'

I began slipping out of the room to join the other men waiting in the hallway. Each of us leaned against the wall beside our respective doors. They couldn't speak English and I couldn't speak Spanish, but that didn't matter. We were in this together.

The hours passed. Jenny pushed. I coached. As night fell I stepped out into the hall bearing a tiny swaddled football. I lifted my newborn son for my new friends to see and called out, '*Es el niño!*' The other dads flashed big smiles and held up their thumbs in the international sign of approval.

Unlike our heated struggle to name our dog, we easily settled on a name for our first-born son. He would be named Patrick for the first of my line of Grogans to arrive in the United States from Ireland. A nurse came into our cubicle and told us a birthing suite was now available. It seemed beside the point to change rooms now, but she helped Jenny into a wheelchair, placed our son in her arms, and whisked us away. The gourmet dinner wasn't all it was cracked up to be.

DURING THE WEEKS leading up to her due date, Jenny and I had had long strategy talks about how best to acclimatise Marley to the new arrival who would instantly knock him off his perch as Most-Favoured Dependant. We wanted to let him down gently. As we converted the spare bedroom into a nursery, we gave Marley full access to the crib and bedding and all the accoutrements of infancy. In the thirty-six hours that Jenny remained hospitalised recuperating after the birth, I made frequent trips home to visit Marley, armed with receiving blankets and anything else that carried the baby's scent.

When I finally brought mother and child home, Marley was oblivious. Jenny placed baby Patrick, asleep in his car carrier, in the middle of our bed and then joined me in greeting Marley out in the garage, where we had an uproarious reunion. Then we brought him into the house with us. Our plan was to just go about our business, not pointing the baby out to him. We would hover nearby and let him gradually discover the presence of the newcomer on his own.

Marley followed Jenny into the bedroom; he clearly had no idea there was a living thing sitting on our bed. Then Patrick stirred and let out a small birdlike chirp. Marley's ears pulled up and he froze. *Where did that come from?* Patrick chirped again, and Marley lifted one paw in the air, pointing like a bird dog. My God, he was *pointing* at our baby boy like a hunting dog would point at . . . *prey.*

Then he lunged. It was not a ferocious 'kill the enemy' lunge; there were no bared teeth or growls. But it wasn't a 'welcome to the neighbourhood, little buddy' lunge, either. Jenny dived for the baby and I for the dog, pulling him back by the collar with both hands. 'Well, that went well,' I said.

Jenny unbuckled Patrick from his car seat; I pinned Marley between my legs and held him tightly by the collar with both fists. Even Jenny could see Marley meant no harm. He was panting with that dopey grin of his; his eyes were bright and his tail was wagging. As I held tight, she gradually came closer, allowing Marley to sniff first the baby's toes, then his feet and calves and thighs. The poor kid was only a day and a half old, and he was already under attack. When Marley reached the diaper, he seemed to enter an altered state of consciousness, a sort of Pampers-induced trance. He had reached the holy land. The dog looked positively euphoric.

'One false move, Marley, and you're toast,' Jenny warned, and she meant it. If he had shown even the slightest aggression towards the baby, that would have been it. But he never did. We soon learned our problem was not keeping Marley from hurting our precious baby boy. Our problem was keeping him out of the diaper pail.

As THE DAYS turned into weeks and the weeks into months, Marley came to accept Patrick as his new best friend. He seemed to understand that this was a fragile, defenceless little human, and he moved gingerly whenever he was near him, licking his face delicately. As Patrick began crawling, Marley would lie quietly on the floor and let the baby scale him like a mountain, tugging on his ears, poking his eyes and pulling out little fistfuls of fur. None of it fazed him. Marley just sat like a statue. He was a gentle giant around Patrick.

Jenny and I settled into a routine. At night-time she would get up with Patrick every few hours to nurse him, and I would take the 6.00 a.m. feeding so she could sleep in. Half asleep, I would pluck him from his crib, change his diaper and make a bottle of formula for him. Then the payoff: I would sit on the back porch with his tiny warm body nestled against my stomach as he sucked on the bottle and I watched the dawn sky turn from purple to pink to blue. When he was fed and I had got a good burp out of him, I would get us both dressed, whistle for Marley and take a morning walk along the water. We invested in a jogging stroller with three large bicycle tyres that allowed it to go through sand and over kerbs. The three of us must have made quite a sight, Marley out in front leading the charge like a mush dog, me in the rear holding us back for dear life, and Patrick in the middle, gleefully waving his arms in the air like a traffic cop. By the time we arrived home, Jenny would be up and have coffee on.

Parenthood suited us well. We settled into its rhythms, celebrated its simple joys, and grinned our way through its frustrations, knowing even the bad days soon enough would be cherished memories. We had everything we could ask for. We had our precious baby. We had our numskull dog. We had our little house by the water. Of course, we also had each other. And that November, my newspaper promoted me to columnist, a coveted position that gave me my own space three times a week to spout off about whatever I wanted. Life was good. When Patrick was nine months old, Jenny wondered aloud when we might want to start thinking about having another baby.

'Oh, gee, I don't know,' I said. We knew we wanted more than one, but I hadn't really thought about a time frame. 'I guess we could just go back off birth control again and see what happens,' I suggested.

'Ah,' Jenny said knowingly. 'The old *Che sarà, sarà* school of family planning.'

So that is what we did. We figured if we conceived anytime in the next year, the timing would be about right. As Jenny did the maths, she said, 'Let's say six months to get pregnant and then nine more months to deliver. That would put two full years between them.'

It sounded good to me. Two years was a long way off. Two years was next to an eternity. Two years was almost not real.

A week later, Jenny was knocked up.

Chapter 7

A Scream in the Night

With another baby growing inside her, Jenny's odd, late-night food cravings returned. One night it was root beer, the next grapefruit. 'Do we have any Snickers bars?' she asked once a little before midnight. It looked as though I was in for another jaunt down to the all-night convenience store. I whistled for Marley, hooked him to his leash, and set off for the corner. In the parking lot, a young woman with teased blonde hair, bright lavender lips and some of the highest heels I had ever seen engaged us. 'Oh, he's so cute!' she gushed. 'Hi, puppy. What's your name, cutie?' Marley, of course, was more than happy to strike up a friendship, and I pulled him tight against me so he wouldn't slobber on her purple miniskirt and white tank top.

As we chatted, I wondered what this attractive woman was doing out in a parking lot along Dixie Highway alone at this hour. She did not appear to have a car. She did not appear to be on her way into or out of the store.

Just then, a car pulled up, and an older man rolled down his window. 'Are you Heather?' he asked. She shot me a bemused smile as if to say, *You do what you have to do to pay the rent.* 'Gotta run,' she said, hopping into the car. 'Bye, puppy.'

'Don't fall too in love, Marley,' I said as they drove off. 'You can't afford her.'

I wasn't the only one witnessing the burgeoning prostitution trade along Dixie Highway. In response to complaints from residents, the police began running stings, positioning undercover women officers on the corner and waiting for would-be johns to take the bait. One bust went down directly in front of our house.

If it had been just the hookers and their customers, we could have made our separate peace, but the criminal activity didn't stop there. Our neighbourhood seemed to grow dicier each day. When Patrick was not quite a year old, murder came to our block. The victim was an elderly woman who lived alone. Hers was the first house as you turned onto Churchill Road off Dixie Highway, directly behind the all-night Laundromat, and I only knew her to wave to as I passed. The attacker was a stranger who snuck into her house and ransacked it for money. Police quickly arrested a drifter who had been seen hanging around the coin laundry; when they emptied his pockets they found his total haul had been sixteen dollars and change. The price of a human life.

The crime swirling around us made us grateful for Marley's bigger-than-life presence in our house. We had a baby now and another on the way. We were no longer so cheerfully cavalier about personal safety. Jenny and I often speculated about just what, if anything, Marley would do if someone ever tried to hurt the baby or us. I tended to think he was a pacifist whose most aggressive attack strategy would be a Slobber Offensive. Jenny placed more faith in him. She was convinced his loyalty to us would translate in a crisis to a fierce primal protectiveness. Then one night he settled the dispute once and for all.

After the eleven o'clock news I let Marley out to pee, checked Patrick in his crib, turned off the lights and crawled into bed beside Jenny, already fast asleep.

Marley, as he always did, collapsed in a heap on the floor beside me, releasing an exaggerated sigh. I was just drifting off when I heard it—a shrill, sustained, piercing noise. I was instantly wide awake, and Marley was, too. He stood frozen beside the bed in the dark, ears cocked. A scream. A woman's scream, loud and unmistakable. There was desperation in it, real terror and it was dawning on me that someone was in terrible trouble.

'Come on, boy,' I whispered, slipping out of bed.

'Don't go out there.' Jenny's voice came from beside me in the dark. I hadn't realised she was awake and listening.

'Call the police,' I told her. 'I'll be careful.'

Holding Marley by the end of his choke chain, I stepped out onto the front porch in my boxer shorts just in time to glimpse a figure sprinting down the street towards the water.

The scream came again, the likes of which I had heard only in horror movies. Other porch lights were flicking on. The two young men who shared a rental house across the street from me burst outside, wearing nothing but cut-offs, and ran towards the screams. I followed, Marley tight by my side. I saw them run up on a lawn a few houses away and then, seconds later, come dashing back towards me.

'Go to the girl!' one of them shouted. 'She's been stabbed.'

'We're going after him!' the other yelled, and they sprinted off down the street in the direction the figure had fled.

I let go of Marley's collar and ran towards the scream. Three doors down I found my seventeen-year-old neighbour Lisa, standing alone in her driveway, bent over, sobbing in jagged raspy gasps. She clasped her ribs, and beneath her hands I could see a circle of blood spreading across her blouse. She was a thin, pretty girl with sand-coloured hair that fell over her shoulders. She lived in the house with her divorced mother, a pleasant woman who worked as a night nurse. I had chatted a few times with the mother, but I only knew her daughter to wave to.

'He said not to scream or he'd stab me,' she said, sobbing; her words gushed out in heaving, hyperventilated gulps. 'But I screamed, and he stabbed me.' She lifted her shirt to show me the puckered wound that had punctured her rib cage. 'I was sitting in my car with the radio on. He just came out of nowhere.' I put my hand on her arm to calm her, and as I did she collapsed into my arms, her legs folding fawnlike beneath her. I eased her down to the pavement and sat cradling her. 'He told me not to scream,' she kept saying.

'You did the right thing,' I said. 'You scared him away.'

It occurred to me that she was going into shock. *Come on, ambulance. Where are you?* I comforted her as I would comfort my own child, stroking her hair, holding my palm against her cheek, wiping her tears away. As she grew weaker, I kept telling her to hang on, help was on the way. 'You're going to be OK,' I said, but I wasn't sure I believed it. Her skin was ashen. We sat alone on the pavement like that for what seemed hours but was in actuality, the police report later showed, about three minutes.

Only gradually did I think to check on what had become of Marley. When I looked up, there he stood, ten feet from us, facing the street, in a determined, bull-like crouch I had never seen before. It was a fighter's stance. His muscles bulged at the neck; his jaw was clenched; the fur between his shoulder blades bristled. He was intensely focused and poised to lunge. I realised in that instant that Jenny had been right. If the assailant returned, I knew without doubt that Marley would fight him to the death before he would let him at us. The sight of him so uncharacteristically guarding us like that brought tears to my eyes. Man's best friend? Damn straight he was.

'The police are coming,' I told the girl. 'Hold on. Please, hold on.'

Soon police officers were swarming around us, and an ambulance crew arrived with a stretcher and wads of sterile gauze. I stepped out of the way, told the police what I could and walked home, Marley ahead of me.

Jenny met me at the door and together we stood in the front window watching the drama unfold on the street. Our neighbourhood looked like the set from a police television drama. A police helicopter hovered overhead, shining its spotlight down on back yards. Cops set up roadblocks and combed the neighbourhood. Their efforts would be in vain; a suspect was never apprehended. My neighbours who gave chase later told me they had not even caught a glimpse of him.

Jenny and I eventually returned to bed, where we both lay awake for a long time.

'You would have been proud of Marley,' I told her. 'It was so strange. Somehow he knew how serious this was. He felt the danger, and he was like a completely different dog.'

'I told you so,' she said. And she had.

It said something about South Florida's numbness to crime that the stabbing of a teenage girl as she sat in her car in front of her home would merit just six sentences in the morning newspaper. The *Sun-Sentinel*'s story made no mention of me or Marley or the guys across the street who set out half naked after the assailant. It didn't mention all the neighbours who turned on porch lights and dialed 911. In South Florida's seamy world of violent crime, our drama was just a minor hiccup. No deaths, no hostages, no big deal.

The knife had punctured Lisa's lung, and she spent five days in the hospital and several weeks recuperating at home. Her mother kept the neighbours apprised of her recovery, but the girl remained inside and out of sight. I worried about the emotional wounds the attack might leave. Would she ever again be comfortable leaving the safety of her home? Our lives had come together for just three minutes, but I felt invested in her as a brother might be in a kid sister. I wanted to respect her privacy, but I also wanted to see her, to prove to myself she was going to be all right.

Then as I washed the cars in the driveway on a Saturday, Marley chained up beside me, I looked up and there she stood. Prettier than I had remembered. Tanned, strong, athletic—looking whole again. She smiled and asked, 'Remember me?'

'Let's see,' I said, feigning puzzlement. 'You look vaguely familiar. Weren't you the one in front of me at the Tom Petty concert who wouldn't sit down?'

She laughed, and I asked, 'So how are you doing, Lisa?'

'I'm good,' she said. 'Just about back to normal.'

'You look great,' I told her. 'A little better than the last time I saw you.'

'Yeah, well,' she said, and looked down at her feet. 'What a night.'

'What a night,' I repeated.

That was all we said about it. She told me about the hospital, the doctors, the detective who interviewed her, the endless fruit baskets, the boredom of sitting at home as she healed. But she steered clear of the attack, and so did I. Some things were best left behind.

'I'm glad you stopped by,' I said.

'I'm glad I did, too,' Lisa answered.

By the time she left, I had a good feeling about this girl. She was strong. She was tough. She would move forward. And indeed I found out years later, when I learned she had built a career for herself as a television broadcaster, that she had.

Chapter 8

A Postpartum Ultimatum

'John.' Through the fog of sleep, I gradually registered my name being called. 'John, wake up.' It was Jenny; she was shaking me. 'I think the baby might be coming.'

I propped myself up on an elbow and rubbed my eyes

'I'm having bad cramps,' she said. 'I've been lying here timing them. We need to call Dr Sherman.'

I was wide awake now. *The baby was coming?* I was wild with anticipation for the birth of our second child—another boy, we already knew from the sonogram. The timing, though, was wrong, terribly wrong. Jenny was twenty-one weeks into the pregnancy, barely halfway through the forty-week gestation period. At twenty-one weeks a foetus can fit in the palm of a hand, and the odds of surviving outside the womb are exceptionally long.

'It's probably nothing,' I said. But I could feel my heart pounding as I speed-dialled the ob-gyn answering service. Two minutes later Dr Sherman called back, sounding groggy himself. 'It might just be gas,' he said, 'but we better have a look.' He told me to get Jenny to the hospital immediately. I raced around the house, throwing items into an overnight bag for her and making baby bottles. Jenny called her friend and coworker Sandy, another new mom who lived a few blocks away, and asked if we could drop Patrick off. Marley was up now, too, stretching, yawning, shaking. *Late-night road trip!* 'Sorry, Mar,' I told him as I led him out to the garage, grave disappointment on his face. 'You've got to hold down the fort.' I scooped Patrick out of his crib, buckled him into his car seat and into the night we went.

At St. Mary's neonatal intensive-care unit, the nurses quickly went to work. They got Jenny into a hospital gown and hooked her to a monitor that measured contractions. Sure enough, Jenny was having a contraction every six minutes. This was definitely not gas.

Dr Sherman ordered an injection of the labour inhibitor Brethine. The contractions levelled out, but two hours later they were back again with a fury, requiring a second shot, then a third.

For the next twelve days Jenny remained hospitalised, poked and prodded by a parade of perinatalogists and tethered to monitors and intravenous drips. I took vacation time and played single parent to Patrick, doing my best to hold everything together—the laundry, the feedings, meals, bills, housework, the yard. Oh, yes, and that other living creature in our home. Poor Marley's status dropped precipitously from second fiddle to not even in the orchestra.

But life wasn't completely bleak for him. On the bright side, I had quickly reverted to my premarriage (read: slovenly) lifestyle. By the power vested in me as the only adult in the house, I suspended the Married Couple Domesticity Act and proclaimed the once-banished Bachelor Rules to be the law of the land. While Jenny was in the hospital, shirts would be worn twice, even three times, barring obvious mustard stains, between washes; milk could be drunk directly from the carton, and toilet seats would remain in the upright position unless being sat on. Much to Marley's delight, I instituted a 24/7 open-door policy for the bathroom. After all, it was just us guys. I got into the habit of turning the bathtub tap on at a trickle while I was in the bathroom so Marley could lap up some cool, fresh water. Jenny would have been appalled, but the way I saw it, it sure beat the toilet.

I tried to fool Jenny into thinking I had everything effortlessly under control. 'Oh, we're totally fine,' I told her, and then, turning to Patrick, I would add, 'aren't we, partner?' To which he would give his standard reply: 'Dada!' and then, pointing at the ceiling fan: 'Fannnnn!' She knew better. One day when I arrived with Patrick for our daily visit, she stared at us in disbelief and asked, 'What in God's name did you do to him?'

'What do you mean, what did I do to him?' I replied. 'He's great. You're great, aren't you?'

'Dada! Fannnnn!'

'His outfit,' she said. 'How on earth—'

Only then did I see. Something was amiss with Patrick's snap-on one-piece. His chubby thighs, I now realised, were squeezed into the armholes, which were so tight they must have been cutting off his circulation. The collared neck hung between his legs like an udder. Up top, Patrick's head stuck out through the unsnapped crotch, and his arms were lost somewhere in the billowing pant legs.

'You goof,' she said. 'You've got it on him upside-down.'

'That's your opinion,' I said.

But the game was up. Jenny began working the phone from her hospital bed, and a couple of days later my sweet, dear aunt Anita, a retired nurse who lived across the state from us, magically appeared, suitcase in hand, and cheerfully went about restoring order. The Bachelor Rules were history.

WHEN HER DOCTORS finally let Jenny come home, it was with the strictest of orders. If she wanted to deliver a healthy baby, she was to remain in bed, as still as possible. The only time she was allowed on her feet was to go to the bathroom. She could take one quick shower a day, then back into bed. No lifting anything heavier than a toothbrush—and that meant her baby, a stipulation that nearly killed her. Complete bed rest, no cheating. Jenny's doctors had successfully shut down the early labour; their goal now was to keep it shut down for the next twelve weeks minimum.

A hospital technician came to our home and inserted a catheter into Jenny's thigh; this she attached to a small battery-powered pump that strapped to Jenny's leg and delivered a continuous trickle of labour-inhibiting drugs into her bloodstream. Jenny was trying to keep her spirits up, but the tedium and the uncertainty about the health of her unborn child were conspiring to drag her down. Worst of all, she was a mother with a fifteen-month-old son whom she was not allowed to lift, to feed when he was hungry, to scoop up and kiss when he was sad. I would drop him next to her on the bed, where he would point to the whirling paddles above and say, 'Mama! Fannnnn!' It made her smile, but it wasn't the same. She was slowly going stir crazy.

Her constant companion through it all, of course, was Marley. He set up camp on the floor beside her, surrounding himself with a wide assortment of toys, just in case Jenny changed her mind and decided to jump out of bed and engage in a little tug of war. There he held vigil, day and night. I would come home from work and find Aunt Anita in the kitchen cooking dinner, Patrick in his bouncy seat beside her. Then I would walk into the bedroom to find Marley standing beside the bed, chin on the mattress, tail wagging, nose nuzzled into Jenny's neck as she read or snoozed, her arm draped over his back. I marked off each day on the calendar to help her track her progress.

When Jenny had a full month of bed rest still to go, Aunt Anita packed her suitcase and kissed us goodbye. She had stayed as long as she could, in fact extending her visit several times, but she had a husband at home who she only half jokingly fretted was quite possibly turning feral as he survived alone. Once again, we were on our own.

I did my best to keep the ship afloat, rising at dawn to bathe and dress Patrick, feed him and take him and Marley for a walk. Then I would drop Patrick at Sandy's house for the day while I worked. I would come home on my lunch hour to make Jenny her lunch, bring her the mail, throw sticks to

Marley and straighten up the house, which was slowly taking on a patina of neglect. I could see dismay in Jenny's eyes. It took all of her self-control not to jump out of bed and whip her home back into shape. I grocery-shopped after Patrick was asleep for the night, sometimes walking the aisles at midnight. We survived on carry-outs, Cheerios and pots of pasta.

Then one day, as we approached Jenny's thirty-fifth week of pregnancy, the hospital technician arrived at our door and said, 'Congratulations, girl, you've made it. You're free again.' She unhooked the medicine pump, removed the catheter, packed up the foetal monitor and went over the doctor's written orders. Jenny was free to return to her regular lifestyle. The baby was fully viable now.

Jenny tossed Patrick over her head, romped with Marley in the back yard, tore into the housework. That night we celebrated by going out for Indian food and catching a show at a local comedy club. The next day the three of us continued the festivities by having lunch at a Greek restaurant. Before the food ever made it to our table, however, Jenny was in full-blown labour. Each contraction nearly doubled her over. We raced home, where Sandy was on standby to take Patrick and keep an eye on Marley. Jenny waited in the car, puffing her way through the pain with shallow breaths as I grabbed her overnight bag. By the time we got to the hospital and checked into a room, Jenny was dilated to seven centimetres. Less than an hour later, I held our new son in my arms. His eyes were open and alert, his cheeks blushed.

'You did it,' Dr Sherman declared. 'He's perfect.'

Conor Richard Grogan, five pounds and thirteen ounces, was born October 10, 1993. I was so happy I barely gave a second thought to the irony that for this pregnancy we had rented one of the luxury suites but had hardly a moment to enjoy it. If the delivery had been any quicker, Jenny would have given birth in the parking lot. I hadn't even had time to stretch out on the Dad Couch.

THESE SHOULD HAVE BEEN the happiest days of our lives, and in many ways they were. We had two sons now, a toddler and a newborn, just seventeen months apart. The joy they brought us was profound. Yet the darkness that had descended over Jenny while she was on forced bed rest persisted. Some weeks she was fine, cheerfully tackling the challenges of being responsible for two lives completely dependent on her. Other weeks, without warning, she would turn glum and defeated, locked in a blue fog that sometimes would not lift for days. We were both exhausted and sleep deprived. Patrick was still waking us at least once in the night, and Conor was up several more times. Seldom did we get more than two hours of uninterrupted sleep at a stretch. Some nights we were like zombies, moving silently past each other with glazed eyes, Jenny to one baby and I to the other.

Complicating the sleep-deprived chaos that was our lives, our new baby had us terribly worried. Already underweight, Conor was unable to keep nourishment down. Jenny would offer him her breast, and he would suckle hungrily. Then, in one quick heave, he would throw it all up. The doctors diagnosed reflux, and while Conor eventually would outgrow the condition and catch up on his weight, for four long months we were consumed with worry over him. Jenny was a basket case of fear and stress and frustration. She nursed him nearly nonstop and then watched helplessly as he tossed her milk back at her. 'I feel so inadequate,' she would say. 'Moms are supposed to be able to give their babies everything they need.' Her fuse was as short as I had seen it, and the smallest infractions—a cupboard door left open, crumbs on the counter—would set her off.

The good news was that Jenny never once took out her anxiety on either baby. In fact, she nurtured both of them with almost obsessive care and patience. The bad news was that she directed her frustration and anger at me and even more at Marley. She had lost all patience with him. Each transgression—and there continued to be many—pushed Jenny a little closer to the edge. Oblivious, Marley stayed the course with his misdeeds and boundless ebullience. I bought a flowering shrub and planted it in the garden to commemorate Conor's birth; Marley pulled it out by the roots the same day and chewed it into mulch. He escaped one day and when he finally returned, he had a pair of women's panties in his teeth. I didn't want to know.

Despite the prescription tranquillisers, Marley's thunder phobia grew more intense and irrational each day. By now a soft shower would send him into a panic. If we were home, he would merely latch onto us and salivate nervously all over our clothes. If we weren't home, he sought safety by digging and gouging through doors and plaster and linoleum. The more I repaired, the more he destroyed. I should have been furious, but Jenny was angry enough for both of us. Instead, I started covering for him. If I found a chewed shoe or book or pillow, I hid the evidence before she could find it.

It was into this volatile environment that I walked one evening. I opened the front door to find Jenny beating Marley with her fists. She was crying uncontrollably and flailing wildly at him, landing glancing blows on his back and shoulders and neck. 'Why? Why do you do this?' she screamed at him. 'Why do you wreck everything?' In that instant I saw what he had done. The couch cushion was gouged open, the fabric shredded and the stuffing pulled out. Marley stood with head down and legs splayed as though leaning into a hurricane. He didn't try to flee or dodge the blows; he just stood there and took each one without whimper or complaint.

'Hey! Hey!' I shouted, grabbing her wrists. 'Come on. Stop!' She was sobbing and gasping for breath. 'Stop,' I repeated.

I stepped between her and Marley and shoved my face directly in front of hers. It was like a stranger's. I did not recognise the look in her eyes. 'Get him out of here,' she said, her voice flat. 'Get him out of here now.'

'OK, I'll take him out,' I said, 'but you settle down.'

'Get him out of here and keep him out of here,' she said in an unsettling monotone.

I opened the front door and he bounded outside, and when I turned back to grab his leash off the table, Jenny said, 'I mean it. I want him gone for good.'

'Come on,' I said. 'You don't mean that.'

'I mean it,' she said. 'You find him a new home, or I will.'

She couldn't mean it. She adored this dog despite his laundry list of shortcomings. She was upset; she was stressed to the breaking point. She would reconsider. For the moment I thought it was best to give her time to cool down.

I walked out the door without another word. In the front yard, Marley raced around, apparently no worse for the pummelling. I knew she hadn't hurt him. I routinely whacked him much harder when I played rough with him, and he loved it, always bounding back for more.

Out in the street, I hooked him to his leash and ordered, 'Sit!' He sat. The incident with Jenny appeared to be behind him; now I hoped it would be behind her, as well. 'What am I going to do with you, you big dope?' I asked him. He leapt up, as though outfitted with springs, and smashed his tongue against my lips.

Marley and I walked for miles that evening, and when I finally opened the front door, he was exhausted and ready to collapse. Jenny was feeding Patrick a jar of baby food as she cradled Conor in her lap. She was calm and appeared back to her old self. Maybe the horrible moment had passed.

Maybe she felt sheepish about her outburst and was searching for the words to apologise. As I walked past her, Marley close at my heels, she said in a calm, quiet voice without looking at me, 'I'm dead serious. I want him out of here.'

OVER THE NEXT SEVERAL DAYS she repeated the ultimatum enough times that I finally accepted that this was not an idle threat. The issue was not going away. I was sick about it. As pathetic as it sounds, Marley had become my soul mate, my near-constant companion, my friend. He was the undisciplined, recalcitrant, nonconformist, politically incorrect free spirit I had always wanted to be, had I been brave enough, and I took vicarious joy in his unbridled verve. No matter how complicated life became, he reminded me of its simple joys. No matter how many demands were placed on me, he never let me forget that wilful disobedience is sometimes worth the price. In a world full of bosses, he was his own master.

The thought of giving him up seared my soul. But I had two children to worry about now and a wife whom we needed. Our household was being held together by the most tenuous of threads. If losing Marley made the difference between meltdown and stability, how could I not honour Jenny's wishes?

I began putting out feelers, asking friends and coworkers if they might be interested in taking on a lovable and lively two-year-old Labrador retriever. Unfortunately, Marley's reputation preceded him.

Each morning I opened the newspaper to the classifieds as if I might find some miracle ad: 'Seeking wildly energetic, out-of-control Labrador retriever with multiple phobias. Destructive qualities a plus. Will pay top dollar.' What I found instead was a booming trade in young adult dogs that had not worked out. Many were purebreds that their owners had spent several hundred dollars for just months earlier. Now they were being offered for a pittance or even for free. An alarming number of the unwanted dogs were male Labs.

The ads were in almost every day, and were at once heartbreaking and hilarious. They were full of sunny euphemisms for the types of behaviour I knew all too well. 'Lively . . . loves people . . . needs room to run . . . spirited . . . one of a kind.' It all added up to the same thing: a dog its master could not control. A dog that had become a liability. A dog its owner had given up on.

Part of me ached with sadness. I was not a quitter; I did not believe Jenny was a quitter, either. We were not the kind of people who pawned off our problems in the classifieds. Marley was undeniably a handful, but in his own flawed way, he was trying. For better or worse, he was our dog. He was a part of our family, and he had returned our affection one hundredfold. Devotion such as his could not be bought for any price.

I was not ready to give up on him.

Even as I continued to make halfhearted enquiries about finding Marley a new home, I began working with him in earnest. My own private Mission: Impossible was to rehabilitate this dog and prove to Jenny he was worthy. Interrupted sleep be damned, I began rising at dawn, buckling Patrick into the jogging stroller, and heading down to the water to put Marley through the paces. Sit. Stay. Down. Heel. Over and over we practised, with my helper Patrick clapping and calling to his big yellow friend, 'Waddy! Hee-O!'

By the time I re-enrolled Marley in obedience school, he was a different dog from the juvenile delinquent I had first shown up with. Yes, still as wild as a boar, but this time he knew I was the boss and he was the underling. This time there would be no lunges towards other dogs, no out-of-control surges across the tarmac, no crashing into strangers' crotches. During eight weekly sessions, I marched him through the commands on a tight leash, and he was happy to cooperate. At our final meeting, the trainer—a relaxed woman who was the antithesis of Miss Dominatrix—called us up and handed us our diploma. Marley had passed basic obedience training, ranking seventh in the class. So what if it was a class of eight? I would take it. Marley, my incorrigible, untrainable, undisciplined dog, had passed. I was so proud I could have cried, and in fact I actually might have had Marley not leapt up and promptly eaten his diploma.

On the way home, I sang 'We Are the Champions' at the top of my lungs. Marley, sensing my joy and pride, stuck his tongue in my ear. For once, I didn't even mind.

ONE MORNING, not long after, I woke up and my wife was back. My Jenny, the woman I loved who had disappeared into that unyielding blue fog, had returned to me. As suddenly as the postpartum depression had swept over her, it swept away again. It was as if she had been exorcised of her demons. They were gone. She was strong, she was upbeat, she was not only coping as a young mother of two, but thriving. Marley was back in her good graces, safely on solid ground. With a baby in each arm, she leaned to kiss him. She threw him sticks and made him gravy from hamburger drippings. She danced him around the room when a good song came on the stereo. Sometimes at night when he was calm, I would find her lying on the floor with him, her head resting on his neck. Jenny was back. Thank God, she was back.

Chapter 9

The Audition

Some things in life are just too bizarre to be anything but true, so when Jenny called me at the office to tell me Marley was getting a film audition, I knew she couldn't be making it up.

'Like for a movie?' I asked.

'Yes, like for a movie, dumbo,' she said. 'A feature-length movie.'

I tried to reconcile the image of our lug-head chewer of ironing boards with the image of Rin Tin Tin leaping across the silver screen, pulling helpless children from burning buildings.

'Our Marley?' I asked one more time, just to be sure.

It was true. A week earlier, Jenny's supervisor at the *Palm Beach Post* had called and said she had a friend who needed to ask a favour of us. The friend was a local photographer named Colleen McGarr who had been hired by a New York City film-production company called the Shooting Gallery to help with a movie they planned to make in Lake Worth, the town just south of us. Colleen's job was to find a 'quintessential South Florida household' and photograph it top to bottom—the bookshelves, the refrigerator magnets, the closets—to help the directors bring realism to the film.

'The whole set crew is gay,' Jenny's boss told her. 'They're trying to figure out how married couples with kids live around here.'

'Sort of like an anthropological case study,' Jenny said.

'Exactly.'

'Sure,' Jenny agreed, 'as long as I don't have to clean first.'

Colleen came over and started photographing, not just our possessions but us, too. The way we dressed, the way we wore our hair, the way we slouched on the couch. She photographed the babies in their cribs. She photographed the quintessentially heterosexual couple's eunuch dog, too. Or at least what she could catch of him on film. As she observed, 'He's a bit of a blur.'

As Colleen clicked away, I couldn't help thinking of the possibilities. Most of the secondary actors and all of the extras for this film would be hired locally. What if the director spotted a natural star amid the kitchen magnets and poster art? Stranger things had happened.

I could just picture the director bent over a large table scattered with hundreds of photographs. Then he freezes over a single snapshot and shouts to his assistants: 'Get me this man! I must have him for my film!' When they finally track me down, I at first humbly demur before finally agreeing to take the role. After all, the show must go on.

Colleen thanked us for opening our home to her and left. She gave us no reason to believe she or anyone else associated with the movie would be calling back. But a few days later when Jenny called me at work to say, 'I just got off the phone with Colleen McGarr, and you are NOT going to believe it,' I had no doubt whatsoever that I had just been discovered. My heart leapt. 'Go on,' I said.

'She says the director wants Marley to try out.'

'Marley?' I asked, certain I had misheard. She didn't seem to notice the dismay in my voice.

'Apparently, he's looking for a big, dumb, loopy dog to play the role of the family pet, and Marley caught his eye.'

'Loopy?' I asked.

'That's what Colleen says he wants. Big, dumb and loopy.'

Well, he had certainly come to the right place. 'Did Colleen mention if he said anything about me?' I asked.

'No,' Jenny said. 'Why would he?'

Colleen picked Marley up the next day. Knowing the importance of a good entrance, he came racing through the living room to greet her at full bore. When he hit the wood floor, he flew into a full skid, which did not stop until he hit the coffee table, went airborne, crashed into a chair, landed on his back, rolled, righted himself, and collided head-on with Colleen's legs.

'Are you sure you don't want us to sedate him?' Jenny asked.

The director would want to see him in his unbridled, unmedicated state, Colleen insisted, and off she went with our desperately happy dog beside her in her red pick-up truck.

Two hours later Colleen and Company were back and the verdict was in: Marley had passed the audition. 'No way!' Jenny shrieked. Our elation was not dampened a bit when Colleen told us that Marley's would be the only non-paying role in the movie.

I asked her how the audition went.

'I got Marley in the car and it was like driving in a Jacuzzi,' she said. 'He was slobbering on everything' When they arrived at production headquarters at the GulfStream Hotel, a faded tourist landmark from an earlier era, Marley immediately impressed the crew by jumping out of the truck and tearing around the parking lot in random patterns as if expecting the aerial bombing to commence at any moment. 'He was just berserk,' she said.

'Yeah, he gets a little excited,' I said.

Marley eventually calmed down enough to convince everyone he could do the part, which was basically just to play himself. The movie was called *The Last Home Run*, a baseball fantasy in which a seventy-nine-year-old nursing-home resident becomes a twelve-year-old for five days to live his dream of playing Little League ball. Marley was cast as the hyperactive family dog of the Little League coach.

On the morning shooting was to begin, we left for the GulfStream Hotel, the boys in their car seats and Marley between them. Our instructions were to arrive by 9.00 a.m., but a block away, the road was barricaded and a police officer was diverting traffic away from the hotel. The filming had been covered in the newspapers, and a crowd of spectators had turned out to gawk. The police were keeping everyone away. We inched forward in traffic, and when we finally got up to the officer I leaned out the window and said, 'We need to get through.'

'No one gets through,' he said. 'Keep moving. Let's go.'

'We're with the cast,' I said.

He eyed us sceptically, a couple in a minivan with two toddlers and family pet in tow. 'I said move it!' he barked.

'Our dog is in the film,' I said.

Suddenly he looked at me with new respect. 'You have the dog?' he asked. The dog was on his checklist.

'I have the dog,' I said. 'Marley the dog.'

'Playing himself,' Jenny chimed in.

The officer moved the barricade and waved us through. 'Right this way,' he said politely. I felt like royalty.

In the parking lot outside the hotel, the film crew was ready for action. Cables crisscrossed the road; camera tripods and microphone booms were set up. Lights hung from scaffolding. Trailers held racks of costumes. Tables of food and drinks were set up in the shade for cast and crew.

Director Bob Gosse greeted us and gave us a quick run-down of the scene to come. A minivan pulls up to the kerb, Marley's make-believe owner, played by the actress Liza Harris, is at the wheel. Her daughter, played by a cute teenager named Danielle from the local performing-arts school, and son, another local budding actor not older than nine, are in the back with their family dog, played by Marley. The daughter opens the sliding door and hops out; her brother follows with Marley on a leash. They walk off camera. End of scene.

'Easy enough,' I told the director. 'He should be able to handle that, no problem.' I pulled Marley off to the side to wait for his cue to get into the van.

'OK, people, listen up,' Gosse told the crew. 'The dog's a little nutty, all right? But unless he completely hijacks the scene, we're going to keep rolling.' He explained his thinking: the goal was to capture Marley behaving as a typical family dog would behave on a typical family outing. Pure *cinéma vérité*. 'Just let him do his thing,' he coached, 'and work around him.'

When everyone was set to go, I loaded Marley into the van and handed his nylon leash to the little boy, who looked terrified of him. 'He's friendly,' I told him. 'He'll just want to lick you. See?' I stuck my wrist into Marley's mouth to demonstrate.

Take one: The van pulls to the kerb. The instant the daughter slides open the side door, a yellow streak shoots out like a giant fur ball being fired from a cannon and blurs past the cameras trailing a red leash.

'Cut!'

I chased Marley down in the parking lot and hauled him back.

'OK, folks, we're going to try that again,' Gosse said. Then to the boy he coached gently, 'The dog's pretty wild. Try to hold on tighter this time.'

Take two. The van pulls to the kerb. The door slides open. The daughter is just beginning to exit when Marley huffs into view and leaps out past her, this time dragging the white-knuckled and white-faced boy behind him.

'Cut!'

Take three: I load Marley into the back of the van with the boy and shut the door. Before Gosse calls 'Action!' he breaks for a few minutes to confer with his assistants. Finally, the scene rolls. The van pulls to the kerb. The door slides open. The daughter steps out. The boy steps out, but with a bewildered look on his face. He peers directly into the camera and holds up his hand. Dangling from it is half the leash, its end jagged and wet with saliva.

'Cut! Cut! Cut!'

The boy explained that as he waited in the van, Marley began gnawing on the leash and wouldn't stop. The crew and cast were staring at the severed leash in disbelief. I, on the other hand, was not surprised in the least. Marley had sent more leashes and ropes to their graves than I could count.

'OK, everybody, let's take a break!' Gosse called out. Turning to me, he asked—in an amazingly calm voice—'How quickly can you find a new leash?' He didn't have to tell me how much each lost minute cost him as his union-scale actors and crew sat idle.

'There's a pet store a half-mile from here,' I said. 'I can be back in fifteen minutes.'

'And this time get something he can't chew through,' he said.

I returned with a heavy chain leash that looked like something a lion trainer might use, and the filming continued, take after failed take. In one scene, Marley was panting so loudly at Danielle's feet as she spoke on the telephone that the sound engineer flipped off his headphones in disgust and complained loudly, 'I can't hear a word she's saying. All I hear is heavy breathing. It sounds like a porn flick.'

'Cut!'

So went day one of shooting. Marley was a disaster, unmitigated and without redemption. Part of me was defensive—*Well, what did they expect for free?* and part was mortified.

At the end of the day one of the assistants, clipboard in hand, told us the shooting line-up was still undecided for the next morning. 'Don't bother coming in tomorrow,' he said. 'We'll call if we need Marley.' And to ensure there was no confusion, he repeated, 'So unless you hear from us, don't show up. Got it?' Yeah, I got it, loud and clear. Gosse had sent his underling to do the dirty work. Marley's acting career was over. It was the old 'Don't call us, we'll call you' routine.

'Marley,' I said when we got home, 'your big chance and you blew it.'

THE NEXT MORNING I was still fretting over our dashed dreams of stardom when the phone rang. It was the assistant, telling us to get Marley to the hotel as soon as possible. 'You mean you want him back?' I asked.

'Right away,' he said. 'Bob wants him in the next scene.'

I arrived thirty minutes later, not quite believing they had invited us back. Gosse was ebullient. He had watched the raw footage from the day before and couldn't have been happier. 'The dog was hysterical!' he gushed. 'Just hilarious. Pure madcap genius!' I could feel myself standing taller, chest puffing out.

'We always knew he was a natural,' Jenny said.

Shooting continued around Lake Worth for several more days, and Marley was lapping up stardom. The crew, especially the women, fawned over him. The weather was brutally hot, and one assistant was assigned the duty of following Marley around with a bowl and a bottle of spring water, pouring him drinks at will. I left him with the crew for a couple of hours while I checked in at work, and when I returned I found him sprawled out like King Tut, paws in the air, accepting a leisurely belly rub from the strikingly gorgeous make-up artist.

Stardom was starting to go to my head, too. I began introducing myself as 'Marley the Dog's handler' and dropping lines such as 'For his next movie, we're hoping for a barking part.'

We remained on the set for four straight days, and by the time we were told Marley's scenes were all completed, Jenny and I both felt we were part of the Shooting Gallery family. Granted, the only unpaid members of the family, but members nonetheless. 'We love you guys!' Jenny blurted out to all within earshot as we herded Marley into the minivan. 'Can't wait to see the final cut!'

But wait we did. One of the producers told us to give them eight months and then call and they'd mail us an advance copy. After eight of months when I called, however, a front-desk person put me on hold and returned several minutes later to say, 'Why don't you try in another couple of months?' I waited and tried, waited and tried, but each time was put off. Eventually I stopped calling, convinced that the project had been abandoned on the editing-room floor on account of the overwhelming challenges of trying to edit that damn dog out of every scene. It would be two full years before I would finally get my chance to see Marley's acting skills.

I was in a video rental store when on a whim I asked the clerk if he knew anything about a movie called *The Last Home Run*. Not only did he know about it; he had it in stock. In fact, as luck would have it, not a single copy was checked out.

Only later would I learn the whole sad story. Unable to attract a national distributor, the Shooting Gallery had to relegate Marley's movie debut to that most ignoble of celluloid fates. *The Last Home Run* had gone straight to video. I didn't care. I raced home with a copy and yelled to Jenny and the kids to gather round the VCR. All told, Marley was on-screen for less than two minutes, but they were two of the livelier minutes in the film. We laughed! We cried! We cheered!

'Waddy, that you!' Conor screamed.

'We're famous!' Patrick yelled.

Marley seemed unimpressed. He yawned and crawled beneath the coffee table. By the time the end credits rolled, he was sound asleep. We waited as the names of all the actors of the two-legged variety had scrolled by. For a minute, I thought our dog was not going to merit a credit. But then there it was, listed in big letters across the screen for all to see: MARLEY THE DOG . . . AS HIMSELF.

Chapter 10

In the Land of Bocahontas

One month after filming ended for *The Last Home Run*, we said goodbye to West Palm Beach and all the memories it held. There had been two more murders within a block of our home, but in the end it was clutter, not crime, that drove us from our little bungalow on Churchill Road. With two children and all the accoutrements that went with them, we were packed to the rafters. Marley was ninety-seven pounds, and he could not turn around without knocking something over.

Besides, Jenny was now working half-time for the *Post*'s feature section, and mostly from home, as she attempted to juggle children and career. It only made sense for us to relocate closer to my office.

Life is full of little ironies, and one of them was the fact that, after months of searching, we settled on a house in the one South Florida city I took the greatest glee in publicly ridiculing. That place was Boca Raton, which, translated from the Spanish, means literally 'Mouth of the Rat'.

Boca Raton was a wealthy Republican bastion. Most of the money in town was new money, and most of those who had it didn't know how to enjoy it without making fools of themselves. Boca Raton was a land of luxury sedans, red sports cars, pink stucco mansions crammed onto postage-stamp lots and walled developments with guards at the gates. The men favoured linen trousers and Italian loafers sans socks and spent inordinate amounts of time making important-sounding cellphone calls to one another. The women were tanned to the consistency of the Gucci leather bags they favoured, their burnished skin set off by hair dyed alarming shades of silver and platinum.

The city crawled with plastic surgeons, and they had the biggest homes of all. For Boca's well-preserved women, breast implants and face-lifts were a virtual requirement of residency. Butt sculpting, nose jobs and tummy tucks rounded out the cosmetic line-up.

In my column I had been poking fun at the Boca lifestyle, starting with the name itself. Residents of Boca Raton never actually called their city Boca Raton. They simply referred to it by the familiar 'Boca'. The Disney movie *Pocahontas* was in the theatres then, and I launched a running spoof on the Indian-princess theme, which I titled 'Bocahontas'. My gold-draped protagonist was a suburban princess who drove a pink BMW, her rock-hard, surgically enhanced breasts jutting into the steering wheel, allowing her to drive hands-free, talking on her cellphone and teasing her hair in the rearview mirror.

My characterisation was cruel. It was uncharitable. It was only slightly exaggerated. Boca's real-life Bocahontases were the biggest fans of those columns, trying to figure out which of them had inspired my fictional heroine. (I'll never tell.) I was frequently invited to speak before social and community groups and invariably someone would stand up and ask, 'Why do you hate Boca so much?' It wasn't that I hated Boca, I told them; it was just that I loved high farce. And no place on earth delivered it quite like the Mouth of the Rat.

So it only made sense that when Jenny and I finally settled on a house, it was located at ground zero of the Boca experience, midway between the waterfront estates of east Boca Raton and the snooty gated communities of west Boca Raton. Our new neighbourhood was in one of the few middle-class sections in the city.

'Are you crazy?' I said to Jenny. 'We can't move to Boca! I'll be run out of town on a rail. They'll serve my head up on a bed of organic mesclun greens.'

'Oh, come on,' she said. 'You're exaggerating again.'

My paper, the *Sun-Sentinel*, was the dominant newspaper in Boca Raton, and because my photograph appeared above my column, I was frequently recognised. I didn't think I was exaggerating. 'They'll skin me alive and hang my carcass in front of Tiffany's,' I said.

But we had been looking for months, and this was the first house that met all our criteria. The public schools were about as good as public schools got in South Florida, and Boca Raton had an excellent park system, including some of the most pristine ocean beaches in the Miami–Palm Beach metro-politan area. With more than a little trepidation, I agreed to go forward with the purchase. The barbarian was about to slip inside the gate.

OUR HOUSE was a 1970s-vintage four-bedroom ranch with twice the square footage of our first home and none of the charm. The place had potential, though, and gradually we put our mark on it. We ripped up the wall-to-wall shag carpeting and installed oak floors. Slowly I turned the bereft front yard into a tropical garden teeming with gingers and heliconias and passion vines that butterflies and passers-by alike stopped to drink in.

The two best features of our new home had nothing to do with the house itself. Visible from our living-room window was a small city park filled with playground equipment beneath towering pines. The children adored it. And in the back yard was an in-ground swimming pool. We hadn't wanted a pool, worrying about the risk to our two toddlers, but the boys—Patrick had just turned three and Conor nineteen months when we arrived—took to the water like a pair of dolphins. A swimming pool in Florida, we soon learned, made the difference between barely enduring the withering summer months and actually enjoying them.

No one loved the back-yard pool more than our water dog, that proud descendant of fishermen's retrievers plying the ocean swells off the coast of Newfoundland. Marley would charge for the water, getting a running start from the family room, and, with one bounce off the brick patio, land in the pool on his belly with a giant flop that sent a geyser into the air and waves over the edge. Swimming with Marley was a potentially life-threatening adventure, a little like swimming with an ocean liner.

One thing our new house did not have was a Marley-proof bunker. It had a two-car garage, but it was unsuitable for housing Marley or any other life form that could not survive temperatures above 150 degrees. The garage had no windows and was stiflingly hot. Besides, it was finished in plasterboard, not concrete, which Marley had already proved himself quite adept at pulverising.

The first time we left him alone in our new house, we shut him in the laundry room, just off the kitchen, with a blanket and a big bowl of water. When we returned a few hours later, he had scratched up the door. The damage was minor, but we knew it didn't bode well. 'Maybe he's just getting used to his new surroundings,' I offered.

'There's not even a cloud in the sky,' Jenny observed sceptically. 'What's going to happen the first time a storm hits?'

The next time we left him alone, we found out. As thunderheads rolled in, we cut our outing short and hurried home, but it was too late. Jenny was a few steps ahead of me, and when she opened the laundry-room door she stopped short and uttered, 'Oh my God.' She said it the way you would if you had just discovered a body hanging from the chandelier.

I peeked in over her shoulder, and it was uglier than I had feared. Marley was standing there, panting frantically, his paws and mouth bleeding. Loose fur was everywhere, as though the thunder had scared the hair right out of his coat. An entire wall was gouged open, obliterated clear down to the studs. Plaster and wood chips and bent nails were everywhere. Electric wiring lay exposed. Blood smeared the floor and the walls. It looked like the scene of a shotgun homicide.

'Oh my God,' I repeated. It was all either of us could say.

After several seconds of just standing there mute, staring at the carnage, I finally said, 'OK, we can handle this. It's all fixable.' Jenny shot me her look; she had seen my repairs. I slipped Marley one of his tranquillisers and worried silently that this latest destructive jag might just throw Jenny back into the funk she had sunk into after Conor's birth. Those blues, however, seemed to be long behind her. She was surprisingly philosophical about it.

'A few hundred bucks and we'll be good as new,' she chirped.

'That's what I'm thinking, too,' I said. 'I'll give a few extra speeches to bring in some cash. That'll pay for it.'

Within a few minutes, Marley was beginning to mellow. His eyelids grew heavy and his eyes deeply bloodshot, as they always did when he was doped up. 'Geez, dog,' I said. 'What are we going to do with you?' Without lifting his head, he gazed at me as if he were trying to tell me something, something important he needed me to understand. 'I know,' I said. 'I know you can't help it.'

THE NEXT DAY Jenny and I took the boys with us to the pet store and bought a giant cage. It was enormous, big enough for a lion to stand up and turn around in. Made out of heavy steel grating, it had two bolt-action barrel locks to hold the door securely shut. This was our answer, our own portable Alcatraz. Conor and Patrick both crawled inside and I slid the bolts shut, locking them in for a moment. 'What do you guys think?' I asked. 'Will this hold our Superdog?'

Conor teetered at the cage door and said, 'Me in jail.'

'Waddy's going to be our prisoner!' Patrick chimed in, delighted at the prospect.

Back home, we set up the crate next to the washing machine. Portable Alcatraz took up nearly half the laundry room. 'Come here, Marley!' I called when it was fully assembled. I tossed a Milk-Bone in and he happily pranced in after it. I closed and bolted the door behind him, and he stood there chewing his treat, unfazed by the new life experience he was about to enter, the one known in mental-health circles as 'involuntary commitment'.

'This is going to be your new home when we're away,' I said cheerfully. Marley stood there panting contentedly, not a trace of concern on his face, and then he lay down and let out a sigh. 'A good sign,' I said to Jenny. 'A very good sign.'

That evening we decided to give the maximum-security dog-containment unit a test run. This time I didn't even need a Milk-Bone to lure Marley in. I simply opened the gate, gave a whistle, and in he walked, tail banging the metal sides. 'Be a good boy, Marley,' I said. As we loaded the boys into the minivan to go out to dinner, Jenny said, 'You know something?'

'What?' I asked.

'This is the first time since we got him that I don't have a queasy feeling leaving Marley alone in the house,' she said. 'I never even realised how much it put me on edge until now.'

'I know what you mean,' I said. 'It was always a guessing game: "What will our dog destroy this time?"'

We had a great dinner out, followed by a sunset stroll on the beach. The boys splashed in the surf and chased seagulls. Jenny was uncharacteristically relaxed. Just knowing Marley was safely secured inside Alcatraz, unable to hurt himself or anything else, was a balm. 'What a nice outing this has been,' she said as we walked up the front sidewalk to our house.

I was about to agree with her when I noticed something in my peripheral vision, something up ahead that wasn't quite right. I turned my head and stared at the window beside the front door. The mini-blinds were shut, as they always were when we left the house. But about a foot up from the bottom of the window the metal slats were bent apart and something was sticking through them.

Something black. And wet. And pressed up against the glass. 'What the—?' I said. 'How could . . . Marley?'

When I opened the front door, sure enough, there was our one-dog welcoming committee, pleased as punch to have us home again. We fanned out across the house, checking every room for telltales of Marley's unsupervised adventure. The house was fine, untouched. We converged on the laundry room. The crate's door stood wide open. I squatted down beside the cage to have a closer look. The two bolt-action locks were slid back in the open position, and—a significant clue—they were dripping with saliva. 'It looks like an inside job,' I said. 'Somehow Houdini here licked his way out of the Big House.'

'I can't believe it,' Jenny said. Then she uttered a word I was glad the children were not close enough to hear.

We always fancied Marley to be as dumb as algae, but he had been clever enough to figure out how to use his long, strong tongue through the bars to slowly work the barrels free from their slots. He had licked his way to freedom. Involuntary commitment was not a concept Marley was going to take lying down.

Whatever false sense of security the contraption had once offered us was gone. Each time we left, even for a half-hour, we wondered whether this would be the time that our manic inmate would bust out and go on another couch-shredding, wall-gouging, door-eating rampage. So much for peace of mind.

MARLEY DIDN'T FIT into the Boca Raton scene any better than I did. Boca had a disproportionate share of the world's smallest, yappiest, most pampered dogs, the kind of pets that the Bocahontas set favoured as fashion accessories. They were precious little things, often with bows in their fur and cologne spritzed on their necks, some even with painted toenails. You would spot them cruising around town in Lexuses, Mercedes-Benzes and Jaguars, perched aristocratically behind the steering wheels on their owners' laps.

With his recently digested obedience certificate under his belt, Marley was fairly manageable on walks, but if he saw something he liked, he would drag Jenny or me behind him at the end of the leash, the noose tightening around his throat, making him gasp and cough. Each time Marley would be roundly snubbed, not only by the Boca mini-dog but by the Boca mini-dog's owner, who would snatch up young Fifi or Cheri as if rescuing her from the jaws of an alligator. Marley didn't seem to mind. The next mini-dog to come into sight, he would do it all over again, undeterred by his previous jilting. As a guy who was never very good at the rejection part of dating, I admired his perseverance.

Outside dining was a big part of the Boca experience, and many restaurants offered alfresco seating beneath palm trees studded with tiny white lights. These were places to see and be seen, to sip caffè lattes and jabber into cellphones as your companion stared vacantly at the sky. The Boca minidog was an important part of the alfresco ambiance. Couples brought their dogs with them and hooked their leashes to the wrought-iron tables where the dogs would contentedly curl up at their feet or sometimes even sit up at the table beside their masters.

One Sunday afternoon Jenny and I thought it would be fun to take the whole family for an outside meal at one of the popular meeting places. 'When in Boca, do as the Bocalites,' I said. We loaded the boys and the dog into the minivan and headed to Mizner Park, the downtown shopping plaza modelled after an Italian piazza with wide sidewalks and endless dining possibilities.

We parked and strolled up to a restaurant with one of the more affordable menus and hovered nearby until a sidewalk table opened up. The table was perfect—shaded, with a view of the piazza's central fountain, and heavy enough, we were sure, to secure an excitable nearly hundred-pound Lab. I hooked the end of Marley's leash to one of the legs, and we ordered drinks all around, two beers and two apple juices.

'To a beautiful day with my beautiful family,' Jenny said, holding up her beer for a toast. We clicked our bottles; the boys smashed their sippy cups together. That's when it happened. So fast, in fact, that we didn't even realise it had happened. All we knew was that one instant we were sitting at a lovely outdoor table toasting the beautiful day, and the next our table was on the move, crashing its way through the sea of other tables, banging into innocent bystanders, and making a horrible, ear-piercing shriek as it scraped over the concrete. In that first split second, it seemed possible that our table was possessed. In the next split second, I saw that it wasn't our table that was haunted, but our dog. Marley was out in front, chugging forward with every ounce of rippling muscle he had, the leash stretched tight as piano wire.

In the fraction of a second after that, I saw just where Marley was heading, table in tow. Fifty feet down the sidewalk, a delicate French poodle, nose in the air, lingered at her owner's side. *Damn*, I remember thinking, *what is his thing for poodles?* Jenny and I both sat there for a moment, drinks in hand, our perfect Sunday afternoon unblemished except for the fact that our table was now motoring its way through the crowd. An instant later we were on our feet, screaming, running, apologising to the customers around us as we went. I was the first to reach the runaway table as it surged and scraped down the piazza. I grabbed on, planted my feet, and leaned back with everything I had. Soon Jenny was beside me, pulling back, too.

When we finally got the table stopped and Marley reeled in, just feet from the poodle and her mortified owner, I turned back to check on the boys, and got my first good look at the faces of my fellow alfresco diners. Men were stopped in mid-conversation, cellphones in their hands. Women stared with opened mouths. It was finally Conor who broke the silence. 'Waddy go walk!' he screamed with delight.

A waiter rushed up and helped me drag the table back into place as Jenny held Marley, still fixated on the object of his desire. 'Let me get some new place settings,' the waiter said.

'That won't be necessary,' Jenny said nonchalantly. 'We'll just be paying for our drinks and going.'

IT WASN'T LONG after our excellent excursion into the Boca alfresco-dining scene that I found a book in the library titled *No Bad Dogs* by the acclaimed British dog trainer Barbara Woodhouse. As the title implied, *No Bad Dogs* advanced the same belief that Marley's first instructor, Miss Dominatrix, held so dear—that the only thing standing between an incorrigible canine and greatness was a befuddled, indecisive, weak-willed human master. Dogs weren't the problem, Woodhouse held; people were. That said, the book went on to describe some of the most egregious canine behaviours imaginable. There were dogs that howled incessantly, dug incessantly, fought incessantly and bit incessantly. There were even dogs that ate their own faeces. *Thank God*, I thought, *at least he doesn't eat his own faeces.*

As I read, I began to feel better about our flawed retriever. I was buoyed to read that there were all sorts of horrid behaviours he did *not* have. He didn't have a mean bone in his body. He wasn't much of a barker. Didn't bite. Didn't assault other dogs, except in the pursuit of love. Considered everyone his best friend.

Then I got to chapter twenty-four, 'Living with the Mentally Unstable Dog'. As I read, I swallowed loudly. Woodhouse was describing Marley with an understanding so intimate I could swear she had been bunking with him in his battered crate. She addressed the manic behaviour patterns, the destructiveness when left alone. She described the attempts by owners of such beasts 'to make some place either in the house or yard dogproof'. She even addressed the use of tranquillisers as a desperate (and largely ineffective) last measure.

In a subsequent chapter, titled 'Abnormal Dogs', Woodhouse wrote with a sense of resignation: 'I cannot stress often enough that if you wish to keep a dog that is not normal, you must face up to living a slightly restricted existence.' *You mean like living in mortal fear of going out for a gallon of milk?*

Woodhouse had nailed our dog and our pathetic, codependent existence. We had it all: the hapless, weak-willed masters; the mentally unstable, out-of-control dog; the trail of destroyed property. We were a textbook case. 'Congratulations, Marley,' I said to him, snoozing at my feet. 'You qualify as subnormal.' He opened his eyes at the sound of his name, stretched and rolled onto his back, paws in the air.

I was expecting Woodhouse to offer a cheery solution for the owners of such defective merchandise, but she ended her book on a dark note: 'Only the owners of unbalanced dogs can really know where the line can be drawn between a dog that is sane and one that is mentally unsound. No one can make up the owner's mind as to what to do with the last kind. I, as a great dog lover, feel it is kinder to put them to sleep.'

Put them to sleep? Gulp. Even Barbara Woodhouse, lover of animals, successful trainer of thousands of dogs their owners had deemed hopeless, was conceding that some dogs should be humanely dispatched to that great canine insane asylum in the sky.

'Don't worry, big guy,' I said, leaning down to scratch Marley's belly. 'The only sleep we're going to be doing around this house is the kind you get to wake up from.'

He sighed dramatically and drifted back to his dreams of French poodles.

AFTER CONOR'S ARRIVAL, everyone we knew assumed we were done having children. In the two-income crowd in which we ran, one child was the norm, two were considered a bit of an extravagance, and three were simply unheard-of. Especially given the difficult pregnancy we had gone through with Conor, no one could understand why we would want to subject ourselves to the process all over again. But parenthood became us. Our two boys brought us more joy than we ever thought possible. They defined our life now. We had come to find our pleasures in spilt apple sauce and tiny nose prints on windowpanes and the soft symphony of bare feet padding down the hallway at dawn.

So when a sonogram finally confirmed our secret hope for a daughter, Jenny draped her arms over my shoulders and whispered, 'I'm so happy I could give you a little girl.' I was so happy, too.

On January 9, 1997, Jenny gave me a late Christmas present: a pink-cheeked, seven-pound baby girl, whom we named Colleen. Our family now felt complete. If the pregnancy for Conor had been a litany of stress and worry, this pregnancy was textbook perfect, and delivering at Boca Raton Community Hospital introduced us to a whole new level of pampered customer satisfaction. Just down the hall from our room was a lounge with a free, all-you-can-drink cappuccino station—so very *Boca*. By the time the baby came, I was so jacked up on frothy caffeine, I could barely hold my hands still to snip the umbilical cord.

WHEN COLLEEN was one week old, Jenny took her outside for the first time. The day was beautiful, and the boys and I were in the front yard, planting flowers. Marley was chained to a tree, happy to lie in the shade. Jenny sat in the grass beside him and placed the sleeping Colleen in a portable bassinet on the ground between them. After several minutes, the boys beckoned for Mom to come see their handiwork, and they led Jenny and me around the garden beds as Colleen napped in the shade beside Marley. We wandered behind some large shrubbery from where we could still see the baby but passers-by on the street could not see us. As we turned back, I stopped and motioned for Jenny to look out through the shrubs. Out on the street, an older couple walking by had stopped and were gawking at the scene in our front yard with bewildered expressions. At first, I wasn't sure what had made them stop and stare. Then it hit me: from their vantage point, all they could see was a fragile newborn alone with a large yellow dog, who appeared to be baby-sitting single-handedly.

We lingered in silence, stifling giggles. There was Marley, panting contentedly, every few seconds pushing his snout over to sniff the baby's head. The poor couple must have thought they had stumbled on a case of felony child neglect. No doubt the parents were out drinking at a bar somewhere. As if he were in on the ruse, Marley shifted positions, rested his chin across the baby's stomach, and let out a long sigh as if he were saying, *When are those two going to get home?* He appeared to be protecting her, and maybe he was, though I'm pretty sure he was just drinking in the scent of her diaper.

Jenny and I stood there in the bushes and exchanged grins. The thought of Marley as an infant caregiver—Doggy Day Care—was just too good to let go. I was tempted to wait there and see how the scene would play out, but then it occurred to me that one scenario might involve a 911 call to the police. We stepped out of the bushes and waved to the couple—and watched the relief wash over their faces.

'You must really trust your dog,' the woman said somewhat cautiously, betraying a belief that dogs had no place that close to a defenceless newborn.

'He hasn't eaten one yet,' I said.

TWO MONTHS after Colleen arrived home I celebrated my fortieth birthday in a most inauspicious manner, namely, by myself. The Big Four-O is supposed to be a major turning point, meriting a blowout celebration. But not for me. We were now responsible parents with three children; Jenny had a new baby pressed to her breast. There were more important things to worry about.

I arrived home from work, and after a quick meal of leftovers, I bathed the boys and put them to bed while Jenny nursed Colleen. By eight thirty, all three children were asleep, and so was my wife. I popped a beer and sat out on the patio, staring into the blue water of the lit swimming pool. As always, Marley was faithfully at my side, and as I scratched his ears, it occurred to me that he was at about the same point in life. We had brought him home six years earlier. In dog years, that would put him somewhere in his early forties now. He had crossed unnoticed into middle age but still acted every bit the puppy. Except for a string of stubborn ear infections that required Dr Jay's repeated intervention, he was healthy. He showed no signs whatsoever of growing up or winding down. I had never thought of Marley as any kind of role model, but sitting there sipping my beer, I was aware that maybe he held the secret for a good life. Never slow down, never look back, live each day with verve.

'Well, big guy,' I said, pressing my beer bottle against his cheek in a kind of interspecies toast. 'It's just you and me tonight. Here's to forty. Here's to middle age.'

I was still moping about my solitary birthday a few days later when an old colleague, Jim Tolpin, called unexpectedly and asked if I wanted to grab a beer the next night, a Saturday. Jim had left the newspaper business to pursue a law degree at about the same time we moved to Boca Raton, and we hadn't spoken in months. 'Sure,' I said. Jim picked me up at six and took me to an English pub, where we quaffed Bass ale and caught up on each other's lives. We were having a grand old time until the bartender called out, 'Is there a John Grogan here? Phone for John Grogan.'

It was Jenny, and she sounded very upset and stressed-out. 'The baby's crying, the boys are out of control, and I just ripped my contact lens!' she wailed into the phone. 'Can you come home right away?'

'Try to calm down,' I said. 'I'll be right home.' I hung up, and the bartender gave me a you-poor-sorry-henpecked-bastard kind of a nod and simply said, 'My sympathies, mate.'

'Come on,' Jim said. 'I'll drive you home.'

When we turned onto my block, both sides of the street were lined with cars. 'Somebody's having a party,' I said.

'Looks like it,' Jim answered.

'Someone even parked in my driveway,' I said when we reached the house. 'If that isn't nerve.'

We blocked the offender in, and I invited Jim inside. I was still griping about the inconsiderate jerk who had parked in my driveway when the front door swung open. It was Jenny with Colleen in her arms. She didn't look upset at all. In fact, she had a big grin on her face. Behind her stood a bagpipe player in a kilt. Then I looked beyond the bagpipe player and saw floating candles in the pool. The deck was crammed with several dozen of my friends, neighbours and coworkers. Just as I was making the connection that all those cars on the street belonged to all these people in my house, they shouted in unison, 'HAPPY BIRTHDAY, OLD MAN!'

My wife had not forgotten after all.

When I was finally able to snap my jaw shut, I took Jenny in my arms, kissed her on the cheek and whispered in her ear, 'I'll get you later for this.'

Chapter 11

Off to Pennsylvania

Shortly after Colleen turned two, I inadvertently set off a fateful series of events that would lead us to leave Florida. And I did it with the click of a mouse. I had wrapped up my column early for the day and, on a whim, decided to check out the website of a magazine I had been subscribing to since we bought our West Palm Beach house. The magazine was *Organic Gardening*, which was launched in 1942 by the eccentric J. I. Rodale and went on to become the bible of the back-to-the-earth movement that blossomed in the 1960s and 1970s.

Rodale had been a New York City businessman specialising in electrical switches when his health began to fail. Instead of turning to modern medicine to solve his problems, he moved from the city to a farm outside the tiny borough of Emmaus, Pennsylvania, and began playing in the dirt. He had a deep distrust of technology and believed that chemical pesticides and fertilisers were gradually poisoning the earth and its inhabitants. He began experimenting with techniques that mimicked nature. On his farm, he built huge compost piles of decaying plant matter, which, once the material had turned to rich black humus, he used as fertiliser and a natural soil builder. He unleashed thousands of ladybirds and other beneficial insects that devoured the destructive ones. His garden flourished and so did his health, and he trumpeted his successes in the pages of his magazine.

By the time I started reading *Organic Gardening*, J. I. Rodale was long dead and so was his son, Robert, who had built his father's business, Rodale Press, into a multimillion-dollar publishing company. The magazine was not very well written or edited; you got the impression it was put out by a group of dedicated gardeners with no professional training as journalists. Regardless, the organic philosophy increasingly made sense to me, especially after Jenny's miscarriage and our suspicion that it might have had something to do with the pesticides we had used. By the time Colleen was born, our Boca Raton yard was a little organic oasis in a suburban sea of chemical weed-and-feed applications and pesticides. Passersby often stopped to admire our thriving front garden, which I tended with increasing passion.

That afternoon in my office, I clicked through the screens at *organicgardening.com* and eventually found my way to a button that said 'Career Opportunities'. I clicked on it, why I'm still not sure. I loved my job as a columnist, loved the daily interaction I had with readers. I loved the newsroom and the quirky, brainy, neurotic, idealistic people it attracted. Still, I began scrolling through the Rodale job postings, idly curious. Midway down the list I stopped cold. *Organic Gardening*, the company's flagship magazine, was seeking a new managing editor. My heart skipped a beat. I had often daydreamed about the huge difference a decent journalist could make at the magazine, and now here was my chance.

That night I told Jenny about the opening, fully expecting her to tell me I was insane for even considering it. Instead she surprised me by encouraging me to send a résumé. The idea of leaving the heat and humidity and congestion and crime of South Florida for a simpler life in the country appealed to her. She missed four seasons and hills. She wanted our kids and, as ridiculous as it sounds, our dog to experience the wonders of a winter blizzard. 'Marley's never even chased a snowball,' she said, stroking his fur with her bare foot.

'Now, there's a good reason for changing careers,' I said.

'You should do it just to satisfy your curiosity,' she said. 'If they offer it to you, you can always turn them down.'

I had to admit I shared her desire to move north again. As much as I had enjoyed our dozen years in South Florida, I dreamed of someday escaping to my own private paradise—a real piece of land where I could dig in the dirt, chop my own firewood, and tromp through the forest, my dog at my side.

I applied, fully convincing myself it was just a lark. Two weeks later the phone rang and it was J. I. Rodale's granddaughter, Maria Rodale. I was so surprised to be hearing from the owner of the company that I asked her to repeat her last name. Maria was convinced she needed a professional journalist to return the magazine to its former glory. She wanted to take on more challenging stories about the environment, genetic engineering and the burgeoning organic movement.

I arrived for the job interview fully intending to play hard to get, but I was hooked the moment I drove out of the airport and onto the first curving, two-lane country road. At every turn was another postcard: a stone farmhouse here, a covered bridge there. Icy brooks gurgled down hillsides, and furrowed farmland stretched to the horizon. At the first payphone I could find, I called Jenny. 'You're not going to believe this place,' I said.

TWO MONTHS LATER the movers had the entire contents of our Boca house loaded into a gigantic truck. An auto carrier arrived to haul off our car and minivan. We turned the house keys over to the new owners and spent our last night in Florida sleeping on the floor of a neighbour's home, Marley in the middle of us. 'Indoor camping!' Patrick shrieked.

The next morning I arose early and took Marley for what would be his last walk on Florida soil. He sniffed and tugged and pranced, happily oblivious to the abrupt change I was about to foist on him. I had bought a sturdy plastic travel crate to carry him on the airplane, and following Dr Jay's advice, I slipped a double dose of tranquillisers down his throat. By the time our neighbour dropped us off at the airport, Marley was exceptionally mellow. We could have strapped him to a rocket and he wouldn't have minded.

In the terminal, the Grogan clan cut a fine form: two wildly excited little boys racing around, a hungry baby in a stroller, two stressed-out parents and one very stoned dog. Rounding out the line-up was the rest of our menagerie: two frogs, three goldfish, a hermit crab, a snail named Sluggy and a box of live crickets for feeding the frogs. As we waited in line at check-in, I assembled the plastic pet carrier. It was the biggest one I could find, but when we reached the counter, a woman in uniform looked at Marley, looked at the crate, looked back at Marley, and said, 'We can't allow that dog aboard in that container. He's too big for it.'

'The pet store said this was the "large dog" size,' I pleaded.

'FAA regulations require that the dog can freely stand up inside and turn fully around,' she explained, adding sceptically, 'Go ahead, give it a try.'

I opened the gate and called Marley, but he was not about to voluntarily walk into this mobile jail cell. Where were the dog biscuits when I needed them? I searched my pockets for something to bribe him with, finally fishing out a tin of breath mints. I took one out and held it in front of his nose. 'Want a mint, Marley? Go get the mint!' and I tossed it into the crate. Sure enough, he took the bait and blithely entered the box.

The lady was right; he didn't quite fit. Even with his nose touching the back wall, his butt stuck out the open door. I scrunched his tail down and closed the gate, nudging his rear inside.

'He's got to be able to turn around,' she said.

'Turn around, boy,' I beckoned to him, giving a little whistle. He shot a glance over his shoulder at me with those doper eyes, his head scraping the ceiling, as if awaiting instructions on just how to accomplish such a feat.

If he could not turn around, the airline was not letting him aboard the flight. I checked my watch. We had twelve minutes left to get through security, down the concourse and onto the plane. 'Come here, Marley!' I pleaded desperately. 'Turn around.' I was about to drop to my knees and beg when I heard a crash, followed almost immediately by Patrick's voice.

'Oops,' he said.

'The frogs are loose!' Jenny screamed, jumping into action.

'Froggy! Croaky! Come back!' the boys yelled in unison.

My wife was on all fours now, racing around the terminal as the frogs stayed one hop ahead of her. Passers-by began to stop and stare.

'Excuse me a second,' I said as calmly as I could to the airline worker, then joined Jenny on my hands and knees.

After doing our part to entertain the early-morning travel crowd, we finally captured Froggy and Croaky. As we turned back, I heard a mighty ruckus coming from the dog crate. Marley had somehow got himself turned around. 'See?' I said to the baggage supervisor. 'He can turn around, no problem.'

'OK,' she said with a frown. 'But you're really pushing it.'

Two workers lifted Marley and his crate onto a dolly and wheeled him away. The rest of us raced for the plane, arriving at the gate just as the flight attendants were closing the hatch.

As we settled into our seats, I finally allowed myself to exhale. We had got Marley squared away. We had captured the frogs. We had made the flight. I could relax now. Through the window I watched a tram pull up with the dog crate sitting on it.

'Look,' I said to the kids. 'There's Marley.' They waved out the window and called, 'Hi, Waddy!'

As the flight attendant went over the safety precautions, I pulled out a magazine. Then I heard it. From below our feet, deep in the bowels of the plane, came a sound, muffled but undeniable. It was a pitifully mournful sound, a sort of primal howl. For the record, Labrador retrievers do not howl. Beagles howl. Wolves howl. Labs do not howl. But now, no question about it, Marley was howling.

The passengers began to look up from their newspapers and novels. A woman across the aisle asked her husband, 'Do you hear that? I think it's a dog.' Jenny stared straight ahead. I stared into my magazine.

'Waddy's sad,' Patrick said.

No, son, I wanted to correct him, *some strange dog we have never seen before and have no knowledge of is sad.*

The jet engines whined and the plane taxied down the runway, drowning out Marley's dirge. I pictured him down below in the dark hold, alone, scared, stoned. The poor guy. I wasn't willing to admit he was mine, but I knew I would be spending the whole flight worrying about him.

The airplane was barely off the ground when I heard another little crash, and Conor said, 'Oops.' I looked down and then furtively glanced around. When I was sure no one was staring, I whispered into Jenny's ear, 'Don't look now, but the crickets are loose.'

WE SETTLED into a rambling house on two acres perched on the side of a steep hill. Our property had a wood where I could chop logs to my heart's content, a small spring-fed creek where the kids and Marley soon found they could get exceptionally muddy, and a white-steepled church on the next hill, visible from our kitchen window.

Our new home even came with a neighbour right out of Central Casting, an orange-bearded bear of a man who lived in a 1790s stone farmhouse and on Sundays enjoyed sitting on his back porch and shooting his rifle into the woods just for fun, much to Marley's unnerved dismay. On our first day in our new house, he walked over with a bottle of homemade wild-cherry wine and a basket of blackberries. He introduced himself as Digger.

As we surmised from the nickname, Digger made his living as an excavator. If we had any holes we needed dug or earth we wanted moved, he instructed, we were to just give a shout and he'd swing by with one of his big machines. 'And if you hit a deer with your car, come get me,' he said with a wink. 'We'll butcher it up and split the meat before the game officer knows a thing.' No doubt about it, we weren't in Boca any more.

Living in the country was at once peaceful, charming—and just a little lonely. After Florida's crowds and queues, I should have been ecstatic about the solitude. Instead, at least in the early months, I found myself darkly ruminating over our decision to move to a place where so few others apparently wanted to live.

Marley, on the other hand, had no such misgivings. For a dog with more energy than sense, what wasn't to like? He raced across the lawn, crashed through the brambles, splashed through the creek. His life's mission was to catch one of the countless rabbits that considered my garden their own personal salad bar. He was about as stealthy as a marching band and never got closer than a dozen feet before his intended prey scampered off into the woods to safety. Fortunately, he was no better at sneaking up on the skunks.

Autumn came and with it a whole new mischievous game: Attack the Leaf Pile. In Florida, trees do not shed their leaves in the fall, and Marley was convinced that the foliage drifting down from the skies now was a gift meant just for him. As I raked the orange and yellow leaves into giant heaps, Marley would sit and watch patiently, biding his time. Only after I had gathered a mighty towering pile would he slink forward, crouched low. Every few steps, he would stop, front paw raised, to sniff the air like a lion on the Serengeti stalking an unsuspecting gazelle. Then, just as I leaned on my rake to admire my handiwork, he would lunge, land in a giant belly flop in the middle of the pile, and, for reasons not clear to me, fiercely chase his tail, not stopping until my neat leaf pile was scattered across the lawn again. Then he would give me a self-satisfied look, as if his contribution were an integral part of the leaf-gathering process.

OUR FIRST CHRISTMAS in Pennsylvania was supposed to be white. Jenny and I had had to do a sales job on Patrick and Conor to convince them that leaving Florida was for the best, and one of the big selling points was the promise of snow. We wantonly spun an image of waking up on Christmas morning to a starkly white landscape, unblemished except for the solitary tracks of Santa's sleigh outside our front door.

In the week leading up to the big day, the three children sat in the window together for hours, their eyes glued on the leaden sky. 'Come on, snow!' the kids chanted. But the clouds would not give it up.

A few days before Christmas, the whole family piled into the minivan and drove to a farm where we cut a spruce tree and enjoyed a free hayride and hot apple cider around a bonfire. It was the kind of classic northern holiday moment we had missed in Florida, but one thing was absent. Where was the damn snow? Jenny and I were beginning to regret how recklessly we had hyped the inevitable first snowfall. As we hauled our fresh-cut tree home, the sweet scent of its sap filling the van, the kids complained about getting gypped.

Christmas morning found a brand-new toboggan beneath the tree, but the view out of our windows remained all bare branches, dormant lawns and brown cornfields. I built a cheery fire in the fireplace and told the children to be patient. 'Maybe little boys and girls in some other place need the snow more than we do.'

'Yeah, right, Dad,' Patrick said.

Three weeks into the new year, the snow finally rescued me from my purgatory of guilt. It came during the night after everyone was asleep, and Patrick was the first to sound the alarm, running into our bedroom at dawn and yanking open the blinds. 'Look! Look!' he squealed. 'It's here!'

The snow was nearly a foot deep and still coming down. Soon Conor and Colleen came chugging down the hall, thumbs in mouths, blankets trailing behind them. Marley was up and stretching, banging his tail into everything, sensing the excitement. I turned to Jenny and said, 'I guess going back to sleep isn't an option,' and when she confirmed it was not, I turned to the kids and shouted, 'OK, snow bunnies, let's suit up!'

For the next half-hour we wrestled with zippers and leggings and hoods and gloves. By the time we were done, the kids looked like mummies. I opened the front door and before anyone else could step out, Marley blasted past us, knocking the well-bundled Colleen over in the process. The instant his paws hit the strange white stuff—*Ah, wet! Ah, cold!*—he had second thoughts and attempted an abrupt about-face. As anyone who has ever driven a car in snow knows, sudden braking coupled with tight U-turns is never a good idea.

Marley went into a full skid before somersaulting headfirst into a snow-drift. When he popped back up a second later, he looked like a giant pow-dered doughnut. Except for a black nose and two brown eyes, he was completely dusted in white. The Abominable Snowdog. Marley did not know what to make of this foreign substance. He jammed his nose deep into it and let loose a violent sneeze. He snapped at it and rubbed his face in it. Then, as if jabbed with a giant shot of adrenaline, he took off at full throttle.

To follow Marley's tracks in the snow was to begin to understand his warped mind. His path was filled with abrupt twists and turns and about-faces, with erratic loops and figure of eights, as though he were following some bizarre algorithm that only he could understand. Soon the kids were taking his lead, spinning and rolling and frolicking, snow packing into every crevice of their outerwear. Jenny came out with mugs of hot cocoa and an announcement: school was cancelled. I knew there was no way I was getting my little two-wheel-drive Nissan out the driveway anytime soon, let alone up and down the unploughed mountain roads, and I declared an offi-cial snow day for me, too.

I scraped the snow from the stone circle I had built that fall for back-yard campfires and soon had a crackling blaze going. The kids glided screaming down the hill on the toboggan, past the campfire and to the edge of the woods, Marley chasing them. I looked at Jenny and asked, 'If someone had told you a year ago that your kids would be sledding right out their back door, would you have believed them?'

'Not a chance,' she said, then wound up and unleashed a snowball that thumped me in the chest. Snow was in her hair, a blush in her cheeks, her breath rising in a cloud above her.

'Come here and kiss me,' I said.

Later, as the kids warmed themselves by the fire, I decided to try a run on the toboggan. I positioned it at the top of the hill and lay back, my feet tucked inside its nose. I began rocking to get moving. Not often did Marley have the opportunity to look down at me, and having me supine like that was tantamount to an invitation. He clambered aboard, straddling me and dropping onto my chest. 'Get off me, you big lug!' I screamed. But it was too late. We were already creeping forward, gathering speed as we began our descent.

'Bon voyage!' Jenny yelled.

Off we went, snow flying, Marley plastered on top of me, licking my face lustily as we careered down the slope. With our combined weight, we had considerably more momentum than the kids had, and we barrelled past the point where their tracks petered out. 'Hold on, Marley!' I screamed. 'We're going into the woods!'

We shot past a large walnut tree, then between two wild cherry trees, miraculously avoiding all unyielding objects as we crashed through the underbrush. It suddenly occurred to me that just up ahead was the bank leading down several feet to the creek, still unfrozen. The bank was steep, nearly a sheer drop-off, and we were going over. I had time only to wrap my arms around Marley, squeeze my eyes shut, and yell, 'Whoaaaaaa!'

Our toboggan shot over the bank and dropped out from beneath us. I felt as if I was in one of those classic cartoon moments, suspended in midair for an endless second before falling to ruinous injury. Only in this cartoon I was welded to a madly salivating Labrador retriever. We clung to each other as we crash-landed into a snowbank with a soft *poof* and slid to the water's edge. I opened my eyes and took stock of my condition. I could wiggle my toes and rotate my neck; nothing was broken. Marley was prancing around, eager to do it all over again. I stood up with a groan and said, 'I'm getting too old for this stuff.' In the months ahead it would become increasingly obvious that Marley was, too.

SOMETIME TOWARDS THE END of that first winter in Pennsylvania I began to notice Marley had moved quietly out of middle age and into retirement. He had turned nine that December, and ever so slightly he was slowing down. One day I walked him down our hill and up the next one, even steeper than ours, where the white church perched on the crest beside an old Civil War cemetery. It was a walk I took often and one that even the previous fall Marley had made without visible effort. This time, though, he was falling behind. I coaxed him along. 'You're not going soft on me, are you?' I asked, leaning over and stroking his face with my gloved hands.

The sun bathed over him, and I noticed just how much grey had crept into his tawny face. His whole muzzle and a good part of his brow had turned from buff to white. Without us quite realising it, our eternal puppy had become a senior citizen.

That's not to say he was any better behaved. Marley was still up to all his old antics, simply at a more leisurely pace. He still stole food. He still swallowed a wide assortment of household objects. Still drank out of the bathtub and trailed water from his gullet. And when thunder rumbled, he still panicked and, if alone, turned destructive. One day we arrived home to find Marley in a lather and Conor's mattress splayed open down to the coils.

Over the years, we had become philosophical about the damage, which had become much less frequent now that we were away from Florida's daily storms. In a dog's life, some cushions would open, some rugs would shred. Like any relationship, this one had its costs. They were costs we came to balance against the joy and amusement and protection and companionship he gave us. We could have bought a small yacht with what we spent on our dog and all the things he destroyed. Then again, how many yachts wait by the door all day for your return? How many live for the moment they can climb in your lap or ride down the hill with you on a toboggan, licking your face?

Marley had earned his place in our family. We accepted him for the dog he was, and loved him all the more for it.

'You old geezer,' I said to him on the side of the road that late-winter day. Our goal, the cemetery, was still a steep climb ahead. But just as in life, I was figuring out, the destination was less important than the journey. I dropped to one knee, running my hands down his sides, and said, 'Let's just sit here for a while.' When he was ready, we turned back down the hill and poked our way home.

Chapter 12

Poultry on Parade

That spring we decided to try our hand at animal husbandry. We owned two acres in the country now; it only seemed right to share it with a farm animal or two. Besides, I was editor of *Organic Gardening*, a magazine that celebrated the incorporation of animals—and their manure—into a healthy, well-balanced garden. 'A cow would be fun,' Jenny suggested.

'A cow?' I asked. 'Are you crazy? We don't even have a barn.'

'How about sheep?' she said. 'Sheep are cute.' I shot her my well-practiced you're-not-being-practical look.

In the end we settled on poultry. For any gardener who has sworn off chemical pesticides and fertilisers, chickens made a lot of sense. They were inexpensive and relatively low-maintenance. They needed only a small coop and a few cups of cracked corn each morning to be happy. Not only did they provide fresh eggs, but, when let loose to roam, they spent their days studiously devouring bugs and ticks, and fertilising with their high-nitrogen droppings as they went. Besides, as Jenny pointed out, they passed the cuteness test.

Chickens it was. Jenny had become friendly with a mom from school who lived on a farm and said she'd be happy to give us some chicks from the next clutch of eggs to hatch. I told Digger about our plans, and he agreed a few hens around the place made sense.

'Just one word of warning,' he said, folding his meaty arms across his chest. 'Whatever you do, don't let the kids name them. Once you name 'em, they're no longer poultry, they're pets.'

'Right,' I said. Chicken farming, I knew, had no room for sentimentality. Hens could live fifteen years or more but only produced eggs in their first couple of years. When they stopped laying, it was time for the stewing pot. That was just part of managing a flock.

Digger looked hard at me, as if divining what I was up against, and added, 'Once you name them, it's all over.'

'Absolutely,' I agreed. 'No names.'

The next evening I pulled into the driveway from work, and the three kids raced out of the house to greet me, each cradling a newborn chick. Jenny was behind them with a fourth in her hands. Her friend, Donna, had brought the baby birds over that afternoon. They were barely a day old and peered up at me with cocked heads as if to ask, 'Are you my mama?'

Patrick was the first to break the news. 'I named mine Feathers!'

'Mine is Tweety,' proclaimed Conor.

'My wicka Wuffy,' Colleen chimed in.

I shot Jenny a quizzical look.

'Fluffy,' Jenny said. 'She named her chicken Fluffy.'

'Jenny,' I protested, 'these are farm animals, not pets.'

'Oh, get real, Farmer John,' she said. 'You know as well as I do that you could never hurt one of these.'

'Jenny,' I said, the frustration rising in my voice.

'By the way,' she said, holding up the fourth chick in her hands, 'meet Shirley.'

Feathers, Tweety, Fluffy and Shirley took up residence in a box on the kitchen counter, a light bulb dangling above them for warmth. They grew at a breathtaking pace. Several weeks after the birds arrived, something jolted me awake before dawn. I sat up in bed and listened. From downstairs came a croaky and hoarse call, like a tubercular cough. It sounded again: *Cock-a-doodle-do!*

I shook Jenny and, when she opened her eyes, asked, 'When Donna brought the chicks over, you did ask her to check to make sure they were hens, right?'

'You mean you can do that?' she asked, and rolled back over, sound asleep.

It's called sexing. Farmers who know what they are doing can inspect a newborn chicken and determine, with about 80 per cent accuracy, whether it is male or female. At the farm store, sexed chicks command a premium price. The cheaper option is to buy 'straight run' birds of unknown gender. You take your chances with straight run, the idea being that the males will be slaughtered young for meat and the hens will be kept to lay eggs. Playing the straight-run gamble, of course, assumes you have what it takes to kill, gut and pluck any excess males you might end up with. As anyone who has ever raised chickens knows, two roosters in a flock is one rooster too many.

As it turned out, Donna had not attempted to sex our four chicks, and three of our four 'laying hens' were males. The thing about roosters is they're never content to play second chair to any other rooster. They will fight endlessly to determine who will dominate the roost.

As they grew into adolescents, our three roosters took to crowing their testosterone-pumped hearts out as I raced to finish their coop in the back yard. Shirley, our one poor, overtaxed female, was getting way more attention than even the most lusty of women could want.

I had thought the constant crowing of our roosters would drive Marley insane, but each morning he slept right through the racket. That's when it first occurred to me that maybe he couldn't hear it.

Marley's ears had caused him problems from an early age. Like many Labrador retrievers, he was predisposed to ear infections, and we had spent a small fortune on antibiotics, ointments, cleansers, drops and veterinarian visits. It had not occurred to me until after we brought the impossible-to-ignore roosters into our house that all those years of problems had taken their toll and our dog had gradually slipped into a muffled world of faraway whispers.

Not that he seemed to mind. Retirement suited Marley just fine, and his hearing problems didn't seem to impinge on his leisurely country lifestyle. If anything, deafness gave him a doctor-certified excuse for disobeying. After all, how could he heed a command that he could not hear? As thick-skulled as I always insisted he was, I swear he figured out how to use his deafness to his advantage. Drop a piece of steak into his bowl, and he would come trotting in from the next room. He still had the ability to detect the dull, satisfying thud of meat on metal. But yell for him to come when he had somewhere else he'd rather be going, and he'd stroll blithely away from you, not even glancing guiltily over his shoulder as he once would have.

'I think the dog's scamming us,' I told Jenny. She agreed his hearing problems seemed selective, but every time we tested him, sneaking up, clapping our hands, shouting his name, he would not respond. And every time we dropped food into his bowl, he would come running.

One day I arrived home from work to find the house empty. Jenny and the kids were out somewhere, and I called for Marley but got no response. I found him in the kitchen up to no good. His back to me, he was standing on his hind legs, his front paws resting on the kitchen table as he gobbled down the remains of a grilled cheese sandwich.

I decided to see how close I could get before he realised he had company. I tiptoed up behind him until I was close enough to touch him. As he chewed the crusts, he kept glancing at the door that led into the garage, knowing that was where Jenny and the kids would enter upon their return. Apparently it had not occurred to him that Dad would be arriving home, too, and just might sneak in through the front door.

'Oh, Marley?' I asked in a normal voice. 'What do you think you're doing?' He just kept gulping the sandwich down, clueless to my presence.

He polished off one sandwich, nosed the plate out of the way, and stretched forward to reach the crusts left on a second plate. 'You are such a bad dog,' I said as he chewed away.

That's when I reached out and tapped him on the butt. I might as well have lit a stick of dynamite. The old dog nearly jumped out of his fur coat. He dropped to the floor, rolling over to expose his belly to me in surrender. 'Busted!' I told him. 'You are so busted.' But I didn't have it in me to scold him. He was old; he was deaf; he was beyond reform. I wasn't going to change him. Sneaking up on him had been great fun, and I laughed out loud when he jumped. Now as he lay at my feet begging for forgiveness I just found it a little sad. I guess secretly I had hoped he'd been faking all along.

I FINISHED the chicken coop, an A-frame plywood affair with a drawbridge-style gangplank that could be raised at night to keep out predators. Donna kindly took back two of our three roosters and exchanged them for hens from her flock.

We let the chickens out each morning to roam the yard, and Marley made a few gallant runs at them, charging ahead, barking for a dozen paces or so before losing steam and giving up. Soon the birds learned that the lumbering yellow beast was no threat whatsoever, and Marley learned to share the yard with these new, feathered interlopers. One day I looked up from weeding in the garden to see Marley and the four chickens making their way down the row towards me as if in formation, the birds pecking and Marley sniffing as they went. It was like old friends out for a Sunday stroll. 'What kind of self-respecting hunting dog are you?' I chastised him. Marley lifted his leg and peed on a tomato plant before hurrying to rejoin his new pals.

Chapter 13

Borrowed Time

A person can learn a few things from an old dog. As the months slipped by and his infirmities mounted, Marley taught us mostly about life's uncompromising finiteness. Jenny and I were not quite middle-aged. It would have been easy to deny the inevitable creep of age, to pretend it might somehow pass us by. Marley would not afford us the luxury of such denial. As we watched him grow grey and deaf and creaky, there was no ignoring his mortality—or ours.

In the brief span of twelve years, he had aged roughly seven years for every one of ours, putting him, in human years, on the downward slope to ninety. His once-sparkling white teeth had gradually worn down to brown nubs. Three of his four front fangs were missing, broken off during crazed panic attacks as he tried to chew his way to safety. His breath, always a bit on the fishy side, had taken on the bouquet of a sun-baked Dumpster. The fact that he had acquired a taste for that little appreciated delicacy known as chicken manure didn't help, either. To our complete revulsion, he gobbled the stuff up like caviar.

His digestion was not what it once had been, and he became as gassy as a methane plant. There were days I swore that if I lit a match, the whole house would go up. Marley was able to clear an entire room with his silent, deadly flatulence, which seemed to increase in direct correlation to the number of dinner guests we had in our home. 'Marley! Not again!' the children would scream, and lead the retreat.

Marley's eyesight had grown fuzzy, and bunnies could now scamper past a dozen feet in front of him without his noticing. He was shedding his fur in vast quantities, forcing Jenny to vacuum every day—and still she couldn't keep up with it. Dog hair insinuated itself into every crevice of our home, every piece of our wardrobe, and more than a few of our meals. He had always been a shedder, but now his hairballs rolled across the wood floors like tumbleweeds on a wind-blown plain.

Most worrisome of all were his hips. Arthritis had snuck into his joints, weakening them and making them ache. He groaned in pain when he lay down, and groaned again when he struggled to his feet. I did not realise just how weak his hips had become until one day when I gave his rump a light pat and his hindquarters collapsed beneath him. Down he went. It was painful to watch.

Climbing the stairs to the first floor was becoming increasingly difficult for him, but he wouldn't think of sleeping alone on the main floor. Marley loved people, loved resting his chin on the mattress and panting in our faces as we slept, loved jamming his head through the shower curtain for a drink as we bathed, and he wasn't about to stop now. Each night when Jenny and I retired to our bedroom, he would fret at the foot of the stairs, whining, yipping, pacing, tentatively testing the first step with his front paw as he mustered his courage for the ascent that not long before had been effortless.

From the top of the stairs, I would beckon, 'Come on, boy. You can do it.' After several minutes of this, he would disappear around the corner to get a running start and then come charging up. Sometimes he made it; sometimes he stalled midflight and had to return to the bottom and try again. On his most pitiful attempts he would lose his footing and slide ingloriously backwards down the steps on his belly. He was too big for me to carry, but increasingly I found myself following him up the stairs, lifting his rear end up each step as he hopped forward on his front paws.

As age took its toll, Marley had good days and bad days. Sometimes it was hard to believe it was the same dog. One evening in the spring of 2002, I took him out for a short walk around the yard. The night was cool and windy. Invigorated by the crisp air, I started to run, and Marley, feeling frisky himself, galloped along beside me. I said to him, 'See, Marl, you still have some of the puppy in you.' We trotted together back to the front door, his tongue out as he panted happily, his eyes alert.

At the porch stoop, Marley tried to leap up the two steps—but his hips collapsed on him as he pushed off, and he found himself stuck, his front paws on the stoop, his belly resting on the steps and his butt collapsed flat on the sidewalk. He flailed his front legs valiantly, trying to get up, but it was no use.

'Come on, Marley!' I called, but he was immobilised. Finally, I grabbed him under the front shoulders so he could get all four legs on the ground. Then, after a few tries, he was able to stand. He backed up, looked apprehensively at the stairs for a few seconds, and loped up and into the house. From that day on, his confidence as a stair climber was shot; he never attempted those two small steps again without first stopping and fretting.

MARLEY REMINDED ME of life's brevity, of its fleeting joys and missed opportunities. He reminded me that each of us gets just one shot at the gold, with no replays. Like everyone else, I had but one life to live. I kept coming back to the same question: What was I doing spending it at a gardening magazine? It wasn't that my job did not have its rewards. I was proud of what I had done with the magazine. But I missed newspapers desperately. I missed the people who read them and the people who write them. I missed the adrenaline surge of writing on deadline and the satisfaction of waking up the next morning to find my in-box filled with emails responding to my words. Mostly, I missed telling stories.

When a former colleague of mine mentioned in passing that the *Philadelphia Inquirer* was seeking a metropolitan columnist, I leapt without a second's hesitation. Columnist positions are extremely hard to come by, and when a position does open up it's almost always filled internally. The *Inquirer* was one of the country's great newspapers. I was a fan, and now the *Inquirer*'s editors were asking to meet me. I wouldn't even have to relocate my family to take the job. The office I would be working in was just forty-five minutes down the Pennsylvania Turnpike, a tolerable commute. I don't put much stock in miracles, but it seemed like an act of divine intervention.

In November 2002, I traded in my gardening togs for a *Philadelphia Inquirer* press badge. I was back where I belonged, in a newsroom as a columnist once again.

THE FOLLOWING YEAR, when school let out for the summer, Jenny packed the kids into the minivan and headed to Boston for a week to visit her sister. I stayed behind to work. That left Marley with no one at home to keep him company and let him out. Of the many little embarrassments old age inflicted on him, the one that seemed to bother him most was the diminished control he had over his bowels. For all Marley's bad behaviour over the years, his bathroom habits had always been sure-fire. It was the one Marley feature we could brag about. From just a few months of age, he never, ever, had accidents in the house, even when left alone for ten or twelve hours.

That had changed in recent months. He no longer could go more than a few hours between pit stops. When the urge called, he had to go, and if we were not home to let him out, he had no choice but to go inside. It killed him to do it, and we always knew the second we walked into the house when he had had an accident. Instead of greeting us at the door in his exuberant manner, he would be standing far back in the room, his head hanging nearly to the floor, the shame radiating off him. We never punished him for it. How could we? He was nearly thirteen, about as old as Labs get. We knew he couldn't help it, and he seemed to know it, too.

Jenny bought a steam cleaner for the carpet, and we began arranging our schedules to make sure we were not away from the house for more than a few hours at a time. With Jenny and the kids away, I knew I would be putting in long days. This was my chance to explore the region I was now writing about. With my long commute, I would be away from home ten to twelve hours a day. There was no question Marley couldn't be left alone that long, or even half that long.

We decided to board him at the local kennel we used every summer when we went on vacation. The kennel was attached to a large veterinarian practice that offered professional care if not the most personal service. Each time we went there, it seemed, we saw a different doctor who knew nothing about Marley except what was printed in his chart. We never even learned their names. Unlike our beloved Dr Jay in Florida, these were strangers— competent strangers but strangers nonetheless.

I dropped Marley off on a Sunday evening and left my cellphone number with the front desk. That Tuesday morning, I was near Independence Hall in downtown Philadelphia when my cellphone rang. 'Could you please hold for Dr So-and-so?' the woman from the kennel asked. It was yet another veterinarian whose name I had never heard before. A few seconds later the vet came on the phone. 'We have an emergency with Marley,' she said.

My heart rose in my chest. 'An emergency?'

The vet said Marley's stomach had bloated with food, water and air and then, stretched and distended, had flipped over on itself, twisting and trapping its contents. With nowhere for the gas and other contents to escape, his stomach had swelled painfully in a life-threatening condition known as gastric dilatation-volvulus. It almost always required surgery to correct, she said, and if left untreated could result in death within a few hours.

She said she had inserted a tube down his throat and released much of the gas that had built up in his stomach, which relieved the swelling. By manipulating the tube in his stomach, she had worked the twist out of it, or as she put it, 'unflipped it', and he was now sedated and resting comfortably.

'That's a good thing, right?' I asked cautiously.

'But only temporary,' the doctor said. 'We got him through the immediate crisis, but once their stomachs twist like that, they almost always will twist again.'

'Like how almost always?' I asked.

'I would say he has a one per cent chance that it won't flip again,' she said. *One per cent? For God's sake*, I thought, *he has better odds of getting into Harvard.*

'One per cent? That's it?'

'I'm sorry,' she said. 'It's very grave.'

If his stomach did flip again—and she was telling me it was a virtual certainty—we had two choices. The first was to operate on him. She said she would open him up and attach the stomach to the cavity wall with sutures to prevent it from flipping again. 'The operation will cost about two thousand dollars,' she said. I gulped. 'And I have to tell you, it's very invasive. It will be tough going for a dog his age.'

'What's the second option?' I asked.

'The second option,' she said, hesitating only slightly, 'would be putting him to sleep.'

'Oh,' I said.

I was having trouble processing it all. Five minutes ago I was walking to the Liberty Bell, assuming Marley was happily relaxing in his kennel run. Now I was being asked to decide whether he should live or die. I had never even heard of the condition she had described. Only later would I learn that bloat was fairly common in some breeds of dogs, especially those, such as

Marley, with deep barrel chests. Dogs who scarfed down their entire meal in a few quick gulps—Marley, once again—also seemed to be at higher risk. 'Can't we just wait and see how he does?' I asked. 'Maybe it won't twist again.'

'That's what we're doing right now,' she said, 'waiting and watching.' She added, 'If his stomach flips again, I'll need you to make a quick decision. We can't let him suffer.'

'I need to speak with my wife,' I told her. 'I'll call you back.'

When Jenny answered her cellphone she was on a crowded tour boat with the kids in the middle of Boston Harbor. We had a choppy conversation over a bad connection. She was only getting snippets. Marley . . . emergency . . . stomach . . . surgery . . . put to sleep.

There was silence on the other end. 'Hello?' I said. 'Are you still there?'

'I'm here,' Jenny said, then went quiet again. We both knew this day would come eventually; we just did not think it would be today. Not with her and the kids out of town where they couldn't even have their goodbyes; not with me ninety minutes away in downtown Philadelphia with work commitments. By the end of the conversation, we decided there was really no decision at all. The vet was right. Marley was fading on all fronts. It would be cruel to put him through a traumatic surgery simply to try to stave off the inevitable. If this was Marley's time, then it was his time, and we would see to it he went out with dignity and without suffering. We knew it was the right thing, yet neither of us was ready to lose him.

I called the veterinarian back and told her our decision. The vet, whom I now knew as Dr Hopkinson, made it easy on me. 'I think it's time,' she said.

'I guess so,' I answered, but I didn't want her to put him down without calling me first. I wanted to be there with him if possible.

'Let's talk in an hour,' she said.

An hour later Dr Hopkinson sounded slightly more optimistic. Marley was still holding his own, resting with an intravenous drip in his front leg. She raised his odds to five per cent. 'I don't want you to get your hopes up,' she said. 'He's a very sick dog.'

The next morning the doctor sounded brighter still. 'He had a good night,' she said. When I called back at noon, she had removed the IV from his paw and started him on a slurry of rice and meat. 'He's famished,' she reported. By the next call, he was up on his feet. 'Good news,' she said. 'One of our techs just took him outside and he pooped and peed.' I cheered into the phone as though he had just taken Best in Show. Then she added,

'He must be feeling better. He just gave me a big sloppy kiss on the lips.' Yep, that was our Marley.

'I wouldn't have thought it possible yesterday,' the doc said, 'but I think you'll be able to take him home tomorrow.' The following evening after work, that's just what I did. He looked terrible—weak and skeletal, his eyes milky and crusted with mucus, as if he had been to the other side of death and back, which in a sense I guess he had. When I thanked the doctor for her good work, she replied, 'The whole staff loves Marley. Everyone was rooting for him.'

I walked him out to the car, my ninety-nine-to-one-odds miracle dog, and said, 'Let's get you home where you belong.' One of the kennel workers helped me lift him into the car, and I drove him home with a box of medicines and strict instructions.

Marley would never again gulp a huge meal in one sitting. His days of playing submarine with his snout in the water bowl were over. From now on, he was to receive four small meals a day and only limited rations of water—a half-cup or so at a time. In this way, the doctor hoped, his stomach would stay calm and not bloat and twist again. He also was never again to be boarded in a large kennel surrounded by the excitement of other dogs. I was convinced, and Dr Hopkinson seemed to be, too, that that had been the precipitating factor in his close call with death.

That night, after I got him home and inside, I spread a sleeping-bag on the floor in the family room beside him. He was not up to climbing the stairs to the bedroom, and I didn't have the heart to leave him alone. I knew he would fret all night if he was not at my side.

'We're having a sleepover, Marley!' I proclaimed, and lay down next to him. I stroked him from head to tail until huge clouds of fur rolled off his back. I wiped the mucus from the corners of his eyes and scratched his ears until he moaned with pleasure.

Jenny and the kids would be home in the morning; she would pamper him with frequent mini-meals of boiled hamburger and rice. It had taken him thirteen years, but Marley had finally merited people food, not leftovers but a stovetop meal made just for him. The children would throw their arms around him, unaware of how close they had come to never seeing him again.

Tomorrow the house would be loud and boisterous and full of life again. For tonight, it was just the two of us, Marley and me. Lying there with him, his smelly breath in my face, I couldn't help thinking of our first night together all those years ago after I brought him home from the breeder, a tiny puppy whimpering for his siblings. I remembered how I dragged his box into the bedroom and the way we had fallen asleep together, my arm dangling over the side of the bed to comfort him. I thought about his puppyhood and adolescence, about the shredded couches and eaten mattresses, about the wild walks along the Intracoastal and the cheek-to-jowl dances with the stereo blaring. I thought about the swallowed objects and purloined pay cheques and sweet moments of canine-human empathy. Mostly I thought about what a good and loyal companion he had been all these years. What a trip it had been.

'You really scared me, old man,' I whispered as he stretched out beside me and slid his snout beneath my arm to encourage me to keep petting him. 'It's good to have you home.'

OVER THE NEXT several weeks, Marley bounced back from the edge of death. The mischievous sparkle returned to his eyes, the cool wetness to his nose, and a little meat to his bones. For all he'd been through, he seemed none the worse off. He was content to snooze his days away, favouring a spot in front of the glass door in the family room where the sun flooded in and baked his fur. On his new low-bulk diet of petite meals, he was perpetually ravenous and was begging and thieving food more shamelessly than ever.

The scare of that summer should have snapped Jenny and me out of our denial about Marley's advancing age, but we quickly returned to the comfortable assumption that the crisis was a one-time fluke, and his eternal march into the sunset could resume once again. Part of us wanted to believe he could chug on for ever. Despite all his frailties, he was still the same happy-go-lucky dog. His daily routine included barking at the mailman, visiting the chickens, staring at the bird feeder, and banging around the house, tail thumping the walls and furniture. Even in old age, some things did not change.

But Marley was living on borrowed time; that much was clear. Another health crisis could come any day, and when it did, I would not fight the inevitable. Any invasive medical procedure at this stage in his life would be cruel, something Jenny and I would be doing more for our sake than his. We loved that crazy old dog, loved him despite everything—or perhaps *because* of everything. But I could see now the time was near for us to let him go.

THAT FALL, a crisis did arrive. I was in the bedroom getting dressed for work when I heard a terrible clatter followed by Conor's scream: 'Help! Marley fell down the stairs!' I came running and found him in a heap at the bottom of the long staircase, struggling to get to his feet. Jenny and I raced to him and ran our hands over his body, gently squeezing his limbs, pressing his ribs, massaging his spine. Nothing seemed to be broken.

'Wow, was he lucky,' I said. 'A fall like that could have killed him.'

'I can't believe he didn't get hurt,' Jenny said. 'He's like a cat with nine lives.'

But he had got hurt. Within minutes he was stiffening up, and by the time I arrived home from work that night, Marley was completely incapacitated, unable to move. He seemed to be sore everywhere, as though he had been worked over by thugs.

The next morning Marley was better, though still hobbling about like an invalid. We got him outside, where he urinated and defecated without a problem. Jenny and I together lifted him up the porch steps to get him back inside. 'I have a feeling,' I told her, 'that Marley will never see the upstairs of this house again.' From now on, he would have to get used to living and sleeping on the ground floor.

I worked from home that day and was upstairs in the bedroom, writing a column on my laptop computer, when I heard a commotion on the stairs. I stopped typing and listened. The sound was instantly familiar, a sort of loud clomping noise as if a shod horse were galloping up a gangplank. I looked at the bedroom doorway and held my breath. A few seconds later, Marley popped his head around the corner and came sauntering into the room. His eyes brightened when he spotted me. *So there you are!* He smashed his head into my lap, begging for an ear rub, which I figured he had earned.

'Marley, you made it!' I exclaimed. 'I can't believe you're up here!'

Later, as I sat on the floor with him and scruffed his neck, he twisted his head around and gamely gummed my wrist in his jaws. It was a good sign, a telltale of the playful puppy still in him. The previous night he had seemed at death's door. Today he was panting and pawing and trying to slime my hands off. Just when I thought his long, lucky run was over, he was back.

I pulled his head up and made him look me in the eyes. 'You're going to tell me when it's time, right?' I said, more a statement than a question. I didn't want to have to make the decision on my own. 'You'll let me know, won't you?'

Chapter 14
Beneath the Cherry Trees

Winter arrived early that year, and as the days grew short and the winds howled through the frozen branches, we cocooned into our snug home. I chopped firewood and stacked it by the back door. Jenny made hearty soups and homemade breads, and the children sat in the window and waited for the snow to arrive. I anticipated the first snowfall, too, but with a quiet sense of dread, wondering how Marley could possibly make it through another tough winter. How would he navigate ice-glazed sidewalks, slippery steps and a snow-covered landscape?

In mid-December, we packed the minivan in preparation for a family vacation to Disney World in Florida. It would be the children's first Christmas away from home, and they were wild with excitement. That evening, in preparation for an early-morning departure, Jenny delivered Marley to the veterinarian's office, where she had arranged for him to spend our week away in the intensive-care unit where the doctors and workers could keep their eyes on him around the clock. After his close call the previous summer, they were happy to give him the extra attention at no extra cost.

That night as we finished packing, both Jenny and I commented on how strange it felt to be in a dog-free zone. There was no oversized canine constantly underfoot, shadowing our every move. The freedom was liberating, but the house seemed cavernous and empty, even with the kids bouncing off the walls.

The next morning, we piled into the minivan and headed south. Ridiculing the whole Disney experience is a favourite sport in the circle of parents I run with. But the whole family had a wonderful time. Of the many potential pitfalls—sickness, fatigue-induced tantrums, lost children—we escaped them all. It was a great family vacation. When we were halfway home on the long drive back north, my cellphone rang. It was the veterinarian's office. Marley was acting lethargic, and his hips had begun to droop worse than usual. He seemed to be in discomfort. The vet wanted our permission to give him a steroid shot and pain medication. Sure, I said. Keep him comfortable, and we'd be there to pick him up the next day.

When Jenny arrived to take him home the following afternoon, on

December 29, Marley looked tired and a little out of sorts but not visibly ill. Within a half-hour of getting him home, however, he was retching, trying to clear thick mucus from his throat. Jenny let him out into the front yard, and he simply lay on the frozen ground and could not or would not budge. She called me at work in a panic. 'I can't get him back inside,' she said. 'He's lying out there in the cold, and he won't get up.' I left immediately, and by the time I arrived home forty-five minutes later, she had managed to get him to his feet and back into the house. I found him sprawled on the dining-room floor, clearly distressed and clearly not himself.

In thirteen years I had not been able to walk into the house without Marley bounding to greet me as if I'd just returned from the Hundred Years' War. Not on this day. His eyes followed me as I walked into the room, but he did not move his head. I knelt down beside him and rubbed his snout. No reaction. His eyes were far away, and his tail lay limp on the floor.

It was becoming obvious this was turning into an emergency. Marley slowly stood up on shaky legs and tried to retch again, but nothing would come out. That's when I noticed his stomach; it looked bigger than usual, and it was hard to the touch. My heart sank; I knew what this meant. I called the veterinarian's office, and described Marley's bloated stomach. The receptionist put me on hold for a moment, then came back and said, 'The doctor says to bring him right in.'

Jenny and I did not have to say a word to each other; we both understood that the moment had arrived. We braced the kids, telling them Marley had to go to the hospital and the doctors were going to try to make him better, but that he was very sick. As I was getting ready to go, I looked in, and Jenny and the kids were huddled around him as he lay on the floor so clearly in distress. The children remained bullishly optimistic that this dog who had been a constant part of their lives would soon be back, good as new. 'Get all better, Marley,' Colleen said in her little voice.

With Jenny's help, I got him into the back of my car. She gave him a last quick hug, and I drove off with him, promising to call as soon as I learned something. He lay on the floor in the back seat with his head resting on the centre hump, and I drove with one hand on the wheel and the other stretched behind me so I could stroke his head. 'Oh, Marley,' I just kept saying.

In the parking lot of the animal hospital, I helped him out of the car, and he stopped to sniff a tree where the other dogs all pee—still curious despite how ill he felt. I gave him a minute, knowing this might be his last time in his beloved outdoors, then led him into the lobby. Just inside the front door, he decided he had gone far enough and gingerly let himself down on the tile floor. The techs brought out a stretcher, slid him onto it, and disappeared into the examining area.

A few minutes later, the vet, a young woman I had never met before, came out and led me into an exam room where she put a pair of X-ray films up on a light board. She showed me how his stomach had bloated to twice its normal size. Just as with the last time, she said she would sedate him and insert a tube into his stomach to release the gas causing the bloating. 'It's a long shot,' she said, 'but I'm also going to try to use the tube to massage his stomach back into place.' It was the same one per cent gamble Dr Hopkinson had given over the summer. It had worked once, it could work again. I remained silently optimistic.

'OK,' I said. 'Please give it your best shot.'

A half-hour later she emerged with a grim face. She had tried three times and was unable to open the blockage. 'At this point,' she said, 'our only real option is to go into surgery.' She paused, and then said, 'Or the most humane thing might be to put him to sleep.'

Jenny and I had been through this decision five months earlier and had already made the hard choice, not to subject Marley to any more suffering. Yet standing in the waiting room, the hour upon me once again, I stood frozen.

I told the doctor I wanted to step outside to call my wife. On the cell-phone in the parking lot, I told Jenny that they had tried everything short of surgery to no avail. We sat silently on the phone for a long moment before she said, 'I love you, John.'

'I love you, too, Jenny,' I said.

I walked back inside and asked the doctor if I could have a couple of minutes alone with him. She warned me that he was heavily sedated. 'Take all the time you need,' she said. I found him unconscious on the stretcher on the floor, an IV shunt in his forearm. I got down on my knees and ran my fingers through his fur, the way he liked. I lifted each floppy ear in my hands—those crazy ears that had caused him so many problems over the years and cost us a king's ransom. I picked up a front paw and cupped it in my hand. Then I dropped my forehead against his and sat there for a long time, as if I could telegraph a message through our two skulls, from my brain to his. I wanted to make him understand some things.

'You know all that stuff we've always said about you?' I whispered.

'What a total pain you are? Don't believe it. Don't believe it for a minute, Marley.' He needed to know that, and something more, too. There was something I had never told him, that no one ever had. I wanted him to hear it before he went.

'Marley,' I said. 'You are a *great* dog.'

I FOUND the doctor waiting at the front counter. 'I'm ready,' I said. My voice was cracking, which surprised me because I had really believed I'd braced myself months earlier for this moment. I knew if I said another word, I would break down, and so I just nodded and signed as she handed me release forms. When the paperwork was completed, I followed her back to the unconscious Marley, and I knelt in front of him again, my hands cradling his head as she prepared a syringe and inserted it into the shunt. 'Are you OK?' she asked. I nodded, and she pushed the plunger. His jaw shuddered ever so slightly. She listened to his heart and said it had slowed way down but not stopped. He was a big dog. She prepared a second syringe and again pushed the plunger. A minute later, she listened again and said, 'He's gone.' She left me alone with him, and I gently lifted one of his eyelids. She was right; Marley was gone.

I walked out to the front desk and paid the bill. She discussed cremation, but I said I would be taking him home. A few minutes later, she and an assistant wheeled out a cart with a large black bag on it and helped me lift it into the back seat. The doctor shook my hand, told me how sorry she was.

In the car on the way home, I started to cry, something I almost never do, not even at funerals. It only lasted a few minutes. By the time I pulled into the driveway, I was dry-eyed again. I left Marley in the car and went inside where Jenny was sitting up, waiting. The children were all in bed asleep; we would tell them in the morning. We fell into each other's arms and both started weeping. I tried to describe it to her, to assure her he was already deeply asleep when the end came, that there was no panic, no trauma, no pain. But I couldn't find the words. So we simply rocked in each other's arms. Later, we went outside and together lifted the heavy black bag out of the car and into the garden cart, which I rolled into the garage for the night.

SLEEP CAME FITFULLY that night, and an hour before dawn I slid out of bed and dressed quietly so as not to wake Jenny. In the kitchen I drank a glass of water—coffee could wait—and walked out into a light, slushy drizzle. I grabbed a shovel and pickaxe and walked to the pea patch, where I had decided to lay him to rest.

The temperature was in the mid-thirties and the ground blessedly unfrozen. In the half-dark, I began to dig. Once I was through a thin layer of topsoil, I hit heavy, dense clay studded with rocks. The going was slow and arduous. I peeled off my coat and paused to catch my breath. After thirty minutes I was in a sweat and not yet down two feet. At the forty-five-minute mark, I struck water. The hole began to fill. Soon a foot of muddy cold water covered the bottom. There was no way I could lay Marley down in that icy swamp. No way.

I abandoned the location and scouted the yard, stopping where the lawn meets the woods at the bottom of the hill. Between two big native cherry trees, their branches arching above me in the grey light of dawn like an open-air cathedral, I sank my shovel. These were the same trees Marley and I had narrowly missed on our wild toboggan ride, and I said out loud, 'This feels right.'

Digging went easily, and I soon had an oval hole roughly two by three feet around and four feet deep. I went inside and found all three kids up, sniffling quietly. Jenny had just told them.

Seeing them grieving—their first up-close experience with death— deeply affected me. Yes, it was only a dog, and dogs come and go in the course of a human life. It was only a dog, and yet every time I tried to talk about Marley to them, tears welled in my eyes. I told them it was OK to cry, and that owning a dog always ended with this sadness because dogs just don't live as long as people do. I told them how Marley was sleeping when they gave him the shot and that he didn't feel a thing. He just drifted off and was gone. Colleen was upset that she didn't have a chance to say a real goodbye to him; she thought he would be coming home. I told her I had said goodbye for all of us. Conor showed me something he had made for Marley, to go in the grave with him. It was a drawing of a big red heart beneath which he had written: *To Marley, I hope you know how much I loved you all of my life. You were always there when I needed you. Through life or death, I will always love you. Your brother, Conor Richard Grogan.* Then Colleen drew a picture of a girl with a big yellow dog and beneath it, with spelling help from her brother, she wrote: *PS—I will never forget you.*

I went out alone and wheeled Marley's body down the hill, where I cut an armful of soft pine boughs that I laid on the floor of the hole. I lifted the heavy body bag off the cart and down into the hole as gently as I could, though there was really no graceful way to do it. I got into the hole, opened the bag to see him one last time, and positioned him in a comfortable, natural way—just as he might be lying in front of the fireplace. 'OK, big guy, this is it,' I said. I closed the bag up and returned to the house to get Jenny and the kids.

As a family, we walked down to the grave. Conor and Colleen had sealed their notes in a plastic bag, and I placed it beside Marley's head. Patrick used his jackknife to cut five pine boughs, one for each of us. One by one, we dropped them in the hole. We paused for a moment, then all together, as if we had rehearsed it, said, 'Marley, we love you.' I picked up the shovel and tossed the first scoop of dirt in. It slapped heavily on the plastic, making an ugly sound, and Jenny began to weep. I kept shovelling. The kids stood watching in silence.

When the hole was half filled, I took a break and we all walked up to the house, where we sat around the kitchen table and told funny Marley stories. One minute tears were welling in our eyes, the next we were laughing. Jenny told the story of Marley going bonkers during the filming of *The Last Home Run*. I told about all the leashes he had severed, all the things he had destroyed and the thousands of dollars he had cost us. We could laugh about it now. To make the kids feel better, I told them something I did not quite believe. 'Marley's spirit is up in dog heaven now,' I said. 'He's in a giant golden meadow, running free. And his hips are good again. And his hearing is back, and his eyesight is sharp, and he has all his teeth. He's back in his prime—chasing rabbits all day long.'

The morning was slipping away, and I still needed to go to work. I went back down to his grave alone and finished filling the hole, gently, respectfully, using my boot to tamp down the loose earth. When the hole was flush with the ground, I placed two large rocks from the woods on top of it, then went inside, took a hot shower, and drove to the office.

IN THE DAYS immediately after we buried Marley, the whole family went silent. The animal that was the amusing target of so many hours of conversation over the years had become a taboo topic. We were trying to return our lives to normal, and speaking of him only made it harder. Colleen in particular could not bear to hear his name or see his photo. Tears would well in her eyes and she would clench her fists and say angrily, 'I don't want to talk about him!'

I resumed my schedule, driving to work, writing my column, coming home again. Every night for thirteen years he had waited for me at the door. Walking in now at the end of the day was the most painful part of all. The house seemed silent, empty, not quite a home any more.

I wanted to write a farewell column to Marley, but I was afraid all my emotion would pour out into a gushy, maudlin piece of self-indulgence. So I stuck with topics less dear to my heart. I did, however, carry a tape recorder with me, and when a thought came to me, I would get it down. I knew I wanted to portray him as he was and not as some impossibly perfect creature. So many people remake their pets in death, turning them into noble beasts that in life did everything for their masters except fry eggs for breakfast. I wanted to be honest. Marley was a funny, bigger-than-life pain in the ass who never quite got the hang of the whole chain-of-command thing. Honestly, he might well have been the world's worst-behaved dog. Yet he intuitively grasped from the start what it meant to be man's best friend.

During the week after his death, I walked down the hill several times to stand by his grave. Partly, I wanted to make sure no wild animals were coming around at night. The grave remained undisturbed, but I could see that in the spring I would need to add soil to fill the depression where it was settling. Mostly I just wanted to commune with him. Standing there, I found myself replaying random snippets from his life. I was embarrassed by how deep my grief went for this dog. I walked around all week with a dull ache inside. It was actually physical, not unlike a stomach virus. I was lethargic, unmotivated.

On New Year's Eve we were invited to a neighbour's house for a party. Friends quietly expressed their condolences, but we all tried to keep the conversation light. This was, after all, New Year's Eve. At dinner, Sara and Dave Pandl, a pair of landscape architects who had moved back to Pennsylvania from California to turn an old stone barn into their home, and who had become our dear friends, sat at one corner of the table with me, and we talked at length about dogs and love and loss. Dave and Sara had put down their cherished Nellie, a border collie, five years earlier and buried her on the hill beside their farmhouse. Dave is one of the most unsentimental people I have ever met, a quiet stoic cut from taciturn Pennsylvania Dutch stock. But when it came to Nellie, he, too, had struggled with deep grief. As Sara said, blinking back her tears, 'Sometimes a dog comes along that really touches your life, and you can never forget her.'

That weekend I took a long walk through the woods, and by the time I arrived at work on Monday, I knew what I wanted to say about the dog that had touched my life, the one I would never forget.

I began the column by describing my walk down the hill with the shovel at dawn and how odd it was to be outdoors without Marley, who for thirteen years had made it his business to be at my side for any excursion. 'And now here I was alone,' I wrote, 'digging him this hole.'

I quoted my father who, when I told him I had to put the old guy down, gave the closest thing to a compliment my dog had ever received: 'There will never be another dog like Marley.'

I gave a lot of thought to how I should describe him, and this is what I settled on: 'No one ever called him a great dog—or even a good dog. He was as wild as a banshee and as strong as a bull. He crashed joyously through life with a gusto most often associated with natural disasters. He's the only dog I've ever known to get expelled from obedience school.' I continued: 'Marley was a chewer of couches, a slasher of screens, a slinger of drool, a tipper of trash cans. As for brains, let me just say he chased his tail till the day he died, apparently convinced he was on the verge of a major canine breakthrough.' There was more to him than that, however, and I described his intuition and empathy, his gentleness with children, his pure heart.

What I really wanted to say was how this animal had touched our souls and taught us some of the most important lessons of our lives. 'A person can learn a lot from a dog, even a loopy one like ours,' I wrote. 'Marley taught me about living each day with unbridled exuberance and joy, about seizing the moment and following your heart. He taught me to appreciate the simple things—a walk in the woods, a fresh snowfall, a nap in a shaft of winter sunlight. And as he grew old and achy, he taught me about optimism in the face of adversity. Mostly, he taught me about friendship and selflessness and, above all else, unwavering loyalty.'

It was an amazing concept that I was only now, in the wake of his death, fully absorbing: Marley as mentor. As teacher and role model. Was it possible for a dog—any dog, but especially a nutty, wildly uncontrollable one like ours—to point humans to the things that really mattered in life? I believed it was. Loyalty. Courage. Devotion. Simplicity. Joy. And the things that did not matter, too. A dog has no use for fancy cars or big homes or designer clothes. Status symbols mean nothing to him. A waterlogged stick will do just fine. A dog judges others not by their colour or creed or class but by who they are inside. A dog doesn't care if you are rich or poor, clever or dull. Give him your heart and he will give you his. It was really quite simple, and yet we humans, so much wiser and more sophisticated, have always had trouble figuring out what really counts and what does not. As I wrote that farewell column to Marley, I realised it was all right there in front of us, if only we opened our eyes. Sometimes it took a dog with bad breath, worse manners and pure intentions to help us see.

I finished my column, turned it in to my editor, and drove home for the night, feeling somehow lighter, as though a weight I did not even know I had been carrying was lifted from me.

WHEN I ARRIVED at work the next morning, the red message light on my telephone was blinking. I punched in my access code and received a recorded warning I had never heard before. 'Your mailbox is full,' the voice said. 'Please delete all unneeded messages.'

I logged on to my computer and opened my email. Same story. The opening screen was filled with new messages, and so was the next screen, and the one after that. The morning email was a ritual for me, a visceral, if inexact barometer of the impact that day's column had made. Some columns brought as few as five or ten responses, and on those days I knew I had not connected. Others brought several dozen, a good day. But this morning there were hundreds, far more than anything I had received before. The headers at the top of the emails said things like 'Deepest condolences,' 'About your loss', or simply 'Marley'.

Animal-lovers are a special breed of human, generous of spirit, full of empathy, perhaps a little prone to sentimentality, and with hearts as big as a cloudless sky. Most who wrote and called simply wanted to express their sympathies, to tell me they, too, had been down this road and knew what my family was going through. Others had dogs whose lives were drawing to their inevitable ends; they dreaded what they knew was coming, just as we had dreaded it, too.

My correspondents wrote and called for another reason, too. They wanted to dispute the central premise of my report, the part in which I insisted Marley was the world's worst-behaved animal. 'Excuse me,' the typical response went, 'but yours couldn't have been the world's worst dog—because mine was.' To make their case, they regaled me with detailed accounts of their pets' woeful behaviour. I heard about shredded curtains, stolen lingerie, devoured birthday cakes, trashed auto interiors, great escapes, even a swallowed diamond engagement ring, which made Marley's taste for gold chains seem positively lowbrow by comparison. My in-box resembled a television talk show, *Bad Dogs and the People Who Love Them*, with the willing victims lining up to proudly brag, not about how wonderful their dogs were but about just how awful. Oddly enough, most of the horror stories involved large loopy retrievers just like mine.

A woman named Nancy clipped my column to save because Marley reminded her so much of her retriever Gracie. 'I left the article on the kitchen table and turned to put away the scissors,' Nancy wrote. 'When I turned back, sure enough, Gracie had eaten the column.'

Wow, I was feeling better by the minute. Marley no longer sounded all that terrible. If nothing else, he certainly had plenty of company in the Bad Dog Club. I brought several of the messages home to share with Jenny, who laughed for the first time since Marley's death. My new friends in the Secret Brotherhood of Dysfunctional Dog Owners had helped us more than they ever would know.

THE DAYS TURNED INTO WEEKS and winter melted into spring. Daffodils pushed up through the earth and bloomed around Marley's grave, and delicate white cherry blossoms floated down to rest on it. Gradually, life without our dog became more comfortable. As time passed, the recollections were more pleasant than painful. Long-forgotten moments flashed in my head with vivid clarity like clips being rerun from old home videos: the way the crew on the movie set had fawned over him; the way he held mangoes in his front paws as he nibbled out the flesh; and the way he begged for his tranquillisers like they were steak bits. Little moments randomly playing out on my mental movie screen at the least likely times and places. Most of them made me smile; a few made me bite my lip and pause.

I was driving to an interview when out of nowhere came an early scene from our marriage: a romantic weekend getaway to a beachfront cottage on Sanibel Island before children arrived. The bride, the groom—and Marley. I had completely forgotten about that weekend, and here it was again, replaying in living colour: driving across the state with him wedged between us, his nose occasionally bumping the gearshift lever into neutral. Bathing him in the tub of our rental place after a day on the beach, suds and water and sand flying everywhere. And later, Jenny and I making love beneath the cool cotton sheets, an ocean breeze wafting over us, Marley's tail thumping against the mattress.

He was a central player in some of the happiest chapters of our lives. Chapters of young love and new beginnings, of budding careers and tiny babies. Of heady successes and crushing disappointments; of discovery and freedom and self-realisation. He came into our lives just as we were trying to figure out what they would become. He joined us as we grappled with what every couple must confront, the sometimes painful process of forging from two distinct pasts one shared future. He became part of our melded fabric, a tightly woven strand in the weave that was us. Just as we had helped shape him into the family pet, he helped to shape us, as well—as a couple, as parents, as animal-lovers, as adults. Despite everything, all the disappointments and unmet expectations, Marley had given us a gift, at once priceless and free. He taught us the art of unqualified love. How to give it, how to accept it. Where there is that, most of the other pieces fall into place.

THE SUMMER after his death Jenny marvelled at how easy it was to keep the house clean without a dog shedding and drooling and tracking in dirt. I admitted how nice it was to walk barefoot in the grass without watching where I stepped. No doubt about it, life without a dog was easier and immensely simpler. We could take a weekend jaunt without arranging boarding. We could go out to dinner without worrying what family heirloom was in jeopardy. The kids could eat without having to guard their plates. I could move around the house without a giant yellow magnet glued to my heels.

Still, as a family, we were not quite whole.

One morning in late summer I came down for breakfast, and Jenny handed me a section of the newspaper folded over to expose an inside page. 'You're not going to believe this,' she said.

Once a week, our local paper featured a dog from a rescue shelter that needed a home. The profile always featured a photograph of the dog, its name and a brief description, written as if the dog were speaking in the first person, making its own best case. It was a gimmick the shelter people used to make the animals seem charming and adorable. We always found the doggy résumés amusing, if for no other reason than the effort made to put the best shine on unwanted animals that had already struck out at least once.

On this day, staring up from the page at me was a face I instantly recognised. Our Marley. Or at least a dog that could have been his identical twin. He was a big male yellow Lab with an anvil head, furrowed brow, and floppy ears cocked back at a comical angle. He stared directly into the camera lens with a quivering intensity that made you just know that seconds after the picture was snapped he had knocked the photographer to the ground and tried to swallow the camera. Beneath the photo was the name: Lucky. I read his sales pitch aloud. This is what Lucky had to say about himself: 'Full of zip! I would do well in a home that is quiet while I am learning how to control my energy level. My new family will need to be patient with me and continue to teach me my doggy manners.'

'My God,' I exclaimed. 'It's him. He's back from the dead.'

'Reincarnation,' Jenny said.

It was uncanny how much Lucky looked like Marley and how much the description fitted him, too. Full of zip? Problem controlling energy? Working on doggy manners? Patience required? We were well familiar with those euphemisms, having used them ourselves. Our mentally unbalanced dog was back, young and strong again, and wilder than ever. We both stood there, staring at the newspaper, not saying anything.

'I guess we could go look at him,' I finally said.

'Just for the fun of it,' Jenny added.

'Right. Just out of curiosity.'

'What's the harm of looking?'

'No harm at all,' I agreed.

'Well then,' she said, 'why not?'

'What do we have to lose?'

JOHN GROGAN

Born: Detroit, March 20, 1957
Home: Pennsylvania
Website: www.marleyandme.com

For years, John Grogan had entertained friends, family and the readers of his newspaper columns with tales of his Labrador Marley's mad antics, and it was partly a desire to set the record straight that inspired the book. 'After Marley died, I figured I owed it to him to tell the whole story. Yes, he was an attention-deficit, hyperactive, nutty dog but he had a pure heart and an incredible gift of canine-human empathy.'

Grogan says that his children were bereft after Marley's death. 'My wife and I had lost a beloved pet but for them it was like saying goodbye to a sibling. He had been close beside them every step of the way, from infancy forward, drooling all over them. A dog is the greatest gift a parent can give a child. Okay, a good education, then a dog.' Grogan found that writing about Marley was therapeutic for the whole family. 'I would read passages aloud to my children as I progressed, and it seemed to help them, too. Mostly, we laughed. Bittersweet is probably the right word.'

> *'Yes, he was an attention-deficit, hyperactive, nutty dog but he had a pure heart . . .'*

Marley proved difficult to replace. At the end of the book, Grogan remembers seeing the description of another Labrador, Lucky, who seemed just like Marley, in the paper. The family were tempted to buy him but it didn't work out. 'When we showed up to meet him, the staff took one look at our young children and told us they would not let us adopt Lucky. He had been seriously abused and was too unpredictable to be around kids. He had a wide host of issues that made Marley look down-right well adjusted.'

The Grogans, who live on a wooded hillside in Pennyslvania, now have a surprisingly calm Labrador retriever named Gracie. 'We all agree she's no Marley—not that there's anything wrong with that.' In spite of the book's massive success, Grogan continues to work as the Pennsylvania columnist for *The Philadelphia Inquirer*. He is also at work on another book, but says he prefers not to talk about it. 'I'm superstitious that way.'

FALSE IMPRESSION

JEFFREY ARCHER

At Wentworth Hall in Sussex a Van Gogh
painting worth $60 million
hangs undisturbed.
A thousand miles away, in downtown
Manhattan, Bryce Fenston, an
unscrupulous and greedy collector,
is plotting to make it his.
Enter Anna Petrescu, art historian,
valuer—and the only one who has the
inside track on Fenston's plans and
the determination to stop him . . .

Victoria Wentworth sat alone at the table where Wellington had dined with sixteen of his field officers the night before he set out for Waterloo.

General Sir Harry Wentworth sat at the right hand of the Iron Duke that night, and was commanding his left flank when a defeated Napoleon rode off the battlefield and into exile. A grateful monarch bestowed on the general the title Earl of Wentworth, which the family had borne proudly since 1815.

These thoughts were running through Victoria's mind as she read Dr Petrescu's report for a second time. When she turned the last page, she let out a sigh of relief. A solution to all her problems had been found, quite literally at the eleventh hour.

The dining-room door opened noiselessly and Andrews, who from second footman to butler had served three generations of Wentworths, deftly removed Victoria's dessert plate.

'Thank you,' she said, and waited until he had reached the door before she added, 'and has everything been arranged for the removal of the painting?' She couldn't bring herself to mention the artist's name.

'Yes, milady,' Andrews replied. 'The picture will have been dispatched before you come down for breakfast.'

'And has everything been prepared for Dr Petrescu's visit?'

'Yes, milady,' repeated Andrews. 'Dr Petrescu is expected around midday on Wednesday, and I have already informed Cook that Dr Petrescu will be joining you for lunch in the conservatory.'

'Thank you, Andrews,' said Victoria. The butler gave a slight bow and quietly closed the heavy oak door behind him.

By the time Dr Petrescu arrived, one of the family's most treasured heirlooms would be on its way to America, and although the masterpiece would never be seen at Wentworth Hall again, no one outside the immediate family need be any the wiser.

Victoria folded her napkin and rose from the table. She picked up Dr Petrescu's report and walked out of the dining room into the marble hall. She paused at the foot of the staircase to admire Gainsborough's full-length portrait of Catherine, Lady Wentworth, who was dressed in a magnificent gown, set off by a diamond necklace and matching earrings. Victoria touched her ear and smiled at the thought that such an extravagant bauble must have been considered quite risqué at the time.

She looked steadfastly ahead as she climbed the wide marble staircase to her bedroom. She felt unable to look into the eyes of her ancestors, brought to life by Romney, Lawrence, Reynolds, Lely and Kneller, conscious of having let them all down. Victoria accepted that before she retired to bed she must finally write to her sister and let her know the decision she had come to.

Arabella was so wise and sensible. If only her beloved twin had been born a few minutes earlier rather than a few minutes later, then she would have inherited the estate and would, without doubt, have handled the problem with considerably more panache.

Victoria closed her bedroom door and placed Dr Petrescu's report on her desk. She spent the next few minutes brushing her hair before slipping on a silk nightgown, which a maid had laid out on the end of the bed. Unable to avoid the responsibility any longer, she sat down at her writing desk and picked up her fountain pen.

WENTWORTH HALL

September 10, 2001

My dearest Arabella,

I have put off writing this letter for far too long, as you are the last person who deserves to learn such distressing news.

When dear Papa died and I inherited the estate, it was some time before I appreciated the full extent of the debts he had run up. I fear my lack of business experience, coupled with crippling death duties, only exacerbated the problem.

I thought the answer was to borrow even more, but that has simply made matters worse. Now, however, I am pleased to tell you that a solution has been found.

On Wednesday, I will be seeing—

Victoria thought she heard the bedroom door open. She wondered which of her servants would have entered without knocking.

By the time Victoria had turned to find out who it was, the intruder was standing by her side.

Victoria stared up at a slim woman, even shorter than herself, whom she had never seen before. The woman smiled at her and Victoria returned her smile, before noticing that she had a kitchen knife in her right hand.

'Who—' began Victoria as the woman's free hand shot out, grabbed her hair and snapped her head back. She felt the thin, razor-sharp blade as it touched the skin of her neck. In one swift movement the knife had sliced open her throat as if she were a lamb sent to slaughter.

Moments before Victoria died, the woman cut off her left ear.

9/11

Anna Petrescu touched the button on the top of her bedside clock. It glowed 5:56 a.m. Her mind had been racing all through the night, until finally she had decided exactly what she must do if the chairman was unwilling to go along with her recommendations. She switched off the alarm, jumped out of bed and headed straight for the bathroom, where she stood under a cold shower a little longer than usual, hoping it would fully wake her. Her last lover—heaven knows how long ago that must have been—had thought it amusing that she always showered before going out for her morning run.

Once she had dried herself, Anna slipped on a white T-shirt and blue running shorts. She zipped up her track-suit top, which still displayed a faded 'P' where the bold blue letter had been unstitched. Anna didn't want to advertise the fact that she had once been a member of the University of Pennsylvania track team. After all, that was nine years ago. Last of all, she pulled on her Nike training shoes, then attached her door key to a thin silver chain that hung round her neck.

Anna double-locked her four-room apartment, walked across the landing and pressed the elevator button. She rode down to the ground floor, then stepped into the lobby and smiled at her favourite doorman, who quickly opened the front door so that she didn't have to stop in her tracks.

'Morning, Sam,' she said, as she jogged out of Thornton House onto East 54th Street and headed towards Central Park.

Every weekday she ran the Southern Loop. At the weekends she would tackle the longer six-mile loop, when it didn't matter if she was a few minutes late. It mattered today.

BRYCE FENSTON also rose before six o'clock that morning, as he too had an early appointment. While he showered, he listened to the morning news.

'Another clear, sunny day, with a gentle breeze heading southeast,' announced a chirpy weather girl as Fenston stepped out of the shower. A more serious voice informed him that the Nikkei in Tokyo was up fourteen points and Hong Kong's Hang Seng down one. London's FTSE hadn't yet made up its mind in which direction to go. He considered that Fenston Finance shares were unlikely to move dramatically either way, as only two people were aware of his little coup. Fenston was having breakfast with one of them at seven, and he would fire the other at eight.

By 6.40 a.m., Fenston was dressed. He glanced at his reflection in the mirror; he would like to have been a couple of inches taller and a couple of inches thinner. Nothing that a good tailor and a pair of Cuban shoes with specially designed insoles couldn't rectify. He would also like to have grown his hair again, but not while so many exiles from his country might still recognise him.

Although his father had been a tram conductor in Bucharest, anyone would have assumed that the immaculately dressed man stepping out of his brownstone on East 79th Street had been born into the Upper East Side establishment. Only those who looked closely would have spotted the small diamond in his left ear—an affectation he believed singled him out from his more conservative colleagues.

Fenston settled down in the back of his limousine. 'The office,' he barked before touching a button in the armrest. A smoked grey screen purred up between him and the driver. Fenston picked up a copy of the *New York Times* from the seat beside him. He was poring over the financial pages when his driver swung onto the FDR Drive, and he had reached the obituaries by the time the limousine came to a halt outside the North Tower. No one would be printing the only obituary he was interested in until tomorrow, but, to be fair, no one in America realised she was dead.

'I have an appointment on Wall Street at eight thirty,' Fenston informed his driver as the man opened the back door for him. 'So pick me up at eight fifteen.' The driver nodded as Fenston marched off in the direction of the lobby. Although there were ninety-nine elevators in the building, only one went directly to the restaurant on the 107th floor.

As Fenston stepped out of the elevator a minute later, the maître d' bowed his head slightly and escorted him to a table. Fenston was not surprised to find Karl Leapman waiting for him. Leapman had never once been late in the ten years he had worked for Fenston Finance. Fenston looked down at a man who had proved, time and again, that there was no sewer he wasn't willing to swim in for his master. But then Fenston was the only person to offer Leapman a job after he'd been released from jail. Disbarred lawyers with a prison sentence for fraud don't expect to make partner.

Even before he took his seat, Fenston began speaking. 'Now that we are in possession of the Van Gogh,' he said, 'how do we rid ourselves of Anna Petrescu without her becoming suspicious?'

Leapman opened a file in front of him and smiled.

NOTHING HAD GONE as planned that morning.

Andrews had instructed Cook that he would be taking up Her Ladyship's breakfast tray as soon as the painting had been dispatched. But the security van turned up forty minutes late, with a cheeky young driver who refused to leave until he'd been given coffee and biscuits. Andrews was only relieved that Her Ladyship hadn't stirred before the driver finally departed. He checked the tray and left the kitchen to take breakfast up to his mistress.

Andrews knocked quietly on the bedroom door with his spare hand, before opening it. When he saw Her Ladyship lying on the floor in a pool of blood, he let out a gasp, dropped the tray and rushed over to the body.

Although it was clear Lady Victoria had been dead for several hours, Andrews did not consider contacting the police until the next in line to the Wentworth estate had been informed of the tragedy. He left the bedroom, locked the door and, for the first time in his life, ran downstairs.

ARABELLA WENTWORTH was serving someone when Andrews called. She put the phone down and apologised to her customer, explaining that she had to leave immediately. She switched the OPEN sign to CLOSED, and locked the door of her antiques shop moments after Andrews uttered the word 'emergency'. It was not an opinion she'd heard him express in the past forty-nine years.

Fifteen minutes later, Arabella brought her Mini to a halt on the gravel outside Wentworth Hall, where Andrews was waiting for her.

'I'm so very sorry, milady,' was all he said before leading his new mistress up the wide marble staircase. When Andrews touched the banister to steady himself, Arabella knew her sister was dead.

Although she was violently sick when she first saw her sister's body, Arabella didn't faint. After a second glance, she grabbed the bedpost. Blood was everywhere, congealing on the carpet, the walls and the writing desk. With a Herculean effort, she staggered to the phone on the bedside table, picked up the receiver, and dialled 999. When the phone was answered with the words, 'Emergency, which service?' she replied, 'Police.'

Arabella replaced the receiver. She was determined to reach the bedroom door without looking back at her sister's body. She failed. This time her eyes settled on the letter addressed 'My dearest Arabella'. She grabbed the unfinished missive, unwilling to share her sister's last thoughts with the local constabulary, then stuffed the epistle into her pocket and walked unsteadily out of the room.

ANNA JOGGED WEST, past the Museum of Modern Art, crossing 6th Avenue before taking a right on 7th. She didn't start the stopwatch on her wrist until she had passed through Artisans' Gate and into Central Park. Once she had settled into her rhythm, Anna focused on the meeting scheduled with the chairman for eight o'clock.

She had been surprised and somewhat relieved when Bryce Fenston had offered her a job only days after she'd left her position as the number two in Sotheby's Impressionist Department. Her boss there had made it only too clear that any thought of progress would be blocked after she'd admitted to being responsible for losing the sale of a major collection to their main rival, Christie's. Anna had spent months nurturing one particular customer into selecting Sotheby's for the disposal of their family's estate, and had naively assumed, when she shared the secret with her lover, that he would be discreet. After all, he was a lawyer.

After the name of the client was revealed in the arts section of the *New York Times,* Anna lost both her lover and her job. It didn't help when the paper reported that Dr Anna Petrescu had left Sotheby's 'under a cloud'.

Bryce Fenston was a regular attendee at all the major Impressionist sales, and he couldn't have missed Anna standing by the side of the auctioneer's podium, acting as a spotter. She resented any suggestion that her striking good looks and athletic figure were the reason Sotheby's regularly placed her in so prominent a position, rather than at the side of the room along with the other spotters.

It had been known for some time that Fenston was amassing one of the great Impressionist collections, along with Steve Wynn, Leonard Lauder, and Takashi Nakamura. For such collectors, what often begins as an innocent hobby can quickly become an addiction. For Fenston, who owned an example of all the major Impressionists except Van Gogh, even the thought of possessing a work by the Dutch master was an injection of pure heroin.

When Fenston read in the *New York Times* that Anna was leaving Sotheby's, he immediately offered her a place on his board with a salary that reflected how serious he was about building his collection. What tipped the balance for Anna was the discovery that Fenston also originated from Romania. He continually reminded Anna that, like her, he had escaped the oppressive Ceausescu régime to find refuge in America.

Within days of Anna's joining the bank, Fenston quickly put her expertise to the test. Most of the questions he asked concerned her knowledge of any large collections still in the hands of old-money families. Anna was puzzled by his obsession with other people's collections, until she discovered that it was Fenston's company policy to advance large loans against works of art. Few banks are willing to consider 'art', no matter what form, as collateral. Bankers do not understand the market and are reluctant to reclaim the assets from their customers, not least because storing the works, insuring them, and often ending up having to sell them, is time-consuming and impractical. Fenston Finance was a rare exception.

One of Anna's assignments was to take a trip to England and value the estate of Lady Victoria Wentworth, who had applied for a large loan from Fenston Finance. The Wentworth collection turned out to be a typically English one, built up by the second earl, an eccentric aristocrat with considerable taste. From his own countrymen he acquired Romney, West, Constable, Stubbs and Morland, as well as a magnificent example of a Turner, *Sunset over Plymouth*.

The third earl showed no interest in anything artistic, so the collection gathered dust until his son, the fourth earl, spent nearly a year taking what used to be known as the Grand Tour before returning to Wentworth Hall in possession of a Raphael, Tintoretto, Titian, Rubens, Holbein and Van Dyck. However, it was Charles, the fifth earl, who, for all the wrong reasons, trumped his ancestors. After an energetic weekend in Paris, his latest mistress convinced him to purchase a painting by an unknown artist. Charlie

Wentworth returned to England with a painting he relegated to a guest bedroom, although many aficionados now consider *Self-Portrait with Bandaged Ear* to be among Van Gogh's finest works.

Anna had already warned Fenston to be wary when it came to purchasing a Van Gogh. She told him there were several fakes hanging in private collections and even one or two in major museums. However, after Anna had studied the provenance that accompanied the *Self-Portrait*, she felt confident enough to advise the chairman that the magnificent work was indeed by the hand of the master.

For Van Gogh addicts, *Self-Portrait with Bandaged Ear* was the ultimate high. Although the maestro painted thirty-five self-portraits, he attempted only two after cutting off his left ear. The other one was on display at the Courtauld Institute in London.

Anna spent a pleasant ten days at Wentworth Hall, valuing the family's collection. When she returned to New York, she advised the board that should a sale ever prove necessary, the assets would more than cover the Fenston Finance's loan of $30 million. Although she had no interest in Victoria Wentworth's reasons for needing such a large sum of money, during her stay, Anna had often heard Victoria speak of the sadness of 'dear Papa's' premature death, the retirement of their trusted estates manager and the iniquity of 40 per cent death duties.

Anna's responsibility did not go beyond valuing the collections of potential clients and then submitting written reports for the board's consideration. She never became involved in the drawing up of any contract. That was exclusively in the hands of the bank's in-house lawyer, Karl Leapman. However, Victoria had let slip that Fenston Finance was charging her 16 per cent compound interest. Anna had quickly become aware that a combination of debt, naiveté and a lack of any financial expertise, were the ingredients on which Fenston Finance thrived. This was a bank that seemed to relish its customers' inability to repay their debts.

Anna lengthened her stride as she passed by the carousel. She had decided she would have to resign if the chairman felt unable to accept her recommendation that morning on the Wentworth collection. She had learned to live with Fenston's vanity and even tolerate his occasional outburst, but she could not condone misleading a client, especially one as naive as Victoria Wentworth. Leaving Fenston Finance after less than a year might not look good on her résumé, but an ongoing fraud investigation would look a lot worse.

'WHEN WILL WE FIND out if she's dead?' asked Leapman.

'I'm expecting confirmation this morning,' Fenston replied.

'Good, because I'll need to be in touch with her lawyer to remind him that in the case of a suspicious death'—he paused—'any settlement reverts to the jurisdiction of the New York State Bar.'

'Strange that none of them ever query that clause in the contract,' said Fenston, buttering another muffin.

'Why should they?' asked Leapman, sipping his coffee. 'After all, they have no way of knowing that they're about to die.'

'And is there any reason for the police to be suspicious?'

'No. You've never met Victoria Wentworth, you didn't sign the contract, and you haven't even seen the painting. It could be years before the police are willing to admit they don't have a suspect.'

'A couple of years will be quite enough,' said Fenston. 'By then, the interest on the loan will be more than sufficient to ensure that I can hold on to the Van Gogh, then sell off the rest of the collection without losing my original investment.'

'It's a good thing I read Petrescu's report when I did,' said Leapman, 'because if Lady Wentworth had gone along with Petrescu's recommendation, there would have been nothing we could do.'

'Agreed,' said Fenston, 'but now we have to find a way of losing Petrescu.'

ARABELLA SAT ALONE in the drawing room, unable to take in what was happening all around her. A cup of Earl Grey tea on the table beside her had gone cold. Several police cars and an ambulance were parked on the gravel outside. People in uniforms and white coats came and went.

There was a gentle tap on the door. Arabella looked up to see an old friend standing in the doorway. Chief Superintendent Renton removed a peaked cap covered in silver braid as he entered the room. Arabella rose from the sofa, her eyes red from crying. The tall man kissed her on both cheeks, then waited for her to sit down before he took his place in the leather wing chair opposite her. Renton offered his condolences, which were genuine. He'd known Victoria for many years.

Arabella thanked him and asked quietly, 'Who could have done such a terrible thing, especially to someone as innocent as Victoria?'

'I'm afraid there doesn't appear to be a logical answer to that question,' the chief superintendent replied. 'Do you feel up to answering some questions, my dear?'

Arabella gave a nod. 'I'll do anything I can.'

'Normally, I would ask if your sister had enemies, but I confess that, knowing her as I did, that doesn't seem possible. However, I must ask if you were aware of any problems Victoria might have been facing. There have been rumours in the village that, following your father's death, your sister was left with considerable debts.'

'I don't know,' Arabella admitted. 'After I married Angus, we only came down from Scotland for a couple of weeks in the summer. It wasn't until my husband died that I returned to Surrey and heard the same rumours. Victoria denied there was any problem, but then she adored Father, and in her eyes he could do no wrong.'

'Can you think of anything that might give some clue as to why . . .'

Arabella rose and, without explanation, walked to a writing desk. She picked up the blood-spattered letter that she had found on her sister's table and handed it across to him.

The chief superintendent read the missive. 'Have you any idea what Victoria could have meant by "a solution has been found"?'

'No,' admitted Arabella, 'but it's possible I'll be able to answer that question once I've had a word with Arnold Simpson.'

'That doesn't fill me with confidence,' Renton said.

Arabella noted his comment but didn't respond. She knew his natural instinct was to mistrust all solicitors.

The chief superintendent took her hand. 'Try not to keep too many secrets from me, Arabella, because I'll need to know everything if we're to find who murdered your sister.'

Arabella didn't reply.

'DAMN,' MUTTERED ANNA when an athletic, dark-haired man jogged past, as he'd done several times during the last few weeks. It annoyed her whenever she was overtaken: she had come ninety-seventh in last year's New York Marathon, so she was rarely passed by anything on two legs. The man didn't glance back—serious runners never did. Anna had once caught a sideways glimpse of him, but he then strode away and all she had seen was the back of his emerald-green T-shirt. She tried to put him out of her mind and focus once again on her meeting with Fenston.

Anna had sent a copy of her report to the chairman's office, recommending that Fenston sell the self-portrait as quickly as possible. She knew a collector in Tokyo who was obsessed with Van Gogh and still had the yen to prove it. Takashi Nakamura was chairman of the largest steel company in Japan, an intensely secretive individual who guarded the details of his private collection with typical Japanese inscrutability. He'd let it be known that his collection was to form part of a foundation that would eventually be left to the nation of Japan. The sale of the Van Gogh would also allow Victoria Wentworth to save face—something the Japanese fully understood. Anna had once acquired a Degas for Nakamura, and she was confident he would offer at least $60 million for the rare Dutch masterpiece. So if Fenston accepted her proposal—and why shouldn't he?—everyone would be satisfied with the outcome.

When Anna passed Tavern on the Green, she checked her watch. She would need to pick up her pace if she hoped to be back in less than twelve minutes. She sprinted down the hill, passed through Artisans' Gate, and jogged off in the direction of her apartment, unaware that she was being closely watched by the man in the emerald-green T-shirt.

JACK DELANEY still wasn't sure if Anna Petrescu was a criminal.

The FBI agent watched her disappear into the crowd, then he resumed jogging through Sheep Meadow. He'd been investigating the woman for the past six weeks. The FBI was also investigating her boss—who, Jack had no doubt, *was* a criminal.

It was nearly a year since Richard W. Macy, Jack's supervising special agent, had assigned him and a team of eight agents to investigate three vicious murders on three continents that had one thing in common: each of the victims had been killed at a time when they also had large outstanding loans with Fenston Finance. Jack quickly concluded that the murders were the work of a professional killer.

Jack cut through Shakespeare Garden as he headed to his small West Side apartment. He had just about completed his file on Fenston's most recent recruit, although he couldn't make up his mind if she was a willing accomplice or a naive innocent.

He had begun his research with Anna's upbringing and discovered that her uncle, George Petrescu, had emigrated from Romania in 1972 to settle in Danville, Illinois. In 1974, within weeks of Ceausescu naming himself President of Romania, George had written to his brother, imploring him to join him in America. Several years later, he renewed his invitation and this time, although Anna's parents refused to leave, they allowed their seventeen-year-old daughter to be smuggled out of Bucharest in 1987, promising she could return the moment Ceausescu had been overthrown. Anna never returned. She wrote home regularly, begging her mother to join them in the States, but she rarely received a response. Two years later she learned that her father had been killed in a border skirmish while attempting to oust the dictator. Her mother repeated that she would never leave her native land.

That much one of Jack's squad members had been able to discover from an essay Anna had written for her high school magazine. One of her classmates had also written about the gentle girl with long fair plaits and blue eyes who knew so few English words that she couldn't recite the Pledge of Allegiance. By the end of her second year, Anna was editing the magazine.

From high school, Anna won a scholarship to Williams University to study art history. A local newspaper recorded that she also won the intervarsity mile against Cornell in a time of four minutes forty-eight seconds. After a PhD at the University of Pennsylvania, Dr Petrescu joined Sotheby's as a graduate trainee. Here Jack's information became somewhat sketchy, as he could allow his agents only limited contact with Anna's former colleagues. No one would discuss what 'under a cloud' meant, although Jack couldn't fathom why, despite her dismissal, she considered joining Fenston Finance. For that part of his enquiry, he had to rely on speculation, because he couldn't risk approaching anyone she worked with at the bank. It was clear, though, that Tina Forster, the chairman's secretary, had become a close friend.

In the short time Anna had worked at Fenston Finance, she had visited several new clients who had taken out large loans, all of whom were in possession of major art collections. Jack feared that it could only be a matter of time before one of them suffered the same fate as Fenston's three previous victims.

He ran onto West 86th Street. Three questions still needed answering. How long had Fenston known Petrescu before she joined the bank? Had they known each other in Romania? And was she the hired assassin?

FENSTON SCRAWLED his signature across the breakfast bill, rose, and, without waiting for Leapman to finish his coffee, marched out of the restaurant. He stepped into an open elevator, but waited for Leapman to press the button for the eighty-third floor.

When the elevator opened, Leapman followed his master out, but then turned the other way and headed for Petrescu's office. He opened her door without knocking to find Anna's assistant, Rebecca, preparing the files for her eight o'clock meeting with the chairman. Leapman barked out instructions and Rebecca immediately went in search of a large cardboard box.

Leapman walked back down the corridor and joined the chairman in his office. 'I don't think Petrescu will leave without putting up a fight,' he said. 'After all, she isn't going to find it easy to get another job.'

'She certainly won't if I have anything to do with it,' said Fenston, rubbing his hands.

'But perhaps it might be wise if I—'

A knock on the door interrupted their exchange. Barry Steadman, the bank's head of security, stood in the doorway. 'Sorry to bother you, Chairman, but there's a FedEx courier here, says he has a package for you and no one else can sign for it.'

Fenston waved the courier in and penned his signature in the little oblong box. Leapman looked on until the courier had departed and Barry had closed the door behind him.

'Is that what I think it is?' he asked quietly.

'We're about to find out.' Fenston ripped open the package.

They both stared down at Victoria Wentworth's left ear.

'And she even sent a bonus,' said Fenston, staring at the antique diamond earring. 'See that Krantz is paid the other half million.'

ANNA FINISHED PACKING just after 7 a.m. She left her suitcase in the hall, intending to pick it up on the way to the airport. Her flight to London was scheduled for 5.40 p.m, arriving at Heathrow the following morning. She only hoped Victoria had read her report and would agree that selling the Van Gogh privately was a simple solution to her problems.

Anna hailed a taxi just after 7.20 a.m. She sat in the back of the cab and checked her appearance in her compact mirror, wanting to look her best for her meeting with the chairman. Her suit and silk blouse would surely make heads turn, although some might be puzzled by her black trainers.

The cab took a right on the FDR Drive as Anna checked her cellphone. There were messages she would deal with after the meeting: one from her secretary—Rebecca, needing to speak to her urgently—and a confirmation of her flight from British Airways.

When her cab drew up outside the entrance to the North Tower, she paid the driver and jumped out to join a sea of workers as they filed through the bank of turnstiles. She took the express elevator, stepped out onto the dark green carpet of the executive floor, and went straight to her office.

TINA FORSTER didn't rise until just after 7 a.m. Her appointment with the dentist wasn't until 8.30, and Fenston had made it clear that she needn't be on time this morning. That usually meant he had an out-of-town appointment or was going to fire someone. If it was the latter, he wouldn't want her hanging around the office, sympathising with the person who had just lost their job. Tina lay soaking in the bath—a luxury she usually only allowed herself at weekends—wondering when it would be her turn to be fired.

She'd been Fenston's personal assistant for more than a year, and although she despised the man, she'd still tried to make herself indispensable. Tina knew she couldn't consider resigning until . . .

The phone rang in her bedroom, but she made no attempt to answer it. She assumed it would be Fenston demanding to know where a particular file was, a phone number, even his diary. 'On the desk in front of you' was usually the answer. She wondered for a moment if it might be Anna, the only real friend she'd made since moving from the West Coast. Unlikely, she concluded, as Anna would be presenting her report to the chairman at eight o'clock.

Tina climbed out of the bath and wrapped a towel round herself. She got dressed, then went to the kitchen to make herself a cup of coffee. She flicked on the television to catch the morning news. A story about a suicide bomber on the West Bank was followed by one about a 320-pound woman who was suing McDonald's. She was about to turn off *Good Morning America* when the quarterback for the San Francisco 49ers appeared on the screen.

It made Tina think of her father.

JACK DELANEY arrived at his office at 26 Federal Plaza just after 7 a.m. He felt depressed as he stared down at the files that littered his desk. Every one of them was connected with his investigation of Bryce Fenston, and he was no nearer to presenting his boss with enough evidence to ask a judge to issue an arrest warrant.

Jack opened Fenston's personal file in the vain hope that he might stumble across some tiny clue that would finally link Fenston to the murders in Marseille, Los Angeles and Rio de Janeiro.

In 1984, thirty-two-year-old Nicu Munteanu had presented himself at the American Embassy in Bucharest, claiming he could identify two spies working in Washington in exchange for an American passport. A dozen such claims proved groundless every week, but in Munteanu's case the information stood up. Within a month, two well-placed officials found themselves on a flight back to Moscow, and Nicu Munteanu landed in New York on February 17, 1985.

Jack had been able to find little intelligence on Munteanu the following year, but the man had suddenly re-emerged with enough money to take over Fenston Finance, a small, ailing bank in Manhattan. Munteanu changed his name to Bryce Fenston and began to accept large deposits from unlisted companies across Eastern Europe. Then, in 1989, the same year Ceausescu and his wife fled from Bucharest following an uprising, the cash flow dried up.

Jack looked out of his window and recalled the FBI maxim: never believe in coincidences, but never dismiss them.

Following Ceausescu's death, the bank appeared to go through a couple of lean years until Fenston met up with Karl Leapman, a disbarred lawyer recently released from prison for fraud. It was not too long before Fenston Finance resumed its profitable ways.

Jack stared down at several photographs of Bryce Fenston. He was described as a brilliant banker and a leading financier, with a magnificent art collection. Jack hadn't yet come to terms with a man who wore an earring, and he was even more puzzled why someone would choose to shave himself bald. Who was he hiding from?

Jack turned to Pierre de Rochelle, the first victim.

Pierre de Rochelle required Fr70 million to pay for his share in a vineyard. His only previous experience of the wine industry seemed to have come from draining the bottles on a regular basis. However, what caught Fenston's attention when he perused the application was that the young man had inherited a chateau in the Dordogne, its every wall graced with Impressionist paintings, including a Degas, two Pissarros, and a Monet of Argenteuil.

The vineyard failed to show a return for four fruitless years, during which time the chateau began to render up its assets, leaving only outlines where the pictures had once hung. By the time Fenston had shipped the last painting to New York to join his private collection, Rochelle's original loan had, with accumulated interest, more than doubled. When his chateau was finally placed on the market, Rochelle took up residence in a small flat in Marseille, drinking himself into a stupor until a friend suggested that Fenston Finance sell his Degas, the Monet and the two Pissarros. He could not only pay off his debt but also take the chateau off the market and reclaim the rest of his collection. This suggestion did not fit in with Fenston's long-term plans.

A week later, the drunken body of Pierre de Rochelle was found slumped in a Marseille alley, his throat sliced open. Four years later, the Marseille police closed the file. When the estate was finally settled, Fenston had sold off all the works, with the exception of the Renoir, the Monet and the two Pissarros; Rochelle's younger brother inherited the flat in Marseille.

Jack knew Chris Adams, Jr's, case history by heart. Chris Adams, Sr, had operated a successful art gallery in Los Angeles. He specialised in the American School so admired by the Hollywood glitterati. His death in a car crash left Chris, Jr, with a collection of Rothkos, Pollocks, Johnses and several Warhol acrylics.

An old school friend advised Chris to invest in the dotcom revolution. Chris, Jr, didn't have any ready cash—just the gallery, the paintings, and *Christina*, his father's old yacht, and even that was half owned by his younger sister. Fenston Finance advanced him a loan of $12 million, allowing the debt to continue mounting without ever troubling their client. That was until Chris, Jr, read in the *Los Angeles Times* that Warhol's *Shot Red Marilyn* had sold for more than $4 million. Christie's in LA assured him he could expect an equally good return for his Rothkos, Pollocks and Johnses. Three months later, Leapman rushed into the chairman's office bearing the latest Christie's sale catalogue. He had placed yellow Post-It notes against seven different lots that were due to come under the hammer. Fenston made one phone call, then booked himself on the next flight to Rome.

Three days later, Chris, Jr, was discovered in the lavatory of a bar with his throat cut. Fenston was on holiday in Italy at the time. The paintings were immediately withdrawn from the Christie's sale while the police carried out their investigations. After eighteen months of dead ends, the file joined the other LAPD cold cases. All Chris's sister ended up with was a model of her father's much-loved yacht.

Jack stared down at the file of Maria Vasconcellos, a Brazilian widow who inherited a lawn full of statues—and not of the garden-centre variety. Moore, Giacometti, Remington, Botero, Calder. Unfortunately, she fell in love with a gigolo, and he suggested—

The phone rang on Jack's desk. 'Our London Embassy is on line two,' his secretary informed him.

'Thanks, Sally,' said Jack, knowing it could only be his friend Tom Crasanti, who had joined the FBI on the same day as he had. 'Hi, Tom, how are you?' he asked.

'In good shape,' Tom replied. 'Even if I'm not as fit as you.'

'Got any good news?'

'No. That's why you're going to have to open another file.'

A cold shiver ran through Jack's body. 'Who is it this time?'

'The lady's name, and Lady she was, is Victoria Wentworth.'

'How did she die?' Jack asked quietly.

'In exactly the same manner as the other three, throat cut, almost certainly with a kitchen knife.'

'What makes you think Fenston was involved?'

'She owed the bank more than thirty million.'

'And what was he after this time?'

'A Van Gogh self-portrait. Value: sixty million dollars.'

'I'll be on the next plane to London.'

ANNA REPLACED her trainers with a pair of black high-heeled shoes, gathered up the files on her desk and walked down the corridor towards the corner suite. A knock on the chairman's door—Anna was surprised when it was immediately pulled open and she came face to face with Karl Leapman.

'Good morning, Karl,' she said, but didn't receive a response.

The chairman looked up from behind his desk and motioned Anna to take the seat opposite him. Leapman took his place on the right slightly behind him, like a cardinal in attendance on the Pope. Anna assumed that Tina would appear at any moment, but the secretary's door remained shut.

Anna glanced up at the Monet on the wall behind the chairman's desk. She shifted uneasily in her chair, trying not to appear fazed by the silence, which was suddenly broken, on Fenston's nod.

'Dr Petrescu,' Leapman began, 'some distressing information has been brought to the attention of the chairman. It would appear that you sent one of the bank's private documents to a client before the chairman had the chance to consider its implications.'

For a moment Anna was taken by surprise, but she quickly recovered. 'If, Mr Leapman, you are referring to my report concerning the loan to the Wentworth estate, you are correct. I did send a copy to Lady Victoria.'

'But the chairman was not given enough time to make a considered judgment before you forwarded that report.'

'Mr Leapman, both you and the chairman were sent my report on September 1st.'

'I never received the report,' said Fenston brusquely.

'And indeed,' said Anna, still looking at Leapman, 'the chairman acknowledged receipt. His office returned the attached form.'

'I never saw it,' stated Fenston.

'Which he initialled,' said Anna, who opened her file, extracted the relevant form and placed it on the desk in front of Fenston.

He ignored it. 'You should have waited for my opinion.'

'I waited for a week, Chairman,' Anna replied, 'during which time you made no comment, despite the fact that I will be flying to London this evening to keep an appointment with Lady Victoria tomorrow. I sent you a reminder two days later.' She placed a second sheet of paper on the chairman's desk.

'But I hadn't read your report,' Fenston said, repeating himself.

Anna took a deep breath. 'My report does no more than advise the board that if we were to sell the Van Gogh, either privately or through one of the auction houses, the amount raised would more than cover the bank's original loan plus interest.'

'But I may have come up with a better solution,' said Fenston.

'If that was the case, as colleagues we could have discussed any difference of opinion.'

'That is an impertinent suggestion,' said Fenston.

'I don't consider it is impertinent, Chairman, to abide by the law,' said Anna calmly. 'It's the bank's legal requirement to report any alternative recommendations to their clients—'

'Your first responsibility,' Fenston shouted, 'is to me.'

'Not if I believe an officer of the bank is breaking the law.'

'Are you trying to goad me into firing you?'

'I have a feeling you are trying to goad me into resigning.'

'Either way,' said Fenston, swivelling round in his chair and staring out of the window, 'it is clear you no longer have a role to play in this bank, as you are not a team player—something they warned me about when you were dismissed from Sotheby's.'

Don't rise, thought Anna. She pursed her lips and stared at Fenston's profile. She was about to reply when she noticed there was something different about him, and then she spotted the new earring. Vanity will surely be his downfall, she thought.

'Chairman, I would like to make one thing absolutely clear. Enticing a colleague to swindle a naive woman out of her inheritance is a criminal offence, as I feel sure Mr Leapman, with all his experience, will be happy to explain to you.'

'Get out, before I throw you out,' screamed Fenston, jumping up from his chair. Anna rose slowly and walked towards the door. 'I want you out of your office in ten minutes. If you are still on the premises after that, security will escort you from the building.'

Anna closed the door quietly behind her.

The first person Anna saw as she stepped into the corridor was Barry, who had clearly been tipped off. Anna walked back to her office with as much dignity as she could muster, despite Barry matching her stride for stride. She passed an elevator that was being held open for someone and wondered who. Surely it couldn't be for her. Anna was back in her office half an hour after she'd left it. This time Rebecca was waiting for her, clutching a large brown cardboard box. 'Don't touch anything,' Barry said. 'Your personal belongings have been packed, so let's go.'

'I'm so sorry,' said Rebecca. 'I tried to call you, but—'

'Don't speak to her,' barked Barry, 'she's outta here.'

Anna smiled. 'It's not your fault,' she said, as her secretary handed her the box. Anna removed her high heels, placed them in the box, pulled on her trainers and headed back into the corridor.

The head of security accompanied his charge on the long walk to the elevator. Then he pressed the down arrow.

They were both waiting for the elevator doors to open when American Airlines Flight 11 out of Boston crashed into the ninety-fourth floor of the North Tower.

RUTH PARISH LOOKED up at the departures monitor on the wall above her desk in an office near Heathrow Airport. She was relieved to see that United's Flight 107 bound for JFK had finally taken off at 1.40 p.m., forty minutes behind schedule.

Ruth had founded Art Locations nearly a decade before. Moving great, and not so great, works of art from one area of the globe to the other allowed her to combine a natural flair for organisation with a love of beautiful objects. She dealt with gallery owners, dealers and private collectors. Over the years, many of her customers had become personal friends. But not Bryce Fenston. Ruth had long ago concluded that the words 'please' and 'thank you' were not in this man's vocabulary. Fenston's latest demand had been to collect a Van Gogh from Wentworth Hall and transport it, without delay, to his office in New York.

When a Mr Andrews, the butler at Wentworth Hall, had rung the previous day to say that the painting would be ready for collection in the morning, Ruth had scheduled one of her high-security air-ride trucks to be at the hall by eight o'clock. Once the painting was unloaded, Ruth supervised every aspect of its packing and safe dispatch to New York. She stood over her senior packer as he wrapped the painting in acid-free glassine paper and placed it into the foam-lined case, then tightened the captive bolts and stencilled FRAGILE on both sides and the number '47' in all four corners. The customs officer checked the shipping papers and export licence. Ruth drove across to the waiting 747 and watched as the red case disappeared into the vast hold. She didn't return to her office until the heavy door was secured in place. She checked her watch and smiled. The plane had taken off at 1.40 p.m.

Putting a call through to Fenston Finance to inform them that the Van Gogh was on its way, she dialled Anna's number in New York and waited for her to pick up the phone.

THERE WAS a loud explosion and the building began to sway. Anna was hurled across the corridor, as if she'd been floored by a heavyweight boxer. She lay on the ground, dazed.

An eerie silence followed, soon replaced by screams of 'Oh my God!' as huge shards of glass, twisted metal and office furniture flew past windows.

It must be another bomb, Anna thought. Everyone who had been in the building in 1993 told stories of what had happened then. Anna remembered the instructions on the stairwell door: 'In case of emergency, do not return to your desk, do not use the elevator, exit by the nearest stairwell.' But first she needed to find out if she could stand up, aware that part of the ceiling had collapsed on her and the building was still swaying. She pushed herself up, and although she was bruised and cut, nothing seemed to be broken.

Anna abandoned what was left of the cardboard box and stumbled towards stairwell C in the centre of the building. Some of her colleagues were also beginning to recover from the shock.

'What are we supposed to do?' asked a cleaner.

'Do we wait to be rescued?' asked a bond dealer.

These were all questions for the security officer, but Barry was nowhere to be seen.

Once Anna reached the stairwell, she joined a group of dazed people, some silent, some crying. No one seemed to have the slightest idea what had caused the explosion. Some were trying to contact the outside world on their cellphones. One who did get through began to relay the conversation he was having with his wife: 'A plane has hit the North Tower,' he announced to them all.

'But where, where?' shouted several voices at once. 'Above us, somewhere in the nineties,' he said.

'But what are we meant to do?' asked the chief accountant.

The younger man repeated the question to his wife. 'The mayor is advising everyone to get out as quickly as possible.'

On hearing this news, all those in the stairwell began their descent. Anna looked back through the glass window and was surprised to see how many people had remained at their desks. She began to count the steps—eighteen to each flight, which meant at least another fifteen hundred before she would reach the lobby. The stairwell became more and more crowded as countless people swarmed out of their offices on each floor. Anna was surprised by how calm the descending queue was.

She heard the first order when she reached the sixty-eighth floor. 'Get to the right, and keep moving,' said an authoritative voice somewhere below her. It was several more floors before she spotted the first fireman heading slowly towards her. He was wearing a baggy fireproof suit and sweating profusely under his helmet, overloaded with coiled ropes and oxygen tanks. Another fireman followed, carrying a vast length of hose, six poleaxes and a large bottle of drinking water. He was sweating so much that from time to time he removed his helmet and poured some water over his head.

Those who continued to leave their offices were mostly silent. Whenever she reached a new landing, Anna stared through the panes of glass at workers who remained at their desks. She even overheard snatches of conversation through the open doors. One of them, a broker on the sixty-second floor, was trying to close a deal before the markets opened at nine o'clock.

More and more firemen were now climbing towards her. Their constant cry: 'Get to the right, keep moving.' The building had stopped swaying. On, on, on Anna went, floor after floor, until even she began to feel tired.

She thought about Rebecca and Tina, and prayed they were both safe. She even began to feel confident that she would eventually wake up from this nightmare, until she heard a voice scream.

'A second plane has hit the South Tower.'

JACK WAS APPALLED by his first reaction when he heard what sounded like a bomb and Sally rushed in to tell him a plane had crashed into the North Tower of the World Trade Center.

'Let's hope it scored a hit on Fenston's office,' he said.

His second thoughts were more professional when he joined Dick Macy, the supervising special agent, along with the rest of the senior agents in the command centre. While others hit the phones in an attempt to make sense of what was happening, Jack told the SSA he was in no doubt that it was an act of terrorism. When a second plane crashed into the South Tower at 9.03 a.m., Macy said, 'Yes, but *which* terrorist organisation?'

Jack's third reaction was delayed, and it took him by surprise. He hoped that Anna Petrescu had managed to escape, but when the South Tower came crashing down fifty-six minutes later, he assumed it would not be long before the North Tower followed suit.

He returned to his computer. Information was flooding in. Jack took a call from one of his agents on the ground. Joe Corrigan reported that Fenston and Leapman had been seen entering a building on Wall Street just before the first plane crash.

'And Petrescu?' Jack asked.

'No idea,' Joe replied. 'She was seen entering the building at seven forty-six and hasn't been seen since.'

'A SECOND PLANE has hit the South Tower,' a lady on the step above Anna repeated.

'It's no accident,' said a voice from behind. 'Air space above the city is a no-fly zone, so it must have been planned.'

Within minutes, conspiracy theories, terrorist attacks and stories of freak accidents were being bandied about. People were masking their worst fears by all talking at once. 'Keep to the right, and keep moving,' was the constant cry from whatever uniform trudged past.

It was somewhere in the lower forties that Anna first smelt smoke. When she reached the next landing, the smoke became denser and quickly filled her lungs. She covered her eyes and began coughing uncontrollably. Those ahead of her slowed to a crawl. The coughing turned into an epidemic. Had they all been trapped?

'Keep moving,' came the order from a fireman heading towards them. 'It gets worse but then you'll be through it.' Anna continued coughing for another three floors, but the smoke was already beginning to disperse.

By the time Anna reached the twenty-fourth floor, several bedraggled stragglers were stopping to take a rest, while others were still refusing to leave their offices, unable to believe that a problem on the ninety-fourth floor could possibly affect them. Anna looked around, hoping to see a familiar face.

'We've got a level three up here,' a battalion commander was saying over his radio, 'so I'm sweeping every floor.' But each floor was the size of a football field.

When Anna reached the twentieth floor, she had to wade through water pouring in from sprinklers and leaking pipes. She stepped over fragments of glass and flaming debris. When she finally reached the teens, her progress became dramatically faster. All the floors below her had been cleared. But by the seventh floor, the water and flotsam were holding her up. She was picking her way through when she heard the sound of a megaphone. 'Keep moving, don't use your cellphones—it slows up those behind you.'

Three more floors had to be negotiated before she found herself in the lobby, paddling through inches of water. More sprinklers jetted from the ceiling, but Anna was already drenched to the skin.

The megaphones were becoming louder by the moment. 'Keep moving, get out of the building, get as far away as you can.' When she reached the turnstiles she found them battered and twisted by wave after wave of firemen transporting their heavy equipment.

Anna joined the tired horde stepping onto an overcrowded escalator. She allowed it to carry her down to the concourse before taking another escalator up to the open promenade. Another voice bellowed, 'Lady, keep movin'.'

'Where to?' she asked desperately.

'Just keep goin'. As far away as possible.'

When she came across fire trucks and ambulances tending to the walking wounded, Anna began jogging for the first time. Her jog turned into a run and then she heard an unfamiliar noise behind her. It sounded like a clap of thunder that seemed to grow louder and louder. She didn't want to look back, but she did.

Anna stood transfixed as she watched the South Tower collapse in front of her eyes, as if it had been constructed of bamboo. In a matter of seconds, the crash threw up dust and debris that mushroomed into dense flames and fumes that advanced through the crowded streets, engulfing everyone.

Anna ran as she had never run before. She wasn't in any doubt she was about to die. She only hoped it would be quick.

FROM THE SAFETY of an office on Wall Street, Fenston watched in disbelief as a second plane flew into the South Tower.

He and Leapman had arrived late for their meeting, just as the first plane crashed. Fenston spent the next hour on a public telephone in the corridor trying to contact someone, anyone, in his office. Leapman was carrying out the same exercise on his cellphone.

When Fenston heard another volcanic eruption, he left the phone and rushed to the window. Leapman joined him. They both stood in silence as they watched the South Tower collapse.

'It can't be long before the North Tower goes,' said Fenston.

'Then I think we can assume Petrescu will not survive.'

'I don't give a damn about Petrescu. If the North Tower goes, then I've lost my Monet, and it isn't insured.'

ANNA BEGAN RUNNING flat out, aware that everything around her was becoming quieter. One by one the screams were dying out, and she knew she had to be next. For the first time in her life Anna understood what it must be like to be pursued by an avalanche at a speed ten times faster than any human could achieve. She lifted her white silk blouse—now black and sodden—over her mouth just moments before she was overtaken by the all-enveloping grey cloud.

A whoosh of air hurled her forward and threw her to the ground, but she still tried desperately to keep moving. She hadn't managed more than a few feet before she began choking uncontrollably. She pushed forward and somehow managed a few more inches. She was about to stop breathing when she touched something warm. Was it alive? 'Help,' she murmured, expecting no response.

'Give me your hand.' His grip was firm. 'Try to stand.'

With his help, Anna somehow pushed herself up. 'Can you see that triangle of light over there?' the voice said, but Anna turned a circle and stared into 360 degrees of black night. Suddenly she let out a muffled yelp of joy when she spotted a ray of sunlight trying to break through the gloom. She took the stranger's hand and they began inching towards a light that grew brighter with every step, until she walked out of hell and back into New York.

Anna turned to the grey ash-coated figure who had saved her life. 'Keep heading towards the light,' he said, and disappeared back into the murky cloud before she could thank him.

FENSTON GAVE UP trying to contact his office only when he saw the North Tower collapse before his eyes. He rushed down the corridor to find

Leapman scrawling SOLD on a 'For Rent' board attached to the door of an empty office.

'Tomorrow there will be ten thousand people after this space,' he explained, 'so at least that's one problem solved.'

'You may be able to replace an office, but what you can't replace is my Monet,' Fenston said ungraciously. He paused. 'And if I don't get my hands on the Van Gogh . . .'

'It should be halfway across the Atlantic by now,' Leapman said.

'Let's hope so, because we no longer have any documentation to prove we even own the painting,' said Fenston, as he stared out of the window at a grey cloud that hung above the ground where the Twin Towers had once proudly stood.

COMING OUT of such darkness, Anna couldn't bear to look up at the glaring sun; even opening her dust-covered eyelids demanded effort. Coughing up dirt and dust with every step, she wondered how much more black liquid could possibly be left in her body.

When she reached the next intersection, she collapsed on the sidewalk and stared up at a street sign—she was on the corner of Franklin and Church. I'm only a few blocks from Tina's apartment, she thought. But as Tina was still somewhere behind her, how could she possibly have survived? Without warning, a bus came to a halt by her side. She clambered on. It stopped on the corner of every block, with no suggestion of anyone paying a fare.

Anna sat on the bus and buried her head in her hands. For the first time she thought about the firemen who had passed her on the stairwell, and of Tina and Rebecca, who must be dead.

When the bus came to a halt near Washington Square Park, Anna almost fell off. Her throat dry, her feet blistered and aching, she stumbled slowly up Waverly Place, trying to remember the number of Tina's apartment. Pausing outside number 273, she grabbed at the familiar wrought-iron balustrade and yanked herself up the steps. She ran her finger down the names by the buzzers: Amato, Kravits, O'Rourke, Forster . . . Forster, Forster, she repeated joyfully, before pressing the little bell. But how could Tina answer her call, when she must be dead? Anna left her finger on the buzzer as if it would bring Tina to life, but it didn't. She finally turned to leave, tears streaming down her dust-caked face, when out of nowhere a voice demanded, 'Who is it?'

Anna collapsed onto the top step. 'Oh, thank God,' she cried, 'you're alive, you're alive.'

'But you can't be,' said a disbelieving voice.

'Open the door,' pleaded Anna, 'and you can see for yourself.'

The click of the entry button was the best sound Anna had heard that day.

'YOU'RE alive,' repeated Tina, as she flung open the door and threw her arms round her friend. 'I was thinking about how you could always make me laugh, and wondering if I'd ever laugh again, when the buzzer sounded.'

'And I was convinced you couldn't have survived.'

'If I had champagne, we could celebrate,' said Tina.

'I'll settle for a coffee, then another coffee, followed by a bath.'

'I do have coffee,' said Tina, who led Anna through to the small kitchen. Anna left a set of grey footprints on the carpet behind her.

Anna sat down at a small wooden table while a soundless television was showing images of the news story. She tried to stay still, aware that anything she touched was immediately smeared with ash and dirt. 'This may sound strange,' she said, 'but I haven't a clue what's going on.'

Tina turned up the sound on the TV. 'Fifteen minutes of that,' she said as she filled the coffeepot, 'and you'll know everything.'

Anna watched the endless replays of the collapse of first the South and then the North Tower.

'And another plane hit the Pentagon?' she asked.

'There was a fourth,' said Tina, as she placed two mugs on the table, 'but no one seems certain where it was heading.'

'Who's responsible for all this?'

Tina filled her mug with black coffee. 'CNN is pointing a finger at Afghanistan and a terrorist group called Al-Qaeda, but I'm not sure as I've never heard of them.' She sat down opposite Anna.

'I thought they were a bunch of religious fanatics interested in taking over Saudi Arabia.' Anna glanced back up at the television. When the South Tower collapsed, she started coughing and shaking ash onto everything.

'Are you OK?' asked Tina, jumping up from her chair.

'Yes, I'll be fine,' said Anna, draining her coffee. 'Would you mind if I turned the TV off? I don't think I can face continually being reminded what it was like to be there.'

'Of course not,' said Tina, who picked up the remote and touched the OFF button. The images melted from the screen.

'I can't stop thinking about all our friends in the building,' said Anna, as Tina refilled her mug. 'I wonder if Rebecca . . .'

'No word from her. Barry is the only person who's reported in.'

'I can believe Barry was the first down the stairs. But who did he call?'

'Fenston. On his mobile.'

'Fenston? How did he manage to escape when I left his office only minutes before the plane hit the building?'

'He'd arrived on Wall Street by then—he and Leapman had an appointment with a potential client.'

'So that's why the elevator door was being held open.'

'The elevator door?' repeated Tina.

'It's not important,' said Anna. 'But why weren't you at work this morning?'

'I had a dental appointment,' said Tina. 'It had been on my calendar for weeks.' She paused. 'The moment I heard the news I never stopped trying to call you on your cellphone, but all I got was a ringing tone. Where were you?'

'Being escorted off the premises. Fenston had just fired me.'

'Fired you?' said Tina in disbelief. 'Why would he fire you?'

'Because in my report to the board, I recommended that Victoria Wentworth should sell the Van Gogh, which would allow her to clear her overdraft and hold on to the rest of the estate.'

'But the Van Gogh was the only reason Fenston ever agreed to that deal,' said Tina. 'I thought you realised that—'

'I also sent a copy of my recommendations to the client, which I considered to be no more than ethical banking practice. And I was just about to fly to England and let Victoria know that I'd even lined up a prospective buyer, a well-known Japanese collector named Takashi Nakamura. Fenston can't make Victoria hand over the Van Gogh unless—'

'I wouldn't be so sure about that,' said Tina. 'Fenston put a call through to Ruth Parish yesterday and ordered her to pick up the painting immediately. I heard him repeat the word "immediately".'

'Before Victoria had a chance to act on my recommendations.'

'Which would explain why he had to fire you before you could get on that plane and upset his plans.'

Anna thumped the table in anger, sending up a small cloud of dust. 'I'm so dumb,' she said. 'I should have seen it coming, and now there's nothing I can do about it.'

'We don't know for certain that Ruth Parish has picked up the painting from Wentworth Hall,' said Tina. 'If she hasn't, you'll still have enough time to call Victoria and advise her to hold onto the picture until you've had a chance to get in touch with Mr Nakamura,' added Tina as her cellphone began ringing. She checked its caller ID. 'It's Fenston,' she warned, flipping open the phone.

'Do you realise who got left behind in the rubble?' Fenston asked before Tina could speak.

'Anna?'

'No,' said Fenston. 'Petrescu is dead.'

'Dead?' Tina stared across the table at her friend.

'Barry confirmed that the last time he saw her she was lying on the floor, so she can't possibly have survived. I already had plans to replace her, but I can't replace my Monet.'

'But—does that also mean we've lost the Van Gogh?'

'No,' said Fenston. 'It should arrive at JFK this evening. Leapman is going to pick it up. I've taken over offices at 40 Wall Street, so tomorrow it will be business as usual.' The line went dead.

'He thinks you're dead,' said Tina, as she snapped her cellphone shut. 'But he's more fussed about losing his Monet.'

'He'll find out soon enough that I'm not,' said Anna.

'Only if you want him to,' said Tina. 'Has anyone else seen you since you got out of the tower?'

'Only looking like this,' said Anna.

'Then let's keep it that way, while we work out what needs to be done. Fenston says the Van Gogh is already on its way to New York and Leapman will pick it up as soon as it lands.'

'Then what can we do?'

'I could try to delay Leapman somehow while you pick up the painting. You could get on the first plane back to London and return the picture to Wentworth Hall.'

'I couldn't do that without Victoria's permission.'

'Good God, Anna, when will you grow up? You've got to start imagining what Fenston would do in your position.'

'He'd find out what time the plane was landing,' said Anna. 'So the first thing I need to do—'

'The first thing you need to do is have a shower, while I find out what time the plane lands and also what Leapman's up to,' said Tina, standing.

Anna drained her coffee and followed Tina into the corridor. Tina opened

the bathroom door and looked closely at her friend. 'See you in about'—
she hesitated—'an hour.'

Anna laughed for the first time that day.

ANNA SLOWLY PEELED off her clothes and dropped them in a heap on the
floor. She removed the silver chain that held her apartment key from round
her neck and placed it on the side of the bath, next to the model of a yacht.
She finally took off her watch. It had stopped at eight forty-six. A few seconds later and she would have been in the elevator.

As Anna stepped into the shower, she watched the water turn from black
to grey, and however hard she scrubbed, the water remained grey. She didn't
emerge until she'd washed her hair three times, but it was going to be days
before anyone realised that she was a natural blonde. Anna didn't bother to
dry herself; she bent down, put the plug in the bath, and turned on the taps.

As she lay soaking, her mind revisited all that had taken place. Eventually,
she stood up, reached for a towel and began to dry herself. Her thoughts were
interrupted by Tina knocking on the door. She walked in and sat on the end of
the bath. 'Change of plan,' she said. 'All aircraft across America have been
grounded until further notice and no incoming flights will be allowed to land,
so by now the Van Gogh will be on its way back to Heathrow.'

Wrapping the towel tightly round herself, Anna stepped out of the bath.
'Then I'll need to call Victoria immediately and tell her to instruct Ruth
Parish to return the painting to Wentworth Hall.'

'Agreed,' said Tina, 'but I've just realised that Fenston has lost something
even more important than the Monet—his contract with Victoria and all the
other paperwork that proves he owns the Van Gogh, along with the rest of
the estate if she fails to clear the debt.'

'But Victoria will be in possession of all the documents.'

'Not if she was willing to destroy them.'

'Victoria would never agree to that,' said Anna.

'Why don't you phone her and find out? If she did feel able to, it would
give you more than enough time to sell the Van Gogh and clear the debt.'

'I don't have her number. Her file is in my office, and I've lost my cellphone and Palm Pilot, even my wallet.'

'I'm sure international directories can solve that problem,' suggested
Tina. 'Why don't you put on a bathrobe? We can sort out some clothes
later.' She turned to leave.

'Tina, can I ask you something?'

'Anything.'

'Why do you continue to work for Fenston, when you obviously detest the man as much as I do?'

Tina hesitated. 'Anything but that,' she eventually replied.

As ANNA PULLED on her friend's bathrobe, she began to speculate on what possible reason Tina could have to go on working for Fenston. After all, Tina was bright enough to pick up a far better job.

She slid her feet into some slippers, placed the key on its chain back round her neck, and put on her one-time watch. Then she opened the bathroom door and walked down the corridor into the kitchen.

Tina handed over her cellphone. 'Time to call Victoria and warn her what you're up to.'

'What am I up to?' asked Anna.

'For starters, ask her if she knows where the Van Gogh is.'

'Locked up in a customs-free zone at Heathrow would be my bet, but there's only one way to find out.' Anna dialled 00.

'International operator.'

'I need a residential number in Surrey, England,' said Anna.

'Name?'

'Wentworth, Victoria.'

There was a long silence before Anna was informed, 'I'm sorry, ma'am, that number is ex-directory. I can't give it out.'

'But this is an emergency,' insisted Anna.

'I'm sorry, ma'am, but I still can't release that number.' The line went dead.

'So what's plan B?' asked Tina.

'No choice but to get myself to England somehow and try to see Victoria so I can warn her what Fenston's up to.'

'Good. Then the next thing to decide is which border you're going to cross.'

Anna frowned. 'What chance have I got of crossing any border, when I can't even go back to my apartment to pick up my things—unless I want the whole world to know I'm alive and kicking?'

'There's nothing to stop me going to your place,' said Tina. 'Tell me what you want and I can pack a bag and—'

'No need to pack,' said Anna. 'Everything I want is ready and waiting in the hallway—don't forget I was expecting to fly to London this evening.'

'Then all I need is the key to your apartment,' said Tina.

Anna unclasped the chain and handed over the key.

'How do I get past the doorman?' asked Tina. 'He's bound to ask who I've come to see.'

'That won't be a problem,' said Anna. 'His name is Sam. Tell him you're visiting David Sullivan and he'll just smile and call for the elevator. Sullivan's got an apartment on the fourth floor and rarely entertains the same girl twice.'

'But that doesn't solve the cash problem. You lost your wallet and credit card, and all I have is about seventy dollars.'

'I took three thousand out of my account yesterday. I've also got five hundred in a drawer beside my bed.'

'And you'll need to take my watch,' said Tina.

Anna took off her broken watch and replaced it with Tina's.

TINA WALKED nervously to the Thornton House entrance, her opening line well prepared. The script changed the moment she saw Sam seated behind the counter, head in hands, sobbing.

'What's the matter?' Tina asked. 'Did you know someone in the World Trade Center?'

Sam looked up. On the desk in front of him was a photo of Anna running in the marathon. 'She hasn't come home,' he said. 'All my others who worked at the WTC returned hours ago.'

Tina put her arms round the old man. How much she wanted to tell him Anna was alive and well. But not today.

ANNA FOUND a couple of maps on a bookshelf in the front room: a copy of *Streetwise Manhattan* and *The Columbia Gazetteer of North America*. She returned to the kitchen and laid the map of New York out on the table.

Once she'd decided on a route out of Manhattan, Anna folded the map and turned her attention to the larger volume. She hoped that it would help her make up her mind which border to cross.

Anna looked up Mexico and Canada in the index, and then began making copious notes. When she finally closed the cover on the thick, blue book, she wasn't in any doubt in which direction she had to go if she hoped to reach England in time.

She was writing detailed notes of everything that needed to be done before she left in the morning when the front door burst open and Tina staggered in—a laptop over one shoulder, dragging a bulky case behind her. Anna ran out to welcome her back.

'Sorry to have taken so long, honey,' Tina said, as she dumped the luggage in the corridor and walked into the kitchen. 'Not many buses going in my direction.' She collapsed into a kitchen chair.

'My turn to make you coffee,' Anna suggested, filling the pot. 'Any trouble at the apartment?'

'Only having to comfort Sam, who obviously adores you. He looked as if he'd been crying for hours. All he wanted to do was talk about you, he didn't seem to care where I was going.' Tina looked at the map books on the table. 'So have you come up with a plan?'

'Yes,' said Anna. 'My best bet will be the ferry to New Jersey and then to rent a car, because according to the news all the tunnels and bridges are closed. But I can't see why I shouldn't make Toronto airport by tomorrow night, in which case I could be in London the following morning.'

'Do you know what time the first ferry sails in the morning?'

'Five o'clock. But who knows if they'll be running at all.'

'I suggest you have an early night. I'll set my alarm for four. You'd better have the bedroom. I'll sleep on the couch.'

'No way,' said Anna, as she poured her friend a fresh mug of coffee. 'You've done more than enough already. If Fenston ever found out what you were up to, he'd fire you on the spot.'

'That would be the least of my problems,' Tina responded.

JACK YAWNED involuntarily. It had been a long day, and he had a feeling that it was going to be an even longer night.

No one on his team had gone home, and they were all beginning to look, and sound, exhausted. The phone on his desk rang.

'Just thought I ought to let you know, boss,' said Joe, 'that Tina Forster, Fenston's secretary, turned up at Thornton House. She took a suitcase and a laptop back to her place.'

Jack sat bolt upright.

'Then Petrescu must be alive,' he said.

'Although she obviously doesn't want us to think so,' said Joe.

'But why?'

'Perhaps she wants us to believe she's missing, presumed dead?' suggested Joe.

'Not us,' said Jack. 'Fenston, would be my bet.'

'Why?'

'I have no idea,' said Jack, 'but I have every intention of finding out. Put an OPS team on Forster's apartment until Petrescu leaves the building.'

'But we don't even know if she's in there,' said Joe.

'She's in there,' said Jack, and put the phone down.

9/12–9/13

During the night, Anna managed to catch only a few minutes of sleep as she considered her future. She was beginning to feel that her best hope was to prove what Fenston was really up to, and she couldn't do that without Victoria's full cooperation, which might include destroying all the relevant documentation, even her report.

Tina knocked on the door just after four. Over breakfast Anna went over her plan with Tina. They decided on some ground rules they should follow. Anna agreed to call Tina only on her home number and always from a public phone booth—never the same one twice. Anna would announce herself as 'Vincent', and the call would never last for more than one minute.

Anna left the apartment at 4.52 a.m., dressed in jeans, a blue T-shirt, a linen jacket and a baseball cap. Few people were out on the streets, and those who were had their heads bowed. No one gave Anna a second glance as she strode along the sidewalk pulling her suitcase, her laptop bag slung over her shoulder. She passed a queue of people who were already waiting to give blood in the hope that more survivors would be found. She was a survivor, but she didn't want to be found.

FENSTON WAS SEATED behind his desk in his new office by seven o'clock that morning. The first call he made was to Ruth Parish. 'Where's my Van Gogh?' he demanded, without bothering to announce who it was.

'Good morning, Mr Fenston,' said Ruth. 'As you know, the aircraft was turned back, following yesterday's tragedy.'

'So where's my Van Gogh?' repeated Fenston.

'Safely locked up in one of our secure vaults in the restricted customs area. Of course, we will have to renew the export licence.'

'Do it today,' said Fenston.

'This morning I had planned to move four Vermeers from—'

'Your first priority is to my painting.'

'But the paperwork might take a few days,' said Ruth. 'I'm sure you appreciate that there's a backlog following—'

'Forget any backlog. The moment the FAA lift their restrictions, I'm sending Karl Leapman to pick up the painting.'

'But my staff are working to clear the extra work caused by—'

'I'll only say this once,' said Fenston. 'If the painting is ready for loading by the time Leapman's plane touches down at Heathrow, I will triple—I repeat, triple—your fee.'

Fenston put the phone down, confident that the only word she'd remember would be 'triple'. He was wrong. Ruth was puzzled that he hadn't made any reference to Anna. Had she survived, and if so, why wasn't she picking up the painting?

Tina had overheard every word of Fenston's conversation with Ruth Parish on the extension in her office. Tina flicked off the phone switch, but left on the screen that was fixed to the corner of her desk. This allowed her to watch everybody who came in contact with the chairman, something that Fenston wasn't aware of, but then he hadn't asked. Fenston would never have considered entering her office when the press of a button would summon her, and if Leapman walked into the room—without knocking, as was his habit—she would quickly flick the screen off.

When Leapman took over the lease, he'd shown no interest in the secretary's office. Tina had said nothing about her technological extras, aware that in time someone was bound to find out, but perhaps by then she would have gathered all the information she needed to ensure that Fenston would suffer an even worse fate than he had inflicted on her.

Fenston pressed the button on the side of his desk and Tina grabbed a notepad and pencil and made her way to his office.

'The first thing I need you to do,' Fenston began, 'is find out how many staff I still have. Make sure they know where we are relocated, so they can report for work without delay.'

'I'll have those names on your desk by midday,' Tina said.

She spent the morning trying to contact the forty-three employees who worked in the North Tower. Tina was able to account for thirty-four of them by twelve o'clock. She placed a provisional list of nine still missing, presumed dead, on Fenston's desk before he went to lunch.

Anna Petrescu was the sixth name on that list.

ANNA FINALLY MADE IT to Pier 11, by cab, bus, foot, and then cab again, only to find a long queue of people waiting patiently to board the ferry to New Jersey. The police were checking the IDs of everyone leaving Manhattan. It was almost one o'clock before Anna reached the front of the queue.

'Why are you going to New Jersey?' enquired one of the police officers.

'A friend of mine in the North Tower is still missing.' Anna paused. 'I thought I'd spend the day with her parents.'

'I'm sorry, ma'am,' said the policeman. 'I hope they find her.'

'Thank you,' said Anna, and carried her bags up the gangway.

'THE FIRST FLIGHTS out of JFK won't be taking off for another couple of days,' said Tina.

'Does that include private aircraft?' asked Fenston.

'There are no exceptions,' Tina assured him. 'I'm trying to get you on what the press are describing as the priority list.'

'Do we have any friends at JFK?' asked Fenston.

'Several,' said Leapman, 'but they've all suddenly acquired a whole lot of rich relations.'

'Try and turn one of our friends into a relation,' said Fenston. 'Someone will want something,' he added. 'They always do.'

'I'LL TAKE ANY car you've got,' said Anna.

'I have nothing available at the moment,' said the weary-looking young man behind the Happy Hire Company desk, whose plastic badge displayed the name HANK. Anna couldn't mask her disappointment.

'I don't suppose you'd consider a van?' Hank ventured. 'It's not exactly the latest model, but if you're desperate . . .'

'I'll take it,' said Anna, well aware of the long queue of customers behind her. Hank placed a form in triplicate on the counter and Anna pushed across her driver's licence, which she had packed along with her passport. 'How long do you require the vehicle?' Hank asked.

'A day, possibly two—I'll drop it off at the Toronto airport.'

Hank swivelled the form around for her signature. 'That'll be sixty dollars and a two-hundred-dollar deposit.'

Anna frowned and handed over $260.

'And I'll also need your credit card.'

Anna slipped another hundred-dollar bill across the counter. The first time she'd ever attempted to bribe someone.

Hank pocketed the money. 'It's the white van in bay thirty-eight,' he told her, handing over a key.

When Anna located bay thirty-eight, she could see why the little two-seater white van was the last vehicle on offer. She placed her case and laptop inside, then checked the dashboard. The mileometer read 98,617. It was clearly coming to the end of its rental life, and another 400 miles to the border might well finish it off.

Anna started the engine, tentatively reversed out of the parking lot, and began to look for signs to the Jersey Turnpike.

'YOU WERE RIGHT, boss,' said Joe, 'Petrescu has left and is headed for Toronto airport.'

'Car or train?' Jack asked.

'Van,' replied Joe. 'I've already fixed a GPS on her rear bumper, so we'll be able to track her night and day.'

'And be sure you have an agent waiting at the airport.'

'He's to let me know where she intends to fly.'

'She'll be flying to London,' said Jack.

'WHAT'S THE LATEST from JFK?' Fenston asked that afternoon.

'They're allowing a few flights out tomorrow,' said Leapman. 'Visiting diplomats, hospital emergencies. But I've managed to secure us a slot for Friday morning. Someone wanted a new Ford Mustang.'

'I would have agreed to a Cadillac.'

ANNA HAD REACHED the outskirts of Scranton by 3.30 p.m., but decided to press on for a couple more hours. She would try to make Buffalo by seven o'clock, then perhaps take a break.

She checked her rearview mirror, suddenly aware of what it must feel like to be a criminal on the run. You couldn't use a credit card or a cellphone, and you looked over your shoulder every few minutes. Anna longed to be back in New York, among her friends, doing the job she loved. She wasn't very good at thinking like a criminal.

LEAPMAN WALKED into Tina's office unannounced. She quickly flicked off the screen on the side of her desk. 'Wasn't Anna Petrescu a friend of yours?' Leapman asked without explanation.

'Yes, she is,' said Tina, looking up from her desk.

'Is?' said Leapman.

'Was,' said Tina, quickly correcting herself.

'So you haven't heard from her?'

'If I had, I wouldn't have left her name on the missing list.'

'Wouldn't you?' said Leapman.

'No, I wouldn't,' said Tina, looking directly at him. 'So perhaps you'll let me know if she gets in touch with you.'

Leapman frowned and left the room.

ALTHOUGH SHE'D DRUNK nothing but coffee since breakfast, it wasn't long before Anna began to feel sleepy. FEEL TIRED? TAKE A BREAK, advised a sign on the side of the highway, which only caused her to yawn. Ahead of her, she spotted a rest stop. Anna glanced at the clock on the dashboard—just after 11 p.m. She decided to catch a couple of hours' rest before tackling the rest of the journey. After all, she could always sleep on the plane.

Anna drove across the rest stop to the farthest corner and parked behind a large twelve-wheeler truck. She made sure all the doors of the van were locked before climbing into the back, using her laptop bag as a pillow. She couldn't have been more uncomfortable but fell asleep within minutes.

'PETRESCU STILL WORRIES me,' said Leapman.

'Why should a dead woman worry you?' asked Fenston.

'Because I'm not convinced she's dead.'

'How could she have survived that?' asked Fenston, looking out of the window at the black shroud that refused to lift its veil from the face of the World Trade Center.

'We did. Perhaps she did. After all, you ordered her off the premises within ten minutes.'

'Barry thinks otherwise.'

'Barry's alive,' Leapman reminded him.

'Even if Petrescu did escape, she still can't do anything,' said Fenston. 'Victoria Wentworth is dead.'

'But that might prove just as convenient for her as it is for us.'

'Then we'll have to make it less convenient.'

A LOUD, REPEATED banging jolted Anna out of a deep sleep. She rubbed her eyes and looked through the windscreen. A man with a pot belly hanging out of his jeans was thumping on the van with a clenched fist. In his other hand he was carrying a can of beer. Anna was about to scream at him when she realised that someone else was trying to wrench open the back door. An ice-cold shower couldn't have woken her any quicker.

Anna scrambled into the driver's seat and turned the key in the ignition. She looked in her side-view mirror and was horrified to see that another forty-ton truck was now stationed behind her, leaving her with almost no room to manoeuvre. She pressed the palm of her hand on the horn, which only encouraged the man holding the beer can to clamber up onto the bonnet and leer at her toothlessly through the windscreen. Anna felt cold and sick. He began licking the glass, while his friend continued trying to force open the back door. The engine finally spluttered into life.

Anna yanked the steering wheel round to give her the tightest possible turns, but the space between the two trucks only allowed her to advance a few feet before she had to reverse. When she shot back, the second man threw himself to one side. Anna crashed into first gear and as the van leaped forward, the pot-bellied man slid to the ground with a thud. Anna rammed into reverse again and was horrified to see the first man's hands reappear on the bonnet as he pulled himself back up onto his feet. He lurched forward and gave her a thumbs-down sign, then shouted to his buddy, 'I get to go first,' and walked to his truck. His mate climbed up into his cab.

It didn't take Anna more than a split second to work out that she was about to become the meat in their next sandwich. She hit the accelerator so hard that the van careered into the truck behind her, then she crashed the gears back into first as she once again thrust her foot down on the accelerator. This time she collided with the corner of the front truck's massive mudguard, which tore off her front bumper as the rear truck ploughed into her, ripping off her rear bumper. The little van came hurtling through the gap and spun round a full 360 degrees before it came to a halt. Anna looked in her mirror to see the two trucks, unable to react in time, crash into each other.

She accelerated across the parking lot and out onto the highway. There she jammed her foot down on the accelerator until it touched the floor, determined to find out the maximum speed the van could manage: sixty-eight miles per hour was the answer. It was more than an hour before she was calm enough to stop looking in her wing mirror every few minutes.

After another hour, as the first shafts of the morning sun appeared through the clouds, she even began to feel hungry and decided to pull in to a café for breakfast. She parked the van, strolled in and took a seat. She perused the menu before ordering eggs, bacon, sausage, pancakes and coffee.

Between mouthfuls, Anna checked her map. She calculated that she had already covered 380 miles, but there were still at least fifty to go before she reached the Canadian border. She checked her watch: 7:55 a.m.

Leaving six dollars on the table, Anna walked across to the phone booth on the far side of the diner. She dialled a 212 number.

AS THE STRANGER entered the lobby, Sam looked up from his desk. The tall, middle-aged man was wearing a smart but well-worn suit, the cloth a little shiny at the elbows. He wore a tie that Sam reckoned had been tied a thousand times.

'Good morning,' Sam said.

'Good morning,' replied the man. 'I'm from the Department of Immigration. I'm checking up on those people who are still missing, presumed dead, following the terrorist attack on Tuesday.'

'Anyone in particular?' asked Sam.

'Yes,' said the man. He placed his briefcase on the counter, extracted a piece of paper containing a list of names, and ran a finger down it. 'Anna Petrescu. This is the last known address we have for her.'

'I haven't seen Anna since she left for work on Tuesday morning,' said Sam, 'though several people have asked about her, and one of her friends took away some of her personal things.'

'What did she take?'

'I don't know,' said Sam. 'I just recognised the suitcase.'

'Do you know her name? Anna's mother is quite anxious.'

'No, I don't know her name,' admitted Sam.

'Would you recognise her if I showed you a photograph?'

'Might,' said Sam.

Once again, the man opened his briefcase. This time he extracted a photo. Sam studied it for a moment. 'Yes, that's her. Pretty girl, but not as pretty as Anna. She was beautiful.'

'GOOD MORNING, sir, my name is Agent Roberts.'

'Morning, Agent Roberts,' replied Jack, leaning back in his chair. 'Have anything to report?'

'I'm standing in a vehicle rest stop somewhere between New York and the Canadian border.'

'And what are you doing there, Agent Roberts?'

'I'm holding a bumper.'

'Let me guess,' said Jack. 'The bumper was attached to a white van driven by the suspect.'

'Yes, sir.'

'And where is the van now?' asked Jack.

'I have no idea, sir. When the suspect drove into the rest stop, I must admit, sir, I also fell asleep. When I woke, the van had left, leaving the bumper with the GPS still attached.'

'Then she's either very clever or she's been in an accident.'

'I agree. What do you think I should do next, sir?'

'Join the CIA,' said Jack.

'HI, IT'S VINCENT, any news?'

'Yep. Ruth Parish has the painting locked up in the secure customs area at Heathrow.'

'Then I'll have to unlock it,' said Anna.

'That might not prove easy,' said Tina. 'Leapman flies out first thing tomorrow morning to pick up the painting, so you've only got twenty-four hours before he joins you.' She hesitated. 'And you have another problem. Leapman isn't convinced you're dead.'

'What makes him think that?'

'He keeps asking about you, so be especially careful. Heaven knows what Fenston would do if he lost the Van Gogh.'

Anna could feel beads of sweat breaking out on her forehead as the line went dead. She checked her watch: thirty-two seconds.

'OUR "FRIEND" at JFK has confirmed a slot at seven twenty tomorrow morning,' Leapman said. 'But I haven't informed Tina.'

'Why not?' asked Fenston.

'Because the doorman at Petrescu's apartment block told me that someone matching Tina's description was seen leaving the building carrying Anna's suitcase.'

Fenston frowned. 'But that would mean—'

'Do you want me to do anything about it?'

'What do you have in mind?' asked Fenston.

'Bug the phone in her apartment for a start. If Petrescu is in contact with her, we'll know exactly what she's up to.'

Fenston didn't reply, which Leapman always took to mean yes.

CANADIAN BORDER 4 MILES declared a sign. Anna smiled—a smile that was quickly removed when she swung round the next corner and came to a halt behind a line of vehicles that stretched as far as the eye could see.

During the next twenty minutes, Anna progressed just one hundred yards, ending up opposite a gas station. She made an instant decision and swung the van across the road, drove past the pumps and parked next to a tree, behind a large sign declaring CAR WASH. Then she retrieved her bags and started out on the four-mile trek to the border.

'I'M SO SORRY, my dear,' said Arnold Simpson, as he looked across his desk at Arabella Wentworth. He smiled benignly at his client and placed his hands on the desk, as if about to offer up a prayer.

'As our family's solicitor,' Arabella said, opening a file on her lap, 'perhaps you can explain how my father and Victoria managed to run up such massive debts and in so short a time.'

Simpson was momentarily lost for words as he searched through the files that littered his desk. 'Ah, yes,' he declared eventually, opening one. 'When your father became a name at Lloyd's in 1971, he signed up for several syndicates, putting up the estate as collateral. For many years, the insurance industry showed handsome returns and your father received a large annual income.' Simpson ran his finger down a list of figures. 'I confess that, like many others, I did not anticipate such an unprecedented run of bad years.'

'And what happened to the large portfolio of stocks and shares that the family had accumulated?'

'They were among the first assets your father had to liquidate to keep his current account in surplus. In fact, at the time of his death, he had run up an overdraft of something like ten million pounds.'

'And how, may I ask, with you as her principal adviser, did Victoria manage to double that debt in less than a year?'

'I am not to blame for that,' snapped Simpson. 'You can direct your anger at the tax man, who always demands his pound of flesh. The Exchequer is entitled to forty per cent of any assets not passed on to a spouse. However, I managed to reach a settlement of eleven million pounds with the inspectors, which Lady Victoria seemed well satisfied with at the time.'

'My sister was a naive spinster who never left home without her father,' said Arabella, 'but still you allowed her to sign a contract with Fenston Finance, which was bound to land her in even more debt.'

'It was that or putting the estate on the market.'

'No, it wasn't,' replied Arabella. 'It only took me one phone call to be told that Christie's would expect the family's Van Gogh to make over thirty million pounds were it to come up for auction.'

'But your father would never have agreed to sell the Van Gogh.'

'You obviously didn't read the contract. Because not only did my sister agree to pay sixteen per cent compound interest on the loan, but you even allowed her to hand over the Van Gogh as collateral. And should there be a dispute, any decision will revert to a New York court.'

'I feel confident,' said Simpson, 'that I can wrap up this—'

'I'll tell you exactly what you can wrap up,' said Arabella, rising. 'All those files concerning the Wentworth estate, and send them to Wentworth Hall.' She stared down at the solicitor. 'And enclose your final account'—she checked her watch—'for one hour of your invaluable advice.'

ANNA WALKED DOWN the road, pulling her suitcase behind her, with the laptop hanging over her left shoulder, aware of passengers in their stationary cars staring as she passed them. She averted her eyes, and when she came to the white line, she stood to one side.

There were two customs officers on duty, sitting in their little boxes, checking everyone's documents much more assiduously than usual. Eventually, the younger of the two beckoned her over and checked her travel documents.

He stared at her quizzically, wondering how far she had trudged. 'What is your reason for visiting Canada?' he asked.

'I'm attending an art seminar at McGill University. It's part of my PhD thesis on the pre-Raphaelite movement,' she said.

'Which artists in particular?' asked the officer casually.

'Rossetti, Holman Hunt and Morris, among others.'

'Who's giving the seminar?'

Anna's cheeks coloured. 'Er, Vern Swanson. From Yale,' said Anna, hoping the man would not have heard of the most eminent expert in the field.

'Good, then I'll get a chance to meet him. If he's coming from New Haven, since there are no flights in and out of the US, this is the only way he can cross the border.'

Anna couldn't think of a suitable response.

'I was at McGill,' said the young man with a smile, as he handed Anna back her passport. 'We're all sorry about what happened in New York.'

'Thank you,' said Anna, and walked across the border.

THE GREYHOUND BUS left Niagara Falls at three o'clock. Two hours later, it came to a halt on the western shore of Lake Ontario. Anna was first down the steps and, without stopping to admire the Toronto skyline, she hailed the first available cab.

'The airport, please, and as fast as possible.'

It took twenty-five minutes to drive the seventeen miles to Lester B. Pearson International Airport. Anna paid the fare and walked quickly into terminal three. She stared up at the departures board as the digital clock flicked over to twenty-eight minutes past five.

The last flight to Heathrow had just closed its gates. Anna cursed. Her eyes scanned the list of remaining flights: Tel Aviv, Bangkok, Sydney, Amsterdam. Amsterdam—how appropriate, she thought. Flight KL692, gate C31, now boarding.

'SHE'S ON HER WAY to Amsterdam,' said Joe.

'Amsterdam?' repeated Jack, tapping his fingers on the desk.

'Yes, she missed the last flight to Heathrow. We already have an agent there. Do you want agents anywhere else?'

'Yes, Gatwick and Stansted,' said Jack.

'Fenston's jet has a slot booked out of JFK at seven twenty tomorrow morning. The only passenger is Karl Leapman.'

'Then they probably plan to meet up. Call Agent Crasanti at our London embassy and ask him to put extra agents at all three airports. I want to know exactly what those two are up to,' Jack said, putting the phone down.

9/14

Leapman was awake long before the limousine was due to pick him up. This was not a day for oversleeping. He climbed out of bed and headed for the bathroom. Once he'd showered and shaved, he didn't bother making himself breakfast. He'd be served coffee and croissants by the stewardess on the bank's private jet. Who in this run-down building would believe that in a couple of hours he would be on a Gulfstream V on its way to London?

He walked across to his half-empty closet and selected his most recently acquired suit, then stood waiting by the window for the limousine to appear, aware that his little apartment was not much of an improvement on the prison cell where he'd spent four years. He looked down on 43rd Street as the incongruous limousine drew up outside the front door.

Leapman climbed into the back, not speaking to the driver. He knew he was nothing more than a bagman, even if the bag today contained one of the most valuable paintings on earth. He despised Fenston, who never treated him as an equal. If Fenston just once acknowledged his contribution to the company, it would be enough.

For more than a decade he had watched as the unsophisticated immigrant from Bucharest had climbed up the ladder of wealth and status—a ladder he had held in place. But that could change overnight. She only needed to make one mistake, and their roles would be reversed. Fenston would end up in prison, and he would have a fortune no one could ever trace.

Forty-five minutes later the limousine turned off the expressway and took the exit to JFK. The driver passed a small terminal building and pulled up beside the steps of the aircraft.

The plane began to taxi even before he'd finished his juice, but he didn't relax until the jet reached its cruising altitude. Then he leaned forward, picked up the phone and dialled Fenston's private line.

'I'm on my way,' he said.

'Call me the moment you land,' was the chairman's response.

TINA FLICKED off the extension to the chairman's phone.

The chairman's jet had taken off from JFK on time that morning. She realised that Anna only had a few hours' start on Leapman, and that was assuming she was even in London.

Tina thought about Leapman returning to New York, that sickly grin plastered on his face as he handed the Van Gogh to the chairman. She continued to download the contracts, having earlier emailed them to her private address—something she only did when Leapman was out of the office and Fenston was fully occupied.

THE FIRST AVAILABLE flight to London Gatwick that morning was due out of Schiphol at ten o'clock. Anna purchased a ticket from British Airways and sat in Caffè Nero sipping coffee until her flight was called.

After crossing the English Channel, the plane touched down at Gatwick thirty-five minutes late. Anna stepped onto English soil aware that it would be only hours before Leapman landed at Heathrow. Once she was through passport control and had retrieved her baggage, she stood in line at the car-rental counter.

She didn't see the smartly dressed young man in the duty-free shop whispering into a cellphone, 'She's landed. I'm on her tail.'

FORTY MINUTES after renting her car, Anna drove through the gates of Wentworth Hall. The pile—Victoria's description of her home—had been built in 1697 by Sir John Vanbrugh, who moved on to create Castle Howard and, later, Blenheim Palace.

The long drive up to the house was shaded by fine oaks of the same vintage as the hall itself. Anna drove past an ornate lake and on past two tennis courts and a croquet lawn, sprinkled with the first leaves of autumn. As she rounded a bend, the great hall, surrounded by a thousand green acres, loomed up to dominate the sky.

Victoria had once told Anna that the house had sixty-seven rooms, fourteen of them guest bedrooms. The bedroom she had stayed in, the Van Gogh room, was about the same size as her apartment in New York.

As she brought the car to a halt, Anna noticed that the crested family flag on the east tower was fluttering at half mast. She stepped out of the vehicle and approached the hall, wondering which of Victoria's many elderly relatives might have died.

The massive oak door was pulled open even before Anna reached the top step. She prayed that Victoria was at home and that Fenston still had no idea she was in England.

'Good morning, madam,' the butler intoned. 'May I help you?'

It's me, Andrews, Anna wanted to say, surprised by his formal tone. He had been so friendly when she stayed at the hall. 'I need to speak to Lady Victoria, urgently.'

'I'm afraid that will not be possible,' replied Andrews, 'but I will find out if Her Ladyship is free. Perhaps you would be kind enough to wait here while I enquire.'

What did he mean, *that will not be possible, but I will find out if Her Ladyship* . . .

As Anna waited in the hall, she glanced up at Gainsborough's portrait of Catherine, Lady Wentworth. She turned to face the morning room, to be greeted with Stubbs's *Actaeon, Winner of the Derby*. If Victoria took her advice, at least she could still save the rest of the collection.

The butler returned at the same even pace. 'Her Ladyship will see you now,' he said, 'if you would care to join her in the drawing room.' He gave a slight bow before leading her across the hall.

Victoria, head bowed, was dressed in mourning black, seated on the sofa. Anna was surprised when she didn't greet her in her usual warm manner. Victoria raised her head, and Anna gasped, as Arabella Wentworth stared coldly up at her. In that second, she realised why the family's crest had been flying at half mast. She tried to take in the fact that she would never see Victoria again, and would now need to convince her sister, whom she had never met before.

'Would you care for some tea, Dr Petrescu?' Arabella asked in a distant voice.

'No, thank you,' Anna said. The mirror image of Victoria did not rise from her place. 'May I ask how Victoria died?'

'I assumed you already knew,' replied Arabella drily.

'I have no idea what you mean.'

'Then why are you here, if it's not to collect the rest of the family silver?'

'I came to warn Victoria not to let them take away the Van Gogh before I had a chance to—'

'They have already taken the painting away,' said Arabella. 'They didn't even have the good manners to wait until after the funeral.'

'I tried to call, but the number is ex-directory,' Anna mumbled incoherently. 'I sent Victoria my report recommending that—'

'Yes, I've read your report. But my new lawyer has already warned me that it could be years before the estate can be settled, by which time we'll have lost everything.'

'I was fired on Tuesday for sending my report to Victoria.'

'Victoria read your report,' Arabella said. 'I have a letter confirming that she was going to take your advice, but that was before her cruel death.'

'How did she die?' Anna asked once more.

'She was murdered in a vile and cowardly fashion,' said Arabella. 'I have no doubt Mr Fenston will fill in the details for you.'

Anna bowed her head. 'I am so sorry,' she said. 'I didn't know. You have to believe me. I had no idea.'

Arabella stood up and walked across to the window. She stood looking out across the lawn and didn't speak for some time. She turned back to see Anna, trembling.

'I believe you,' Arabella said eventually. 'I originally assumed that it was you who was responsible for this evil charade. I see now that I was wrong. But, sadly, it's all to late. There's nothing we can do now.'

'I'm not so sure about that,' Anna said, looking at Arabella with fierce determination in her eyes. 'But if I'm to do anything, I'll have to ask you to trust me as much as Victoria did.'

'What do you mean, "trust you"?' said Arabella.

'Give me a chance to prove that I wasn't responsible for your sister's death. Let me retrieve your Van Gogh. It has to be in England still, because Fenston has sent a Mr Leapman to pick it up. He'll be landing at Heathrow in a few hours' time.'

'But even if you managed to get your hands on the painting, how would that solve the problem?'

Anna outlined the details of her plan and was pleased to see Arabella nodding from time to time. She ended by saying, 'I'll need your backing, otherwise what I have in mind could get me arrested.'

Arabella remained silent for some time before she said, 'You're a brave young woman, and I wonder if you realise just how brave. But if you're willing to take such a risk, so am I, and I'll back you to the hilt.'

Anna smiled. 'Then can you confirm who collected the Van Gogh?'

Arabella rose from the sofa and crossed the room to the writing desk. She picked up a business card. 'Ruth Parish,' she read, 'of Art Locations.'

'Just as I thought,' said Anna. 'I'll leave immediately.' She stepped forward and thrust out her hand, but Arabella didn't respond. Instead, she took her in her arms. 'If I can do anything to help you avenge my sister's death . . .'

'Anything?'

'Anything,' repeated Arabella.

'When the North Tower collapsed, all the documentation concerning Victoria's loan was destroyed, including the original—'

'You don't have to spell it out,' said Arabella.

ANNA HEADED BACK towards the M25, looking for a sign to Heathrow. She checked the clock on the dashboard. It was almost 2 p.m., so she had missed any chance of calling Tina, who would now be at her desk on Wall Street. But she did need to make another call if there was to be the slightest chance of succeeding.

As she drove through the village of Wentworth, she tried to recall the pub where Victoria had taken her to dinner. When she saw the familiar crest flapping in the wind, also at half-mast, Anna swung into the Wentworth

Arms and parked. She walked through reception and into the bar.

'May I use your phone?' she asked the barmaid. 'I need to make a call.'

'Of course, love. It's just to your right.'

Anna dialled a number she could never forget. The phone rang twice before a voice announced, 'Good afternoon, Sotheby's, Mark Poltimore speaking.'

'Mark, it's Anna, Anna Petrescu.'

'Anna, what a pleasant surprise. We've all been anxious about you. Where were you on Tuesday?'

'Amsterdam,' she replied.

'Thank God for that. Terrible business. And Fenston?'

'Not in the building at the time,' said Anna, 'and that's why I'm calling. He wants your opinion on a Van Gogh.'

'Authenticity or price?' asked Mark. 'Because when it comes to provenance, I bow to your superior judgment.'

'I would like a second opinion on its value,' said Anna.

'Is it one we would know?'

'*Self-Portrait with Bandaged Ear*,' said Anna.

'The Wentworth *Self-Portrait*?' queried Mark. 'I've known the family all my life and had no idea they were considering selling the painting.'

'I didn't say they were,' said Anna.

'Are you able to bring the painting in for inspection?'

'I'd like to, but I don't have secure enough transport. I was hoping you might be able to help.'

'Where is it now?' asked Mark.

'In a bonded warehouse at Heathrow.'

'That's easy enough. We have a daily pick-up from Heathrow. Would tomorrow afternoon be convenient?'

'Today, if possible. You know what my boss is like.'

'Hold on. I'll just need to find out if they've already left.' The line went silent, although Anna could hear her heart thumping. Mark came back on the line. 'You're in luck. Our handler is picking up some other items for us around four.'

'Could they call Ruth Parish before the van is due to arrive?'

'Sure. You'd come to Sotheby's first if you ever considered selling the *Self-Portrait,* wouldn't you, Anna?'

'Of course.'

'I can't wait to see it,' said Mark.

Anna replaced the receiver, appalled by how easily she could now lie. She was also becoming aware just how simple it must have been for Fenston to deceive her.

She drove out of the Wentworth Arms, aware that everything now depended on Ruth Parish being in her office. Once she reached the M25, Anna remained in the slow lane as she went over all the things that could go badly wrong. Was Ruth aware that Anna had been fired? Had Fenston told her she was dead? Anna was so deep in thought that she nearly missed her exit for Heathrow.

She headed for the cargo depots just off the Southern Perimeter Road and parked her car in a visitor's space directly outside the offices of Art Locations. She sat for some time, trying to compose herself. Why didn't she just drive off? She didn't need to become involved or even consider taking such a risk. She then thought about Victoria and the role she had unwittingly played in her death.

'Get on with it, woman,' Anna said out loud, and finally opened the car door. She took a deep breath and strolled across the tarmac towards the entrance, then pushed through some swing doors into the reception area. 'Is Ruth around?' she asked cheerily.

'No,' said the receptionist, 'but I'm expecting her back at any moment.'

'Then I'll wait,' Anna said with a smile. She took a seat and picked up a copy of *Newsweek*.

Ruth finally walked through the doors at 3.22 p.m. 'Any messages?' she asked the receptionist.

'No,' replied the girl, 'but a lady is waiting to see you.'

Anna held her breath as Ruth swung round.

'Anna,' she exclaimed. 'It's good to see you.' First hurdle crossed. 'I wondered if you'd still be on this assignment after the tragedy in New York.' Second hurdle crossed. 'Especially when your boss told me that Mr Leapman would be coming to collect the picture.' Third hurdle crossed. 'You look a bit pale,' continued Ruth. 'Are you all right?'

'I'm fine,' said Anna, stumbling over the fourth hurdle, but at least she was still on her feet.

'Where were you on the eleventh? I would have asked Mr Fenston, but he never gives you a chance to ask anything.'

'Covering a sale in Amsterdam,' Anna replied, 'but Karl Leapman called me last night and asked me to fly over and double-check that everything was in place.'

'We're more than ready for him,' said Ruth testily, 'but I'll drive you to the warehouse and you can see for yourself.'

Anna nodded agreement and followed her out of the building. They crossed to where Ruth's Range Rover stood waiting, and Anna opened the passenger door and climbed in.

'Terrible business, Lady Victoria,' said Ruth, as she swung the car round and headed for the south end of the cargo terminal. 'The press are making a real meal of the murder—mystery killer, throat cut with a kitchen knife—but the police still haven't arrested anyone.'

Anna remained silent, the words 'throat cut' and 'mystery killer' reverberating in her mind.

Ruth pulled up outside an anonymous-looking concrete building, which Anna had visited several times in the past. She checked her watch: 3.40 p.m. Ruth flashed a security pass to the guard, who unlocked the three-inch steel door. The long grey concrete corridor always felt like a bunker to Anna. At a second security door, Ruth entered a six-digit number. She pulled open the heavy door, allowing them to enter a square concrete room.

The wooden shelves were stacked with Art Locations's distinctive red packing cases. Ruth checked her inventory before walking across the room and tapping a crate showing the number 47 stencilled in all four corners.

Anna strolled across to join her. She also checked the inventory: number 47, Vincent Van Gogh, *Self-Portrait with Bandaged Ear*, 24 by 18 inches. 'Everything seems to be in order,' she said.

The guard reappeared at the door. 'Sorry to interrupt you, Ms Parish, but there are two security men from Sotheby's outside, say they've been instructed to pick up a Van Gogh for valuation.'

'Do you know anything about this?' Ruth asked Anna.

'Oh, yes. The chairman instructed me to have the Van Gogh valued for insurance purposes before it's shipped. Mark Poltimore will only need the piece for about an hour. Sotheby's will send it straight back.'

'Mr Leapman didn't mention this in his email,' said Ruth.

'Frankly,' said Anna, 'Leapman's such a philistine, he wouldn't know the difference between Van Gogh and Van Morrison.' She paused. 'If you're in any doubt, why don't you call and have a word with Fenston? That should clear the matter up.'

'And have my head bitten off again?' said Ruth. 'No, thank you. I think I'll take your word for it. That's assuming you will take responsibility for signing the release order?'

'Of course. That's no more than my fiduciary duty.'

Ruth looked relieved and said to the guard, 'It's number forty-seven.' They both accompanied him as he removed the red packing case and carried it out to the Sotheby's security van.

'Sign here,' said the driver.

Anna stepped forward and signed the release document.

'It had better be back before Mr Leapman lands,' said Ruth, 'because I don't need to get on the wrong side of that man.'

'Would you be happier if I accompanied the painting to Sotheby's?' asked Anna. 'Perhaps I can speed up the process.'

'Would you be willing to do that?' asked Ruth.

'It might be wise given the circumstances,' said Anna, and she climbed into the front of the van and took a seat.

Ruth waved as the van disappeared through the perimeter gate and joined the late-afternoon traffic on its journey into London.

BRYCE FENSTON'S GULFSTREAM V executive jet touched down at Heathrow at 7.22 p.m., and Ruth was waiting on the tarmac. She had alerted customs with all the relevant details so that the paperwork could be completed just as soon as Anna returned.

For the past hour, Ruth had spent more and more time looking towards the main gate, willing the security van to reappear. She had rung Sotheby's, and was assured that the painting had arrived. But that was over two hours ago.

The fuselage door opened and the steps unfolded onto the ground. Karl Leapman stepped onto the tarmac and shook hands with Ruth before joining her in the back of an airport limousine for the short journey to the private lounge. He didn't bother to introduce himself. 'Any problems?' he asked.

'None that I can think of,' replied Ruth, as the driver pulled up outside the executive building. 'We've carried out your instructions to the letter. We'll begin loading the moment the captain has finished refuelling— shouldn't be more than an hour.'

'I'm glad to hear it,' said Leapman, pushing through the swing doors. 'We have a slot booked for eight thirty.'

'Then perhaps it might be more sensible if I left you to oversee the transfer. I'll report back the moment the painting is on board.'

Leapman nodded and sank back in a chair. Ruth turned to leave.

'Can I get you a drink, sir?' asked the barman.

'Scotch on the rocks,' said Leapman, scanning the dinner menu.

As Ruth reached the door, she turned and said, 'When Anna comes back, would you tell her I'll be over at customs?'

'Anna?' exclaimed Leapman, jumping out of his chair.

'Yes, she's been around for most of the afternoon.'

'Doing what?' Leapman demanded, advancing towards Ruth.

'Just checking over the manifest,' Ruth said, trying to sound relaxed, 'and making sure Mr Fenston's orders were carried out.'

'What orders?' barked Leapman.

'To send the Van Gogh to Sotheby's for insurance valuation.'

'The chairman gave no such order. Petrescu was fired three days ago. Who does she deal with at Sotheby's?'

'Mark Poltimore,' Ruth said, running across to the phone. She quickly looked up Poltimore's number on her Palm Pilot and began dialling. 'Mark?' she said.

Leapman snatched the phone from her. 'Poltimore?'

'Speaking.'

'My name is Leapman. I'm the—'

'I know who you are, Mr Leapman,' said Mark.

'Good. I understand you are in possession of our Van Gogh.'

'Was, would be more accurate,' replied Mark, 'until Dr Petrescu informed us you'd had a change of heart and wanted the canvas taken back to Heathrow for immediate transport to New York.'

'And you went along with that?' said Leapman, his voice rising.

'We had no choice, Mr Leapman. After all, it was Dr Petrescu's name on the manifest.'

'Hi, it's Vincent.'

'Hi. Is it true what I've just heard?'

'What have you heard?'

'That you've stolen the Van Gogh.'

'Have the police been informed?'

'No, he can't risk that. He's sending someone to London to track you down, but I can't find out who it is.'

'Maybe I won't be in London. I'm going home.'

'And is the painting safe?'

'Safe as houses.'

'Good. But he will be attending your funeral this afternoon.'

The phone went dead. Fifty-two seconds.

Anna replaced the receiver, even more concerned about the danger she was placing Tina in. What would Fenston do if he were to discover the reason she always managed to stay one step ahead of him? She walked over to the departures desk.

'Do you have any bags to check in?' asked the woman behind the counter. Anna heaved the red packing case off the luggage cart and onto the scales. She then placed her suitcase next to it.

'You're quite a bit over the weight, madam,' she said. 'I'm afraid there will be an excess charge of thirty-two pounds.' Anna took the money out of her wallet while the woman attached a label to her suitcase and fixed a sticker on the crate. 'Gate 43,' she said, handing her a ticket. 'Boarding in about thirty minutes.' Anna began walking towards the gate.

Whoever Fenston was sending to London to track her down would be landing long after she had flown away. But Anna knew that they only had to read her report carefully to work out where the picture would be ending up. She just needed to be certain that she got there before they did. But first she had to make a couple of phone calls: one to tell the car hire company to pick up her car outside Art Locations, and the second to someone she hadn't spoken to for more than ten years to warn him that she was on her way.

Anna joined a long queue waiting to be checked through security.

'She's heading towards Gate 43,' said a voice, 'and will be departing on Flight BA 272 to Bucharest.'

FENSTON squeezed himself into a line of dignitaries as President Bush and Mayor Giuliani shook hands with a select group who were attending the service at Ground Zero.

He hung around until the President's helicopter had taken off and then walked across to the other mourners. He listened as the names were read out, each was followed by the single peal of a bell.

Greg Abbot. Kelly Gullickson. He studied the faces of the relations and friends who had gathered in memory of their loved ones.

Anna Petrescu. Fenston knew that Petrescu's mother lived in Romania and wouldn't be travelling to the service. He wondered which of the huddled strangers was Uncle George from Danville, Illinois.

Rebecca Rangere. He glanced across at Tina. Tears filled her eyes.

The priest delivered a prayer, then made the sign of a cross. 'In the name of the Father, the Son and the Holy Ghost,' he declared.

'Amen,' came back the unison reply.

TINA LOOKED across at Fenston, not a tear shed, just the familiar movement from one foot to the other—the sign he was bored. While others gathered in groups to sympathise and pay their respects, Fenston left without commiserating with anyone.

Tina stood among a group of mourners, although her eyes remained on Fenston. His driver was holding open the back door for him. Fenston climbed into the car and sat next to a woman Tina had never seen before. Neither spoke until the driver had returned to the front seat and the smoked-glass screen rose behind him. Then the car eased into traffic and disappeared out of sight.

THE WOMAN seated next to Fenston was dressed in a grey trouser suit. Anonymity was her most important asset. She had never once visited Fenston at his office or apartment, even though she had known him for almost twenty years. She'd first met Nicu Munteanu when he was bagman for President Nicolae Ceausescu.

Fenston's primary responsibility during Ceausescu's reign was to distribute vast sums of money into bank accounts around the world—backhanders for the dictator's loyal henchmen. When they ceased to be loyal, the woman seated next to Fenston eliminated them, and he redistributed their assets. Fenston's speciality was money laundering. Her speciality was to dispose of the bodies—her chosen instrument, a kitchen knife.

In 1985, Ceausescu decided to send his private banker to New York to open an overseas branch for him. For the next four years, Fenston lost touch with the woman seated next to him, until in 1989 Ceausescu was arrested by his countrymen, tried and executed. Among those who avoided the same fate was Olga Krantz, who crossed seven borders before she slipped into America to become one of countless illegal immigrants who live off cash payments from unscrupulous employers.

Fenston was one of the few people alive who knew Krantz's true identity. He'd first watched her on television when she was fourteen years old and representing Romania in a gymnastics competition. Krantz came second to her teammate Mara Moldoveanu, and the press were already tipping them for the gold and silver at the next Olympics. Unfortunately, Moldoveanu died in tragic circumstances, when she fell from the beam attempting a double somersault and broke her neck. Krantz, the only other person in the gymnasium at the time, vowed to win the gold medal in her memory.

Krantz pulled a hamstring only days before the Olympic team was selected. Like all athletes who don't quite make the grade, her name quickly disappeared from the headlines. Fenston assumed he would never hear of her again, until one morning he saw her coming out of Ceausescu's office. The short, sinewy woman had lost none of her agile movement, and no one could forget those steel-grey eyes. A few well-placed questions and Fenston learned that Krantz was now head of Ceausescu's personal protection squad. Her particular responsibility: breaking selected bones of those who crossed the dictator. Having perfected the routines she moved on to cutting throats.

Ceausescu had paid her well. Fenston paid her better. In twelve years, her fee had risen to $1 million.

Fenston extracted a folder from his briefcase and handed it to Krantz. She studied five recent photographs of Anna Petrescu.

'Where is she at the moment?' asked Krantz, still unable to disguise her mid-European accent.

'London,' replied Fenston, passing her a second file.

She extracted a single colour photograph. 'Who's he?'

'He's more important than the girl,' replied Fenston. 'He's irreplaceable. But don't kill the girl until she's led you to the painting.'

'And my payment for kidnapping a man who has lost an ear?'

'One million dollars, and the girl the same, but only after I have attended her funeral for the second time.' Fenston tapped the screen in front of him and the driver pulled in to the kerb. 'I've instructed Leapman to deposit the cash in the usual place.'

Krantz opened the door, got out of the car and disappeared into the crowd.

9/15–9/16

'Goodbye, Sam,' said Jack, as his cellphone began to ring. He'd just finished checking out Anna's apartment. Back out on East 54th Street, he pressed the green button. 'What have you got for me, Joe?'

'Petrescu landed at Gatwick,' said Joe. 'She rented a car and drove straight to Wentworth Hall.'

'How long was she there?' Jack walked towards 5th Avenue.

'Thirty minutes, no more. She made a phone call before travelling on to

Heathrow, where she met up with Ruth Parish. Around four, a Sotheby's van turns up, picks up a red packing case—'

'No prizes for guessing what's inside,' said Jack. 'Where did the van go?'

'They delivered the painting to their West End office. And Petrescu went along for the ride. Two porters unloaded the picture. She followed them in.'

'How long before she came back out?'

'Twenty minutes, and she was carrying the red case. She hailed a taxi, put the painting in the back and disappeared.'

'Disappeared? What do you mean, disappeared?'

'Most of our guys are working round the clock trying to identify terrorist groups that might have been involved in Tuesday's attacks. But we picked her up again a few hours later.'

'Where?' asked Jack, calming down.

'Gatwick Airport. Mind you,' said Joe, 'an attractive blonde carrying a red packing case does have a tendency to stand out in a crowd.'

'Where was she heading?'

'Bucharest.'

'Why take a priceless Van Gogh to Bucharest?'

'On Fenston's instructions, would be my bet,' said Joe. 'It's his home town as well as hers, and I can't think of a better place to hide the picture.'

'Then why send Leapman to London if it wasn't to pick up the painting?'

'A smokescreen?' said Joe. 'That would also explain why Fenston attended her funeral.'

'Or she's no longer working for him, and she's stolen the Van Gogh.'

'Why would she risk that, when he wouldn't hesitate to come after her?'

'I don't know, but there's only one way I'm going to find out.' Jack touched the red button on his phone, hailed a cab and gave the driver an address on the West Side.

FENSTON SWITCHED OFF the recorder and frowned. Both of them had listened to the tape for a third time.

'When are you going to fire the bitch?' Leapman asked.

'Not while she's the one person who can lead us to the painting,' Fenston replied.

Leapman scowled. 'And did you pick up the only word in their conversation that matters? "*Going*." If she'd used the word "coming"—"I'm coming home"—it would have been New York.'

Fenston raised an eyebrow. 'So it has to be Bucharest.'

JACK SAT BACK in the cab seat and tried to work out what Petrescu's next move might be. He still couldn't make up his mind if she was a professional criminal or a complete amateur. And where did Tina Forster fit into the equation? Was it possible that Fenston, Leapman, Petrescu and Forster were all working together?

But if Petrescu had branched out on her own, surely she realised that it would only be a matter of time before Fenston caught up with her? Although, Jack had to admit, Petrescu was now on her own ground and didn't seem to have any idea how much danger she was in. But why steal a painting worth millions that she couldn't hope to dispose of without her former colleagues finding out? It just didn't add up.

As the taxi swung into Central Park, Jack tried to make sense of all that had happened during the past few days. He hadn't found it difficult to obtain a search warrant while Anna remained on the missing list. Sam had burst into tears at the mention of her name and had accompanied him to her apartment and even opened the door.

Jack had walked round the tidy rooms while Sam remained in the hall-way. He didn't learn a great deal more than he already knew. An address book confirmed her uncle's number in Illinois and her mother's address in Bucharest. Perhaps the only surprise was a Picasso drawing in the hallway, signed in pencil by the artist. He couldn't believe she'd stolen it and then left it in the hall for everyone to admire. Or was it a bonus from Fenston?

He returned to the main room and glanced at a photo on the corner of the writing desk of what must have been Anna with her parents. He opened a box file to discover a bundle of letters that he couldn't read. Most were signed 'Mama', although one or two were from someone called Anton. He had looked back up at the photo and couldn't help thinking that if his mother had seen the picture, she would have invited Anna back to sample her Irish stew.

'Damn,' said Jack, loud enough for the cab driver to ask, 'What's the problem?'

'I forgot to phone my mother.'

'Then you're in big trouble. I should know, I'm Irish too.'

Is it that obvious? thought Jack. Mind you, he should have called to let her know he wouldn't make 'Irish stew night', when he usually joined his parents to celebrate the natural superiority of the Gaelic race over all God's other creatures.

His father had wanted Jack to be a lawyer. After twenty-six years with the NYPD, he had come to the conclusion that the only people who made a profit out of crime were the lawyers. Despite his advice, Jack signed up for the FBI only days after he graduated from Columbia with a law degree. His father grumbled about it every Saturday, and his mother kept asking if he was ever going to make her a grandmother.

Jack enjoyed every aspect of the job, from the first moment he arrived at Quantico, to joining the New York field office, to being promoted to senior investigating officer. Macy had made it clear he hoped Jack would take over once he was transferred back to Washington, DC. But before that could happen, Jack had to put in jail a man who was turning any thoughts of promotion into fantasies. And so far he hadn't so much as landed a glove on Bryce Fenston.

He phoned his secretary. 'Sally, book me on the first available flight to London with a connection to Bucharest. I'm on my way home to pack.'

THE RULES were simple. Krantz stole a new cellphone every day. She'd phone the chairman, speak in their native tongue, and dispose of the phone. That way, no one could ever trace her.

Fenston was sitting at his desk when the little red light flashed on his private line. Only one person had that number.

'Where is she?' the caller asked.

'Bucharest' was all he said.

Krantz dropped today's cellphone into the Thames and hailed a cab. 'Gatwick Airport.'

WHEN JACK CAME down the steps at Heathrow, he wasn't surprised to find Tom Crasanti on the runway. A car was parked behind his old friend, the back door held open by another agent.

Neither of them spoke until the car was on the move.

'Where's Petrescu?' was Jack's first question.

'She's landed in Bucharest,' said Tom. 'She wheeled the painting out of customs on a baggage trolley.'

'That woman's got style.'

'Agreed, but perhaps she has no idea what she's up against.'

'I suspect she's about to find out,' said Jack, 'because if she stole the painting, I won't be the only person looking for her.'

'Then there's no time to waste. We've got a helicopter to take you to Gatwick, and they're holding up the flight to Bucharest.'

'How did you manage that?' asked Jack.

'The ambassador called the Foreign Office. I don't know what he said, but try not to forget that we don't have an official presence in Bucharest. You'll be on your own.'

ANNA STEPPED onto the concourse of Otopeni, Bucharest's international airport, in the early hours of Saturday morning, pushing a trolley laden with a wooden crate, a suitcase and a laptop. She stopped in her tracks when she saw a man rushing towards her.

Anna stared at him suspiciously. He was about five foot nine, balding, with a ruddy complexion and a thick black moustache. He must have been over sixty. He wore a tight-fitting suit, which suggested he'd once been slimmer. He came to a halt in front of her.

'I'm Sergei,' he announced in his native tongue. 'Anton told me you asked to be picked up. He has booked you into a hotel downtown.' Sergei pushed Anna's trolley to his waiting taxi, a yellow Mercedes that had 300,000 miles on the clock. Anna stepped into the car, while he loaded her luggage in the boot and then took his place behind the wheel.

Anna stared out of the window and thought how the city had changed since her birth. This thrusting, energetic capital demanded its place at the European table. Modern office buildings and a fashionable shopping centre had replaced the drab communist grey-tiled façade of only a decade ago.

Sergei drew up outside a small hotel tucked away down a narrow street. He lifted the red crate out of the boot while Anna took the rest of the luggage and headed into the hotel.

'I'd like to visit my mother first thing,' said Anna, once she'd checked in at the desk.

Sergei looked at his watch. 'I'll pick you up around nine. That will give you the chance to grab a few hours' sleep.'

'Thank you,' said Anna.

He watched as she walked away and disappeared into the elevator, carrying the red crate.

JACK HAD FIRST spotted the woman when he was standing in line to board the plane. It is a basic surveillance technique: hang back, just in case you are being followed. The trick is not to let the pursuer realise that you are on to them. Act normal, never look back.

Jack climbed the steps of the plane. He didn't look back.

WHEN ANNA STROLLED out of her hotel a few minutes after 9 a.m., she found Sergei standing by his Mercedes, waiting for her.

'Good morning, Sergei,' she said, as he opened the back door.

'Good morning, madam. You still wish to visit your mother?'

'Yes,' replied Anna. 'She lives at—'

Sergei waved a hand to make it clear that he knew where to go.

Anna smiled with pleasure as he drove through the centre of town past a magnificent fountain that would have graced a lawn at Versailles. But by the time her driver had reached the neglected outpost of Berceni, Anna realised that the new régime still had a long way to go to achieve the 'prosperity-for-all' programme they had promised the voters. She saw many of her country-men downcast in the degradation that surrounded them.

Anna had tried so many times to convince her mother to join her in America. She missed her dreadfully. The first decision she had made after she joined Sotheby's was to open a separate bank account for her mother in Bucharest, to which she transferred $400 on the first day of every month.

'I'll wait for you,' said Sergei, as the taxi finally came to a halt outside a dilapidated block of flats in Piata Resitei.

'Thank you,' said Anna, as she looked out at the prewar estate where she was born.

She walked up the litter-strewn, potholed path. The elevator didn't respond to Anna's button-pressing—nothing changed. She couldn't under-stand why her mother hadn't moved years ago; she had sent more than enough money for her to rent a comfortable apartment on the other side of town. Anna's feeling of guilt grew the higher up she climbed. She had for-gotten just how dreadful it was. When eventually she reached the sixteenth floor, she stopped to catch her breath before knocking on the door that hadn't seen a splash of paint since she'd last stood there.

A frail, white-haired lady, dressed in black, pulled the door open a few inches. Mother and daughter stared at each other, until suddenly Elsa Petrescu flung open the door and threw her arms round her daughter.

Her mother continued to cling to Anna as she led her into the flat. Inside it was spotless, but nothing had changed. The sofa and chairs, the unframed black and white family photographs, the rug so worn it was hard to make out the pattern.

'Anna, Anna, so many questions to ask,' her mother said, clutching her daughter's hand. 'Where do I begin?'

The sun was setting before Anna had responded to every one of her mother's questions, and then she begged once again, 'Please, Mama, come back with me and live in America.'

'No,' her mother replied, 'all my friends and all my memories are here. I am too old to begin a new life.'

Anna looked round the room. 'But why haven't you spent some of the money I've been sending to you each month?'

'I have,' she said firmly. 'But not on myself, because I want for nothing.'

'Then what have you spent it on?'

'Anton,' said her mother. 'I expect you heard he's a professor now. He was released from jail and they gave him back his old job at the academy.'

'Is he still painting?' Anna asked.

'Yes, but his main responsibility is to teach the graduates.'

'So what does he do with the money?' Anna asked.

'He buys canvases and brushes his pupils can't afford, so your generosity is put to good use.' She paused. 'Anton was your first love, Anna, yes?'

Anna wouldn't have believed that her mother could still make her blush. 'Yes,' she admitted, 'and I suspect I was his.'

'He's married now, and they have a little boy called Peter.' She paused again. 'Do you have a young man?'

'No, Mama.'

'Is that what brings you back home? Are you running away from something, or someone?'

'What makes you ask that?'

'There is a sadness in your eyes, and fear,' she said, looking up at her daughter, 'which you could never hide as a child.'

'I do have one or two problems,' admitted Anna, 'but nothing that time won't sort out.' She smiled. 'In fact, I think that Anton might be able to help me with one of them and I'm going to join him at the academy for a drink. Do you have any message you want passed on?'

Her mother didn't reply. She had quietly dozed off. Anna rearranged the rug on her lap and kissed her on the forehead. 'I'll be back tomorrow, Mama,' she whispered.

ANNA RETURNED to her hotel, and after a quick shower and change of clothes, her newly acquired chauffeur took her to the Academy of Art on Piata Universitatii.

The building had lost none of its elegance or charm, and when Anna climbed the steps to the massive sculptured doors, memories of her teenage art classes came flooding back. She glanced at a poster outside the main lecture theatre that announced: THE INFLUENCE OF PICASSO ON 20TH-CENTURY ART: PROFESSOR ANTON TEODORESCU. TONIGHT 7 P.M.

Anna gingerly pushed open the door, pleased to find that the presentation had come to an end, and that her first love was collecting his slides and putting them in an old briefcase. Tall and angular, with a mop of curly dark hair, his ancient corduroy jacket and open-neck shirt gave him the air of a perpetual student. Anna made her way to the front.

Anton glanced up over his spectacles. 'Anna,' he exclaimed, grinning widely. 'Was Sergei at the airport to pick you up?'

'Yes, thank you,' said Anna, kissing him on both cheeks. 'Where did you meet him?'

'In jail,' admitted Anton. 'He was lucky to survive Ceausescu. And have you visited your sainted mother?'

'I have. She's still living in conditions no better than a jail.'

'I agree, but at least your dollars allow my students—'

'I know,' said Anna, 'she's already told me.'

'You can't begin to know, so let me show you some of the results of your investment.' Anton took Anna by the hand and guided her to a long corridor crammed with paintings in every medium.

'This year's prize-winning students,' he told her, holding out his arms like a proud father. 'Each entry has been painted on a canvas supplied by you. In fact, one of the awards is the Petrescu Prize.' He paused. 'How appropriate if you were to select the winner.'

'I'm flattered,' said Anna, as she strolled up and down the canvas-filled walls, pausing occasionally to study an image closely. She finally stopped in front of an oil entitled *Freedom*, depicting the sun rising over Bucharest.

'You haven't lost your touch,' said Anton, smiling. 'Danuta Sekalska is this year's star pupil, and she's to continue at the Slade in London, if only we can raise enough money to cover her expenses.' He looked at his watch. 'Do you have time for a drink?'

'I certainly do,' replied Anna, 'because I confess there's a favour I need to ask of you.' She paused. 'In fact, two favours.'

Anton led her down to the senior common room, where they were greeted by the sound of good-humoured chatter as tutors sat around enjoying coffee.

Anton poured two cups. 'Black, if I remember,' he said. Heads turned as Anton guided his former pupil to a place by the fire. 'Now, what can I do for you, Anna, because I am unquestionably in your debt.'

'It's my mother,' she said quietly. 'I can't get her to spend a cent on her-self. She could do with a new carpet, sofa, a TV and even a telephone, not to mention fresh paint on that front door.'

'You think I haven't tried? Where do you imagine you get your stubborn streak from? I even suggested she move in with us.' Anton took a long draught of his coffee. 'But I promise I'll try again. What's the second favour?'

'You'll need to think long and hard about it.'

Anton put down his coffee and listened carefully as Anna explained her plan in detail.

'How much time have I got?' he asked when she'd finished.

'Three, perhaps four days.'

'And if I'm caught?'

'You'd probably go back to jail,' admitted Anna.

'And you?'

'The canvas would be shipped to New York and used as evidence against me. If you need any more money for—'

'No, I'm still holding more than eight thousand dollars of your mother's money. A dollar goes a long way in Romania.'

'Can I bribe you? I'll pay for your pupil to go to the Slade.'

Anton thought for a moment. 'You'll be back in three days.'

'Four at the most,' said Anna.

'Then let's hope I'm as good as you think I am.'

'IT'S VINCENT.'

'Where are you?'

'Visiting my mother.'

'Don't hang about. The stalker knows where you are.'

'Then I'm afraid he'll miss me again.'

'I'm not even convinced the stalker's a man. I saw Fenston talking to a woman in his car while I was attending your funeral. It worries me that I've never seen her before.'

'Describe her.'

'Five foot, slim, dark-haired.'

'There will be a lot of people like that where I'm going.'

'And are you taking the painting with you?'

'No, I've left it where no one can give it a second look.'

The phone went dead.

LEAPMAN PRESSED the OFF button. 'Where no one can give it a second look,' he repeated.

'*Can*, not *will*?' said Fenston. 'It must still be in the crate.'

'Agreed, but where's she off to next?'

'To a country where people are five foot, slim and dark-haired,' said Fenston.

'Japan,' said Leapman. 'She's going to try to sell your painting to the one person who won't be able to resist it.'

'Nakamura,' said Fenston.

JACK HAD CHECKED IN at what was ambitiously described on a neon sign as the Bucharesti International. He spent most of the night either turning the radiator up because it was so cold or turning it off because it was so noisy. He skipped breakfast, fearing it might be as unreliable as the radiator.

He hadn't spotted the woman again since he'd stepped onto the plane, so either he'd made a mistake or she was a professional. But he was no longer in any doubt that Anna was working independently. He had already decided the most likely place he'd catch up with her would be when she visited her mother. This time he'd be waiting for her. He wondered if the woman he'd seen when he stood in line for the plane had the same idea and, if so, was she Fenston's retriever or did she work for someone else?

He walked to a kiosk and purchased a guidebook entitled *Everything You Need to Know About Bucharest*. There wasn't a single paragraph devoted to the Berceni district, although Piata Resitei appeared on the foldout map. Jack worked out that Anna's birthplace must be about six miles north of the hotel. He decided he would walk the first three miles, not least because he needed the exercise, but also because it would give him a better chance to discover if he was a surveillance target.

Jack left the International at 7.30 a.m. and set off at a brisk pace.

ANNA ALSO HAD a restless night, finding it hard to sleep while the crate was under her bed. She was beginning to have doubts about Anton taking on an unnecessary risk. They'd agreed to meet at the academy at eight o'clock, an hour no self-respecting student would admit existed.

When she stepped out of the hotel, the first thing she saw was Sergei in his old Mercedes parked by the entrance. He jumped out of the car. 'Good morning, madam,' he said, as he loaded the red crate back into the boot.

'Good morning, Sergei,' Anna replied. 'I would like to go back to the academy, where I'll be leaving the crate.' Sergei nodded and opened the passenger door for her.

On the journey over to the Piata Universitatii, Anna learned that Sergei had a wife, that they had been married for more than thirty years and had a son who was serving in the army. Anna was about to ask if he'd ever met her father when she spotted Anton standing on the bottom step of the academy. Sergei stopped the car, went round to the boot and unloaded the crate.

'Is that it?' asked Anton, viewing it suspiciously. Anna nodded and Anton joined Sergei as he carried the crate up the steps. He opened the front door for the old man and they disappeared inside the building.

Anna kept checking her watch and looking back towards the entrance. Was Fenston's stalker watching her even now? Had he worked out where the Van Gogh was? The two men finally reappeared carrying an identical but unmarked wooden crate, which Sergei placed in the boot.

'Thank you,' said Anna, before kissing Anton on both cheeks. 'I'll be back in three, four days at the most, when I'll happily take the painting off your hands and no one will be any the wiser.'

JACK DIDN'T LOOK back, but once he'd walked the first mile, he slipped into a large supermarket and disappeared behind a pillar. He waited for her to walk by. She didn't. He bought a bacon and egg baguette and walked back onto the road. As he munched his breakfast, he tried to work out why he was being followed. Who did she represent? What was her brief? Was she hoping he would lead her to Anna? Or was he just paranoid?

Once he was out of the city centre, Jack rechecked his map, turned left at the next corner and hailed a cab.

ANNA ASKED her driver—as she now thought of Sergei—to take her back to the same block of flats they'd visited the previous day. She knew her mother would have risen by six to be sure everything had been dusted and polished.

When Sergei parked at the end of the litter-strewn path to the Piata Resitei, Anna told him that she expected to be about an hour and then wanted to go to Otopeni Airport.

JACK TOOK a seat in the cab, opened his map and pointed to Piata Resitei. The driver shrugged in disbelief and set out on a journey no tourist had ever requested before.

The taxi slipped out into the middle lane and both of them checked the rearview mirror. Had he lost her, or was she in one of three taxis he could see following them? She was a pro; he had the feeling she knew exactly where he was going.

Jack knew that every major city has its run-down districts, but he had never experienced anything quite like Berceni, with its grim, high-rise concrete blocks on every desolate corner. The taxi was already slowing when Jack spotted another yellow Mercedes parked by the kerb, in a street that hadn't seen two taxis in the same year.

'Drive on,' he said sharply, tapping the driver firmly on the shoulder and waving frantically forward.

'But this is place you ask for,' insisted the driver.

'Keep moving,' shouted Jack.

The puzzled driver shrugged and accelerated past.

'Turn at the next corner,' said Jack, pointing left. The driver nodded, now looking even more perplexed. He awaited his next instruction. 'Turn round, and stop at the end of the road.'

Once the driver had parked, Jack got out of the car and walked slowly to the corner, cursing his error. He wondered where the woman was, because she clearly hadn't made the same mistake. He should have anticipated that Anna might already be there.

Jack stared up at the grey concrete block and swore he'd never complain about his cramped West Side apartment again. He had to wait forty minutes before Anna emerged from the building. He remained still as she walked back down the path to her taxi.

As the taxi drove off, Jack jumped back into his own cab and, pointing frantically, said, 'Follow them, but keep your distance until the traffic is heavier.' He wasn't even sure that the driver understood what he said. The two yellow cabs must have looked like camels in a desert as they drove through the empty streets. Jack cursed again. Even an amateur would have spotted him by now.

'YOU DO REALISE that someone is following us?' Sergei said as he drove off.

'No, but I'm not surprised.' Anna felt cold and sick now that Sergei had confirmed her worst fear. 'Did you get a look at them?'

'Only a glimpse,' Sergei replied. 'A man, around thirty, thirty-five, slim, dark hair; not much else, I'm afraid.'

Anna shivered. So Tina had been wrong when she'd thought the stalker was a woman.

Sergei checked his rearview mirror. 'I could lose him.'

'Not much point. He already knows where I'm going.'

Once they reached the airport, Anna handed Sergei a twenty-dollar bill and told him which flight she was to return on. 'Would you pick me up?' she asked.

'Of course,' promised Sergei as the cab came to a halt.

'Is he still following us?' Anna asked.

'Yes,' Sergei replied, and jumped out of the car. A porter helped him load the crate and her suitcase onto a trolley. 'I'll be here when you return,' Sergei assured Anna before she disappeared into the terminal.

JACK'S CAB screeched to a halt behind the yellow Mercedes. He leaped out and ran to the driver's window, waving a ten-dollar bill. Sergei wound down the window slowly and took the money.

'The lady in your cab, do you know where she's going?'

'Yes,' replied Sergei, stroking his thick moustache.

Jack peeled off another ten-dollar bill, which Sergei happily pocketed.

'Well, where?' demanded Jack.

'Abroad,' replied Sergei, putting the car in gear and driving off.

Jack cursed, ran back to his cab, paid the fare and walked quickly into the airport. Moments later he spotted Anna heading towards the escalator. By the time he had reached the top of the escalator, she was in the café. She'd taken a seat in the far corner, where she could observe everything and everybody. Not only was *he* being followed, but now the person he was following was also looking out for him.

He retraced his steps and checked the departures board. There were only five international flights that day.

Jack always carried his passport and credit cards with him in case of just such an emergency. He dismissed Moscow, as it was due to depart in forty minutes, and New Delhi and Berlin weren't scheduled to leave until the early evening. He also considered Hong Kong unlikely, although it departed in just under two hours, while the London flight left fifteen minutes later. It had to be London, he decided, but he would purchase two tickets, one for Hong Kong and a second for London. If she didn't appear at the departure gate for Hong Kong, he would board the flight to Heathrow. He wondered if her other pursuer was considering the same options.

Once Jack had purchased both tickets and explained twice that he had no luggage, he took a seat among those passengers awaiting their flight to

Moscow. He called the hotel manager at the Bucharesti International on his cellphone and asked for his bags to be packed and left in reception, where they would be collected later. His suggestion that they add twenty dollars to his bill elicited the response, 'I'll deal with it personally, sir.'

Flight 3211 to Moscow was already boarding when Anna strolled by and took her place among those waiting to board Cathay Pacific Flight 017 to Hong Kong. Jack slipped back down to the concourse and kept out of sight while he waited for its final call.

All three of them boarded the Boeing 747 bound for Hong Kong. One in first class, one in business and one in economy.

9/17–9/18

'I'm sorry to interrupt you, milady, but a large box of documents has been delivered by Simpson and Simpson, and I wondered where you wished me to put it.'

Arabella looked up from the writing desk. 'Andrews, do you remember when I was a child and you were second butler?'

'I do, milady,' said Andrews, sounding somewhat puzzled.

'And every Christmas we used to play Hunt the Parcel?'

'We did indeed, milady.'

'And one Christmas you hid a box of chocolates. Victoria and I spent an entire afternoon trying to find them—but we never did.'

'Yes, milady. Your father promised me sixpence if I didn't reveal where they were hidden. His Lordship hoped to spend a peaceful Christmas afternoon enjoying a glass of port and a leisurely cigar.'

'Can you still recall where you hid them?'

'Yes, milady, and for all I know, they are still there.'

'Good, because I should like you to put the box that Simpson and Simpson have just delivered in the same place.'

'As you wish, milady.'

'And next Christmas, Andrews, should I attempt to find them, you must be sure not to let me know where they are hidden.'

'And will I receive sixpence on this occasion, milady?'

'A shilling, but only if no one finds out where they are.'

ANNA HAD SETTLED herself into a window seat at the back of economy. If the man Fenston had sent to track her down was on the plane, as she suspected he was, at least she now knew what she was up against. She had begun to think about him and how he'd discovered that she would be in Bucharest. How did he know her mother's address? And was he already aware that her next stop was Tokyo?

She had watched from the check-in counter as he ran up to Sergei's taxi. It had been her phone calls to Tina that had given her away. She felt confident her friend must have become an unwitting accomplice. Leapman was well capable of tapping her phone.

Anna had purposely dropped clues in her last two conversations to find out if there was an eavesdropper, and they must have been picked up: *going home* and *there will be a lot of people like that where I'm going*. Next time she would plant a clue that would send Fenston's man in completely the wrong direction.

JACK HAD SAT in business class sipping a Coke and trying to think logically. He was pursuing a woman who seemed to have stolen a $60-million painting. If Petrescu had stolen the painting, the other person pursuing her was clearly employed by Fenston to follow Anna until she found out where the picture was. But how did she always know where Anna would be? And did she now realise that he too was following Anna?

He found himself falling into a trap that he regularly warned his junior officers to be wary of. Don't be lulled into believing that the suspect is innocent. You must always assume they are guilty, and occasionally be surprised. He didn't remember his instructor saying anything about what to do if you found the suspect attractive.

But if Anna was about to try to sell the picture in Hong Kong, where would she deposit such a huge sum of money? Was she willing to live in Bucharest for the rest of her life?

And then Jack remembered that she had visited Wentworth Hall.

KRANTZ HAD SAT ALONE in first class. She always flew first class, because it allowed her to be the last on, and first off, any flight.

But now that someone else was following Petrescu, she would have to be even more cautious. After all, she couldn't afford to kill her with an audience watching, even an audience of one.

Krantz was puzzled by who the tall, dark-haired man could be. He was certainly a professional because she hadn't spotted him before, or after, his crass mistake with the taxis. She hoped he was an American, because if she had to kill him, that would be a bonus.

ANNA CHECKED her watch as the plane descended into Chek Lap Kok Airport. Her onward connection wasn't scheduled for another couple of hours. She would use any spare time to pick up a guide to Tokyo, a city she had never visited before.

Once they'd come to a halt at the terminal gate, Anna progressed slowly down the aisle, waiting for other passengers to rescue their bags from the overhead lockers. She looked around, wondering if Fenston's man was watching her.

She stepped off the aircraft and joined a handful of travellers turning left for 'Other Destinations', while the majority of passengers turned right. When she walked into the transit area, she was greeted by a neon-lit city and strolled from shop to shop admiring the latest fashions, electrical equipment, cellphones and jewellery. A book store displayed foreign newspapers and the latest best sellers. She strolled across to the travel section, where her eyes settled on the section on Japan.

JACK SLIPPED into an electrical shop from where he had a clear sight line of his quarry. All he could make out was that she was standing below a large, multicoloured TRAVEL sign, turning pages.

'Can I assist you, sir?' asked the lady behind the counter.

'Not unless you have a pair of binoculars,' said Jack, not taking his eyes off Anna.

'Several,' replied the assistant. 'May I recommend this particular model?' She placed a pair of binoculars on the counter.

'Thank you,' said Jack. He picked them up and focused them on Anna. She was still turning the pages of the same book, but he couldn't make out the title. 'I'd like to see your latest model,' he said, placing the binoculars back on the counter. 'One that could focus on a street sign at a hundred metres.'

The assistant extracted another pair from a display cabinet. 'These are Leica, top-of-the-line. You could identify the label on the coffee they're serving in the café opposite.'

Jack focused on the bookshop. Anna was replacing the book she had been reading, only to pick up the one next to it. He had to agree with the assistant, the binoculars were state-of-the-art. He could make out the word

'Japan' and even the letters TOKYO that were displayed above the shelf Anna was taking so much interest in. Anna closed the book, smiled and headed across to the counter.

'They are good, yes?' said the assistant.

'Very good,' said Jack, 'but I'm afraid they're out of my budget. Thank you,' he added before leaving the shop.

Anna was paying for her purchase when Jack headed off in the opposite direction. He joined a queue at the far end of the concourse.

When he reached the front, he asked for a ticket to Tokyo.

'Yes, sir. Which flight—Cathay Pacific or Japan Airlines?'

'When do they leave?' asked Jack.

'Japan Airlines departs in forty minutes. Cathay's Flight 301 is due to take off in an hour and a half.'

'Japan Airlines, please,' said Jack, 'business class.'

The sales assistant printed the ticket and said, 'If you proceed to Gate 71, Mr Delaney, boarding is about to commence.'

Jack walked back towards the coffee shop. Anna was sitting at the counter, engrossed in the book she had just purchased. He spent the next few minutes purchasing goods from shops he wouldn't normally have visited. He ended up with an overnight bag filled with clothes and toiletries, then hung around the pharmacy, waiting to see if Anna was about to move.

'Last call for passengers on Japan Airways Flight 416 to Tokyo. Please proceed immediately to Gate 71.'

Anna turned another page of her book, which convinced Jack that she must be booked onto the Cathay Pacific flight leaving an hour later. This time he would be waiting for her. He followed the signs for Gate 71 and was among the last to board the aircraft.

KRANTZ ONLY LET Anna out of her sight after she'd watched her board Cathay Pacific Flight 301. Upon entering the aircraft, Krantz turned left and took her usual window seat in the front row. She knew that Anna was seated at the back of economy, but she had no idea where the American was. Had he missed the flight?

JACK'S PLANE touched down at Narita International Airport, Tokyo, thirty minutes late, but he wasn't too anxious. Once he had cleared customs, his first stop was the enquiry desk, where he asked what time the Cathay flight was due to land. He was told it would be in just over forty minutes.

He then tried to work out in which direction Petrescu would go once she had cleared customs. Her first choice of transport, if she was still in possession of the crate, would surely have to be a taxi. Having checked out every possible exit, Jack returned to the arrivals hall. Above him, to his left, was a mezzanine floor, which overlooked the hall. He walked up the stairs and inspected the two telephone booths fixed to the wall. If he stood behind the second one, he could look down without being spotted. Jack checked the arrivals board. Flight CX 301 was due in twenty minutes. Easily enough time for him to carry out his final task.

He left the airport and stood in the taxi queue. When he reached the front, he climbed into the green Toyota and instructed the driver to park on the other side of the road.

'Wait here until I return,' he added, leaving his new bag on the back seat. 'I should be about thirty minutes. And keep the meter running.'

Jack returned to find that Flight CX 301 had just landed. He took his place behind the phone booth and waited to see who would be first through the door.

The indicator board flicked over. Passengers on Flight CX 301 were now in the baggage hall. Jack began to concentrate.

He didn't have long to wait. Krantz was first. She nestled in behind a melee of waiting locals before she risked turning round. But her blonde crew cut made Jack's task a lot easier.

While Jack kept one eye on the thin, short, muscular woman with the blonde crew cut, he turned back repeatedly to check on the new arrivals who were now swarming through the exit in little clusters. Gingerly, he took a step forward, praying that the blonde wouldn't look up.

He slipped a hand into an inside pocket, slowly removed his cellphone, flicked it open and focused it towards the crowd below him. For a moment he couldn't see her, then a man stepped forward and Jack's quarry was exposed for a split second. *Click*, then Jack switched his attention to the new arrivals. As he turned back, a mother bent to pick up a child and she was exposed again, *click*, and just as suddenly disappeared from view. Jack turned to watch as Anna came through the swing doors. He closed his phone, hoping that one of the images would he enough for the tech guys to identify the woman with the crew cut.

It wasn't only Jack's head that turned when the slim, blonde American strode into the arrivals hall pushing a cart laden with a suitcase and a wooden crate. He stepped back into the shadows the moment she paused to check the exit boards before turning right. Taxi it was.

Jack knew that Petrescu would have to join a long queue before she could hope to get a cab, so he allowed both women to leave the airport before he came down from the balcony. He took a circuitous route back to his taxi and was relieved to see the green Toyota waiting, meter ticking.

He climbed into the back and said to the driver, 'See the blonde with a crew cut, seventh in line? I want you to follow her, but she mustn't know.'

His eyes returned to Petrescu, who was fifth in the queue. When she reached the front, she turned and walked slowly to the back again. Clever girl, thought Jack, as he waited to see how Crew Cut would react.

He tapped his driver on the shoulder, and said, 'Don't move,' when the blonde stepped into a taxi, which drove off round the corner. Jack knew she'd be parked a few yards away, waiting for Petrescu to reappear. Eventually, Anna reached the front of the queue again. Jack told his driver, 'Follow that woman.'

'But it isn't the same woman,' queried the taxi driver.

'I know,' Jack said. 'Change of plan.'

As Petrescu's taxi drove past him and onto the freeway, Jack watched an identical vehicle slip in behind her. At last it was Jack's turn to be the pursuer and not the pursued. For the first time, he was thankful for the notorious snarl-ups and traffic jams that are the accepted norm for anyone driving into the city centre from Narita Airport. He never lost sight of either taxi.

It was another hour before Petrescu's taxi came to a halt outside the Hotel Seiyo in the Ginza district. A bellboy stepped forward to help with her luggage. Jack didn't consider entering the hotel until some time after Petrescu and the crate had disappeared inside. Crew Cut was secreted in the far corner of the lobby, with a view of the staircase and elevator. The moment he spotted her, Jack retreated outside. While he waited for Anna to reappear, he dialled through to London. He tried not to think what time it was.

'Where are you?' asked Tom.

'Tokyo.'

'What's Petrescu doing there?'

'I wouldn't be surprised if she isn't trying to sell a rare painting to a well-known collector.'

'Have you found out who the other interested party is?'

'No,' said Jack, 'but I did manage to get a couple of images of her at the airport. I'm sending the pictures to you now.' He keyed a code into his cell-phone and the images appeared on Tom's screen moments later.

'They're a bit blurred, but I'm sure the guys can clean them up. Any other information?'

'She's around five foot, slim, with a blonde crew cut and the shoulders of a swimmer. I've got a feeling she may be Russian.'

'Or even Romanian?' suggested Tom.

'Oh God, I'm so dumb,' said Jack. 'And the truth is, I think both parties are well aware of my existence.'

'Then I'd better find out who the crew cut is pretty fast.'

TINA TURNED on the switch under her desk. The little screen in the corner came alive. Fenston was on the phone. She flicked up the switch to his private line and listened.

'You were right,' said a voice, 'she's in Japan.'

'Then she probably has an appointment with Nakamura. All his details are in your file.' Fenston put the phone down.

Tina was confident that the voice fitted the woman she had seen in the chairman's car. She must warn Anna.

Leapman walked into the room.

ANNA STEPPED OUT of the shower and put on the white bathrobe that hung behind the door. She sat on the bed and opened her laptop to access a file. *Takashi Nakamura, industrialist. BSc in engineering. Tokyo University 1966–70, UCLA 1971–3, MA Economics. Joined Maruha Steel Company 1974. Director 1989, Chief Executive Officer 1997, Chairman 2001.* Anna scrolled down to Maruha Steel. Last year's balance sheet showed profits of more than $400 million. Mr Nakamura owned 22 per cent of the company and, according to *Forbes*, was the ninth richest man in the world.

Nakamura had made statements over the years, saying that his valuable Impressionist collection belonged to the company. Although Christie's never made such matters public, it was well known that Nakamura had been the under-bidder for Van Gogh's *Sunflowers* in 1987, when he was beaten by Yasuo Goto, chairman of Yasuda Fire and Marine Insurance Company, whose hammer bid was $39,921,750.

Anna unpacked her suitcase and selected a smart blue suit with a skirt that fell just below the knees, a cream shirt and low-heeled navy shoes; no make-up, no jewellery. While she pressed her clothes, Anna thought about the man she had met only once, and wondered if she had made any lasting impression on him. She dressed and checked herself in the mirror. Exactly what a Japanese businessman would expect a Sotheby's executive to wear.

Anna looked up his number on her laptop and dialled.

'*Hai, Shacho-Shitso desu,*' announced a high-pitched voice.

'Good afternoon, my name is Anna Petrescu. Mr Nakamura may remember me from Sotheby's.'

'Are you hoping to be interviewed?'

'Er, no, I simply want to speak to Mr Nakamura.'

'One moment, please. I will see if he is free to take your call.'

How could she expect him to remember her after only one meeting?

'Dr Petrescu, how nice to hear from you. I hope you are well?'

'I am, thank you, Nakamura-san.'

'Are you in Tokyo? Because if I am not mistaken it is after midnight in New York.'

'I am, and I wondered if you would be kind enough to see me.'

'You weren't on the interview list, but you are now. I have half an hour at four o'clock. Would that suit you?'

'Yes, that would be just fine,' said Anna.

Anna replaced the receiver and for some time didn't move. She tried to recall his exact words. What had his secretary meant when she asked, 'Are you hoping to be interviewed,' and why did Mr Nakamura say, 'You weren't on the interview list, but you are now'? Was he expecting her call?

JACK LEANED forward to take a closer look. Two bellboys were coming out of the hotel carrying the wooden crate. One of them spoke to the driver of the front taxi in line, who jumped out and carefully placed the crate in the boot. Jack rose from his chair and checked the taxi rank: four cars waiting. He calculated he could reach the second taxi in about twenty seconds.

He looked back at the hotel's sliding doors, wondering if Petrescu was about to appear. But the next person who caused the doors to open was Crew Cut, who slipped past the doorman and onto the main road. Jack knew she would sit in a taxi well out of sight, waiting for both of them.

Seconds later, Petrescu appeared, dressed as if she was about to attend a board meeting. The doorman escorted her to the front taxi and the driver eased out onto the road and joined the afternoon traffic.

Jack was seated in the back of the second taxi before the doorman had a chance to open the door for him.

'Follow that cab,' Jack said to the driver, 'and if you don't lose it, you can double the fare.' The taxi shot off. 'But don't make it too obvious,' he added, aware that Crew Cut would be in one of the numerous green vehicles ahead.

Petrescu's taxi turned left at Ginza and headed north towards the business district of Marunouchi, then turned left at the next set of lights. Jack repeated, 'Don't lose her.' Both cabs came to a halt at the next red light. Petrescu's taxi was indicating right and, when the light turned green, several other cars followed. Jack knew Crew Cut would be in one of them. As they swung onto the three-lane highway, Jack could see a string of green lights awaiting them. He swore under his breath. He preferred red lights; stopping and starting was better when you needed to remain in contact with a mark.

They all moved through the first green light and then the second, but as they passed in front of the Imperial Palace gardens, the third light turned amber just as Petrescu's taxi crossed the intersection. 'Go, go,' shouted Jack, but the driver came meekly to a halt and a police car drew up beside them. Jack stared ahead.

When the light returned to green, Petrescu's cab was long gone. It was bad enough he'd lost her, but the thought that Crew Cut was still on her tail caused Jack to curse the patrol car just as it turned right and drifted away.

KRANTZ WATCHED attentively as the green taxi edged across to the inside lane and drew up outside a modern white marble building. The sign above the entrance, MARUHA STEEL COMPANY, was in Japanese and English.

Krantz allowed her taxi to pass in front of the building before she asked the driver to draw up to the kerb, where she watched in the rearview mirror as Anna stepped out and walked to the back of the taxi. Her driver joined her and opened the boot, just as the doorman came running down the steps to assist with the luggage. Krantz continued to watch as the doorman carried the wooden crate up the steps and into the building.

Once they were out of sight, Krantz paid her fare, stepped out of the taxi and slipped into the shadows. She was satisfied that the American no longer posed a threat and wondered briefly if he was still roaming around Hong Kong in search of Petrescu, or the picture, or both.

It was beginning to look as if the painting had reached its destination; there had been a full page on Nakamura in the file Fenston had given her. If Petrescu reappeared with the crate, she must have failed, which would make it that much easier for Krantz to carry out her assignment. If she walked out without it, Krantz would need to make an instant decision.

The taxi driver came back out, climbed into his cab, and swung onto the street in search of his next customer. There was no sign of Petrescu.

As Krantz waited, her eyes settled on an establishment on the opposite side of the road that she had only been able to read about before but had always wanted to visit: the Nozaki Cutting Tool Shop. She crossed the road and, while keeping a wary eye on the Maruha Company's front door, stared into the window like a child for whom Christmas had come early. Left-handed scissors, Swiss Army knives and long-bladed tailor's shears all played second fiddle to a ceremonial Samurai sword. Krantz could not risk carrying her preferred weapon of death on a plane, so she was left with no choice but to pick up a local product in whichever country Fenston needed a client account closed indefinitely.

After she made her purchase, she left the shop to return to the anonymity of the shadows on the other side of the road. She removed the rice paper from her latest acquisition and slipped the blade into a sheath that had been tailor-made to fit on the inside of her jeans. It fitted like a gun in a holster.

THE RECEPTIONIST could not hide her surprise when the doorman appeared carrying a wooden crate, which he propped against the wall.

Anna offered no explanation, only her name.

'Mr Nakamura is interviewing another candidate at the moment,' the receptionist said, 'but should be free shortly.'

'Interviewing them for what?' asked Anna.

'I have no idea,' said the girl, seeming equally puzzled that an intervie-wee needed to ask such a question.

Anna sat down beside the crate and waited. Punctuality is an obsession with the Japanese, so she was not surprised when a smartly dressed woman appeared at two minutes to four, bowed and invited Anna to follow her.

'Yes, please,' said Anna, picking up the wooden crate.

The secretary led Anna down a long corridor, passing several doors that displayed no name or title. When they reached the last door, she knocked quietly, opened it and announced, 'Dr Petrescu.'

Mr Nakamura rose from behind his desk and came forward to greet Anna, whose mouth was wide open. A reaction that was not caused by the short, slim, dark-haired man who looked as if he had his suits tailored in Paris or Milan. It was Mr Nakamura's office that had caused Anna to gasp. The room was a perfect square and one wall was a single pane of glass. Anna stared out onto a tranquil garden, a stream winding from one corner to the other, crossed by a bridge and bordered by willow trees, whose branches cascaded over the rails.

On the wall behind the chairman's desk was a magnificent painting, duplicating exactly the same scene. Anna closed her mouth and turned to face her host.

Mr Nakamura smiled, delighted with the effect his Monet had created, but his first question shocked her. 'How did you manage to survive Nine Eleven, when, if I recall correctly, your office was in the North Tower?'

'I was very lucky, although some of my colleagues . . .'

Mr Nakamura raised a hand. 'I apologise,' he said. 'How tactless of me. Shall we begin the interview by asking you the provenance of the paintings in the room? Starting with the Monet?'

'*Willows at Vetheuil*. Its previous owner was a Mr Clark of Sangton, Ohio. Christie's sold the oil for twenty-six million dollars, but I had no idea you were the purchaser.'

Mr Nakamura revealed a smile of pleasure.

Anna turned to the opposite wall and paused. 'I have for some time wondered where that particular painting ended up,' she said. 'It's a Renoir, of course. *Madame Duprez and Her Children*, also known as *The Reading Lesson*. It was sold in Paris by Roger Duprez, whose grandfather purchased it from the artist in 1868.' Anna turned to the final piece. 'Easy,' she declared, smiling. 'It's one of Manet's late Salon works, probably painted in 1871, entitled *Dinner at the Café Guerbois*.'

Nakamura bowed. 'The position is yours.'

'The position, Nakamura-san?' said Anna.

'You are not here for the job of chief executive officer of my foundation?'

'No. Although I am flattered that you would consider me, I actually came to see you on a completely different matter.'

The chairman nodded, clearly disappointed, and then his eyes settled on the wooden crate.

'A small gift,' said Anna, smiling.

'If that is the case, I cannot open your offering until you have left.' Anna nodded, well aware of the custom. 'Please have a seat. Now, what is your real purpose in visiting me?' he asked as he leaned back in his chair and stared at her intently.

'I believe I have a painting that you will be unable to resist.'

'As good as the Degas pastel you purchased on my behalf?'

'Oh yes,' she said, a little too enthusiastically.

'Artist?'

'Van Gogh.'

Nakamura smiled an inscrutable smile. 'Title?'

'*Self-Portrait with Bandaged Ear.*'

'I presume it has to be the Wentworth *Self-Portrait*, purchased by the fifth Earl. What figure do you have in mind?' he asked.

'Sixty million dollars,' said Anna without hesitation.

For a moment, the inscrutable face appeared puzzled. 'Why is such an acknowledged masterpiece so underpriced?' he asked eventually. 'There must be some conditions attached.'

'The sale must not be made public,' said Anna in reply.

'That has always been my custom.'

'You will not resell the work for at least ten years.'

'I buy pictures,' said Nakamura. 'I sell steel.'

'During the same period of time, the painting must not be displayed in a public gallery.'

'Who are you protecting, young lady?' asked Nakamura without warning. 'Bryce Fenston or Victoria Wentworth?'

Anna didn't reply. She now understood why her boss at Sotheby's had once said that you underestimate this man at your peril.

'It was impertinent of me to ask such a question,' said Nakamura. 'I apologise,' he added, as he rose from his place. 'Perhaps you would be kind enough to allow me to consider your offer overnight.' He bowed low, indicating that the meeting was over.

'Of course, Nakamura-san,' she said, returning the bow.

'Please drop the "san", Doctor. In your chosen field, I am not your equal.'

She wanted to say, *Please call me Anna; in your chosen field, I know nothing*—but she lost her nerve.

Nakamura glanced at the wooden packing case. 'I will look forward to finding out what is in the box. Perhaps we can meet again tomorrow, after I've had more time to consider your proposition.'

'Thank you, Mr Nakamura.'

'Shall we say ten o'clock? I will send my driver to pick you up.'

Anna gave a farewell bow and Mr Nakamura returned the compliment. He walked to the door and as he opened it, added, 'I only wish you *had* applied for the job.'

KRANTZ WAS STILL in the shadows when Petrescu came out of the Maruha Steel building. The meeting must have gone well because a chauffeur-driven limousine was waiting for her and there was no sign of the crate.

Krantz was left with two choices. She was confident Petrescu would be returning to the hotel for the night, while the painting must still be in the building. She made her choice.

ANNA SAT BACK in the chairman's car and relaxed for the first time in days, confident that even if Mr Nakamura didn't agree to $60 million, he would still make a realistic offer. Otherwise why put his car at her disposal and invite her to return the following day?

When Anna was dropped outside the Seiyo, she went straight to the reception desk and picked up her key before heading towards the elevator. If she had turned right instead of left, she would have walked straight past a frustrated American.

Jack's eyes never left her as she stepped into an empty elevator. She was on her own. No sign of the package and, perhaps more significant, no sign of Crew Cut, who must have made the decision to stay with the painting rather than with its courier. Jack had to decide quickly what he would do if Petrescu reappeared with her bags and left for the airport. At least he hadn't unpacked this time.

KRANTZ HAD BEEN standing in different shadows for nearly an hour, only moving with the sun, when the chairman's limousine returned and parked outside the entrance to Maruha Steel. A few moments later, Mr Nakamura's secretary appeared with a man in a red uniform carrying the wooden crate. The driver opened the boot for the doorman to place the painting inside and listened as the secretary passed on the chairman's instructions. The chairman needed to make several calls to America and England and would therefore be staying in the company flat overnight. He had seen the picture and wanted it to be delivered to his home in the country.

Krantz checked the traffic. She knew she'd get just one chance, and then only if the lights were red. She was thankful it was a one-way street. She knew that the lights at the far end would remain on green for forty-five seconds as about thirteen cars crossed the intersection. She moved stealthily down the sidewalk, like a cat, aware that she was about to risk one of her nine lives.

The black limousine emerged onto the street. The light was green, but there were fifteen cars ahead of him. Krantz stood exactly opposite where she thought the vehicle would come to a halt. When the light turned red, she fell onto her right shoulder and rolled under the car. She gripped the two sides of the outer frame firmly and, spread-eagled, pulled herself up—one of the advantages of being four foot eleven and weighing less than a hundred pounds.

When the light turned green and the car moved off, she was nowhere to be seen.

The limousine drove at an uneven pace through the city, and it was another twenty minutes before the driver turned off into the hills. A few minutes later, another turn, a much smaller road and far less traffic. When they stopped at a crossroads, Krantz listened attentively. A passing lorry was holding them up.

She slowly released her right arm, which was almost numb, unsheathed the knife from her jeans and thrust the blade into the right-hand rear tyre until she heard a loud hissing sound. As the car moved off, she fell to the ground and didn't move an inch until she could no longer hear the engine. She rolled over to the side of the road and watched the limousine as it drove higher up the hill. As soon as it had disappeared out of sight, she pushed herself up and began jogging slowly towards the brow of the hill. Coming into view was a magnificent mansion, which dominated the surrounding landscape.

When Krantz came over the rise, she saw the chauffeur on one knee, staring at the flat tyre. As she approached, he looked up and smiled. Krantz returned the smile and jogged up to his side. He was about to speak when with one swift movement Krantz kicked him in the throat, then in the groin. He collapsed on the ground like a puppet whose strings had been cut.

Krantz ran to the front of the limousine and removed the keys from the ignition before returning to the back to unlock the boot. The lid swung up and her eyes settled on the crate. She grabbed a screwdriver from the tool kit in the boot, wedged it into a corner of the crate and wrenched the lid open, then tore at the bubble wrap. When the last remnant had been removed, she stared down at the prize-winning painting by Danuta Sekalska entitled *Freedom*.

JACK WAITED for another hour, one eye on the door for Crew Cut, the other on the elevator for Petrescu, but neither appeared. Yet another hour passed, by which time he was convinced that Anna must be staying overnight. He walked wearily up to reception and asked if they had a vacant room.

'How many nights will you be staying with us, sir?'

Jack would have liked to have been able to answer that question.

9/19–9/20

When Anna woke the next morning, the first thing she did was to phone Wentworth Hall.

'It's going to be a close-run thing,' warned Arabella, once Anna had imparted her news.

'What do you mean?'

'Fenston has issued a bankruptcy order against the estate, giving me fourteen days to clear the debt or he'll put Wentworth Hall on the market. If Nakamura finds out, it will weaken your bargaining position.'

'I'm seeing him at ten o'clock this morning,' said Anna. 'I would call you back when I find out his decision, but it will be the middle of the night.'

'I don't care what time it is,' said Arabella, 'I'll be awake.'

Once Anna had put the phone down, she bathed, dressed and took the elevator to the lobby to wait for the chairman's limousine.

Jack was already in a taxi when the car drew up and she appeared at the entrance. He was determined he wasn't going to lose her a second time.

KRANTZ HAD also spent the night in the centre of Tokyo, but not in a hotel bed. She had slept in the cab of a crane, some 150 feet above the city. She was confident that no one would come looking for her there. She stared down as the sun rose over the Imperial Palace, then checked her watch. It was 5.56 a.m. Time to descend.

She joined the early-morning commuters as they disappeared underground and made their way to work. Seven stops later she emerged in the Ginza and quickly slipped back into the Seiyo, a regular guest who never booked in and never stayed overnight.

Krantz positioned herself in the corner of the lounge, where she had a perfect sight line of the elevators. It was a long wait, but patience was developed over hours of practice—like any skill.

THE CHAUFFEUR closed the door behind her. He was not the same driver as the night before, Anna noted. He stepped in and drove off without a word.

When the chauffeur opened the door again, Anna could see that Mr Nakamura's secretary was waiting for her.

'Good morning, Dr Petrescu. Nakamura-san is looking forward to seeing you.' Anna followed her through reception and down the corridor.

Nakamura rose from behind his desk and bowed. Anna returned the compliment before he ushered her into a chair on the opposite side of the desk. He sat down. Yesterday's smile had been replaced by a grim visage.

'Dr Petrescu,' he began, 'it seems that when we met yesterday, you were less than frank with me.'

Anna felt her mouth go dry.

'You did not tell me, for instance, that you no longer work for Fenston Finance, having been dismissed for conduct unworthy of a bank officer.' Anna tried to breathe regularly. 'You also failed to inform me of the distressing news that Lady Victoria had been murdered, at a time when she had run up debts with your bank of over thirty million dollars. You also forgot to mention the small matter of the New York police being under the illusion that you are missing, presumed dead. But perhaps most damning was your failure to let me know that the painting you were attempting to sell is, to use police jargon, stolen goods. Perhaps there is a simple explanation for such sudden amnesia?'

Anna wanted to jump up and run out of the room, but she couldn't move. Her father had always told her: 'When you've been found out, confess.' She confessed everything. In fact, she even let him know where the painting was hidden. He didn't speak for some time. Anna sat and waited to be escorted from a building for the second time in just over a week.

'I am bound to ask how you intend to square the circle with your former boss. It is clear to me that Mr Fenston is more interested in holding on to such a valuable asset than having the debt cleared.'

'But that's the point. Once the overdraft has been cleared, the Wentworth estate can sell the painting to whoever they wish.'

Mr Nakamura nodded. 'Assuming that I accept your version of events, and if I was still interested in purchasing the *Self-Portrait*, I would want to make some conditions of my own.'

Anna nodded.

'First, the painting would be purchased directly from Lady Arabella only after legal tenure had been established.'

'I can see no objection to that,' said Anna.

'Second, I would expect the work to be authenticated by the Van Gogh Museum in Amsterdam.'

'That causes me no problems,' said Anna.

'Third—as I do believe I am, to use that ghastly American expression, in the driving seat—I offer fifty million dollars, which will both clear Lady Arabella's debt and leave enough to cover taxes.' Nakamura smiled for the first time. 'I am advised that Mr Fenston has recently issued a bankruptcy order against your client. It might be years before any legal action can be settled, and my London lawyers confirm that Lady Arabella is in no position to consider such crippling legal costs.'

Anna took a deep breath. 'If I accept your terms, in return I would expect some gesture of goodwill.'

'And what do you have in mind?'

'You will place ten per cent, five million dollars, in escrow with Lady Arabella's solicitors in London, to be returned if you do not wish to purchase the original.'

'No, Dr Petrescu.' Nakamura shook his head. 'However, I am willing to place five million with *my* London lawyers.'

'Thank you,' said Anna, unable to disguise a sigh of relief.

'But,' Nakamura continued, 'I would also expect a gesture of goodwill in return.' He rose from behind his desk and Anna got to her feet nervously. 'You will give serious consideration to taking up the appointment as the CEO of my foundation.'

Anna smiled and offered her hand. 'To use another ghastly American expression, Mr Nakamura, we have a deal.'

'One more thing before you go,' said Nakamura, picking up an envelope from his desk. 'Would you be kind enough to pass on this letter to Miss Danuta Sekalska, a huge talent that I can only hope will be allowed to mature?' He accompanied Anna back to the waiting limousine, making no reference to why his regular driver was in the hospital, recovering from serious injuries.

But then the Japanese have always considered that some secrets are best kept in the family.

ONCE THE TEMPORARY chauffeur had dropped Anna back at the Seiyo, she couldn't wait to check out. She picked up her key, ran up to her room and called Arabella, who sounded wide awake.

Then she exchanged her more formal attire for a T-shirt, jeans and trainers. Although checkout was at noon, she still had enough time to make one more call. Anna needed to plant the clue.

The ringing tone continued for some time before a sleepy voice answered.

'Who's this?'

'Vincent. You can go back to sleep after you've heard my news.'

'You've sold the painting?'

'How did you guess?'

'Congratulations. So where are you going next?'

'To pick it up where it's always been,' said Anna, before hanging up.

'WHO THE HELL is this?' Fenston fumbled for the bedside light as he tried to keep his eyes shut.

'Vincent's just made a call.'

'And where was she calling from this time?' asked Fenston, his eyes suddenly wide open.

'Tokyo.'

'So she must have seen Nakamura.'

'Sure has,' said Leapman, 'and claims she's sold the painting.'

'Did she say where she was going next?'

'To pick it up where it's always been.'

'Then it has to be in London,' said Fenston.

'How can you be so sure?' asked Leapman.

'Because if she had taken the painting to Bucharest, why not take it on to Tokyo? No, she left the picture in London,' said Fenston adamantly, '"where it's always been".'

'I'm not so sure,' said Leapman.

'Then where do you think it is?'

'In Bucharest, "where it's always been", in the red crate.'

'No, the crate was just a decoy. Now that Petrescu thinks she's sold the painting, her next stop will be to pick it up. And this time Krantz will be waiting for her.' Fenston slammed the phone down.

ANNA CHECKED out of the hotel and took a train to the airport. She assumed that once she boarded the shuttle, the same man would be following her, and she intended to make his task as easy as possible. He would already have been informed of her next stop.

She didn't know that her pursuer was sitting eight rows behind her.

KRANTZ OPENED a copy of the *Shinbui Times*, ready to raise it and cover her face should Petrescu look round. She dialled the number and waited for ten rings. On the tenth ring the call was picked up. She didn't speak.

'London' was the only word Fenston uttered.

Krantz dropped the cellphone out of the window and watched as it landed in front of an oncoming train.

IMMEDIATELY HER TRAIN came to a halt at the airport terminal, Anna jumped out and went straight to the British Airways desk. She enquired about an economy fare to London, although she had no intention of purchasing the ticket. She checked the departures board. There were ninety minutes between the two flights. Anna walked slowly towards Gate 91B, window-shopping all the way, and arrived just before boarding. She selected her seat carefully, sitting next to a small boy.

'Would those passengers in rows . . .' The child screamed and ran away, a harassed parent chasing after him.

JACK HAD ONLY been distracted for a moment, but she was gone. Had she boarded the plane or turned back? Perhaps she had worked out that *two* people were following her. Jack's eyes searched the concourse below him. They were now boarding business class and she wasn't anywhere to be seen. He checked the remaining passengers in the lounge, and he wouldn't have spotted the other woman if she hadn't touched her hair, no longer a blonde crew cut, now a black wig.

Krantz walked to the ladies' washroom behind where Petrescu had been sitting. She emerged a few moments later and returned to her seat. When they called final boarding, she was among the last to hand over her ticket.

Jack waited until the gate closed, now painfully aware that both women were obviously on the flight to London. But there had been something about Anna's manner since she'd left the hotel . . . almost as if, this time, she wanted to be followed.

The door of the men's washroom opened and Anna stepped out.

WHEN ANNA BOARDED the flight for Bucharest an hour later, she felt confident that she had shaken off Fenston's man. She had perhaps overdone it a little, but even Anna was surprised by how much fuss the little boy had made when she'd pinched him on his calf.

As the wheels lifted off Japanese soil, Anna's only real concern was for Tina. By this time tomorrow, Fenston and Leapman would realise that Anna had fed them false information. Anna feared that losing her job might end up the least of Tina's problems.

AS SHE STEPPED out of the airport at Bucharest, Anna was delighted to see a smiling Sergei standing by his yellow Mercedes. He opened the back door for her. 'Where to?' he asked.

'First, I need to go to the academy,' she told him.

Anna would have liked to share with Sergei all she had been through, but she still didn't feel she knew him well enough to risk it. Not trusting people was another experience she didn't enjoy.

Sergei dropped her at the bottom of the steps. She no longer needed to ask him to wait. The student working at the reception desk told Anna that Professor Teodorescu's lecture on attribution was about to begin, so she made her way to the lecture theatre and slipped into a seat at the end of the second row, just as the lights dimmed.

'Attribution and provenance,' began Anton, 'are the cause of more discussion and disagreement among art scholars than any other subject. There is no doubt that several of the world's most popular galleries currently display works that were not painted by the artists whose names are on the frame.'

As Anton turned to display a slide, his eyes rested on Anna. She smiled at him, but to her surprise he fixed her with a stare.

'This great city,' Anton continued, 'has produced its own scholar in the field of attribution. Some years ago, when we were students, we used to have long nighttime discussions about painting. We would meet up at our favourite rendezvous, *Koskies,* at *nine o'clock*, following the evening lecture.' He turned his attention back to the picture displayed on the screen. 'This is a portrait known as *The Madonna of the Pinks . . .*'

Anna left immediately. She could not mistake that look of fear in Anton's eyes, a look so obvious to those who've had to survive in a police state.

ANNA GLANCED AROUND Koskies. It hadn't changed much. The same plastic tables, the same plastic chairs, and probably the same wine that couldn't find an exporter. She ordered two glasses of the house red.

She looked up to see a tall man coming towards her. For a moment she couldn't be sure it was Anton. The advancing man was dressed in an army greatcoat with a woollen scarf topped off by a fur hat with ear flaps.

Anton took the seat opposite her and removed his hat.

'Do you have the painting?' asked Anna, unable to wait a moment longer.

'Yes,' said Anton. 'The canvas never left my studio,' he added before sipping his wine. 'Though I confess I'll be glad to be rid of the man. I went to jail for less and I haven't slept for four days.'

'I'm so sorry,' said Anna. 'I shouldn't have placed you in danger. What makes it worse is I have to ask you for another favour. You told me you kept eight thousand dollars of my mother's money.'

'Yes, most Romanians stash the cash under their mattress, in case there's a change of government in the middle of the night.'

'I need to borrow some of it. I'll refund the money just as soon as I get back to New York.'

'It's your money, Anna, you can have every last cent.'

'No, it's my mother's, but don't let her know, or she'll assume I'm in financial trouble and start selling off the furniture.'

Anton didn't laugh. 'But you *are* in trouble, aren't you?'

Anna rose. 'Not as long as I take the painting off your hands.'

Anton drained his glass and left a few coins on the table, then he pulled his hat back on and followed her out of the bar.

Anna looked up and down the street before she joined Anton, who was whispering intently to Sergei.

'Will you have time to visit your mother?' Anton asked, as Sergei opened the back door of the car.

'Not while someone is watching my every move.'

'I didn't see anyone,' said Anton.

'You don't see him,' said Anna. 'You feel him.' She paused. 'And I was under the illusion that I'd got rid of him.'

'You haven't,' said Sergei, as they drove off.

No one spoke for the rest of the short journey to Anton's home. Once Sergei had brought the car to a halt, Anton led Anna quickly up the stairs to an attic room crowded with canvases. Her eyes were immediately drawn to the painting of Van Gogh, his left ear bandaged. She smiled. The picture was in its familiar frame, safely back inside the open red crate.

'Couldn't be better,' she said. 'Now all I have to do is make sure it ends up in the right hands.'

Anton was on his knees in the far corner, lifting up a floorboard. He extracted a thick envelope, which he slipped into an inside pocket. He then returned to the wooden crate and hammered the lid back in place. He lifted the crate and led Anna back down the stairs.

Anna opened the front door, pleased to see Sergei waiting by the open boot. Anton placed the crate in the boot and Sergei slammed the lid closed. Anton turned to Anna and handed the thick envelope to her.

'Thank you,' she said, giving him another envelope in exchange.

He looked at the name and said, 'I'll see she gets it. Whatever it is you're up to,' he added, 'I hope it works out.'

He kissed her on both cheeks before disappearing into the house.

'Where will you stay tonight?' asked Sergei, as Anna joined him in the front of the car.

Anna told him.

9/21

When Anna woke, Sergei was sitting on the bonnet of the car, smoking a cigarette. Anna blinked and rubbed her eyes. She got out of the back seat and stretched her legs. The red crate was still in place.

'Good morning,' said Sergei. 'I hope you slept well?'

She laughed. 'Better than you, it seems.'

'After twenty years in the army, sleep becomes a luxury,' said Sergei. 'But please do join me for breakfast.' He retrieved a tin box from under the driver's seat and removed the lid to reveal its contents: two bread rolls, a boiled egg, a hunk of cheese, an orange and a flask of coffee.

'Where did this come from?' asked Anna.

'Last night's supper,' explained Sergei, 'prepared by my wife.'

'How will you explain why you didn't go home?'

'I'll tell her the truth,' said Sergei. 'I spent the night with a beautiful woman.' Anna blushed. 'But I fear I am too old for her to believe me,' he added. 'So what do we do next? Rob a bank?'

'Only if you know one with fifty million dollars in loose change,' said Anna. 'Otherwise I have to get that crate on the next flight to London, so I need to find out when the freight depot opens.'

'When the first person turns up.' Sergei removed the shell from the egg and handed it to Anna. 'Usually around seven.'

Anna took a bite. 'Then I'd like to be there by seven.'

'I don't think so.'

'What do you mean?' asked Anna, sounding anxious.

'When a woman like you has to spend the night in a car, there has to be a reason. So perhaps it would be unwise for you to be seen checking in a red crate this morning.' He paused, but Anna didn't comment. 'You know, when I was a colonel in the army, and I needed something done I didn't want anyone to know about, I chose a corporal to carry out the task. That way, no one took the slightest interest. I think today I will be your corporal.'

'But what if you're caught?'

'Then I'll have done something worthwhile for a change. Do you think it's fun being a taxi driver when you've commanded a regiment? Do not concern yourself, dear lady. One or two of my boys work in the customs shed, and if the price is right, they won't ask too many questions.'

Anna took five twenty-dollar bills out of the envelope.

'No, no,' he said, throwing his hands in the air. 'We are not trying to bribe the chief of police, just a couple of local boys.' He took one of the twenty-dollar notes.

Anna laughed. 'And when you sign the manifest, Sergei, be sure your signature is illegible.'

He looked at her closely. 'I understand, but then I do not understand. You keep out of sight. All I need is your plane ticket.'

Anna handed over her ticket to London. Sergei climbed into the driver's seat, turned on the engine and waved goodbye.

Anna watched as the car disappeared around the corner with the painting, her luggage, and her ticket to London. All she had as security was a hunk of cheese, a roll and a flask of cold coffee.

FENSTON PICKED UP the receiver on the tenth ring.

'I'm in Bucharest,' she said. 'The red crate was loaded onto a flight to London, which will be landing at Heathrow around four this afternoon.'

'And the girl?'

'I don't know what her plans are, but when I do—'

'Just be sure to leave the body in Bucharest.' The phone went dead.

Krantz walked out of the airport, placed the recently acquired cellphone under the wheel of a truck, and waited for it to move off before she slipped back into the terminal. Petrescu wouldn't fool her a second time.

AFTER THIRTY MINUTES, Anna began to feel anxious. After fifty, close to panic. An hour after he'd left, Anna even wondered if Sergei worked for Fenston. A few minutes later, an old yellow Mercedes came round the bend.

Sergei smiled. 'You look relieved,' he said, as he opened the front door for her and handed back her ticket.

'No, no,' said Anna, feeling guilty.

'The package is booked for London, on the same flight as you.' He climbed back behind the wheel. 'But you'll have to be careful. The American is there waiting.'

'He's not interested in me,' said Anna, 'only the package.'

'But for another twenty dollars he'll know where it's going.'

'I don't care any longer,' said Anna without explanation.

Sergei looked puzzled but didn't question her as he eased the Mercedes onto the highway and continued to the airport.

'I owe you so much,' said Anna.

'Four dollars, plus gourmet meal. I'll settle for five.'

Anna took out Anton's envelope, removed all but five hundred dollars, and resealed it. When Sergei came to a halt at the taxi stand outside the terminal, Anna passed him the envelope. 'Five dollars,' she said.

'Thank you, ma'am,' he replied.

'Anna,' she said, and kissed him on the cheek. She didn't look back, but if she had, she would have seen an old soldier crying.

WHEN TINA STEPPED out of the elevator, she spotted Leapman leaving her office. She slipped into the washroom, her heart beating frantically as she considered the consequences. Did he now know that she could overhear every phone conversation while watching everything that was going on in the chairman's office? But worse, had he found out that she had been emailing confidential documents to herself for the past year? Tina tried to remain calm as she walked back to her office.

She sat and flicked on the screen. She felt ill. Leapman was talking to Fenston. The chairman was listening intently.

JACK WATCHED as Anna kissed the driver on the cheek. He thought about the fact that the two of them had stayed awake all night while she had slept. If he'd dozed off, even for a moment, Jack feared that Crew Cut would have moved in, although he hadn't spotted her since she boarded the plane for London.

The crate was booked on the next flight to London. Already loaded on board, the cargo manager assured him. But would she be on the same flight? If the Van Gogh was in the red crate, what was in the crate that Petrescu had delivered to Nakamura's office? Jack had no choice but to wait and see if she boarded the same plane.

SERGEI WATCHED as Anna walked to the airport entrance, pulling her suitcase. He would call Anton later, to let him know he had delivered her safely. Anna turned to wave, so he didn't notice a customer climb into the Mercedes until he heard the door close.

Sergei glanced up at his rearview mirror. 'Where to, madam?'

'The old airport,' she said.

'I didn't realise it was still in service,' he ventured, but she didn't reply

Sergei took the next exit. He checked in the mirror again. There was something familiar about the woman. At the crossroads, Sergei turned left onto the old airport road. It was deserted—nothing had flown out of there since Ceausescu had attempted to escape in 1989. He glanced up at the mirror once more, and suddenly it all came back to him. The hair had been longer and blonde, but those eyes hadn't changed—eyes that registered nothing when she killed.

His platoon had been surrounded and marched to the nearest prisoner-of-war camp. He could still hear the cries of his young volunteers, some of whom had only just left school. And then, once they had told her everything they knew, or nothing at all, she would slit their throats while staring into their eyes. Each night she left with the same parting words: 'I haven't decided which of you will be next.'

Three of his men had survived, but only because a new set of prisoners, with more up-to-date information, had been captured. Her last victim had been Anna's father, one of the bravest men he'd ever known. When they were finally repatriated, Sergei had assured Anna's mother that her husband died bravely on the battlefield. Why should he pass his nightmare on to her?

Then Anton said he'd had a call from Captain Petrescu's daughter; she was coming to Bucharest and would he . . . someone else he hadn't passed his secret on to.

Once the hostilities had ceased, rumour concerning Krantz was rife. She was in jail, she had escaped to America, she'd been killed. He thought that she would never show her face in Romania again, because so many former comrades would line up for the privilege of cutting her throat. So why had she returned? What could be in that crate to make her take such a risk?

Sergei slowed down when he reached a stretch of runway covered in weeds and potholes. He kept one hand on the wheel, while the other slowly reached under the seat for a gun he hadn't used since Ceausescu had been executed. 'Where do you want me to drop you?' he asked, as if they were in the middle of a busy street.

She didn't reply. His eyes glanced up into the mirror. She was watching his every move.

Sergei eased out the gun. He was about to hit the brakes when a hand grabbed his hair and jerked back his head. His foot came off the accelerator and the car slowed to a halt.

'Where is the girl going?' she said, pulling his head back even further so that she could look into his eyes.

'What girl?' he managed to say as the knife touched his skin.

'Don't play games with me, old man. The girl at the airport.'

'She didn't say.' Another inch.

'She didn't say, even though you drove her everywhere?' she shouted, the knife now piercing the skin as warm blood began to trickle down his neck. 'Where—was—she—going?'

'I don't know,' Sergei screamed, as he raised the gun, pointed it towards her head and pulled the trigger.

The bullet ripped into Krantz's shoulder and threw her backwards, but she never let go of his hair. Sergei pulled the trigger again, but there was a full second between the two shots. Just long enough for her to slit his throat in a single movement.

LEAPMAN WASN'T ASLEEP when his phone rang, but he knew there was only one person who would consider calling him at such an ungodly hour.

He picked up the phone. 'Good morning, Chairman.'

'Krantz has located the painting.'

'Where is it?' asked Leapman.

'It was in Bucharest, but it's now on its way back to Heathrow. The plane lands just after four, London time.'

'I'll have someone standing by to pick it up and put it on the first flight to New York. Where's Petrescu?'

'No idea, but Krantz is at Bucharest airport, waiting for her.'

Leapman heard the click. Fenston never said goodbye.

He climbed out of bed and thumbed through his phone book until he reached the P's. He checked his watch and dialled her office.

'Ruth Parish.'

'It's Karl Leapman. We've found our painting. It's in the cargo hold of a flight from Bucharest, due to land outside your front door shortly after four o'clock this afternoon.' He paused. 'Just make sure you're there to pick it up. And don't mislay it a second time.' Leapman put the phone down.

RUTH PARISH and four of her carriers were already on the tarmac when Flight 019 from Bucharest landed at Heathrow. Once the aircraft had been cleared for unloading, the customs official's car, Ruth's Range Rover, and an Art Locations security van drove up and parked within twenty metres of the cargo hold. If Ruth had looked up, she would have seen Anna's smiling face in her tiny window at the back of the aircraft. But she didn't.

Ruth stepped out of her car and joined the customs officer. She had earlier informed him that she wished to transfer a painting from an incoming flight to an onward destination.

When the hold eventually opened, they both walked forward together. The customs officer addressed the chief loader, who gave instructions to his two men in the hold. The men disappeared into the darkness. By the time they reappeared, Anna was heading towards passport control.

'That's it,' said Ruth, when the two loaders reappeared, carrying a red crate. The customs official nodded. A forklift truck moved forward, extracted the crate expertly from the hold and lowered it slowly to the ground. It was driven across to the Art Locations van, where two of Ruth's carriers loaded the crate on board.

Anna had reached the baggage area by the time the security van began its circuitous journey. When the driver came to a halt, he parked beside a United Airlines plane bound for New York.

Ruth then watched the process in reverse. The back door of the security van was unlocked, the painting placed on a forklift truck, driven to the side of the hold, raised and accepted on board by two handlers before it disappeared into the bowels of the aircraft.

Ruth waited until the plane had taken off before she phoned Leapman in New York. Her message was simple: 'The package is on its way.'

JACK WAS PUZZLED. He had watched Anna stroll into the arrivals hall, exchange some dollars at Travelex, and then join the queue for a taxi. Jack's cab was already waiting on the other side of the road, engine running, as he waited for Anna's cab to pass.

'Where to, guv?' asked the driver.

'I'm not sure,' admitted Jack, 'but my first bet would be cargo.'

He assumed that Anna would ask the cab driver to go straight to the cargo depot and retrieve the crate that he had seen her taxi driver dispatch at Bucharest, but instead of turning right when the large blue CARGO sign loomed up, Anna's taxi continued west down the M25.

'I'm so stupid,' Jack said.

'I wouldn't want to venture an opinion on that, sir, but it would help if I knew where we was goin'.'

Jack laughed. 'I think you'll find it's Wentworth.'

Jack tried to relax, but every time he glanced out of the rear window he could have sworn that another black cab was following them. A shadowy figure was seated in the back. Why was she still pursuing Anna, when the painting must have been in cargo?

When his driver turned off the M25 and took the road to Wentworth, the taxi Jack had imagined was following them continued straight on.

'You're not stupid, after all, guv, because it looks as if it could be Wentworth.'

'No, but I am paranoid,' admitted Jack.

'Make up your mind, sir' the driver said, as Anna's taxi swung through the gates of Wentworth Hall and disappeared up the drive. 'Do you want me to keep followin' her?'

'No,' said Jack. 'But I'll need a local hotel for the night.'

'They ought to be able to fix you up at the Wentworth Arms.'

'Then let's find out,' said Jack.

'Right you are, guv.'

Jack sat back and dialled a number on his cellphone.

'American Embassy.'

'Tom Crasanti, please.'

WHEN KRANTZ CAME to following the operation, the first thing she felt was a stabbing pain in her right shoulder. She managed to raise her head off the pillow as she tried to focus on the small, white-walled room—a bed, a table, a chair, one sheet, one blanket, a bedpan. It could only be a hospital, but not of the private variety, because the exit had bars across the door.

Krantz tried to piece together what had happened to her. She could remember the taxi driver's gun pointing at her heart. She'd had just enough time to turn—an inch, no more. No one had been that close before. He had to be a pro, an ex-policeman, perhaps, possibly a soldier. But then she must have passed out.

JACK CHECKED in to the Wentworth Arms and booked a table for dinner at eight. After a shower and a change of clothes, he looked forward to devouring a large, juicy steak.

Even though Anna was safely ensconced at Wentworth Hall, he didn't feel he could relax while Crew Cut might be hovering somewhere nearby.

He sat in the lounge enjoying a Guinness. Long before the hall clock struck eight, Tom walked in, looked around and spotted his old friend. Jack rose to greet him and apologised for dragging him down to Wentworth.

'As long as this establishment can produce a decent Tom Collins, you'll not hear me complain,' Tom said, turning to the barman. They went to sit by the fire, where they were soon joined by the head waiter who took their orders for dinner. They both chose steak.

Tom extracted a thick file from his briefcase. 'Let's begin with the important news,' he said, opening the file. 'We've identified the woman in the photograph you sent from Tokyo. Her name is Olga Krantz. The agency was under the illusion that she was dead. We lost contact with her in 1989, when she ceased to be one of Ceausescu's personal bodyguards. We're now convinced she works exclusively for Fenston.'

'That's one hell of a leap of logic,' suggested Jack, as the barman appeared with a Tom Collins and another half pint of Guinness.

'Not if you consider the facts,' said Tom, before sipping his drink. 'Um, not bad . . . both Krantz and Fenston worked for Ceausescu, and Krantz removed anyone who posed a threat.'

'Still circumstantial.'

'Until you discover her chosen method of disposal.'

'A kitchen knife?' suggested Jack.

'You've got it,' said Tom.

'Which means Anna is being lined up as her next victim?'

'No—because Krantz was arrested in Bucharest this morning by the local police.'

'It's hard to believe they got within a mile of her,' said Jack. 'I kept losing her even when I knew where she was.'

'Krantz was unconscious at the time. It seems she was involved in a quarrel with a taxi driver.He had had his throat cut, while she ended up with a bullet in her right shoulder. The police have taken her to a secure hospital. We thought you might be able to throw some light on what caused the fight.'

'Krantz would have been trying to find out which plane Anna was on, but that taxi driver would never have told her. He protected her like a father.'

'Whatever. With luck, Krantz will spend the rest of her life in jail. And it turns out that our taxi driver, Colonel Sergei Slatinaru, was a hero of the resistance.' Tom packed the file back into his briefcase. 'So there's no longer any reason for you to worry about Dr Petrescu's safety.'

A waiter arrived to accompany them their table in the dining room.

'I won't relax until Krantz is dead,' said Jack, settling into his chair. 'Until then, I'll remain anxious for Anna.'

'Anna? Are you two on first-name terms?' asked Tom, as he took his seat opposite Jack.

'Hardly, though we may as well be. I've spent more nights with her than any of my recent girlfriends.' Jack waited a moment while the waiter served him his Caesar salad and placed a bowl of leek and potato soup in front of Tom. 'Have you found out anything else about Anna?' he continued.

'Not a lot,' admitted Tom, 'but I can tell you that one of the calls she made from Bucharest airport was to the New York Police Department. She asked them to take her name off the missing list, said she'd been in Romania visiting her mother. She also called her uncle in Danville, Illinois, and Lady Arabella Wentworth.'

'Then her meeting in Tokyo must have gone belly up.'

'You're going to have to explain that one to me,' said Tom.

'She had a meeting in Tokyo with a steel tycoon called Nakamura, who has one of the world's largest collections of Impressionist paintings in the world, so the concierge at the Seiyo informed me.' Jack paused. 'She obviously failed to sell Nakamura the Van Gogh, which would explain why she sent the painting back to London and allowed it to be forwarded to New York.'

'She doesn't strike me as someone who gives up that easily,' said Tom. 'By the way, the Happy Hire Company is also looking for her. They claim she abandoned one of their vehicles on the Canadian border, minus its bumpers, with not one light working.'

'Hardly a major crime,' said Jack.

'Are you falling for this girl?' asked Tom.

Jack didn't reply as their waiter cleared their plates. A moment later, he reappeared by the table. 'Two steaks, one rare, one medium,' he said.

'Mine's rare,' said Tom.

'Did you get any further with Leapman?' Jack asked, when the waiter had placed both plates on the table and left.

'Oh yes,' said Tom. 'He's an American citizen, second generation, and studied law at Columbia. After graduation he worked for several banks and then became involved in a share fraud.' He paused. 'He served a two-year sentence and was banned for life from working in any financial institution.'

'But he's Fenston's right hand?'

'Fenston's possibly, but not the bank's. Leapman's name doesn't appear on their books. He pays taxes on his only known income, a monthly cheque from an aunt in Mexico.'

'Any Romanian connection?'

'None that we're aware of,' said Tom. 'Straight out of the Bronx and into a suit.'

'Leapman may yet turn out to be our best lead,' said Jack. 'If we could only get him to testify—'

'Not a hope,' said Tom. 'I suspect he's more frightened of Fenston than he is of us.' He picked up his glass and drank from it. 'So when do you fly back to the States? I only ask as I want to know when I can return to my day job.'

'Tomorrow, I suppose,' said Jack. 'With Krantz locked up, Macy will want to know if I'm any nearer to linking her with Fenston.'

As they continued to eat, neither of them noticed the two men in coats who were talking to the head waiter. Now they walked purposefully across the dining room.

'Good evening, gentlemen,' said the taller of the two men. 'My name is Detective Sergeant Frankham, and this is Detective Constable Ross. I'm sorry to disturb your meal, but I need to have a word with you, sir.' He touched Jack on the shoulder. 'I'm afraid I must ask you to accompany me to the station.'

'On what charge?' demanded Jack, putting down his knife and fork.

'And on whose authority—' began Tom.

'I don't think you need to involve yourself, sir.'

'I'll decide about that,' said Tom, as he removed his FBI badge from an inside pocket. He was about to flick the leather wallet open when Jack said, 'Let's not create a scene, Tom. No need to get the Bureau involved. I'll go to the police station and sort this out.'

Reluctantly, Tom placed his FBI badge back in his pocket.

As Jack stood up, the sergeant grabbed his arm and handcuffed him.

'Hey, is that really necessary?' demanded Tom.

'Tom, don't get involved,' said Jack in a measured tone. 'Just stick around—I'm sure I'll be back in time for coffee.'

WHEN TINA HEARD her door open, she didn't look up. There was only one person who never bothered to knock before entering her office.

'I presume you know Petrescu tried to steal the Van Gogh?'

'I'd heard,' said Tina, as she continued typing.

'Don't play games with me,' said Leapman. 'You think I don't know that you listen in on every phone conversation the chairman has?' Tina stopped typing and looked up at him. 'Perhaps the time has come to let Mr Fenston know about the switch that allows you to spy on him.'

'Are you threatening me, Mr Leapman?' asked Tina. 'Because if you are, I might have a word with the chairman about the weekly calls you receive from a Mr Pickford.'

Leapman took his hands off the table and stood up straight.

'I feel sure your probation officer will be interested to learn that you've been harassing staff at a bank you don't work for, don't have an office in, and don't receive a salary from.'

Leapman took a pace backwards, hesitated, then left without another word. When the door closed, Tina was shaking so much she had to grip the armrests of her chair.

ONCE JACK HAD been checked in by the desk sergeant, the two detectives accompanied him to an interview room. Detective Sergeant Frankham asked him to take a seat on the other side of the table and extracted a long form from a file. 'Name?' he began.

'Jack Fitzgerald Delaney,' Jack replied.

'Date of birth?'

'November 22nd, 1963.'

'Occupation?'

'Senior investigating officer with the FBI, New York field office.'

The officer dropped his pen. 'Do you have some ID?'

Jack produced his FBI badge and identity card.

'Thank you, sir.' Frankham turned to his colleague. 'Would you see Agent Delaney is offered a coffee? This may take time.'

DS Frankham turned out to be right, because it was another hour before an older man entered the room. He was dressed in a tailored uniform, with silver braid on his cap. He took a seat opposite Jack.

'Good evening, Mr Delaney, my name is Chief Superintendent Renton. Now that we have been able to confirm your identity, perhaps you'd be kind enough to answer a few questions.'

'If I can,' said Jack.

'We received a complaint from a usually reliable source that you have, for the past week, been following a lady without her prior knowledge. This is an offence in England under the 1997 Protection from Harassment Act. However, I feel sure you have an explanation.'

'Dr Petrescu is part of an ongoing investigation, which my department has been involved in for some time.'

'Would that investigation have anything to do with the death of Lady Victoria Wentworth?'

'Yes,' replied Jack.

'And is Dr Petrescu a suspect in that murder?'

'No. In fact, we had thought she might be the next victim. Fortunately the murderer has been apprehended in Bucharest.'

'And you didn't share this information with us?' said Renton. 'Even though you must have been aware that we were conducting a murder inquiry?'

'I apologise, sir. I only found out myself a few hours ago. I'm sure our London office planned to keep you informed.'

'Mr Tom Crasanti has briefed me, I suspect because his colleague was under lock and key. He did assure me that you will keep us fully informed of future developments.' The chief superintendent rose from his place. 'Good night, Mr Delaney. I can only hope you have a pleasant flight home.'

'Thank you, sir,' said Jack, as Renton left the room. A few moments later, DS Frankham returned and Jack followed him out of the building.

Tom was waiting for him outside. 'The condemned man is to be given a chance to redeem himself,' Tom said.

'What do you have in mind?' asked Jack.

'We've both been invited to join Lady Arabella and Dr Petrescu for breakfast at Wentworth Hall tomorrow morning—and by the way, Jack, I see what you mean about Anna.'

9/22–9/23

Jack emerged from the Wentworth Arms just after 7.30 a.m. to find a Rolls-Royce by the entrance. A chauffeur opened the back door. 'Good morning, sir. Lady Arabella asked me to say how much she is looking forward to meeting you.'

'Me too,' said Jack, as he climbed into the back.

'We'll be there in a few minutes,' the chauffeur assured him.

After the long drive from the wrought-iron gates at the entrance to the estate, the Rolls came to a halt at the hall and the chauffeur walked round to open the passenger door.

Jack stepped out to see a butler on the top step.

'Welcome to Wentworth Hall, sir,' he said. 'If you would be good enough to follow me, Lady Arabella is expecting you.'

The butler led Jack through to the drawing room. 'Mr Delaney, milady,' he announced.

'Good morning, Mr Delaney,' said Arabella. 'I think we owe you an apology. You are so obviously not a stalker.'

Jack stared at Anna, who also looked suitably embarrassed, and then turned towards Tom, who couldn't remove the grin from his face.

Andrews reappeared at the door. 'Breakfast is ready, milady.'

WHEN SHE WOKE the second time, a young doctor was changing the dressing on her shoulder.

'How long before I'm recovered?' was her first question.

The doctor cut a length of bandage. 'Three or four days. But I wouldn't be in a hurry to get discharged. Your next stop is Jilava.'

Krantz could never forget the stone-walled, rat-infested building that she had visited every night to question prisoners before being driven back to the warmth of her well-furnished dacha. No one had ever escaped from Jilava, not even Ceausescu.

After the doctor left, Krantz discovered that there were always six guards, covering three eight-hour shifts. The first group clocked in at the hospital at six o'clock, the second at two, and the night shift came on at ten. Krantz discovered that one of them was lazy and spent half the night asleep. Another was always sneaking off to have a cigarette on the fire escape. The third, a philanderer, was never more than a few paces from one of the nurses. The fourth spent most of his time grumbling about how little he was paid. The other two guards were older, and remembered her only too well from the past régime.

But even they were entitled to a meal break.

JACK SAT DOWN to eggs, bacon, devilled kidneys, mushrooms and tomatoes, followed by toast, marmalade and coffee.

'You must be hungry after such an ordeal,' remarked Arabella.

'If it hadn't been for Tom, I might have had to settle for prison rations.'

'And I fear I am to blame,' said Anna. 'Because I fingered you,' she added with a grin.

'Not true,' said Tom. 'You can thank Arabella for having Jack arrested and Arabella for having him released.'

'But there is one thing I still don't understand,' said Anna, 'despite Tom filling us in with all the finer details. Why did you continue to follow me once you were convinced I was no longer in possession of the painting?'

'Because I thought the woman who murdered your driver would then follow you to London.'

'Where she planned to kill me?' said Anna quietly.

Jack nodded.

'Thank God I never knew,' said Anna, pushing her breakfast aside.

'But by then she'd already been arrested for murdering Sergei?' queried Arabella.

'That's right,' said Jack. 'But I didn't know that until I met up with Tom.'

'So the FBI had been keeping an eye on me at the same time?' said Anna, turning to Jack, who was buttering toast.

'For some considerable time,' admitted Jack. 'At one point, we wondered if you were the assassin. An art consultant would be a good front, especially if she was also an athlete who was born in Romania.' He took a sip of coffee. 'We were about to close your file when you stole the Van Gogh.'

'I didn't steal it,' said Anna sharply.

'She retrieved it, with my blessing,' interjected Arabella.

'And are you hoping Fenston will agree to sell the painting so that you can clear the debt? Because if he did, it would be a first.'

'No,' said Arabella, a little too quickly. 'That's the last thing I want.'

Jack looked puzzled.

'Not until the police solve the mystery of who murdered your sister,' interjected Anna.

'We all know who murdered my sister,' said Arabella sharply.

'Knowing it is not the same as proving it,' said Jack.

'So Fenston has got away with murder,' said Anna.

'More than once, I suspect,' admitted Jack. 'There are now five murders that have the Krantz trademark. But we've had a tiny break. When Krantz was taken to the secure hospital, the only thing they found on her, other than the knife and a little cash, was a key with NYRC 13 stamped on it. If we could find out what it opened, it might connect Krantz to Fenston.'

'Krantz murdered Victoria and Sergei?' said Anna.

'Without a doubt,' said Jack.

'And Colonel Sergei Slatinaru was your father's commanding officer,' said Tom. 'As well as being a close friend.'

'I'll do anything I can to help,' said Anna, close to tears. 'Do you want me to stay in England while you continue your investigation?'

'No, I need you to return to New York,' said Jack. 'Let everyone know you're safe and well. Even look for a job. Just don't give Fenston any reason to become suspicious.'

'Do I stay in touch with my former colleagues?' asked Anna. 'Fenston's secretary, Tina, is one of my closest friends.'

'Are you sure about that?' said Jack. 'How do you explain the fact that Fenston always knew where you were, if Tina wasn't telling him?'

'I can't, but I know she hates Fenston and her life must be in danger.'

'If that's the case,' suggested Tom, 'all the more reason for you to make contact with her as soon as possible.'

Jack nodded his agreement.

'I'm booked on a flight later this morning,' said Anna. 'Stansted.'

'Me too,' said Jack. 'Heathrow.'

'Well, one of you is going to have to change your flight,' suggested Tom.

'Not me,' said Jack. 'I'm not going to be arrested for stalking again.'

'I need to know if I'm still under investigation,' said Anna. 'Because if I am, you can go on following me.'

'No,' said Jack. 'When Arabella's sister was murdered, you had an unimpeachable witness as your alibi.'

'And who was that, may I ask?'

'Me,' replied Jack. 'Following you around Central Park.'

'You run in Central Park?' said Anna.

'Every morning around the loop,' said Jack. 'I overtook you several times during the last six weeks.'

Anna stared at him. 'The man in the green T-shirt. You're not bad.'

'And you're not so—'

'I'm sorry to break up this meeting of the Central Park joggers' club,' said Tom, as he pushed back his chair, 'but I ought to get back to my office.'

Jack smiled. 'I'd settle for a lift to the Wentworth Arms.'

'You got it,' said Tom.

'And now that I feel safe to join you at Heathrow, where shall we meet?' asked Anna, rising from her place.

'Don't worry,' said Jack. 'I'll find you.'

LEAPMAN WAS DRIVEN to JFK to pick up the painting an hour before the plane was due to land. That didn't stop Fenston from calling him every ten minutes on the way to the airport, which became every five once the limousine was on its way back with the red crate stowed in the boot.

Fenston was pacing up and down his office by the time Leapman was dropped outside the building and waiting in the corridor when Barry Steadman and the driver stepped out of the elevator carrying the red crate.

'Open it,' ordered Fenston, long before the crate had been propped against the wall in his office. Barry and the driver undid the special clamps before extracting the long nails in the rim, while Fenston and Leapman looked on. Barry lifted the painting out carefully and leaned it up against the chairman's desk. Fenston began to tear off the bubble wrap with his bare hands, until he could at last see what he'd been willing to kill for.

Fenston gasped. 'It's even more magnificent than I'd expected. Truly a masterpiece. I know exactly where I'm going to hang my Van Gogh.' He looked up at the wall behind his desk, where a massive photograph of George W. Bush shaking hands with him at Ground Zero filled the space.

JACK WAS WAITING for her when she checked in. Anna took a little time to relax with a man she couldn't forget had been following her for the last nine days, but by the time they climbed the steps to the aircraft, Jack knew she was a Knicks fan, liked spaghetti and Dustin Hoffman, while Anna had found out that he also supported the Knicks, that his favourite artist was Fernando Botero, and nothing could replace his mother's Irish stew.

She managed to nod off on the flight, and woke about an hour before they were due to land to find Jack asleep on her shoulder. She sat up sleepily and accepted a cup of tea from the stewardess.

Jack straightened up. 'So what's the first thing you're going to do now that you've miraculously risen from the dead?' he asked after a while.

'Find out if anyone wants to employ me. And you?'

'I'll have to let my boss know I'm no nearer to nailing Fenston, which will be greeted with one of his two favourite maxims: 'Raise your game, Jack,' or 'Step it up a notch.' '

'That's hardly fair, now that Krantz is behind bars.'

'No thanks to me,' said Jack. 'And then I'll have to face up to an even fiercer wrath than the boss's when I try to explain to my mother why I didn't turn up for her Irish stew night. My only hope of redemption is to discover what NYRC stands for.' Jack put a hand in his top pocket. 'Thanks to modern technology, Tom was able to produce an exact copy, even though the original is in Romania.' He handed the facsimile across to Anna.

Anna turned the small key over in her hands. 'New York Racing Club, New York Rowing Club, anything else?'

'New York Racquet Club, but if you come up with any others, let me know, because I intend to find out before Monday.'

'Perhaps you could slow down enough on your morning run to let me know if you've cracked it.'

'I was rather hoping to tell you over dinner tonight,' said Jack.

'I can't. I'm sorry, Jack, much as I'd love to, I'm having dinner with Tina. Six o'clock tomorrow morning suit you?'

'That means I'll have to set my alarm for six thirty if we're going to meet up about halfway round.'

'I'll be out of my shower by then.'

'I'll be sorry to miss that,' said Jack.

LEAPMAN STRODE into the chairman's office without knocking.

'Have you seen this?' Leapman asked, placing the *New York Times* on the chairman's desk and jabbing a finger at an article from the international section.

Fenston studied the headline: ROMANIAN POLICE ARREST ASSASSIN, then read the article. 'Find out how much the chief of police wants.'

'It may not prove to be that easy.' Leapman frowned. 'And there's another matter you should consider. You ought to have the Van Gogh insured, after what happened to the Monet.'

'I never insure my paintings. I don't need the IRS to find out how much my collection is worth, and in any case it's never going to happen twice.'

'It already has,' said Leapman.

Fenston scowled and didn't reply for some time. 'All right, but make it Lloyd's of London, and keep the book value below twenty million,' he said eventually. 'The last thing I need is to have the Van Gogh with an asset value of a hundred million while I'm still hoping to get my hands on the rest of the Wentworth collection.'

KRANTZ WET her bed and then explained to the doctor about her weak bladder. He authorised periodic visits to the bathroom, but only when accompanied by at least two guards.

These regular little outings gave Krantz an opportunity to study the floor layout, but also served another purpose. Once the guards had locked Krantz into her cubicle, she sat on the seat and extracted a condom from her rectum, which she then washed in the toilet water. She undid the knot at the top and pulled out a roll of tightly wrapped twenty-dollar bills. She extracted two from the roll, tucked them into her arm sling, and then carried out the whole process in reverse.

Krantz pulled the chain, then the guard opened the door and Krantz was escorted back to her room. She spent the rest of the day sleeping.

JACK SAT in the back of the taxi and phoned his boss to let him know that he was back in New York.

Macy said, 'Why don't you take the rest of the week off, Jack? You've earned it.'

'It's Saturday,' Jack reminded him.

'So I'll see you first thing Monday morning,' said Macy.

Jack decided to call his mother.

'Will you be coming home for supper tonight?' she asked. He could almost smell the meat stewing in the background.

'Would I miss it, Ma?'

'You did last week.'

'Ah, yes, I meant to call you, but something came up.'

'Will you be bringing this something with you tonight?' Jack hesitated, a foolish mistake. 'Is she a good Catholic girl?'

'No, Mother, she's a divorcée, three ex-husbands, two of whom died in mysterious circumstances. Oh, and she has five children, not all by the three husbands, but you'll be glad to know only four are on hard drugs—the other's in jail.'

'Does she have a regular job?'

'Oh, yes, Ma, it's a cash business. She services most of her customers on the weekends, but she assures me that she can always take an hour off for a bowl of Irish stew.'

'So what does she really do?' asked his mother.

'She's an art thief. Specialises in Van Gogh and Picasso.'

'Then she'll be an improvement on the last one, who specialised in losing your money.'

'Goodbye, Mother,' said Jack. 'I'll see you tonight.'

He ended the call to find a text message from Anna on his cellphone, using her ID for Jack: *Switch your brain on, Stalker. Got the obvious R. U R 2 slow 4 me.*

THE NIGHT SHIFT spent their first two hours marching up and down the corridor, every few minutes unlocking her door, switching on the bare bulb and checking that she was 'present'. After that it lapsed to every half an hour.

At 4.05 a.m., when the two older guards went off for their meal break, Krantz pressed the buzzer by her bed. The grumbler with money problems and the chain smoker accompanied her to the bathroom. When she entered the lavatory, one remained in the corridor, while the other stood guard outside the cubicle. Krantz extracted two more notes and then pulled the lavatory chain. The guard opened the door. She smiled and slipped the notes into his hand. He quickly put them in his pocket before rejoining his chain-smoking colleague in the corridor. They accompanied Krantz back to her room and locked her in.

Twenty minutes later, the other two guards returned from their meal break. One of them unlocked her door to make sure she was there. The check completed, he walked back into the corridor, locked the door and joined his colleague for a game of backgammon.

Krantz concluded that her one chance of escaping would be between four o'clock and 4.20 in the morning, when the two older guards took their meal break—the philanderer, the smoker and the dozer would be otherwise occupied, and her unwitting accomplice would be only too happy to accompany her to the bathroom.

JACK SCOURED the New York telephone directory in search of NYRC. Other than the three he had already come up with, he couldn't spot Anna's 'obvious one.' He switched on his laptop and Googled the words 'new york racquet club'. He was able to retrieve several photographs of an elegant building on Park Avenue. No doubt the only way he was going to get past the front door was if he looked like a member. Never embarrass the Bureau.

Once Jack had unpacked and showered, he selected a dark suit with a faint stripe, a blue shirt and a tie for this particular outing. He took a cab to 370 Park Avenue and admired the magnificent four-storey Renaissance revival architecture. He walked up the steps to an entrance with the letters NYRC discreetly etched into the glass and strolled up to the reception desk.

'May I help you, sir?' asked a young man.

'I'm not sure,' Jack admitted. He took the replica key out of his pocket and placed it on the countertop. 'Ever seen one of these?'

The young man picked up the key. 'No, sir, can't say I have. It could well be a safety deposit box key, but not one of ours.'

'Any suggestions?' asked Jack, trying to keep desperation out of his voice.

'No, sir. Not unless it was before my time. I've been here eleven years, but Abe might be able to help.'

An older man appeared from an office at the back. 'And what is it that I might be able to help with?' he said.

'A key,' said the young man. 'This gentleman wants to know if you've seen one like it.' He passed the key to Abe.

'It's certainly not one of ours,' Abe confirmed, 'but I know what the R stands for, because it must have been nearly twenty years ago, a young man came in and asked if this was the Romanian Club.'

'Of course,' murmured Jack, 'how stupid of me.'

'He couldn't read English,' continued Abe, 'so I had to look up the address for him. The only reason I remember is because the club was on Lincoln.' He glanced at Jack. 'Named after him,' he explained. 'Some place in Queens, I think.'

JACK STEPPED into a liquor store on the corner of Lincoln and Harris. 'I'm looking for the Romanian Club,' he told the woman behind the counter.

'Closed years ago. It's a guest house now.' She looked him up and down. 'But I don't think you'll wanna stay there.'

'Any idea of the number?' asked Jack.

'No, but it's halfway down the other side of the street.'

Jack thanked the woman. Back on Lincoln, he tried to judge where the halfway mark might be, when he spotted a faded ROOMS FOR RENT sign. He looked down a short flight of steps to see an even more faded sign: NYRC, FOUNDED 1919. Jack descended the steps and entered a dingy, unlit hall. There was a small reception desk straight ahead, and behind it an old man enveloped in cigarette smoke was reading the *New York Post*.

'I need a room for the night,' said Jack, trying to sound as if he meant it.

The old man gave Jack's suit a disbelieving look. 'That'll be seven dollars,' he said, 'in advance.'

'And I'll also need somewhere to lock my valuables.'

'That'll be another dollar—in advance.'

Jack handed over eight dollars in return for a key.

'Number three, boxes at the end of the corridor,' the man said, passing him a second key. He returned his attention to the *Post*.

Jack walked down the corridor until he reached a wall lined with safety deposit boxes. He opened his box and peered into it. It must have been about eight inches wide and a couple of feet deep. He glanced back towards the front counter before moving further down. Then he removed the replica key from an inside pocket and opened box 13. He stared inside and tried to remain calm, although his heart was pounding. He locked the box and walked back out to the street.

In his apartment, Jack attempted to calculate how many hundred-dollar bills must have been stuffed inside box 13. By the time he called Dick Macy, he'd measured a space out on the kitchen table and used several five-hundred-page paperbacks to assist him in his calculation.

'I thought I told you to take the rest of the weekend off,' said Macy.

'I've found the box that NYRC 13 opens.'

'What was inside?'

'Hard to be certain. I'd say around two million dollars.'

'Your leave is cancelled,' said Macy.

ANNA SET OUT on her morning run just before 6 a.m. Sam rushed from behind the reception desk to open the door for her—a Cheshire cat grin hadn't left his face from the moment she'd arrived back.

Anna wondered at what point Jack would catch up with her. She had to admit, he'd been in her thoughts a lot and she hoped their relationship might stray beyond a professional interest.

She spotted Jack jogging under Artists' Gate. 'Been waiting long, Stalker?' she asked as she strode past him.

'No,' he replied once he'd caught up. 'I've already been round twice, so I'm treating this as a cooling-down session.'

'Cooling down already, are we?' said Anna, as she accelerated away. It was only a few seconds before he was back and she decided that her only hope would be to distract him. 'Have you worked out what R stands for?'

'You tell me,' said Jack.

'Romania would be my bet,' said Anna, almost out of breath.

'You should have joined the FBI,' said Jack, slowing down.

'So where is the Romanian Club?'

'In a run-down neighbourhood in Queens,' replied Jack.

'And what did you find when you opened the box?'

'About two million dollars.'

'Two million?' repeated Anna. 'What sort of person keeps two million in cash in a safety deposit box in Queens?'

'A person who can't risk opening a bank account.'

'Krantz,' said Anna.

'So now it's your turn. Did anything come out of your dinner with Tina?'

'Fenston thinks the latest addition to his collection is magnificent. But, more important, when Tina took in his morning coffee, there was the *New York Times* on his desk, open at page seventeen. International Section.' Anna extracted the article from her pocket and passed it over to Jack.

Jack read the headline. 'Sharp girl, your friend Tina. I take back everything I said. She's on our team.'

'No, Stalker, she's on *my* team,' said Anna, accelerating through Strawberry Fields as she always did, with Jack striding by her side.

LEAPMAN HAD SELECTED a Sunday because it was the one day of the week Fenston didn't go into the office.

He sat in his apartment eating a TV dinner. When he'd eaten every last scrap, he returned to his bedroom and put on a grey track suit, then he reached under the bed and pulled out a gym bag. Next he opened a drawer that contained a carton of Marlboros and extracted a packet. His final act was to place his hand under the drawer and remove a key taped to the base.

He double-locked the door of his apartment and walked one block before hailing a yellow cab. He gave the driver an address. This would be the last time he carried out this particular chore for Fenston, a man who had taken advantage of him every day for the last decade. During that time, Leapman had deposited more than five million dollars into box 13 at the guesthouse in Lincoln Street, and he knew it would always be a one-way journey—until she made a mistake. He knew this would be his one chance.

'You can drop me on the corner,' Leapman said.

The driver came to a halt. 'Twenty-three dollars.'

Leapman passed three tens through the grille. 'I'll be back in five minutes. If you're still around, you'll get another fifty.'

'I'll be around,' came back the immediate reply.

Leapman grabbed the empty gym bag and stepped out of the cab. He reached number 61 and stopped for a moment to check that no one was taking any interest in him. Why would they? He descended the steps and pushed open a door.

The caretaker looked up and, when he saw who it was, nodded and turned his attention back to the racing page. Leapman placed the packet of Marlboros on the counter. Every man has his price.

He peered into the gloom of a corridor lit only by a naked forty-watt bulb. He knew exactly where her box was located. He looked back; one of the Marlboros was already glowing in the dark.

He took the key out of his track-suit pocket, placed it in the lock and turned it. He unzipped the bag. It took him less than a minute to empty the box, fill the bag with the bills and then zip the bag back up. He picked up the bag, momentarily surprised by how heavy it was, and walked back to the counter where he laid the key. 'I won't be needing this again,' he told the old man, who didn't allow this sudden break in routine to distract him from his study of the odds at Belmont for the four o'clock.

Leapman climbed back up the steps to Lincoln Street. He began to walk quickly, relieved to see the cab was still waiting for him.

He had covered about twenty yards when, out of nowhere, he was surrounded by a dozen men dressed in jeans and blue nylon windbreakers with the letters 'FBI' printed in bold yellow on their backs. Two cars entered Lincoln, one from each end, and came to a screeching halt in a semicircle round the suspect. The taxi sped away.

'Read him his rights,' said one officer, as another handcuffed him, while a third relieved him of his gym bag.

'You have the right to remain silent . . .' which Leapman did.

Once his rights had been recited to him, Leapman was led off to one of the cars and unceremoniously dumped in the back, where Agent Delaney was waiting for him.

ON THE MORNING of the fourth day, Krantz heard the clock on the nearby church strike four times. She then heard one of the guards say, 'We're off for our supper.' The chain smoker coughed but didn't respond. Krantz lay still until she could no longer hear their departing footsteps. She pressed the buzzer by her bed and a key turned in the lock.

'Where's your mate?' Krantz asked.

'He's having a drag,' said the guard. 'Don't worry, he'll get his share.'

She climbed out of bed. Another guard was lolling in a chair, half asleep, at the other end of the corridor. The smoker and the philanderer were nowhere to be seen.

The guard accompanied her into the bathroom. Krantz disappeared into the cubicle, peeled off two more twenty-dollar bills and folded them in the palm of her right hand. Once she'd pulled the chain, her guard unlocked the door. He smiled in anticipation as she walked back out into the corridor. The guard seated at the far end of the corridor didn't stir.

Krantz nodded towards the linen closet. Her personal minder pulled open the door and they both slipped inside. Krantz immediately opened the palm of her hand. Just as the guard went to grab the bills, she dropped one on the floor. He bent down to pick it up and the full force of her knee came crashing up into his groin. As he fell forward, Krantz grabbed him by the hair and sliced open his throat with the doctor's scissors. Not the most efficient of instruments, but the only thing she had been able to lay her hands on. With all the strength she could muster, she bundled him into the laundry chute, then dived in behind him.

They both bounced down the spacious metal tube and landed with a thud on a pile of towels in the laundry room. Krantz leaped up, grabbed the smallest overall from a peg on the wall, pulled it on and ran to the door. She peered out into the corridor. The only person in sight was a cleaner, on her knees polishing the floor. Krantz walked past her, pushed open the door and ran up one flight of steps. She pulled up a window on the ground floor and climbed out into a flowerbed. It was pouring with rain.

9/24

One of Anna's golden rules when she woke in the morning was not to check the messages on her cellphone until she had showered, dressed, had breakfast, and read the *New York Times*. But as she had broken every one of her golden rules over the last two weeks, she checked her messages even before she got out of bed. One from Stalker asking her to call, which made her smile, and one from Mr Nakamura, which made her frown—only four words: *Urgent, please call. Nakamura.*

Heart pounding, she dialled Nakamura's number in Tokyo.

'*Hai, Shacho-Shitso desu,*' announced the receptionist.

'Mr Nakamura, please. It's Anna Petrescu calling.'

'Ah, yes, he is expecting your call.'

'Good morning, Dr Petrescu.'

'Good afternoon, Mr Nakamura.' Anna's heartbeat quickened.

'I just wanted to let you know that I have, as you requested, deposited five million dollars with my lawyers in London. So I would like to view the Van Gogh as soon as possible.'

'I could fly to Tokyo,' Anna assured him, 'but I would first have to go to England and pick up the painting.'

'That may not prove necessary. I have a meeting with Corus Steel in London scheduled for Wednesday, and would be happy to fly over a day earlier, if that was convenient for Lady Arabella.'

'I'm sure that will be just fine,' said Anna. 'I'll need to contact Arabella, then call your secretary to confirm the details.'

'Excellent,' said Nakamura. 'Then I'll look forward to seeing you both tomorrow evening.'

ALTHOUGH IT WAS the third time Fenston had read the article, a smile never left his face. He couldn't wait to share the news with Leapman. He glanced at the clock on his desk, just before ten. Leapman was never late. Where was he?

Tina had already warned him that Mr Jackson, from Lloyd's of London, was in the waiting room, and the front desk had just called to say that Chris Savage of Christie's was on his way up.

'As soon as Savage appears,' said Fenston, 'send them both in and then tell Leapman to join us.'

'I haven't seen Mr Leapman this morning,' said Tina.

'Well, I want him in here the moment he arrives.' Fenston reread the headline, KITCHEN KNIFE KILLER ESCAPES.

There was a knock on the door and Tina ushered both men into the office. 'Mr Jackson and Mr Savage,' she said.

Fenston shook hands with a short, balding man in a navy pin-striped suit, who introduced himself as Bill Jackson. Fenston nodded at Savage, whom he had met at Christie's on occasion. He was wearing his trademark bow tie.

'I wish to make it clear from the outset,' began Fenston, 'that I only want to insure this one painting,' he said, gesturing towards the Van Gogh, 'for twenty million dollars.'

'Despite the fact it might fetch five times that amount under the hammer?' Savage turned to study the picture.

'That's a far lower premium,' interjected Jackson. 'Assuming our security boys consider the painting adequately protected.'

'Just stay where you are, Mr Jackson, and decide for yourself.' Fenston entered a six-digit code on the keypad next to the light switch, then left the room. The moment the door closed, a metal grille appeared from out of the ceiling and eight seconds later was clamped to the floor, covering the Van

Gogh. At the same time, an alarm emitted an ear-piercing sound.

Jackson pressed his hands over his ears and turned to see a second grille barring his exit. A few seconds later, the alarm stopped and the metal grilles slid up. Fenston marched back in, looking pleased with himself.

'Impressive,' said Jackson. 'How many people know the code?'

'Only two of us,' said Fenston, 'my chief of staff and myself, and I change the sequence once a week.'

'And that window, is there any way of opening it?'

'No, it's double-glazed bulletproof glass.'

'And the alarm . . .'

'Connected to Abbott Security. They have an office in the building and guarantee to be on this floor in two minutes.'

'What we in the business call triple-A,' said Jackson, 'which means the premium can be kept to one per cent or, in real terms, around two hundred thousand dollars. I can complete the paperwork as soon as Mr Savage confirms a value of twenty million.'

'That shouldn't be too difficult,' said Fenston. 'He's already assured us that the Wentworth Van Gogh is worth nearer one hundred million.'

'The Wentworth Van Gogh most certainly is,' said Savage, 'but the only part of this work that's original is the frame. The painting is a fake.'

'*A fake?*' repeated Fenston, staring up at his painting. 'But it came from Wentworth Hall. How can you be sure?'

'The wrong ear is bandaged,' said Savage emphatically. 'Van Gogh cut off his left ear but he painted the self-portrait while looking in a mirror, which is why the right ear is bandaged. I must confess, though,' he added, 'that whoever painted this particular version is a fine artist.'

'Get me Leapman,' Fenston screamed at the top of his voice, causing Tina to come running into the room.

'He's just arrived,' she said. 'I'll tell him you want him.'

The man from Lloyd's and the Christie's expert left discreetly. Leapman came rushing in.

'The painting's a fake,' shouted Fenston.

Leapman stared at the picture. 'Then I know who's responsible.'

'Petrescu,' Fenston said, spitting out the name.

'Not to mention her partner, who has been feeding Petrescu with information since the day you fired her.'

'You're right,' said Fenston, and turning towards the open door he shouted 'Tina' at the top of his voice. She came running back into the room.

'You see that picture?' he said, unable even to look at the painting. Tina nodded. 'I want you to put it in its packing case and then dispatch it to Wentworth Hall, along with a demand for—'

'Thirty-two million, eight hundred and ninety-two thousand dollars,' said Leapman.

'And once you've done that,' said Fenston, 'collect your personal belongings, because you're fired, you little bitch.'

Tina began shaking as Fenston rose from behind his desk. 'But before you leave, tell your friend Petrescu that I still haven't removed her name from the "missing, presumed dead" list.'

ANNA FELT that her lunch with Ken Wheatley could have gone better. The deputy chairman of Christie's had made it clear that the unfortunate incident that had caused her to resign from Sotheby's was not yet considered by her colleagues in the art world to be 'a thing of the past'. And it didn't help that Bryce Fenston was telling anyone who cared to listen that she had been fired for conduct unworthy of an officer of the bank. Wheatley admitted that no one much cared for Fenston. However, they felt unable to offend such a valuable customer, which meant that her re-entry into the auction house arena wasn't going to prove that easy. There wasn't anything suitable at the moment for someone with her qualifications, was how Ken euphemistically put it, but he promised to keep in touch.

When Anna left the restaurant, she hailed a cab. Perhaps her second meeting would prove more worth while. 'Twenty-six Federal Plaza,' she told the driver.

JACK WAS STANDING in the New York field office lobby waiting for Anna. When she arrived, a guard requested her driver's licence, which he checked before ticking her name on his clipboard. Jack opened the door for her.

'Not my idea of a first date,' said Anna, as she stepped inside.

'Nor mine,' Jack tried to reassure her, 'but my boss wanted you to be in no doubt how important he considers this meeting.'

He whisked Anna to the nineteenth floor, where Dick Macy was waiting in the corridor to greet her.

'How kind of you to come in, Dr Petrescu,' Macy said, as if she'd had a choice. He led her through to his office and ushered her into a comfortable chair on the other side of his desk. 'I cannot stress how important we at the Bureau consider your assistance.'

'Why do you need *my* assistance?' asked Anna. 'I thought you had arrested Leapman.'

'We released him this morning,' said Macy. 'Leapman signed an agreement with the prosecutor to ensure that if he cooperates, he'll end up with only a five-year sentence. He claims he can show a direct financial link between Fenston and Krantz, but he needs to return to their Wall Street office so he can get his hands on all the documents.'

'He could be double-crossing you,' said Anna. 'Most of the documents were destroyed when the North Tower collapsed.'

'True,' said Macy, 'but he's also agreed to appear as a government witness, should the case come to trial.'

'Then let's be thankful that Krantz is safely locked up, otherwise your star witness wouldn't even make it to the courthouse,' Anna said.

Macy looked across at Jack, unable to mask his surprise. 'You haven't read today's *Times,* Anna?' he asked.

'No,' she replied, having no idea what he was talking about.

Macy opened a file and passed the article about Krantz's escape from the high-security in Bucharest across to her.

'I'm going to be looking over my shoulder for the rest of my life,' said Anna, long before she'd reached the last paragraph.

'I don't think so,' said Jack. 'Krantz won't be in a hurry to return to America now that she's joined nine men on the FBI's most wanted list. She'll also realise that we've circulated a detailed description of her to every port of entry, as well as Interpol.'

'But that won't stop Fenston seeking revenge.'

'Why should he bother?' asked Jack. 'Now that he's got the Van Gogh, you're history.'

'But he hasn't got the Van Gogh,' said Anna, bowing her head.

'What do you mean?' asked Jack.

'I had a call from Tina. She warned me that Fenston had the painting valued for insurance. Something he's never done before.'

'But why should that cause any problems?' asked Jack.

Anna raised her head. 'Because it's a fake.'

'A fake?' both men said in unison.

'Yes, that's why I had to fly to Bucharest. I was having a copy made by an old friend who's a brilliant portrait artist.'

'So that's why you sent the red crate back to London, even allowing it to be intercepted by Art Locations and delivered on to New York,' said Macy.

Anna nodded.

'You must have realised you'd be found out,' said Jack.

'In time, yes,' said Anna. 'That's the point. All I needed was enough time to sell the original before Fenston discovered what I was up to.'

'But did you succeed?' asked Macy.

'Yes,' said Anna. 'Nakamura agreed to purchase the original for fifty million dollars, more than enough for Arabella to clear her sister's debts while holding on to the rest of the estate. He's already deposited five million dollars with his London solicitors and has agreed to pay the balance once he's inspected the original.'

'Have you got enough time?' asked Macy.

'I'm flying to London this evening,' said Anna, 'and Nakamura plans to join us at Wentworth Hall tomorrow night.'

'It's going to be close,' said Jack.

'Not if Leapman delivers the goods tonight,' said Macy.

'Am I allowed to know what you're up to?' asked Anna.

'No, you are not,' said Jack firmly. 'You catch your plane to England and close the deal, while we get on with our job.'

'Does your job include keeping an eye on Tina?' asked Anna quietly. 'She was fired this morning.'

'For what reason?' enquired Macy.

'Because Fenston found out she was keeping me informed of everything he was up to while I was chasing round the world.'

'Dr Petrescu,' said Macy, 'If Fenston is in possession of a fake, where's the original?'

'At Wentworth Hall. Once I'd retrieved the painting from Sotheby's, I took it straight to Arabella in a cab. The only thing I came away with was the red packing case and the painting's original frame.'

'And you carried out the whole deception right in front of Jack's eyes.'

'Sure did,' said Anna with a smile.

'So where was the Van Gogh while two of my most experienced agents were having breakfast with you and Lady Arabella?'

'In the Van Gogh bedroom,' replied Anna, 'just above them.'

'That close,' said Macy.

KRANTZ WAITED until the tenth ring before she heard a click and a voice enquired, 'Where are you?'

'Over the Russian border,' she replied.

'Good. I have another assignment for you. Wentworth Hall. And I'll double your fee.'

'I couldn't go back there. It's too much of a risk.'

'You may not think so when I tell you whose throat I want you to cut.'

'I'm listening,' she said, and Fenston revealed the name of his next victim. 'You'll pay me two million dollars for that?'

'Three, if you manage to kill Petrescu at the same time. And four, if she's a witness to the first throat being cut.'

A long silence followed. 'I'll need two million in advance.'

'The usual place?'

'No,' she replied, and gave him a numbered account in Moscow.

FENSTON PUT the phone down and buzzed through to Leapman. 'I need to see you—now.'

After a moment, there was a knock on the door.

'She's escaped. She's on her way to Moscow,' said Fenston.

'Is she planning to return to New York?'

'She can't risk it while security remains on such high alert.'

'That makes sense.' Leapman tried not to sound relieved.

'Meanwhile, I've given her another assignment,' said Fenston.

Leapman listened in disbelief as he revealed Krantz's next victim, and why it would be impossible for her to cut off the left ear.

'And has the impostor been dispatched back to Wentworth Hall?' asked Fenston, as Leapman stared up at the blown-up photograph of the chairman shaking hands with George W. Bush, returned to its place of honour behind Fenston's desk.

'Yes. Art Locations picked the canvas up this afternoon,' replied Leapman. 'I also had a word with our lawyer in London. The sequestration order is being heard on Wednesday, so if the original isn't returned by then, the estate automatically becomes yours and we can start selling off the collection until the debt is cleared.'

'If Krantz does her job, the debt will never be cleared,' said Fenston, 'which is why I want you to put the collection up for auction immediately. Divide the pictures between Christie's, Sotheby's, Phillips and Bonhams, and sell them all at the same time.'

'But that would flood the market and bring the prices down.'

'How sad,' said Fenston, smiling. 'In which case I will be left with no choice but to put Wentworth Hall on the market and dispose of everything down to the last suit of armour. By the time I finish with Lady Arabella, she'll not only be penniless but, knowing the British press, humiliated.'

'And Petrescu?'

'She happens to be in the wrong place at the wrong time,' said Fenston, unable to hide a smirk.

'So Krantz will kill two birds with one stone,' said Leapman, as he turned to leave. 'Good luck with your speech, Chairman.'

'My speech?' said Fenston.

'I thought you were addressing the bankers' dinner tonight.'

'Damn, you're right. Where did Tina put my speech?'

AT 7.16 P.M., Leapman switched the light off in his office and closed, but didn't lock, his door. He stepped into an empty elevator, aware that the only office light still shining was coming from under the chairman's door. Whisked to the ground floor, he walked to reception and signed out. A woman standing behind him stepped forward to sign herself out as Leapman took a pace backwards, his eyes never leaving the two guards behind the desk. One was supervising the steady flow of people exiting the building, while the other was dealing with a delivery. Leapman kept retreating until he reached the empty elevator. He backed in and stood to one side so that the guards could no longer see him, then he pressed button 32. Less than a minute later, he stepped out into the silent corridor.

The only light came from under the chairman's door. He opened his own door, stepped inside and locked it. He sat down behind his desk and waited patiently in the darkness.

FENSTON TOSSED a loan application to one side and began thumbing through the latest Christie's catalogue, a smile appearing on his lips when he realised how much his own collection was increasing in value. He glanced up at the clock on his desk: 7.43 p.m. If he didn't hurry he was going to be late for his own speech at the bankers' dinner. He picked up the catalogue and walked quickly to the door. He entered a six-digit code on the pad next to the light switch and stepped out into the corridor. Eight seconds after he'd locked his door, he heard the security grilles slam into place.

He rode down in the elevator and, when the doors slid open, he walked to reception and signed himself out: 7.48 p.m.

As he strolled through the lobby, he could see his driver waiting at the bottom of the steps. He climbed into the back seat.

'Excuse me, sir,' said the driver, 'are you going to the bankers' dinner?'

'Yes, we'd better get a move on,' said Fenston.

'It's just that'—the driver picked up a gold-embossed card from the passenger seat— 'the invitation says "dinner jacket", sir.'

'Damn,' said Fenston. Normally, Tina would have put out his dinner jacket. He jumped out of the car and took the steps up to the entrance of the building two at a time, bypassing reception, not bothering to sign back in.

When he stepped out of the elevator, the first thing he noticed was a beam of light under his office door. He could have sworn he'd switched the light off after he'd set the alarm. He was about to enter the code when he heard a noise from inside.

Fenston hesitated, wondering who it could be. He slipped into the adjoining office and quietly closed the door. He sat down in his secretary's chair and began to look for the switch Leapman had alerted him to. He found it under the desk and flipped it on. When the screen lit up, Fenston stared in disbelief. Leapman was sitting at his desk, a thick file in front of him. He was turning the pages, while occasionally photographing a sheet with what looked like a high-tech camera.

Several thoughts flashed through Fenston's mind. Leapman must be collecting material so that he could blackmail him; he was peddling information to a rival bank; the Internal Revenue Service had put a squeeze on him . . . Fenston settled for blackmail. Next he pondered his alternatives before finally choosing something he considered worthy of Leapman.

He threw a switch to stop all outgoing or incoming calls from his office, then slipped back into the corridor to enter the correct code, 170690, on the pad by his office, as if he was leaving. He then turned his key in the lock and silently pushed open the door, then pulled it closed again.

The deafening alarm was set off, but Fenston still waited until the grilles had clamped into place. He then entered last week's code, 170680, opened the door and slammed it closed.

Fenston ran back to the adjoining office and dialled the emergency number for Abbott Security.

A voice announced, 'Duty officer, Security.'

'My name is Bryce Fenston, chairman of Fenston Finance. The alarm has been triggered. I must have entered last week's code by mistake, and I want to let you know that it's *not* an emergency.'

'Can you repeat your name, sir?'

'Bryce Fenston,' he shouted above the noise of the alarm.

'Thank you, Mr Fenston. We'll get someone up to the thirty-second floor as quickly as possible.'

'No hurry. The office won't open until seven tomorrow.'

'With your permission, then, Mr Fenston, we'll change your category from emergency to priority. There will still be an after-hours call-out charge of five hundred dollars. However, if you report to the front desk, and sign our alarm roster, the charge is automatically cut to two fifty and your status lowered to routine, in which case we couldn't come to your assistance until we've dealt with all priority and emergency calls.'

'That won't be a problem,' said Fenston.

Once he'd stepped out of the elevator on the ground floor, he hurried out through the front door and down the steps to the waiting car.

The driver closed the door behind Fenston and returned to the front seat, puzzled. His boss still wasn't wearing a dinner jacket.

JACK DELANEY parked his car on Broad Street just after nine thirty and settled back to wait. Leapman had told the FBI man to expect him some time between ten and eleven, when he would hand over their camera containing enough evidence to ensure a conviction.

Jack was half asleep when he heard the siren. He checked his watch: 11.15 p.m. Leapman had warned Jack not to keep him to the minute. But that was before he had rung Jack's office a few minutes after seven to say that Fenston had told him something far more damning than any document. But he didn't want to reveal the information over the phone.

The sound of the siren was now only a couple of blocks away.

Jack got out of the car and strolled down to the building in which Leapman was working. An ambulance came to a screeching halt in front and three paramedics jumped out onto the sidewalk with a stretcher and an oxygen cylinder. Jack watched them as they charged up the steps.

He turned his attention to the reception desk, where a guard—pointing to something on his clipboard—was talking to an older man, probably his supervisor, while a second guard was occupied on the telephone. Several people strolled in and out of the elevators, not surprising in the heart of a city where finance is a twenty-four-hour occupation. When the paramedics reappeared, wheeling their patient on the stretcher, everyone stood aside. Jack strolled up the steps to take a closer look. As an NYPD siren blared in the distance, Jack stared at the pallid face of a stricken man, whose eyes were glazed over as if they'd been caught in the blaze of a headlight. One look at that face and Jack didn't need to be told that Leapman wasn't going to be speaking to anyone for a very long time.

Jack paused at the reception desk to show his FBI badge. He jabbed at the elevator button marked 32. When the doors opened, he ran down the corridor to find a security guard and two engineers in red overalls, along with a cleaner, standing by an open door.

'Who are you?' demanded the guard.

'FBI,' said Jack, producing his badge as he strode into the room. The first thing he saw was a blown-up photograph of Fenston shaking hands with George W. Bush. His eyes quickly settled on the one thing he was looking for, resting on a pile of spread-out papers beside an open file.

'What happened?' demanded Jack authoritatively.

'Some guy got himself trapped in this office for over three hours and must have set the alarm off.'

'It wasn't our fault,' jumped in one of the engineers, 'we were told to downgrade the call.'

Jack walked over to the desk, his eyes scanning the papers. He glanced up to find all four men staring at him. Jack looked directly at the security guard. 'Go to the elevator, wait for the cops, and bring them straight to me.' The guard disappeared into the corridor. 'And you three, out. This may be a crime scene, and I don't want you disturbing any evidence.' The men turned to leave and Jack grabbed the camera and dropped it into one of the pockets of his trench coat.

9/25

The taxi drew up outside the discreet entrance of a bank that prided itself on having few customers. The letters G and Z were chiselled in the white marble cornice. Krantz paid the fare and waited until the cab was out of sight before she entered the building.

The Geneva and Zurich Bank was an establishment that specialised in catering to the needs of a new breed of Russians who had reinvented themselves following the demise of communism. These oligarchs could afford the anonymity of a number when it came to finding out the details of what they were worth.

Krantz walked up to an old-fashioned wooden counter, no queues, no grilles, where a row of smartly dressed men in grey suits waited to serve. They wouldn't have looked out of place in either Geneva or Zurich.

'How may I assist you?' asked the clerk Krantz selected.

'One zero seven two zero nine five nine,' she said.

He tapped the code into his computer and the figures flashed up on the screen. 'May I see your passport?'

Krantz handed over one of the passports she had collected from a safety-deposit box in her hotel.

'How much is there in my account?' she asked.

'How much do you think there should be?' he replied.

'Just over two million dollars.'

'And what amount do you wish to withdraw?'

'Ten thousand in dollars, and ten thousand in roubles.'

He pulled out a tray from under the counter and counted out the notes slowly before passing across two neatly sealed plastic wallets, with no hint of where they had come from and no paperwork to suggest a transaction had even taken place.

Krantz picked up the two wallets, placed them in an inside pocket, and walked slowly out of the bank. She hailed the third available taxi. 'The Kalstern,' she said. Ten minutes later, she handed over four hundred roubles, stepped out of the cab and joined a group of tourists peering at a window, hoping to find some memento to prove to the folks back home they had visited the wicked communists. In the centre of the window was displayed the most popular item: a four-star general's uniform with cap, belt, holster and three rows of campaign medals. No price tag attached, but Krantz knew the going rate was twenty dollars. Next to the general stood a KGB colonel, ten dollars.

Krantz entered the shop. Sitting behind a large wooden desk, littered with papers, empty cigarette cartons, and a half-eaten salami sandwich, sat an overweight man in a baggy brown suit.

He offered a weak smile. 'How can I help?' he asked.

Krantz told him what she required. The proprietor burst out laughing. 'That wouldn't come cheap, and could take time.'

'I need the uniform by this afternoon,' said Krantz.

'That's not possible,' he said with a shrug of his shoulders.

Krantz removed a wad of cash from her pocket and peeled off a hundred-dollar bill. 'This afternoon,' she repeated.

The proprietor raised his eyebrows. 'I may have a contact.'

Krantz placed another hundred on the desk. 'I also need her passport.'

'Impossible.'

Krantz placed a further two hundred on the table.

'But I feel sure some arrangement could be made.' He paused. 'At the right price.' He rested his hands on his stomach.

'A thousand if everything is available by this afternoon.'

'I'll do my best,' said the proprietor.

'I feel sure you will,' said Krantz. 'Because I'm going to knock off a hundred dollars for every fifteen minutes after'—Krantz looked at her watch—'two o'clock.'

WHEN ANNA'S TAXI drove through the gates of Wentworth Hall, she was surprised to see Arabella waiting on the top step with a shotgun under her arm. The butler opened the taxi door as his mistress walked to greet her.

'How nice to see you,' said Arabella, kissing her on both cheeks. 'You've arrived just in time for tea.'

Anna accompanied Arabella into the house, while an under-butler removed her suitcase from the taxi. As she stepped into the hall, she paused to allow her eyes to move slowly round the walls from picture to picture.

'Yes, it is nice to have one's family around one,' said Arabella, 'even if this might be their last weekend in the country.'

'What do you mean?' asked Anna apprehensively.

'Fenston's lawyers delivered a letter reminding me that should I fail to repay their client's loan in full by midday tomorrow, I must be prepared to pension off all the family retainers.'

'He plans to dispose of the entire collection at the same time? But that doesn't make sense. He wouldn't even clear his original loan.'

'He would, if he then put the hall up for sale,' said Arabella.

'He wouldn't—' began Anna.

'He would. So we can only hope that Mr Nakamura remains infatuated with Van Gogh, because frankly he's my last hope.' She led Anna through to the drawing room.

'Come and sit down,' said Arabella as a maid entered carrying a silver tray. She had begun to lay up for tea by the fire when Andrews entered.

'Milady,' he said, 'there's a gentleman at the door with a package. He said he couldn't release it without your signature.'

Arabella followed Andrews out of the room. When she returned, the smile of moments before had been replaced by a grim expression.

'Is there a problem?' asked Anna.

'Come and see for yourself,' replied Arabella.

Anna followed her into the hall, where she found Andrews and the under-butler removing the casing of a red crate that Anna had hoped she had seen for the last time. They both watched as Andrews neatly removed the bubble wrap to reveal a canvas that Anna had last seen in Anton's studio.

'But what shall we do with him?' asked Arabella. The butler gave a discreet cough. 'You have a suggestion, Andrews?'

'No, milady,' Andrews replied, 'but I thought you would want to know that your other guest is proceeding up the drive.'

'The man clearly has a gift for timing,' said Arabella, as she quickly checked her hair in the mirror. 'Andrews, has the Wellington Room been prepared for Mr Nakamura?'

'Yes, milady. And Dr Petrescu will be in the Van Gogh room.'

The butler walked down the steps at a pace that would ensure he reached the gravel just as the Lexus came to a halt. Andrews opened the back door of the limousine to allow Mr Nakamura to step out. He was clutching a small square package.

'The Japanese always arrive bearing a gift,' whispered Anna, 'but under no circumstances open it in his presence.'

'Lady Arabella,' said Mr Nakamura, bowing low at the door, 'it is a great honour to be invited to your magnificent home.'

'You honour my home, Mr Nakamura,' said Arabella.

Nakamura turned to Anna and bowed. 'How nice to see you again, Dr Petrescu.'

'And you too, Mr Nakamura,' said Anna. 'I hope you had a pleasant flight.'

'Yes, thank you. We even landed on time, for a change,' said Nakamura, who didn't move as his eyes roamed around the hall. 'You will please correct me, Anna, should I make a mistake. Gainsborough?' he queried, as he admired the full-length portrait of Catherine, Lady Wentworth. Anna nodded, before Nakamura moved on 'Landseer, Morland, Romney, Stubbs, but then, I am stumped—is that the correct expression?'

'It is,' confirmed Arabella, 'and you were stumped by Lely.'

'Ah, Sir Peter, and what a fine-looking woman'—he paused—'a family trait,' he said, turning to face his host.

'And I can see, Mr Nakamura, that your family trait is flattery,' teased Arabella in return.

Nakamura burst out laughing. 'Lady Arabella, if every room is the equal of this, it may prove necessary for me to cancel my meeting with those dullards from Corus Steel.' His gaze swept the room and ended on the portrait propped up against the wall.

'Quite magnificent,' he finally said. 'The work of an inspired hand, but not the hand of Van Gogh.'

'How can you be so sure, Nakamura-san?' asked Anna.

'Because the wrong ear is bandaged,' replied Nakamura.

'But everyone knows Van Gogh cut off his left ear,' said Anna.

Nakamura smiled. 'And you know only too well,' he added, 'that Van Gogh painted the original while looking in a mirror, which is why the bandage ended up on the wrong ear.'

'I do hope that someone is going to explain all this to me later,' said Arabella as she led her guests to the drawing room.

KRANTZ RETURNED to the shop at 2 p.m. She was pleased to see the proprietor with a bulky plastic bag on his desk. He paused for a moment, then pulled out the red outfit Krantz had requested. She held the uniform up against her shoulders. The previous owner was at least three or four inches taller than Krantz but only a few pounds heavier; nothing that a needle and thread wouldn't remedy.

'And the passport?' asked Krantz.

Once again the proprietor's hand dipped into the carrier bag and he offered up a Soviet passport. 'She has a three-day layover, so she probably won't discover that it's missing until Friday,' he said.

'It will have served its purpose long before then,' Krantz said, as she began to turn the pages of the official document.

Sasha Prestakavich, she discovered, was three years younger than Krantz and eight centimetres taller. When Krantz reached the page where Sasha Prestakavich's photo had once been, the proprietor produced a Polaroid camera from under the counter. 'Smile,' he said. She didn't.

A few seconds later an image spewed out. Next, a dollop of glue to fix the new picture in place. His final act was to drop a needle and thread into the carrier bag. Krantz was beginning to realise that this was not the first occasion he had supplied such a service. She placed the uniform and the passport back in the carrier bag before handing over a wad of bills.

The proprietor checked the notes carefully. 'Do come and visit us again,' he suggested.

Once she was back on the street, she hailed a taxi, gave the driver an address and told him the exact entrance where she wished to be dropped off. When the cab drew up by a side door marked STAFF ONLY, she paid the fare and went straight to the ladies' room. She locked herself in a cubicle, where, with the aid of the needle and thread supplied by the shop proprietor, she raised the hemline of the skirt by a couple of inches and made a couple of tucks in the waist. She then stripped off all her outer garments before trying on the uniform—not a perfect fit, but fortunately the company she was proposing to work for was not known for its sartorial elegance.

When Krantz emerged, her eyes settled on a woman dressed in an identical uniform. She walked to the counter and asked, 'Have you got a spare seat on any of our London flights?'

'That shouldn't be a problem,' the company representative replied. 'Can I see your passport?' Krantz handed over the document. According to the database, Sasha Prestakavich was on a three-day layover. Krantz was handed a crew pass. 'Be sure you're among the last to check in, just in case we have any latecomers.'

Krantz walked across to the international terminal and once she'd been checked through customs, hung around in duty free until she heard the final boarding call for Flight 413 to London. By the time she arrived at the gate, the last passengers were checking in.

Krantz had chosen a seat in the back of the aircraft so that few of the passengers would notice her, only the crew. She needed to be adopted by one of them long before they touched down.

'Domestic or international?' asked the senior stewardess, soon after the aircraft had reached its cruising height.

'Domestic,' replied Krantz.

'Ah, that's why I haven't seen you before.'

'I've only been with the company for three months.'

'That would explain it. My name's Nina.'

'Sasha,' said Krantz, giving her a warm smile.

Trying to relax when she couldn't lean on her right shoulder meant that Krantz remained awake for most of the flight. She used these hours getting to know Nina. By the time they landed, the senior stewardess would unwittingly play a role in her deception.

Krantz remained in her seat until the last passenger had left the aircraft. She then joined the crew as they disembarked and headed in the direction of the terminal. Krantz never left the senior stewardess's side during the long walk down endless corridors, while Nina offered her opinion on everything from Putin to Rasputin.

When the Aeroflot crew finally reached passport control, Nina guided her charge past the long line of passengers and on towards the exit marked CREW ONLY. Krantz tucked in behind Nina, who didn't stop chatting even when she'd handed over her passport. The official turned the pages and checked the photograph. 'Next.'

Krantz handed over her passport. Once again, the official looked carefully at the photograph and then at the person it claimed to represent. He even smiled as he waved her through, before turning his attention to the second officer, who was next in line.

'Will you be joining us on the bus?' asked Nina, as they strolled out of the airport and onto the pavement.

'No,' said Krantz. 'I'm being met by my boyfriend.'

Nina said goodbye before crossing the road in the company of the second officer.

'Who was that?' her colleague asked. Nina told him.

ANDREWS CAREFULLY PLACED the Van Gogh on an easel in the centre of the drawing room.

'What do you think?' said Arabella, as she took a step back to admire the self-portrait.

'Don't you feel that Mr Nakamura might consider it a little . . .' ventured Anna, not wishing to offend her host.

'Crude, blatant, obvious? Which word were you searching for, my dear?' asked Arabella. 'Let's face it, I'm strapped for cash and running out of time, so I don't have a lot of choice.'

'No one would believe it, looking at you,' said Anna, as she admired the long, rose silk taffeta gown and diamond necklace Arabella was wearing, making Anna feel somewhat casual in her short black Armani dress.

'It's kind of you to say so, my dear, but if I had your looks and your figure, I wouldn't cover myself with other distractions.'

Anna smiled, admiring the way Arabella had put her at ease.

'When do you think he'll make a decision?' asked Arabella.

'Like all great collectors, he'll make up his mind within moments. It will take him about eight seconds to decide if he wants to own this painting,' she said, looking directly at the Van Gogh.

'Let's drink to that,' said Arabella.

Andrews stepped forward, proffering a silver tray that held three glasses. 'A glass of champagne, madam?'

'Thank you,' said Anna, removing a long-stemmed flute. When Andrews stepped back, her gaze fell on a turquoise and black vase. 'It's quite magnificent,' she said.

'Mr Nakamura's gift,' said Arabella. 'Most embarrassing. By the way, I do hope I haven't committed a *faux pas* by putting it on display while Mr Nakamura is still a guest in my home.'

'Certainly not,' said Anna. 'Mr Nakamura will be flattered. The piece survives, even shines in this room. There is only one rule when it comes to real talent,' she added. 'Any form of art isn't out of place as long as it's displayed among its equals. I have no doubt that in his own country, whoever made this is considered a master.'

'Not exactly a master,' said a voice from behind them.

Arabella and Anna turned at the same time to see that Mr Nakamura had entered, dressed in a dinner jacket.

'Not a master?' queried Arabella.

'No,' said Nakamura. 'In this country, you honour those who achieve greatness by making them knights or barons, whereas we in Japan reward such talent with the title "national treasure".'

'How immensely civilised,' said Arabella as Andrews offered Nakamura a glass of champagne. 'I simply love it, and whatever Mr Fenston manages to prise away from me over the coming years, I shall never allow him to get his hands on my national treasure.'

'Perhaps it won't be necessary for him to prise anything away,' said Mr Nakamura, turning to face the Van Gogh as if he'd seen it for the first time. Arabella held her breath while Anna studied the expression on his face.

Nakamura turned to Arabella. 'There are times when it is a distinct advantage to be a millionaire. It does allow one to indulge in collecting other people's national treasures.'

Anna wanted to cheer but simply raised her glass. Mr Nakamura returned the compliment. Tears were flooding down Arabella's cheeks. 'I don't know how to thank you,' she said.

'Not me,' said Nakamura, 'Anna. Without her courage, this would not have been brought to such a worthwhile conclusion.'

'I agree,' said Arabella, 'which is why I shall ask Andrews to return the self-portrait to Anna's bedroom, so that she can be the last person to appreciate it before its long journey to Japan.'

'How appropriate,' he said. 'But if Anna were to become the CEO of my foundation, she could see it whenever she wished.'

Anna was about to respond when Andrews re-entered the drawing room and announced, 'Dinner is served, milady.'

'WASN'T THERE anything on the film that would assist us?' asked Macy.

'Nothing,' replied Jack. 'Leapman had only been in the office long enough to photograph eight documents.'

'And what do those eight documents tell us?'

'Nothing we didn't already know. Mainly contracts confirming that Fenston is still fleecing customers in different parts of the world. My only hope is that the NYPD has enough evidence to press charges in the Leapman case.'

'Any news from the hospital about his chances of recovery?' asked Macy.

'Not great,' admitted Jack. 'While he was in Fenston's office he suffered a stress stroke caused by high blood pressure. Frankly, his doctor is describing him as a vegetable.'

'The police want to know if we have an agent called Delaney, and if so did he remove a camera from the crime scene.'

'It was FBI property,' said Jack, trying not to smile.

'Not if it was evidence in a criminal investigation, as you well know, Jack. Why don't you send them a set of the photos Leapman took and try to be more cooperative?'

'But what do they have to offer in exchange?'

'A copy of a photograph with your name on the back.' The supervisor pushed across his desk a print of Fenston shaking hands with George W. Bush when he visited Ground Zero. Jack recalled the blown-up version on Fenston's wall. 'How come the NYPD has a copy of this?'

'They found it on Leapman's desk. He was obviously going to hand it over to you yesterday evening, along with an explanation of what he'd written on the back.'

Jack was considering the words, 'Delaney, this is all the evidence you need,' when the phone on Macy's desk buzzed.

He picked it up and listened. 'Put him on,' said Macy, as he replaced the receiver and flicked a switch that would allow them both to follow the conversation.

'Hi, Dick. It's Tom Crasanti, calling from London. We think Krantz has slipped into England.'

'That's not possible,' said Jack. 'How could she hope to get through passport control?'

'By posing as an Aeroflot stewardess, it would seem,' said Tom. 'My contact at the Russian Embassy called to warn me that a woman had entered Britain using a fake passport under the name of Sasha Prestakavich.'

'But why did they assume Prestakavich is Krantz?' asked Jack.

'They didn't,' said Tom. 'All they could tell me was that the suspect befriended Aeroflot's senior stewardess while on their daily flight to London. She then fooled her into accompanying her through passport control. The copilot asked who the woman was, and when he was told that her name was Sasha Prestakavich, he said that wasn't possible because he travelled with her regularly and this woman certainly wasn't Prestakavich.'

'That still doesn't prove it's Krantz,' pressed Macy.

'But the copilot,' continued Tom, 'alerted Aeroflot's security. It didn't take them long to discover that Sasha Prestakavich's passport had been stolen, along with her uniform. They asked me to fax over a photograph of Krantz, which I did. He then forwarded a copy to the copilot at his London hotel, who confirmed that it was the fake stewardess.'

'Good work, Tom,' said Macy, 'but why would Krantz chance going to England at this particular time?'

'To kill Petrescu would be my bet,' said Tom.

'I agree,' said Macy. He leaned forward. 'Now listen carefully, Tom. I need you to get in touch with Chief Superintendent Renton of the Surrey CID. Warn him that we think Krantz is about to strike again, and the target could well be someone else at Wentworth Hall. He won't want that to happen twice on his watch.'

'Yes, sir,' came back the reply from London.

Macy flicked off the speaker phone. 'And, Jack, I want you to take the next flight to London. If Krantz is even thinking about harming Petrescu, let's make sure we're waiting for her.'

Jack frowned but didn't respond.

'You look apprehensive,' said Macy.

'I can't see why a photo of Fenston shaking hands with the president is "all the evidence you need".' He paused. 'Although I think I've worked out why Krantz is willing to risk returning to Wentworth Hall a second time.'

'And why's that?' asked Macy.

'She's going to steal the Van Gogh painting,' said Jack, 'then somehow get it to Fenston.'

'So Petrescu isn't the reason Krantz has returned to England.'

'No, she isn't,' said Jack, 'but once Krantz discovers she's there, you can assume that she'll consider killing Anna a bonus.'

KRANTZ, DRESSED in a black skin-tight track suit, circled the estate twice before deciding where to enter the grounds. She climbed the perimeter wall in seconds, then ran along the long drive until Wentworth Hall came into view. She waited for the moon to disappear behind a cloud, before running the thirty or forty yards to a little copse of trees by the river, where she had a clear view of the front of the house.

She estimated the distance between the copse and the north end of the house to be 100 yards. With the moon throwing out such a clear light, she knew that there was only one form of movement that would go unobserved.

She fell to her knees before lying flat on the grass. She first placed one arm in front of her, followed by one leg, the second arm, then the second leg, and finally she eased her body forward. When Krantz was within ten yards, she checked the windows of the large room where the most noise was coming from. Although the heavy curtains were drawn, she spotted one affording a slight chink. When she reached the window, she pushed herself up onto her knees until one eye was in line with the gap.

A man dressed in a dinner jacket was on his feet, a glass of champagne in one hand as if proposing a toast. At one end of the table sat a lady in a long dress with her back to the window. Krantz almost smiled when she saw who was at the other end of the table. When Petrescu retired to bed later that night, Krantz would be waiting for her, hidden in the place Petrescu would least expect. Her eyes moved around the room, searching for the other throat Fenston had sent her to cut.

'Lady Arabella, I thank you for your hospitality. Tonight will remain memorable for many reasons. Not least, that I will leave Wentworth Hall tomorrow with one of the finest examples of Van Gogh's work, as well as one of the most talented professionals in her field, who has agreed to be the CEO of my foundation.'

Krantz decided that it was time to move on.

She crept slowly towards the north end of the building, where the massive cornerstones formed perfectly proportioned footholds. She climbed up onto the first-floor balcony in less than two minutes. With the aid of her knife, she slipped the bolt on the first window. Once inside, she switched on a slimline pen torch. The square of light moved across the bedroom wall, illuminating picture after picture, and although Hals, Hobbema and Van Goyen would have delighted most connoisseurs' eyes, Krantz passed quickly over them in search of another Dutch master. She had covered five bedrooms by the time Arabella invited her guests to join her in the drawing room for coffee. There were still another nine rooms to consider, and Krantz was aware she was running out of time.

She moved swiftly to the next room, where someone who believed in fresh air had left a window wide open. She switched on her torch just as Mr Nakamura placed his coffee cup back on the table. 'I think it is time for me to retire, Lady Arabella,' he said, 'in case those dull men of Corus Steel feel I have lost my edge.'

Krantz thought she heard a door close, and returned quickly to the balcony. She needed the use of her knife to secure entry into the next room. She moved stealthily across the floor, coming to a halt at the end of a four-poster bed. She switched on the torch, expecting to be greeted by a blank wall. But not this time.

The insane eyes of a genius stared at her. The insane eyes of an assassin stared back.

Krantz smiled. She switched off her torch, crawled under the four-poster, lay flat on her back on the carpet and waited.

NAKAMURA BOWED before accompanying Anna up the staircase, stopping occasionally to admire Arabella's ancestors.

'You will forgive me, Anna,' he said, 'for taking my time, but I may not be given the opportunity of meeting these gentlemen again.'

Anna smiled as she left him to admire the Romney of Mrs Siddons. Down the corridor, she opened the door to the Van Gogh room and switched on the light by the side of the bed, stopping for a moment to admire the portrait of the great artist. She closed the door, took off her dress and hung it in the wardrobe, then disappeared into the bathroom.

When Krantz heard the sound of a shower, she slid out from under the bed, pulled back the covers on the side of the bed away from the lamp, and climbed carefully in. Neatly replacing the blanket and cover over her head, Krantz lay flat and didn't move a muscle. She was so slight that she barely made an impression in the half-light. She heard a switch being flicked off—the bathroom light.

Krantz extracted the knife and gripped the handle firmly. Anna slipped under the covers and immediately turned on her side to switch off the bedside light. She lowered her head onto the soft goose-feather pillow.

She was drifting off to sleep when Krantz leaned across and touched her back. Was she dreaming? Anna wondered, as she lay in that semiconscious state before sleep. It wasn't possible that someone else could be in her bed. That was when she felt the cold steel of a blade between her thighs and suddenly she was wide awake, a thousand thoughts rushing through her mind.

She was about to throw the blanket back and dive to the floor, when a voice said, 'Don't even think about moving, not even a muscle; you have a six-inch knife between your legs, facing upwards. If you as much as murmur, you'll live just long enough to wish you were dead.'

Anna tried not to move, although she couldn't stop trembling.

'There is a light on your side of the bed,' said Krantz. 'Lean across, very slowly, and turn it on.'

Anna leaned over and switched on the light.

'Good,' said Krantz. 'Now I'm going to pull back the blanket. Push yourself up onto your knees and turn to face the wall.'

Anna pushed herself up slowly onto her knees and inched round until she stared up at Van Gogh.

'Take hold of the painting on both sides of the frame and lower it off its hook down onto the pillow.'

Anna managed to find the strength to bring the portrait to rest.

'Now I'm going to place the tip of the knife on the back of your neck. Don't give a second's thought to any sudden movement, because I can kill you in less than three seconds.'

A moment later, the knife was pressed against the nape of Anna's neck.

'Lift the picture off the pillow, then turn to face me. The blade will never be less than a few inches from your throat.'

Anna lifted the picture off the pillow and moved her knees round inch by inch, until she came face to face with Krantz. When Anna first saw her, she was momentarily taken by surprise. Krantz was so small and slight, but she had got the better of Sergei, so what chance did Anna have?

'Now I want you to turn the picture round to face me, and don't take your eye off the knife,' she added, as she pulled back the blade from Anna's throat and raised it above her head. 'Grip the frame firmly,' she said, 'because your friend Van Gogh is about to lose more than his ear.'

'But why?' cried Anna, unable to remain silent any longer.

'Mr Fenston wanted you to be the last person to see the masterpiece before it was destroyed.'

'But why?' Anna repeated.

'As Mr Fenston couldn't own the painting himself, he wanted to be sure that Mr Nakamura couldn't either. What a pity you won't have the chance to tell Lady Arabella what Mr Fenston has in mind for her. Her death, unlike yours, will be a long and lingering one.' Krantz paused. 'I fear that time is running out, both for you and Mr Van Gogh.'

Krantz suddenly plunged the blade into the canvas. She sliced through Van Gogh's neck and, with all the power she could muster, completed an uneven circle, finally removing the head of Van Gogh and leaving a ragged hole in the centre of the canvas.

Van Gogh's head fell onto the sheet. As Krantz sat back to enjoy her moment of triumph, Anna brought the heavy frame crashing down towards her head. But Krantz turned, raised an arm, and deflected the blow onto her left shoulder. Anna jumped off the bed and began to run towards the door before Krantz dived at her, thrusting the tip of the blade into her leg. Anna fell, only inches from the door handle, blood spurting in every direction. Before she could turn the handle, Krantz grabbed her by the hair and pulled her down. The last words Anna heard her utter were: 'This time it's personal.'

Krantz was about to perform a ceremonial incision when the bedroom door was flung open by a woman dressed in a shimmering silk gown and carrying a shotgun.

Krantz was momentarily transfixed as she looked up at Lady Victoria Wentworth. Hadn't she already killed this woman? Was she staring at a ghost? She hesitated, while still holding the knife to Anna's throat.

Arabella raised the gun as Krantz eased backwards, dragging her quarry towards the open window. Arabella cocked the trigger. 'Another drop of blood,' she said, 'and I'll blow you to smithereens.'

Without warning, Krantz let go of Anna's hair and threw herself sideways out of the open window, landing on the balcony. Arabella raised the gun and fired, blowing away the window and leaving a gaping hole. She rushed over to the smouldering gap and shouted, 'Now, Andrews,' as if she was ordering a beat at a pheasant shoot to commence. A second later, the security lights floodlit the front lawn so that it looked like a football field with a single player advancing towards the goal.

Arabella's eyes settled on the diminutive black figure zigzagging across the lawn. She pulled the gun butt firmly into her shoulder, took aim and squeezed the trigger. Krantz fell to the ground, but managed to crawl on towards the fence.

'Damn,' said Arabella, 'I only winged her.' She ran down the stairs and shouted, 'Two more cartridges, Andrews.'

Andrews opened the front door and simultaneously passed Her Ladyship two cartridges. Arabella quickly reloaded before charging onto the lawn. The small black figure changed direction, but Arabella was beginning to make ground on Krantz with every stride. She came to a halt in the middle of the lawn, took aim, and was about to squeeze the trigger when three police cars and an ambulance came speeding up the drive, their headlights blinding her so that she could no longer see her quarry.

The first car screeched to a halt almost at Arabella's feet. 'Good evening, Chief Superintendent,' she said, placing a hand across her forehead as she tried to shield her eyes.

'Good evening, Arabella,' he replied, as if he had arrived a few minutes late for one of her parties. 'Is everything all right?'

'It was until you turned up. How did you get here so quickly?'

'You've got your American friend, Jack Delaney, to thank for that. We've had the place under surveillance for the past hour.'

'If you'd given me a couple more minutes, I'd have finished her off and been quite happy to face the consequences.'

'I have no idea what you're talking about,' said the chief superintendent, just as Mr Nakamura appeared in his dressing gown.

'I think that Anna—'

'Oh, my God,' said Arabella. Running back to the house, she dashed up the staircase to the guest bedroom. She found Andrews kneeling on the floor, winding a bandage expertly around Anna's leg.

Mr Nakamura came running through the door. 'For many years, Arabella, I have wondered what took place at an English country-house party.' He paused. 'Well, now I know.'

Arabella burst out laughing and turned to find him staring at the mutilated canvas. 'Oh my God,' she said, setting eyes on what was left of her inheritance. 'That bastard Fenston has beaten us all.'

Anna rose slowly and sat on the end of the bed. 'I don't think so,' she said. Arabella looked puzzled. 'But you have Andrews to thank for that.'

'Andrews?' repeated Arabella.

'Yes. He warned me that Mr Nakamura would be leaving first thing in the morning and suggested that it might be appropriate for him to remove the painting during dinner. This would allow his staff time to transfer the frame onto the original and to have the picture packed and ready.' Anna paused. 'I think I recall his exact words: "If you were to allow me to replace the masterpiece with the fake, I feel confident that Her Ladyship would be none the wiser."'

It was one of the rare occasions during the past forty-nine years that Andrews had witnessed the Lady Arabella rendered speechless.

'I think you should fire him on the spot for insubordination,' said Nakamura, 'then I can offer him a job. Were you to accept,' he said, turning to Andrews, 'I would double your present salary.'

'Not a hope,' said Arabella, before the butler could respond. 'Andrews is one national treasure I will never part with.'

9/26

Mr Nakamura woke a few minutes after six, when he thought he heard the bedroom door close. He spent a few moments thinking over what had taken place the previous evening, trying to convince himself it hadn't all been a dream.

He pushed back the sheets and lowered his feet onto the carpet, to find a pair of slippers had been left by the side of the bed. He placed his feet in the slippers, put on a dressing gown and walked to the chair where he'd left his dinner jacket, evening dress shirt and the rest of his clothes. He had intended to pack before leaving, but they were no longer there. He tried to recall if he had already put them in his suitcase. He opened the lid to discover that his dress shirt had been washed, ironed and packed and his dinner jacket was pressed and hanging up in his suit carrier.

He walked into the bathroom to find the large bath three-quarters full. Then he recalled the door closing, with just enough force to wake him without disturbing any other guest. He took off his dressing gown and stepped into the bath.

ANNA CAME OUT of the bathroom and started to get dressed. She was putting on Tina's watch when she first saw the envelope on the bedside table. Had Andrews delivered it while she was in the shower? She felt sure it hadn't been there when she woke. 'Anna' was scrawled on it in Arabella's unmistakable, bold hand.

WENTWORTH HALL

September 26, 2001

Dearest Anna,

How do I begin to thank you? Ten days ago you told me that you wished to prove you had nothing to do with Victoria's tragic death. Since then, you have done so much more, and even ended up saving the family's bacon.

Anna burst out laughing at the quaint English expression, causing two slips of paper to fall out of the envelope and onto the floor. Anna bent down to pick them up. The first was a cheque made out to 'Anna Petrescu' for £1 million. The second . . .

ONCE NAKAMURA was dressed, he picked up his cellphone and dialled a number in Tokyo. He instructed his finance director to deposit $45 million by electronic transfer with his bank in London. He had already given his lawyers instructions to transfer the full amount to Coutts & Co in the Strand, where the Wentworth family had maintained an account for two centuries.

As he walked down the marble staircase, he spotted Andrews in the hall supervising the moving of the red crate to the front door.

Arabella bustled out of the breakfast room as her guest reached the bottom step. 'Good morning, Takashi,' she said. 'I do hope that, despite everything, you managed some sleep.'

'Yes, thank you, Arabella,' he replied, as Anna limped down behind him.

'I don't know how to thank you,' said Anna. 'And I know that Tina—' she continued, when there was a rap on the front door. Andrews walked sedately across the hall and pulled it open. 'Good morning, sir,' he said.

Arabella smiled at her unexpected guest. 'Good morning, Jack,' she said. 'I hadn't realised you were joining us for breakfast. Have you spent the night at our local police station?'

'No, Arabella, I did not, but I'm told that you should have,' replied Jack with a grin.

'Hello, my hero,' said Anna, giving Jack a kiss. 'You arrived just in time to save us all.'

'Not quite fair,' chipped in Arabella, 'as it was Jack who tipped off the local constabulary in the first place.'

Anna smiled and, turning to Nakamura, said, 'This is my friend Jack Fitzgerald Delaney.'

'No doubt christened John,' suggested Mr Nakamura, as he shook hands.

'Names chosen by an Irish mother, or perhaps you were born on November the 22nd, 1963?'

'Guilty on both counts,' admitted Jack.

Arabella led her guests to the breakfast room and Anna explained to Jack why she had a bandage round her leg. Arabella invited Nakamura to take the place on her right and said to Jack, 'Come and sit on my left, young man, and you can forget any thought of food until you've explained why I'm not on the front page of the *Daily Mail* following my heroic efforts last night.'

'I have no idea what you're talking about,' said Jack, as Andrews poured him a cup of coffee. 'But I can tell you that a woman, approximately five foot tall, with a gunshot wound, spent the night at Belmarsh prison.'

'From which, no doubt, she will escape,' suggested Arabella.

'I can assure you, no one has ever escaped from Belmarsh.'

'But they'll end up having to send her back to Bucharest.'

'Unlikely,' said Jack, 'as there's no record of her entering the country.'

'Well, if that's the case, I'll allow you to help yourself to a small portion of mushrooms.'

'Which I can highly recommend,' said Mr Nakamura, as he rose from his place, 'but I fear I must now leave you, Arabella, if I am not to be late for my meeting.'

Everyone left the table to join Mr Nakamura in the hall. Andrews was standing by the front door, organising the packing of the red crate into the boot of a limousine.

'I think,' said Mr Nakamura, 'that to describe my visit to Wentworth Hall as memorable would be classic English understatement.' He smiled, taking one last look at Gainsborough's portrait of Catherine, Lady Wentworth. 'Correct me if I am wrong, Arabella, but isn't that the necklace you were wearing last night?'

'It is indeed. Her Ladyship was an actress, which would be the equivalent today of being a lap dancer, so heaven knows from which of her many admirers she acquired such a bauble. But I'm not complaining. I have *her* to thank for the necklace.'

'And the earrings,' said Anna.

'Earring, sadly,' said Arabella, touching her right ear.

'Earring,' repeated Jack as he looked up at the painting. 'I'm so dumb. It's been staring me in the face all the time.'

'What has been staring you in the face?' asked Anna.

'Leapman wrote on the back of a photograph of Fenston with George W. Bush: "This is all the evidence you need."'

'All the evidence you need for what?' asked Arabella.

'To prove that it was Fenston who murdered your sister,' replied Jack.

'I fail to see a connection between Catherine, Lady Wentworth, and the President of the United States,' said Arabella.

'The same mistake I made,' said Jack. 'The connection is not between Lady Wentworth and Bush, but between Lady Wentworth and Fenston. And the clue has been staring us in the face.'

Everyone looked up at the Gainsborough portrait.

'They're both wearing the same earring,' Anna said quietly. 'I missed it completely. I saw Fenston wearing the earring on the day he fired me, but I just didn't make the connection.'

'Leapman realised its significance,' said Jack. 'He'd worked out that it was the evidence we needed to secure a conviction.'

Andrews coughed.

'You're quite right, Andrews,' said Arabella. 'We mustn't keep Mr Nakamura any longer. The poor man has suffered quite enough family revelations for one day.'

'True,' said Mr Nakamura. 'However, I would like to congratulate Mr Delaney on a remarkable piece of detection.'

'Slow, but he gets there in the end,' said Anna, taking his hand.

Mr Nakamura smiled as Arabella accompanied him down to his car, while Jack and Anna waited on the top step.

'Well done, Stalker,' said Anna. 'I agree with Mr Nakamura, that wasn't a bad piece of detective work.'

Jack smiled. 'But how about your efforts as a rookie agent? Did you ever discover why Tina—'

'I thought you'd never ask, though I confess I also missed clues that should have been obvious, even to an amateur.'

'Like what?' asked Jack.

'A girl who happens to support the 49ers, has a considerable knowledge and love of art, whose hobby was sailing a boat called *Christina* that had been named after the owner's two children.'

'She's Chris Adams's daughter?' said Jack.

'And Chris Adams, Jr.'s, sister. After her brother had his throat cut, she had to drop out of law school. She changed her name, moved to New York, took a secretarial course and waited for Fenston's secretary to resign.'

'And held on to her position until she was fired the other day,' Jack reminded her, as Nakamura bowed low to Arabella before climbing into the back of his limousine.

'And even better news, Stalker,' continued Anna, as she returned Mr Nakamura's wave. 'Tina downloaded every document that might implicate Fenston onto her personal computer. She kept contracts, letters, personal memos. So I have a feeling that it won't be long before you can finally close the file on Mr Bryce Fenston.'

'Thanks to you and Tina,' said Jack. He paused. 'But she lost everything.'

'Not everything,' said Anna, 'because you'll be happy to know that Arabella has given her a million dollars for the part she played in saving the Wentworth estate.'

'A million dollars?'

'Not to mention the million pounds she's presented to me. '"For the labourer is worthy of his hire" was how Arabella expressed it.'

'St Luke,' said Jack. '"And in the same house remain, eating and drinking such things as they give: for the labourer is worthy of his hire."'

'Impressive,' said Anna. 'Perhaps I'll let you join me for lunch in first class on the flight home.'

He turned to her and smiled. 'I'd much rather you came to dinner with me on Saturday evening.'

'Your mother's Irish stew night? Now that's better than first class. I'd certainly be up for that.'

'But there's something I have to tell you,' said Jack, as Mr Nakamura's car disappeared down the drive and out of the gates.

'And what's that?' asked Anna, turning back to face him.

'My mother is under the illusion that you've already been married three times, you have five children, not necessarily by the three husbands, four of them are on hard drugs, and the other one is currently serving a jail sentence.' He paused. 'She also thinks that you work in a far older profession than art consultancy.'

Anna burst out laughing. 'But what will you tell her when she discovers that none of it's true?'

'You're not Irish,' said Jack.

JEFFREY ARCHER

Born: April 15, 1940
Homes: London and Cambridgeshire
Passions: art, athletics, cricket

RD: You're thought of as one of Britain's best storytellers. Where do you think that ability comes from?

JA: I think storytelling is a God-given gift. You can't acquire the ability to tell a good story. Otherwise everybody would be doing it.

RD: How does the process start for you?

JA: Well, with *False Impression*, it came from something I read in the *New York Times* after 9/11. There was a list published of people missing, presumed dead. But some had in fact disappeared because of financial or matrimonial problems, some because they were involved in crime. I thought it would be interesting to turn that on its head, to have someone disappear because they wanted to do something good.

RD: The art angle in the book is interesting, particularly as you have been a collector yourself for many years. Would you invest in a Van Gogh and, if so, which one?

JA: I'd have done that years ago if I could have afforded to. They now sell for silly prices. The estimate for the latest one coming up in two months' time at Sotheby's in New York, is $40 million. I love the the classic one of the bed, the table and the chair.

RD: Now that you've regained your freedom, have your priorities changed? Are there things you cherish more?

JA: Time, possibly. But that may just be because one is getting older, and there are things one wants to do. I work now as hard as I've ever worked.

RD: What would you like to achieve in the next few years?

JA: I'm working on a collection of short stories, which I hope will come out in a year's time, and then I want to write a big, big novel, which will probably take me two years. I'm getting mentally prepared for it now.

RD: Is it more rewarding to write a big novel like *Kane and Abel*?

JA: Yes, but it's thrilling, too, to write a story that you feel has got speed and pace and excitement. That's pretty hard to do.

RD: Do you miss the political arena?

JA: No. My generation's gone. We had our day. I'm still involved in the sense that I read about it all the time, I'm fascinated by it and obviously retain a large number of friends in the political world. But I'm no longer in the centre.

RD: What drew you to it in the first place?

JA: I think I loved the idea that it was never-ending. However much energy you put in, however much you did, it just went on and on. I liked the energy of it.

RD: That's interesting, because by becoming more of a full-time writer you're moving to a life that's almost completely opposite in style.

JA: Totally opposite, because one is secluded. It's very lonely. You're on your own: you, the pen, the pad, that's it. Politics is a very clubby thing; lots of people involved, trying to rub along together. You're quite right, it is a weird combination.

RD: If you were in power, what one thing above all, would you like to change about Britain today—if you could even do the impossible?

JA: I'd have got the pensions thing sorted out thirty years ago. The problem we're going to face is that everyone is going to be living to a hundred. It doesn't take a great economic brain to work out the problems that that brings. We're living longer lives . . .

RD: What will you do with the longer life?

JA: I shall go on writing. I exercise in the gym every day. I'm also doing a lot of charity work, a lot of auctioneering. And I'm sure there'll be other challenges.

RD: Is there any other kind of work that you'd have liked to have done?

JA: I'd love to have Seb Coe's job, to be in charge of bringing the Olympics here. I love the Games and have been to them seven or eight times. Seb's doing it all so brilliantly, though, that we can all sit and admire from the sidelines.

RD: Your life has gone from one extreme to the other—triumph to disaster and back again—which of them do you think has taught you more?

JA: (Long pause) It's about equal. Well, except the good thing about disaster is that you've got somewhere to come back from. Which forces you to get up and start working again.

RD: Do you have any ambitions for your children?

JA: I think it's very dangerous to do so. My son was running at one point, very well indeed, and looked as though he might join the British Olympic team. And then he got pleurisy. And I was so disappointed . . . but what it taught me was not to expect anything. I hope they'll be decent, nice kids. Can't ask more than that. And that they'll be healthy. Most problems in life come from not being well or being in debt. Both those things I would hope they'll never have to worry about.

RD: And if you had to sum yourself up in a word?

JA: Energy, probably.

JACQUOT AND THE ANGEL © 2005 Martin O'Brien
Published by Headline

THE HARD WAY © Lee Child 2006
Published by Bantam Press

MARLEY & ME © 2005 by John Grogan
Published by Hodder & Stoughton

FALSE IMPRESSION © Jeffrey Archer 2005
Published by Macmillan

Illustrations and Photos:
Pages 4 & 5: Martin O'Brien © Gavin Shaw; Lee Child © Sigrid Estrada; John Grogan ©
Jenny Vogt; Jeffrey Archer © Paul Stuart.
Jacquot and the Angel: 6–8: Images: Photographer's Choice. Page 172 © Gavin Shaw;
page 173 © J. Lilly/Garden World Images.
The Hard Way: 174–5: images: Stone and the Imagebank; page 317 © Sigrid Estrada.
Marley & Me: 318–20: images: Hodder & Stoughton; page 429 © Jenny Vogt.
False Impression: 430–2: images: illustrator: Stuart Williams @ the organisation; page 574:
© Paul Stuart.
Dustjacket spine: Stuart Williams @ the organisation.

Printed and bound by GGP Media GmbH, Pössneck, Germany

242/06